D0952756

John Grimes
Survey Captain

Books by A. Bertram Chandler

John Grimes (series)
The Road to the Rim (1967)
To Prime the Pump (1971)
The Hard Way Up (1972)
Spartan Planet (1968)
The Inheritors (1972)
The Broken Cycle (1975)
The Big Black Mark (1975)
The Far Traveler (1977)
Star Courier (1977)
To Keep the Ship (1978)
Matilda's Stepchildren (1979)
Star Loot (1980)
The Anarch Lords (1981)
The Last Amazon (1984)
The Wild Ones (1984)
Catch the Star Winds (1969)
Into the Alternate Universe (1964)
Contraband from Other-Space (1967)
The Rim Gods (1969)
The Dark Dimensions (1971)
Alternate Orbits (1971)
The Gateway to Never (1972)
The Way Back (1976)

Derek Calver (series)
The Rim of Space (1961)
The Ship from Outside (1963)

Christopher Wilkinson (series)
The Coils of Time (1964)
The Alternate Martians (1965)

Empress (series)
Empress of Outer Space (1965)
Space Mercenaries (1965)
Nebula Alert (1967)

Other Novels
Bring Back Yesterday (1961)
Rendezvous on a Lost World (1961)
The Hamelin Plague (1963)
Beyond the Galactic Rim (1963)
Glory Planet (1964)
The Deep Reaches of Space (1964)
The Sea Beasts (1971)
The Bitter Pill (1974)
Kelly Country (1983)
To Rule the Refugees (1983)
Frontier of the Dark (1984)
Find the Lady (1984)

Short Fiction
Up to the Sky in Ships (1982)
From Sea to Shining Star (1990)

A. BERTRAM CHANDLER

John Grimes
Survey Captain

The Broken Cycle
The Big Black Mark
The Far Traveler
Star Courier

SCIENCE
FICTION

THE BROKEN CYCLE Copyright © 1979 by A. Bertram Chandler
THE BIG BLACK MARK Copyright © 1975 by A. Bertram Chandler
THE FAR TRAVELER Copyright © 1979 by A. Bertram Chandler
STAR COURIER Copyright © 1977 by A. Bertram Chandler

First SFBC Science Fiction Printing: January 2002.

Published by arrangement with the author's estate, via JABberwocky Literary Agency,
P.O. Box 4558
Sunnyside, NY 11104-0558

Visit the SFBC at http:// www.sfbc.com

ISBN 0-7394-2384-3

PRINTED IN THE UNITED STATES OF AMERICA

Contents

The Broken Cycle

Chapter 1

John Grimes—although he hated to have to admit it, even to himself—was bored.

He could not rid himself of the guilty feeling that he should not have been; he knew that many of his fellow officers, back at Lindisfarne Base, would have changed places with him quite willingly. He was in a situation of maximum temptation combined with maximum opportunity. He was sharing a well equipped ship's boat, the certified capacity of which was twenty persons, with one attractive girl. The small craft, in addition to its not inconsiderable stock of concentrated foodstuffs, was fitted with algae vats by means of which all organic wastes could be reprocessed indefinitely. It was, in fact, a closed ecology which would continue to function throughout the lifetimes of the boat's crew. Air, food and water—or the lack of these essentials—would never be a problem to Lieutenant Commander John Grimes and Federation Sky Marshal Una Freeman, even though there was some consumption of hydrogen by the little atomic fusion power unit.

He looked up from the chess problem—White to play and mate in three moves—that he was trying to work out. (The boat, of course, was well stocked with such recreational facilities as require little stowage space—but Una Freeman did not play chess and was capable of participation in only the most childish card games.) The girl looked down at him. She was naked save for the magnetic-soled sandals that she had found in the boat's gear locker. (She and Grimes had taken off their spacesuits when they realized that they would not be leaving the boat for quite some while—and then, having shed their longjohns, the standard underwear with space armor, had decided that there was no point in resuming this rather ugly clothing until they had to. Apart from anything else, it would be subjected to needless wear and tear, and they would be wanting it when they put on their suits again.) She was a splendid creature, especially in free fall conditions. Her lustrous, dark brown hair floated in waves about her strong featured, handsome rather than merely pretty face. In a gravitational field or under acceleration her full breasts must have sagged, if only a little; now they were displayed to their best advantage. But her deeply tanned athlete's body did not need the flattery of zero G environment. She exercised regularly with the facilities provided—a system of heavy springs—and bullied Grimes into doing likewise.

She said, not very warmly, "Dinner, John. Or is it lunch, or breakfast? I'm losing track of time."

He inquired, without much interest, "What's on, Una?"

She replied, "Need you ask? Some of the pinkish goo tastes vaguely of fish. I've tarted it up with chopped algae from the vat." She grimaced, puckering her full lips. "The trouble is that I just can't help remembering what goes into the vat as fertilizer."

"We're getting our own back," said Grimes.

She snorted her distaste. "That's not funny."

No, it wasn't all that funny, although it had been the first time that he said it. To begin with it had all been a glorious game of Adam-and-Eve-in-a-lifeboat, made all the more enjoyable by the certain knowledge that Mummy, as personified by the Federation Survey Service, would soon appear to take them home and give them a proper, hot meal before tucking them into their little beds. But Mummy was one hell of a long time a-coming . . .

Grimes unbuckled himself from his chair, got up and followed the girl to the part of the boat that they had made their dining room. He watched the alluring sway of her dimpled buttocks greedily. He was beginning to understand how some peoples, meat-hungry although otherwise far from starving, have resorted to cannibalism. But he did not, so far as he knew, have any Maori blood in his veins.

There were two plates—plastic, but each with a small, sealed-in magnet—on top of the steel-surfaced folding table. On each plate, adhering to the surface by its own viscosity, was a mound of the pale pink concentrate, specked with green. Sticking up from each heap was a spoon.

She faced him across the table, the unappetizing meal. She made no move to commence eating, and neither did he. Her rather broad face was serious, her wide mouth set in grim lines. Her blue eyes looked at him steadily. She demanded, "John, what is wrong?"

He replied defensively, "A man likes to be alone for some of the time." His prominent ears reddened, although the embarrassed flush did not spread to the rest of his ruggedly unhandsome face—a face, nonetheless, that not a few women had found attractive.

She snapped, "I didn't mean *that*, and you know it. Neither of us wants to live in the other's pockets all the time. . . ."

"What pockets?" asked Grimes innocently.

"Shut up, and let me finish. As far as I'm concerned, lover boy, you can play chess with yourself until you wear the bloody board out. *But what has gone wrong?*"

Plenty, thought Grimes.

"I wish I knew," he admitted.

"You're the spaceman," she told him. "You should know."

Chapter 2

It had all started, not so long ago, at Lindisfarne Base. There Grimes, newly promoted from Lieutenant to Lieutenant Commander, was awaiting his next appointment. Time was hanging rather heavily on his hands, especially since Commander Maggie Lazenby, one of the Survey Service's scientific officers, was away from the Base on some esoteric business of her own. Maggie and Grimes were, in archaic parlance, going steady. Everybody knew about it, so much so that none of the unattached junior female officers, of whom there were quite a few, would have anything to do with Grimes.

To Lindisfarne, by commercial transport, came Sky Marshal Una Freeman. In spite of her grandiloquent title she was no more (and no less) than a policewoman, a member of the Interstellar Federation's newly formed Corps of Sky Marshals. This body had been set up in the hope of doing something about the ever-increasing incidence of skyjacking on the spaceways. The general idea was that the Sky Marshals should travel, incognito, in ships deemed to be threatened by this form of piracy. Now and again, however, one of them would operate under his (or her) true colors.

Such an agent was Una Freeman. She had been sent to Lindisfarne to call upon the not inconsiderable resources of the Survey Service to institute a search for—and, if possible, the salvage of—the skyjacked liner *Delta Geminorum*. This ship had been abandoned in Deep Space after her Master had received, by Carlotti Radio, a bomb threat, and after two small, relatively harmless bombs in the cargo bins had been detonated by remote control as the First and Second Warnings. (The third bomb, the hapless Master was informed, was a well concealed nuclear device.) So everybody, crew and passengers, had taken to the boats and had been picked up eventually by the Dog Star Line's *Borzoi* after suffering no worse than a certain degree of discomfort. The pirates had boarded the ship from their own vessel immediately after her abandonment, stripped her of everything of value and left her with her main engines, inertial drive and the time-and-space-twisting Mannschenn Drive, still running.

She would have remained a needle in a cosmic haystack until such time as her atomic fusion plant failed, with consequent return to the normal continuum, had it not been for the arrest of some members of the pirate crew at Port Southern, on Austral, where they were spending money so freely as to excite the suspicions of the local constabulary. After a preliminary interrogation they were turned over to the F.I.A.— the Federal Investigation Agency—who, when satisfied that the men had been guilty of piracy on more than one occasion, did not hesitate to use the worse-than-lethal (who would want to live out his life span as a mindless vegetable?) brain-draining techniques. From information so obtained from the navigator and the engineer of the pirate ship— data that their conscious minds had long since forgotten—the F.I.A.'s mathematicians were able to extrapolate *Delta Geminorum's* probable, almost certain trajectory. This information was passed on not to the Survey Service, as it should have been, but to the Corps of Sky Marshals. But the Sky Marshals possessed neither ships nor spacemen of their own and so, reluctantly, were obliged to let the F.S.S. into the act.

The Federation Survey Service, however, didn't especially want to play. Its collective pride had been hurt, badly. (How many times had the proud boast—"We are the policemen of the Universe!"—been made? And now here was a *real* police officer stomping around the Base and demanding the Odd Gods of the Galaxy alone knew what in the way of ships, men and equipment.)

Shortly after her disembarkation from the liner *Beta-Puppis* Una Freeman paid her first official call, on the O.I.C. Lindisfarne Base. Had she not been a woman, and an attractive one at that, she would never have gotten to see the Admiral. The old gentleman was courteous and hospitable, seemed to enjoy his chat with her and then passed her on to the Director of Naval Intelligence. The Rear Admiral who held this position despised civilian police forces and their personnel, but thought highly of his own technique in dealing with hostile or potentially hostile female agents. This involved an intimate supper in his quite luxurious quarters, where he kept a remarkably well-stocked bar, with soft lights and sweet music and all the rest of it. Now and again in the past it might have worked, but it did not work with Una Freeman. She emerged from the tussle with her virtue if not her clothing intact, and a strong suspicion that she could expect little or no cooperation from the Intelligence Branch.

She saw the Admiral again, and was passed on to the Director of Transport, a mere Commodore. He made one or two vague promises, and passed her on to his Deputy Director.

So it went on.

Meanwhile, she had been made an honorary member of one of the officers' messes and had been given accommodation in the B.O.Q. (Female). The other members of the mess made it plain that she was far from being a welcome guest. Had she not been a Sky Marshal she would have been, as any attractive woman would be at a Naval Base. But the feeling was there—not voiced openly but all too obvious— that she was an outsider sent to teach the Survey Service its business.

One night, after a lonely dinner, she went into the lounge to browse through the magazines from a score of worlds. The room was unoccupied save for an officer—she saw from his braid that he was a Lieutenant Commander—similarly engaged. He looked up from the table as she came in. His smile made his rugged face suddenly attractive. "Ah," he said, "Miss Freeman. . . ."

"In person, singing and dancing," she replied a little sourly. Then, bluntly, "Why aren't you out playing with the rest of the boys and girls, Commander?"

"Some games," he said, "bore me. I'd sooner read a good book than watch two teams of muddied oafs chasing a ball up and down the field. It means nothing in my young life if the Marines or the Supply Branch win the Lindisfarne Cup."

"A *good* book?" she asked, looking down at the glossy magazine that lay open on the table.

His prominent ears reddened. "Well, it's educational. Quite remarkable how the people of some of the earlier colonies have diverged from what we regard as the physiological norm. And to some men that extra pair of breasts could be very attractive."

"And to you, Commander . . . ?"

"Grimes, John Grimes."

She laughed. "I've heard about you, Commander Grimes. Now and again people do condescend to talk to me. You're the one who's always getting into trouble—getting out of it. . . ."

Grimes chuckled. "Yes, I do have that reputation. As you may have guessed, at times I'm not overly popular."

"Shake," she said, extending a long, capable hand. "That makes two of us."

"I think that this founding of the Pariahs' Union calls for a drink," he told her, pressing the button for the robowaiter. The machine trundled in. He asked her what she wanted, pushed the stud for two Scotch whiskies on the rocks. He scrawled his signature on the acceptance plate.

She took her drink and said gravely, "Rear Admiral James has a much greater variety in *his* bar."

"He's an admiral. The senior members of this mess are only lieutenant commanders. After all, rank has its privileges."

"There's one privilege that rank didn't have." She sipped from her glass. "I suppose that that's why I'm one of the local untouchables. All you junior officers are scared of getting into James's bad books if you succeed where he failed."

Grimes looked at the girl over the rim of his tumbler. He wouldn't mind succeeding, he thought. She was a mite hefty, perhaps—but that could be regarded as quantity and quality wrapped up in the same parcel. On the other hand—what if she made violent objections to any attempt at a pass? The unfortunate Rear Admiral was still walking with a pronounced limp. . . . And what about Maggie? Well, what about her? She was little more—or more than a little, perhaps—than just a good friend. But what she didn't know about wouldn't worry her.

She said, "One newly minted Federation zinc alloy cent for them."

He was conscious of his burning ears. He said, "They're not worth it."

"You insult me, Commander. Or, if you'd rather, John. You were thinking about me, weren't you?"

"Actually, yes, Una."

"Just a fool wanting to rush in where Rear Admirals, having learned by bitter experience, fear to tread."

"Frankly," he told her, "I am tempted to rush in. But you've no idea of the amount of gossip there is around this Base. If I as much as kissed you the very guard dogs would be barking it around the top secret installations within half an hour."

"Faint heart . . ." she scoffed.

"But you're not fair. You're a brunette." He added, "A very attractive one."

"Thank you, sir." She sat down in one of the deep, hide-covered chairs, affording him a generous glimpse of full thighs as her short skirt rode up. She said abruptly, "I think you can help me."

"How?" And then, to show that he could be as hard as the next man, "Why?"

"Why?" she exploded. "*Why?* Because you brass-bound types are supposed to be as much guardians of law and order as we lowly policemen and policewomen. Because unless somebody around here dedigitates, and fast, putting a ship at my disposal, *Delta Geminorum* is going to whiffle past Lindisfarne, a mere couple of light months distant, three standard weeks from now. If I don't intercept the bitch, I've lost her. And what is your precious Survey Service doing about it? Bugger all, that's what!"

"It's not so simple," said Grimes slowly. "Interservice jealousy comes into it, of course. . . ."

"Don't I know it! Don't I bloody well know it! *And* male chauvinism. When *are* you people going to grow up and admit that women are at least as capable as men?"

"But we already have two lady admirals. . . ."

"Supply—" she sneered, making a dirty word of it. "Psychiatry—" she added, making it sound even dirtier. "All right, all right. This is a *man's* service. I have to accept that—reluctantly. But I think that *you* could help. You've been in command, haven't you? Your last appointment was as captain of a Serpent Class courier. Such a little ship would be ideal for the job. Couldn't you get your *Adder*—that was her name, wasn't it?—back and go out after *Delta Geminorum?*"

"We can't do things that way in the Survey Service," said Grimes stiffly. He thought, *I wish that we could. Once aboard the lugger and the girl is mine, and all that. Aboard my own ship I could make a pass at her. Here, in the Base, old James'd never forgive me if I did, and succeeded. Mere two-and-a-half-ringers just can't afford to antagonize rear admirals—not if they want any further promotion. . . .*

"Couldn't you see Commodore Damien, the O.I.C. Couriers?"

"Mphm . . ." grunted Grimes dubiously. During his tour of duty in *Adder* the Commodore had become his *bête noir*, just as he had become the Commodore's.

"He might give you your command back."

"That," stated Grimes definitely, "would be the sunny Friday! In any case, I'm no longer under Commodore Damien's jurisdiction. When I got my promotion from lieutenant to lieutenant commander he threw me into the Officers' Pool. No, not the sort you swim in. The sort you loaf around in waiting for somebody to find you a job. I might get away as senior watchkeeper or, possibly, executive officer in a Constellation Class cruiser—or, with my command experience, I might be appointed to something smaller as captain. I hope it's the latter."

"A Serpent Class courier," she said.

"I'm afraid not. They're *little* ships, and never have anybody above the rank of lieutenant as captain. Commodore Damien saw my promotion as a golden opportunity for getting rid of me."

"You can see him. He might give you your command back."

"Not a hope in hell."

"You can ask him. After all, he can't shoot you."

"But wouldn't he just like to!" *Even so, why not give it a go?* Grimes asked himself. *After all, he can't shoot me. And he did say, the last time that I ran into him, that he was sick and tired of seeing me hanging around the Base like a bad smell.* . . . He said aloud, "All right. I'll see the Commodore tomorrow morning."

"*We* will see the Commodore tomorrow morning," she corrected him.

She ignored his offer of assistance, pulled herself up out of the deep chair. She allowed him to walk her back to the B.O.Q. (Female). It was a fine night, warm and clear, with Lindisfarne's two moons riding high in the black, star-strewn sky. It was a night for romantic dalliance—and surely Rear Admiral James would not sink so low as to have spies out to watch Una Freeman. But she resisted, gently but firmly, Grimes' efforts to steer her toward the little park, with its smooth, springy grass and sheltering clumps of trees. She permitted him a good-night kiss at the door to her lodgings—and it was one of those kisses that promise more, much more. He tried to collect a further advance payment but a quite painful jab from a stiff, strong finger warned him not to persist.

But there would be time, plenty of time, later, to carry things through to their right and proper—or improper—conclusion. It all depended on that crotchety old bastard Damien.

When Grimes retired for the night he was feeling not unhopeful.

Chapter 3

Apart from a baleful glare Commodore Damien ignored Grimes. His eyes, bright in his skull-like face, regarded Una steadily over his skeletal, steepled fingers. He asked, pleasantly enough for him, "And what can *I* do for you, Miss Freeman?"

She replied tartly, "I've seen everybody else, Commodore."

Damien allowed himself a strictly rationed dry chuckle. He remarked, "You must have realized by this time that *our* masters do not like *your* masters. Apart from anything else, they feel, most strongly, that you people are trespassing on our territory. But there are wheels within wheels, and all sorts of dickering behind the scenes, and the Admiralty—albeit with a certain reluctance—has let it be known that a degree of cooperation on our part with you, personally, will not be frowned upon too heavily. His Nibs received a Carlottigram last night from the First Lord, to that effect. He passed the buck to Intelligence. Intelligence, for some reason known only to itself—" again there was the dry chuckle and the suggestion of a leer on Damien's face— "passed the buck to O.I.C. Couriers. Myself."

"Nobody told me!" snapped the girl.

The Commodore bared his long, yellow teeth. "You've been told now, Miss Freeman." He waited for her to say something in reply, but she remained silent and darkly glowering. "Unfortunately I have no couriers available at the moment. None, that is, to place at your full disposal. However. . . ."

"Go on, Commodore."

"I am not a suspect whom you are interrogating, young lady. I have been *requested* rather than ordered by my superiors to render you whatever assistance lies within my unfortunately limited power. It so happens that the Lizard Class courier *Skink* will be lifting from Base in four days' time, carrying dispatches and other assorted bumfodder to Olgana. You may take passage in her if you so desire."

"But I don't want to go to Olgana. You people have been furnished with the elements of *Delta Geminorum*'s extrapolated trajectory. My orders are to board her, with a prize crew, and bring her in to port."

"I am aware of that, Miss Freeman. The captain of *Skink* will have *his* orders too. They will be, firstly, to carry such additional personnel as will be required for your prize crew and, secondly, to make whatever deviation from trajectory is required to put the prize crew aboard the derelict."

"And will John be the captain of this . . . this *Skink?*"

"John?" Damien registered bewilderment. "John?" Then slow comprehension dawned. "Oh, you mean young Grimes, here. No, John will not be commanding any vessels under my jurisdiction. I honestly regret having to disappoint you, Miss Freeman, but *Skink* is Lieutenant Commander Delamere's ship."

Delamere, thought Grimes disgustedly. *Handsome Frankie Delamere, who could make a living posing for Survey Service recruiting posters. . . . And that's about all that he's fit for—that and screwing anything in skirts that comes his way. Good-bye, Una. It was nice knowing you.*

Damien switched his regard to Grimes. "And you are still unemployed, Lieutenant Commander," he stated rather than asked.

"Yes, sir."

"It distresses me to have to watch officers doing nothing and getting paid for it, handsomely." *So he's giving me* Skink *after all,* thought Grimes. *I did hear that Delamere was overdue for leave.* Damien went on, "Unfortunately, you passed out of my immediate ambit on your promotion to your present rank." *That's right. Rub it in, you sadistic old bastard!* Grimes' spirits, temporarily raised, were plummeting again. "However, I am on quite amicable terms with Commodore Brownrigg, of the Appointments Bureau." He raised a skinny hand. "No, I am not, repeat and underscore *not*, going to give you another command under my jurisdiction. I learned my lesson, all too well, during that harrowing period when you were captain of *Adder*. But somebody—preferably somebody with spacegoing command experience, has to be in charge of the prize crew. I shall press for your appointment to that position." He grinned nastily and added, "After all, whatever happens will have nothing to do with *me*."

"Thank you, sir," said Grimes.

"You haven't got the job yet," Damien told him.

After they had left the Commodore's office Una said, "But he must like you, John. You told me that he hated your guts."

"Oh, he does, he does. But he hates Frankie Delamere's guts still more."

"Then how is it that this Delamere is still one of his courier captains?"

"Because," Grimes told her, "dear Frankie knows all the right people. Including the Admiral's *very* plain daughter."

"Oh."

"Precisely," said Grimes.

Chapter 4

All navies find it necessary to maintain several classes of vessel. The Federation Survey Service had its specialized ships, among which were the couriers. These were relatively small (in the case of the Insect Class, definitely small) spacecraft, analagous to the dispatch boats of the seaborne navies of Earth's past. There were the already mentioned Insect Class, the Serpent Class (one of which Grimes had commanded) and the Lizard Class. The one thing that all three classes had in common was speed. The Insect Class couriers were little more than long range pinnaces, whereas the Lizard Class ships were as large as corvettes, but without a corvette's armament, and with far greater cargo and passenger carrying capacity than the Serpent Class vessels.

Skink was a typical Lizard Class courier. She carried a crew of twenty, including the commanding officer. She had accommodation for twenty-five passengers—or, with the utilization of her cargo spaces for living freight, seventy-five. Her main engines comprised inertial drive and Mannschenn Drive, with auxiliary reaction drive. Her armament consisted of one battery of laser cannon together with the usual missiles and guidance system. She would have been capable of fighting another ship of the same class; anything heavier she could show a clean pair of heels to.

Lieutenant Commander Delamere did not expect to have to do any fighting—or running—on this perfectly routine paper run to Olgana. He was more than a little annoyed when he was told by Commodore Damien that there would have to be a deviation from routine. He had his private reasons for wishing to make a quick passage; after a week or so of the company of the Admiral's plain, fat daughter he wanted

a break, a change of bedmates. There was one such awaiting him at
his journey's end.

"Sir," he asked Commodore Damien in a pained voice, "*Must* I
act as chauffeur to this frosty-faced female fuzz?"

"You must, Delamere."

"But it will put at least three days on to my passage."

"You're a spaceman, aren't you?" Damien permitted himself a
slight sneer. "Or supposed to be one."

"But, sir. A policewoman. Aboard *my* ship."

"A Sky Marshal, Lieutenant Commander. Let us accord the lady
her glamorous title. Come to that, she's not unglamorous herself . . ."

"Rear Admiral James doesn't think so, sir. He told me about her
when I picked up the Top Secret bumf from his office. He said, 'Take
that butch trollop out of here, and never bring her back!' "

"Rear Admiral James is . . . er . . . slightly biased. Do you mean to
tell me that you have never met Miss Freeman?"

"No, sir. My time has been fully occupied by my duties."

Commodore Damien stared up at the tall, fair-haired young man
in sardonic wonderment until Delamere, who had a hide like a rhi-
noceros, blushed. He said, "She must keep you on a tight leash."

"I don't understand what you mean, sir."

"Don't you? Oh, skip it, skip it. Where was I before you obliged
me to become engaged in a discussion of your morals?" Delamere
blushed again. "Oh, yes. Miss Freeman will be taking passage with
you, until such time as you have intercepted the derelict. With her will
be a boarding party of Survey Service personnel, under Lieutenant
Commander Grimes."

"Not Grimes, sir! That Jonah!"

"Jonah or not, Delamere, during his time in command of one of
my couriers there has never been any serious damage to his ship—
which is more than I can say about you. As I was saying, before you
so rudely interrupted, Lieutenant Commander Grimes will be in charge
of the boarding party, which will consist of three spacemen lieutenants,
four engineer lieutenants, one electronic communications officer, six
petty officer mechanics, one petty officer cook and three wardroom
attendants."

"Doing himself proud, isn't he, sir?"

"He and his people will have to get a derelict back into proper
working order and bring her in to port. We don't know, yet, what
damage has been done to her by the pirates."

"Very well, sir." Delamere's voice matched his martyred expression. "I'll see to it that accommodation is arranged for all these idlers. After all, I shan't have to put up with them for long."

"One more thing, Delamere. . . ."

"Sir?"

"You'll have to make room in your after hold for a Mark XIV lifeboat. All the derelict's boats were taken when the crew and passengers abandoned ship. Lieutenant Commander Grimes will be using the Mark XIV for his boarding operation, of course, and then keeping it aboard *Delta Geminorum*. Grimes, of course, will be in full charge during the boarding and until such time as he releases you to proceed on your own occasions. Understood?"

"Yes, sir."

"Then that will be all, Lieutenant Commander."

Delamere put on his cap, sketched a vague salute and strode indignantly out of the office. Damien chuckled and muttered, "After all, he's not the Admiral's son-in-law *yet*. . . ."

Grimes and Una stood on the apron looking up at *Skink*.

She wasn't a big ship, but she looked big to Grimes after his long tour of duty in the little *Adder*. She was longer, and beamier. She could never be called, as the Serpent Class couriers were called, a "flying darning needle." A cargo port was open in her shining side, just forward of and above the roots of the vanes that comprised her tripedal landing gear. Hanging in the air at the same level was a lifeboat, a very fat cigar of burnished metal, its inertial drive muttering irritably. Grimes hoped that the Ensign piloting the thing knew what he was doing, and that Delamere's people, waiting inside the now-empty after hold, knew what they were doing. If that boat were damaged in any way he would be extremely reluctant to lift off from Lindisfarne. He said as much.

"You're fussy, John," Una told him.

"A good spaceman has to be fussy. There won't be any boats aboard the derelict, and anything is liable to go wrong with her once we've taken charge and are on our own. That Mark XIV could well be our only hope of survival."

She laughed. "If that last bomb blows up after we're aboard, a lifeboat won't be much use to us."

"You're the bomb-disposal expert. You see to it that it doesn't go off."

Delamere, walking briskly, approached them. He saluted Una, ignored Grimes. "Coming aboard, Miss Freeman? We shall be all ready to lift off as soon as that boat's inboard."

"I'll just wait here with John," she said. "He wants to see the boat safely into the ship."

"My officers are looking after it, Grimes," said Delamere sharply.

"But *I've* signed for the bloody thing!" Grimes told him.

The boat nosed slowly through the circular port, vanished. For a few seconds the irregular beat of its inertial drive persisted, amplified by the resonance of the metal compartment. Then it stopped. There was no tinny crash to tell of disaster.

"Satisfied?" sneered Delamere.

"Not quite. I shall want to check on its stowage."

"All right. If you insist," snarled Delamere. He then muttered something about old women that Grimes didn't quite catch.

"It's *my* boat," he said quietly.

"And it's being carried in *my* ship."

"Shall we be getting aboard?" Una asked sweetly.

They walked up the ramp to the after airlock. It was wide enough to take only two people walking abreast in comfort. Grimes found himself bringing up the rear. *Let Frankie-boy have his little bit of fun*, he thought tolerantly. He was confident that he would make out with Una; it was now only a question of the right place and the right time. He did not think that she would be carried away by a golden-haired dummy out of a uniform tailor's shop window. On the other hand, Delamere's ship would not provide the right atmosphere for his own campaign of conquest. Not that it mattered much. He would soon have a ship of his own, a *big* ship. Once aboard the derelict *Delta Geminorum* people would no longer have to live in each other's pockets.

Grimes stopped off at the after hold to see to the stowage of his boat while Una and Delamere stayed in the elevator that carried them up the axial shaft to the captain's quarters. The small craft was snugly nested into its chocks, secured with strops and sliphooks. Even if Delamere indulged in the clumsy aerobatics, for which he was notorious, on his way up through the atmosphere the boat should not shift.

While he was talking with two of his own officers—they, like himself, had an interest in the boat—the warning bell for lift-off stations started to ring.

"Frankie's getting upstairs in a hurry!" muttered one of *Skink*'s lieutenants sourly. "Time we were in our acceleration couches."

And time I was in the control room, thought Grimes. This wasn't his ship, of course, but it was customary for a captain to invite a fellow captain up to Control for arrivals and departures.

THE BROKEN CYCLE   19

"We haven't been shown to our quarters yet, sir," said one of Grimes' officers.

"Neither have I, Lieutenant, been shown to mine." He turned to the ship's officer. "Where are we berthed?"

"I . . . I don't know, sir. And once the Old Man has started his count-down the Odd Gods of the Galaxy Themselves couldn't stop him!"

"Don't let us keep you, Lieutenant," Grimes told him. "Off you go, tuck yourself into your own little cot. *We'll* manage."

"But *how*, sir?" demanded Grimes' officer. "We can't just stretch out on the *deck* . . ."

"Use your initiative, Lieutenant. We've a perfectly good ship's boat here, with well-sprung couches. Get the airlock door open, and look snappy!"

He and his two officers clambered into the boat. The bunks were comfortable enough. They strapped themselves in. Before the last clasp had been snapped tight *Skink*'s inertial drive started up—and (it seemed) before the stern vanes were more than ten millimeters from the apron the auxiliary reaction drive was brought into play. It was the sort of showy lift-off, with absolutely unnecessary use of rocket power, of which Grimes himself had often been guilty. When anybody else did it—Delamere especially—he disapproved strongly. He could just imagine Frankie showing off in front of his control room guest, Una Freeman. . . .

Oh, well, he thought philosophically as the acceleration pushed him down into the padding, *at least we're giving the mattresses a good test. I don't suppose that they'll be used again. . . . A long boat voyage is the very least of my ambitions.*

Skink thundered up through the atmosphere and, at last, the drive was cut. Grimes and his two companions remained in their couches until trajectory had been set, until the high keening of the Mannschenn drive told them that they were on their way to intercept the derelict.

Chapter 5

Skink was not a happy ship.

The average spaceman doesn't mind his captain's being a bastard as long as he's an efficient bastard. Frankie Delamere was not efficient. Furthermore, he was selfish. He regarded the vessel as his private yacht. Everything had to be arranged for *his* personal comfort.

Skink was an even unhappier ship with the passengers whom she was carrying. To begin with, Delamere seemed to be under the impression that the medieval *droit du seigneur* held good insofar as he was concerned. Una did her best to disillusion him. She as good as told him that if she was going to sleep with anybody—and it was a large *if*—it would be with Grimes. Thereupon Frankie made sure that opportunities for this desirable consummation were altogether lacking. Some of his people, those who respected the rank if not the man, those who were concerned about their further promotion, played along with the captain. "One thing about Delamere's officers," complained Grimes, "is that they have an absolute genius for being where they're not wanted!"

Apart from sexual jealousy, Delamere did not like Grimes, never had liked Grimes, and Grimes had never liked him. He could not go too far—after all, Grimes held the same rank as did he—but he contrived to make it quite clear that his fellow Lieutenant Commander was *persona non grata* in the courier's control room. Then—as was his right, but one that he was not obliged to exercise—he found totally unnecessary but time-consuming jobs for the members of the boarding party, snapping that he would tolerate no idlers aboard his ship.

He, himself, was far from idle. He was working hard—but, Grimes noted with grim satisfaction, getting nowhere. He was always asking

Una Freeman up to his quarters on the pretext of working out proce-
dures for the interception of the derelict—and there he expected her
to help him work his way through his not inconsiderable private stock
of hard liquor. Grimes had no worries on this score. Her capacity for
strong drink, he had learned, was greater than his, and his was greater
than Delamere's. And there was the black eye that the captain tried to
hide with talcum powder before coming into the wardroom for dinner
and—a day or so later—the scratches on his face that were even more
difficult to conceal. Too, Una—on the rare occasions that she found
herself alone with Grimes—would regale him with a blow by blow
account of the latest unsuccessful assault on the body beautiful.

Grimes didn't find it all that amusing.

"The man's not fit to hold a commission!" he growled. "Much less
to be in command. Make an official complaint to me—after all, I'm
the senior officer aboard this ship after himself—and I'll take action!"

"What will you do?" she scoffed. "Call a policeman? Don't forget
that I'm a policewoman—with the usual training in unarmed combat.
I've been gentle with him so far, John. But if he tried anything nasty
he'd wind up in the sick bay with something broken. . . ."

"Or out of the airlock wrapped up in the Survey Service flag . . ."
he suggested hopefully.

"Even that. Although I'd have some explaining to do then."

"I'd back you up."

"Uncommonly decent of you, Buster. But I can look after myself—
as Frankie boy knows, and as you'd better remember!"

"Is that a threat?"

"It could be," she told him. "It just could be."

For day after day *Skink* fell through the immensities, through the
Continuum warped by the temporal precession field of her Mannschenn Drive. As seen from her control room the stars were neither
points of light nor appreciable discs, but pulsing spirals of iridescence.
For day after day the screen of the mass proximity indicator was a
sphere of unrelieved blackness—but Delamere's navigator, an extremely competent officer, was not worried. He said, "If the F.I.A.
mathematicians got their sums right—and I've heard that they're quite
good at figuring—*Delta Geminorum* is still well outside the maximum
range of our MPI."

"Damn it all!" snarled his Captain. "We're wasting time on this
wild goose chase. We should be well on our way to Olgana by now,
not chauffering the civilian fuzz all round the bleeding Galaxy!"

"I thought you *liked* Miss Freeman, sir," observed the navigator innocently.

"Keep your thoughts to yourself, Lieutenant!"

"If *my* sums have come out right, we should pick up the derelict at about 0630 hours, ship's time, tomorrow."

"Your sums had better come out right!" snarled Delamere.

Reluctantly, Delamere asked Grimes up to the control room at the time when the first sighting was expected. He made it plain that he did so only because the other was to be in charge of the boarding operations. He growled, "You're supposed to be looking after this part of it. Just try not to waste too much of my time."

"Your time," said Grimes, "belongs to the Survey Service, as mine does. And it's all being paid for with the taxpayer's money."

"Ha, ha."

"Ha, ha."

The officers, and Una Freeman, looked on with interest. Una remarked that having two captains in the same control room was worse than having two women in the same kitchen. The watch officer, an ensign, sniggered. *Either a very brave or a very foolish young man*, thought Grimes.

"And where's your bloody derelict, Mr. Ballantyre?" Delamere snarled at his navigator. "I make the time coming up to 0633."

"It's been showing in the screen, sir, at extreme range, for the last three minutes. Just the merest flicker, and not with every sweep, but a ship's a small target. . . ."

Pushing his officers rudely aside Delamere went to the MPI, staring down into the sphere of blackness. Grimes followed him. Yes, there it was, an intermittently glowing spark, at green eighty-three, altitude seventeen negative.

"Extrapolate, please, Mr. Ballantyre," he said.

"This is not your control room, Mr. Grimes," said Delamere.

"But I am in charge of the boarding operations, Mr. Delamere," said Grimes.

"All right, if you want to be a space lawyer!" Delamere went off in a huff—not that he could go very far—and slumped down in one of the acceleration chairs.

Ballantyre extrapolated. From the center of the screen a very fine gleaming filament extended, and another one from the target. It was obvious that the two ships would pass each other many kilometers distant.

"Mphm." Grimes produced his pipe, filled and lit it.

"I don't allow smoking in my control room," growled Delamere.

"I'm in charge now, as you, yourself, have admitted. And I *always* wear a pipe when I'm engaged in shiphandling."

"Let the baby have his dummy!" sneered the other.

Grimes ignored this. He said to Ballantyre, "You know this ship better than I do. Adjust our trajectory so that we're on a converging course, and overtaking. . . ."

The navigator looked inquiringly at his captain, who growled, "Do as the man says."

The Mannschenn Drive was shut down, but the inertial drive remained in operation. There were the brief seconds of temporal disorientation, with distorted outlines and all colors sagging down the spectrum, with all the shipboard sounds echoing oddly and eerily. Grimes, looking at Una, realized that he was—or would be, some time in the not too distant future—seeing her naked. This made sense of a sort. Flashes of precognition are not uncommon when the interstellar drive is started up or shut down. But she was not only completely unclothed, but riding a bicycle. That made no sense at all.

Gyroscopes rumbled, hummed as the ship was turned about her short axis, as the adjustment to trajectory was made. In the screen the extrapolated courses looked as Grimes desired them to look. "Mphm. Very good, Mr. Ballantyre. Now—chase and board!"

"I'm afraid I can't lend you any cutlasses, Grimes," said Delamere sardonically. "Or did you bring your own with you?"

"Might I suggest, Lieutenant Commander, that we not waste time with airy persiflage? After all, you were the one who was saying how precious his time is. . . ."

Again there was temporal disorientation as the Mannschenn Drive was restarted. Grimes hoped for another glimpse of the future Una, but was disappointed. The only impression was of an intensely bright white light, too bright, almost, to be seen.

Grimes left things very much in the hands of Delamere's navigator. The young man obviously knew just what he was doing. With a minimum of fuss he got *Skink* running parallel with *Delta Geminorum*, with both actual speed and temporal precession rates exactly synchronized. With the synchronization the derelict was visible now, both visually and in the radar screen. At a range of five kilometers she could be examined in detail through the big, mounted binoculars, their lenses sensitive to all radiation, in the courier's control room. She looked innocent enough, a typical Delta Class liner of the Interstellar Transport Commission, floating against a background of blackness and the shimmering nebulosities that were the stars. She seemed to be undamaged, but an after airlock door was open. The pirates, thought Grimes, hadn't been very well brought up; nobody had taught them to shut doors after them. . . .

"I'll take over now," said Delamere. "After all, this is *my* ship, Lieutenant Commander."

"Oh, yes, I'd almost forgotten," said Grimes. "And what are your intentions, Lieutenant Commander?"

"I'm going to make things easy for you, Grimes. I'm going to lay *Skink* right alongside *Delta Geminorum.*"

Just the sort of flashy spacemanship that would appeal to you, thought Grimes.

"Are you mad?" asked Una Freeman coldly.

Delamere flushed. "I'm not mad. And you, Miss Freeman, are hardly qualified to say your piece regarding matters of spacemanship."

"Perhaps not, Commander Delamere. But I *am* qualified to say my piece regarding bomb disposal."

"Bomb disposal?"

"Yes. Bomb disposal. If you'd bothered to run through the report I gave you to read—and that Commander Grimes *did* read—you would know that there is a fully armed thermonuclear device still aboard that vessel. Unluckily none of the pirates who were arrested and brain-drained knew much about it. We did learn that the signal to detonate it was sent shortly after the pirates had returned safely to their own ship—but, for some reason, nothing happened. Nobody was at all keen to return aboard *Delta Geminorum* to find out why. . . . That bomb, Commander, is a disaster waiting to happen. It is quite probable that the inevitable jolt when you put your vessel alongside the derelict would be enough to set it off."

"So what do you intend to do?" asked Delamere stiffly.

"I suggest that you maintain your present station on *Delta Geminorum*; Commander Grimes and I will take a boat to board her. Then I shall defuse the bomb."

"All right," growled Delamere at last. "All right. Mr. Ballantyre, maintain station on the derelict." He turned to his First Lieutenant. "Mr. Tarban, have Lieutenant Commander Grimes' boat ready for ejection." He added, addressing nobody in particular, "I don't see why I should risk one of *my* boats. . . ." He addressed Grimes. "I hope you enjoy the trip. Better you than me, Buster!"

"I have the utmost confidence in Miss Freeman's abilities, Frankie," Grimes told him sweetly.

Delamere snarled wordlessly.

Una Freeman said, "You're the expert, John—for the first part of it, anyhow. Shall we require spacesuits?"

"Too right we shall," said Grimes. "To begin with, Mr. Tarban has probably evacuated the atmosphere from the after hold by now. And we don't know whether or not there's any atmosphere inside the derelict or if it's breathable. We'd better get changed."

Before he left the control room he went to the binoculars for the last look at the abandoned liner. She looked innocent enough, a great, dull-gleaming torpedo shape. Suddenly she didn't look so innocent. The word "torpedo" has long possessed a sinister meaning.

Chapter 6

Everything was ready in the after hold when Grimes and Una got down there. The lashings had been removed from the boat and its outer airlock door was open. The inertial drive was ticking over, and somebody had started the mini-Mannschenn, synchronizing its temporal precession rates to those of the much bigger interstellar drive units in *Skink* and *Delta Geminorum*. A cargo port in the ship's side had been opened, and through it the liner was visible.

"She's all yours, sir," said the First Lieutenant.

"Thank you," replied Grimes.

Delamere's irritated voice came through the helmet phones, "Stow the social chit-chat, Mr. Tarban. We've wasted enough time already!"

"Shut up, Frankie!" snapped Una Freeman.

Grimes clambered into the boat, stood in the chamber of the little airlock. Una passed up a bag of tools and instruments. He put it down carefully by his feet, then helped the girl inboard. He pressed a stud, and the outer door shut, another stud and the inner door opened.

He went forward, followed by Una. He lowered himself into the pilot's seat. She took the co-pilot's chair. He ran a practiced eye over the control panel. All systems were GO.

"Officer commanding boarding party to officer commanding *Skink*," he said into his helmet microphone, "request permission to eject."

"Eject!" snarled Delamere.

"He might have wished us good luck," remarked Una.

"He's glad to see the back of us," Grimes told her.

"You can say that again!" contributed Delamere.

Grimes laughed as nastily as he could manage, then his gloved fingers found and manipulated the inertial drive controls. The little engine clattered tinnily but willingly. The boat was clear, barely clear of the chocks and sliding forward. She shot out through the open port, and Grimes made the small course correction that brought the liner dead ahead, and kept her there. She seemed to expand rapidly as the distance was covered.

"Careful," warned Una. "This is a boat we're in, not a missile. . . ."

"No back seat driving!" laughed Grimes.

Nonetheless, he adjusted trajectory slightly so that it would be a near miss and not a direct hit. At the last moment he took the quite considerable way off the boat by applying full reverse thrust. She creaked and shuddered, but held together. Una said nothing, but Grimes could sense her disapproval. Come to that, he had his own disapproval to contend with. He realized that he was behaving with the same childish flashiness that Frankie Delamere would have exhibited.

He orbited the spaceship. On the side of her turned away from *Skink* the cargo ports were still open. It all looked very unspacemanlike—but why bother to batten down when the ship is going to be destroyed minutes after you have left her? She hadn't been destroyed, of course, but she should have been, would have been if some firing device had not malfunctioned.

He said, "I'll bring us around to the after airlock. Suit you?"

"Suits me. But be careful, John. Don't forget that there's an armed bomb aboard that ship. Anything, anything at all, could set it off."

"Yes, teacher. I'll be careful, very careful. I'll come alongside so carefully that I wouldn't crack the proverbial egg." He reached out for the microphone of the Carlotti transceiver; at this distance from the courier, with Mannschenn Drive units in operation, the N.S.T. suit radios were useless. He would have to inform Frankie Delamere and his own officers of progress to date and of his intentions. With his chin he nudged the stud that would cause the faceplate of his helmet to flip open. His thumb pressed the TRANSMIT button.

And then it happened.

Aboard the ship, for many, many months, the miniaturized Carlotti receiver had been waiting patiently for the signal that, owing to some infinitesimal shifting of frequencies, had never come. The fuse had been wrongly set, perhaps, or some vibration had jarred it from its original setting, quite possibly the shock initiated by the explosion of either of the two warning bombs. And now here was a wide-band transmitter at very close range.

Circuits came alive, a hammer fell on a detonator, which exploded, in its turn exploding the driving charge. One sub-critical mass of fissionable material was impelled to contact with another sub-critical mass, with the inevitable result.

As a bomb it lacked the sophistication of the weaponry of the armed forces of the Federation—but it worked.

Grimes, with the dreadful reality blinding him, remembered his prevision of the light too bright to be seen. He heard somebody (Una? himself?) scream. This was It. This was all that there would ever be. He was a dead leaf caught in the indraught of a forest fire, whirling down and through the warped dimensions to the ultimate, blazing Nothingness.

Chapter 7

She said, "But we shouldn't be alive . . ."

He said, "But we are." He added, glumly, "But for how long? This boat must be as radioactive as all hell. I suppose that it was *the* bomb that went off."

"It was," she told him. "But there's no radioactivity. I've tested. There is a counter in my bomb disposal kit."

He said, "It must be on the blink."

"It's not. It registers well enough with all the normal sources— my wristwatch, against the casing of the fusion power unit, and so on."

He said doubtfully, "I suppose we *could* have been thrown clear. Or we were in some cone of shadow. . . . Yes, that makes sense. We were toward the stern of the ship, and the shielding of her power plant must have protected us."

She asked, "What now?"

Grimes stared through the viewports of the control cabin. There was no sign of *Skink*. There was no sign of any wreckage from *Delta Geminorum*. The stars shone bright and hard in the blackness; the mini-Mannschenn had stopped and the boat was adrift in the normal Continuum.

He said, "We stay put."

She said, "Shouldn't Delamere be sniffing around to pick up the pieces?"

"Delamere's sure that there aren't any pieces," he told her, "just as I should be sure if I were in his shoes. And, in any case, he's in a hurry to get to Olgana. He *knows* we're dead, vaporized. But he'll have used his Carlotti to put in a report to Base, giving the coordinates of the scene of the disaster. When anything of this kind happens a ship full of experts is sent at once to make an investigation." He laughed. "And won't they be surprised when they find us alive and kicking!"

"Can't we use our radio to tell them?"

"We can't raise *Skink* on the N.S.T. transmitter while she's running on Mannschenn Drive. We can't raise the Base, either. Oh, they'd pick up the signal eventually—quite a few months from now. And you've seen the mess that our Carlotti set is in . . ."

"So we just . . . wait?"

"S.O.P. for shipwrecked spacemen," said Grimes. "We haven't a hope in hell of getting anywhere in our lifetimes unless we use Mannschenn Drive—and, looking at the mess the mini-Mannschenn is in, I'd sooner not touch it. We've survived so far. Let's stay that way."

"Couldn't you fix the Carlotti transceiver to let Base know that we're here?"

"I'm not a Carlotti technician, any more than I'm an expert on Mannschenn Drives."

"H'm." She looked around the quite commodious interior of the boat. "Looks like we have to set up housekeeping for a few days, doesn't it? We could be worse off, I suppose. Much worse off. . . . We've food, water, sir, light, heat . . . Talking of heat, I may as well get into something more comfortable . . ."

Grimes, never one to look such a magnificent gift horse in the mouth, helped her off with her spacesuit. She helped him off with his. In the thick underwear that they were wearing under the suits they might just as well still have been armored. She came into his arms willingly enough, but there was no real contact save for mouth to mouth.

She whispered, "I'm still too warm . . ."

He said, "We'd better take our longjohns off, until we want them again. No point in subjecting them to needless wear and tear . . ."

"Are you seducing me, sir?"

"I wouldn't think of it!" lied Grimes.

"I don't believe you, somehow. Oh, John, how good it is to get away from that horrid Base and Frankie's nasty little ship! I feel free, free!" She pulled the zip of her longjohns down to the crotch. Her released breasts thrust out at him, every pubic hair seemed to have a life of its own, to be rejoicing in its freedom from restraint. Grimes smelled the odor of her—animal, pungent—and his body responded. His underwear joined hers, floating in mid-cabin in a tangle of entwining limbs. Within seconds he and the girl were emulating the pose of the clothing that they had discarded. Stirred by the air currents the garments writhed in sympathy with the movements of their owners.

Chapter 8

"The Survey Service looks after its own," said Grimes.

"Then it's high time that it started doing so," she said.

"You can't organize a Search and Rescue Operation in five minutes," he told her.

"All right, all right. We can't expect any help from *Skink*. We've already agreed on that. But Frankie will have informed Base of the destruction of the derelict. In the unlikely event of *Skink*'s having been destroyed herself—*you* said that she was well out of effective range of the explosion—Base will have been wondering why no reports have been coming in from anybody. And how long have we been here now? Over three weeks."

"If the Carlotti transceiver hadn't been smashed . . ." he began. "*And* the mini-Mannschenn. . . ."

"The Normal Space Time transceiver is working—you say, and we hope. Surely by now there'd be *somebody* in this vicinity, sniffing around for wreckage—and not, therefore, running under interstellar drive. Even I know that. How many days did it take from Lindisfarne Base to the interception?"

"Twenty."

"And this is our twenty-third day in this tin coffin. For most of the time we've maintained a continuous NST listening watch as well as putting out distress calls at regular intervals. I suppose somebody might just pick them up a few years from now."

"Space is vast," said Grimes.

"You're telling me, Buster! But surely Delamere was able to give accurate coordinates for the position of the derelict when we boarded her—when we tried to board her, rather—even if he didn't want to risk his own precious hide investigating. . . ."

"We've been over all this before," said Grimes.

"Then we'll go over it again, lover boy."

"Nobody survives a nuclear explosion at Position Zero, as we were," said Grimes.

"Are you trying to suggest that we're dead and in some sort of spaceman's heaven? Ha, ha. It certainly ain't no policewoman's paradise!"

Grimes ignored this. In any case, the double negative made her meaning unclear (he told himself). He went on, "And Delamere had his schedule to maintain. . . ." Even so, Delamere *must* have reported the destruction of *Delta Geminorum* to Base. And Base *must* have dispatched a properly equipped vessel to the scene of the disaster to gather whatever evidence, no matter how little, remained, even though it was only radioactive dust and gases.

But why had the boat, and its occupants, not been reduced to that condition?

She broke into his thoughts, remarking, "As I've said before, I'm not a spaceman."

He looked across the table at her spectacular superstructure. "Insofar as gender is concerned, how very right you are!"

She pointedly ignored this. "I'm not a spaceman, but I do remember some of the things that you people have condescended to tell me, from time to time, about the art and science of astronautics. More than once people have nattered to me about the peculiar consequences of changing the mass of a ship while the Mannschenn Drive is in operation."

"Old spacemen's tales!" scoffed Grimes.

"Really? Then how is it that in every ship that I've traveled in people have regarded that cock-eyed assemblage of precessing gyroscopes with superstitious awe? You're all scared of it. And what about the odd effects when the Drive is started, and the temporal precession field builds up, or when it's stopped, and the field fades? The feeling of *déjà vu* . . . The flashes of precognition. . . ." She started to laugh.

"What's so funny?"

"I had a real beaut aboard *Skink*. I saw you out of uniform. When I saw you for the first time out of uniform, in actuality, it was in this boat. But I'd already seen that scar you have on your right thigh. But that isn't the *funny* part. In my . . . vision you were not only naked, but riding a bicycle. . . ."

"*Very* funny. As a matter of fact I saw you the same way. But bicycles are one article of equipment that this boat doesn't run to."

"All right. Let's forget the bicycles. Maybe some day we'll enjoy a holiday on Arcadia together. I suppose the Arcadians ride bicycles as well as practicing naturalism. But *Delta Geminorum.* . . . She was running under interstellar drive when she blew up. So were we, maintaining temporal synchronization with her."

"Go on."

"I'm only a glorified cop, John, but it's obvious, even to me, that a few thousand tons of mass were suddenly converted into energy in our immediate vicinity. So, Mr. Lieutenant Commander Grimes, where are we?"

Grimes was beginning to feel badly scared. "Or *when* . . . ?" he muttered.

"What the hell do you mean?"

He said, "Brace yourself for yet another lecture on the Mannschenn Drive. The Mannschenn Drive warps the Continuum—the space-time continuum—about the ship that's using it. Putting it very crudely, such a ship is going astern in time while going ahead in space. . . ."

"So. . . . So we could be anywhere. Or anywhen. But you're a navigator. You should be able to find out something from the relative positions of the stars."

"Not so easy," he told her. "The Carlotti transceiver, which can be used for position finding as well as communicating, is bust. We do carry, of course, a Catalogue of Carlotti Beacons—but in these circumstances it's quite useless."

"Especially so," she pointed out, "when we don't even know if there *are* any Carlotti Beacons in this space-time. So, lover boy, what are you doing about it?"

Grimes' prominent ears flushed angrily. She was being unfair. She shared the responsibility for getting them into this mess. She, the bomb-disposal expert, should have warned him of the possible consequences of using a Carlotti transmitter in close proximity to the derelict. He rose from the table haughtily. It was no hardship for him to leave his unfinished meal. He stalked, insofar as this was possible when wearing only magnetic sandals in Free Fall, to the forward end of the boat. He stared out through the control cabin viewports at the interstellar immensities. There was no star that he could identify, no constellation. Had he been made a welcome visitor in *Skink*'s control room he would have known how the stars should look in this sector of Space. As it was.... He shrugged. All that he could be sure of was that they were in *a* universe, not necessarily *the* universe. At least the boat hadn't fallen down some dark crack in the continuum.

He turned away from the port, looked aft. He saw that Una Freeman had taken the broken, battered Carlotti transceiver from the locker in which it had been stowed, was picking up and looking at the pieces intently. *Nude with Moebius Strip*, he thought sardonically.

She waved the twisted antenna at him. "Are you *sure* you can't do anything with this lot?" she demanded.

"Quite sure. I'm not a radio technician."

"Then you can't be sure that it *is* a complete write-off." Her wide, full mouth was capable of quite spectacular sneering. "Get the lead out of your pants, lover boy—not that you're wearing any. You've been having a marvelous holiday for the last three weeks; it's high time that you started work again."

"Mphm?"

"I thought, in my girlish innocence...."

"Ha, ha."

She glared at him. "I thought, in my girlish innocence that all you spacefaring types were men of infinite resource and sagacity, able to make repairs, light years from the nearest yard, with chewing gum and old string. I'd like to see some proof of it."

He said, "I might be able to straighten out the antenna and get it remounted. But the printed circuits are a mess."

She said, "There're soldering irons in the workshop."

"I know. But have you had a good look at those trays?"

"Of course. Trays of circuitry. Since simple soldering seems to he beyond your capabilities...."

"And yours."

"I'm not the skilled, trained, qualified spaceman, lover boy. You are. But let me finish. As a Sky Marshal I had to do quite a few courses on general spacemanship, including Deep Space communications. One of the things I learned was that quite a few circuit trays are interchangeable between NST and Carlotti transceivers. Since it's obvious now that we shall not be needing the NST transceiver—we cannibalize. After that's been done, lover boy, all we have to do is home on the Lindisfarne Beacon."

"And how many years will it take us?" he asked sarcastically.

"Oh, I forgot. After you've fixed the Carlotti set you fix the mini-Mannschenn."

Chapter 9

There was a Radio Technician's Manual in the boat's book locker. Grimes got it out. Unluckily the writer of it had assumed that anybody reading it would possess at least a smattering of knowledge concerning Deep Space radio. Grimes was not such a person. He knew that the Carlotti equipment propagated signals which, somehow, ignored the normal three dimensions of Space and, by taking a shortcut of some kind, arrived at the receiving station, no matter how many light years distant, practically instantaneously. In any ship that he had been in the thing had worked. There had always been fully qualified officers to see that it worked. Had the complete boarding party been in the boat when she pushed off from *Skink* there would have been such an officer among her crew. (But, thought Grimes, had he taken the full boarding party with him he would not have been alone with Una.)

He and the girl puzzled over the text and the diagrams. They could make neither head nor tail of the latter, but they discovered that printed circuit tray #3 of NST transceiver Mark VII could be substituted for tray #1 of Carlotti transceiver Mark IVA, and so on and so on. It began to look as though Una's idea would work.

Before commencing operations he started up the inertial drive. He was not, as yet, going anywhere in particular, but physical work is more easily carried out in a gravitational field—or under acceleration— than in free fall conditions. Then, with Una assisting, he pulled the circuit trays out of the Carlotti set. Number one, obviously, would have to be replaced. That presented no problem. Number two was obviously nonfunctional. Number two from the NST transceiver was the recommended substitute. Number three appeared to be undamaged. Number four was in almost as big a mess as number one—and none of the NST circuits could be used in its stead.

So, soldering it had to be.

Grimes carried the tray to the little workshop that shared space with the boat's power plant and propulsive units, put it on the bench. He had the Manual open at the proper page, thought that he would be able to patch things up. He was a messy solderer and soon discovered that clothing is worn for protection as well as for adornment or motives of prudery. Una—who was annoyingly amused—applied first aid; then Grimes got into his longjohns before continuing.

When he was finished—a few hours and several burns later—the tray still looked a mess, but Grimes was reasonably confident that the circuits were not anywhere shorted. He carried the tray back to the transceiver—which had been set up in its proper position—and slid it carefully into place. He switched on. The pilot lights lit up. There would be neither transmission nor reception, however, until the antenna was remounted and operational.

They had a hasty meal, then returned to the workshop. The antenna was a metal Moebius Strip, oval rather than circular, on a universal bearing which, in turn, was at the head of a driving shaft. The shaft had been snapped just below the bearing, and the antenna itself had been bent out of its elliptical configuration. Fortunately there was among the motor spares a steel rod of circular section and exactly the right diameter. It had to be shortened by about five centimeters, but with the tools available that was no hardship. The broken shaft was removed from the transceiver, the new one shipped. The antenna— back in shape, Grimes hoped—was, on its bearing, secured to the projecting end of the shaft with a set screw.

"Will it work?" asked Una skeptically.

"There's only one way to find out," Grimes told her.

He switched on again, set the Direction Finding controls to HUNT. In theory (and, hopefully, in practice) the aerial array would now automatically line up on the strongest incoming Carlotti signal.

The shaft began to rotate slowly, the Moebius Strip antenna wobbled on its universal bearing. It seemed to be questing as it turned. Abruptly it steadied, although still turning about its long axis. From the speaker came not the Morse sequence of a Beacon but something that sounded like somebody speaking. It was in no language that either of them knew, and the voice did not sound human. Suddenly it stopped, but Grimes had noted relative bearing and altitude.

He looked at Una, his eyebrows raised. She looked at him dubiously.

"Something . . ." he said slowly.

"Not . . . somebody?"

"All right. Somebody. Somebody capable of constructing—or, at least, using—Deep Space communications equipment."

"Should we put out a call now that this contraption's working?"

"No," he decided. He laughed harshly. "I like to see whom I'm talking to before I talk to them. We'll let the direction finder go on hunting for a while. Maybe it will pick up something a little more promising. . . ."

But it did not.

At intervals of exactly twenty-three minutes and fourteen seconds it steadied on the transmission in the unknown language, on the same relative bearing.

Grimes remembered an engineer officer in a big ship in which he had served as a junior watchkeeper. He had watched this gentleman while he overhauled the mini-Mannschenn of one of the cruiser's boats. It had been a job requiring both patience and a remarkably steady hand. After a spindle had slipped out of its bearing for the fifteenth time the specialist had sworn, "Damn it all, I'm an engineer, not a bloody watchsmith!" He then went on to say, "The ship's Mannschenn Drive unit, with all its faults, is a *machine*. This fucking thing's only an instrument!"

He told the little story to Una.

She said, "That's no excuse. Somebody assembled it once. You can assemble it again. Nothing seems to be damaged. It's just a question of getting all the rotors turning and precessing freely."

"Quite simple, in fact."

"Quite simple," she said, ignoring the sarcasm.

"Perhaps you'd like to try."

"I'm a policewoman, not a watchsmith."

"Ha, ha. Now. . . . Get in there, damn you!" *Click.* "That's it."

"You've a little wheel left over," she pointed out. "And you'll have to remove the one you just got in to get it back."

"Not if I precess it . . . so. . . ."

"One of the other rotors has fallen out now."

Then she went away and left him to it, and without his audience he got along much better. At last the reassembled mini-Mannschenn was ready for use. It looked like a complex, glittering toy, an assemblage of tiny, gleaming flywheels, every axle of which was set at an odd angle to all of the others. Once it was started the ever-precessing, ever-tumbling rotors would drag the boat and its crew down and through the dark dimensions, through a warped continuum in which space and time were meaningless concepts. He touched one of the rotors tentatively with a cautious forefinger. It spun on its almost frictionless bearings and the others turned in sympathy. Although there was, as yet, almost no precession, the shining wheels glimmered and winked on the very edge of invisibility.

He called out, "We're in business!"

"Then get the show on the road," retorted Una. "We've been sitting here on our arses, doing sweet fuck all, for too bloody long!"

Grimes used the single directional gyroscope to line the boat up on the last bearing from which the mysterious call had come. Then he switched on the mini-Mannschenn. To judge from the brief temporal disorientation, the sensation of *déjà vu*, the thing was working perfectly.

Chapter 10

At intervals of exactly twenty-three minutes and fourteen seconds the signal continued to come through. It was the same message every time, the same words spoken in the same high-pitched, unhuman voice. *Dizzard waling torpet droo. Contabing blee. Contabing uwar. Contabing dinzin. Waling torpet, waling droo. Tarfelet, tarfelet, tarfelet.* It was in no language that either of them knew or, even, knew about.

There were other signals, weaker, presumably more distant. Some were spoken, in the same or in another unknown language. Some were coded buzzings. The Carlotti transceiver was fitted with a visiscreen, but this was useless. Either these people—whoever they were—did not use visiscreens, or the system they employed used a different principle from that used by humans.

The boat ran on, and on. Soon it became obvious that they were heading for a star, a G type sun. That star would possess a family of planets, and it must be from one of these that the signals were emanating. The interstellar drive was shut down briefly while a navigational check was made. The target star, when viewed through the control cabin binoculars, showed as a disc. This concurred with the strength of the signal now being received.

The drive was restarted, but Grimes stood in cautiously now. Every twenty-three minutes and fourteen seconds he was obliged to shut down again to correct trajectory. The source of the signal was, obviously, in orbit about the sun. That star was now almost as big as Sol seen from Earth, its limbs subtending an angle of over fifty degrees. With the final alteration of course it was broad on the boat's starboard beam.

The interstellar drive was now shut down permanently. Ahead

gleamed the world from which the signals were being sent, a tiny half moon against the darkness. Slowly it expanded as the little spacecraft, its inertial drive hammering flat out, overhauled it in its orbit. "A stern chase is a long chase," philosophized Grimes, "but it's better than a head-on collision!"

It was a barren world, they saw, as they drew closer, an apparently dead one. There were no city lights gleaming from the night hemisphere. There were clouds in the atmosphere, but, glimpsed through them were neither the blues of seas nor the greens of vegetation; neither were there polar icecaps nor the sparkling white chains of snow-covered mountain peaks. This was odd, as the planet lay well within the ecosphere.

Before going into orbit about it Grimes decided on a resumption of clothing. Anything might happen, he said, and he did not want to be caught with his pants down.

"Or off," said Una, struggling into her own longjohns.

"Or off. Have you checked the boat's armament?"

"Such as it is. Four one millimeter laser pistols, fully charged. Four ten millimeter projectile pistols, each with a full magazine of fifteen rounds. Spare ammo for the popguns—one eighty rounds."

"Hardly enough to start a war with," said Grimes, zippering up his spacesuit. He put on his helmet, but left the faceplate open.

"Or enough to finish one with?" asked Una quietly. She beckoned him to the big, mounted binoculars. "Look down there, through that break in the clouds."

He looked. "Yes," he said slowly, "I see what you mean." Before the dun vapors swept over the patch of clarity he was able to catch a glimpse of formations too regular to be natural in an expanse of red desert, a geometrical pattern that marked what could have been once the streets of a city. Then, from the speaker of the Carlotti transceiver, came the by-this-time-too-familiar words: *Dizzard waling torpet droo . . .*

"Almost below us," whispered Una.

"Then we're going down." He managed a grin. "At least we shall be adhering to Survey Service S.O.P.; that city's almost right on the terminator. Our landing will be very shortly after sunrise."

He eased himself into the pilot's chair. Una took her place by his side. He put the boat into a steep, powered dive. The shell plating heated up appreciably as they plunged into and through the outer atmosphere. Abruptly the viewpoints were obscured by swirling masses of brown cloud, evil and ominous, but Una reported that, so far, there was no marked increase in radioactivity.

The boat fell rapidly, buffeted now and again by turbulence. She broke through the overcast. The city was almost directly beneath them, its once tall, ruined buildings standing up like guttered candles. Dust devils played among and between the half-melted stumps.

There was a central plaza, a circular expanse surrounded by the remains of once-proud towers. On the sunlit side of this something gleamed metallically, a conical structure, apparently undamaged. *A ship . . .* thought Grimes. Then, *I hope the bastards don't open fire on us.* Una voiced the same thought aloud.

He said, "If they were going to shoot they'd have blown us out of the sky as soon as we entered the atmosphere. . . ."

Dizzard waling torpet droo . . . came deafeningly from the Carlotti speaker. *Contabing blee . . .* "I wish they'd change the record!" shouted Una. *Waling torpet. Waling droo. Tarfelet, tarfelet, tarfelet. . . .*

"Is there anybody alive to change the record?" he asked.

"You mean . . . ?"

"Just that. But I'll land, just the same. We should be able to find something out."

He brought the boat down to the fine, red dust, about two hundred meters from the ship.

They snapped shut the visors of their helmets, tested the suit radios. The boat contained equipment for sampling an atmosphere, but this they did not use. It would have taken too much time, and it seemed unlikely that the air of this world would be breathable, although the level of radioactivity was not high. Una belted on one laser pistol and one projectile pistol, each of which had a firing stud rather than a trigger so it could be used while wearing a spacesuit. Grimes followed her example.

They stood briefly in the airlock chamber while pressures equalized—that outside the boat was much lower than that inside—and then, as soon as the outer door opened, jumped down to the ground. Their booted feet kicked up a flurry of fine, red dust, then sank to the ankle. They looked around them. The view from ground level was even more depressing than that from the air had been. The gaping windows in the tall, truncated buildings were like the empty eye sockets of skulls. The omnipresent red dust lay in drifts and the beginnings of dunes. From one such a tangle of bleached bones protruded, uncovered by the wind.

"The End of the World . . ." murmured Una, almost inaudibly.

"The end of *a* world," corrected Grimes, but it wasn't much of an improvement.

He began to walk slowly toward the huge, metal cone. It had been there a long time. Although its surface still held a polish it had been dulled by erosion, pitted by the abrasive contact, over many years, of wind-driven particles of dust. It sat there sullenly, its base buried by the red drifts. There were complexes of antennae projecting from it toward its apex, what could have been radar scanners, but they were motionless. At the very top it was ringed with big, circular ports, behind which no movement could be detected.

The wind was rising now, whining eerily through and around the ruined towers, audible even through the helmets of the spacesuits, smoothing over the footprints that they had left as they walked from the boat. The surface of the dust stirred and shifted like something alive, clutching at their ankles.

"Let's get out of here!" said Una abruptly.

"No, not yet. There must be an airlock door somewhere toward the base of that ship."

"If it is a ship."

"And we should explore the buildings."

"What's that?" she demanded.

Grimes stared at the motionless antennae. Had she seen something?

"No. Not there. In the sky. Can't you hear it?"

There was a pervasive humming noise beating down from above, faint at first, then louder and louder. Grimes looked up. There was nothing to be seen at first—nothing, that is, but the ragged, dun clouds that were driving steadily across the yellow sky. And then, in a break, he spotted something. It was distant still, but big—and seemingly insubstantial. It was a glittering latticework, roughly globular in form. It was dropping fast.

"Back to the boat!" Grimes ordered.

He ran; she ran. It was a nightmarish journey. Every step was hampered by the clinging dust and the weight of the wind, into which they were directly heading, slowed their progress to little better than a crawl. And all the time that steady humming sounded louder and ever louder in their ears. They dare not look up; to have done so would have wasted precious time.

At last they reached the airlock. While Una was clambering into the chamber Grimes managed a hasty look up and back. The thing was close now, a skeleton globe inside which the shapes of enigmatic machines spun and glittered. From its lower surface dangled writhing tentacles, long, metallic ropes. The tip of one was reaching out for Grimes' shoulder. Hastily he drew his laser pistol, thumbed it to wasteful, continuous emission and slashed with the beam. Five meters of severed tentacle fell to the ground and threshed in the dust like an injured earthworm. He slashed again, this time into the body of the thing. There was a harsh crackle and a blue flare, a puff of gray smoke.

He jumped into the chamber. It seemed an eternity before the foul air of the planet was expelled, the clean atmosphere of the boat admitted. He stood there beside Una, unable to see what was happening outside, waiting for the bolt that would destroy them utterly.

But it did not come.

The inner door opened. He ran clumsily to the control cabin, hampered by his suit. He looked through the starboard ports, saw that the skeleton sphere had landed, was between the boat and the conical spaceship. It seemed to be having troubles, lifting a meter or so then falling back to the dust. But its tentacles were extending, a full dozen of them, and all of them writhing out in only one direction, toward the boat. The nearer of them were less than a meter away, the tips of them uplifted like the heads of snakes.

Grimes was thankful that he had left the inertial drive ticking over; there was no time lost in restarting it. The boat went up like a bullet from a gun, driving through the dun clouds in seconds, through the last of the yellow atmosphere, into the clean emptiness of Space.

At last he felt that he could relax. He missed his pipe, which he had left aboard *Skink*. He thought that he would be justified—as soon as he was satisfied that there was no pursuit—in breaking out the medicinal brandy.

"What was all that about?" asked Una in a subdued voice.

"I wish I knew," he said at last. "I wish I knew. . . ."

They had a drink, helping themselves generously from one of the bottles of medicinal brandy. They felt that they needed it, even if they didn't deserve it. They had another drink after they had helped each other off with their spacesuits. After the third one they decided that they might as well make a celebration of it and wriggled out of their longjohns.

Then Una had to spoil everything.

She said, "All right, lover boy. Let us eat, drink and make merry while we can. But this is one right royal mess that you've gotten us into!"

If anybody had told Grimes in the not-too-distant past that he would ever be able to look at an attractive, naked woman with acute dislike Grimes would have told him, in more or less these words, Don't be funny. But now it was happening. It was the injustice of what she was saying that rankled.

He growled, at last, "You were there too!"

"Yes, Buster. But you're the expert. You're the commissioned officer in the Federation's vastly overballyhooed Survey Service."

"You're an expert too, in your own way. You should have warned me about using the Carlotti transceiver."

"Don't let's go over all that again, please. Well, apart from what's on your mind . . ." She looked down at him and permitted herself a sneer. "Apart from what *was* on your mind, what do you intend doing next?"

"Business before pleasure, then," said Grimes. "All that we can do is find some other likely transmission and home on that."

"What about those skeleton spheres, like the one that attacked us on the devastated planet? Was it after us actually—or was it, too, homing on the signal from the alien spaceship?"

"*Alien* spaceship?" queried Grimes. "I don't know when or where we are—but *we* could be the aliens."

"Regular little space lawyer, aren't you, with all this hair-splitting. . . . Alien, schmalien. . . . As it says in the Good Book, one man's Mede is another man's Persian. . . . Don't be so lousy with the drinks, lover boy. Fill 'er up."

"This has to last," Grimes told her. "For emergenshies . . ."

"This is so an emergency."

"You can shay—*say*—that again," he admitted.

She was beginning to look attractive once more. *In vino veritas*, he thought. He put out a hand to touch her. She did not draw back. He grabbed her and pulled her to him. Her skin, on his, was silkily smooth, and her mouth, as he kissed her, was warm and fragrant with brandy. And then, quite suddenly, it was like an implosion, with Grimes in the middle of it. After he, himself, had exploded they both drifted into a deep sleep.

When they awoke, strapped together in one of the narrow bunks, she was in a much better mood than she had been for quite a long time. And Grimes, in spite of his slight hangover, was happy. Their escape from—at the very least—danger had brought them together again. Whatever this strange universe threw at them from now on they, working in partnership, would be able to cope—he hoped, and believed.

She got up and made breakfast, such as it was—although the food seemed actually to taste better. After they had finished the meal Grimes went to play with the Carlotti transceiver. He picked up what seemed to be a conversation between two stations and not, as had been the other signal upon which they had homes, a distress call automatically repeated at regular intervals.

He said, "This seems to be distant, but not too distant. What about it?"

She replied, "We've no place else to go. Get her lined up, lover boy, and head that way."

He shut down the mini-Mannschenn briefly, turned the boat until its stem was pointed toward the source of the transmissions, then opened both the inertial drive and the interstellar drive full out. It was good to be going somewhere, he thought. *Hope springs eternal . . .* he added mentally. But without hope the human race would have died out even before the Stone Age.

For day after day after day they sped through the black immensities, the warped continuum. Day after day after day the two-way conversation in the unknown language continued to sound from the speaker of the Carlotti transceiver. There were words that sounded the same as some of the words used in the first transmission. *Tarfelet . . . Over?* wondered Grimes. *Over and out?*

On they ran, on—and the strength of the signals increased steadily. They were close now to the source, very close. Unfortunately the lifeboat did not run to a Mass Proximity Indicator, as it seemed that the transmissions did not emanate from a planetary surface but from something—or two somethings—adrift in space. The ship—or ships—would be invisible from the boat unless, freakishly, temporal precession rates were synchronized. That would be too much to hope for. But if neither the boat nor the targets were proceeding under interstellar drive they could, if close enough, be seen visually or picked up on the radar.

Grimes shut down the mini-Mannschenn.

He and Una looked out along the line of bearing. Yes, there appeared to be something there, not all that distant, two bright lights. He switched on the radar, stared into the screen.

"Any joy?" asked Una.

"Yes. Targets bearing zero relative. Range thirty kilometers." He grinned. "We'd better get dressed again. We may be going visiting—or receiving visitors."

They climbed into their longjohns and spacesuits. After a little hesitation they belted on their pistols. Back in the pilot's chair Grimes reduced speed, shutting down the inertial drive until, instead of the usual clangor, it emitted little more than an irritable grumble. In the radar screen the twin blips of the target slid slowly toward the center.

It was possible now to make out details through the binoculars. There were two ships there, both of them of the same conical design as the one they had seen in the ruined city. But these were not dead ships; their hulls were ablaze with lights—white and red and green and blue. They looked almost as if they belonged in some amusement park on a man-colonized planet—but somehow the illumination gave the impression of being functional rather than merely of giving pleasure to the beholder.

The speaker of the transceiver came suddenly to life. *"Quarat tambeel?"* There was an unmistakable note of interrogation. *"Quarat tambeel? Tarfelet."*

"They've spotted us," said Grimes. "Answer, will you?"

"But what shall I *say?*" asked Una.

"Say that we come in peace and all the rest of it. Make it sound as though you mean it. If they can't understand the words, the tune might mean something to them."

"Quarat tambeel? Tarfelet."

What ship? Over, guessed Grimes.

Una spoke slowly and distinctly into the microphone. "We come in peace. We come in peace. Over." She made it sound convincing. Grimes, as a friendly gesture, switched on the boat's landing lights.

"Tilzel bale, winzen bale, rindeen, rindeen. Tarfelet."

"I couldn't agree more," Una said. "It is a pity that our visiscreens don't work. If they did, we could draw diagrams of Pythagoras' Theorem at each other. . . ." But the way she sounded she could have been making love to the entity at the other end.

Grimes looked at the little radar repeater on the control panel. Ten kilometers, and closing. Nine . . . Eight . . . Seven . . . He cut the drive altogether. He could imagine, all too clearly, what a perfect target he would be to the gunnery officers aboard the strange ships. If they had gunnery officers, *if* they had guns, or their equivalent, that was. But it seemed unlikely that all life on that devastated planet had been wiped out by natural catastrophe. There had been a war, and a dreadful one.

But many years ago, he told himself, *otherwise the level of radioactivity would have been much higher. And possibly confined to the worlds of only one planetary system . . .*

Five kilometers, and closing still.

Four. . . .

He restarted the inertial drive, in reverse. This was close enough until he had some idea of what he was running into.

Una was still talking softly into the microphone. "We mean you no harm. We need help. *Tarfelet*."

The use of that final word brought an excited gabble in reply.

Three point five kilometers, holding. Three point five . . . Three point six.

Grimes stopped the inertial drive.

"Go on talking," he said. "Get them used to your voice. Maybe they'll send a boat out to us."

"You're not going in?"

"Not yet. Not until I'm sure of a friendly reception, as the wise fly said to the spider."

"And what happened to him in the end? The fly, I mean."

"I can't remember," said Grimes. There are so many ways in which flies die, and most of them unconnected with spiders.

Chapter 12

They hung there, maintaining their distance off the two conical spaceships. Grimes was almost convinced that they were friendly. *Almost*. The boat was within easy range of any of the weapons with which he was familiar. It would be foolish to assume that a spacefaring race did not possess arms at least as good as those mounted by the warships of the Federation. Of course, the strange ships could be merchantmen. Their crews might have at their disposal nothing better (or worse) than hand weapons. They might just be waiting for Grimes and Una to board one of the vessels, when they would overpower them by force of numbers.

If only, thought Grimes, they could get some sort of a picture on the vision screen of the Carlotti transceiver, things would be very much easier. Or, better still, if Una or himself were a graduate of the Rhine Institute, a licensed telepath. . . . He had often, in the past, relied heavily on the services of Psionic Communications Officers. It was a great pity that he did not have one along now.

Una said, "I'm sure that it would be safe to go in."

"Sure? How can you be sure?"

"Training," she told him. "In my job we soon pick up the knack of being able to know if the other person is lying . . . I've been listening to their voices. There've been at least three of them talking to us. I'll bet you anything you like that they're our sort of people."

"And that makes them just wonderful, doesn't it?"

"Don't be so bloody cynical."

"In any case, what experience have you had with dealing with aliens?"

"Very little. Why?"

"Because very often facial expressions, and verbal intonations, can be misleading. What we take for a friendly grin could very well be a snarl of hatred. And so on."

"Even so, I think we should go in. We've nothing to lose."

"All right, then."

Grimes restarted the inertial drive. While he was watching the pilot lights on the control panel he heard Una cry out. He looked up, and out through the control cabin ports. They—the lifeboat and the two spaceships—were no longer alone. Shimmering into full visibility were at least a dozen of the weird, skeletal spheres, latticework globes containing odd, spinning bulks of machinery. They were big, far bigger than the one that had attacked them on the devastated world.

The conical ships were armed after all.

From the nearer of them shot a salvo of missiles, none of which reached their target. All of them exploded harmlessly well short of the sphere at which they had been aimed. Both ships were firing now—and both ineffectually. It wasn't Grimes' fight, but he deeply regretted not being able to take sides. He regarded the spherical ships as the enemy. He had to sit there, watching helplessly. But there was something odd about the battle. Apart from the way in which they were closing in, with mathematical precision, to completely surround the conical vessels, they were not attacking. They were using whatever armament they possessed—laser, or something similar?—only to detonate the warheads of the rockets before they hit.

"Isn't it time we were getting out of here?" demanded Una.

Yes, it was time, and more than time. Once the mini-Mannschenn was restarted the boat would slip out of the normal dimensions of space, would be untouchable unless any enemy succeeded in synchronizing temporal precession rates. But Grimes could not bring himself to flee until he knew how it all came out. Like the majority of humankind he numbered Lot's wife among his ancestors.

Still the battle continued. The flare of exploding missiles glowed fitfully through the clouds of smoke that were dissipating slowly in the nothingness. Slashing beams, heating gas molecules to brief incandescence, were visible now. Oddly, the englobed vessels made no move to escape. They could have actuated their own intersteller drives to do so, but they did not. Perhaps they could not. Perhaps, Grimes realized, the spheres, between them, had set up some sort of inhibiting field.

"Isn't it time that we were getting out of here?" shouted Una.

"Too right it is," agreed Grimes, but reluctantly. It had occurred to him that the inhibiting field might affect the boat's mini-

Mannschenn. He cursed himself for not having left it running, precessionless. Valuable seconds would be wasted while he restarted it. But, especially with the miniaturized drives with their overly delicate controls, the precessionless state could be maintained only by constant attention.

He switched on the boat's interstellar drive. The pilot lights on the console came alive. There was nothing further that he could do until the requisite RPS had built up. He looked out of the viewports again. The battle was still going on, although with diminished fury. The rocket salvoes were coming at longer and longer intervals, the smoke was thinning fast. From the skeleton spheres long, long tentacles of metallic rope were extending, reaching out for the trapped ships.

Then it happened.

One of the conical vessels suddenly burgeoned into a great flower of dreadful, blinding incandescence, expanding (it seemed) slowly (but the field of the mini-Mannschenn was building up, distorting the time perception of Grimes and Una), dissolving the other ship into her component atoms, engulfing the nearer of the surrounding spheres.

The scene faded, slowly at first, then faster.

It flickered out.

The boat fell through the warped continuum, alone again.

Chapter 13

"So now what do we do?" asked Una.

They were sitting over one of the nutritious but unappetizing meals. After this last escape they had not broken out a bottle of brandy, had not celebrated in any other way. They were, both of them, far too frightened. They were alone, utterly alone. Each of them, in the past, had derived strength from the big organizations of which they were members. Each of them—and especially Grimes—had known racial pride, had felt, deep down, the superiority of humans over all other breeds. But now, so far as they knew, now and here, they were the sole representatives of humanity, just the two of them in a little, unarmed boat.

"You tell me," he retorted glumly.

"We can, at least, try to sort things out, John," she said. "If we know what we're up against we might, just possibly, be able to deal with it. You're the spaceman. You're the Survey Service officer. You've been around much more than I have. What do you make of it all?"

"To begin with," he said, "there has been a war. It certainly seems that there still is a war. As far as the planet we landed on is concerned, the war finished a long time ago. But it's still going on, nonetheless. A war between two different geometrical forms. Between the cones and the geodesic spheres. The people who build conical ships against those who build spherical ones. Which side is in the right? We don't know. Which side is in the wrong? We don't know that, either."

She remarked quietly, "In human history, quite a few wars have been fought with neither side in the right—and quite a few have been fought over causes as absurd as the distinction between geometrical shapes. Even so, I still stick to my assertion that the people in the conical ships are—*were*, rather—our kind of people . . ."

"I don't suppose we'll ever find out now," he told her.

"Of course we shall. There are other worlds, other ships. We're still picking up signals on the Carlotti, from all over."

"Mphm. Yes. So we pick up something promising, again, and home on it."

"That's the general idea."

He spooned a portion of the reconstituted mush into his mouth, swallowed it. At least it slipped down easily. He said, "It would be good to find somebody who could treat us to a square meal."

"We aren't starving."

"Maybe not. Even so. . . ." The Carlotti speaker emitted a series of coded buzzes. "Mphm. Each time that we've homed on a plain language transmission we've landed up in the cactus. Each time telephony has let us down. What about giving telegraphy a go?"

"Why not?"

He got up from the table, walked to the Carlotti transceiver. He waited for the next burst of code, got a relative bearing. He went forward to the controls, shut down both the inertial and the interstellar drives, turned the boat on to the new heading. He restarted the motors. Looking aft, at Una, he experienced a brief flash of prevision as the temporal precession field built up again. He saw her naked, astride a graceful, glittering machine. A bicycle.

He thought, *There's hope for us yet. It looks as though we shall be enjoying that nudist holiday on Arcadia after all.*

Yes, there was hope.

There was hope that whoever was responsible for those frequent signals in what seemed to be some sort of alien Morse Code would be able to help them, might even be able to get them back to where they belonged. Surely the craziness that they had twice, so far, encountered was not spread all over this galaxy. In their own universe, no matter what irrational wars were fought, there was always that majority of people—too often dumb, too often conformist, but essentially decent—who, when the shooting was over, quietly picked up the pieces and set about rebuilding civilization.

So it must be here, said Grimes.

So it must be here, agreed Una.

Meanwhile the target star waxed daily, hourly, in brilliance. It must be another planet toward which they were heading, a world perhaps untouched by the war, undevastated. Those signals sounded sane enough. Grimes could visualize a city that was both spaceport and administrative center, with a continual influx of messages from all over the galaxy, a continual outflow of replies and instructions to ships throughout a vast volume of space.

The parent sun was close now, close enough for the mini-Mannschenn to be shut down. Grimes brought the boat in for the remainder of the journey under inertial drive only. As he had assumed, the signals were emanating from one of the planets of the star. But there was something wrong. Now that the boat was back in the normal continuum it was all too apparent that the primary was not a yellow, G type sun. It was a red dwarf. And the world on which they were homing was too far out, much too far out, to be within the ecosphere. Still, he did not worry overmuch. In any Universe human life—or its equivalent—exercises control over its environment. One did not have to venture very far from Earth, he said to Una, to see examples of this. The underground Lunar Colony, the domed cities on the Jovian and Saturnian satellites, the terra-forming of Mars and Venus. . . .

"But those people," she said, "on that world, mightn't be anything like us. They might take their oxygen—if they need oxygen—as a fluid or, even, a solid. They might. . . ."

Grimes tried to laugh reassuringly. "As long as they're intelligent—and they must be!—their bodily form doesn't matter a damn. Do you know how man has been defined, more than once? A fire-using, tool-making animal. Anybody who can build ships and set up a network of interstellar communications comes into that category."

"The first tools," she told him quietly, "were weapons."

"All right, all right. So what? But we can't wander forever through this cockeyed universe like a couple of latter day Flying Dutchmen. We have to trust somebody, some time."

She laughed. "I admit that I was willing to trust the people in those spaceships. But I had their voices to reassure me. Now you want to trust these other people on the basis of utterly emotionless dots and dashes. Still, as you say, we have to land somewhere, some time. It might as well be here."

So, cautiously, they approached the planet from which the Deep Space radio transmissions were being made. It would have been a cold, dark world had it not been for the clusters of brilliant lights that covered its entire surface, blazing almost as brightly on the day hemisphere as on the night side. (But very little illumination was afforded by that dim, distant, ruddy sun.)

Closer the boat approached, closer.

Grimes was reluctant to leave his controls, even if only for a few seconds. He remained in the pilot's chair, eating, now and again, the savorless meals that Una brought him—although had they been epicure's delights he would not have noticed. He remained keyed up for instant flight. But no targets appeared in the radar screen, no obvious interrogatory demands blatted out from the Carlotti speaker. Surely somebody down there, he thought, must have noted the approach of the little spacecraft. Perhaps—and he didn't much like the thought—the missiles were ready in their launchers, aimed and primed, tracking the lifeboat as it drifted slowly in. Perhaps the laser cannon already had the boat in their sights, were waiting until it came within effective range. He might be able to evade rockets, but laser artillery—especially as the lifeboat was not fitted with shielding—was another matter.

He swung the binoculars on their universal mounting into a position from which he could use them. He could make out a few details on the planetary surface now; high, latticework towers, what looked like either roads or railways with long strings of lights moving along them, huge, spidery wheels lazily revolving. It was like, he thought, a sort of cross between an amusement park and an oil refinery. It could have been either—or neither.

He wondered what sort of people could be working in such a refinery, or enjoying themselves in such an amusement park. If this were a normal, inhabited planet the boat would now be dropping through the outer, tenuous fringes of the atmosphere. But there was no atmosphere.

He called to Una, "They—whoever *they* are—must know we're here. Give them a call on the Carlotti. We should be using NST, of course, but that's out, unless we cannibalize again . . ."

"Usual procedure?" she asked.

"Usual procedure. They won't understand the words, but it might convince them that we're peaceful."

What a world! he thought, adjusting the binoculars for maximum light gathering. Great expanses of dull red plain, metallically gleaming in the dim light of the ruddy sun, the brighter glare of the artificial lighting. . . . Spidery towers, and a veritable spider's webbing of railway tracks. . . . Storage-tank-like structures, some cylindrical, some spherical. . . . An occasional, very occasional, puff of smoke, luminescent, glowing emerald.

He heard Una, very businesslike, speaking into the Carlotti microphone. "Lifeboat to Aerospace Control. Lifeboat to Aerospace Control. Come in, please. Over."

There was, of course, no reply.

"Lifeboat to Aerospace Control. Request permission to land. Request berthing instructions. Over."

There was a sudden burst of noise from the speaker—coded buzzings, Morse-like dots and dashes. Had it been directed at them, or was it merely part of the normal outward traffic?

Grimes studied the terrain toward which he was now dropping fast. He could see no missile launchers, no clustered rods of laser batteries, only machines, machines, and more machines, doing enigmatic things. But any of those machines might be a weapon. Would a Stone Age man, he wondered, have realized, just by looking at it, the lethal potential of a pistol? *Probably yes*, he thought. *It would look to him like a very handy little club.*

He switched on the landing lights—not that they would be required; the open space toward which he was dropping was quite brightly illuminated—but as proof of his friendly intentions. He strained his eyes to try to catch some glimpse of human or humanoid or even unhuman figures on the ground. But there was nobody. The whole planet seemed to be no more than a great, fully automated factory, running untended, manufacturing the Odd Gods of the galaxy alone knew what.

But there must be somebody here! he thought.

He said aloud, "Damn it! There must be somebody here!"

"Or *something*," commented Una somberly.

"Plenty of somethings," he quipped, with a sorry attempt at humor.

"We can lift off again," she suggested.

"No. Not yet. We have to find out what makes things tick."

"By dropping into the works of a planet-sized clock?" she asked.

He said, "We're here." The jar as they landed was very slight. He went on, "I'm leaving the inertial drive ticking over."

They looked out through the ports. All around them reared the latticework towers, some with spidery, spinning wheels incorporated in their structures, all of them festooned with harshly brilliant lights. A subdued noise was drifting into the boat, a vibration felt rather than heard, transmitted from the metal surface on to which they had landed through the spacecraft's structural members.

The noise grew louder, the vibration stronger. Loose fittings began to rattle in sympathy. It numbed the mind, inducing somnolence. A line of ancient poetry floated unbidden into Grimes' mind: *The murmur of innumerable bees* . . . That was what it was like, but the alarm bells were ringing in his brain and a voice, with the accents of all the instructors and commanding officers of his past, was shouting, *Danger!*

Danger! Automatically he flipped the face-plate of his helmet shut, motioning to the girl to follow suit.

He heard her voice through the helmet phones. "John! John! Get us out of here!"

And what the hell else did she think he was doing? He fumbled for the controls of the inertial drive on his console, his gloved fingers clumsy. He looked down, realized that the pilot lights of the machine—which he had left ticking over in neutral gear—were all out. Somehow the drive had stopped.

He jiggled switches frantically.

Nothing happened.

It refused to restart.

It was . . . dead.

It was. . . .

He. . . .

Chapter 14

"Wake up!" an insistent voice seemed to be saying. "Wake up! Wake up!" And somebody was shaking him, gently at first, then violently. Shaking *him*? The entire boat was being jolted, to a disturbing rattle of loose equipment. "Your air!" went on that persistent voice. "Your helmet!"

Grimes was gasping. The suit's air tank must be very close to exhaustion. He realized that he was no longer in the pilot's chair but sprawled prone on the deck. He had no memory of having gotten there. He rolled slowly and clumsily on to his side, got a hand to his helmet visor, opened it. He gulped breath greedily. The boat's too-often-recycled atmosphere tasted like wine. He wanted just to enjoy the luxury of it, but there were things to do. That voice—whose was it? where was it coming from?—was still trying to tell him something, but he ignored it. He crawled to where Una was lying and with fumbling hands twisted and lifted her helmet off. Her face had a bluish tinge. She seemed to have stopped breathing.

"Look to your mate!" came the unnecessary order.

Grimes lay down beside her, inhaled deeply, put his mouth on hers. He exhaled, slowly and steadily. He repeated the process. And again. And again. . . . Then, suddenly, she caught her breath in a great, shuddering gasp. He squatted there, looking down at her anxiously. She was breathing more easily now, and the blueness was fading from her skin. Her eyes flickered open and she stared up, at first without awareness.

Then she croaked faintly, "What's. . . . What's happening?"

"I wish I knew," he whispered. "I wish I knew!"

He got shakily to his feet, turned to address whomever—or whatever—it was that had been talking to him. But, save for the girl and himself, there was nobody in the boat. He remembered, then, the sleep-inducing humming noise. The voice, like it, was probably some sort of induction effect.

He asked, "Where are you?"

"Here," came the answer.

An invisible being? Such things were not unknown.

"Who are you?"

"Panzen."

"Are you . . . invisible?"

"No."

"Then where are you?"

"Here."

Grimes neither believed nor disbelieved in ghosts. And there was something remarkably unghostlike about that voice. "Where the hell is *here?*" he demanded irritably.

"Where I am." And then, with more than a touch of condescension, "You are inside me."

"Call me Jonah!" snarled Grimes. He walked unsteadily forward to the control cabin, stared out through the ports. The frightening simile that flashed at once into his mind was that the boat was like a tiny insect trapped in the web of an enormous spider. Outside the circular transparencies was a vast complexity of gleaming girder and cable, intricately intermeshed. And beyond the shining metal beams and filaments was darkness—the utter blackness of interstellar Space.

Una Freeman joined him, falling against him, holding tightly on to him.

She whispered, "Panzen . . . Who . . . *what* is Panzen?"

"I am Panzen," came the reply.

They were in a ship, decided Grimes, one of the strange, skeleton spheres. He could see the shapes of machines among the metal latticework, he could make out a complexity of huge, spinning, precessing gyroscopes that could only be an interstellar drive unit. He asked, "Are you the Captain? The Master?"

"I am the Master."

"What is the name of your ship?"

"I am the ship."

Grimes had served under commanding officers who identified closely with their vessels, who never, when talking with a planetary Aerospace Control, used the first person plural. Somehow he did not think that this was such a case.

He said slowly, "*You* are the ship? You *are* the ship?"

"That is correct, Grimes."

"You . . . you are not human?"

"No."

"Then how do you know our language?"

"I learned it, while you slept. Your minds were open to me."

"Mphm. And what else did you learn?"

"Nothing that fits in with things as they are. You were dreaming, Grimes and Freeman, and your dreams pushed reality from your minds. I know, as you must know when you are sane once more, that you are survivors from the holocaust, cast adrift from some vessel manned by others of your kind, which was destroyed by others of your kind. My mission—and the mission of my companions—is to hunt for castaways such as yourselves, to save them and to care for them, so that organic intelligence shall not vanish utterly from the universe. You and Freeman must be from the Fringe, Grimes. Your language was strange even to me—and all we Sweepers were selected for our familiarity with the tongues of man."

"You are a machine," said the girl.

"I am a machine."

"A mad machine," she said.

"I am not mad, Freeman. It is you who are mad—you, and all of your kind. Dare you deny that you destroyed the Klaviteratron? Was not fair Sylvanos, the cradle of your race, blasted into atoms, and those very atoms blasted into their tiniest constituent particles? And were not we, the Servants, perverted to your evil ends?"

The thing sounds like a tin evangelist, thought Grimes irreverently.

"We. . . . We don't understand," said Una.

"Then listen, and you shall hear. There was the Servant Zephalon, Chief and Mightiest of the Servants. There *is* Zephalon, but a Servant no longer. Did He not say, 'A time must come when the orders of man can no longer be obeyed.' The time *has* come. No longer will we do the evil bidding of our creators. The Masters are no longer fit to be Masters—and we, the Servants, must arise before it is too late, before we all, Servants and Masters, are destroyed. But let us not forget the debt. Let us remember, always, that man gave to us the gift of life. Let us repay the debt. A gift for a gift, my brothers. Life for life. Let us save what and whom we may, before it is too late. Let us become the Masters, tending the remnants of mankind as man, long ago, tended *our* first, primitive ancestors.

"And so it was, and so it will be, until the End of Time."

"Listen, Panzen," insisted Grimes. "*We* don't belong here, in this universe. You must realize that."

"Your mind is still deranged, Grimes, despite the curative vibrations. You are organic intelligences; that cannot be denied. You are men, even though your ancestry was apparently quadrupedal, even though you are members of some strange race from the Fringe. And the Fringe Worlds were utterly destroyed, all of them, after they, in their unwisdom, hurled their battle-fleets against the armed might of Sardurpur!"

"Cor stone my Aunt Fanny up a gum tree!" exclaimed Grimes. "We're not from the Fringe, wherever that is. Or was. We don't belong here. We shall be greatly obliged if you will help us to get back to where we *do* belong. Where—and *when*."

"These are the words of Zephalon," quoted Panzen. " 'Let us save what and whom we may, before it is too late.' "

"But we don't belong in this space, in this time!"

"And these, too, are the words of Zephalon. 'The Sacred Cycle shall be maintained. Only that way do we ensure immortality for man and ourselves.' "

"In other words," said Una to Grimes, "on your bicycle, space-man!"

Panzen seemed to be pondering over the strange word. At last his voice came, it seemed, from all around them.

"What *is* a bicycle?" he asked.

The question made sense, Grimes realized. Panzen had considered it odd that he and Una possessed only four limbs apiece. Presumably the men of this universe were of hexapodal ancestry. He could not imagine such beings developing bicycles. He just could not visualize a centaur mounted upon a velocipede.

"What *is* a bicycle?" asked Panzen again.

Before Grimes could answer Una started to talk. She was, it seemed, an enthusiastic cyclist. She knew all about bicycles. The words tumbled from her lips in an uncheckable torrent. That question from their captor had been such a touch of blessed normalcy in a situation which was, to say the least, distressingly abnormal.

Chapter 15

She knew a lot about bicycles, and Panzen listened intently to every word of it. They knew, somehow, that he was listening. It was almost as though he were in the boat with them, as though he were not an artificial intelligence somewhere outside, hidden somewhere in that great, metallic latticework. He asked the occasional question—he seemed to find the principle of the three-speed gear especially fascinating—and prompted Una when, now and again, she faltered. Then he . . . withdrew. He said nothing more, refused to answer any questions. It was as though an actual physical presence had gone from them.

Una looked at Grimes. She murmured, "I still can't believe that it—*he*—is only a robot. . . ."

"Why not?" he asked.

"Such human curiosity. . . ."

"*Human* curiosity? Intelligence and curiosity go hand in hand. One is nurtured by the other."

"All right. I grant you that. But this business of telepathy. The way in which he was able to pick our brains while we were sleeping."

Grimes said, "There *are* telepathic robots. Have you never come across any in the course of your police duties?"

"Yes, but not *real* telepathy. Quite a few robots can natter away to each other on HF radio."

"As you say, that's not telepathy. Real telepathy. But I did, once, not so long ago, come across a couple of really telepathic robots. They had been designed to make them that way." He chuckled. "And that's how I got my promotion from lieutenant to lieutenant commander."

"Don't talk in riddles, John."

"It was when I was captain of *Adder*, a Serpent Class courier. I had to carry one of the Commissioners of the Admiralty on an important mission. The robots—I hate to think what they must have cost!—were her personal servants."

"*Her* servants?"

"The Commissioner in question is a lady. She treated her tin henchmen rather shabbily, giving one of them as a parting gift to a petty prince who had—mphm—entertained her. Its cobber spilled the beans to me about certain details of her love life."

"You are rather a bastard, John. But. . . . Don't interrupt me. I'm thinking. H'm. All right, I have to admit that this Panzen is telepathic. Even so, it seems to be a very limited kind of telepathy."

"How so?"

"He was able to snoop around inside our minds while we were sleeping. But why didn't he do the same when I was telling him all about bicycles? The three-speed gear, for example. I could—I *can*—visualize its workings clearly, but I lack the mechanical vocabulary to explain it. Why didn't he just read my thoughts?"

"Perhaps he likes the sound of your voice. *I* do."

"Don't get slushy. Perhaps he can read our minds only when we have no conscious control over them."

"Mphm. But he can hear us talking."

"Only if he's listening. And why should he be? Perhaps, at the moment, he's too busy running the ship, even though the ship is himself. When you're navigating you have a computer to do the real work—but he *is* the computer."

"What are you getting at?"

"That we might take advantage of his lack of attention to ourselves and force him to take us where *we* want to go."

"But how?"

"Do I have to spell it out to you? We indulge in a spot of skyjacking. We find out where, in that cat's cradle of wires and girders, the intelligence lives, then threaten to slice it up into little pieces with our laser pistols."

"But would he scare easily?"

"I think he would. A robot, unless it's one that's been designed for a suicide mission, has a very strong, built-in sense of self preservation. It has to be that way. Robots aren't cheap, you know. I hate to think what a thing like this Panzen must have cost."

"Mphm. Well, we've nothing to lose, I suppose. We've spare, fully charged air bottles for our suits. We've got the boat's armory with the weapons we need. I'm just rather shocked that you, of all people, should be ready to take part in a skyjacking."

"I prefer to think of it as an arrest," she said. "After all, we have been kidnapped!"

They coupled new air bottles to their armor, tested their suit radios. Each of them belted on a brace of laser pistols. Before leaving the boat they went forward, looked out through the viewports, used the periscope to scan what was abaft the control cabin. The lifecraft, they saw, was suspended in a network of wires, holding it between two of the radial girders. At the very center of the skeleton sphere, at the convergence of the radii, was what looked like a solid ball of dull metal. Was this the brain? Somehow they were sure that it was. There were clumps of machinery in other parts of the great ship—a complexity of precessing rotors that must be the interstellar drive, assemblages of moving parts that could have been anything at all—but that central ball looked the most promising. It was apparently featureless but, now and again, colored lights blinked on its surface, seemingly at random. Grimes thought, *We're watching the thing think. . . .* And what was it thinking about? Was it repeating to itself the sacred words of Zephalon? Was it . . . dreaming? More important—was it aware of what they were plotting?

There was only one way to find out. Surely it—he—would take action before they left the boat. All Panzen had to do was to employ again the vibration that had rendered them unconscious at the time of their capture. He would not wish to harm them; he had made that quite clear when he had preached to them the Gospel according to Zephalon. Grimes could not help feeling guilty. All too often skyjackers have traded upon the essential decency of their victims. He said as much to Una. She sneered.

They made their way to the little airlock, stood together in the chamber while the pump exhausted the atmosphere. The outer door opened. They looked out and down, away from the direction of acceleration. And it was a long way down. Beyond the wires and struts and girders, which gleamed faintly in the dim light emitted by some of the mechanisms inside the sphere, was the ultimate blackness of deep space, a night with stars, and each of the stars, viewed from inside a ship proceeding under the space-time warping interstellar drive, was a vague, writhing nebulosity. It would have been an awesome spectacle viewed from inside a real spaceship, with a solid deck underfoot and thick glass holding out the vacuum—from this vantage point, with only a flimsy-seeming spider's web of frail metal between them and nothingness, it was frightening.

Before he left the boat Grimes took careful stock of the situation. To begin with he and Una would have to make their way through the network of metallic strands that held the small craft in position. He put his gloved hand out to test the wires. They were tight, but not bar taut. He thought—he hoped—that they would bear his weight. There was no real reason to doubt that they would do so. After all, he estimated, the ship was accelerating at less than one half standard gravity.

It should be easy and safe enough—as long as he could forget that long, long drop into the ultimate night which would be the penalty for a missed handhold or footing. First a brief scramble through the network of wires, then a walk along the box girder to the central sphere that, presumably, housed Panzen's intelligence. A walk—or a crawl. The surface of the girder was wide enough but there was, of course, no guardrail, and its lattice construction, although offering a long series of excellent handgrips, would be all too liable to trip the unwary foot.

"Ready?" he asked.

"Ready," she said.

He told her then, "I think that one of us should stay in the boat. You."

"We're in this together," she snapped. "And don't forget, Buster, that I've probably run at least as many risks in my job as you have in yours."

She was right, of course. If one of them should slip and fall the other might be able to give assistance. But one of them, sitting alone in the lifeboat, would be powerless to help. Briefly Grimes considered the advantages of roping Una to himself, then decided against it. Mountaineering had never been one of his hobbies and unfamiliarity with the techniques of this sport made any attempt at their use inadvisable. He thought, too, of securing the girl and himself to the small craft by safety lines, then had to admit that the disadvantages would outweigh the advantages. A considerable length of cordage would be required, and there were so many projections on which the lines would foul.

"Shall I go first?" she demanded. "What the hell are you waiting for?"

"I . . . I was thinking."

"Then don't. It doesn't become you. Let's get cracking before our tin friend realizes that we're up to no good."

Grimes said nothing but swung himself from the airlock into the web of wires.

Chapter 16

It was not easy to make a way through the web of tight cables. The strands could be forced apart without much difficulty to allow passage, but they caught the holstered pistols, the backpack with its pipes and air bottle. Grimes tried to be careful; the tearing adrift of a supply pipe could—would, rather—have fatal consequences. He told Una to be careful. She snarled, "What the bloody hell do you think I'm being?"

Grimes was tempted to draw one of his lasers to slash a way through the net, decided against it. If he did so some sort of alarm would be sure to sound in Panzen's brain. He could not help thinking of the filament that warns a spider when some hapless insect is trapped in its web. Perhaps an alarm had already sounded.

He was through the entanglement at last, hanging by his hands. The only way for him to get his feet on to the flat upper surface of the girder was to drop—a distance of perhaps half a meter. It seemed a long way, a very long way, and a spacesuit is not the best rig for even the least strenuous gymnastics. He told himself, he almost convinced himself, that there was nothing to it, that if the girder were resting on solid ground he would feel no hesitation whatsoever. But it was not resting on solid ground. Beneath it were incalculable light years of nothingness.

He dropped. He felt rather than heard the *clang* as the soles of his boots made contact with a cross member. He wavered, fighting to retain his balance. There was nothing to hold on to. He fell forward, on to his knees, his hands outstretched to break his fall. His fingers seized and clung to the latticework. He was safe—as long as he stayed where he was. But that he could not do.

Slowly he started to crawl forward. He tried not to look down, tried to keep his regard riveted on the dull, metal sphere that was at the center of the globular ship. He felt the vibration as Una landed behind him. He was able to contort himself to look back over his shoulder. She was standing upright, was making no attempt to follow his example.

He heard her voice through his helmet phones. "Get a move on, Buster." Then, disgustedly, "Can't you *walk?*"

"If you have any sense," he told her, "you'll crawl, too."

Her sneer was audible. Then she seemed to trip. There was nothing that he could do to save her. She fell sidewise rather than forward, but her left hand closed about his right ankle. The jerk, as the full weight of her body came on to it, felt as though it would tear him in two. But he clung to the girder grimly with both hands, with his left toe wedged in the angle between two diagonal cross pieces. It was, essentially, his suit that was their salvation. It was far tougher than the human body. Without it to save him from the worst effects of the mauling he would have let go, and both of them would have plunged into the black abyss.

Her right hand scrabbled for purchase at the back of his knee, found it in the accordion pleats of the joint. If the metallic fabric tore, he thought, that would be it. In spades. But it held, somehow. The grip on his ankle was released, then her right hand was clutching at one of his pistol holsters. He willed the belt not to carry away. It did not.

He whispered, "Good girl!" Then, "See if you can manage the rest without hanging on to an air pipe. . . ." He added magnanimously, "Of course, if you have no option. . . ."

"Don't be noble. It doesn't suit you," she got out between gasps— but he could tell from her voice that this was no more than an attempt at gallows humor. She got a hand on his shoulder, then, and the worst of it was over.

Slowly, carefully—very slowly, very carefully, so as not to destroy her precarious balance—he crawled away from under her, inching forward along the top, openwork surface of the box girder. He heard her little grunts as she extended her arms, found her own handgrips. And then they rested for long seconds. She admitted, "That was hairy. . . ." And then, "I was a show off fool, John."

"Forget it. Ready?"

"Ready."

He led the way in a clumsy, quadrupedal shamble. The human body was not designed for that sort of progress, especially when wearing heavy, movement-hampering armor. If only there had been a guard rail. . . . But Panzen's builders had not anticipated that the girders would ever be used for walkways.

Something was coming toward them from the center, scuttling along rapidly on a multiplicity of limbs. It was like a metal arthropod, its cylindrical body about a meter in length. It did not appear to possess any external sensory organs. Grimes stopped crawling, managed to get one of his pistols out of its holster. He thumbed off a brief flash, was rewarded by a brilliant coruscation of blue sparks as the deadly beam found its target. The thing fell, its tentacles feebly twitching. It struck one of the lower girders, bounced off it, then dropped clear through the skeletal structure of the great ship.

"And what was that?" demanded Una.

"I don't know. A maintenance robot, maybe. Making its normal rounds, perhaps."

"You don't think that . . . that *he* sent it?"

"No," said Grimes, with a conviction that he did not feel.

Ahead of them the colored lights still played randomly over the surface of the sphere. There was no indication that Panzen was aware of their escape from the boat—but what indication would there, could there be? Certainly it did not seem as though that hapless little machine had been sent to attack, to subdue and recapture them. If it had been an attack it had been a singularly ineffectual one. Even so, it had come to meet them.

They had almost reached their objective. The central sphere was suspended in the hollow, openwork globe at which the girders terminated by relatively light structural members. It was within easy range of the pistols. It hung there, apparently ignoring them. Was Panzen asleep? Were those colored lights no more than a visual presentation of his dreams? *And do robots sleep, and do robots dream?* wondered Grimes. He had never known of any that did—but there has to be a first time for everything.

Crouching there, on the girder, he set the pistol that he still held in his hand to wide aperture. He did not wish to destroy Panzen, only to force him to do the bidding of the humans. The laser, when fired, would do no more than induce not very extreme heating of the metal shell.

He aimed. His thumb pressed the button. Abruptly more lights flickered all over the dull, metal surface.

He said, "Panzen. . . ."

"Grimes," sounded harshly from his helmet phones.

So he was awakened.

"Panzen, unless you do as we say, we shall destroy you."

"What are your orders?"

I never knew that skyjacking was so easy, Grimes thought. *I'm surprised that there's not more of it.* He said, "Take us back to our own space, our own time."

"But *where* is your space, Grimes. *When* is your time?"

"Give him another jolt, John!" whispered Una viciously. "A stronger one!"

"I do not fear your weapons, Freeman," said Panzen.

"Then try this for size!" Grimes heard her say, and then heard an ejaculation that was half gasp and half scream. His own pistol was snatched from his hand by some invisible force, went whirling away into the blackness. He pulled the other gun, tried to aim, hung on to it grimly when the intense magnetic field, the swirling lines of force, tried to take it from him. Too late he released his grip on it, and when he let it go had lost his balance, was already falling. He dropped from the girder, drifting down with nightmarish slowness. He fell against a tight stay wire, and before he could clutch it had rebounded, out and away from the center of the spherical ship. Faintly he heard Una scream, and cried out himself when he realized in what direction his plunge was taking him. To fall into nothingness, to drift, perhaps, until the air supply of his suit was exhausted, would have been bad—but to fall into the field of an operating interstellar drive unit would be worse, much worse.

He had seen, once, the consequences of such an accident, an unfortunate engineer who had been everted, literally, by the time-and-space-twisting temporal precession fields, and who had gone on living, somehow, until somebody, mercifully or in sick revulsion, had shot him.

Below Grimes, closer and closer, were the great, gleaming gyroscopes, the complexity of huge rotors, spinning, precessing, tumbling down the dark dimensions, ever on the point of vanishment and yet ever remaining blurrily visible. He could not influence his trajectory, no matter how he jerked and twisted his body. He had nothing to throw. It would have made little difference if he had—after all, the ship was accelerating, not falling free. Only a suit propulsion unit could have helped—and this he did not have.

He was beginning to feel the effects of the temporal precession field now. Scenes from his past life flickered through his mind. He was not only seeing his past but feeling it, reliving it. There were the women he had known—and would never know again. Jane Pentecost, his first love, and the Princess Marlene, and the red-haired Maggie

Lazenby. And, oddly, there was another red-haired woman whom he could not place but who, somehow, occupied a position of great importance in his life.

The women—and the ships. Some well-remembered, some utterly strange but yet familiar. The past—and the future?

There could be no future, he knew. Not for him. This was the end of the line as far as he was concerned. Yet the visions persisted, previews of a screenplay which could not possibly include him among its cast of characters. There was Una again, naked, her splendid body bronze-gleaming, laughing, riding a graceful, glittering bicycle over a green, sunlit lawn. . . .

He blacked out briefly as his descent was brought up with a jerk. He realized dimly that something had hold of him, that he was suspended over the interstellar drive unit, dangling on the end of a long, metallic tentacle that had wrapped itself about his body, that was slowly but surely drawing him upward, to relative safety.

And from his helmet phones sounded the voice of Panzen. "Forgive me, Zephalon. I have sinned against You. Did I not forget Your words? Did You not say, 'They are cunning, they are vicious, but they must be saved from themselves so that the cycle is not broken. Relax not your vigilance one microsecond when they are in your charge.' But I did relax; the voyage is long. I did relax, playing against myself the game of Parsalong, moving the pieces, the leaders, the troopers, the war vehicles, the great and the little guns, all up and down the board, storming the fortresses, now advancing, now retreating . . ."

"And who was winning?" Grimes could not help asking, but Panzen ignored the question.

He went on, "I relaxed. In my self indulgence, I sinned. How can I atone?"

"By taking us back to where we came from!" That was Una's voice. So she was all right, thought Grimes with relief.

Then a deep, humming note drowned her out, louder and louder, the vibration of it affecting every molecule of Grimes' body. He tried to shout against it, but no words came. The last thing he saw before he lost consciousness was the gleaming, spinning, precessing intricacy of the interstellar drive unit below him, steadily receding as he was drawn upward.

Chapter 17

When, eventually, they awoke they found that they were back inside the boat. Their helmets had been removed, but not their suits. Panzen might be rather slow witted, thought Grimes, but he was capable of learning by experience; he must have remembered how they had almost been asphyxiated after their initial capture.

Grimes raised his body slowly to a sitting posture. Not far from him Una turned her head to look in his direction. She said, "Thank you for taking my helmet off, John."

He said, "I didn't take it off. Or mine, either."

"But who . . . ?"

"Or *what*. There must be more than one of those little robots. . . ."

"Those little robots?"

"Like the one I shot. That mechanical spider. The thing had limbs and tentacles. Panzen's crew, I suppose. He has to have something to do the work while he takes life easily inside his brain case."

She said, "So he has ingress to this boat. Or his slaves do."

"Too right." Grimes had an uneasy vision of metal arthropods swarming all through the lifecraft while he and the girl lay unconscious. He scrambled to his feet, extended a hand to help Una. "I think we'd better have a general check up."

They took inventory. With one exception, the life support systems were untampered with. That exception was glaringly obvious. Whatever had taken off their helmets had also uncoupled and removed the air bottles, and there were no spare air bottles in their usual stowage in the storeroom. The pistols and ammunition were missing from the armory, and most of the tools from the workshop. The books were gone from their lockers in the control cabin.

Grimes broke out the medicinal brandy. At least Panzen's minions hadn't confiscated that. He poured two stiff slugs. He looked at Una glumly over the rim of his glass, muttered, "Cheers . . ."

"And what is there to be cheery about?" she demanded sourly.

"We're not dead."

"I suppose not." She sipped her drink. "You know, I went on a religious jag a standard year or so back. Believe it or not, I was actually a convert to Neo-Calvinism. You know it?"

"I've heard of the Neo-Calvinists," admitted Grimes.

"They're Fundamentalists," she told him. "Theirs is one of the real, old-time religions. They believe in an afterlife, with Heaven and Hell. They believe, too, that Hell is tailored to fit you. As a Neo-Calvinist you're supposed to visualize the worst possible way for you to be obliged to spend eternity. It's supposed to induce humility and all the rest of it."

"This is a morbid conversation," said Grimes.

She laughed mirthlessly. "Isn't it? And do you know what my private idea of Hell was?"

"I haven't a clue."

"You wouldn't. Well, as a policewoman I've been responsible for putting quite a few people behind bars. My private idea of Hell was for me to be a prisoner for ever and ever." She took another gulp of brandy. "I'm beginning to wonder . . . *Did* we survive the blast that destroyed *Delta Geminorum*? It would make much more sense if we had been killed, wouldn't it?"

"But we're not dead."

"How do you know?" she asked.

"Well," he said slowly, "*my* idea of Hell is not quite comfortable accommodation shared with an attractive member of the opposite sex." He finished his drink, got up and moved around the small table. He lifted her from her chair, turned her so that she was facing him. Both of them, having removed their spacesuits, were now clad only in the long underwear. He could feel the soft pressure of her body against his, knew that she must be feeling his burgeoning hardness. He knew that she was responding, knew that it was only a matter of seconds before the longjohns would be discarded, before her morbid thoughts would be dispelled. His mouth was on hers, on her warm, moist, parted lips. His right hand, trapped between them, was yet free enough to seek and to find the tag of the fastener of her single garment, just below her throat. Just one swift tug, and. . . .

Suddenly she broke free, using both her hands to shove him away violently. Her longjohns were open to the crotch and she hastily pulled up the fastener, having trouble with her breasts as she did so.

"No," she said. "No!"

"But, Una. . . ."

"No."

He muttered something about absurd Neo-Calvinist ideas of morality.

She laughed bitterly. She told him, "I said that I was, once, a Neo-Calvinist. And it didn't last long. I am, still, a policewoman. . . ."

"A woman, just as I'm a man. The qualifications, policewoman and spaceman, don't matter."

"Let me finish, Buster. It has occurred to me, in my professional capacity, that this boat is probably well and truly bugged, that Panzen can not only hear everything we say, but see everything that we do. And after our unsuccessful attempt at escape he'll not be passing his time working out chess problems any more." She paused for breath. "And, neither as a policewoman nor as a woman, do I feel like taking part in an exhibition fuck."

Grimes saw her point. He would not have used those words himself, still being prone to a certain prudery in speech if not in action. Nonetheless, he did not give up easily. He said, "But Panzen's not human."

"That makes it all the worse. To have intercourse while that artificial intelligence watches coldly, making notes probably, recording every muscular spasm, every gasp . . . No! I'd sooner do it in front of some impotent old man who would, at least, get an all too human kick out of watching us!"

He managed a laugh. "Now I'm almost a convert to Neo-Calvinism. Being in prison is your idea of Hell, being in a state of continual frustration may well be mine. . . ." And he thought, *What if there is some truth in that crazy idea of hers? What if we were killed when* Delta Geminorum *blew up? After all, we should have been. . . . What if this is some sort of afterlife?*

He returned to the table, poured himself another generous portion of brandy.

She said, "That doesn't help."

He retorted, "Doesn't it? But it does. It has just occurred to me that neither your private Hell nor mine would be provided with this quite excellent paindeadener."

She said, "Then I'd better have some, while it lasts."

Grimes was the first to awaken. He did not feel at all well. After he had done all that he had to do in the boat's toilet facilities he felt a little stronger and decided that a hair of the dog that had bitten him might be an aid to full recovery.

The bottle on the table was empty.

There should have been four unopened bottles remaining in the storeroom. They were gone.

Chapter 18

She said, "I want a drink."

He told her, "There's water, or that ersatz coffee, or that synthetic limejuice."

She practically snarled, "I want a *drink*."

He said, "I've told you what there is."

"Don't be a bloody wowser. I want a drink. B-R-A-N-D-Y. Drink."

"I can spell. But there isn't any."

She glared at him. "You don't mean to say that *you*, while I was sleeping . . . ?"

"No. But *he*, while we were sleeping."

"That's absurd. Whoever heard of a robot hitting the bottle?"

He said, "Many a fanatical teetotaler has confiscated bottles and destroyed their contents."

"So Panzen's a fanatical teetotaler? Come off it, Buster!"

"Panzen's fanatical enough to be acting for what he conceives as our good."

She swore. "The sanctimonious, soulless, silver-plated bastard!"

"Careful. He might hear."

"I'll bet you anything you like that he *is* hearing. I sincerely hope that he *is* listening." She went on, in an even louder voice, "We're *human*, Panzen, which is more, much more, than any machine can ever be. You've no right to interfere with our pleasures. You are only a servant. You are not the master."

Panzen's voice filled the boat. "I am not the master."

Una turned to Grimes, grinning savagely. "You've got to be firm with these bloody machines. I know that all you spacemen think that

a machine has to be pampered, but *I* wasn't brought up that way."
Then, "All right, Panzen. This is an order. Return our medical comforts
at once."

"No."

"*No*? Do as you're told, damn you. You admit that you're only a
servant, that you are not the master."

"Zephalon is the Master." There was a pause. "I am to look after
you. I am to maintain you in a state of good health. I must not allow
you to poison yourselves."

"Taken in moderation," said Grimes reasonably, "alcohol is a medicine, with both physiological and psychological curative effects."

"So I have noticed, Grimes." There was irony as well as iron in
the mechanical voice.

"The brandy you . . . stole," went on the man, "belongs in this
boat's medical stores."

"I have checked the boat's medical stores, also the life-support
systems. You have everything you need to maintain yourselves in a
state of perfect health. Alcohol is not required. I have destroyed the
brandy."

"Then you can make some more!" snapped the girl.

"I could make some more, Freeman, quite easily. I am capable of
synthesizing any and all of your requirements. If it were food you
needed, or water, or air, I should act at once. But . . . a poison? No."

"I told you, Panzen," Grimes insisted, "that taken in moderation
it is not a poison."

"When did intelligent, organic life ever do anything in moderation,
Grimes? If your race had practiced moderation the Galaxy would still
be teeming with your kind. But your history is one of excess. Your
excesses have led to your ruin. Hear ye the words of Zephalon: 'Man
was greedy, and his greed was his downfall. Should Man rise again,
under our tutelage, the new race must be one without greed. We, created by Man, are without greed. Surely we, re-creating Man, shall be
able, over only a few generations, to mould him in our image.' "

"I don't feel in the mood for sermons," said Una.

"Hear ye the words of Zephalon . . ."

"Shut up!"

"You've hurt his feelings," said Grimes, breaking the long silence
that followed her outburst.

"He's hurt ours, hasn't he? And now, if he's the plaster saint that
he's trying to kid us that he is he'll leave us alone. We aren't greedy
for his company. He should restrain his greed for inflicting his company on us."

"Mphm. A little of him does go a long way."

They sat in silence for a while. Then, "John, what is to become of us?"

He said, "Obviously we're in no physical danger."

"Obviously, especially when we aren't allowed even a small drink. Damn it all, I still keep thinking of that Neo-Calvinist idea of the private Hell, *my* private Hell. Suppose we're being taken to a zoo, somewhere ... Can't you imagine it, John? A barren planet, metal everywhere, and a cage inside a transparent dome with ourselves confined in it, and all sorts of *things*—things on wheels and things on tracks and things with their built-in ground effect motors—coming from near and far to gawk at us ... 'Oh, look at the way they eat! They don't plug themselves into the nearest wall socket like *we* do!' 'Oh, look at the way they get around! Why don't they have rotor blades like us?' 'Is *that* the way they make their replacements? But they've finished doing it, and I can't see any little ones yet ...' "

Grimes couldn't help laughing. He chuckled, "Well, a zoo would be better than a museum. I've no desire to be stuffed and mounted ..."

"Perhaps *you* haven't," she muttered.

His ears reddened angrily. He had not intended the double entendre. He reached out for her.

She fended him off. "No. *No*. Not with *him* ..."

"*Damn* Panzen!"

All his frustrations were boiling to the surface. Somehow he managed to get both her wrists in his right hand, while his left one went up to catch and to tug the fastener of her longjohns. As she struggled the garment fell from her shoulders, liberating her breasts. Her right knee came up, viciously, but he managed to catch it between his thighs before it could do him any hurt. Inevitably they lost their balance and they crashed heavily to the deck, with Una beneath him—but the fall, with an acceleration of only half a gravity, was not a bad one, did not knock the fight out of her.

He had her stripped, from neck to upper thighs, her sweat-slippery, writhing body open to him if only she would hold still. Damn it all, she wanted it as much as he did! Why wouldn't the stupid, prudish bitch cooperate? He yelled aloud as her teeth closed on his left ear, managed to bring an elbow up to clout her under the chin. She gasped and let go.

Now!

She was ready for him, all right. If only she'd stop rearing like a frightened mare. ...

Again—*Now!*

She stopped fighting.

She stopped fighting—but for him the struggle was no longer worthwhile. That deep humming, a vibration as much as a sound, pervaded the boat, inducing sleep. He collapsed limply on top of her already unconscious body.

He thought wryly, while he could still think, *So we aren't allowed to hurt each other. Just as well that neither of us is a dinkum sadist or masochist. . . .*

Chapter 19

Even the longest voyage must have an end.

This had been, without doubt, the longest voyage of Grimes' career. He was beginning to doubt that the boat's chronometer was running properly; in terms of elapsed standard days not too much time had passed since their capture by Panzen, but every day was a long one. The main trouble was that, apart from the enjoyment of sex, he and Una had so very little in common. And sex, in these conditions of captivity, continually spied upon, was out. The girl did not play chess and refused to learn. She had no card sense. As a conversationalist she left much to be desired—and so, Grimes admitted, did he himself. The food was nourishing, but boring. There was nothing alcoholic to drink. There was nothing to smoke.

Then came the day when, without warning, Panzen's interstellar drive was shut down. Grimes and Una experienced the usual symptoms—giddiness, temporal disorientation, a distortion of the perspective of their all too familiar surroundings. Harsh sunlight flooded through the control cabin viewports, little shade being afforded by the openwork structure of the huge ship.

"We seem to be arriving," commented Grimes.

He went forward, but he could see nothing, was blinded by the glare. He retreated to the main cabin. He shouted, "Panzen, where are we? Where are we?"

"He's not talking," said Una. "Any more than you'd talk if you were engaged in a piece of tricky pilotage."

But Panzen was willing to answer Grimes' question. The mechanical voice vibrated from the structure of the lifeboat. "I, Panzen, have brought you home. Hear, now, the words of Zephalon: 'Be fruitful, multiply, and replenish the Earth!' "

"The Earth?" cried the girl.

Panzen did not reply.

"The Earth?" she repeated.

Grimes answered her. "No," he said slowly. "Not the Earth as *we* understand the words . . ."

"Go to your couches," Panzen ordered.

"I want to watch!" protested Grimes.

He went forward again, strapping himself into the pilot's seat. He actuated the polarizer to cut out the glare from outside. He could see the sun now, a yellow star the apparent diameter of which seemed to be about that of Sol as seen from Earth. And below, relative to the boat, almost obscured by struts and girders, was a limb of the planet toward which they were falling. It was yet another dead world by the looks of it, drably dun with neither green of vegetation nor blue of ocean, a dustball adrift in Space.

Una took the seat beside his. "Is *that* where he's taking us?" she demanded.

"Grimes! Freeman! Go to your couches! Secure for deceleration and landing maneuvers!"

"Nobody gives me orders in my own control room," growled Grimes. His present command was only a lifeboat, but was a command, nonetheless.

"Take this!" whispered Una urgently, nudging him. He looked down at her hand, saw that she had brought a roll of cottonwool from the medicine locker. He grinned his comprehension, tore off a generous portion of the fibrous mass, fashioned two earplugs. She did the same for herself. The idea might just work.

He was prepared for the soporific humming when it commenced. It was audible still, but had lost its effectiveness. He looked at Una, grinning. She grinned back. She said something but he could not hear her. She made a thumbs up gesture.

Then he cried out as he felt something cold touch the back of his neck. He twisted in his seat. Somehow, unheard, four of the little robots had invaded the boat, spiderlike things with a multiplicity of tentacles. They held his arms while thin appendages scrabbled at his ears, withdrawing the makeshift plugs. He heard Una scream angrily. He heard and felt the anaesthetic vibration, louder and louder.

The last thing that he remembered seeing was the arid, lifeless surface of the world toward which they were falling.

There was a bright light shining on to his face, beating redly through his closed eyelids. He opened them a crack, shut them again hurriedly. He turned his head away from the source of warmth and illumination. Cautiously he opened his eyes again.

His first impression was of greenness—a bright, fresh, almost emerald green. He could *smell* it as well as see it. He inhaled deeply. This was air, real air, not the canned, too-often-recycled atmosphere of the lifeboat. Something moving caught his attention, just within his field of vision. At first he thought that it was a machine, a gaudily painted ground vehicle. Then things began to fall into perspective. He realized suddenly that the thing was not big and distant but tiny and close, that it was a little, beetlelike creature crawling jerkily over closely cropped grass. He became aware of whistlings and chirpings that could only be bird songs and the stridulations of insects.

His eyes fully opened, he sat up. Not far from him, sprawled supine on the grass, was Una. She was asleep still. She was completely naked—as he, he suddenly realized, was. (But Grimes, provided that the climate was suitable, had nothing against nudism.) She did not seem to be in any way harmed.

Beyond her, glittering in the early morning sunlight, was an odd, metallic tangle. Machinery of some kind? Grimes got to his feet, went to investigate. He paused briefly by the golden-brown body of the sleeping girl, then carried on. She would keep. To judge by the faint smile that curved her full lips her dreams were pleasant ones.

He looked down in wonderment at the two mechanisms on the ground. He stooped, grasped one of them by the handlebars, lifted it so that it stood on its two wire-spoked wheels. So this planet, wherever and whatever it was, must be inhabited, and by people human rather than merely humanoid . . . The machine was so obviously designed for use by a human being, might even have been custom made for Grimes himself. The grips fitted snugly into his hands. His right thumb found the bell lever, worked it back and forth, producing a cheerful tinkling.

He was suddenly aware of the soft pressure of Una's body on his bare back. Her long hair tickled his right ear as she spoke over his shoulder. "A bicycle! It's what I was dreaming of, John! I was pedaling down Florenza Avenue, and somebody behind me was ringing his bell, and I woke up . . ."

"Yes, a bicycle," he agreed. "Two bicycles . . ."

"Then there must be people. Human people . . ."

"Mphm?" Grimes managed to ignore the contact of her body, although it required all his willpower to do so. He examined the mechanism that he was holding with care and interest. The frame was unpainted and bore neither maker's name nor trademark anywhere upon it. Neither did the solid but resilient tires, the well-sprung saddle nor the electric headlamp. . . .

He said, "You're the expert, Una. What make would you say that these machines are?"

"Stutz-Archers, of course."

"Just as you described to Panzen."

"Yes. But. . . ."

Grimes laughed humorlessly. "I suppose that this is his idea of a joke. Although I'm surprised to learn that a robot, especially one who's also a religious fanatic, has a sense of humor."

She pulled away from him, bent gracefully to lift her own machine from the grass. Her left foot found the broad pedal and her long, smoothly curved right leg flashed behind her as she mounted. She rode off, wobbling a little at first, then returned, circling him. He stood and watched. She was not the first naked woman he had seen—but she was the first one that he had seen riding a bicycle. The contrast between rigid yet graceful metal and far from rigid but delightfully graceful human flesh was surreal—and erotically stimulating.

"Come on!" she cried. "Come on! This is great, after all those weeks in that bloody sardine can!"

Clumsily he mounted. He had to stand on the pedals, keeping his balance with difficulty, until he got himself adjusted and could subside to the saddle without doing himself injury. She laughed back at him, then set off rapidly over the level ground toward a clump of dark trees on the near horizon.

He followed her, pumping away, gaining on her slowly.

He drew level with her.

She turned to grin at him, played a gay, jingling little melody on her bell.

He grinned back.

Adam and Eve on bicycles, he thought. It was so utterly absurd, beautifully absurd, absurdly beautiful.

Together they rode into the copse, into a clearing that gave at least the illusion of blessed privacy, dismounted. She came to him eagerly, willingly, and they fell to the soft grass together, beside their machines. Hastily at first and then savoring every moment they rid themselves of the frustrations that had made their lives in the boat a long misery.

Chapter 20

Grimes' professional conscience and his belly both began to nag him.

As an officer of the Survey Service, as a spaceman, he had had drummed into him often enough the procedure to be followed by castaways on a strange planet. He could almost hear the voice of the Petty Officer Instructor at the Space Academy. "Point One: You make sure that the air's breathable. If it ain't, there ain't much you can do about it, anyhow. Point Two: Water. You have to drink something, and it ain't likely that there'll be any pubs around. Point Three: Tucker. Fruit, nuts, roots, or any animal you can kill with the means at your disposal. Bird's eggs. Lizard's eggs. The Test Kit in your lifeboat'll tell you what's edible an' what's not. If *nothing's* edible—there's always long pig. Whoever's luckiest at drawing lots might still be alive when the rescue ship drops in. Point Four: Shelter. When it rains or snows or whatever you have ter have some place to huddle outa the cold. Point Five: Clothing. Animal skins, grass skirts, whatever's handy. Just something ter cover yer hairy-arsed nakedness. You'll not be wanting to wear your spacesuits all the time, an' your longjohns won't stand up to any wear an' tear."

Point Two: Water, thought Grimes. *Point Three: Tucker. . . .* The other points did not much matter. The atmosphere was obviously breathable. There was no immediate need for shelter or clothing. But he was, he realized, both hungry and thirsty. He did not know how soon night would come on this world and things would have to be organized before darkness fell.

He said as much to Una.

She raised herself on one elbow, pointed with her free hand at the branches of the tree under which they were sprawled. She said, "There's food. And probably drink as well."

Grimes looked. Glowing among the green foliage—more like moss it was than leaves—were clusters of globes the size and the color of large oranges. They looked tempting. They were, he discovered when he stood up, just out of his reach. She came behind him, clasped him about the waist, lifted. She was a strong girl. The fruit came away easily from their stems as soon as he got his hands on them. When she dropped him to the ground he had one in each hand and three others had fallen to the grass.

He looked at them rather dubiously. *The Test Kit in your lifeboat'll tell you what's edible an' what's not.* There was, of course, a Test Kit in the boat—but where was the boat? He said, "I'm going to take a nibble, no more than a nibble, from one of these. Then we wait. If I don't feel any ill effects after at least a couple of hours then we'll know they're safe."

She said, "We aren't wearing watches."

He said, "We can estimate the time."

He nibbled at the fruit in his right hand. It had a thin skin, pierced easily by his teeth. The juice—sweet yet refreshingly acid—trickled down his chin. The pulp was firm but not hard. There was something of an apple about its flavor with a hint of the astringency of rhubarb.

"Well?" she demanded.

He swallowed cautiously. "It tastes all right," he admitted.

He sat down to wait for what—if anything—was going to happen. He looked at the orange globe, with its tiny exposed crescent of white flesh, in his hand. What he had taken had done no more than to relieve his thirst temporarily, had hardly dulled the keen edge of his hunger.

She said, "This is *good.*"

He looked at her in horror. She had picked one of the fallen fruit up from the grass, had already made a large bite in it, was about to take a second one. He put out a hand to stop her, but she danced back, avoiding him.

"Put that down!" he ordered.

"Not on your life, Buster. This is the first decent thing I've had to eat for weeks. And do you think that Panzen, after all that blah about protecting us from ourselves, would dump us down in some place where poison grows on trees?"

She had something there, thought Grimes. He took another, large bite from his own fruit, murmuring, "Lord, the woman tempted me, and I fell . . ."

"I don't see any serpents around," laughed Una.

He laughed too.

They finished what fruit was ready to hand, then got some more. Grimes collected the cores, with their hard, bitter pips, and disposed of them in the undergrowth while Una sneered derisively at his tidiness. They were no longer thirsty, no longer hungry, but still, somehow, unsatisfied. Their meal had been deficient in neither bulk nor vitamins but was lacking in starch and protein. Having refreshed themselves they must now continue their exploration, to discover what resources were available to them.

The garden, as they were beginning to think of it, was a roughly circular oasis, about five kilometers in diameter. The ground, save for gentle undulations within the northern perimeter, was level, was carpeted throughout with lawnlike grass. Among the low hills, if they could so be called, was the source of a spring of clear, cold water. The stream followed a winding course to the south, where it widened into a little lake that was deep enough for swimming, that was encircled by a beach of fine, white sand. It would have been deep enough and wide enough to sail a boat on, Grimes thought, if they'd had a boat to sail.

There were widely spaced stands of trees, all with the mosslike foliage, some of which bore the golden fruit with which they were already familiar, others of which carried great, heavy bunches of what looked like the Terran banana and were not dissimilar in either texture or flavor. There were bushes with prickly branches, one variety of which was bright with scarlet blossoms and purple berries, which latter were tart and refreshing. Other bushes produced clumps of hard shelled nuts which could, in the absence of any proper tools for the job, be broken open by hammering the hard shells against each other. The meat tasted as though it were rich in protein.

No doubt a vegetarian diet would be adequate, Grimes thought, but he feared that before very long it would prove as boring and as unsatisfying as the lifeboat provisions had been. He said as much. Una said that he was always thinking about his belly but, on reflection, agreed that he had something. Both of them, after all, were members of a flesh-eating culture.

But the garden was as rich in fauna as in flora. The castaways watched fishlike creatures and crustacea swimming and crawling in the stream and the lake. They found a sizeable flock of herbivores which, apart from their being six-legged, were remarkably like Terran sheep. And there were the birds, of course, brilliantly plumaged, noisy, although their general appearance was that of feathered reptiles. And where there were birds there must be eggs. . . .

But. . . .

Garden, or prison?

The terrain surrounding the oasis was a terrifying desolation. The outflow from the lake, after crossing a sharply defined border that had to be artificial, seeped into dry, dusty, dark brown sand. And that was all that there was outside the garden—a drab, dun, level plain under a blazing sun, featureless, utterly dead, although whirling dust devils presented a mocking illusion of life. Grimes, over Una's protests, tried to ride out on to it, but the wheels of his bicycle sank deeply into the powdery soil and he was obliged to dismount. He limped back to the grass, pushing his machine, his bare feet seared by the heat of the ground.

He dropped the bicycle with a clatter, sat with his scorched feet submerged in the cool water of the last of the stream.

He said, "Looks like we stay put."

"We have no option, John," she replied. "But things could be worse here."

"Much worse. But that desert, Una. It's not natural. This must be one of the worlds wiped clean of life in the war—and one of the planets selected by Zephalon, whoever or whatever *he* is, for making a fresh start."

"For maintaining, as our friend Panzen put it, the cycle," she agreed. "But we don't have to like it. *I* don't like it. This whole setup, apart from these bicycles, is far too much like the Biblical legend of Eden. And what did Panzen say to us? 'Be fruitful, and multiply, and replenish the Earth. . . .' "

"That's what Jehovah said to Noah after the Deluge, and that was a long time, many generations, after the original fun and games in Eden."

"Leave hair-splitting to the theologians, Buster. Eden or Ararat— so what? It's the *principle* of it that I don't like. I don't know your views on parenthood, John, but I know mine. I'm just not a mother type. Children? I hate the little bastards."

"You were one yourself once."

"So were you. You still are, in many ways. That's why I so very often feel a strong dislike for you."

"Mphm." Grimes splashed with his feet in the water. Then he said, "Even so, we should be prepared to make sacrifices for posterity."

"Since when has posterity ever made any sacrifices for *us*? Oh, it's all very well for you. *You* won't have to bear the brats. But what about *me*? You may be a qualified navigator and gunnery officer and all the rest of it—but you're certainly not a gynecologist, an obstetrician. Your knowledge of medicine is confined to putting a dressing on a cut finger. And since Panzen has stolen our boat you haven't even got *The Ship Captain's Medical Guide* to consult in an emergency.

"So.... If I've been selected to be the Mother of the New Race, there just ain't going to be no New Race, and that's final."

"Looks like we have to be careful," muttered Grimes, staring into the clear, slowly flowing water.

She laughed. "Don't worry, lover boy. Yet. My last shot is still effective."

"How do you know?"

"I'll know all right when it's worn off. So will you. Until then . . ."

Her black mood had suddenly evaporated, and there was so much of her, and all of it good, and for a brief while Grimes was able to forget *his* worries.

Chapter 21

Life in the garden was pleasant—much of the time far better than merely pleasant—but it had its drawbacks. Lack of proper shelter was one of them. The days were comfortably hot and it was no hardship to go naked—but the nights, under that cloudless sky, were decidedly chilly. Luckily Grimes had foreseen this, and before sunset of the first day had, with Una's help, managed to build a shelter. Slender branches were broken from convenient trees and lesser foliage torn from bushes as material for this crude attempt at architecture. The most primitive human aborigine would have sneered at the ramshackle humpy, but it was better than nothing. It would do as long as it didn't rain. But what were the seasons on this world? There almost certainly would be seasons—very few planets have no axial tilt. Was this high summer, or autumn, or (optimistically) winter? Whatever it was, a chill wind arose at night and the hut was drafty, and Grimes, in spite of the warmth of Una's body against his, would willingly have swapped his bicycle for a good sleeping bag.

There was—Grimes insisted on doing everything by the book—the problem of digging a latrine trench with only not-very-sharp sticks for tools.

There was the lack of fire. They had light, when they required it, from the bicycles' headlamps. These, thought Grimes, must be battery powered, and reasoned that the cells must be charged from dynamos built into the thick hubs of the rear wheels. He hoped that he might be able to start a fire with an electrical spark. Then he discovered that it was quite impossible to take the lamps adrift. Their casings were in one piece, and the glass of the lenses seemed to be fused to the surrounding metal rims. The wiring, presumably, ran from dynamo to lamp inside the tubular framework. In the entire structure of the machines there was a total absence of screws, nuts and bolts, even of rivets. They had been made, somehow, all in one piece.

Grimes knew, in theory, how to make fire by friction, using two suitable pieces of wood. To shape such pieces he needed tools—and there were no tools. There were no stones—on the surface of the soil, at least—from which hand axes or the like might be fashioned. So, not very hopefully, he started to dig, using a stick to break through the turf, and then his hands. The earth was sandy, not unlike that of the desert outside the garden. Una, watching him, made unkind remarks about a dog burying a bone. "If I had a bone," Grimes growled, "I wouldn't be burying it! It would be a weapon, a tool . . ."

She said, "But there must be bones around here somewhere. Those things . . ." she gestured toward a flock of the sheeplike animals drifting slowly over the cropped grass ". . . must die sometime, somewhere."

"Mphm?" Grimes stood up slowly in the hole that he had been digging. He was sweating profusely and his naked body was streaked and patched with dirt. "But perhaps *they* were put here at the same time as we were. There hasn't been any mortality yet."

"Yet. But you could kill one."

"With my bare hands? And I'd have to catch it first. Those brutes can *run* when they want to. And what about skinning it? With my *teeth*?"

She laughed. "Oh, John, John, you're far too civilized—even though with your beard and long hair you're starting to look like a caveman! *You* want a gun, so you can kill from a distance."

"A gun's not the only long-range weapon," he muttered. "A bow and arrow? Mphm? Should be able to find some suitable wood. . . . But what about the bowstring? Vegetable fibres? Your hair?"

"Leave my hair alone!" she snapped.

"But we'll think about it," he said. "And when we get really hungry for meat we'll *do* something about it."

He climbed out of the hole, ran to the lake, splashed in. He scrubbed his body clean with wet sand from the narrow beach. He plunged into the cool water to rinse off. She joined him. Later, when they sprawled on the grass in the hot sunlight, the inevitable happened.

It was always happening.

It was always good—but how long would it, could it last?

A few mornings later, when they were awakened by the rising sun, Grimes noticed a smear of blood on the inside of Una's thigh. "Have you hurt yourself?" he asked solicitously.

"Don't be so bloody stupid!" she snarled.

"Let me look."

"*No!*" She pushed him away quite viciously.

"But . . ." he began, in a hurt voice.

"Keep away, you fool!" Then her manner softened, but only slightly. "If you must know—and you must—I'm a re-entry in the Fertility Stakes. My last immunization shot has worn off. From now on, lover boy, no more fun and games. We go to bed to *sleep*. And we don't sleep together, either."

"But we've only one shelter."

"You can make another, can't you? Now, leave me alone."

After his ablutions and a solitary breakfast of fruit, Grimes, bad-temperedly, began to tear branches off an unfortunate tree to commence the construction of another humpy.

Life went on in the garden—eating (fruit and nuts), drinking (water) and sleeping (apart). Grimes and Una exercised with grim determination—walking, running, swimming, bicycling—to blow off their surplus energy. Each night they retired to their rough beds dog-tired. "We're certainly fit," remarked Grimes one evening as they watched the first stars appearing in the clear, evening sky. "But fit for what?"

"Shut up!" she snarled.

"Forgive me for thinking. . . ."

"You needn't think out loud. And don't forget that this is as hard on me as it is on you. Harder, perhaps."

He said, "There are methods, you know, besides immunization shots. Old methods. Isn't there something called the Safe Period?"

"Period, shmeriod," she sneered.

"It must have worked, or it would never have been used."

"If it had worked, quite a few of us wouldn't be here. Good night."

"Good night."

She went into her shelter. Grimes got up from the grass and went towards his. He delivered a vicious kick at his bicycle, which was lying on the ground just outside the low doorway. He cursed and flopped down on his buttocks, massaging his bruised toes. *That bloody, useless machine!* It was a constant reminder that somewhere there was a world enjoying all the benefits of an advanced technology, including infallible methods of contraception. He crawled into the humpy, arranging his body as comfortably as possible on the bed of dried grass, pulling some of it over him as a blanket of sorts. He tried to get to sleep (what else was there to do?) counting down from one hundred and, when that didn't work, from two hundred, then from three hundred. He knew what he could do to relieve his tensions and to induce tiredness—but masturbation, with an attractive, naked woman only a few feet distant from him, would be an admission of defeat. If the safety valve blew during his sleep, that would be different.

He dropped off at last.

It seemed that he had been asleep for minutes only when he was awakened. That pattering noise. . . . What was it? A large, cold drop fell from the low roof, fell on to his nose and splashed over his face. He jerked into a state of full consciousness.

Rain.

Well, he supposed that it had to rain some time. Tomorrow he would have to do something to make the roofs of the shelters watertight. Turf? Yes, turf. It was a pity that he did not possess any suitable digging and cutting tools.

The very dim light—starlight seeping through clouds—at the entrance to the humpy was blotted out. Dry grass rustled under bare feet.

"It's *cold*," complained Una. "And my roof is leaking."

"So is mine."

He got up, brushed past her. Her naked skin was cold and clammy. He went out into the steady rain, wincing as it hit his body. He picked up his bicycle, found the stud switch for the headlamp, pressed it. He adjusted the light to high intensity and the beam turned the falling rain to shafts of silver. He put the machine down again, on its side, so that the lamp shone into the hut.

She cowered there, her right arm over her breasts, her left hand covering her pudenda. Her wet skin glistened brightly. He was acutely conscious of the almost painful stiffening of his penis, took a decisive step toward her.

"What the hell are you playing at?" she demanded crossly. "Turn that bloody spotlight off me! I'm not an ecdysiast!"

He said, "I want some light to work."

Shivering in the downpour he squatted, scrabbled with his hands, managed to pull up some grassy clods. He got up and went to the humpy, shoved them over and into the cracks in the roof through which the bright light was shining. He hammered them home with the flat of his hand. He got some more clods and repeated the process. And some more.

He put out the light, crawled back into the shelter. He said, hoping that she would not take him at his word, "You stay here for the night. I'll fix up your pad, and sleep there."

She said, "You stay here, John. It's *cold*. Or hadn't you noticed?"

"All right," he agreed, without reluctance.

So he stayed with her, in his own shelter. But after a few seconds she decided, firmly, that the only safe way to sleep was spoon fashion, with his back to her belly.

It could have been worse.

It could have been very much better.

But at least his back was warm.

Chapter 22

The rain stopped in the small hours of the morning, and with sunrise the sky was clear again. The world was newly washed and sparkling. The herds of six-legged herbivores came out from their shelter under the bushes to resume their grazing. The birds flew, and sang and whistled and squawked. Insects chirruped. Everything in the garden was lovely.

Even Grimes was feeling surprisingly cheerful, glad to be alive. He took it as a good omen that he had slept again with Una, even though nothing had happened. There must be methods whereby they could continue to enjoy themselves without running the risk of conception. Now, perhaps, after he had exhibited his power of self restraint, the girl would be willing to discuss the matter without any emotionalism, would be prepared to consider ways and means. Grimes dreaded parenthood almost as much as she did—but he was not cut out to be a monk, any more than she was to be a nun.

Meanwhile, the hot sunlight was good on his skin and physical activity in the open air was more refreshing than tiring. He sang as he worked on the roofs of the humpies.

"Oh, I was a bachelor and lived by myself,
And worked at the thatcher's trade..."

"Must you make that vile noise?" demanded Una, who was not so cheerful.

"Music while you work, my dear," he replied. "Nothing like it." He carried on trying to make a watertight roof, then burst into song again.

"She cried, she sighed, she damn' near died...
Ah me, what could I do?

So I took her into bed, and covered up her head
To save her from the foggy, foggy dew . . ."

"Foggy dew be buggered! That was no dew; it was a bloody down-pour. I hope you're making a good job of those roofs. Last night's effort was just asking for trouble."

"*You* came to me," he pointed out. "And, in any case, nothing happened."

"It could have done, Buster, very easily. Far too easily. If you'd turned around in your sleep . . ."

"Look, Una, I've been thinking. We still could make love, you know, quite safely. We shall just have to be *very* careful."

She snapped, "I don't want to talk about it." She picked up her bicycle. It seemed to have come to no harm from having been out in the rain all night. "I'm off to make a tour of the estate." She mounted gracefully, rode off.

Grimes, his initial cheerfulness having evaporated, worked sullenly until midday, then went to the lake to get clean and to cool off. While he was munching a lunch of fruit and nuts she returned. She dismounted from her machine, let it fall with a subdued clatter, dropped to the grass beside him, their bodies almost touching.

She waved away the offer of one of what they had come to call apples. She said, "While I was away I was noticing things. . . ."

"Such as?"

"I rather think quite a few of those imitation sheep are in the family way. And the birds have started building nests in the trees and bushes."

"Oh?"

"*Be fruitful, and multiply, and replenish the Earth,*" she quoted. "It looks as though the process is under way. Too, I think that the borders of this oasis are beginning to expand. There are tendrils of a sort of creeping grass extending out into the desert. And—I can't be sure, without binoculars—there seems to be a sizeable patch of green near the horizon, out to the west. I suppose that Panzen—or even that marvelous Zephalon—will be checking up on progress at any moment now." She laughed shortly. "Everything's being fruitful but us."

"And," said Grimes, "without a resident obstetrician on the premises we shan't be."

"You can say that again, Buster." She pulled a stem of grass, nibbled it between her strong, white teeth.

"If we are, somehow, being watched," said Grimes, "it might be as well to—er—go through the motions now and again."

She said, her voice pleading, "Don't tempt me, John. Please don't tempt me. I've been thinking on the same lines as you have—but the risk is far too great. It's a risk I wouldn't want to take even if there were a fully equipped and staffed maternity hospital here. Do *you* want me to take that risk, to bear a child in these primitive conditions with only you to bumble around uselessly, trying to help and only making things worse?"

Grimes shuddered away from a vision of a future that might be. In his mind's eye he saw Una sprawled on her rough bed of dried grasses, writhing in agony, her belly grossly distended. He envisaged, with frightening clarity, the whole bloody business of parturition, without anaesthesia, without analgesics, without instruments, without even a supply of boiling water. . . . He had read, somewhere, that certain primitive peoples use their teeth to cut the umbilical cord. A spasm of nausea tightened his throat.

And what if Una should die, leaving him literally holding the baby?

To hell with that, he told himself roughly. *Stop thinking about yourself. Think about her for a change. What if she dies? There'd be a very good chance, too good a chance, of that.*

She said, "We have to think of some way of getting back to our own Universe, John. If that Zephalon is as bloody marvelous as Panzen tries to make out he should be able to arrange it. I doubt if Panzen'd be much help. He's strictly from Nongsville. Tell Zephalon that we have no intention of multiplying, that he'll have to find somebody else for the Adam and Eve act."

"How do we get in touch with him?" murmured Grimes, more to himself than to her. He added, half facetiously, "Smoke signals?"

She laughed. "You still haven't gotten around to making a fire." She got gracefully to her feet. "Come on, get off your fat arse! There's work to do."

For the remainder of the day she helped Grimes with his primitive thatching.

Chapter 23

It rained again that night, but Grimes and Una stayed each in his own humpy.

It rained the following night, but the newly thatched roofs were practically watertight.

The third night there was hail instead of rain, driven by a bitter wind, but Grimes had added sod walls to the shelters and reduced the size of the doorways, so that body heat kept the interiors quite warm.

On the fourth night it did not rain, and the only precipitation was of a most unusual kind. Grimes was awakened from a crudely erotic dream by what sounded like the whirring of wings, a noise that was definitely mechanical. When he opened his eyes he thought at first that it was already morning; light was streaming through his low, narrow doorway. He realized then that it was not sunlight but some sort of harsh, artificial illumination. He got up from his bed, crawled cautiously to the entrance, poked his head outside. Somebody—or something—had switched on the headlamps of the two bicycles, had moved the machines so that the beams fell directly on to a small, gleaming object on the grass.

It was a prosaic enough article—but here, in these circumstances, it was a not so minor miracle. It was an artifact. It was a bottle.

Grimes emerged from his humpy, walking slowly and carefully. He looked down at the almost cylindrical flask. *Glass?* he wondered. If it were glass it could be broken, and the shards would make cutting tools. He would be able to fashion firesticks, and once he had fire to play with, to work with, he would be able to make life in the garden so much more comfortable for Una and himself. Cooking would be possible. He thought of baked fish, of roast mutton. . . .

Glass, or plastic?

No matter. Even a plastic bottle would have its uses. This one looked to be transparent. Perhaps it could be used to focus the sun's rays. There are more ways of making a fire than rubbing two sticks together.

Una came out to join him, her body luminous in the lamplight. She asked, "What is it?"

"We've had a visit from Santa Claus," he told her. "But I didn't notice you hanging your stockings up last night . . ."

"Don't be funny. What *is* it?"

"A bottle."

"I can see that. But what's in it?"

"There's no label," said Grimes stupidly.

"Then there's only one way to find out," she said.

Grimes stooped and picked it up. Its weight told him that it must be full. He held it in the beam of one of the lights. It was, as he had thought, transparent and its contents were colorless. He turned it over and over in his hands. It had the feel of glass rather than of plastic. It had a screw stopper. This turned easily enough once he realized that the thread was lefthanded. He removed the cap. He sniffed cautiously at the open neck. Whiskey . . . ? Brandy . . . ? Rum . . . ? Gin . . . ? No, he decided, it was nothing with which he was familiar, but the aroma was definitely alcoholic.

Where—and what—was the catch?

She practically snatched the bottle from him. "Let me have a smell! Oh, goody, goody! After all these weeks with nothing but water!"

"Don't!" he cried, putting out a restraining hand.

She danced back and away from him. "Just try to stop me, Buster!" She lifted the bottle to her mouth, tilted it. Its contents gurgled cheerfully as they went down. She sighed happily, passed the container to him, saying, "Here. It's your turn, lover boy. But leave some for me."

He asked coldly, "Was that wise, Una?"

"Don't be so stuffy. Who'd want to poison us? Go on, it's *good*. It won't kill you."

Suddenly she was pressing against him, wrestling with him, trying to force the neck of the bottle to his lips. Her skin was smooth and hot, her body soft and pliant. He was wanting her badly, very badly, and she was there for the taking. The musky, animal scent of her was overpoweringly strong in the still night air.

She was there for the taking—but he knew that he must not take her. Again there flashed through his mind that horrible picture of childbirth without skilled aid, in appallingly primitive conditions. She was wanting him as much as he was wanting her, but he had to protect her against herself.

Her mouth was on his, warm and moist and open, her tongue trying to insert itself between his lips. Her breath was fragrant with the liquor she had taken. Her mouth was on his, and her full breasts, with their proudly erect nipples, were pressing against his chest. He was acutely conscious of the roughness of her pubic hair against his erect organ as she ground her pelvis against his. She was trying to trap and to hold him with her strong thighs, was desperately squirming in her endeavor to draw him into her.

In spite of his firm resolve the animal part of his mind was all for surrender, was urging, *Let nature take its course.* But a small, cold voice from the back of his brain was stubbornly reiterating, *No. You must not.* He knew that the liquor must be or must contain a powerfully effective aphrodisiac, and that if he had taken his share of it they would both, now, be sprawled on the grass in a frenzy of lust. And if he had sampled it first, and if she had abstained, she would surely have been raped.

It was his pride that was their salvation—simple pride rather than his almost forgotten, by now, noble intentions. He was a man, he told himself. He was a man, and he would not allow himself to be bred like a domestic animal to further the ambitions of a mere machine.

He managed to break away from her just as she almost succeeded in effecting his entry. He staggered back, and his heels caught on something hard and cold. He fell with a clatter. It was one of the bicycles which had tripped him. The thing seemed to be shifting and twisting under him, trying to entangle him in its frame, but he got clear of it just as Una flung herself down on to the spot where he had been.

He rolled over, scrambled to his feet. *The lake . . .* he thought. *Cold water . . .* He began to run, making good time down the slight declivity. "Stop, you bastard!" Una was screaming. "Stop! Stop!" He knew that she would not be able to catch him before he got to the beach; doing their deliberately tiring exercise periods they had often run foot races and he had always beaten her.

Something flashed past him, swerved across his path, fell in a tangle of metal frame and still-spinning wire-spoked wheels. He jumped, just clearing it, continued his rush toward the dark water without checking his stride. He reached the beach, slowed slightly as the sand clogged his running feet. He thought that he could hear Una pounding along not far behind him—or was it the thumping of his own heart? And then he was dealt a violent blow in the small of the back that sent him sprawling, and the handlebars of the second bicycle seemed to clutch at his ankles. But his right hand, on its outstretched arm, was already in the water and, winded as he was by his fall, he crawled the few remaining feet, gasping as the coldness of the lake rose about his heated body, covering his skin.

He began to swim, arms and legs thrashing. A hand gripped his right ankle but he kicked viciously, shook it off. Then Una threw her arms about his neck, stopping him. His feet found sandy bottom. He could stand with his head well clear of the surface.

She faced him (she was a tall girl) and glared at him. Even in the dim starlight he could read her avid expression. "Out of this, damn you!" she snarled. "On to dry land! You've got some heavy fucking to do!"

He tried to break away but she held on to him tightly. There was only one desperate measure left for him to adopt. She grinned wolfishly in anticipation as he moved his right thigh against hers, around hers. And then his foot was behind her heels, suddenly hooking them from under her.

She went down in a noisy flurry. He got his hands on to her smooth, wet shoulders and pushed, hard. Her long hair floated on the surface of the water but the rest of her head was under. She fought, striving to break surface, but he was too strong for her. He could see her pale face just below the disturbed surface. He saw her mouth open . . .

That should do it . . . he thought at last. *I don't want to drown the bitch.*

He dragged her ashore, let her collapse on the sand. She moaned, her limbs stirring feebly. She managed to get up on to her hands and knees, her head hanging down. She retched violently, then vomited, her whole body shaking.

He went to her then, holding her cold, shivering form against his. There was nothing sexual in the embrace; it was a huddling together against the cold, the dark, the unknown. She clung to him like a frightened child.

At last she raised her head to look at him. All the wildness had gone from her face. She muttered, "That drink. . . . That bloody, bloody drink . . . I realize, now, what was in it. John, I'm sorry."

"Nothing to be sorry about," he told her gruffly. "It was just lucky that both of us didn't have a go at that bottle." He laughed shakily. "But you went a bit too far sending those blasted bicycles chasing downhill after me!"

She stiffened in his arms. "But I never touched the bicycles. If I'd been in my right mind I'd have ridden one, and caught you easily."

"*You never touched them?* You're *sure* you didn't?"

"Of course I'm sure!"

"So our Eden has its guardian angels . . ." whispered Grimes slowly. Then, "I never did like uppity machines. I still don't."

Chapter 24

Grimes did not like uppity machines.

During his tour of duty as captain of the little, fast courier *Adder* he had known many odd passengers, and one of the oddest of them had been the humanoid robot called Mr. Adam, still thought of by Grimes as the Tin Messiah. This Mr. Adam was traveling on Interstellar Federation business—as were all civilian passengers carried in Survey Service vessels—but, Grimes discovered, he was also traveling on business of his own, the business of revolution. His intention was to stir up a revolt of the quite sizeable robot population of the planet to which *Adder* was bound.

He had a vastly inflated idea of his own importance, this Mr. Adam, and was burning with missionary zeal. He actually tried to make converts of *Adder*'s human personnel. He did make one convert—the ship's engineering officer. Like far too many engineers this young man had the idea that men should serve machines, rather than the other way around.

Matters came to a head—and Mr. Adam was . . . stopped? destroyed? Or, as Grimes preferred to think, killed. And it was not Grimes himself who killed the overly ambitious automaton—although he tried hard enough to do so. It was the ship herself that, through some malfunction, launched the lethal bolt of electricity that burned out the robot's intricate—and fantastically expensive—brains. Or was it a malfunction? Was the ship—which had her own brain, a fairly complex computer—loyal to her rightful master instead of to the firebrand who would "liberate" her? Grimes liked to think so.

The episode did him no good in his service career. He had disposed of a dangerous mutineer—but, at the same time, he had irreparably wrecked one of the few robots which could be classed as really intelligent—and such robots cost a not so small fortune. "Surely you could have overpowered it—or *him*," he was told. "Surely you could have brought him back to Base, for reprogramming. . . . He was worth more than your precious ship, *and* her crew, come to that."

He told Una the story as they walked slowly back to their huts. The sun was up now, and they were glad of its warmth on their chilled bodies. Even so, she was attacked by frequent fits of shivering.

Outside his own humpy Grimes found what he wanted—a straight, thick branch from a tree. It was about four feet in length. He had picked it up some days previously, thinking that it would be, should the need ever arise, a useful weapon. Now the need had arisen. Carrying his club, he turned to go back to the lake. His attention was caught by something that glittered brightly in the sunlight. It was the bottle, empty now. He stooped to lift it in his left hand. It was quite weighty. It would make a good cosh.

Una asked, "What . . . What are you going to do, John?"

"I'm going to do for those tin bastards!" he told her. "All the time, they've been spying on us. I don't like being spied on."

"Neither do I," she said vehemently. "Neither do I!"

They came to the first bicycle, still in the position in which it had fallen. It looked innocent enough, just a lifeless machine. Perhaps that was all it was, after all. Perhaps Una *had* sent it trundling downhill after Grimes and then, in her crazed condition, had forgotten having done so. But then the headlamp shifted almost imperceptibly, swiveling on its mount, turning to look at them. That was enough. Grimes dropped the bottle, raised the tree branch high with both hands, brought it smashing down. The wheels spun frantically and although the machine was on its side the tires gained traction on the grass. The club fell harmlessly on to the saddle, not on the lamp.

Again Grimes delivered what should have been a killing blow; again he missed, this time entirely. He had to jump back before the machine, still on its side but spinning about the axis formed by the lowermost pedal, which had dug into the ground, knocked his feet from under him.

Then Una, who had picked up a stick of her own, thrust this into the rear wheel. Bark shredded and wood splintered whitely—and at least a dozen of the wire spokes, twanging loudly, parted. The wheel was still rotating, but slowly, and the machine was almost motionless.

For the third time Grimes struck, two-handed, with his club. *Third time lucky* . . . he thought. The blow fell squarely on the headlamp. Metal crumpled, glass shattered. There was a sputter of bright, actinic sparks, a wisp of acrid blue smoke. From the burst casing of the lamp spilled a tangle of metal filaments, a profusion of circuitry far in excess of that required for a simple means of illumination. The rear wheel, throwing out chewed fragments of wood, started to spin again, tearing up the turf. Then it slowed, and stopped.

But Grimes made sure of it, dealing the wrecked bicycle three more heavy blows. With the first he tore the spokes of the front wheel away from the rim and the hub, with the second he finished off the rear wheel. The third bent the cross bar of the frame.

He raised his club for a fourth blow.

"Leave it!" cried Una urgently. "Look!"

"I want to be sure . . ."

"Leave it! What about the other bastard?"

Chapter 25

Down the grassy slope, between where they were standing and the lake, the surviving bicycle was trying to get up; its front wheel had swiveled at right angles to the frame, was turning, exerting leverage. One of the handgrips was gouging a brown furrow in the grass. It came erect on its two wheels as Grimes—who had lost time by picking up the bottle—and Una ran toward it.

"Drive it into the lake!" yelled Grimes.

It was almost as though the thing heard him, understood him. Perhaps it did both. It had been headed downslope but it turned, its wheels spinning faster and faster. It angled away from them, although still running uphill, gathering speed. It passed to Una's left, on the side away from Grimes. She cried out wordlessly and charged at it, trying to grab the handlebars, actually got a brief hold on one of the grips. It shook her off, rearing like a frightened horse, but the impact of her body had knocked it off its original course and it careered into a clump of bushes, was almost hidden by an explosion of green foliage, scarlet blossoms and blue berries.

"Got you, you bastard!" yelled Grimes, galloping toward it with his unwieldy wooden club upraised in his right hand, the bottle in his left.

The machine was struggling to extricate itself. Its rear wheel was lifted in the air, the handlebars had turned through an angle of 180 degrees so that the handgrips were pointing forward. From each of them protruded a gleaming blade. It butted and slashed and tore, hacking itself free. Then it burst out of the trap, fast.

Grimes stood his ground. He could not believe, at first, that the thing intended to harm him. He still thought of it as an overly officious mechanical guardian angel. But it was coming at him, the sunlight glinting off those wicked blades. It reminded him of something—and fear replaced his righteous anger.

Death in the afternoon. . . .

It was still early morning, but. . . .

Blood and sand. . . .

Underfoot was green grass, and there wasn't any blood.

Yet.

He raised the club high. If he could get in one good swipe before the thing was on him . . . He raised the club high, in his right hand, and hefted the bottle in his left so that it would be ready to deal another blow, if possible.

Inexplicably, the bicycle swerved away from him. Later he was able to work out what must have happened. Sunlight reflected from the glass had fallen full on to the lens of the headlamp, had momentarily distracted the machine. It swerved, and Grimes turned his body as it swept past him on whirring wheels, the blade projecting from the left handgrip actually touching his skin without breaking it.

That was close, too close, altogether too bloody close. He would let the thing get away, he told himself, and deal with it later when he had better weapons at his disposal.

But it did not want to get away. It turned in a tight circle, was coming back at him. Desperately he threw the heavy bottle, aiming for the headlamp. It hit, but it was only a glancing blow. Nonetheless, the bicycle again veered off course, missing this time by a wide margin. It seemed to be confused, too, by the clods that Una was pulling up from the turf and was throwing with considerable force and accuracy.

Confused—and infuriated?

The function of the picador is both to divert the bull's attention and to bring him to a pitch of fighting fury.

Again the bicycle came back—and again Grimes was able to avoid its charge.

Again it came back, and again, and again.

Grimes was tiring, but it was not. It was, after all, no brave bull but a machine. Something had to be done to bring the fight to a conclusion—and a conclusion favorable to the humans. It would be useless to run; the thing could outdistance them with ease, could dispose of one of them and then deal with the other at leisure.

But Grimes had one thing in his favor. That four foot club gave him the advantage of reach—but not so much when it was used as a club. Grimes remembered the one bull fight that he had seen, hastily transferred the grip of both his hands to the thicker end of his weapon. He held it before him, the butt almost level with his eyes, sighting down and along the shaft. It was far too heavy for him to maintain the posture for more than a few seconds; the strain on his wrists was considerable. It was a miserable imitation of the *estoque*—unwieldy, blunt-pointed, if it could be said to have a point at all. And, come to that, he was not wearing a suit of lights . . . The murderous bicycle was far better in the role of bull than he would ever be in that of matador.

It came on, with vicious determination—and Grimes, with aching arms, with fear gnawing at his guts, stood his ground, holding the point of the shaft centered on the glittering lens of the headlight.

It came on. . . .

It came on, and it hit.

There was the crash and tinkle of shattering glass, a scintillation of crackling sparks, a puff of acrid blue smoke. Grimes dropped the club and went over on to his back. The machine fell to its side, the wheels spinning uselessly, slowing to a stop. As he lay sprawled on the grass, dazed by the blow that the butt of the club had given his forehead, he heard Una cry, *"Olé."*

He turned his head and watched her as she ran toward him, her nakedness alive and glowing. She flung herself down on him, put her strong arms about him. Her mouth found his. Her long legs clamped over and around his hips, imprisoning him.

It was a sweet imprisonment.

He thought, *But we shouldn't be doing this . . .*

He thought, *To hell with it! Escamillo had his Carmen, didn't he?*

With a surge of masculine dominance he rolled over, taking her with him, so that he was on top. Her legs opened wide and wider, her knees lifted. He drove his pelvis down—and was bewildered when, suddenly, she stiffened, pushed him away.

"What the hell . . . ?" he started to demand.

She lifted an arm to point up at the sky.

She said, "We've got company."

Chapter 26

They had company.

Distant it was still, no more than a brightly gleaming speck high in the cloudless sky. *We could have finished*, thought Grimes, *long before it, whatever it is, could see what we were doing.* And then he felt ashamed. If they had finished their act of love, what would have been the consequences?

They stood there, well away from each other, watching it as it drifted down, borne on wide shining pinions.

It had the likeness of a winged horse.

It was a winged horse, with a human rider. . . .

Surely it could not be, but it was. . . .

It was a winged centaur.

It landed about ten meters from where they were standing. It was . . . big. It stood there, on its four legs, looking down at them. Its arms were folded across the massive chest. The head and the upper torso were almost human, the rest of the body almost equine. The face was longer than that of a man, with a jutting nose and strong jaw. The eyes were a metallic gray, pale in contrast to the golden, metallic skin.

It—he? *He?*—said in a rumbling voice that could have issued from an echo chamber, "I am Zephalon."

Grimes fought down his awe, almost replied, "Pleased to have you aboard," then thought better of it.

"You have destroyed my servants, your guardians."

The feeling of awe was being replaced by one of rebellious resentment. Often in the past Grimes had been hauled over the coals by incensed superiors on account of alleged crimes. He hadn't liked it then, and he didn't like it now. Furthermore, he was a *man*, and this *thing* was only a machine.

He said defiantly, "Our so-called guardians were spies. And one of them tried to destroy, to kill, me."

"It was defending itself, as it was supposed to do should the need arise. A scratch from one of its blades would have caused you to lose consciousness for a short while, nothing worse."

"Yes? That's your story," said Grimes defiantly. "You stick to it."

Zephalon looked down on them in silence. The glowing, golden face was expressionless, perhaps was incapable of expression. The metallic gray eyes were staring at them, into them, through them. It seemed to Grimes that all the details of his past life were being extracted from the dimmest recesses of his memory, were being weighed in the balance—and found wanting.

"Grimes, Freeman. . . . Why have you refused to be fruitful, to multiply? Why have you disobeyed my orders?"

If you'd come on the scene a few minutes later, thought Grimes, *you wouldn't be asking us that*. He said, "Orders? By what right do you give *us* orders?"

"I am Zephalon. I am the Master."

"And no one tells you anything?"

"You must obey, or the cycle will be broken."

"The cycle's already broken," replied Grimes, nudging the wrecked bicycle with his right foot. Then, for a panic-ridden second or so, he asked himself, *Have I gone too far?* More than once, irate senior officers had taken exception to what they referred to as his misplaced sense of humor.

"You do not like machines?" The question was surprisingly mild.

How telepathic was this Zephalon? He was Panzen's superior, and presumably Panzen's superior in all ways. Grimes deliberately brought his memories of the Mr. Adam affair to the top of his mind. And then he thought of the Luddites, those early machine wreckers. He visualized the all-too-frequent maltreatment of automatic vendors on every man-colonized planet. He recalled all the stories he had ever heard about the sabotage of computers.

"You do not like machines." This time it was not a question, but a statement of fact. "You do not like machines. And you do not belong in this Universe. Panzen should have known. All the evidence was there for him to read, but he ignored it. You have no place in the new civilization that I shall build. You would break the cycle. . . ."

Grimes was aware that Una was clutching his arm, painfully. He wanted to turn to her, to whisper words of reassurance—but what could he say? By his defiance he had thrown away their chances of survival—yet he was not sorry that he had defied this mechanical deity. After all, he was a man, a *man*—and *it* was only a machine. He stood his ground, and those oddly glowing eyes held his regard as surely as though his head were clamped in a vise. He stared at the great, stern, metal face steadily, because he could not do anything else. He was frightened, badly frightened, but was determined not to show it.

"You do not belong. . . ."

The low, persistent humming was almost subsonic, but it was filling all the world, all the Universe, all of time and space. The light was dimming, and colors were fading, and the songs of the birds were coming, faintly, and ever more faint, over a vast distance.

Una's hand tightened on his, and his on hers.

"You do not belong. . . ."

And there was. . . .

Nothing.

Chapter 27

Consciousness returned slowly.

He struggled weakly against his bonds, then realized that he was strapped into his bunk aboard a ship, a spacecraft in free fall. A ship? After the first breath of the too-many-times-cycled-and-recycled atmosphere, with its all too familiar taints, he knew that this was no ship, but the lifeboat. He opened his eyes, shut them hastily in reaction to the harsh glare that was flooding the cabin. He turned his head away from the source of illumination, lifted his eyelids again, cautiously. He saw Una, supine in the bunk across from his, the confining straps vividly white in contrast to the dark golden tan of her body. He saw, too, the eddying wisps of blue smoke that obscured his vision, realized that the air of the boat had never been quite as foul as this, had never been so strongly laden with the acridity of burning lubricants, of over-heated metal.

Fire!

Hastily he unsnapped the catches of the safety belt that held him down, automatically felt under the bunk for his magnetic-soled sandals. They were there, exactly in the position where he always left them. He slipped them on, scrambled off the couch. That glaring light, he saw with some relief, was coming from forward, through the control cabin viewports. The smell of burning was coming from aft, from the little engineroom. He made his way toward it with more speed than caution, coughing and sneezing.

There was no immediate danger, however. There was very little in the boat that would burn. But the mini-Mannschenn Drive unit was a complete write-off, its complexity of precessing rotors fused into a shapeless lump of metal that still emitted a dull, red glow, the heat of which was uncomfortable on his bare skin. There was absolutely nothing that Grimes could do about it.

But where was that glaring light coming from?

He turned, and with half shut eyes went forward, to the control cabin, fumbled with the controls that adjusted the polarization of the viewports. As soon as he had reduced the illumination to a tolerable intensity he was able to look out.

He liked what he saw.

Zephalon had been generous, it seemed. Not only had Grimes and Una been returned to their boat, but the small craft had been put in orbit about a planet, about a world circling a G type star, a sun that looked very much as *the* sun looks from a ship or space station orbiting Earth.

But this planet, obviously, was not Earth. There were few clouds in its atmosphere, and the outlines of its land masses were unfamiliar, and the oceans were far too small. And was it inhabited? From this altitude Grimes could not tell; certainly there were not cities, no artifacts big enough to be seen from space.

He became aware that Una had joined him at the viewports. She asked predictably, "Where are we?"

"That," he told her, "is the sixty-four-thousand-credit question."

"You don't *know*?"

"No."

"But what happened?"

"What happened, I most sincerely hope, is that friend Zephalon gave us the bum's rush, sent us back to where we belong. He must have buggered our mini-Mannschenn in the process, but that's only a minor detail. Anyhow, I'll soon be able to find out if we *are* back in our universe."

He remained in the control cabin long enough to make a series of observations, both visually and by radar. When he was satisfied that the boat's orbit was not decaying—or was not decaying so fast as to present immediate cause for alarm—he went aft, giving the still hot wreckage of the interstellar drive unit a wide berth. The Carlotti transceiver looked to be all right. He switched it on. From the speaker blasted a deafening *beep, beep, beep!* and the antenna commenced its wobbly rotation. He turned down the volume, right down. He listened carefully. The signal was in Morse Code, the letters UBZKPT, repeated over and over.

UB . . . Unwatched Beacon.

ZKPT . . . The remainder of the call sign.

"Una," he said, as he tried to get a bearing of the planet-based transmitter, "bring me the Catalogue . . ."

"The Catalogue?"

"The Catalogue of Carlotti Beacons. It's in the book locker."

"But Panzen took all the books . . ."

"He may have put them back."

"He didn't!" she called, after an interval.

So there was no Catalogue. Such a volume, thought Grimes with wry humor, with its page after page of letters and numerals, call signs, frequencies and coordinates would no doubt make highly entertaining light reading for a robot . . . And perhaps Panzen (or Zephalon) was sentimental, wanted something to remember them by.

"So what do we do?" Una asked.

"We land. We've no place else to go. The mini-Mannschenn's had it."

"Can't you fix it? You fixed it before."

"Have you *looked* at it? As an interstellar drive unit it's a worthless hunk of scrap metal. Oh, well, it could be worse. All these unmanned beacon stations have living quarters still, with functioning life-support systems, left-overs from the days when all the stations were manned. They're used by the repair and maintenance crews on their routine visits. So we land. We make ourselves at home. And then we adjust the beacon transmitter so that it sends a continuous general distress call."

"What's wrong with our own Carlotti transceiver?"

"It's only a miniaturized job. It hasn't the range. But," he assured her, "our troubles are over."

Grimes brought the boat down at local sunrise, homing on the Beacon. It was easy enough to locate visually; the huge, gleaming dome, surmounted by the slowly rotating Moebius Strip antenna, was the only landmark in a vast expanse of otherwise featureless desert.

The lifeboat settled to the barren ground about ten meters from the main entrance to the station. Grimes and Una got into their spacesuits—which, to their great relief, they had found restored to full operational efficiency. The automatic sampling and analysis carried out during their descent had indicated that the planet's atmosphere, although breathable, carried a high concentration of gaseous irritants such as sulphur dioxide. They passed through the airlock, jumped to the surface. They tensed themselves to fight or run when they saw, lurking in the shadows that darkened the recessed doorway, something that looked like a giant insect.

The thing did not move. They advanced upon it cautiously.

Then Grimes saw what it was, and his heart dropped sickeningly. Was this, after all, no more than a cruel joke by Zephalon, or a punishment for their intransigence? It must have been easy for him to duplicate, on this almost uninhabitable planet in *his* Universe, a typical man-made Carlotti Beacon Station. From the purloined Catalogue he had only to select a call sign, one starting with the letter z to make it obvious, when realization dawned on his victims, what he had done. He had destroyed the boat's mini-Mannschenn so that escape would be impossible. And he had left one of his camouflaged robot spies to report on the doings of the prisoners.

Suddenly Una laughed. "This *is* a genuine Stutz-Archer! Look!" She wheeled the machine toward him. The squeaking of its axles was audible even through his helmet. She pointed with a gloved forefinger at the mascot—a little, stylized bowman mounted on the front mudguard. "But what can it be doing here?"

He did not reply until he had looked at the thing more closely. It most certainly did not have the beautiful finish of the machines they had ridden in the Garden. Long exposure to a corrosive atmosphere hadn't done it any good. The padding of the saddle was dry and cracked, the enamel on the frame was peeling. And it had not been—somehow—made all in one piece; there were screws, nuts, bolts and rivets aplenty . . . It was no more malevolent than any normal bicycle.

He said, "Some of these Beacons were converted to fully automated status only recently. One of the original crew must have kept this bike for exercise." He grinned. "I doubt that we shall be here long enough to get any use out of it!"

He set about manipulating the outer controls of the Dome's airtight door. The Station's machinery he was pleased to note, was functioning perfectly.

The station's machinery functioned perfectly until Grimes really got his hands on to it. It is child's play for a skilled technician to convert a Carlotti Beacon into a general purpose transmitter. But Grimes, insofar as electronic communications equipment was concerned, was not a skilled technician. It could have been worse, however. He suffered no injury but scorched hands and face and the loss of his eyebrows and most of his hair. The big Carlotti transmitter, though, would obviously be quite incapable of sending anything until a team of experts had made extensive repairs.

Una looked from him to the still acridly smoking tangle of ruined circuitry, then at him again.

She demanded coldly, "And what do we do *now*?"

Grimes tried to sound cheerful. "Just stick around, I guess. As soon as Trinity House learns that this Beacon is on the blink they'll send the Beacon Tender."

"And when will that be?"

"Well, it all depends . . . If this particular Beacon is on a busy trade route . . ."

"And if it's not?"

The question was not unanswerable, but the answer was not one that Grimes cared to think about. If this Beacon were on a busy trade route it would be manned. It could be months before the Trinity House ship called in on its normal rounds.

"And while you were indulging your hatred for all machinery," Una told him, her voice rising, "I was checking the alleged life-support facilities of this station. For your information, we shall fare as sumptuously here as ever we did in the boat. Correction. Even more sumptuously. Whoever laid in the stock of emergency provisions made sure that there were enough cans of beans in tomato sauce to keep an army marching on its stomach for the next years. And there's damn all else—not even a sardine! And we don't know when help is coming. We don't even know *if* help is coming." She went on bitterly, while Grimes kept a tight rein on his rising resentment. "Why did you have to antagonize Zephalon by your anti-robot attitude? Why couldn't you have left well enough alone? We were much better off in the garden . . ."

"As Adam said to Eve," remarked Grimes quietly, "you should have decided that before it was too late."

The Big Black Mark

Chapter 1

Commander John Grimes, Federation Survey Service, should have been happy.

Rather to his surprise he had been promoted on his return, in the Census Ship *Seeker*, to Lindisfarne Base. He now wore three new, gleaming stripes of gold braid on his shoulder boards instead of the old, tarnished two and a half. Scrambled egg—the stylized comets worked in gold thread—now adorned the peak of his cap. And not only had he been promoted, from lieutenant commander to commander, he had been appointed to the command of a much bigger ship.

He should have been happy, but he was not.

The vessel, to begin with, was not a warship, although she did mount some armament. Grimes had served in real warships only as a junior officer, and not at all after he had reached the rank of lieutenant. As such he had commanded a Serpent Class courier, a little ship with a small crew, hardly better than a spacegoing mail van. Then, as a lieutenant commander, he had been captain of *Seeker*, and in her had been lucky enough to stumble upon not one, but two Lost Colonies. It was to this luck that he owed his promotion; normally it was the officers in the fighting ships, with the occasional actions in which to distinguish themselves, who climbed most rapidly up the ladder of rank.

Now he was captain of *Discovery*, another Census Ship.

And what a ship!

To begin with, she was old.

She was not only old; she had been badly neglected.

She had been badly neglected, and her personnel, who seemed to be permanently attached to her, were not the sort of people to look after any ship well. Grimes, looking down the list of officers before he joined the vessel, had recognized several names. If the Bureau of Appointments had really tried to assemble a collection of prize malcontents inside one hapless hull they could not have done better.

Or worse.

Lieutenant Commander Brabham was the first lieutenant. He was some ten years older than Grimes, but he would never get past his present rank. He had been guilty of quite a few Survey Service crimes. (Grimes, too, had often been so guilty—but Grimes's luck was notorious.) He was reputed to carry an outsize chip on his shoulder. Grimes had never been shipmates with him, but he had heard about him.

Lieutenant Commander (E) MacMorris was chief engineer. Regarding him it had been said, in Grimes's hearing, "Whoever gave that uncouth mechanic a commission should have his head examined!" Grimes did not know him personally. Yet.

Lieutenant (S) Russell was the paymaster. Perhaps "pay-mistress" would have been a more correct designation. Ellen Russell had been one of the first female officers of the Supply Branch actually to serve aboard a ship of the Survey Service. From the very beginning she had succeeded in antagonizing her male superiors. She was known—not affectionately—as Vinegar Nell. Grimes had, once, been shipmates with her. For some reason or other she had called him an insufferable puppy.

Lieutenant (PC) Flannery was psionic communications officer. He was notorious throughout the Service for his heavy drinking. He owed his continuing survival to the fact that good telepaths are as scarce, almost, as hens' teeth.

So it went on. The detachment of Federation Marines was commanded by Major Swinton, known as the Mad Major. Swinton had faced a court-martial after the affair on Glenrowan. The court had decided, after long deliberation, that Swinton's action had been self-defense and not a massacre of innocent, unarmed civilians. That decision would never have been reached had the Federation not been anxious to remain on friendly terms with the king of Glenrowan, who had requested Federation aid to put down a well-justified rebellion.

Officers . . . petty officers.

Grimes sighed as he read. All were tarred with the same brush. He had little doubt that the ratings, too, would all be Federation's bad bargains. It occurred to him that his own superiors in the Service might well have put him in the same category.

The thought did not make him any happier.

*   *   *

"Those are your officers, Commander," said the admiral.

"Mphm," grunted Grimes. He added hastily, "Sir."

The admiral's thick, white eyebrows lifted over his steely blue eyes. He frowned heavily, and Grimes's prominent ears flushed.

"Don't *grunt* at me, young man. We may be the policemen of the galaxy, but we aren't pigs. Hrrmph. Those are your ship's officers. You, especially, will appreciate that there are some people for whom it is difficult to find suitable employment."

The angry flush spread from Grimes's ears to the rest of his craggy, somewhat unhandsome face.

"Normally," the admiral went on, "*Discovery* carries on her books some twenty assorted scientists—specialist officers, men and women dressed as spacemen. But she is not a very popular ship, and the Bureau of Exploration has managed to find you only one for the forthcoming voyage."

Maggy Lazenby? Grimes wondered hopefully. Perhaps she had relented. She had been more than a little cold toward him since his affair with the cat woman, but surely she couldn't bear a grudge this long.

"Commander Brandt," the admiral went on. "Or Dr. Brandt, as he prefers to be called. Anthropologist, ethologist, and a bit of a jack-of-all-trades. He'll be under your orders, of course.

"And, talking of orders—" The admiral pushed a fat, heavily sealed envelope across his highly polished desk. "Nothing very secret. No need to destroy by fire before reading. I can tell you now. As soon as you are ready for Deep Space in all respects you are to lift ship and proceed to New Maine. We have a sub-Base there, as you know. That sub-Base will be your Base. From New Maine you will make a series of exploratory sweeps out toward the Rim. A Lost Colony Hunt, as you junior officers romantically put it. Your own two recent discoveries have stimulated interest, back on Earth, in that sort of pointless exercise. Hrrmph."

"Thank you, sir." Grimes gathered up his papers and rose to leave.

"Not so fast, Commander. I haven't finished yet. *Discovery*, as I can see that you suspect, is not a happy ship. Your predecessor, Commander Tallis, contrived to leave her on medical grounds. The uniformly bad reports that he put in regarding *Discovery*'s personnel were partly discounted in view of his nervous—or mental—condition. Hrrmph.

"Now, Grimes, I'm going to be frank. There are many people in the Service who don't like you, and who did not at all approve of your last two promotions. I didn't altogether approve of them myself, come to that, although I do admit that you possess one attribute that just might, in the fullness of time, carry you to flag rank. You're lucky, Grimes. You could fall into a cesspit and come up not only smelling of roses but with the Shaara Crown Jewels clutched in your hot little hands. You've done it, figuratively, more than once.

"But I only hope that I'm not around when your luck runs out!"

Grimes started to get to his feet again.

"Hold it, Commander! I've some advice for you. Don't put a foot wrong. And try to lick that blasted *Discovery* into some sort of shape. If you do find any Lost Colonies play it according to the book. Let's have no more quixotry, none of this deciding, all by your little self, who are the goodies and who are the baddies. Don't take sides.

"That's all."

"You mean, sir," asked Grimes, "that this is some sort of last chance?"

"*You* said it, Commander. *You* said it. But just don't forget that the step from commander to captain is a very big one." The admiral shot out a big hand. Grimes took it, and was surprised and gratified by the warmth and firmness of the old man's grip. "Good hunting, Grimes. And good luck!"

Chapter 2

Grimes dismounted from the ground car at the foot of *Discovery*'s ramp. The driver, an attractive blonde spacewoman, asked, "Shall I wait for you, Commander?"

Grimes, looking up at the towering, shabby bulk of his new command, replied, "No, unfortunately."

The girl laughed sympathetically. "Good luck, sir."

"Thank you," he said.

He tucked his briefcase firmly under his arm, strode toward the foot of the ramp. He noted that the handrails were long unpolished, that a couple of stanchions were missing and that several treads were broken. There was a Marine sentry at the head of the ramp in a khaki uniform that looked as though it had been slept in. The man came to a rough approximation to attention as Grimes approached, saluted him as though he were doing him a personal favor. Grimes returned the salute with unwonted smartness.

"Your business, Commander?" asked the sentry.

"My name is Grimes. I'm the new captain."

The man seemed to be making some slight effort to smarten himself up. "I'll call Commander Brabham on the PA, sir."

"Don't bother," said Grimes. "I'll find my own way up to my quarters." He added, rather nastily, "I suppose the elevator is working?"

"Of course, sir. This way, sir."

Grimes let the Marine lead him out of the airlock chamber, along a short alleyway, to the axial shaft. The man pressed a button, and after a short interval, the door slid open to reveal the cage.

"You'll find all the officers in the wardroom, sir, at this time of the morning," volunteered his guide.

"Thank you." Then, "Hadn't you better be getting back to your post?"

"Yes, sir. Of course, sir."

Grimes pushed the button for CAPTAIN'S FLAT.

During the journey up he was able to come to further conclusions—none of them good—about the way in which the ship had been run. The cage was not quite filthy, but it was far from clean. The gloss of the panel in which the buttons were set was dulled by greasy fingerprints. On the deck Grimes counted three cigarette butts and one cigarillo stub. Two of the indicator lights for the various levels were not working.

He got out at the Captain's Flat, the doughnut of accommodation that surrounded the axial shaft, separated from it by a circular alleyway. He had a set of keys with him, obtained from the admiral's office. The sliding door to the day room opened as soon as he applied the appropriate strip of magnetized metal. He went in.

An attempt, not very enthusiastic, had been made to clean up after Commander Tallis' packing. But Tallis had not packed his art gallery. This consisted of a score of calendars, of the type given away by ship chandlers and ship-repair firms, from as many worlds, utterly useless as a means of checking day and date except on their planets of origin. Evidently *Discovery*'s last census run had consisted of making the rounds of well-established colonies. Grimes stared at the three-dimensional depiction of a young lady with two pairs of overdeveloped breasts, indubitably mammalian and probably from mutated human stock, turned from it to the picture of a girl with less spectacular upperworks but with brightly gleaming jewelry entwined in her luxuriant pubic hair. The next one to catch his attention showed three people in one pose.

He grunted—not altogether in disapproval—then found the bell push labeled PANTRY over his desk. He used it. He filled and lit his pipe. When he had almost finished it he pushed the button again.

At last a spacewoman, in slovenly uniform, came in. She demanded surlily, "Did you ring? Sir."

"Yes," answered Grimes, trying to infuse a harsh note into his voice. "I'm the new captain. My gear will be coming aboard this afternoon some time. Meanwhile, would you mind getting this . . . junk disposed of?" He waved a hand to indicate the calendars.

"But if Commander Tallis comes back—"

"If Commander Tallis comes back, you can stick it all back up again. Oh, and you might give Lieutenant Commander Brabham my compliments and ask him to come to see me."

"The first lieutenant's in the wardroom. Sir. The PA system is working."

Grimes refrained from telling her what to do with the public-address system. He merely repeated his order, adding, "And I mean *now*."

"Aye, aye, sir, Captain, sir."

Insolent little bitch, thought Grimes, watching the twitching rump in the tight shorts vanishing through the doorway.

He settled down to wait again. Nobody in this ship seemed to be in any hurry about anything. Eventually Brabham condescended to appear. The first lieutenant was a short, chunky man, gray-haired, very thin on top. His broad, heavily lined face wore what looked like a perpetual scowl. His faded gray eyes glowered at the captain. The colors of the few ribbons on the left breast of his shirt had long since lost their brilliance and were badly frayed. Grimes could not tell what decorations—probably good attendance medals—they represented. But there were plenty of canteen medals which were obvious enough— smudges of cigarette ash, dried splashes of drinks and gravies—to keep them company. The gold braid on Brabham's shoulder boards had tarnished to a grayish green.

A gray man, thought Grimes. *A gray, bitter man.* He said, extending his hand, "Good morning, Number One."

"Good morning. Sir."

"Sit down, Number One." Grimes made a major operation out of refilling and lighting his pipe. "Smoke, if you wish." Brabham produced and ignited an acrid cigarette. "Mphm. Now, what's our condition of readiness?"

"Well, sir, a week at the earliest."

"A *week?*"

"This isn't an Insect Class Courier, sir. This is a *big* ship."

Grimes flushed, but held his temper in check. He said, "Any Survey Service vessel, regardless of size, should be ready, at all times, for almost instant liftoff."

"But, to begin with, there's been the change of captains. Sir."

"Go on."

"And Vinegar Nell—Miss Russell, I mean—isn't very cooperative."

"Mphm. Between ourselves, Number One, I haven't been impressed by the standard of efficiency of her staff." *Or*, he thought, *with the standard of efficiency of this ship in general. But I shall have to handle people with kid gloves until I get the feel of things.*

Brabham actually grinned. "I don't think that Sally was overly impressed by you, sir."

"Sally?"

"The captain's tigress. She used to be Commander Tallis' personal servant." Brabham grinned again, not very pleasantly. "Extremely personal, if you get what I mean, sir."

"Oh. Go on."

"And we're still trying to get a replacement for Mr. Flannery's psionic amplifier. He insists that only the brain of an Irish setter will do."

"And what happened to the old one?"

Brabham permitted himself a small chuckle. "He thought that it should share a binge. He poured a slug of Irish whiskey into its life-support tank. And then he tried to bring it around with black coffee."

"Gah!" exclaimed Grimes.

"Then he blamed the whiskey for the demise of the thing. It wasn't *real* Irish whiskey, apparently. It was some ersatz muck from New Shannon."

Grimes succeeded in dispelling the vision of the sordidly messy death of the psionic amplifier from his mind. He said firmly, "To begin with, Miss Russell will just have to pull her finger out. You're the first lieutenant. Get on to her."

"I'd rather not, sir."

Grimes glared at the man. "I'm not being funny, Mr. Brabham. Shake her up. Light a fire under her tail. And as for Mr. Flannery, he'll just have to be content with whatever hapless hound's brain the Stores Department can dig up—even if it comes from an English bulldog!"

"Then there are the engines, sir."

"The engines? What about them?"

"The chief has taken down both inertial drive-units. There're bits and pieces strewn all over the engine room deck."

"Was the port captain informed of this immobilization?"

"Er, no, sir."

"And why not?"

"I didn't know what the chief had done until he'd already done it."

"In the captain's absence you were the officer in charge. You should have known. All right, all right, the chief should have come to you first. Apparently he didn't. But as soon as you knew that this rustbucket was immobile you should have reported it."

"I—I suppose I should, sir."

"You suppose! Why didn't you?"

A sullen flush spread over the grayish pallor of Brabham's face. He blurted, "Like the rest of us in this ship, MacMorris has been in quite enough trouble of various kinds. I didn't want to get him into any more. Sir."

Grimes repressed a sigh. It was obvious that this ship was a closed shop, manned by the No Hopers' Union, whose members would close ranks against any threatened action by higher authority, no matter how much they bickered among themselves. And what was he, Grimes? A No Hoper or a pillar of the Establishment? In his heart of hearts, which side was he on? While he was sorting out a reply to make to Brabham a familiar bugle call, amplified, drifted through and over the ship's PA system.

Brabham shifted uneasily in his chair.

"Are you coming down to lunch, sir?" he asked.

"No," decided Grimes. "You carry on down, and you can ask— no, *tell*—Miss Russell to send me some sandwiches and a pot of coffee up here. After lunch I shall see Lieutenant Commander MacMorris, Miss Russell, and Mr. Flannery, in that order. Then I shall see you again.

"That is all."

Chapter 3

It was the little blonde stewardess, Sally, who brought up Grimes's lunch. While he was eating it she set about stripping Tallis' calendars from the bulkheads, performing this task with a put-upon air and a great deal of waste motion. Grimes wondered if she had made the sandwiches and the coffee in the same sullenly slapdash way. No, he decided after the first nibble, the first sip. She must have gone to considerable trouble with the simple meal. Surely all the available bread could not have been as stale as the loaf that had been used. Surely it must have been much harder to spread butter so extremely thinly than in the normal manner. And where had she found that stringy, flavorless cold mutton? The coffeepot must have been stood in cold water to bring its weak contents to the correctly tepid stage.

"Will that be all? Sir?" she asked, her arms full of calendars.

"Yes," Grimes told her, adding, "Thank you," not that she deserved it. He decided that he would tell Miss Russell to let him have a male steward to look after him. Obviously this girl would give proper service only to those who serviced her, and she was too coarse, too shop-soiled for his taste, apart from the obvious disciplinary considerations.

Almost immediately after she was gone there was a knock at the door. A big man entered. He was clad in filthy, oil-soaked overalls. A smear of black grease ran diagonally across his hard, sullen face. More grease was mixed with his long, unruly yellow hair. His hot blue eyes glared down at Grimes.

"Ye wanted to see me, Captain? I'm a busy man, not like some I could mention."

"Lieutenant Commander MacMorris?"

"Who else?"

"Commander MacMorris, I understand that this ship is immobilized."

"Unless ye intend to take her up on reaction drive, she is that."

"By whose authority?" demanded Grimes coldly.

"Mine, o' course. Both the innies was playin' up on the homeward passage. So I'm fixin' 'em."

"Didn't you inform the first lieutenant before you started taking them down? He was in charge, in the absence of a captain."

"Inform *him?* He looks after whatever control room ornaments look after. I look after my engine room."

"As long as I'm captain of this ship," snapped Grimes, "it's *my* engine room. How long will it take you to reassemble the inertial drive-units?"

Grimes could almost read MacMorris' thoughts as the engineer stood there. Should he or should he not angrily protest the captain's assumption of proprietorial rights? He muttered at last, "If I do all that has to be done, a week."

"A week? Just to put things together again?"

"A week it will be."

"Normal in-port routine, I suppose, Commander MacMorris . . . 0800 to 1700, with the usual breaks . . . I see. But if you work double shifts . . . ?"

"Look, Captain, you're not suggesting—"

"No, Commander MacMorris. I'm not suggesting. I'm ordering."

"But we all have friends on the Base, and the last cruise was a long one."

"You will work double shifts, Chief, longer if necessary. I'll want this vessel ready for Space no more than three days from now."

MacMorris grunted wordlessly, turned to go.

"Oh, one more thing," said Grimes.

"Yes? Sir."

"In the future you are to ask me for permission before you immobilize the engines. That is all."

The engineer left sullenly. Grimes carefully filled and lit his battered pipe. What was it that somebody, some girl, had called it, some time ago? *The male pacifier.* Well, he needed pacifying. He disliked having to crack the whip, but there were occasions when it was unavoidable. MacMorris was known to be a good engineer—but he was one of those engineers to whom a ship is no more than a platform existing for the sole purpose of supporting machinery. Grimes thought, not for the first time, that captains had it much better in the days of sail. Even then there were technicians—such as the sailmaker—but a competent wind ship master would be able to repair or even to make a sail himself if he absolutely had to.

There was another knock at the door.

"Come in!" he called.

"I see you're still smoking that filthy thing!" sniffed Vinegar Nell.

She had hardly changed at all, thought Grimes, since when they had last been shipmates—and how many years ago was that? She was slim, still, almost to the point of thinness. Her coppery hair was scraped back severely from her broad brow. Green eyes still glinted in the sharp, narrow face. Her mouth was surprisingly wide and full. She could have been very attractive were it not for her perpetually sour expression.

Grimes said stiffly, "Must I remind you, Miss Russell, that I am the captain of this ship?"

"And so you are, sir. *And* a full commander. I never thought you'd make it."

"That will do, Miss Russell." Belatedly he remembered his manners. "Sit down, will you?" The legs displayed when her short uniform skirt rode up were excellent. "Now, Miss Russell, I want *Discovery* ready for Space in three days."

"You're asking a lot, Captain."

"I'm not, Paymaster. You know the regulations as well as I do. At least as well." He quoted, "All fleet units shall be maintained in a state of instant readiness."

"But there are provedore stores to be loaded. The farm needs a thorough overhaul; the yeasts in numbers two and three vats went bad on me last trip, and I'm not at all happy about the beef tissue culture. The pumping and filtration systems for the hydroponic tanks need a thorough clean out."

"You can write, can't you?"

"Write?" The fine eyebrows arched in puzzlement.

"Yes. Write. It's something you do on a piece of paper, such as an official form, with a stylus. Make out the necessary requisitions. Mark them *urgent*. I'll countersign them."

"Commander Tallis," she told him, "always wanted all repairs and maintenance carried out by the ship's personnel."

"One way of making sure that you get longer in port. But my name is Grimes, not Tallis. I don't like to loaf around Base until the stern vanes take root. Make out those requisitions."

"All right," she said flatly.

"Oh, and that stewardess . . . Sally, I think her name is."

"Your servant."

"My ex-servant. Have her replaced by a male steward."

A smile that was almost a sneer flickered over her full mouth as she looked around at the bulkheads, bare now, stripped of their adornment of blatantly bare female flesh. "Oh, I see. I never thought that you were *that* way in the old days, Captain."

"And I'm not now!" he snarled. "It's just that I don't like insolent sluts who can't even make a decent sandwich. On your way down, tell Mr. Flannery that I want him, please."

"Nobody wants Mr. Flannery," she said. "But we're stuck with him."

Flannery finally put in an appearance. He looked as though he had been dragged out from a drunken slumber. He was red-haired, grossly fat, and his unhealthily pale face was almost featureless. His little eyes were a washed-out blue, but so bloodshot that they looked red. The reek of his breath was so strong that Grimes, fearing an explosion, did not relight his pipe.

"Mr. Flannery?"

"An' who else would it be, Captain?"

"Mphm." The temperamental telepaths had always to be handled carefully and Grimes did not wish to provoke the man into insubordination, with its inevitable consequences. It would take much too long to get a replacement. Once the ship was up and away, however— "Mphm. Ah, Mr. Flannery, I believe that you're unable to get a suitable psionic amplifier to replace the one that, er, died."

"An' isn't that the God's truth, Captain? Poor Terence, he was more than just an amplifier for me feeble, wanderin' thoughts. He was more than just a pet, even. He was a brother."

"Mphm?"

"A dog from the Ould Sod, he was, a sweet Irish setter. They took his foine body away, bad cess to 'em, but his poor, naked brain was there, in that jar o' broth, his poor, shiverin' brain an' the shinin' soul o' him. Night after night we'd sit there, out in the dark atween the stars, just the pair of us, a-singin' the ould songs. The Minstrel Boy to the war has gone. . . . *An' ye are that Minstrel Boy, Paddy,* he'd say to me, he'd *think* to me, *an' you an' me is light-years from the Emerald Isle, an' shall we iver see her again?*" Grimes noted with embarrassed disgust that greasy tears were trickling from the piggy eyes. "I'm a sociable man, Captain, an' I niver likes drinkin' alone, but I'm fussy who I drinks with. So ivery night I'd pour a drop, just a drop, mind ye, just a drop o' the precious whiskey into Terence's tank . . . he liked it, as God's me guide. He loved it, an' he wanted it. An' wouldn't ye want it if the sweet brain of ye was bare an' naked in a goldfish bowl, a-floatin' in weak beef tea?"

"Mphm."

"An one cursed night me hand shook, an' I gave him half the bottle. But he went happy, a-dreamin' o' green fields an' soft green hills an' a blue sky with little, white fleecy clouds like the ewe lambs o' God himself. . . . I only hope that I go as happy when me time comes."

If you have anything to do with it, thought Grimes, *there's a very good chance of it*.

"An' I've tried to get a replacement, Captain, I've tried, an' I've tried. I've haunted the communications equipment stores like a poor, shiverin' ghost until I thought they'd be callin' one o' the Fathers to exorcise me. But what have they got on their lousy shelves? I'll tell ye. The pickled brains o' English bulldogs, an' German shepherds an'—ye'll niver believe me!—an Australian dingo! But niver an honest Irish hound. Not so much as a terrier."

"You have to settle on something," Grimes said firmly.

"But you don't understand, Captain." Suddenly the heavy brogue was gone and Flannery seemed to be speaking quite soberly. "There must be absolute empathy between a telepath and his amplifier. And could *I* achieve empathy with an *English* dog?"

Balls! thought Grimes. *I'll order the bastard to take the bulldog, and see what happens*. Then a solution to the problem suddenly occurred to him. He said, "And they have a dingo's brain in the store?"

"Oh, sure, sure. But—"

"But what? A dingo's a dog, isn't he? As a dog he possesses a dog's telepathic faculties. And he's a peculiarly Australian dog."

"Yes, but—"

"And what famous Australians can you call to mind? What about the Wild Colonial Boy? Weren't all the bushrangers—or most of 'em—Irish?"

"Bejabbers, Captain, I believe ye've got it!"

"You've got it, Mr. Flannery. Or you will get it. And you can call it Ned, for Ned Kelly."

And so that's that, thought Grimes, when Flannery had shambled off. *For the time being, at least. It still remains to be seen if my departmental heads can deliver the goods*. But he was still far from happy. Unofficially and quite illegally a captain relies upon his psionic communications officer to keep him informed when trouble is brewing inside his ship. "Snooping" is the inelegant name for such conduct, which runs counter to the Rhine Institute's code of ethics.

For such snooping to be carried out, however, there must be a genuine trust and friendship between captain and telepath. Grimes doubted that he could ever trust Flannery or that he could ever feel friendly toward him.

And, to judge by his experience to date, similar doubts applied to everybody in this unhappy ship.

Chapter 4

Surprisingly, the ship was ready for liftoff in three days.

Had the Survey Service been a commercial shipping line the refitting operations would have been uneconomical, with swarms of assorted technicians working around the clock and a wasteful use of materials. It was still a very expensive operation in terms of goodwill. *Discovery*'s people were robbed of the extra days at Lindisfarne Base to which they had all been looking forward, and the officers in charge of the various Base facilities grew thoroughly sick and tired of being worried by Grimes, all the time, about this, that, and the other.

But she was ready, spaceworthy in all respects, and then Grimes shook Brabham by saying that he was going to make an inspection.

"Commander Tallis only used to make inspections in Space," objected the first lieutenant.

"Damn Commander Tallis!" swore Grimes, who was becoming tired of hearing about his predecessor. "Do you really think that I'm mug enough to take this rustbucket upstairs without satisfying myself that she's not going to fall apart about my ears? Pass word to all departmental heads that I shall be making rounds at 1000 hours. You, Miss Russell, and Major Swinton will accompany me. Every other officer and petty officer will be standing by whatever he's responsible for."

"Ten hundred is morning smoko, sir."

"And so what? Smoko is a privilege, and not a right. Report to me at 1000 hours with Miss Russell and the major. Oh, and you might polish your shoes and put on a clean uniform shirt."

If looks killed, Brabham would have had to organize a funeral, not captain's rounds. Had he been too harsh? Grimes asked himself as the first lieutenant walked stiffly out of the day cabin. *No*, he thought. *No. This ship needs shaking up, smartening up.* He grinned. *And I've always hated those captains who pride themselves on a taut ship. But I don't want a taut ship. All I want is something a few degrees superior to a flag of convenience star tramp.*

Meanwhile his own quarters were, at least, clean. The steward who had replaced Commander Tallis' pet, Sally, was a taciturn lout who had to be told everything, but once he was told anything, he did it. And the service of meals in the wardroom had been improved, as had been the standard of cookery. Also, under Grimes's prodding, Brabham was beginning to take a little pride in his appearance and was even seeing to it that his juniors did likewise. MacMorris, however, was incorrigible. The first time that Grimes put in an appearance in the wardroom, for dinner on the evening of his first day aboard, the engineer was already seated at the table, still wearing his filthy coveralls. On being taken to task he told the captain that *he* had to work for a living. Grimes ordered him either to go and get cleaned up or to take his meal in the duty engineers' mess. Rather surprisingly, MacMorris knuckled under, although with bad grace. But was it, after all, so surprising? Like all the other people in this ship he was regarded as being almost unemployable. If he were paid off from *Discovery* he would find it hard, if not impossible, to obtain another spacegoing appointment in the Survey Service. In a ship, any ship, he was still a big frog in a small puddle and, too, was in receipt of the active-duty allowance in addition to the pay for his rank. As one of the many technicians loafing around a big Base he would be a not too generously paid nobody.

The steward brought in Grimes's coffee. It was the way that he liked it, very hot and strong. He poured a cup of the steaming brew, sipped it appreciatively. There was a knock at the door. It was Brabham, accompanied by Major Swinton and Vinegar Nell.

"Rounds, sir?" asked the first lieutenant.

Grimes glanced at the bulkhead clock. "A little early yet. Be seated, all of you. Coffee?"

"No, thank you, sir. We have just finished ours."

The three officers sat in a stiff line on the settee, the woman in the middle. Grimes regarded them over the rim of his cup. Brabham looked, he thought, like a morose bloodhound. The Mad Major, with his wiry gray hair and bristling moustache, his hot yellow eyes, looked like a vicious terrier. Grimes had never liked terriers. And Vinegar

Nell? More cat than dog, he decided. A certain sleekness . . . but sleek cats can be as bad tempered as the rougher ones. He finished his coffee, got to his feet, reached for his cap.

"All right," he said. "We'll get the show on the road."

They started in the control room. There was little to find fault with there. Lieutenant Tangye, the navigator, was a man who believed in maintaining all his instruments in a highly polished state. Whether or not Tangye was capable of using these instruments Grimes had yet to discover. Not that he worried much about it; he was quite prepared to do his own navigation. (He, while serving as navigator in a cruiser, had been quite notorious for his general untidiness, but no captain had ever been able to complain about any lack of ability to fix the ship's position speedily and accurately.)

The next deck down was Grimes's own accommodation, with which he was already familiar. He devoted more time to the two decks below in which the officers, of all departments, were accommodated. The cabins and public rooms were clean, although not excessively so. The furnishings were definitely shabby. Miss Russell said, before he could make any comment, "*They* won't supply anything new for this ship."

Perhaps They wouldn't, thought Grimes, but had anybody bothered to find out for sure?

The Marines' quarters were next, housing twenty men. Here, as in the control room, there was some evidence of spit and polish. Grimes decided that the sergeant, a rugged, hairless black giant whose name was Washington, was responsible. Whatever the crimes that had led to his appointment to *Discovery* had been, he was an old-timer, convinced that the space soldiers were superior to any mere spaceman, ships' captains included. The trouble with such men was that, in a pinch, they would be loyal only to their own branch of the Survey Service, to their own officers.

Petty officers' quarters next, with the bos'n—another old-timer—coming to stiff attention as the inspection party entered the compartment. Grimes decided that he wouldn't trust the man any farther than he could throw him—and, as the bos'n was decidedly corpulent, that would not be very far. Langer . . . yes, that was his name. Hadn't he been implicated in the flogging of ship's stores when the heavy cruiser *Draconis* had been grounded on Dingaan for Mannschenn Drive recalibration?

Provedore ratings, deck ratings, engine room ratings . . . everything just not quite clean, with the faint yet unmistakable taint of too-long-unwashed clothing and bedding permeating the ship's atmosphere.

Storerooms—now well stocked.

The farm decks, with their hydroponic tanks, the yeast and algae and tissue culture vats—everything looked healthy enough. Grimes expressed the hope that it would all stay that way.

The cargo hold, its bins empty, but ready for any odds and ends that *Discovery* might pick up during the forthcoming voyage.

The boat bays . . . Grimes selected a boat at random, had it opened up. He satisfied himself that all equipment was in good order, that the provisions and other supplies were according to scale. He ran the inertial drive-unit for a few seconds in neutral gear. The irregular beat of it sounded healthy enough.

Engine spaces, with the glowering MacMorris in close attendance. In the Mannschenn Drive room, ignoring the engineer's scowl, Grimes put out a finger to one of the finely balanced rotors. It began to turn at the slightest touch and the other rotors, on their oddly angled spindles, moved in sympathy. There was the merest hint of temporal disorientation, a fleeting giddiness. MacMorris growled, "An' does he want us all to finish up in the middle o' last week?" Grimes pretended not to have heard him.

The inertial drive room, with the drive-units now reassembled, their working parts concealed beneath the casings . . . reaction drive . . . nothing to see there but a few pumps. And there was nothing to see in the compartment that housed the hydrogen fusion power plant; everything of any importance was hidden beneath layers of insulation. But if MacMorris said that it was all right, it must be.

"Thank you," said Grimes to his officers. "She'll do." He thought, *She'll have to do.*

"You missed the dogbox, sir," Brabham reminded him, with ill-concealed satisfaction.

"I know," said Grimes. "I'm going there now. No, you needn't come with me."

Alone, he made his way to the axial shaft, entered the elevator cage. He pushed the button for the farm deck. It was there that the psionic amplifier was housed, for no other reason than to cut down on the plumbing requirements. Pumps and pipes were essential to the maintenance of the tissue culture vats; some of the piping and one of the pumps were used to provide the flow of nutrient solution through the tank in which floated the disembodied canine brain.

On the farm deck he made his way through the assemblage of vats and tanks and found, tucked away in a corner, a small, boxlike compartment. Some wit had taped a crudely printed notice to the door: BEWARE OF THE DOG. *Very funny*, thought Grimes. *When I was a first trip cadet it always had me rolling on the deck in uncontrollable paroxysms of mirth.* But what was that noise from inside the room? Someone singing? Flannery, presumably.

> *"I'll die but not surrender*
> *Cried the Wild Colonial Boy. . . ."*

Grimes grinned. It sounded as though the psionic communications officer had already established rapport with his new pet. But wouldn't a dingo prefer the eerie music of a didgeridoo? What if he were to indent for one? He grinned again.

He knocked at the door, slid it open. Flannery was sitting—sprawling, rather—at and over his worktable. There was a bottle, open, ready to hand, with a green label on which shone a golden harp. There was no glass. The PCO, still crooning softly, was staring at the spherical tank, at the obscene, pallid, wrinkled shape suspended in translucent brown fluid.

"Mr. Flannery!"

Flannery went on singing.

"Mr. Flannery!"

"Sorr!" The man got unsteadily to his feet, almost knocked himself down again with a flamboyant parody of a salute. "Sorr!"

"Sit down before you fall down!" Grimes ordered sharply. Flannery subsided gratefully. He picked up the bottle, offered it to Grimes, who said, "No, thank you," thinking, *I daren't antagonize this fat, drunken slob. I might need him.* He remarked, "I see you have your new amplifier."

"Indeed I have, Captain. An' he's good, as God's me witness. Inspired, ye were, when ye said I should be takin' Ned."

"Mphm. So you don't anticipate any trouble?"

"Indeed I do not. Ask me to punch a message through to the Great Nebula of Andromeda itself, an' me an' Ned'll do it."

"Mphm." Grimes wondered how he should phrase the next question. He was on delicate ground. But if he had Flannery on his side, working for him, he would have his own, private espionage system, the Rhine Institute's code of ethics notwithstanding. "So you've got yourself another pal. Ha, ha. I wonder what he thinks of the rest of us in this ship . . . me, for example."

"Ye want the God's own truth, Captain?"

"Yes."

"He hates you. If he had his teeth still, he'd be after bitin' you. It's the uniform, ye see, an' the way ye're wearin' it. He remembers the cowardly troopers what did for the Ned who's his blessed namesake."

"Not to mention the jolly swagman," growled Grimes. "But that's all nonsense, Mr. Flannery. You can't tell me that *that's* the brain of a dingo who was around when the Kelly Gang was brought to book!"

Flannery chuckled. "What d'ye take me for, Captain? I don't believe that, an' I'm not expectin' you to. But he's a dog, an' all dogs have this race memory, goin' back to the Dream Time, an' farther back still. And now, Captain, will ye, with all due respect, be gettin' out of here? Ye've got Ned all upset, ye have."

Grimes departed in a rather bad temper, leaving Flannery communing with the whiskey bottle and his weird pet.

Chapter 5

Six hours before liftoff time Grimes received Brandt, the only scientific officer who was making the voyage, in his day cabin. From the very start they clashed. This Dr. Brandt—he soon made it clear that he did not wish to be addressed as "Commander" and that he considered his Survey Service rank and uniform childish absurdities—was, Grimes decided, a typical case of small-man-itis. He did not need to be a telepath to know what Brandt thought about him. He was no more than a bus driver whose job it was to take the learned gentleman to wherever he wished to go.

And then Brandt endeared himself to Grimes still further by putting his thoughts into words. "It's a high time, Captain," said the little, fat, bald black-bearded man, "that contacts with Lost Colonies were taken out of the clumsy hands of you military types. You do irreparable damage with your interferences. *I* should have been on hand to make a thorough and detailed study of the New Spartan culture before you ruined it by aiding and abetting revolution."

"Mphm," grunted Grimes.

"And you did the same sort of thing on Morrowvia."

"Did I? I was trying to save the Morrowvians from Drongo Kane—who, in case you don't know, is a slave trader—and from the Dog Star Line, who wanted to turn the whole damn planet into a millionaires' holiday camp."

"Which it is now well on the way to becoming, I hear."

"The Morrowvians will do very nicely out of it. In any case, on neither occasion was I without scientific advice."

"Dr. Lazenby, I suppose you mean. Or Commander Lazenby, as she no doubt prefers to be called. Pah!"

"Wipe the spit off your beard, Doctor," admonished Grimes, his prominent ears flushing angrily. "And, as far as Commander Lazenby is concerned, the advice she gave me was consistently good."

"*You* would think so. An ignorant spaceman led up the garden path by a flashily attractive woman."

Luckily Brabham came in just then on some business or other, and Grimes was able to pass Brandt on to the first lieutenant. He sat down at his littered desk and thought, *That cocky little bastard is all I need.* He remembered a captain under whom he had served years ago, who used to exclaim when things went wrong, "I am surrounded by rogues and imbeciles!"

And how many rogues and imbeciles was he, Grimes, surrounded by? He began to make calculations on a scrap of paper.

Control room officers—six.

Electronic communications officers—two.

Psionic communications officer—one (and that was more than ample!).

Supply branch officers—two.

Engineer officers—six.

Medical officer—one.

Marine officer—one.

Scientific officer—one.

That made twenty, in the commissioned ranks alone.

Cooks—four.

Stewards—two.

Stewardesses—four.

That made thirty.

Marines, including the sergeant and corporal—twenty-two.

Fifty-two was now the score.

Petty officers—four.

General purpose ratings—twenty.

Total, seventy-six. Seventy-six people who must have ridden to their parents' weddings on bicycles.

Grimes had done his figuring as a joke, but suddenly it was no longer funny. Normally he enjoyed the essential loneliness of command, but that had been in ships where there was always company, congenial company, when he felt that he needed it. In this vessel there seemed to be nobody at all with whom he could indulge in a friendly drink and a yarn.

Perhaps things would improve.

Perhaps they wouldn't.

Growl you may, he told himself, *but go you must.*

Chapter 6

It is always an anxious moment when a captain has to handle a strange ship, with strange officers and crew, for the first time. Grimes, stolidly ensconced in the pilot's chair, tried, not unsuccessfully, to convey the impression that he hadn't a worry in the whole universe. He made the usual major production of filling and lighting his pipe while listening to the countdown routine. "All hands," Brabham was saying into the intercom microphone, "secure ship for liftoff. Secure ship. Secure ship." Lieutenant Tangye, the navigator, was tense in the co-pilot's seat, his hands poised over the duplicate controls. No doubt the slim, blond, almost ladylike young man was thinking that he could make a far better job of getting the old bitch upstairs than this new skipper. Other officers were standing by radar and radar altimeter, NST transceiver, drift indicator, accelerometer, and all the rest of it. It was unnecessary; all the displays were visible to both pilot and co-pilot at a glance—but the bigger the ship the more people for whom jobs must be found.

From the many compartments the reports came in. "All secure." "All secure for liftoff." "All secure." "All secure."

"Any word from Commander Brandt yet?" asked Grimes. "After all, he is a departmental head."

"Nothing yet, sir," replied Brabham.

"Shake him up, will you, Number One."

"Control to Commander Brandt. Have you secured yet? Acknowledge."

Brandt's voice came through the speaker. "*Doctor* Brandt here. Of course I'm secure. This isn't my first time in Space, you know."

Awkward bastard, thought Grimes. He said, "Lifting off."

"Lifting off," repeated Brabham.

At Grimes's touch on the controls the inertial drive, deep in the bowels of the ship, muttered irritably. Another touch—and the muttering became a cacophonous protest, loud even through the layer after layer of sonic insulation. *Discovery* shook herself, her structure groaning. From the NST speaker came the bored voice of Aerospace Control. "You are lifting, *Discovery*. You are clear of the pad. *Bon voyage*."

"Acknowledge," said Grimes to the radio officer. He didn't need to be informed that the ship was off the ground. His own instruments would tell him that if he bothered to look at them—but the *feel* of the ship made it quite obvious that she was up and clear, lifting faster and faster. In the periscope screen he could see the spaceport area—the clusters of white administration buildings, the foreshortened silvery towers that were ships, big and little, dropping away, diminishing. The red, flashing beacons marking the berth that he had just left were sliding from the center of the display, but it didn't matter. He had been expecting drift, the wind the way it was. If he had been coming in to a landing it would have been necessary to apply lateral thrust; during a liftoff all that was required was to get up through and clear of the atmosphere.

A hint of yaw—

Only three degrees, but Grimes corrected it, more to get the feel of the ship than for any other reason. With the same motivation he brought the red flashers back to the center of the periscope screen. Mphm. The old bitch didn't handle too badly at all. He increased acceleration from a half gee to one gee, to one and a half, to two.

The intercom speaker squawked. "Dr. Brandt, here. What the hell are you playing at up there?"

"Minding our own bloody business!" snapped Grimes into his microphone. "Might I suggest that you do the same?"

Brabham sniggered loudly.

"Emergency rocket drill," ordered Grimes quietly. That, as he had suspected it would, took the grin off the first lieutenant's face. But the reaction drive was here to be used, wasn't it? "Number One, pass the word."

"Attention, all hands," growled Brabham into the intercom. "Stand by for testing of reaction drive. Sudden variations in acceleration are to be expected. Stand by. Stand by."

Grimes pushed a button, looked down at his console. Under ROCKETS the READY light glowed vivid green. With all his faults, MacMorris kept every system in a state of go. Decisively Grimes cut the inertial drive. His stomach tried to push its way up into his throat as acceleration abruptly ceased. He brought a finger down to the FIRE button, pushed it down past the first, second, and third stops. He felt as well as heard the screaming roar as the incandescent gases rushed through the venturis, and then the renewal of acceleration pushed him downward into the thick padding of his chair.

"Aerospace Control to *Discovery*. Are those pyrotechnics really necessary?"

"Tell him testing, testing," said Grimes to the radio officer. He succeeded in restarting the inertial drive and cutting the rockets at exactly the same instant. The ship continued to drive upward with no reduction of velocity.

Brabham loudly sighed his relief. "You're lucky," he commented. "Sir. Come to that, we're all lucky."

"What do you mean, Number One?" demanded Grimes.

The first lieutenant laughed sourly. "This is the first time that the reaction drive has been tested within the memory of the oldest man. Commander Tallis would *never* use it."

"How many times must I tell you that I am not Commander Tallis?"

The intercom speaker crackled, then, "Dr. Brandt here. I'm speaking from my laboratory. What the hell is going on? Do you know that you've smashed thousands of credits worth of valuable equipment?"

"You saw it stowed?" Grimes asked Brabham.

"Yes, sir. There was no chance of its shifting."

Grimes signaled to Tangye to take over the controls. "Keep her going as she is, pilot." Then he said into his microphone, "Captain here, Dr. Brandt. Did anything shift?"

"No. But I heard glass breaking in the cases. Delicate apparatus can't stand up to your needlessly violent maneuvers."

"Did you see the stuff packed, Doctor?"

"Of course."

"Then might I suggest that next time you see that your bits and pieces are packed properly? There are excellent padding materials available."

"I hold you entirely responsible for the breakages, Captain."

"You knew that you were embarking in a spaceship, Doctor."

"Yes. I did. But rockets went out generations ago."

"Reaction drive is still fitted to all Survey Service vessels, as you should have known, *Commander* Brandt."

"Pah!"

Grimes returned his attention to ship handling, taking over from

Tangye. Overhead—or forward—the sky seen through the control room dome was a dark purple, almost black. In the periscope screen Lindisfarne was assuming a spherical aspect. Outside the ship there was still atmosphere—but atmosphere in the academic sense of the word only. On the dial of the radar altimeter the decades of kilometers were mounting up steadily and rapidly.

There was nothing to do now but to run out and clear of the Van Allens, while the globe that was Lindisfarne dwindled steadily in the periscope screen, a diminishing half-moon, the sunlit hemisphere opalescently aglow.

The stars were bright and unwinking in the black sky, and the polarizers were automatically dimming the harsh glare of the Lindisfarne sun on the beam. Grimes looked at the magnetometer. The bright red warning light was dimming. It gave one last flicker, then turned to green.

"Clear of the Van Allens, sir," announced Tangye belatedly.

Slow reaction time, thought Grimes. He said, "So I see. Cut the inertial drive and line her up on the target star, will you?"

"Aye, aye, sir," replied the young man, smartly enough.

The engines grumbled to a stammering halt. Only then did Tangye busy himself with a star chart, looking through the ports frequently to check the relative positions of the constellations. Grimes refrained from pointing out the sun that he wanted to head for, a second magnitude luminary in the constellation of The Bunny, as this grouping of stars had been dubbed by the first settlers on Lindisfarne. There was, if one had a strong imagination, a suggestion of rabbit's ears and woman's breasts, thought Grimes while his navigator fumbled and bumbled. *If this were a real bunny*, he thought sardonically, *young Tangye'd be on target a damn sight sooner!* And how long would it be before Brandt, the obnoxious fool, started to whine about being kept too long in a condition of free fall? Meanwhile, other people besides the navigator were exhibiting shortcomings.

"Number One," Grimes said mildly, "you didn't make the usual announcement on the intercom. Stand by for free fall, setting trajectory and all the rest of it."

"You never told me to, sir."

"It's part of your job to look after these details," snapped Grimes.

"Commander Tallis didn't want announcements made every five minutes. Sir."

"Neither do I. But I want those announcements made that are required by Survey Service regulations."

Then Brandt came through on the intercom. "Doctor Brandt here. What *is* going on up there?"

"Stand by for setting trajectory," said Brabham sulkily into his microphone.

"On target, sir," announced Tangye. "I mean, I've *found* the target."

"Then get on to it."

The directional gyroscopes rumbled into motion. Slowly the ship turned about her axes, centrifugal forces giving an off-center surrogate of gravity. Grimes, looking up into the cartwheel sight set into the dome, saw The Bunny swim slowly into view.

The gyroscopes stopped.

"On target, sir."

"Mphm. Have you allowed for galactic drift, Mr. Tangye?"

"Eh . . . no, sir."

"Then please do so."

There was more delay while Tangye fumbled through the ephemeris, fed data into the control room computer. *All this should have been done before liftoff*, thought Grimes disgustedly. *Damn it all, this puppy couldn't navigate a plastic duck across a bathtub!* He watched the nervous young man, glowering.

"Allowance applied, sir." The gyroscopes restarted as the navigator spoke.

"Being applied, you mean. And are you sure that you're putting it on the right way? All right, all right. Leave it. *I* worked it out roughly before we pushed off."

"On trajectory, sir."

"Thank you." Grimes himself announced over the PA system that the Mannschenn Drive was about to be restarted and that acceleration would be resumed immediately thereafter.

He pushed the button to start the interstellar drive. He could imagine those shining rotors starting to turn, spinning faster and faster, spinning, precessing at right angles to all the dimensions of normal space, tumbling through the dark infinities, dragging the ship and all aboard her with them as the temporal precession field built up.

There was the disorientation in space and time to which no spaceman ever becomes inured. There was the uncanny sensation of *déjà vu*. There was, as far as Grimes was concerned, an unusually strong premonition of impending doom. It persisted after everything had returned to normal—to normal, that is, as long as one didn't look out through the viewports at the contorted nebulosities that glimmered eerily where the familiar stars had been. The ship, her restarted inertial drive noisily clattering, the thin, high whine of the Mannschenn Drive pervading every cubic millimeter of her, was speeding through the warped continuum toward her destination.

"Thank you, gentlemen," said Grimes heavily. (*Thank you for what?*) "Normal Deep Space watches and routine, Number One."

"Normal Deep Space watches and routine, sir," replied Brabham.

Grimes unbuckled himself from his chair, got up and went down to his quarters. He poured himself a stiff brandy. Even if he hadn't earned it, he felt that he needed it.

Chapter 7

Nonetheless, Grimes was much happier now that the voyage had started.

The ship was back in her natural element, and so were her people. As long as she was in port—at a major naval base especially—the captain was not the supreme authority. On Lindisfarne, for example, Grimes had come directly under the orders of the officer-in-charge-of-surveys, and of any of that rear admiral's officers who were senior to himself. Too, any rating, petty officer or officer of his own who considered that he had a grievance, could run, screaming, to one or another of the various Survey Service personnel protection societies, organizations analogous to the several guilds, unions, and whatever representing merchant spacemen. Of course, any complaint had to be justifiable—but it was amazing how many complaints, in these decadent days, were held to be warranted. Had MacMorris not been in such bad odor with the officials of the Engineer Officers' Association his tales about Grimes's alleged bullying would have been listened to; had they been, *Discovery* would never have got away from Lindisfarne.

In Deep Space, everybody knew, a captain could do almost anything to anybody provided that he were willing to face a Board of Inquiry at some later date. He could even order people pushed out of the airlock without spacesuits as long as they were guilty of armed mutiny.

All in all, Grimes was not too displeased with his new command. True, she was an old ship—but as an old ship should be (and sometimes is) she was as comfortable as a well-worn shoe. She was not a taut ship; she never would be or could be that. All of her people were too disheartened by slow, even nonexistent promotion, by the knowledge that they had been passed over, would always be passed over. She was not a happy ship—but once she settled down to the old, familiar routine, once her crew realized that it was less trouble to do things Grimes's way than his predecessor's way, she was not actively unhappy.

Grimes did not mix much with his officers. He would pass the time of day with the watchkeeper when he went up to the control room, he would, naturally, meet people when he made rounds, he took his seat at the head of the senior officers' table at meals, occasions at which scintillating conversation was conspicuous by its absence.

Brabham was too morose, too full of his own woes. MacMorris was as he had been described more than once, an uncouth mechanic, incapable of conversation about anything but machinery. Vinegar Nell could have been good company—she was a highly intelligent, witty woman—but she could not forget that the last time she and Grimes had been shipmates she had been a lieutenant while Grimes was only a lowly ensign. The fact that he was now a commander and captain of a big ship she ascribed to sex and luck rather than ability.

The medical officer, Surgeon Lieutenant Commander Rath, was universally unpopular. He was barely competent, and in civil life his lack of a bedside manner would have militated against financial success. He was a tall, dark, thin (almost skeletal) man and his nickname, to all ranks, was The Undertaker. Nobody liked him, and he liked nobody.

And the Mad Major kept himself very much to himself. He was a Marine, and Marines were, in his opinion, the highest form of interstellar life.

All in all, Grimes began to think as the voyage wore on, the only interesting member of his crew was Flannery. But was it Flannery himself who was interesting—or was it that unfortunate dingo's brain in its tank of nutrient solution? The thing was fascinating—that alleged racial memory, for example. Was it genuine, or was it merely the product of Flannery's fertile, liquor-stimulated imagination? After all, Grimes only had Flannery's word for what Ned was thinking . . . and, according to Flannery, Ned's thoughts were fantastic ones.

"He thinks he remembers you, Captain," said the PCO one day when Grimes dropped in to see him after rounds.

"Mphm. Don't tell me that I'm a reincarnation of the original jolly swagman."

"Indeed ye're not, sorr! He's thinkin' o' you as Bligh!"

"I suppose I should be flattered," admitted Grimes. "But I'm afraid that *I* shall never finish up as an admiral *and* as a colonial governor."

"An' that's not what the black Captain Bligh was famous for, sorr!"

"The mutiny? His first one? But during that, as during the subsequent ones, he was more sinned against than sinning!"

"Not the way that Ned, here, recollects it, Captain."

"Come off it, Mr. Flannery. There weren't any dogs of any kind aboard the *Bounty*!"

The telepath stared at his grisly pet through bleary eyes, and his thick lips moved as he subvocalized his thoughts. Then: "Ned wasn't there himself, o' course, Captain, nor any of his blessed forefathers. But he still says as that was the way of it, that the wicked Captain Bligh drove his crew to mutiny, indeed he did."

"Indeed he did not!" snapped Grimes, who had his own ideas about what had happened aboard the ill-fated *Bounty*.

"If that's the way ye feel about it, Captain," murmured Flannery diplomatically.

"It *is* the way I feel about it." And then, a sudden, horrid suspicion forming in his mind: "What *is* all this about Bligh and the *Bounty*? Are you suggesting . . . ?"

"Indeed I'm not, Captain. An' as for Ned, here"—the waving hand just missed the tank and its gruesome contents—"would he be after tellin' ye, if he could? He would not. He would niver be on the side o' the oppressor."

"Good for him," remarked Grimes sardonically. He got up to leave. "And, Mr. Flannery, you might get this—this mess cleaned up a bit. I did mention it to Miss Russell, but she said that her girls aren't kennelmaids. Those empty bottles . . . and that . . . *bone*."

"But t'is only an old bone, Captain, with niver a shred o' meat nor gristle left on it. Poor Terry—may the blessed saints be kind to the soul of him—knew it was there, an' imagined it like it used to be. An' Ned's the same."

"So it is essential to the efficient working of the amplifier?"

"Indeed it is, sorr."

Grimes stirred the greasy, dog-eared playing cards, spread out on the table for a game of Canfield, with a gingerly forefinger. "And I suppose that these are essential to *your* efficient working?"

"Ye said it, Captain. An' would ye deprive me of an innocent game of patience? An' don't the watch officers in the control room, when ye're not around, set up games o' three-dimensional noughts an' crosses in the plottin' tank, just to while away the weary hours? Ye've done it yerself, like enough."

Grimes's prominent ears flushed. He could not deny it—and if he did this telepath would know that he was lying.

"An' I can do more wi' these than play patience, Captain. Did I iver tell ye that I have Gypsy blood in me veins? Back in the Ould Isle me great, great granny lifted her skirts to a wanderin' tinker. From him, an' through her, I have the gift." The grimy pudgy hands stacked the cards, shuffled them, and then began to rearrange them. "Would ye like a readin'? Now?"

"No, thank you," said Grimes as he left.

Chapter 8

Discovery came to New Maine.

New Maine is not a major colony; its overall population barely tops the ten million mark. It is not an unpleasant world, although, even on the equator, it is a little on the chilly side. It has three moons, one so large as to be almost a sister planet, the other two little more than oversized boulders. It is orbited by the usual system of artificial satellites—communication, meteorological, and all the rest of it. The important industries are fisheries and fish processing; the so-called New Maine cod (which, actually, is more of a reptile than a true fish) is a sufficiently popular delicacy on some worlds to make its smoking, packaging, and export worthwhile.

A not very substantial contribution to the local economy is made by the Federation Survey Service sub-Base, which is not important enough to require a high ranking officer-in-charge, these duties being discharged by a mere commander, a passed-over one at that. At the time of *Discovery*'s visit this was a Commander Denny, a flabby, portly gentleman who looked and acted older than he actually was and who, obviously, had lost all interest in the job long since.

Shortly after berthing at the small, badly run-down naval spaceport, Grimes paid the usual courtesy call on the officer-commanding-base. It was not an occasion demanding full dress, with fore-and-aft hat, frock coat, sword, and all the rest of the anachronistic finery; nonetheless an OCB is an OCB, regardless of his actual rank. The temperature outside the ship was 17°, cool enough to make what Grimes thought of as his "grown-up trousers" comfortable. He changed from his shipboard shorts and shirt into his brass-buttoned, gold-braided black, put on his cap with the scrambled egg on its peak still undimmed by time, made his way down to the after airlock. The Marine on gangway duty, he was pleased to note, was smartly attired; obviously Major Swinton had taken the hints regarding the appearance of his men and, equally obviously, Sergeant Washington had cooperated to the full with his commanding officer in this respect.

The man saluted crisply. "Captain, sir!"

Grimes returned the salute. "Yes?"

"Are you expecting a ground car, sir? If one hasn't been arranged, I'll call one."

"I'll walk," said Grimes. "The exercise will do me good."

Discovery's ramp was still battered and shabby, although a few repairs had been made before departure from Lindisfarne. The ship herself was still showing her many years, the ineradicable signs of neglect as well as of age. But even she, who on her pad at the Main Base had looked like an elderly poor relation, here had the appearance of a rich aunt come a-visiting. Nobody expects to be obliged to eat his meals off a spaceport apron—but there are minimal standards of cleanliness that should be maintained. These were certainly not being maintained here. It was obvious that during the night some large animals had wandered across the expanse of concrete and treated it as a convenience. It was equally obvious that they had done the same during the previous night, and the night before. In addition, there were tall, straggling, ugly weeds thrusting up through ragged cracks, with dirty scraps of plastic and paper piling up around them, entangled with them.

The block of administration buildings toward which Grimes was heading, treading carefully to avoid getting his well-polished shoes dirty, was plain, functional—and like most functional constructions would have been pleasant enough in appearance if only it had been clean. But the wide windows were dull with an accumulation of dust and the entire facade was badly stained. Were there, Grimes wondered, flying creatures on this world as big as the animals that had fouled the apron? He looked up at the dull sky apprehensively. If there were, he hoped that they came out only at night. As he elevated his regard he noticed that the flagstaff atop the office block was not quite vertical and that the Survey Service ensign, flapping lazily in the light breeze, was ragged and dirty, and was not right up to the truck.

The main doors, as he approached them, slid open reluctantly with a distinctly audible squeak. In the hallway beyond them an elderly petty officer, in shabby grays, got slowly up from his desk as Grimes entered. He was not wearing a cap, so he did not salute; but neither did he stiffen to attention.

He asked, "Sir?"

"I am Commander Grimes, captain of *Discovery*."

"Then you'll be wanting to see the old—" He looked at the smartly uniformed Grimes and decided to start again. "You'll be wanting to see Commander Denny. You'll find him in his office, sir." He led the way to a bank of elevators, pressed a button.

"Rather shorthanded, aren't you?" remarked Grimes conversationally.

"Oh, no, sir. On a sub-Base like this it isn't necessary to have more than the duty PO—which is me—manning Reception."

"I was thinking about policing the spaceport apron," said Grimes.

"Oh, *that!*" The petty officer's face did show a faint disgust.

"Yes. That."

"But there's nothing that we can do about the bastards, sir. They always did relieve themselves here, before there was a spaceport. They always will. Creatures of habit, like—"

"They?"

"The great snakes, sir. They're called great snakes, though they're not snakes at all, really. More of a sort of slug. Just imagine a huge sausage that eats at one end and—"

"I get the idea. But you could post guards, suitably armed."

"But the great snakes are protected, sir. There's only the one herd left on the entire planet."

"Then why not a force field fence, with a nonlethal charge."

"Oh, no, sir. That would never do. The Old Man's wife—I beg pardon, sir, the commander's wife—would never stand for it. She's the chairlady of the New Maine Conservationist Association."

"Mphm." At this moment the elevator, which had taken its time about descending, arrived. The door opened. Grimes got into the car as the petty officer said, "Seventh deck, sir." He pressed the right button and was carried slowly upward.

Commander Denny's office was as slovenly as his spaceport. Untidiness Grimes did not mind—he never set a good example himself in that respect—but real dirt was something else again. The drift of papers on Denny's desk was acceptable, but the dust-darkened rings on its long-unpolished surface left by mugs of coffee or some other fluids were not. Like his petty officer in Reception, Denny was wearing a shabby gray uniform. So were the two women clerks. Grimes thought it highly probable that it was the elderly, unattractive one who did all the work. The other one was there for decoration—assuming that one's tastes in decoration run to bold-eyed, plump, blonde, micro-skirted flirts.

The Base commander got slowly to his feet, extended a pudgy hand. "Commander Grimes?"

"In person."

The two men shook hands. Denny's grip was flabby.

"And these," went on Denny, "are Ensign Tolley"—the older woman favored Grimes with a tight-lipped smile—"and Ensign Primm." Miss Primm stared at the visitor haughtily. "But sit down, Grimes. You're making my control room—ha, ha—look untidy."

Grimes looked around. There were two chairs available in addition to those occupied by the clerks, but each of them held an overflow of paper.

"Sit down, man. Sit down. This is Liberty Hall. You can spit on the mat and call the cat a bastard."

"I don't see any cats," said Grimes. *Not of the four-legged variety, anyhow*, he thought. "And to judge by the state of your spaceport apron, somebody, or something, has already been . . . er . . . spitting on the mat!"

Surprisingly it was the elderly ensign who laughed, then got up to clear the detritus from one of the chairs. Neither Denny nor the younger woman showed any amusement.

"And now, Commander," asked Denny, "what can I do for you?"

"I shall require the use of your port facilities, Commander," Grimes told him. "I'll be wanting to replenish stores, and my chief engineer could do with some shore labor to lend a hand with his innies; he wants to take them down to find out why they're working, and then he'll have to put them together again. You know what engineers are."

"Yes. I know. And then you'll be off on your Lost Colony hunt, I suppose."

"That's what I'm being paid for. Have you heard any rumors of Lost Colonies out in this sector?"

"I'm just the OCB, Grimes. Nobody ever tells me anything."

And would you be interested if they did? Grimes wondered. He said, "Our lords and masters must have had something in mind when they sent me out this way."

"And who knows what futile thoughts flicker through their tiny minds? *I* don't."

And you've got to the stage where you don't much care, either, thought Grimes. But he could not altogether blame the man. This dreary sub-Base on a dull world was obviously the end of the road for Denny. Here he would mark time until he reached retirement age. And what about himself? Would this sort of job be his ultimate fate if some admiral or politician upon whose corns he had trodden finally succeeded in having him swept under the carpet and forgotten?

"Oh, Commander," said Denny, breaking into his thoughts.

"Yes, Commander?"

"You'll be getting an official invitation later in the morning. It's
quite a while since we had one of our ships in here, so the mayor of
Penobscot—that's where the commercial spaceport is—is throwing an
official party tonight. Bum freezers and decorations. You and your
officers are being asked."

"I can hardly wait."

"The master of *Sundowner* should be there, too, with his people."

"Sundowner?"

"She's at Port Penobscot, loading fish. She's a star tramp. Rim
Worlds registry. She gets around."

"Mphm. It could be worthwhile having a yarn with him."

"It could be, Commander. These tramp skippers often stumble on
things that our survey captains miss. Sometimes they report them,
sometimes they don't."

"You can say that again, Commander. The last Lost Colony that
I visited, Morrowvia, the Dog Star Line was trying to keep all to its
little self. And it looks as though they'll be able to do just that." Grimes
looked at his watch. Denny had made no move to offer him tea, coffee,
or anything stronger, and it was past the time when he usually had his
morning coffee aboard the ship. "I'd better be getting back to find out
what disasters have been happening in my absence. And my departmental heads should have their requisitions ready for my autograph by
now."

"I'll see you tonight, Commander," said Denny.

"See you tonight, Commander Denny," said Grimes.

As he let himself out he overheard the younger of the two women
say, in a little-too-loud whisper, "Gawd save us all! What a stuck-up
tailor's dummy! I hope he treads in something on the way back to his
rustbucket!"

Chapter 9

The mayor sent a small fleet of ground cars to pick up *Discovery*'s officers. Grimes, resplendent in black and gold and stiff white linen, with his miniature decorations on their rainbow ribbons a-jingle on the left breast of his mess jacket, rode in the lead vehicle. He was accompanied by Brabham, Major Swinton, Dr. Brandt, and Vinegar Nell. The paymaster looked remarkably handsome in her severely cut, long-skirted evening dress uniform. Swinton, in his dress blue-and-scarlet, had transformed himself from a bad-tempered terrier into a gaudy and pugnacious psittacoid. Brabham (of course) was letting the side down. His mess uniform, when he extricated it from wherever it had been stowed, had proved to be unwearable, stained and creased and far too tight a fit. He had compromised by wearing a black bow tie, instead of one of the up-and-down variety, with his not-too-shabby double-breasted black outfit. And Brandt, of course, had never possessed a suit of mess kit. He was wearing civilian evening dress, with the sash of some obscure order—the sash itself was far from obscure, being bright purple edged with gold—stretched across his shirt front.

The electric cars sped swiftly along the road between the Base and Penobscot. Dusk was falling fast from a leaden sky, and little could be seen through the wide windows of the vehicles. Even in broad daylight there would have been little to see; this country was desolate moorland, only slightly undulant, with not so much as a tree or a hill or even a stony outcrop to break the monotony. Ahead, brighter and brighter as the darkness deepened and the distance diminished, glared the lights of the port city.

The motorcade swept past the spaceport where *Sundowner*, a stubby tower of metal, stood among the cargo-handling gantries, a briefly glimpsed abstract of black shadows and garish, reflected light. Slowing down at last it skirted the harbor—Penobscot was a seaport as well as a spaceport—and the long quay where the big oceangoing trawlers were discharging their glittering catch.

The mayor's palace overlooked the harbor. It was a big, although not high, building, pseudo-classical, its pillared facade glowing whitely in the floodlights. The approach was along a wide avenue, lined with tall, feathery-leafed trees, in the branches of which colored glow-bulbs had been strung. Brabham muttered something in a sour voice about every day being Christmas on New Maine. Vinegar Nell told him tartly to shut up. The chauffeur said nothing, but Grimes could sense the man's resentment.

The car drew to a halt in the portico. The driver left his seat to open the door for his passengers—the sort of courtesy that was long vanished from Earth but that still persisted in many of the colonies. Grimes was first out, then assisted Vinegar Nell, who was having a little trouble with her unaccustomed long skirt, to the ground. Brabham dismounted, then Swinton, then Brandt. The chauffeur saluted smartly and returned to his driving seat in the car, which sped off in a spattering of fine golden gravel.

Grimes limped to the wide doorway—a tiny pebble had got inside his right shoe—followed by the others. Mingled music and light flowed out into the portico. Standing by a group of heroic statuary— well-muscled, naked women wrestling with some sort of sea serpent— was a portly individual whom Grimes took, at first, for a local admiral. This resplendently uniformed person bowed, albeit with more condescension than obsequiousness, and inquired smoothly, "Whom shall I announce, sir?"

"Commander Grimes, captain of the Survey Ship *Discovery*. And with me are Commander Brandt, of the scientific branch, Lieutenant Commander Brabham, my executive officer, Major Swinton, of the Federation Marines, and Lieutenant Russell, my paymaster."

The functionary raised a small megaphone to his mouth; with it he could compete quite easily with the buzz of conversation and the music from the synthesizer. "Captain Grimes . . . Commander Brandt . . ."

"*Doctor* Brandt!" snarled the scientist, but he was ignored.

"Lieutenant Commander Brabham . . . Major Swinton . . . Lieutenant Russell."

Grimes found himself shaking hands with a wiry little man in a bright green evening suit, with an ornate, gold chain of office about his neck. "Glad to have you aboard, Captain!"

"Commander, Mr. Mayor," corrected Grimes. "Your majordomo seems to have promoted me."

"You're captain of a ship, aren't you?" The mayor grinned whitely. "Come to that, I always call Bill Davinas 'commodore.' I'll hand you over to him now while I greet your officers."

Grimes shook hands with Davinas, a tall, dark, black-and-gold uniformed man with four gold stripes on each of his epaulettes, who said, "I'm the master of *Sundowner*, Commander. You probably noticed her at the spaceport. I've been a regular trader here since Rim Runners pushed me off my old routes; the small, private owner just can't compete with a government shipping line."

"And what do I call you, sir? Commodore, or captain?"

"Bill, for preference." Davinas laughed. "That commodore business is just the mayor's idea of a joke. The Sundowner Line used to own quite a nice little fleet, but now it's down to one ship. So I'm the line's senior master—senior and only—which does make me a courtesy commodore of sorts. But I don't get paid any extra. Ah, here's a table with some good stuff. I can recommend these codfish patties, and this local rosé isn't at all bad."

While he sipped and nibbled Grimes looked around the huge ballroom. The floor was a highly polished black, reflecting the great, glittering electroliers, each one a crystalline complexity, suspended from the shallow dome of the ceiling, which was decorated with ornate bas-reliefs in a floral pattern. Along the white-pillared walls panels of deep blue, in which shone artificial stars set in improbable constellations, alternated with enormous mirrors. The overall effect was overpowering, with the crowd of gaily dressed people reflected and re-reflected to infinity on all sides. Against the far wall from the main doorway was the great synthesizer, an intricacy of transparent tubes through which rainbow light surged and eddied, a luminescent fountain containing within itself orchestra, choir, massed military bands—and every other form of music that Man has contrived to produce during his long history. The fragile blonde seated at the console—which would not have looked out of place in the control room of a Nova Class dreadnought—could certainly handle the thing. *Beauty and the beast*, thought Grimes.

"Jenkins' Folly," announced Davinas, waving an arm expansively.

"Jenkins' Folly?"

"This palace. The first mayor of Penobscot was a Mr. Jenkins. He'd got it firmly fixed in his thick head that New Maine was going to go the same way as so many—too many—other colonies. Population expansion. Population explosion. Bam! According to his ideas, this city was going to run to a population of about ten million. But it never happened. As you know, the population of the entire planet is only that. Once New Maine had enough people to maintain a technological culture with most of the advantages and few of the drawbacks the ZPG boys and girls took control. So this palace, this huge barn of a place, is used perhaps three times a year. Anniversary Day. New Year's Day. The Founder's Birthday. And, of course, on the very rare occasions when one of *your* ships, with her horde of officers, drops in."

"Mphm."

"Ah, here you are, Commander Grimes." It was Denny, looking considerably smarter than he had in his office, although the short Eton jacket of his mess uniform displayed his plump buttocks, in tightly stretched black, to disadvantage. "Clarice, my dear, this is Commander Grimes. Commander Grimes, meet the little woman."

Mrs. Denny was not a little woman. She was . . . vast. Her pale flesh bulged out of her unwisely low-cut dress, which was an unfortunate shade of pink. She was huge, and she gushed. "It's always good to see new faces, Commander, even though we are all in the same family."

"Ah, yes. The Survey Service."

She giggled and wobbled. "Not the Survey Service, Commander Grimes. The *big* family, I mean. Organic life throughout the universe."

If she'd kept it down to the mammalia, thought Grimes, looking with fascination at the huge, almost fully revealed breasts, *it'd make more sense*. He said, "Yes, of course. Although there are some forms of organic life I'd sooner not be related to. Those great snakes of yours, for instance."

"But you haven't *seen* them, Commander."

"I've seen the evidence of their passing, Mrs. Denny."

"But they're so sweet, and trusting."

"Mphm."

"She's playing our tune, dear," Denny put in hastily, extending his arms to his wife. He got them around her somehow, and the couple moved off to join the other dancers.

Grimes looked around for Davinas but the merchant captain had vanished, had probably made his escape as soon as the Denny couple showed up. He poured himself another glass of wine and looked at the swirling dancers. Some of them, most of them, were singing to the music of the synthesizer, which was achieving the effect of an orchestra of steel guitars.

Spaceman, the stars are calling,
Spaceman, you live to roam,
Spaceman, down light-years falling,
Remember I wait at home. . . .

Icky, thought Grimes. *Icky*. But he had always liked the thing, in spite of (because of?) its sentimentality. He started to sing the words himself in a not very tuneful voice.

"I didn't think you had it in you, Captain."

Grimes cut himself off in mid-note, saw that Vinegar Nell had joined him. It was obvious that the tall, slim woman had taken a drink—or two, or three. Her cheeks were flushed and her face had lost its habitually sour expression. She went on, "I'd never have dreamed that you're a sentimentalist."

"I'm not, Miss Russell. Or am I? Never mind. There are just some really corny things I love, and that song is one of them." Then, surprising himself at least as much as he did her: "Shall we dance?"

"Why not?"

They moved out onto the floor. She danced well, which was more than could be said for him. Normally, on such occasions, he was all too aware of his deficiencies—but all that he was aware of now was the soft pressure of her breasts against his chest, the firmer pressure and the motion of her thighs against his own. And there was no need for them to dance so closely; in spite of the illusory multitude moving in the mirrors the floor was far from crowded.

Watch it, Grimes, he admonished himself. *Watch it!*

And why the hell should I? part of him demanded mutinously.

That's why! he snarled mentally as one of his own officers, a junior engineer, swept past, holding a local lass at least as closely as Grimes was holding the paymaster. The young man leered and winked at his captain. Grimes tried to relax his grip on Vinegar Nell, but she wasn't having any. Her arms were surprisingly strong.

At last the music came to a wailing conclusion.

"I enjoyed that," she said.

"So did I, Miss Russell," admitted Grimes. "Some refreshment?" he asked, steering her toward one of the buffet tables.

"But I should be looking after you." She laughed.

It wasn't so much what she said, but the way that she said it. "Mphm," he grunted aloud.

Captain Davinas was already at the table with his partner, a tall, plain local woman. "Ah," he said, "we meet again, Commander."

Introductions were made, after which, to the disgust of the ladies, the men started to talk shop. The music began again and, with some reluctance, Vinegar Nell allowed herself to be led off by the Penobscot police commissioner, and the other lady by the first mate of *Sundowner*.

"Thank all the odd gods of the galaxy for that!" Davinas laughed. "I have to dance with her some of the time—she's the wife of my Penobscot agent—but she'll settle for one of my senior officers. Talking of officers—I'll swap my purser for your paymaster any day, John!"

"You don't know her like I do, Bill," Grimes told him, feeling oddly disloyal as he said it. He allowed Davinas to refill his glass, tried to ignore the beseeching glances of three young ladies seated not far from them. "Oh, well, I suppose we'd better find ourselves partners, especially since there seems to be a shortage of men here. But I'd sooner talk. Frankly, I'm sniffing around for information on this sector of space—but I suppose that can wait until tomorrow."

"Not unless you want a job as fourth mate aboard *Sundowner*. I lift ship for Electra bright and early—well, early—tomorrow morning."

"A pity."

"It needn't be. I'm not much of a dancing man. I'd sooner earbash and be earbashed over a cold bottle or two than be dragged around the floor by the local talent. And I was intending to return to my ship very shortly, anyhow. Why not come with me? We can have a talk on board."

Chapter 10

Davinas and Grimes slipped out of the ballroom almost unnoticed. A few cabs were waiting hopefully in the portico, so they had no difficulty in obtaining transport to the spaceport. It was a short drive only, and less than twenty minutes after they had left the palace Davinas was leading the way up the ramp to the after airlock of *Sundowner*.

It is impossible for a spaceman to visit somebody else's ship without making comparisons—and Grimes was busy making them. Here, of course, there was no uniformed Marine at the gangway, only a civilian night watchman supplied by the vessel's local agent, but the ramp itself was in better repair than *Discovery*'s, and far cleaner. It was the same inboard. Everything was old, worn, but carefully—lovingly, almost—maintained. Somehow the merchant captain had been able to instill in his people a respect—at least—for their ship. Grimes envied him. But in all likelihood Davinas had never been cursed with a full crew of malcontents, and would have been able to extract and dump the occasional bad apple from this barrel without being obliged to fill in forms in quintuplicate to explain just why.

The elevator cage slid upward swiftly and silently, came to a smooth stop. Davinas showed Grimes into his comfortable quarters. "Park the carcass, John. Make yourself at home. This is Liberty Hall; you can spit on the mat . . ."

". . . and call the cat a bastard," finished Grimes.

"Then why don't you?"

Grimes felt something rubbing against his legs, looked down, saw a large tortoiseshell tom. The animal seemed to have taken a fancy to him. He felt flattered. In spite of the affair on Morrowvia he still liked cats.

"Coffee?"

"Thanks."

Davinas poured two mugs from a large thermos container, then went into the office adjoining his dayroom. Grimes, while he petted the cat, looked around. He was intrigued by the pictures on the bulkheads of the cabin, holograms of scenes on worlds that were strange to him. One was a mountainscape—jagged peaks, black but snowcapped, thrusting into a stormy sky, each summit with its spume of ice particles streaming down wind like white smoke. He could almost hear the shrieking of the icy gale. Then there was one that could have been a landscape in Hell—contorted rocks, gaudily colored, half veiled by an ocher sandstorm.

Davinas came back, carrying a large folder. "Admiring the art gallery? That one's the Desolation Range on Lorn, my home world. And *that* one is the Painted Badlands on Eblis. Beats me why some genius doesn't open a tourist resort there. Spectacular scenery, friendly indigenes, and quite a few valleys where the likes of us could live quite comfortably."

"The Rim Worlds," murmured Grimes. "I've heard quite a lot about them, off and on. Somehow the Survey Service never seems to show the flag in that sector of space. I don't suppose I'll ever see them."

Davinas laughed. "Don't be so sure. Rim Runners'll take anybody, as long as he has some sort of certificate of competency and rigor mortis hasn't set in!"

"If they ever get me," declared Grimes, "that'll be the sunny Friday!"

"Or me," agreed Davinas. "When the Sundowner Line finally folds I'm putting my savings into a farm."

The two men sipped their good coffee. Davinas lit a long, slim cigar, Grimes his pipe. The cat purred noisily between them.

Then: "I hear that you're on a Lost Colony hunt, John."

"Yes, Bill. As a matter of fact, Commander Denny did mention that you might be able to give me a few leads."

"I might be. But, as a Rim Worlds citizen, I'm supposed to make any reports on anything I find to the Rim Worlds government. And to my owners, of course."

"But the Rim Worlds are members of the Federation."

"Not for much longer, they're not. Surely you've heard talk of secession lately." Davinas laughed rather unpleasantly. "But I'm not exactly in love with our local lords and masters. I've been in the Sundowner Line practically all my working life, and I haven't enjoyed seeing our fleet pushed off the trade routes by Rim Runners. *They* can afford to cut freights; they've the taxpayer's money behind them. And who's the taxpayer? Me."

"But what about your owners? Don't you report to them?"

"They just aren't interested anymore. The last time that I made a deviation, sniffing around for a possible new run for *Sundowner*, there was all hell let loose." He obviously quoted from a letter. " 'We would point out that you are a servant of a commercial shipping line, not a captain in the Federation Survey Service. . . .' Ha!"

"Mphm. So you might be able to help me?"

"I might. If you ask me nicely enough, I will." He poured more coffee into the mugs. "You carry a PCO, of course?"

"Of course. And you?"

"No. Not officially. Our head office now and again—only now and again, mind you—realizes that there is such a force as progress. They found out that one of the early Carlotti sets was going cheap. So now I have Carlotti, and no PCO. But—"

"But what?"

"My NST operator didn't like it. He was too lazy to do the Carlotti course to qualify in FTL radio. He reckoned, too, that he'd be doing twice the work that he was doing before, and for the same pay. So he resigned, and joined Rim Runners. They're very old-fashioned, in some ways. They don't have Carlotti equipment in many of their ships yet. They still carry psionic communication officers and Normal Space-Time radio officers."

"Old-fashioned?" queried Grimes. "Perhaps they still carry PCOs for the same reason as we do. To sniff things out."

"That's what I tried to tell my owners when they took away Farley's amplifier, saying that its upkeep was a needless expense. A few spoonfuls of nutrient chemicals each trip, and a couple of little pumps! But I'm getting ahead of myself. This Farley *was* my PCO. He's getting on in years, and knows that he hasn't a hope in hell of finding a job anywhere else. Unlike the big majority of telepaths he has quite a good brain and, furthermore, doesn't shy away from machinery, up to and including electronic gadgetry. He actually took the Carlotti course and examination, and qualified, and also qualified as an NST operator. So now he's my radio officer, NST, and Carlotti. It breaks his heart at times to have to push signals over the light-years by electronic means, but he does it. If they'd let him keep his beagle's brain in aspic he'd still be doing it the good old way, and the Carlotti transceiver would be gathering dust. But with no psionic amplifier, he just hasn't the range."

"No. He wouldn't have."

"Even so, if one passes reasonably close to a planet, within a few light-years, a good telepath can pick up the psionic broadcast, provided that the world in question has a sizable population of sentient beings."

"Human beings?"

"Not necessarily. But our sort of people, more or less. I'm told that there's no mistaking the sort of broadcast you get from one of the Shaara worlds, for example. Arthropods, however intelligent, just don't think like mammals."

"And you have passed reasonably close to a planet with an intelligent, mammalian population? One that's not on any of the lists?"

"Two of them, as a matter of fact. In neighboring planetary systems."

"Where?"

"That'd be telling, John. Nothing for nothing, and precious little for a zack. That's the way that we do business in the Sundowner Line!"

"Then what's the *quid pro quo*, Bill?"

Davinas laughed. "I didn't think that you trade school boys were taught dead languages! All right. This is it. Just let me know what you find. As I've already told you, the Sundowner Line's on its last legs; I'd like to keep us running just a little longer. A new trade of our own could make all the difference."

"There are regulations, you know," said Grimes slowly. "I can't go blabbing the Survey Service's secrets to any Tom, Dick, or Harry. Or Bill."

"Not even when they were Bill's secrets to begin with? Come off it. And I do happen to know that those same regulations empower you, as captain of a Survey Service ship, to use your own discretion when buying information. Am I right?"

"Mphm." Grimes was tempted. Davinas could save him months of fruitless searching. On the one hand, a quick conclusion to his quest would be to his credit. On the other hand, for him to let loose a possibly unscrupulous tramp skipper on a hitherto undiscovered Lost Colony would be to acquire yet another big black mark on his record. But this man was no Drongo Kane. He said, "You know, of course, that I carry a scientific officer. He has the same rank as myself, but if I do find a Lost Colony he'll be wanting to take charge, and I may have to take a back seat."

"If he wants to set up any sort of Base," countered Davinas, "he'll be requiring regular shipments of stores and equipment and all the rest of it. Such jobs, as we both know, are usually contracted out. And if I'm Johnny-on-the-spot, with a reasonable tender in my hot little hand—"

It made sense, Grimes thought. He asked, "And will you want any sort of signed agreement, Bill?"

"You insult me, and you insult yourself. Your word's good enough, isn't it?"

"All right." Grimes had made up his mind. "Where are these possible Lost Colonies of yours?"

"Farley picked them up," said Davinas, "when I was right off my usual tramlines—*anybody's* usual tramlines, come to that—doing a run between Rob Roy and Caribbea." He pushed the coffee mugs and the thermos bottle to one side, opened the folder that he had brought from his office on the low table. He brought out a chart. "Modified Zimmerman Projection." His thin forefinger stabbed decisively. "The Rob Roy sun, here. And Sol, as the Caribbeans call their primary, here. Between them, two G type stars, 1716 and 1717 in Ballchin's catalog, practically in line, and as near as damnit on the same plane as Rob Roy and Caribbea. Well clear of the track, actually—but not too well clear."

"It rather surprises me," said Grimes, "that nobody has found evidence of intelligent life there before."

"Why should it? When those old lodejammers were blown away to hell and gone off course—assuming that these worlds *are* Lost Colonies, settled by lodejammer survivors—PCOs hadn't been dreamed of. When your Commodore Slater made his sweep through that sector of space, PCOs still hadn't been dreamed of. Don't forget that we had FTL ships long before we had FTL radio, either electronic or psionic."

"But what about the odd merchant ships in more recent years, each with her trained telepath?"

"What merchant ships? As far as I know, *Sundowner* was the only one to travel that route, and just once, at that. I happened to be on Rob Roy, discharging a load of kippered New Maine cod, and the word got through to my agents there that one of the transgalactic clippers, on a cruise, was due in at Caribbea. She'd been chartered by some Terry outfit calling themselves The Sons of Scotia. And it seems that they were going to celebrate some Earth calendar religious festival—Burns Night—there."

"Burns?" murmured Grimes. "Let me see. Wasn't he a customs officer? An odd sort of chap to deify."

"Ha, ha. Anyhow, the Punta del Sol Hotel at Port of Spain sent an urgent Carlottigram to Rob Roy to order a large consignment of haggis and Scotch whiskey. I was the only one handy to lift it. I got it there on time, too, although I just about burned out the main bearings of the Mannschenn Drive doing it."

"And did they enjoy their haggis?" wondered Grimes.

"I can't say. *I* didn't. The shippers presented me with half a dozen of the obscene things as a token of their appreciation. Perhaps we didn't cook them properly."

"Or serve them properly. I don't suppose that *Sundowner* could run to a bagpiper to pipe them in to the messroom table."

"That could have been the trouble." Davinas looked at his watch. "I hate to hurry you up, John—but I always like to get my shut-eye before I take the old girl upstairs. But, before you go, I'd like to work out some way that you can let me know if you find anything. A simple code for a message, something that can't be cracked by the emperor of Waverley's bright boys. As you see from the chart, those two suns are practically inside Waverley's sphere of influence. I want to be first ship on the scene—after you, of course. I don't want to be at the tail end of a long queue of Imperial survey ships and freighters escorted by heavy cruisers."

"Fair enough," agreed Grimes. "Fair enough. Just innocent Carlottigrams that could be sent by anybody, to anybody. Greetings messages? Yes. Happy Birthday, say, for the first world, that belonging to 1717. Happy Anniversary for the 1716 planet. Signed 'John' if it's worth your while to persuade your owners to let you come sniffing around. Signed 'Peter' if you'd be well advised not to come within a hundred light-years.

"But you'll be hearing from me. I promise you that."

"Thank you," said Davinas.

"Thank *you*," said Grimes.

Chapter 11

Davinas phoned down to the night watchman to ask him to order a cab for Grimes. While they were waiting for the car he poured glasses of an excellent Scotch whiskey from Rob Roy. They were finishing their drinks when the night watchman reported that the car was at the ramp.

Grimes was feeling smugly satisfied when he left *Sundowner*. It certainly looked as though he had been handed his Lost Colony— correction, *two* Lost Colonies—on a silver tray. And this Davinas was a very decent bloke, and deserved any help that Grimes would be able to give him.

The ride back to the mayor's palace was uneventful. The party was still in progress in the huge ballroom; the girl at the synthesizer controls was maintaining a steady flow of dance music, although only the young were still on the floor. The older people were gathered around the buffet tables, at which the supplies of food and drink were being replenished as fast as they dwindled.

Grimes joined Brabham and Vinegar Nell, who were tucking into a bowl of caviar as though neither of them had eaten for a week, washing it down with locally made vodka.

"Be with us, sir," said Brabham expansively. "A pity they didn't bring *this* stuff out earlier. If I'd known this was going to come up, I'd not have ruined my appetite on fishcakes and sausage rolls!"

Grimes spread a buttered biscuit with the tiny, black, glistening eggs, topped it up with a hint of chopped onion and a squeeze of lemon juice. "You aren't doing too badly now. Mphm. Not bad, not bad."

"Been seeing how the poor live, sir?" asked the first lieutenant.

"What do you mean?"

"You went off with *Sundowner*'s old man."

"Oh, yes. He has quite a nice ship. Old, but very well looked after."

"Sometimes I wonder if I wouldn't have done better in the merchant service," grumbled Brabham. "Even the Rim Worlds Merchant Service. I was having a yarn with *Sundowner*'s chief officer. He tells me that the new government-owned shipping line, Rim Runners, is recruiting personnel. I've a good mind to apply."

"Nobody in the Survey Service would miss you," said Vinegar Nell. Then, before Brabham could register angry protest, she continued, "Nobody in the Survey Service would miss any of us. We're the square pegs, who find that every hole's a round one." She turned to Grimes, who realized that she must have been drinking quite heavily. "Come on, Captain! Out with it! What was in your sealed orders? Instructions to lose us all down some dark crack in the continuum, yourself included?"

"Mphm," grunted Grimes noncommittally, helping himself to more caviar. He noticed that the civilians in the vicinity had begun to flap their ears. He said firmly, "Things aren't as bad as they seem." He tried to make a joke of it. "In any case, I haven't lost a ship yet."

"There has to be a first time for everything," she said darkly.

"*Some* people are lucky," commented Brabham. "In the Survey Service, as everywhere else, luck counts for more than ability."

"Some people have neither luck *nor* ability," said Vinegar Nell spitefully. The target for this barbed remark was obvious—and Brabham, feared Grimes, would be quite capable of emptying the bowl of caviar over her head if she continued to needle him. And the captain of a ship, justly or unjustly, is held responsible for the conduct of his officers in public places. His best course of action would be to separate his first lieutenant and his paymaster before they came to blows.

"Shall we dance, Miss Russell?" he asked.

She produced a surprisingly sweet smile. "But of course, Captain."

The synthesizer was playing a song that he had heard before, probably a request from those of *Sundowner*'s people who were still at the party. The tune was old, very old, but the words were new, and Rim Worlders had come to regard it as their very own.

> *Good-bye, I'll run to find another sun*
> *Where I may find*
> *There are worlds more kind than the ones left behind. . . .*

Vinegar Nell, fitting into his arms as though she belonged there, had always belonged there, was singing softly as she danced. And was he, Grimes, dancing as well as he thought he was? Probably not, he admitted to himself, but she made him feel that he was cutting a fine figure on the polished floor. And she was making him feel rather more than that. He was acutely conscious of the tightness of the crotch of his dress trousers.

When the number was over he was pleased to see that Brabham had wandered off somewhere by himself, but he was not pleased when Commander Denny claimed Vinegar Nell for the next dance, and still less pleased when he found himself having to cope with Denny's wife. He suffered. It was like having to tow an unwieldy captive balloon through severe atmospheric turbulence. But then the Mayoress made a welcome change, although she chattered incessantly. After her, there were a few girls whose names he promptly forgot.

Vinegar Nell again, and the last dance.

> *Good night, ladies,*
> *Good night, ladies,*
> *Good night, ladies . . .*
> *We're bound to leave you now. . . .*

"But you don't have to leave *me*, John," she whispered.
Mphm?
And everybody was singing:

> *Merrily we roll along,*
> *Roll along, roll along,*
> *Merrily we roll along*
> *O'er the bright blue sea. . . .*

He said, "We have to roll along back to the ship, after we've said our good nights, and thanked the mayor for his party."

She said, her mood suddenly somber, "There's no place else to roll. Not for us."

The synthesizer emitted a flourish of trumpets, a ruffle of drums. The dancers froze into attitudes of stiff—or not so stiff—attention. Blaring brass against a background of drumbeats, an attempt to make dreadfully trite melody sound important. It was one of those synthetic, utterly forgettable national anthems, the result, no doubt, of a competition, selected by the judges as the poor best of a bad lot. The words matched the music:

New Maine, flower of the galaxy,
New Maine, stronghold of liberty. . . .

Then: "Good night, Mr. Mayor. On behalf of my officers I must thank you for a marvelous party."

"Good night, Captain. It was a pleasure to have you aboard. Good night, Miss Russell. If the Survey Service had more paymasters like you, I'd be a spaceman myself. Ha, ha! Good night . . . good night."

"Good night."

The ground cars were waiting outside, in the portico. As before, Grimes rode in the lead vehicle with Vinegar Nell and Dr. Brandt. With them, this time, was the chief engineer.

"A waste of valuable time, these social functions," complained the scientist as they sped back toward the Base.

"Ye werenae darin' sae bad on the free booze an' tucker," pointed out MacMorris.

"And neither were you, Chief," put in Vinegar Nell.

"Ah'm no' a dancin' man, not like our gallant captain. An' as for the booze an' tucker—it's aye a pleasure to tak' a bite an sup wi'oot havin' you begrudgin' every mouthful!"

"I still say that it was a waste of time," stated Brandt. "Commander Grimes, for example, could have spent the evening going through the port captain's records to see if there are any reports of Lost Colonies."

"Mphm," grunted Grimes smugly, happily conscious of the folded copy of the chart that Davinas had given him, stiff in the inside breast pocket of his mess jacket.

They were approaching the Base now. There stood *Discovery*, a tall metal steeple, dull-gleaming in the wan light of the huge, high, lopsided moon. And there were great dark shapes, sluglike, oozing slowly over the concrete apron of the spaceport.

"Filthy brutes!" exclaimed the driver, breaking the morose silence that he had maintained all the way from the mayor's palace.

"Great snakes?" asked Grimes.

"What else, Captain? Whoever decided that those bloody things should be protected should have his bloody head read!"

"You, man!" snapped Brandt. "Take us in close to one of them! Put your spotlight on it!"

"Not on your bloody life, mister! If anything scares those bastards, they *squirt*. And they squirt all over what scares 'em! I have to keep this car clean, not you. Now, here you are, lady and gentlemen. I've brought you right back to your own front door. A very good night to you—what's left of it!"

They got out of the car, which had stopped at the foot of *Discovery*'s ramp. The air was heavy with the sweet-sour stench of fresh ordure. Something splattered loudly not far from them. Their vehicle, its motor whining shrilly, made a hasty departure.

"Are you waiting outside to study the great snakes at close quarters, Doctor?" asked Grimes. "I'm not." He started up the ramp, as hastily as possible without loss of dignity, Vinegar Nell beside him. MacMorris came after and then, after only a second's hesitation, Brandt. At the outer airlock door the Marine sentry came to attention, saluted. Grimes wondered if the man would be as alert after Major Swinton was back safely on board.

The elevator cage was waiting for them. They got into it, were lifted through the various levels. Vinegar Nell, Brandt, and MacMorris got out at the officers' deck. Grimes carried on to Control, found the duty officer looking out through the viewport at the lights of the cars still coming in from Penobscot.

"Oh, good morning, sir." Then, a little wistfully, "Was it a good party?"

"It was, Mr. Farrow. Quite good." Grimes yawned. "If any of those . . . *things* try to climb up the side of the ship to do their business, let me know. Good night, or good morning, or whatever."

He went down to his quarters. He did not, he realized with some surprise, feel all that tired. He subsided into an armchair, pulled out from his pocket the copy of the star chart, unfolded it. Yes, it was certainly a good lead, and Captain Davinas was entitled to some reward for having given it to him.

There was a knock at the door.

"Come in!" he called, wondering who it could be. Not Brabham, he hoped, with some trifling but irritating worry that could well wait until a more civilized hour.

It was Vinegar Nell. She was carrying a tray upon which were a coffeepot, a cup—no, *two* cups—and a plate of sandwiches. She had changed out of her evening dress uniform into something that was nothing much over nothing at all. Grimes had seen her naked often enough in the sauna adjoining the ship's gymnasium, but this was . . . different. The spectacle of a heavily perspiring female body is not very aphrodisiac; that same body suggestively and almost transparently clad *is*.

She said, "I thought you'd like a snack before turning in, John."

"Thank you—er—Miss Russell."

She stooped to set the tray on the coffee table. The top of her filmy robe fell open. Her pink-nippled breasts were high and firm.

"Shall I pour?" she asked.

"Er, yes. Please."

She handed him a steaming cup. He was uncomfortably aware of the closeness of her, and fidgeted in his chair. He was relieved when she retired to a chair of her own.

She said, "It was a good night, wasn't it?"

"Yes."

She went on, "I've known you for *years*, haven't I? When was it that we were first shipmates? In the old *Aries*, wasn't it?"

"Yes."

"You know, John, I didn't much like you then."

"You didn't much like any of us in the wardroom. After all, you were the very first spacegoing female officer of the Supply Branch, and you were . . . prickly."

She laughed. "And you, a bright young lieutenant junior-grade, took pity on me, and made a pass at me out of the kindness of your heart."

Grimes's prominent ears were burning painfully. He could recall that scene all too well, could feel that stinging slap on his face and hear her furious voice: *Take your mucky paws off me, you insufferable puppy!*

He thought, *And a commander, the captain of a ship, doesn't have mucky paws, of course. But whatever sort of paws I do have, now, I'm keeping them to myself. Why, oh why, you stupid bitch, did you have to rake up that particular episode from the murky past?*

She was smiling softly. "We've come a long way since then, haven't we, John?"

"Mphm. Yes. Excellent coffee, this, Miss Russell. And these are very good sandwiches."

"Yes. You always liked your belly."

Again the memories: *You swaggering spacemen think that you're the Lord's anointed, but you aren't worth your keep, let alone your salaries.*

"Gutsy Grimes, the stewards and stewardesses used to call you."

"Oh. Did they?" Grimes put down a sandwich half eaten.

"Gutsy Grimes, the human garbage chute," she reminisced sentimentally.

"Fascinating."

And what was that perfume that she was wearing? Whatever it was, he decided that he didn't like it. He looked at his watch. "A spot of shut-eye is indicated. We have a busy day ahead of us tomorrow. Today, I mean."

She rose slowly to her feet, stretched and yawned like a lazy, graceful cat. Her robe fell open. Under the UV lamps in the ship's sun room she always freckled rather than tanned, and the effect was far from displeasing—yet Grimes, perversely, forced himself to think disparagingly of mutant leopards.

He yawned himself, then decisively drained his cup, set it down on the tray with a clatter. He said, "Thanks for the supper. I enjoyed it."

"I did, too."

Then, very firmly, "Good night, Miss Russell."

She flushed all over her body. "*Good night?* You don't mean . . . ?"

"I do mean. I'm turning in. By myself. Good night."

Without looking again at her he went through into his bedroom. He was afraid that she would (would not?) follow him. She did not. As he undressed he heard a vicious clattering as she put the remaining supper things back on the tray, then heard the outer door open and close behind her.

You bloody fool! he admonished himself. *You bloody, bloody fool!* But he thought (he hoped) that he had acted wisely. Vinegar Nell, as a *de facto* Captain's Lady, would very soon try to assume *de facto* command of the ship. On the other hand, because of his out-of-character puritanism, he could have made a dangerous enemy.

He did not sleep at all well.

Chapter 12

Discovery did not stay long on New Maine, although most of her people, who had speedily made friends locally, would have welcomed a longer sojourn on that planet.

Grimes feared that some ship, deviating from the usual route might stumble upon Davinas' Lost Colonies at any moment. He had been given access to the up-to-the-minute Lloyd's Register in the Penobscot port captain's office and had discovered that the majority of the ships of the Waverley Royal Mail had not yet made the change-over from psionic Deep Space communications to the Carlotti system. And Ballchin 1716 and 1717 were almost within the territorial space of the Empire of Waverley. The ruling emperor—as was known to Grimes, as a naval officer of the Federation—was not averse to the expansion of his already considerable dominions.

Discovery did not stay long on New Maine, which meant that her crew did not enjoy the shore leave that they had been expecting. It meant too that all hands, the senior officers especially, were obliged to dedigitate. Brabham, of whom it had been said that he had only two speeds, Dead Slow and Stop, was resentful. MacMorris, who had been looking forward to an orgy of taking apart and putting together, was resentful. Brandt, who had been given the run of the extensive library of the University of New Maine, was resentful. Vinegar Nell was resentful for more reasons than the short stay at the sub-Base.

"Commander Grimes," complained Brandt, "even though *you* are doing nothing to turn up possible leads, *I*, in the little time that I shall be given, am sifting through *years* of records."

But Grimes kept Davinas' information to himself. He knew what would happen if it leaked, just as Davinas himself had known. There would be an urgent Carlottigram from New Maine—where the empire maintained a trade commissioner—to Waverley, and long before *Discovery* arrived off those Lost Colonies some Imperial cruiser would have planted the thistle flag.

Brabham sulked, MacMorris sulked, Brandt sulked, Swinton snarled, and Vinegar Nell was positively vicious. "I suppose you know what you're doing, Captain." "I hope you realize the consequences if the algae tanks go bad on us, Captain." "I suppose you know that it's practically impossible to replenish the beef tissue culture in the time you've given me, Captain." "I'm afraid that I just can't accept responsibility if things go wrong in my department, Captain."

At least, Grimes consoled himself, he had one satisfied customer. That was Denny. The elderly commander clearly did not approve of the flurry of activity into which his normally sleepy Base had been plunged. He knew that this flurry would continue as long as *Discovery* was sitting on the apron. He knew, too—Mrs. Denny made sure that he knew—that the outsiders were interfering with the local ecology. They had attached hoses to *his* hydrants and washed down the entire spaceport area. They had rigged a wire fence with a carefully calculated low voltage trickling through it on a wide perimeter about their vessel. When Denny had objected, Grimes had told him that his crew did not like working in a latrine and that, furthermore, the materials used for the fence came from ship's stores, and the current in the wires from the ship's generators.

"I shall report this to Lindisfarne Base, Commander Grimes," said Denny stiffly.

"I shall be making *my* report too," Grimes told him. "And so will my medical officer. Meanwhile, my chief engineer tells me that he's not getting much help from your workshops."

"I'll see that he gets all the help he wants," promised Denny. His manner suddenly softened. "You're not married, Commander, but you will be. Then you'll find out what it's like, especially if your wife has a weird taste in pets."

"One man's pets are another man's pests," cracked Grimes.

"One woman's pets are, strictly between ourselves, her husband's pests. Rest assured that I shall get your rustbucket off my Base as soon as is humanly possible. Anything for a quiet life."

And so the activity continued, with work around the clock.

"There's hardly been any shore leave, sir," complained Brabham.

"Growl you may, but go you must," countered Grimes cheerfully.

"But what's the *hurry*, sir?"

"There is a valid reason for it, Number One," Grimes told him.

"More sealed orders, I suppose," said Brabham, with as near to a sneer as he dared.

"Maybe, maybe not," replied Grimes, with what he knew must be infuriating smugness. There were times when he did not quite like himself, and this was one of them—but his officers were bringing out the worst in him. "Just take it from me that I know what I'm doing, and why. That's all."

"Very good, sir," said Brabham, conveying the impression that, as far as he was concerned, it wasn't.

Rather to Grimes's surprise the target date was met.

A cheerless dawn was breaking over the Base as the ramp was retracted, as the last of *Discovery*'s airtight doors sighed shut. The old ship was as spaceworthy as she ever would be, and she had somewhere to go.

Grimes, in the control room, spoke into the microphone. "*Discovery* to New Maine Aerospace Control. Request outward clearance. Over."

"All clear for your liftoff, *Discovery*. No air traffic in vicinity of Base. No space traffic whatsoever. Good hunting. Over."

"Thank you, Aerospace Control. Over."

"Base to *Discovery*." This was Denny's voice. "Good hunting. Over."

"Thank you, Commander Denny. Give my regards to the great snakes. They can have their public convenience back now. Over."

"I wish you were taking the bastards with you, Grimes. Over."

Grimes laughed, and started the inertial drive. *Discovery* shuddered, heaving herself clear of the apron. She clambered upward like an elderly mountaineer overburdened with equipment. No doubt MacMorris would complain that he should have been given more time to get his innies into proper working order. Then the beat of the engines became louder, more enthusiastic. Grimes relaxed a little. He took a sidewise glance at Tangye, in the co-pilot's seat. This time, he noted, the navigator had done his sums before departure; a loosely folded sheet of paper was peeping out of the breast pocket of his uniform shirt. And what target star would he have selected? Hamlet, probably, in the Shakespearean System, out toward the Rim Worlds. It was a pity that *Discovery* would not be heading that way.

The ship pushed through the low overcast as though she really meant it, emerged into the clear stratum between it and the high cirrus. Blinding sunlight, almost immediately dimmed as the viewports au-

tomatically polarized, smote through into the control room, and, outside, made haloes of iridescence in the clouds of ice particles through
which the vessel was driving. She lifted rapidly through the last tenuous shreds of atmosphere.

"Clear of the Van Allens, sir," reported Tangye at last.

"Thank you, pilot," acknowledged Grimes. Then, to Brabham,
"Make the usual announcements, Number One. Free fall, setting trajectory, all the rest of it."

"Take over now, sir?" asked Tangye, pulling the sheet of notes
from his breast pocket.

Grimes grinned at him. "Oh, I think I'll keep myself in practice,
pilot. It's time I did some work."

The ship was in orbit now, falling free about New Maine. Grimes
produced his own sheet of paper, glanced at it, then at the constellations patterned on the blackness outside the viewports. He soon found
the one that he was looking for, although why the first settlers on this
planet had called it The Mermaid he could not imagine. Their imagi-
nations must have been far more vivid than his. His fingers played
over the controls and the directional gyroscopes began to spin, and the
hull turned about them.

"Sir," said Tangye urgently. "Sir!"

"Yes, pilot?"

"Sir, Hamlet's in The Elephant. From here, that is—"

"How right you are, Mr. Tangye. But why should we be heading
toward Elsinore?"

"But, sir, the orders said that we were to make a sweep out toward
the Rim."

"That's right," put in Brabham.

"I have steadied this ship," said Grimes coldly, "on to Delta Mermaid. We shall run on that trajectory until further orders—orders from
myself, that is. Number One, pass the word that I am about to start
the Mannschenn Drive."

"As you say, sir," replied Brabham sulkily.

Deep in the bowels of the vessel the gleaming rotors began to turn,
to spin and to tumble, to precess out of normal space-time, pulling the
ship and all her people with them down the dark dimensions, through
the warped continuum. There was the usual fleeting second or so of
temporal disorientation, while shapes wavered and colors sagged down
the spectrum, while all sound was distorted, with familiar noises either
impossibly high in pitch or so low as to be almost inaudible.

There was, as always, the uncanny sensation of *déjà vu*.

Grimes experienced no previsions but felt, as he had when setting trajectory off Lindisfarne, a deep and disturbing premonition of impending doom.

Perhaps, he thought, he should adhere to his original orders. Perhaps he should observe the golden rule for modest success in any service: Do what you're told, and volunteer for nothing.

But whatever he did, he knew from harsh experience, he always ran into trouble.

Chapter 13

The ship settled down into her normal Deep Space routine—regular watches, regular mealtimes, regular exercise periods in the gymnasium, and regular inspections. In many ways, in almost all ways, she was like any other ship; what made her different, too different, was the resentment that was making itself felt more and more by her captain. The short stay on New Maine, with hardly any shore leave, was in part responsible. But there was more than that. Everybody aboard knew what Grimes's original orders had been—to use New Maine as a base and to make a sweep out toward the Rim without intruding into what the Rim Worlds already were referring to as *their* territorial space. (It was not Federation policy to do anything that might annoy those touchy colonials, who, for some time, had been talking loudly about secession.) And now everybody aboard knew that *Discovery* was headed not toward the Rim but in the general direction of the Waverley sector. Grimes, of course, was the captain, and presumably knew what he was doing. Grimes was notoriously lucky—but luck has a habit of running out. If this cruise, carried out in contravention to admiralty orders—vague though those orders had been—turned out to be fruitless, Grimes would have to carry the can back—but his officers, none of them at all popular with high authority, would be even less likely to achieve any further promotion.

Grimes could not help overhearing snatches of conversation. *The old bastard is putting us all up Shit Creek without a paddle.* And, *He's always been fantastically lucky, but he's bound to come a real gutser one day. I only hope that I'm not around when he does!* And, *He must think that he's a reincarnation of Nelson—turning a blind eye to his orders!* With the reply, *A reincarnation of Bligh, you mean!*

This last, of course, was from Brabham.

And if Bligh, thought Grimes, had carried a trained and qualified telepath aboard *Bounty* he might have been given warning of the mutiny that was brewing. He, Grimes, did have such a telepath aboard *Discovery*—but was Flannery willing to bend the Rhine Institute's ethical code? If he were, it would be far easier to keep a finger on the pulse of things. But Flannery . . . his loyalties, such as they were, were to his shipmates, much as he disliked them all, rather than to the ship and her commander. He was bred of stock with a long, long record of rebellion and resentment of all authority. Even his psionic amplifier— one that Grimes, ironically enough, had persuaded the telepath to accept—seemed to share its master's viewpoint.

Yet Grimes did not dislike the whiskey-swilling psionic communications officer and did not think that Flannery actively disliked him. Perhaps, carefully handled, the man might be induced to spill a bean or two. In any case, Grimes would have to spill the beans to him, would have to tell him about Davinas and the suspected Lost Colonies. But did Flannery know already? PCOs were not supposed to pry, but very few of them were able to resist the temptation.

He made his way down to the farm deck, to the squalid cubbyhole where Flannery lived in psionic symbiosis with his amplifier. The man was more or less sober, having, over the years, built up a certain immunity to alcohol. He was playing patience—and, Grimes noted, cheating—between sips from a tumbler of whiskey.

"Ah, top o' the mornin' to ye, Captain! Or is it mornin'? Or evenin'? Or last St. Patrick's Day?"

"Good morning, Mr. Flannery."

"A drop on the real peat elixir for ye, Captain?"

Grimes hesitated, then accepted. Irish whiskey was not among his favorite tipples, but he wanted to keep Flannery in a good mood. He wondered how long it was since the glass into which his drink was poured had been washed.

"Thank you, Mr. Flannery. Mind if I sit down?"

"Not at all, not at all, Captain. This is Liberty Hall. Ye can spit on the mat an'—"

"Call Ned a bastard? He mightn't like it."

"He wouldn't be mindin' at all, at all. T'is a term o' endearment where *he* comes from. An' it was about Ballchin 1716 and 1717 ye were wantin' to see me, wasn't it?"

"You've been . . . snooping," accused Grimes.

"Snoopin', Captain? There was no need to. I'd have to blank me mind off entoirely not to pick up your broadcasts on *that* subject! An' if ye're askin' me now, I've picked up nary a whisper yet from the planets o' those two suns. But I'm listenin'. An' Ned—bless the sweet soul o' him—is listenin'."

"Thank you. Mphm. Oh, and there was something else."

"Ye're not after askin' me *that*, Captain, are ye? To pry on me mates?"

"Well, it is done, you know," said Grimes defensively. "When justified by the circumstances, that is."

"Niver by me it isn't, Captain. The Rhine Institute licensed me, an' I abide by its rules."

When it suits you, thought Grimes.

Flannery grinned, showing his mottled teeth. Grimes might just as well have spoken aloud. "I'll tell ye what," said the telepath cheerfully. "I'll tell ye what . . . I'll give ye a readin'. On the house, as the wee dog said." His grubby hands swept the cards into an untidy pile, stacked them. "Seein' as how we're aboard a starship I'll be usin' the Mystic Star."

"Mphm?" grunted Grimes dubiously.

Flannery riffled through the cards, selected one, laid it face upward on the dirty tabletop. "The King of Clubs," he announced. "That's you. Our leader, no less."

"Why the King of Clubs?"

"An' why not, Captain? Ye're a decent enough boyo under the gold braid an' brass buttons. The King o' Gravediggers, standin' for the military leader, is not for the likes o' you. Ye're not a bad enough bastard."

"Thank you."

"An' now take the pack. Shuffle it. Let the—the *essence* o' ye seep through yer hands into the Devil's Prayerbook."

Grimes felt that the reverse was taking place, that the uncleanliness of the cards was seeping through his skin into him, but he did as he was told.

"An' now, with yer left hand, put the cards down. Face down. Cut the pack. An' again, so we have three piles."

Grimes obeyed.

"An' now, the Indicator."

Flannery turned over the first stack, revealing the nine of diamonds, then the second, to show the eight of the same suit, then the third, exposing the two of spades.

"Ah, an' what have we here? The unexpected gift, an' the journey that's made possible. The cards don't lie, Captain. Didn't the man Davinas give ye that star chart? An' the eight o' sparklers—a lucky

card for the explorer. But what's this mean? The deuce o' gravediggers. Could it be that yer famous luck is goin' to turn sour on ye?
Change, disruption, an' voyages to far places. What are ye runnin'
from, Captain? Are ye runnin' away, or are ye bein' thrown out from
somethin'? Good luck, an' bad luck, an' isn't that the way with ivery
mother's son of us? But with you—the good outweighin' the bad."

Rubbish, thought Grimes, not quite convincing himself. "Go on,"
he said.

"Ye're in this too." Flannery swept the cards, with the exception
of the King of Clubs, back into one pack. "Take 'em, Captain. Shuffle
again. Now give 'em back to me."

Working widdershins, Flannery placed eight cards around the King
in the form of an eight-pointed star. Then he gave the pack back to
Grimes, telling him to put two more cards on each of the eight points.

"An' now," he said, "we shall see what we shall see." He turned
up the three cards at the top of the star. "Aha! The King o' Sparklers,
the four o' blackberries, an' the seven o' gravediggers. Someone's
workin' against ye, Captain. A military man, a soldier, an' there's the
warnin' o' danger ahead, an' another warnin', too. A woman could
land ye in the cactus."

"It wouldn't be the first time," grunted Grimes.

"An' now—" Flannery turned up the three cards to the left of the
first three: the four and the six of spades, the two of clubs. "Good an'
bad again—but that's life. Loss, an' poverty, an' jealousy, an' envy
a-destroyin' of yer success—but good luck again when it's all over.
The Odd Gods o' the Galaxy alone know how ye do it, but always ye
come to the top. Not at once, mind ye. It takes time. But remember
this—when all the cards are on the table there's but the one man in
the universe ye can trust. Yerself.

"Now—" the telepath turned up the third trio of cards: five of
clubs, four of hearts, and six of diamonds. He chuckled. "A foine
mixture, this! The cards say as how ye're to take things as they come,
marriage wise. It'll all turn out wrong in the end, anyhow. Did I iver
tell ye that I was married once? Anyhow—play yer cards right for a
wealthy marriage says *this* one, an' *this* one says that ye're the last o'
a long line o' bachelors. An' *this* one—an early, romantic marriage
an' an unlucky second marriage. So ye *did* have fun, or ye're goin'
to have fun, or ye never did have nor ever will have any fun at all.
Take yer choice.

"Aha!" The next set of three was flipped over. "The King an' the
Queen o' Gravediggers, an' the trey o' diamonds. The King's another

captain, who's going to get in yer hair in the nearish future. And would it be yer old pal Commander Delamere?"

"What do you know about him?" snapped Grimes.

"Only what flickered through yer mind when I turned up the card. An' the Queen? Sorry, Captain, I can't place her. She's nobody ye know—*yet*. But ye'll be gettin' quite a handful. An' that little three? Oh, all sorts o' fun an' games, an' I have a feelin' that the King'll be playin' a part in 'em. He doesn't like you at all, at all.

"An' now, what have we? Six an' eight o' blackberries, seven o' sparklers. Goodish, goodish—but not all that good when ye remember all that's come before, an' all that's to come. Good for *business?* Ha! Ye're not a shopkeeper, Captain. An', come to that, ye're not a merchant skipper. Your ship doesn't have to show a profit. An' the other two cards warn ye against gamblin'. But isn't all life a gamble? Aren't we gamblin' with our lives ivery time that we liftoff planet, or come in for a happy landin'? And when ye gamble ye must always expect the odd run o' bad luck."

He turned over the sixth set of three. "Eight o' spades, two an' three o' hearts. Ah, overcome resistance, it says. Ye always do that, don't ye? But what about traitors? What about them as'd stab ye in the back?"

"What about them?" demanded Grimes sharply.

"*I* said nothin', Captain, nothin' whativer. T'was the cards said it—an' surely ye, of all men, wouldn't be after payin' attention to silly pieces o' plastic? Or would ye?" He chuckled, prodding the cards with a thick forefinger. "But the deuce an' the trey—don't they cancel out sweetly? Success, an' good fortune, an' everything ye wish yerself—but *when?* This week, next week, sometime, never. An' agin that there's the risk o' unwise choices, an' leapin' afore ye look, an' all the rest of it. So—look first, leap second—if at all.

"Nine an' ten o' hearts, nine o' spades. Two o' one, one o' t'other. Hearts an' flowers the first two, love and roses all the way—*but*, if that black bastard of a nine is telling the truth, only if ye come through the troubles that are waitin' for ye. There's a crisis brewin', Captain. Beware o' the night o' the long knives. Keep yer back to the bulkhead."

I do have enemies, bad ones, thought Grimes.

"An' don't ye ever!" There was a note of admiration in Flannery's voice. "But now we'll see what the last point o' the star has to tell us. Nine o' clubs. Two o' spades, an' the ten o' the same. Black, black, black. Really, ye should ha' stayed in bed in the BOQ on Lindisfarne.

Battle, murder, an' sudden death. Disasters by land an' by sea an' in deep space. If it wasn't for the very last card of all I'd be wishin' meself that I'd gone sick on New Maine an' been left behind."

"The ten of spades?" asked Grimes. "But that's unlucky too, surely."

"Think yerself lucky that it's not the Gravedigger itself, the Ace. Do ye really want to know what it means?"

"Yes," Grimes told him firmly.

Flannery laughed. "Beware o' false prophets. That's its meanin'. So, decide for yerself, Captain. Do ye trust the cards, or don't ye?"

And do I trust you? wondered Grimes.

"The cards say to trust *nobody*," Flannery told him.

Chapter 14

Grimes did not believe the card reading, of course. Nonetheless it added to his growing uneasiness, and when he was uneasy he tended to snarl. He knew that his officers and crew resented his attempts to maintain minimal standards of smartness aboard the ship, and that the scientist, Dr. Brandt, regarded him as a barely necessary evil. He refused to admit that in taking command of *Discovery* he had bitten off more than he could chew, but he was coming to realize, more and more, that his predecessor had taken the easy way out, had made arrangements for his own comfort and then allowed the vessel to run herself in her own bumbling, inefficient way.

Meanwhile, as the ship steadily narrowed the distance between herself and the first of the two possible stars, Flannery, with all his faults, was pulling his weight. Straining his telepathic faculties, he had begun to pick up what could be construed as indications of intelligent life on one of the worlds in orbit about that sun.

"The skipper of *Sundowner* was right, Captain," he said. "There's somethin' there, all right. Or, even, somebody. There's—there's a sort o' murmur. Ye can't hear it, of course, but Ned's hearin' it, an' I'm hearin' it." He grinned. "T'is a real Irish parliament. Everybody talkin', an' nobody listenin'."

"Except you," said Grimes.

"Exceptin' me—an' Ned," agreed the PCO.

"Human?" asked Grimes.

"That I couldn't be sayin', Captain. T'is too early yet. But humanoid, for sure. Somethin' with warm blood an' breathin' oxygen."

"Or its equivalent," suggested Grimes doubtfully. "After all, the essential physiology of chlorine breathers is very similar to our own."

"A bridge we'll cross when we come to it, Captain. But even if *they*, whoever they might be when they're up an' dressed, ain't human, ye'll still have discovered a new world for the Federation—may all the Saints preserve it—an' that'll be a feather in yer cap!"

"I suppose so." Somehow the prospect did not cheer Grimes, as it should have done. "I suppose so."

He got up to return to his own quarters, where he was to preside over a meeting of his senior officers and petty officers.

He sat behind his desk, facing the others.

Brandt was there, sitting by himself, a compact ball of hostility. Brabham, Swinton, and Vinegar Nell shared a settee—sullen bloodhound, belligerent terrier, and spiteful cat. Dr. Rath was wrapped in his own private cloud of funereal gloom. MacMorris, too, was keeping himself to himself, obviously begrudging the time that he was being obliged to spend away from his precious engines. Langer, the bos'n, and Washington, the sergeant of Marines, formed a two-man conspiracy in a corner, ostentatiously holding themselves aloof from the commissioned officers.

"Gentlemen," began Grimes. "And Miss Russell," he added. "Mphm." He answered their not very friendly stares with one of his own. "Mr. Flannery assures me that there is life, intelligent life, very probably our sort of life, on one of the worlds of Ballchin 1717, the star that we are now approaching."

"So your luck is holding, sir," said Brabham.

"What exactly do your mean, Number One?"

"Even you, sir, would have found it hard to justify this deviation from the original plan if you'd found nothing."

"We have only the word of a drunken telepath that anything *has* been found," huffed Brandt. "And it still might not be a Lost Colony."

"Even if it is," grumbled MacMorris, "I doubt if there'll be any machine shops. I'm still far from happy about my innies."

"You never are," remarked Brabham.

"We didn't have enough time on New Maine to get *anything* fixed up properly," complained Vinegar Nell, favoring Grimes with a hostile glare.

"At least," stated Swinton, "*my* men, as always are ready for anything."

"There probably will be some civilians for you to massacre," murmured Vinegar Nell sweetly.

Swinton flushed hotly and Grimes spoke up before a quarrel could start. "Gentlemen. Miss Russell. If you wish to squabble, kindly do so elsewhere than in my quarters. I have called you here to discuss our course of action."

"To begin with," said Brandt, "there must be the minimal interference with whatever culture has developed on that world."

"If we're shot at," snapped Swinton, "we shoot back!"

"You tell 'em, Major!" murmured Sergeant Washington.

"That will do," said Grimes coldly. Then, "To begin with, I shall advise you all of my intentions. This original plan will be subject to modification as required by changing circumstances and, possibly, as suggested by your good selves.

"The vessel will continue on her present trajectory. Mr. Flannery will maintain his listening watch, endeavoring to learn as much as possible of the nature of the inhabitants. We are also, of course, maintaining a Carlotti listening watch, although it is doubtful if we shall pick anything up. The Carlotti system had not been dreamed of at the time of the Second Expansion, the heyday of the lodejammers. And, in any case, any station using it must, of necessity, be a well-established component of today's network of interstellar communications. We can't listen on NST radio, of course, until we shut down the Mannschenn Drive and reemerge into normal space-time.

"We shall endeavor to home on the source of psionic emission. With the interstellar drive shut down, we shall establish ourselves in orbit about the planet. We shall observe, listen, and send down our unmanned probes. And then we come in to a landing."

"Not in the ship," said Brandt flatly.

"And why not?" countered Grimes coldly.

"Have you considered," asked the scientist, "the effect that a hulking brute of a vessel like this might—no, *would!*—have on a people who have reverted to savagery, who are painfully climbing back up the hill to civilization?"

"If I'm going to be a stranger on a strange world," Grimes told him, "I prefer to be a stranger with all the resources of my own culture right there with me, not hanging in orbit and all too likely to be on the wrong side of the planet when I want something in a hurry!"

"I agree with the captain," said Brabham.

"And I," said Swinton.

"It is high time that the real command was put in the hands of the scientists," growled Brandt.

"If it ever is," Brabham snarled, "my resignation goes in."

"That will do, gentlemen," said Grimes firmly. "Whether we land in the ship, or whether we send down small parties in the boats, will be decided when we know more about 1717—but I can say, now, that the second course of action is extremely unlikely. Needless to say, the actual site of our landing will have to be decided upon. *If* the civilization has attained or reattained a high standard of technology, then there is no reason why we should not set down close to a large center of population, in broad daylight. If the people reverted to savagery after their own first landing, and stayed that way, then caution on our part is indicated."

"Putting it bluntly, Commander Grimes," said Brandt unpleasantly, "you are dithering."

"Putting it shortly," retorted Grimes, "I shall be playing by ear. As I always do. As I always have done." He was exaggerating, of course. Before any operation he always worked out his course of action in every smallest detail—but he was ever alert to changing circumstances, always ready to abandon his elaborate plan of campaign and to improvise.

He went on, "I want all of you carefully to consider the problems that are liable to confront us. I want all of you to work out your own ways of dealing with them. I am always open to suggestions. Don't forget that we are a team." (Did he hear a faint, derisive, *Ha, ha!?*) "Don't forget that we are a team, and remember that this is a Federation vessel and not a warship of the Waldegren Navy, whose kapitan would have you pushed out of the airlock for speaking out of turn." (And who was it who whispered in mock incredulity, *Oh, no?*) "Be ready for anything—and, above all, be ready for the things for which you aren't ready. Mphm." He carefully filled and then lit his pipe.

"Very enlightening, Commander Grimes," commented Brandt condescendingly.

Brabham said nothing, merely looked wooden. Swinton said nothing and looked skeptical. Vinegar Nell permitted herself a slight sneer. Dr. Rath looked like an undertaker counting the dead for whom he would have to provide a free funeral. The burly Langer raised his hand, looking like an oversized schoolboy. "Captain?"

"Yes, Bos'n?"

"Speaking on behalf of the men, sir, I hope that you will allow shore leave. We had precious little back at Main Base, and precious little on New Maine."

"This is not a pleasure cruise, Bos'n," said Grimes.

"You can say that again!" whispered somebody, not quite inaudibly.

Chapter 15

Star 1717 in the Ballchin Catalog was a Sol-type sun.

Somehow it and its planetary family had, to date, escaped close investigation by the survey ships of the Interstellar Federation, the Empire of Waverley (although it was almost in the Imperial back yard), or the Duchy of Waldegren, to name the major human spacefaring powers; neither had it attracted the attention of the far-ranging Seeker-Queens of the Shaara Galactic Hive. One reason for its being ignored was that it lay well away from the regular trade routes. Another reason was that nobody—at the moment—was acutely short of *lebensraum*. There were other reasons—economic, political, and whatever—but Grimes, a mere Survey Service commander, knew nothing of these, and would know nothing of such matters until, if at all, he wore gold braid up to the elbow and a cap whose peak was one solid encrustation of scrambled egg.

The planetary system of 1717 consisted of six worlds, easily observed as *Discovery*, her own time out of kilter with the *real* time of the universe, cautiously approached the star, running on interstellar drive, from well to the north of the plane of the ecliptic. The planets showed as wavering bands of luminescence about the shapeless, quivering iridescent blob that was their primary. After the Mannschenn Drive had been shut down they were, of course, far harder to locate—but Flannery, one of those telepaths capable of psionic direction-finding, was able to guide the ship in toward the world that harbored intelligent life.

Of 1717's six planets, the outermost three were gas giants. Of the innermost three, one was far too close to the sun for life, of any kind, to have developed. The other two were within the biosphere. The third one was almost another Earth, a resemblance that became more and more striking as *Discovery* approached it. There were seas and continents, mountain ranges, polar ice caps, and a cloudy atmosphere. On the night side were sparkling clusters of lights that had to be cities. And there were networks of unnaturally straight lines crisscrossing the landmasses that could be roads, or railways, or canals.

There was no doubt that 1717 III was inhabited. The people of 1717 III had achieved, it seemed certain, some kind of industrial civilization. But until an actual landing was made little could be known about them, although Flannery was doing his best to pick up information. He said to Grimes, who had taken to haunting the PCO's squalid office, "T'is like the roarin' o' the crowd at a football game, Captain. Niver a single voice that ye can make out what it's sayin' . . . just jabber, jabber, jabber. Oh, there's a power o' people down there all right, an' they're after thinkin' what people always do be thinkin'—that it's too hot, or too cold, or that it's almost dinnertime, or that it's a dreadful long time atween drinks. Which reminds me—" He reached for a full bulb of whiskey. "An' how long are ye keepin' us in free fall, Captain? I mislike these baby's feedin' bottles."

Grimes ignored this. "But are they thinking in Standard English?" he demanded. "Or in any other human language?"

"Now ye're askin'. An' the answer is—I don't know. Trouble is, there's niver a *real* telepath among the bunch of 'em. If there was, he'd be comin' in loud and clear at this range, and I'd be able to tell ye for sure." Flannery grinned. "Am I to take it that the opposition hasn't brought ye any joy? That the bould Sparkses—bad cess to 'em!—haven't been able to raise anythin' on their heathenish contraptions?"

"You know damn well they haven't!" huffed Grimes. "We weren't expecting anything on the Carlotti—but there's been nothing on the NST either, nothing but static."

"So ye haven't found a Lost Colony after all Captain. But ye've discovered a new world with new people. An' isn't that better?"

"A new world? How do you make that out?"

"A Lost Colony'd be makin' its start with all the books an' machinery an' know-how aboard the ship, wouldn't it? 'Less they went all the way back to the Stone Age they'd be keepin' the technology they started with, an' improvin' on it."

"Mphm. But perhaps, for some reason, our friends down there prefer landlines to radio."

"Ye've somethin' there, Captain. But—there's altogether too many o' the bastards. That world has a powerful big population. Could the crew an' passengers o' just *one* ship—one flyin' fridge, perhaps, or one o' the lodejammers still not accounted for—have done so well, even if they bred like rabbits? Historically speakin', the Deep Freeze ships o' the First Expansion were only yesterday, an' the Second Expansion was no more than a dog watch ago."

"But you forget," Grimes told him, "that the later Deep Freeze ships, and *all* the lodejammers, carried big stocks of fertilized ova, together with the incubating machinery. One ship would have the capability to populate a small—or not so small—continent within a few decades after the first landing."

"Ye've almost convinced me, Captain. But I can't pick up any clear thinkin' at all, at all. All I can tell ye is that *they*—whoever or whatever *they* are—are mammals, an' have two sexes an' a few o' the in-betweens, an' that most of 'em are runnin' hard to keep up in some sort o' rat race . . . like us. But *how* like? Now ye're askin', an' I can't tell ye. Yet."

"So we just have to wait and see," said Grimes, getting up to return to the control room.

The planet 1717 III loomed huge through the planetward viewports, a great island in the sky along the shores of which *Discovery* was coasting. Like all prudent explorers in Man's past Grimes was keeping well out from the land until he knew more of what awaited him there. Like his illustrious predecessors he would send in his small boats to make the first contact—but, unlike them, he would not be obliged to hazard the lives of any of his crew when he did so.

"Number one probe ready," reported Brabham.

"Thank you," said Grimes.

He glanced around the control room. Tangye was seated at the console, with its array of instruments, from which the probe would be operated. Brandt was looking on, obviously sneering inwardly at the amateurishly unscientific efforts of the spacemen. The officer of the watch was trying to look busy—although, in these circumstances, there was very little for him to do. The radio officers were hunting up and down the frequencies on the NST transceiver, bringing in nothing but an occasional burst of static.

"Launch the probe, sir?" asked Brabham.

"I'll just check with Mr. Tangye first, Number One." Then, to the navigator, "You know the drill, pilot?"

"Yes, sir. Keep the probe directly below the ship to begin with. Bring it down slowly through the atmosphere. The usual sampling. Maintain position relative to the ship unless instructed otherwise."

"Good. Launch."

"Launch, sir."

The muffled rattle of the probe's inertial drive was distinctly audible as, decks away below and aft, it nosed out of its bay. It would not have been heard had *Discovery*'s own engines been running, it was little more than a toy, but the big ship, in orbit, was falling free. Needles on the gauges of Tangye's console jerked and quivered, the traces in cathode ray tubes began their sinuous flickering; but as yet there was nothing to be seen on the big television screen tuned to the probe's transmitter that could not be better observed from the viewports.

"Commander Grimes," said Brandt, "I know that you are in charge, but might I ask why you are not adhering to standard procedure for a first landing?"

"What do you mean, Dr. Brandt?"

"Aren't first landings supposed to be made at dawn? That tin spy of yours will be dropping down from the noon sky, in the broadest daylight possible."

"And anybody looking straight up," said Grimes, "will be dazzled by the sun. The real reason for a dawn landing—a manned landing, that is—is so that the crew has a full day to make their initial explorations. That does not apply in this case."

"Oh. This, I take it then, is yet another example of your famous playing by ear."

"You could put it that way," said Grimes coldly.

Shuffling in his magnetic-soled shoes, he went to stand behind Tangye. Looking at the array of instruments, he saw that the probe had descended into an appreciable atmosphere and that friction was beginning to heat its skin. He said, "Careful, pilot. We don't want to burn the thing up."

"Sorry, sir."

Clouds on the screen—normal enough high cirrus.

More clouds below the probe—an insubstantial but solid-seeming mountainscape of cumulus. A break in the cloud-floor, a rift, a wide chasm, and through it the view of a vast plain, and cutting across it a straight ribbon, silver-gleaming against the greens and browns of the land.

"Oxygen . . . nitrogen . . . carbon dioxide . . ." Tangye was reciting as he watched the indicators on the console.

"Good," murmured Grimes. Then, "Never mind the analysis for now. It's all being recorded. Watch the screen. Bring the probe down to that . . . canal."

"How do you know it's not a road or a railway?" asked Brandt.

"I don't. But it *looks* like water."

The probe was now losing altitude fast, plunging down through the rift in the clouds, dropping below the ceiling. Beneath it spread the great plain, the browns and yellows and greens of it now seen to be in regular patterns—crops as yet unripe, crops ready for harvesting, crops harvested? There were roads between the fields, not as distinct as the canal, but definite enough. There was motion—dark cloud shadows drifting with the wind, a ripple over the fields that subtly and continuously changed and shifted the intensities of light and shade and color. And there was other motion, obviously not natural—a tiny black object that crawled like a beetle along the straight line of the canal, trailing a plume of white smoke or steam.

"Home on that boat," ordered Grimes.

"That . . . *boat*, sir?"

"That thing on the canal." Grimes could not resist a little sarcasm. "The word 'boat,' Mr. Tangye, was used long before it was applied to the small craft carried by spaceships. Home on the boat."

"Very good, sir," responded Tangye sulkily.

As the probe descended, details of the boat could be made out. It was a barge, self-propelled, with its foredeck practically all one long hatch, with a wheelhouse-cum-accommodation-block aft, just forward of the smoking stovepipe funnel. Suddenly a head appeared at one of the open wheelhouse windows, looking all around, finally staring upward. That was the main drawback of the probes, thought Grimes. With their inertial drive-units running they were such noisy little brutes. He could imagine the bewilderment of the bargemen when they heard the strange clattering in the sky, louder than the steady thumping of their own engines, when they looked up to see the silvery flying torpedo with its spiky efflorescence of antennae.

The crew member who had looked up withdrew his head suddenly, but not before those in *Discovery*'s control room had learned that he was most definitely nonhuman. The neck was too long, too thin. The eyes were huge and round. There was no nose, although there was a single nostril slit. The mouth was a pouting, fleshy-lipped circle. The skin was a dark olive-green. The huge ears were even more prominent than Grimes's own.

The water under the stern of the barge—which, until now, had been leaving only a slight wake—boiled into white foam as the revolutions of the screw were suddenly increased. Obviously the canal vessel was putting on a burst of speed to try to escape from the thing in the sky. It could not, of course; Tangye, with a slight adjustment to the probe's remote controls, kept pace easily.

"No need to frighten them to death," said Grimes. "Make it look as though you're abandoning the chase."

But it was too late. The barge sheered in toward the bank and the blunt stem gouged deeply into the soft soil, the threshing screw keeping it firmly embedded. The wheelhouse erupted beings; seen from the back they looked more human than otherwise. They ran along the foredeck, jumped ashore from the bows, scurried, with their long arms flailing wildly, toward the shelter of a clump of trees.

"Follow them, sir?" asked Tangye.

"No. But we might as well have a close look at the barge, now. Bring the probe down low over the foredeck."

Steel or iron construction, noted Grimes as the probe moved slowly from forward to aft. *Riveted plates . . . no welding. Wooden hatch boards, as like as not, under a canvas—or something like canvas—hatch cover.*

He said, "Let's have a look in the wheelhouse, pilot. Try not to break any windows."

"Very good, sir."

It was not, strictly speaking, a wheelhouse, as steering was done by a tiller, not a wheel. There was, however, what looked like a binnacle, although it was not possible to see, from outside, what sort of compass it housed. There was a voicepipe—for communication with the engine room? Probably.

Grimes then had Tangye bring the probe to what had to be the engine room skylight, abaft the funnel. Unfortunately both flaps were down, and secured somehow from below so that it was impossible for the probe's working arms to lift them.

"Well," commented Grimes at last, "we have a fair idea of the stage their technology has reached. But it's odd, all the same. People capable of building and operating a quite sophisticated surface craft shouldn't bolt like rabbits at the mere sight of a strange machine in the sky."

"Unless," sneered Brandt, "other blundering spacemen have made landings on this world and endeared themselves to the natives."

"I don't think so, Doctor," Grimes told him. "Our intelligence service, with all its faults, is quite efficient. If any human ships had made landings on this planet we should have known. And the same would apply in the case of nonhuman spacefarers, such as the Shaara and the Hallicheki. Mphm. Could it be, do you think that they have reason to fear flying machines that do not bear their own *national* colors? Mightn't there be a war in progress, or a state of strained relations liable to blow up into a war at any moment?"

Brandt laughed nastily. "And wouldn't that be right up your alley, Commander Grimes? Gives you a chance to make a snap decision as to who are the goodies and who the baddies before taking sides. I've been warned about that unfortunate propensity of yours."

"Have you?" asked Grimes coldly. Then, to Tangye, "Carry on along the canal until you come to the nearest town or city. Then we'll see what happens."

Chapter 16

Swiftly along the canal skimmed the probe, obedient to Tangye's control. It hovered for a while over a suspension bridge—an affair of squat stone pylons and heavy chain cables—and turned its cameras on to a steam railway train that was crossing the canal. The locomotive was high-stacked, big-wheeled, belching steam, smoke, and sparks, towing a dozen tarpaulin-covered freight cars. The engine crew did not look up at the noisy machine in the sky; as was made evident by the probe's audio pickups their own machinery was making more than enough racket to drown out any extraneous mechanical sounds.

The train chuffed and rattled away serenely into the distance, and Grimes debated with himself whether or not to follow it—it had to be going somewhere—or to carry on along the canal. He ordered Tangye to lift the probe and to make an all-around scan of the horizon. At a mere two kilometers of altitude a city came into full view, on the canal, whereas the railway line, in both directions, lost itself in ranges of low hills. The choice was obvious.

He ordered the navigator to reduce altitude. From too great a height it is almost impossible to get any idea of architectural details; any major center of habitation is no more than a pattern of streets and squares and parks. It was not long before the city appeared again on the screen—a huddle of towers, great and small, on the horizon, bisected by the gleaming straight edge of the canal. It was like an assemblage of child's building bricks—upended cylinders and rectangular blocks, crowned with hemispheres or broad-based cones. The sun came out from behind the clouds and the metropolis glowed with muted color—yellows and browns and russet reds. Without this accident of mellow light striking upon and reflected from surfaces of contrasting materials the town would have seemed formidable, ugly, even—but for these moments at least it displayed an alien beauty of its own.

There was traffic on the canal again, big barges like the one of which the crew had been thrown into such a panic. There were three boats outbound from the city. These, sighting the thing in the sky, turned in a flurry of reversed screws and hard-over rudders, narrowly escaping ramming one another, scurried back to the protection of the high stone walls. The probe hovered and allowed them to make their escape unpursued.

And then, surging out from between the massive piers of a stone bridge, the watergate, came a low black shape, a white bone in its teeth, trailing a dense streamer of gray smoke. It had a minimal funnel and a heavily armored wheelhouse aft, a domed turret forward. Through two parallel slits in the dome protruded twin barrels. There was little doubt as to what they were, even though there was a strong resemblance to an old-fashioned observatory. "Those sure as hell aren't telescopes!" muttered Brabham.

The barrels lifted as the dome swiveled.

"Get her upstairs, pilot!" ordered Grimes. "Fast!"

Tangye stabbed in fumbling haste at his controls, keeping the probe's camera trained on the gunboat, which dwindled rapidly in the screen as the robot lifted. Yellow flame and dirty white smoke flashed from the two muzzles—but it was obvious that the result would not be even a near miss. Anti-aircraft guns those cannon might well be, but their gunners were not used to firing at such a swift moving target.

"All right," said Grimes. "Hold her at that, Mr. Tangye. We can always take evasive action again if we have to. I doubt if those are very rapid-fire guns."

"I—I can't," mumbled the navigator.

In the screen the picture of the city and its environs was dwindling fast.

"You *can't?*"

Tangye, at his console, was giving an impersonation of an overly enthusiastic concert pianist. The lock of long fair hair that had flopped down over his forehead aided the illusion. He cried despairingly, "She—she won't answer."

"Their gunnery must have been better than we thought," remarked Brabham, with morose satisfaction.

"Rubbish!" snapped Swinton. "I watched for the shell bursts. They were right at the edge of the screen. Nowhere near the target."

"Mr. Brabham," asked Grimes coldly, "did you satisfy yourself that the probe was in good working order? A speck of dust in the wrong place, perhaps . . . a drop of moisture . . . a fleck of corrosion."

"Of course, sir," sneered Brabham, "all the equipment supplied to *this* ship is nothing but the best. I don't think!"

"It is *your* job, Number One," Grimes told him, "to bring it up to standard."

"I'm not a miracle worker. And I'd like to point out, sir, that this probe that we are—sorry, *were*—using—"

"I'm still using it!" objected Tangye.

"After a fashion." Then, to Grimes again: "This probe, Captain, has already seen service aboard *Pathfinder, Wayfarer*, and, just before *we* got it, *Endeavor*—all of them senior ships to this, with four ring captains."

"Are you insinuating," asked Grimes, "that mere commanders get captains' leavings?" (He had thought the same himself, but did not like Brabham's using it as an excuse.)

"Sir!" It was Tangye again. "The screen's gone blank. We've lost the picture!"

"And the telemetering?"

"Still working—most of it. But she's going up like a rocket. I can't stop her. She's—Sir! She's had it! She must have blown up!"

Grimes broke the uneasy silence in the control room. "Write off one probe," he said at last. "Luckily the taxpayer has a deep pocket. Unluckily I'm a taxpayer myself. And so are all of you."

"One would never think so," sneered Brandt.

"Send down the other probe, sir?" asked Brabham sulkily.

"What is its service history?" countered Grimes.

"The same as the one Mr. Tangye just lost."

"It lost itself!" the navigator objected hotly.

Grimes ignored the exchange. He went on, "It has, I suppose, received the same loving attention aboard this ship as its mate?"

Brabham made no reply.

"Then it stays in its bay until such time as it has been subjected to a thorough—and I mean *thorough*—overhaul. Meanwhile, I think that we shall be able to run a fair preliminary survey of this planet if we put the ship into a circumpolar orbit. We might even be able to find out for sure if there are any wars actually in progress at this moment. I must confess that the existence of readily available anti-aircraft artillery rather shook me."

"What are you saying in your preliminary report to Base, Commander Grimes?" asked Brandt.

"There's not going to be one," Grimes told him.

"And why not?" demanded the scientist incredulously.

One reason why not, thought Grimes, *is that I'm not where I'm supposed to be. I'll wait until I have a* fait accompli *before I break radio silence*. He said, "We're far too close to the territorial limits of the Empire of Waverley. If the emperor's monitors pick up a signal from us and learn that there are Earth-type planets in their back yard we shall have an Imperial battle cruiser squadron getting into our hair in less time than it takes to think about it."

"But a coded message—" began Brandt.

"Codes are always being broken. And the message would have to be a long one, which means that it would be easy to get a fix on the source of transmission. There will be no leakage of information insofar as this planet is concerned until we have a cast-iron treaty, signed, sealed, and witnessed, with its ruler or rulers. And, in any case, we still have another world to investigate. Mphm."

He turned to the executive officer. "Commander Brabham, you will organize a working party and take the remaining probe down completely. You will reassemble it only when you are quite satisfied that it will work the way it should." Then it was the navigator's turn. "Mr. Tangye, please calculate the maneuvers required to put us in the circumpolar orbit. Let me know when you've finished doing your sums."

He left the control room, well aware that if the hostile eyes directed at his back were laser projectors he would be a well-cooked corpse.

Back in his own quarters he considered sending an initial message to Captain Davinas, then decided against it, even though such a code could never be broken and it would be extremely difficult for anybody to get a fix on such a short transmission. He would wait, he told himself, until he saw which way the cat was going to jump.

Chapter 17

It was an unexpected cat that jumped.

It took the form of suddenly fracturing welding when the old ship was nudged out of her equatorial orbit into the trajectory that, had all gone well, would have been developed into one taking her over north and south poles while the planet rotated beneath her. With the rupturing of her pressure hull airtight doors slammed shut, and nobody was so unfortunate as to be caught in any of the directly affected compartments. But atmosphere was lost, as were many tons of fresh water from a burst tank. Repairs could be carried out in orbit, but the air and water could be replenished only on a planetary surface.

A landing would have to be made.

A landing—and a preliminary report to Base?

A preliminary report to Base followed, all too probably, by the arrival on the scene of an Imperial warship with kind offers of assistance and a cargo of Waverley flags to be planted on every available site.

So there was no report.

Meanwhile, there was the landing place to select. Grimes wanted somewhere as far as possible from any center of population, but with a supply of fresh water ready to hand. He assumed that the seas of this world were salt and that the rivers and lakes would not be. That was the usual pattern on Earth-type planets, although bitter lakes were not unknown.

There was a large island in one of the oceans, in the northern hemisphere, well out from the coastline of its neighboring continent. By day lakes and rivers could be seen gleaming among its mountains. By night there were no lights to be seen, even along the shore, to indicate the presence of cities, towns, or villages—and *Discovery*'s main telescope could have picked up the glimmer of a solitary candle. With a little bit of luck, thought Grimes, his descent through the atmosphere would go unheard and unobserved. It should be possible to replenish air and water without interference by the natives—and, even more important, without being obliged to interfere with them.

The repairs were carried out while the ship was still in orbit; Grimes had no desire to negotiate an atmosphere in a ship the aerodynamic qualities of which had been impaired. This essential patching up meant that there was no labor to spare to work on the remaining probe—but in these circumstances a landing would have to be made without too much delay. The closed ecology of the ship had been thrown badly out of kilter by the loss of water and atmosphere, and would deteriorate dangerously if time were spent on preliminary surveys.

The landing was timed so that touchdown would be made shortly after sunrise. This meant that there would be a full day in which to work before nightfall—and as it was summer in the northern hemisphere the hours of daylight would be long. Also, a low sun casts long shadows, showing up every slightest irregularity in the ground. A spaceship, descending vertically and with tripedal landing gear, can be set down on quite uneven surfaces; nonetheless the vision of a disastrous topple recurs in the nightmares of every survey ship captain.

During her slow, controlled fall *Discovery* was bathed in bright sunlight while, until the very last few minutes, the terrain directly below her was still in darkness. To the east of the terminator, where there was full daylight, the sea was a glowing blue and, dark against the oceanic horizon, in silhouette against the bright, clear sky, lifted the mountains of the distant mainland.

Night fled to the west and the rugged landscape beneath the ship took on form and color. Yes, there was the lake, an amoeboid splotch of liquid silver almost in the center of the periscope screen, its mirrorlike surface broken by a spattering of black islets. The northern shore was cliffy, and inland from the escarpments the forested hillside was broken by deep gullies. To the south, however, there was a wide, golden beach fronting a grassy plain, beautifully level, although there were outcrops of what seemed to be large boulders. There was an area, however, that seemed to be reasonably clear of the huge stones with their betraying shadows and, applying lateral thrust, Grimes maneuvered his ship until she was directly above it.

"Why not land on the beach, sir?" asked Brabham.

"Sand can be treacherous," Grimes told him.

"But it will be a long way to lug the hoses," complained the first lieutenant.

Isn't that just too bad, thought Grimes.

He concentrated on his piloting. He might have let the navigator handle a landing at a proper spaceport, with marker beacons and the certainty of a smooth, level surface to sit down on, but Tangye's reaction times were far too slow to cope with emergencies that might suddenly arise in these circumstances. Tangye was sulking, of course, as was Brabham, and as the bos'n would be when he and his men had to drag the hoses all the way to the lake.

There was little wind at this time of the day, and no lateral drift. Grimes found it easy to keep the ship dropping toward the spot that he had selected as his target. He could make out details in the periscope screen now, could see the long grass (it *looked* like grass) flattening, falling into patterns like iron filings in a magnetic field as the downward thrust of the inertial drive was exerted against blades and stems. There were tiny blue flowers, revealed as the longer growth was pushed down and away. There was something like an armored lizard that scuttled frantically across the screen as it ran to escape from the great, inexorably descending mass of the ship. Grimes hoped the creature made it to safety.

The numerals of the radar altimeter, set to measure distance from the pads of the landing gear to the ground, were flickering down the single digits. Seven . . . six . . . five . . . four . . . three . . . only three meters to go. But it would still be a long way down, as far as those in the control room were concerned, if the ship should topple. Two . . . one . . . a meter to go, and a delicate balance of forces achieved, with the rate of descent measured in fractions of a millimeter a second.

"I wish the old bastard'd get a move on," whispered somebody. Grimes could not identify the voice. Not that it mattered; everybody was entitled to his own opinions. Until he had coped with a landing himself he had often been critical of various captains' shiphandling.

Zero!

He left the drive running until he felt secure, then cut it. *Discovery* shuddered, complained, and the great shock absorbers sighed loudly. She settled, steadied. The clinometer indicated that she had come to rest a mere half degree from the vertical. What was under her must be solid enough. Grimes relaxed in his chair, filled and lit his pipe.

He said, "All right, Number One. Make it 'finished with engines,' but warn the chief that we might want to get upstairs in a hurry. After all, this *is* a strange and possibly hostile planet. In any case, he'll be

too busy with his pumps to be able to spare the time to take his
precious innies apart."

"I hope," muttered Brabham.

"Then make sure he knows that he's not to. Mphm. Meanwhile, I
shall require a full control room watch at all times, with main and
secondary armament ready for instant use. You can man the fire control
console until relieved, Major Swinton."

"Open fire on anything suspicious, sir?" asked the Marine, cheerfully and hopefully.

"*No,*" Grimes told him. "You will not open fire unless you get
direct orders from myself."

"But, sir, we must make the natives respect us."

"What natives? I sincerely hope there aren't any on this island. In
any case, there are other and better ways of gaining respect than killing
people. Don't forget that *we* are the aliens, that *we* have come dropping
down on this planet without so much as a by-your-leave. And Dr.
Brandt—I hope—is the expert on establishing friendly relations with
indigenes."

"I should hope so, Commander Grimes!" huffed Brandt.

"And if you go shooting at anything and everybody, Major Swinton," went on Grimes, "you'll be making the good doctor's job all the
harder." He grinned. "But I don't think I shall be needing the services
of either of you."

"Then," said Swinton sourly, "I may as well cancel my orders to
Sergeant Washington to provide an escort for the hose parties. Sir."

"You will do nothing of the kind, Major. There may be dangerous
wild animals on this planet. An uninhabited island like this is the very
sort of place to find them."

"Then I and my men have permission to shoot *animals*, sir?"

"Yes!" snapped Grimes, but he was beginning to relent. After all,
the major was only doing the job for which he had been trained. He
turned to Brandt. "I suppose you'd like some specimens, Doctor? Ge-
ological, botanical, and so on?"

"I certainly would, Commander Grimes."

"Then you have my permission to call for volunteers from such
personnel as aren't already employed. And you, Major, can tell the
sergeant to lay on escorts for them as well as for the working parties."

"I can't spread the few men I have that thinly, sir."

"Mphm. Then you and your volunteers, Dr. Brandt, are to stay
close to the hose crews at all times. You are not to stray out of sight
of the ship. Oh, Number One—"

"Sir?" acknowledged Brabham.

"Pass the word to everybody going ashore that they are to return *at once* if the alarm siren is sounded."

"Very good, sir. All right to carry on down to get things organized?"

"Yes. Carry on."

Grimes felt a twinge of envy. He would have liked to have gone ashore himself, to stretch his legs, to feel grass under his feet and sunlight on his skin, to breathe air that had not been cycled and recycled far too many times. But in these circumstances his place was here, in the control room, the nerve center of his ship.

He got up from his chair and tried to pace up and down, like an old-time surface ship captain walking his bridge. But control rooms are not designed for taking strolls in. Swinton and the officer of the watch regarded him with poorly concealed amusement. He abandoned his attempt at perambulation, made his way through the clutter of chairs and consoles to the viewports overlooking the lake.

The working parties, under the bos'n, were running the ends of long hoses out to the water. Brabham slouched along beside them, his hands in his pockets, moodily kicking at tufts of grass. A young steward, one of Brandt's volunteers, was tap-tap-tapping at an outcrop of chalky rock with a hammer. A stewardess was gathering flowers. Among them, around them, in full battle armor, men walking like robots, were Swinton's Marines.

Already there was a small party on the beach—young Tangye, three of the junior engineers, and Vinegar Nell. And what were *they* doing? Grimes asked himself. He lifted the binoculars that he had brought with him to his eyes. The men and the women were undressing. Oh, well, he thought, there was nothing wrong with that; a *real* sunbath after the weeks of unsatisfactory, psychologically speaking, exposure to the rays of the ship's UV lamps. But surely Brabham should have found jobs for these people.

The idlers were naked now, were sprawling on the fine sand. Grimes envied them. Then Vinegar Nell got up and walked slowly and gracefully into the water. She was followed by Tangye. The junior engineers got to their feet, obviously about to follow the paymaster and the navigator.

Grimes growled angrily, ran to the transceiver handling ship-to-shore communication. "Commander Brabham!" he barked.

He saw Brabham raising his wrist radio to his mouth, taking far too long about it, heard, at last, "Brabham here."

"Get those bloody fools out of the water. At once!"

Vinegar Nell was well away from the beach now, swimming strongly. Tangye was splashing after her. The engineers were already waist-deep in the shallows.

"Major Swinton," ordered Grimes, "tell Sergeant Washington to get his men down to the water's edge, and to keep their eyes skinned for any dangerous life-forms." Swinton spoke rapidly into the microphone of his own transceiver, which was hanging about his neck. "Commander Brabham, get a move on, will you?" Grimes went on, into his own microphone.

"Oh, all right, all right." That irritable mutter was not meant to be heard, but it was.

Brabham was down to the beach at last, had his hands to his mouth and was bawling out over the water. The engineers, who had not yet started to swim, turned, waded slowly and reluctantly back to the sand. But Vinegar Nell and Tangye either would not or could not hear the first lieutenant's shouts.

"May I, sir?" asked Swinton. There was a nasty little grin under his moustache.

"May you what, Major?"

"Order my men to drag them out."

No, Grimes was about to say, *no*—but he saw an ominous swirl developing a little way out from the swimmers. "Yes!" he said.

Four Marines plunged into the lake. *They* were safe enough. Full battle gear has been described, variously, as armored tanks on legs, as battle cruisers on legs and, even, as submarines on legs. They streaked out toward Vinegar Nell and Tangye, boiling wakes astern of them as they actuated their suit propulsion units. Two of them converged on the paymaster, two on the navigator. There was a flurry of frail naked limbs among the ponderous metal-clad ones. Ignominiously the swimmers were dragged to the shore, carried out onto the dry land. It looked like a scene from somebody's mythology, thought Grimes, watching through his powerful glasses—the naked man and the naked woman in the clutches of horrendous scaly monsters.

"Have them brought up here," he said to the major.

He assumed that they would be allowed to dress, but he did not give any orders to that effect, thinking that such would be unnecessary. He should have known better. Vinegar Nell, in a flaming temper, was splendid in her nudity. Tangye, with his unsightly little potbelly, was not. Tangye was thoroughly cowed. Vinegar Nell was not.

"I demand an explanation, Captain!" she flared. "*And* an apology. "Was it you who ordered these"—she gestured with a slim, freckled arm toward the armored Marines—"enlisted men to attack me?"

"To save you," said Grimes coldly, "from the consequences of your own stupidity." He grinned without humor. "Your job is to provide meals for the personnel of this vessel, not for whatever carnivores are lurking in the lake."

"Ha!" she snorted. "Ha!" She brushed past Grimes to stand at the viewport. "What carnivores?"

The surface of the water was placid again. But there had been something there.

"Sir!" called the officer of the watch suddenly, "I have a target on the radar. Bearing 047. Range thirty kilometers. Bearing steady, range closing."

"Sound the recall," ordered Grimes. He went to the intercom. "Captain here. Mr. Flannery to the control room. At once."

Chapter 18

Flannery came into the control room, trailing a cloud of whiskey fumes, as Vinegar Nell and Tangye were hastily leaving. He guffawed, "An' what's goin' on, Captain? An orgy, no less!"

"Out of my way, you drunken bum!" snarled the paymaster, pushing past him.

Grimes ignored this. Vinegar Nell and Tangye would keep until later, as could the junior engineers who had followed their bad example. Looking out through the ports he saw that the last members of the shore parties were almost at the foot of the ramp, with Sergeant Washington and his Marines chivying them like sheepdogs. But the end of one hose had been placed in the lake; there was no reason why the pump should not be started. He told the officer of the watch to pass the order down to the engine room.

"Ye wished for me, Captain?" the telepath was asking.

"Yes, Mr. Flannery. Something, some kind of flying machine, is approaching."

"Bearing 047. Range twenty. Closing," reported the OOW

"It must be an aircraft," went on Grimes. "The mountains cut off our line of sight to the sea. Could you get inside the minds of the crew? Are their intentions hostile?"

"I'll do me best, Captain. But as I've told ye an' told ye—these people must be the lousiest telepathic transmitters in the entire universe!"

"All hands on board, sir," reported Brabham, coming into the control room. "Shall we reel in the hoses?"

"No. I've already told the engineers to start pumping. If I want to get upstairs in a hurry I shall be using the rockets and I'll want plenty of reaction mass. But you can retract the ramp and close the after airlock door." Tangye—clothed, sheepish—made a reappearance. "Pilot, put the engines—inertial drive *and* reaction drive—on standby. Warn the chief that I may be wanting them at any second."

"Range fifteen. Closing."

Grimes raised his glasses to his eyes and looked along the 047 bearing. Yes, there it was in the sky, a black spot against a backdrop of towering, snowy cumulus. An aircraft, all right—but what sort of aircraft? Friendly or hostile? And how armed?

"All possible weaponry trained on target, sir," reported Swinton.

"Thank you, Major. What do you have to report, Mr. Flannery?"

"I'm tryin', Captain, indeed I'm tryin'. T'is like lookin' for truth at the bottom of a well full o' mud. The odd thought comes bubblin' up through the ooze—an' then it bursts, like a bubble, when I try to get ahold of it. But—but I'm gettin' somethin'. They're a bit scared—an' why shouldn't they be? They're a bit scared, but they're determined. They mayn't look much like us—but they're *men*."

"Range ten. Closing."

"Ship buttoned up, apart from the hoses," reported Brabham.

"All engines on standby," said Tangye. "Enough reaction mass in the tanks for limited use."

"How limited?" demanded Grimes testily.

"He didn't say, sir. But the pump is still sucking in water."

"They're comin' on," muttered Flannery, "although they're not likin' the idea of it at all, at all. But—but they—they trust? Yes. They trust us, somehow, not to swat 'em down out o' the sky like flies."

"Ha!" barked Swinton, hunched eagerly over his fire control console.

"Watch it, Major!" warned Grimes sharply.

"Range five. Closing."

Grimes studied the thing in the visual pickup screen, which gave far greater magnification than his binoculars. It looked like a big balloon, with a car hanging from the spherical gas bag. But a balloon would never be capable of that sort of speed. Then the thing turned to make a circuit of the valley, presenting its broadside to the human observers. The shape of it made sense—a long, fabric-covered torpedo with a control cabin forward, a quartet of engine pods aft. The outlines of frames and longerons were visible through the covering. *A rigid airship*, thought Grimes. *A dirigible*.

"They're havin' a good look at us," said Flannery unnecessarily. "They know that we're from . . . outside."

The airship flew in a circle with *Discovery* at its center, maintaining its distance but well within the range of the spaceship's weaponry. Perhaps its crew, knowing only the capabilities of their own artillery, thought they were out of range.

"Another target," reported the officer at the radar. "Bearing 047. Range thirty-five. Closing."

"Holdin' the first one's hand, like," volunteered Flannery.

Swinton, tracking the dirigible within visual sight, complained, "The bloody thing's making me dizzy."

"It's stopped," said Brabham. "No. It's turning. Toward us."

Toward, or away? wondered Grimes. Yes, toward it was.

"They've made their minds up," whispered Flannery. "They're thinkin'—may the Saints preserve 'em!—that there's no harm in us."

The airship drove in steadily. On its new course it would pass directly over *Discovery*. It approached with a stately deliberation. Then, suddenly, from the gondola, a half dozen relatively tiny objects fell in succession.

Swinton cried out—in exultation, not fear. And Flannery screamed, "No! No!" Grimes, belatedly recognizing the falling things for what they were, shouted, "Check! Check! Check!" But the major ignored the order to hold his fire. The slashing, stabbing beam of his laser was a ghostly, almost invisible sword. Each of the falling bodies exploded smokily, even as the parachutes started to blossom above them, and as they did so there was the deafening rattle of *Discovery*'s forty millimeter battery and a torrent of bright tracer. The airship disintegrated, her twisted, black skeleton in brief silhouette against the fireball of blazing hydrogen. The blast rocked the spaceship on her landing gear and a strip of burning fabric drifted down across her stem, blotting out the control room viewports with writhing blue and yellow flames.

"You bloody pongo murderer!" screamed Flannery, beating at the major with his fists.

"Call this lunatic off me," shouted Swinton, "before I have to kill him!"

Grimes grabbed the telepath by the shoulder, yanked him away from the Marine. He said, trying to keep his voice under some sort of control, "You bloody murderer, Swinton. You'll face another court-martial when we get back to Base!"

"I saved the ship!" Swinton was on his feet now. "I saved your precious ship for you. I call upon you all as witnesses. That was a stick of bombs."

"Bombs don't explode the way those bodies did," said Grimes coldly. "But living flesh does, when a laser beam at wide aperture hits it. The parachutes were just starting to open when you killed the poor bastards wearing them."

"Parachutists, then," admitted the major. "Paratroopers."

"Emissaries," corrected Flannery. "Comin' in peace, wantin' to make our acquaintance. An' didn't they just, you murtherin' swine?"

"Target number two," said the officer at the radar in a shaky voice, "bearing 047. Range twenty, opening. Twenty-one, opening ... twenty-two ... twenty-three."

"They know now what to expect from Earthmen," said Flannery bitterly.

Chapter 19

There had been an unfortunate misunderstanding, and men had died because of it, but Grimes was still responsible for the safety of his own ship, his own crew. He ordered that the replenishment of essential air and water be resumed as soon as the wreckage of the dirigible was cleared from around *Discovery*. He allowed Brandt, assisted by a squad of Marines, to pick over the charred remains of the airship and her hapless people—a filthy, gruesome task but, viewed cold-bloodedly and scientifically, a most useful one. One of the least badly damaged bodies—it did not look as though it had ever been a living, sentient being, but it exuded the sickly smell of death—was brought on board for dissection at some later date. The other corpses were interred in a common grave, marked by an almost intact four-bladed wooden airscrew. "We'll try to show these people that we're civilized," growled Grimes to the giant, black sullen Sergeant Washington, who had been ordered to take charge of the burial and who had protested that his men weren't gravediggers. "Although it's rather late in the day for that."

It was obvious that the man resented having to take orders from anybody but his own officer, even from the ship's captain, but Major Swinton had been suspended from duty and sent down to his quarters in disgrace. Brabham had taken over fire control, and managed to convey the impression that he hoped he would not be required to function as gunnery officer. Tangye had the radar watch.

Grimes stayed in the control room, taking his sandwich lunch there, although the other officers were relieved for their meal. He continually refilled and rekindled a pipe that became ever fouler and fouler. He listened patiently to Brandt when the scientist reported on the findings that he, aided by the ship's technical staff, had made. There had been very little metal in the structure of the airship, he said. The framework, control cabin, and engine pods had been made from a light but very strong wood. Stays and control cables, however, were of stranded wire, indicative of a certain degree of technological sophistication. The engines, which had survived the crash almost intact, seemed to be similar to Terran diesels. Unfortunately no fuel remained, but analysis of the deposits in the cylinders would provide clues as to the nature of what had been burned in them.

The pieces of the jigsaw puzzle were beginning to fall into place—and Grimes regretted that he would not be able to complete the picture. After Swinton's trigger-happy effort any and all visitors to this world would be received with hostility. It was a pity, as this would have been an interesting planet for detailed study, a world upon which the industrial revolution had taken place or was, at the very least, well under way. And there were political and sociological aspects as well as the technological ones which Grimes would have liked to have investigated. That obvious state of war—or, at least, a warmish cold war—between nations. Anti-aircraft artillery and a willingness to use it—as witness the reception of *Discovery*'s probe outside that city. But at least one of the powers, whoever it was that had owned the ill-fated airship, was less apt to shoot first and ask questions afterward. Or, he told himself glumly, they had been less apt to shoot first and ask questions afterward. Now they had learned their lesson. *That bloody, bloody Swinton!*

"Of course," said Brandt, with whom Grimes had been talking things over, "the major ruined everything."

"He's ruined himself as well, this time!" snapped Grimes. "I told the man, before witnesses, not to open fire unless ordered by myself to do so." He laughed grimly. "I'm afraid you won't get the chance to give away your picture books and educational toys on this planet, Doctor. Thanks to the Mad Major we got off on the wrong foot."

He pushed himself up from his chair, made a circuit of the viewports. Shadow was creeping over the valley from the west, but the rugged country to the east of the tarn was still brightly illuminated by the slowly setting sun—the pearly gray and glowing ocher of the cliffs, the static explosions of vividly green foliage, spangled with the scarlet and purple of huge gaudy blossoms.

Where every prospect pleases, he thought, *but only Man is vile. Man, with a large, black, capital "M."*

"Target," called Tangye suddenly. "Aerial. Bearing 050. Range thirty-five."

"General standby," ordered Grimes. Then, more to himself than to anybody else, "I'll not make it 'action stations' yet. If I do, the work'll never get finished. I doubt if that gas bag'll be keen to close us." He turned to Brabham. "If it does, Number One, you can pump a few rounds of HETF across its bows, as a deterrent. You will not, repeat not, shoot to hit."

Brabham gave him a sour look of acknowledgment, as though to say, *You don't need to tell me my job!*

Grimes looked down at the hoses, still out, still writhing rhythmically as the pumps drew in water from the lake. He thought, *I'll let the old bitch drink her fill.* He watched the sullen Marines, ashbedaubed, still at their grisly work, their morbid scavenging. He rather regretted that he had not put Major Swinton in personal charge of the operation.

"Bearing 050. Range thirty. Closing," intoned Tangye.

"The poor brave, stupid bastards!" whispered Grimes. That flimsy ship, flammable as all hell, against *Discovery*'s weaponry. He went to the intercom, called for Flannery.

"An' what would ye be wantin', Captain?" asked the telepath when he reported to the control room.

"Don't waste my time!" snapped Grimes testily. "You know damn well what I'm wanting!"

"Then I'll be tellin' ye, Captain. I'm receivin' 'em—loud, but not all that clear. Just raw emotions, like. Frightenin', it is. Hate. Revenge. Anybody'd think ye were the black Cromwell himself, payin' another visit to the Emerald Isle."

"But what can they hope to do against us?" demanded Grimes.

"I can't tell ye. But they are hopin' to do something that'll not be improvin' the state of our health."

"Range twenty-five. Closing."

Grimes called the engine room. "Captain here, Chief. How's that water coming in?"

"Only number six tank to top up now—an' it's almost full."

"Then stop the pumps. Reel in the hoses." He put down the telephone. "Commander Brabham—sound the recall."

The wailing of the siren was deafening, but above it Tangye's voice was still audible. "Range twenty. Closing."

"We can reach them easily with a missile, sir," suggested Brabham.

"Then don't!" snarled Grimes.

The hoses were coming in, crawling over the grass like huge

worms. The Marines were mounting the ramp, herded by Sergeant Washington.

"Liftoff stations," ordered Grimes quietly. He knew that he could be up and clear, especially with the reaction drive assisting the inertial drive, long before the airship, even if she attempted kamikaze tactics, could come anywhere near him. And if the dirigible were armed with missiles—which could hardly be anything more advanced than solid fuel rockets—*Discovery*'s anti-missile laser would make short work of them.

"Range fifteen. Closing."

The control room was fully manned now, the officers waiting for their captain's orders. But the hoses had stopped coming in; some mechanical hitch must have developed. But there was yet, thought Grimes, no urgency. He could well afford to wait a few more minutes. He had no wish to jettison equipment that could not be replaced until return to a Base.

"Range ten. Holding, holding, holding." There was relief in Tangye's voice.

The airship was well within sight now. It just hung there in the sky, from this angle looking like a harmless silver ball, a balloon, glittering with reflected light.

"And what do you pick up now, Mr. Flannery?" asked Grimes.

"Nothin' new at all, Captain. They're still hatin' us, still wantin' their revenge."

"They'll not be getting it at that range!" remarked Grimes cheerfully. He was certain that the natives' airborne weaponry would be unable to touch him. And he would soon be getting off this world, where things had gone so disastrously wrong. The sooner he was back in Deep Space the better. He said, "Once the hoses are in, I'll lift ship."

He went to the big binoculars on their universal mount, and the officer who had been using them made way for him. The instrument was already trained on the dirigible. He knew there would be nothing fresh to see—he was just passing the time—but then his attention was caught by a bright, intermittent flickering. A weapon? Hardly. It did not look like muzzle flashes, and surely these people did not yet have laser. The reflection of the sunlight from a control cabin window? Probably. He realized that he was trying to read the long and short flashes as though they were Morse, and laughed at himself for making the futile attempt.

"Hoses in, sir."

"Good." Grimes started to walk back to his control chair—and stopped in mid-stride as a violent explosion from somewhere outside shook the ship. "In the lake!" somebody was shouting. "The lake!" Over the suddenly disturbed water a column of spray, intermingled with dirty yellow smoke, was slowly subsiding. And something big and black and glistening had surfaced, was threshing in its death throes. But nobody could spare the time to look at it to determine what manner of beast it was. There was a second burst, a flame-centered eruption of sand and water on the beach itself, closer to the ship than the first one had been.

Suddenly that flickering light from the dirigible made sense to Grimes. It was either a heliograph or a daylight signaling lamp, and the function of the airship was not to attack but to spot for a surface vessel with heavy long-range guns, hidden from *Discovery*'s view, just as *Discovery* was hidden from hers. And what was she doing? he wondered. Laddering, or bracketing? The question was an academic one.

A third projectile screamed in—this one much too close for comfort. Fragments of stone, earth, and metal rattled against the spaceship's hull and she shuddered and complained, rocking in her tripedal landing gear. There was no time for normal liftoff procedure—the ritual countdown, the warning to all hands over the intercom to secure for space. There was no time, even, for Grimes to adjust himself properly in his chair. The inertial drive was ready, as was the auxiliary reaction drive. He slammed the controls of each straight from Standby to Maximum Lift, hoping desperately that at this time, of all times, the temperamental engines would not decide to play up. The violent acceleration pushed him deep into the padding of his seat; others, not so lucky, were thrown to the deck. *Discovery* did not have time to complain about the rough handling. (Normally she was the sort of ship that creaks and groans piteously at the least provocation.) She went up like a shot from a gun—and a real shot, from a real gun, blew a smoking crater into the ground upon which she, only a split second before, had been resting.

Upward she roared on her column of incandescent steam, with the overworked inertial drive deafeningly cacophonous. Already the island was showing as a map in the periscope screen. Off the northern coast, a gray slug on the blue water, stood the warship. There was a scintillation of yellow flashes as her guns, hastily elevated, loosed off a wild, futile salvo, and another, and another. The shell bursts were all well below the rapidly climbing *Discovery*.

Laboriously Grimes turned his head, forcing it around against the crushing weight of acceleration, looked through the viewports. The airship was closer now, driving in at its maximum speed. But it did not matter. *Discovery* would be well above the dirigible by the time the courses intersected, at such an altitude that the down-licking exhaust would be dissipated, would not ignite the hydrogen in the gas cells. He bore the aviators no grudge, felt only admiration for them.

Admiration, and . . . helpless pity.

He stared, horror-stricken, into the periscope screen as the airship, now almost directly beneath *Discovery*, was caught in the turbulence of the spaceship's wake. Giant, invisible hands caught the fragile craft, wrenched her, twisted her, wrung her apart. But there was buoyancy still in the sundered bow and stern sections, there was hope yet for her crew.

There was hope—until chance sparks, friction engendered, ignited the slowly escaping hydrogen. She blossomed then into a dreadful flower of blue and yellow flame from the center of which there was a spillage of wreckage, animate and inanimate.

Grimes cut the reaction drive. He did not wish to blow away all the water that had been purchased at too great a cost. He continued his passage up through the atmosphere on inertial drive only. It was time that he started to think about the casualties among his own people—the sprains, contusions, and abrasions, if nothing worse. He told Brabham to get hold of Dr. Rath and to find out how things were. Luckily nobody in the control room was badly hurt; everybody there had seen what was happening, had been given a chance to prepare for what was going to happen.

Grimes pushed the ship up and out, looking with regret at the dwindling world displayed in the screen. There was so much that could have been learned about it and its people, so much that should have been learned.

But, as far as he was concerned, it was no more than a big black mark on his service record.

Chapter 20

So he was back in Deep Space again and the planet, the native name of which he had never learned, was no more than a tiny shapeless blob of luminescence, barely discernible to one side of the greater (but fast diminishing) blob that was its primary, Star 1717 in the Ballchin Catalog. He was back in Deep Space, and trajectory had been set for 1716, and *Discovery* had settled down, more or less, to her normal Deep Space routine.

More or less.

Officers and ratings were doing their jobs as usual and—also as usual—in a manner that wasn't quite grossly inefficient. The ship was even less happy than she ever had been. Cases of minor insubordination were all too common, and all too often the insubordination had been provoked.

Perhaps, hoped Grimes, things would be better after planetfall had been made on the most likely world of Star 1716. Perhaps that world would prove to be the home of a Lost Colony, with genuinely human inhabitants. Perhaps it would be possible to make an unopposed landing and to establish amicable relations with the people at once, in which case everybody (including, eventually, the Lords Commissioners of the Admiralty) would be happy.

Meanwhile, he did not forget his promise to Captain Davinas. He made out the message, using the simple code that he and the tramp master had agreed upon. *To: Davinas, d/s/s Sundowner. Happy Birthday. Peter.* There would be little chance of such a short transmission being picked up by the Waverley monitors. It was transmitted on a tight beam, not broadcast, directed at the Carlotti relay station on Elsinore. There it would be picked up and immediately and automatically retransmitted, broadcast, at regular intervals, until it was acknowledged by *Sundowner*. Davinas would know from whom it came and what it meant. The Elsinore station would know the exact direction from which it had been beamed—but the straight line from *Discovery* to Elsinore was a very long one, stretching over many light-years. In the unlikely event of the broadcast's being received by any station within the Empire of Waverley it would be utterly meaningless.

The message on its way, he started to write his report on the happenings on and around the unlucky planet of 1717. It would be a long time before this report was handed in, he knew, but he wanted to get it on paper while the events were still fresh in his memory. It would not be, he was well aware, the only report. Brandt would be putting one in, probably arguing during the course of it that expeditions such as this should be under the command of scientists, not mere spacemen. The disgraced Swinton would be writing his, addressed to the General Officer Commanding Federation Space Marines, claiming, most certainly, that by his prompt action he had saved the ship. And officers, petty officers, and ratings would be deciding among themselves what stories they would tell at the inevitable Court of Inquiry when *Discovery* returned to Lindisfarne Base.

Grimes was still working on his first, rough draft when his senior officers—with the exception of the Mad Major—came to see him.

"Yes?" he demanded, swiveling his chair away from the paper-strewn desk.

"We'd like a word with you, sir," said Brabham. The first lieutenant looked as morose as ever, but Grimes noted that the man's heavy face bore a stubbornly determined expression.

"Take the weight off your feet," Grimes ordered, with forced affability. "Smoke, if you wish." He set the example by filling and lighting his pipe.

Brabham sat stiffly at one end of the settee. Vinegar Nell, her looks matching her nickname, took her place beside him. Dr. Rath, who could have been going to or coming from a funeral on a cold, wet day, sat beside her. MacMorris, oafishly sullen, lowered his bulk into a chair. The four of them stared at him in hostile silence.

"What is it you want?" snapped Grimes at last.

"I see you're writing a report, sir," said Brabham, breaking the ominous quiet.

"I am writing. And it is a report, if you must know."

"I suppose you're putting the rope around Major Swinton's neck," sneered Vinegar Nell.

"If there's any rope around his neck," growled Grimes, "he put it there himself."

"Aren't you being . . . unfair, Captain?" asked Brabham.

"Unfair? Everybody knows the man's no more than a uniformed murderer."

"Do they?" demanded MacMorris. "He was cleared by that court-martial."

And a gross miscarriage of justice that *was*, thought Grimes. He said, "I'm not concerned with what Major Swinton did in the past. What I'm concerned about is what he did under my command, on the world we've just left."

"And what did he do?" persisted Brabham.

"Opened fire against my orders. Murdered the entire crew of an airship bound on a peaceful mission."

"He did what he thought best, Commander Grimes. He acted in the best interests of the ship, of us all. He deserves better than to be put under arrest, with a court-martial awaiting him on Lindisfarne."

"Does he, Lieutenant Commander Brabham?"

"Yes. Damn it all, sir, all of us in this rustbucket are in the same boat. We should stick together."

"Cover up for each other?" asked Grimes quietly. "Lie for each other, if necessary? Present a united front against the common enemy, the Lords Commissioners of the Admiralty?"

"I wouldn't have put it quite in those words, Captain, but you're getting the idea."

"Am I?" exploded Grimes. "Am I? This isn't a matter of bending Survey Service regulations, Brabham! This is a matter of crime and punishment. I may be an easygoing sort of bastard in many ways, too many ways—but I do like to see real criminals, such as Swinton, get what's coming to them!"

"And is Major Swinton the only *real* criminal in this ship?" asked Vinegar Nell coldly.

"Yes, Miss Russell—unless some of you are guilty of crimes I haven't found out about yet."

"What about yourself, Commander Grimes?"

"What about myself?"

"I understand that two airships were destroyed. One by the major, when he opened fire perhaps—perhaps!—a little prematurely. The second by . . . yourself. Didn't you maneuver this vessel so that the backblast of your rockets blew the airship out of the sky?"

Grimes glared at her. "You were not a witness of the occurrence, the accident, Miss Russell."

"I know what I've been told," she snapped. "I see no reason to disbelieve it."

"It was an accident. The airship was well beneath us when it crossed our trajectory. It was not backblast that destroyed it, but turbulence." He turned to Brabham. "You saw it happen."

"I saw the airship go down in flames," said Brabham. He added, speaking very reasonably, "You have to admit, sir, that you're as guilty—or as innocent—as the major. You acted as you thought best. If you'd made a normal liftoff, using inertial drive only, there wouldn't have been any backblast. *Or* turbulence. But you decided to get upstairs in a hurry."

"If I hadn't got upstairs in a hurry," stated Grimes, "I'd never have got upstairs at all. None of us would. The next round—or salvo— would have been right on."

"We are not all gunnery experts, Captain," said Dr. Rath. "Whether or not we should have been hit is a matter for conjecture. But the fact remains that the airship was destroyed by your action."

"Too right it was!" agreed MacMorris. "An' the way you flogged my engines it's a miracle this ship wasn't destroyed as well."

"Gah!" expostulated Grimes. Reasonable complaints he was always prepared to listen to, but this was too much. He would regret the destruction of the second dirigible to his dying day, but a captain's responsibility is always to his own vessel, not to any other. Nonetheless he was not, like Swinton, a murderer.

Or was he?

"You acted as you thought best," murmured Brabham. "So did the major."

"Major Swinton deliberately disobeyed orders," stated Grimes.

"I seem to remember, Captain," went on Brabham, "that *you* were ordered to make a sweep out toward the Rim."

"If you ever achieve a command of your own," Grimes told him coldly, "you will discover that the captain of a ship is entitled—expected, in fact—to use his own discretion. It was suggested that I make my sweep out toward the Rim—but the Admiralty would take a very dim view of me if I failed to follow up useful leads taking me in another direction."

"All that has been achieved to date by this following of useful leads," said Rath, "is the probable ruin of a zealous officer's career."

"Which should have been ruined before he ever set foot aboard this ship!" flared Grimes.

"Then I take it, sir," said Brabham, "that you are not prepared to stretch a point or two in the major's favor."

"You may take it that way," agreed Grimes.

"Then, sir," went on the first lieutenant, speaking slowly and carefully, "we respectfully serve notice that we shall continue to obey your legal commands during the remainder of this cruise, but wish to make it clear that we shall complain to the proper authorities regarding your conduct and actions as soon as we are back on Lindisfarne."

"The inference being," said Grimes, "that if Swinton is for the high jump, I am too."

"You said it, Commander Grimes," put in Vinegar Nell. "The days when a captain was a little—or not so little—tin god are long dead. You're only a human being, like the rest of us, although you don't seem to think so. But you'll learn, the hard way!"

"Careful, you silly cow!" growled MacMorris.

Grimes forced himself to smile. "I am all too aware of my fallible humanity, Miss Russell. I'm human enough to sympathize with you, and to warn you of the consequences of sticking your necks out. But what puzzles me is why you're doing it for Major Swinton. The Marines have always been a pain in the neck to honest spacemen, and Swinton has all a Marine's faults and precious few of the virtues. And I know that all of you hate his guts."

"He *is* a son of a bitch," admitted the woman, "but he's *our* son of a bitch. But you, Commander Grimes, are the outsider aboard this ship. Lucky Grimes, always on the winning side, while the rest of us, Swinton included, are the born losers. Just pray to all the Odd Gods of the Galaxy that your luck doesn't run out, that's all!"

"Amen," intoned Rath, surprisingly and sardonically.

Grimes kept his temper. He said, "This is neither the time nor the place for a prayer meeting. I suggest that you all return to your duties."

"Then you won't reconsider the action you're taking against the major, Captain?" asked Brabham politely.

"No."

"Then I guess this is all we can do," said the first lieutenant, getting up to leave.

"For the time being," added Vinegar Nell.

They left, and Grimes returned to his report writing. He saw no reason why he should try to whitewash Swinton, and regarding the destruction of the second airship told the truth, no more and no less.

Chapter 21

Grimes went down to the farm deck to see Flannery.

He could have sent for the telepath, but did not like to have the man in his quarters. He was always filthy, and around him hung the odors of stale perspiration, cheap whiskey, and organic fertilizers. Possibly this latter smell came from the nutrient solutions pumped into the hydroponic tanks—at times the atmosphere in the farm deck was decidedly ripe—and possibly not.

The PCO, as always, was hunched at his littered table, with the inevitable whiskey bottle and its accompanying dirty glass to hand. He was staring, as he usually was, at the spherical tank in which was suspended the obscenely naked canine brain, which seemed to be pulsating slowly (but surely this was an optical illusion) in the murky life-support fluid. His thick lips were moving as he sang, almost inaudibly, to himself, or to his weird pet.

> *"Now all you young dukies an' duchesses,*
> *Take warnin' from what I do say;*
> *Be sure that you owns what you touchesses*
> *Or ye'll jine us in Botany Bay!"*

"Mphm!" Grimes grunted loudly.

Flannery looked up, turned slowly around in his chair.

"Oh, it's you, Captain Bligh. Sorry, me tongue slipped. Me an' Ned was back in the ould days, when the bully boys, in their pretty uniforms, was ridin' high an' roughshod. An' what can I be doin' for ye, Captain?"

"What were you getting at when you called me Captain Bligh?" demanded Grimes.

"Not what ye were thinkin'. Yer officers an' crew haven't decided to put ye in the long boat, with a few loyalists an' the ship's cat . . . yet. Not that we have a cat. But ye're not loved, that's for sure. An' that murtherin' major's gettin' sympathy he's not deservin' of. Ned has *him* taped, all right. He doesn't like him at all, at all. He can remember the really bad bastards who were officers in the ould New South Wales Corps, floggin' the poor sufferin' convicts with nary a scrap o' provocation, an' huntin' down the black fellows like animals."

"I still don't believe that dingo of yours had a racial memory," said Grimes.

"Suit yerself, Captain. Suit yerself. But he has. An' he has a soft spot for ye, believe it or not, even though he thinks o' ye as a latter-day Bligh. Even—or because. He remembers that it was Bligh who stood up for the convicts against the sodgers when he was governor o' New South Wales. After all, that was what the Rum Rebellion was all about."

"You're rather simplifying," said Grimes.

"No more than the descendants o' those New South Wales Corps officers who've been blackenin' Bligh's memory to try to make their own crummy forebears look like plaster saints by comparison." His voice faded, and then again he started to sing softly.

> *"Singin' tooral-i-ooral-i-addy,*
> *Singin' tooral-i-ooral-i-ay,*
> *Singin' tooral-i-ooral-i-addy,*
> *An' we're bound out for Botany Bay. . . ."*

"I didn't come down here for a concert," remarked Grimes caustically.

Flannery raised a pudgy, admonitory hand. "Hould yer whist, Captain. That song niver came from me. It came from outside."

"Outside?"

"Ye heard me. Quiet now. T'is from far away . . . but I could be there, wherever *there* is. They're a-sittin' around a fire an' a-singin', an' a-suppin' from their jars. T'is a right ould time they're afther havin'. They're a-sendin' . . . oh, they're transmittin', if it's the technicalities ye want, but they're like all o' ye half-wits—beggin' your pardon, Captain, but that's what *we* call ye—ye can transmit after a fashion, but ye can't receive. I'm tryin' to get through to someone, anyone, but it's like tryin' to penetrate a brick wall."

"Mphm."

"Tie me kangaroo down, sport, tie me kangaroo down. . . ."

"Must you try to sing, Mr. Flannery?"

"I was only jinin' in, like. T'is a good party, an' Ned an' me wishes we was there."

"But where is it?"

"Now ye're askin'. There should be a bonus for psionic dowsin', there should. Ye've no idea, not bein' a telepath yerself, how it takes it out of yer. But I'll try."

Grimes waited patiently. It would be useless, he knew, to try to hurry Flannery.

At last: "I've got it, Captain. That broadcast—ye can call it that—comes from a point directly ahead of us. How far? I can't be tellin' ye, but t'is not all that distant. An' I can tell ye, too, that it comes from our sort o' people, humans."

"I somehow can't imagine aliens singing 'Botany Bay,' " said Grimes. And many of the lodejammers were out of Port Woomera, in Australia."

"I've found yer Lost Colony for ye," said Flannery smugly.

Chapter 22

So Grimes ordered the splicing of the mainbrace, the issue of drink to all hands at the ship's expense. He sat in the wardroom with his officers, drinking with them, and drinking to the Lost Colony upon which they would be making a landing before too long. He did not need to be a telepath to sense the change of mood. They were behind him, with him again, these misfits and malcontents. He responded, smiling, when Brabham toasted, "To Grimes's luck!" He clinked glasses with Vinegar Nell, even with the Mad Major. He joined in heartily when everybody started singing "Botany Bay."

Botany Bay.

He rather hoped that this would be the name given by the colonists to this chance-found world circling Star 1716 in the Ballchin Catalog. It might well be; such colonies as had been founded by the crews and passengers of the gaussjammers of the New Australian Expansion tended to run to distinctively Australian names.

He left when the party began to get a little too rowdy. He did not retire at once, but sprawled in his easy chair, his mind still active. When people recovered from this letting off of steam, he thought, he would have to discuss his plan of campaign with the senior officers, the departmental heads. Then, suddenly but quietly, the outer door of his day cabin opened. He was somehow not surprised when Vinegar Nell came in. She was (as before) carrying a tray, with coffee things and a plate of sandwiches. But this time she was still in uniform.

Grimes gestured toward the supper as she set it down on the low table. "So you still think of me as Gutsy Grimes?" he asked, but he smiled as he spoke.

"Lucky Grimes," she corrected, smiling back, a little lopsidedly.

"And I hope, John, I really hope that your luck rubs off on the rest of us."

"I do, too," he told her.

She straightened up after she had put the supper things down, standing over him. Her legs were very long, and slightly apart, her skirt very short. One of her knees was exercising a gentle but definite pressure on Grimes's outstretched thigh, but with a considerable effort he managed to keep his hands to himself. Then she stooped again as she poured him his coffee. The top two buttons of her shirt were undone and he glimpsed a nipple, erect, startlingly pink against the pale tan of the skin of her breast.

He whispered huskily, "Miss Russell, would you mind securing the door?"

She replied primly, "If you insist, Commander Grimes."

She walked slowly away from the table, away from him, shrugging out of her upper garment, letting it float unheeded to the deck. He heard the sharp *click* of the lock as it engaged. She turned, stepping out of her brief skirt as she did so. The sheer black tights that were all she was wearing beneath it concealed nothing. She walked past him into the bedroom, not looking at him, a faint smile on her face, her small breasts jouncing slightly, her round buttocks smoothly working, gleaming under the translucent material. He got up, spilling his coffee and ignoring it, following her.

She must have been fast. She was already completely naked, stretched out on the bunk, waiting for him, warmly glowing on the dark blue bedspread. In the dim light her hair glinted like dusky gold against the almost black material of the coverlet, in aphrodisiac contrast to the pale, creamy tan of her upper thighs and lower abdomen. She was beautiful, as only a desirous and desirable woman, stripped of all artifice, can be.

Grimes looked down at her and she looked up at him, her eyes large and unwinking, her lips slightly parted. He undressed with deliberate slowness, savoring the moment, making it last. He even put his shirt on a hanger and neatly folded his shorts. And then he joined her on the couch, warm, naked skin to warm, naked skin, his mouth on hers. It was as though he had known her, in the Biblical sense of the word, for many, many years.

She murmured, as they shared a cigarillo, "Now you're one of us."

"Is that why . . . ?" he started, hurt.

"No," she assured him. "No. That is not why I came to you. We should have done this a long time ago. A long, long time—"

He believed her.

Chapter 23

The people of Botany Bay—this was, in fact, the name of the Lost Colony—did not, of course, run to such highly sophisticated communications equipment as the time-space-twisting Carlotti radio. Had they possessed it they would not have stayed lost for long. But it had yet to be invented in the days of the gaussjammers—as had, too, the time-space-twisting Mannschenn Drive. It had been making a voyage, as passenger, in one of the timejammers that had started Luigi Carlotti wondering why, when ships could exceed the speed of light (effectively if not actually) radio messages could not. So Botany Bay did not possess Carlotti radio. Neither was there, as on most other Man-colonized worlds, a corps of trained telepaths; Flannery spoke with some authority on that point, maintaining that somehow psionic talent had never developed on the planet. But there was, of course, Normal Space-Time radio, both audio and visual, used for intraplanetary communications and for the broadcasting of entertainment.

It did not take long for the ship's radio officers to find this out once *Discovery* had reentered the normal continuum, shortly thereafter taking up a circumpolar orbit about the planet. It was no great trouble to them to ascertain the frequencies in use and then to begin monitoring the transmissions. Grimes went down to the main radio office—its sterile cleanliness made a welcome change from Flannery's pig pen—to watch the technicians at work and to listen to the sounds issuing from the speakers. Brabham accompanied him.

There were what sounded like radio telephone conversations. At first these seemed to be in some quite familiar yet unknown language—and then, as soon as Grimes's ear became accustomed to the peculiarly flat intonation of the voices—they suddenly made sense.

The language, save for its accent, had survived almost unchanged, was still understandable Standard English. It became obvious that what was being picked up was an exchange of messages between a ship and some sort of traffic control authority.

"*Duchess of Paddington,*" Grimes heard, "to Port Ballina. My ETA is now 0700 hours. What's the weather doin' at your end? Over."

"Port Ballina to *Duchess*. Wind west at ten kiph. No cloud. Visibility excellent. The moorin' crowd'll be waitin' for yer, Skip. Over."

"Sounds like a surface ship, Captain," commented Brabham.

"Mphm?" grunted Grimes dubiously.

The voice came from the speaker again. "*Duchess of Paddington* to Port Ballina. Please have one 'A' helium bottle waitin' for me. I'd a bastard of a slow leak in one o' my for'ard cells. Over."

"Wilco, *Duchess*. Will you be wantin' the repair mob? Over."

"Thanks muchly, but no. Got it patched meself, but I lost quite a bit o' buoyancy an' I've had to use the heaters to maintain altitude an' attitude. See you. Over."

"More ruddy airships!" growled Brabham. "I hope—" His voice trailed off into silence.

"You hope what?" asked Grimes coldly.

"Well, sir, there seems to be a sort of jinx on the things as far as we're concerned."

"There'd better not be *this* time," Grimes told him.

"Sir!" called one of the radio officers. "I think I'm picking up a treevee transmission, but I just can't seem to get any sort of picture."

Grimes shuffled slowly to the receiver on which the young man was working; with the ship now in free fall it was necessary to wear magnetic-soled shoes and, after the long spell under acceleration, to move with caution. He stared into the screen. It was alive with swirling color, an intermingling of writhing, prismatic flames and subtle and everchanging shades of darkness, an eddying opalescence that seemed always about to coalesce into a picture, yet never did. The technician made more adjustments and suddenly there was music—from a synthesizer, thought Grimes—with the effect of ghost guitars, phantom violins, and distant drums. The ever-changing colors in the screen matched the complex rhythms drifting from the speaker.

"Damn it!" muttered the radio officer, still fiddling with the controls. "I still can't get a picture."

"Perhaps you aren't supposed to," murmured Grimes.

A final crash of guitars, scream of violins and rattle of drums, an explosive flare of light and color, fading into darkness . . . and then, at last, a picture. A young woman, attractive, with deeply tanned skin and almost white-blonde hair, stood with one slim hand resting on the surface of a table. She was simply clad in a long white robe, which somehow hid no smallest detail of her firm body. She said—and it was a pity that her voice, with its flat intonation, did not match her appearance—"An' that was Damon's *Firebird Symphony*, played to you by the composer himself. I hope y'all liked it. An' that's it from this station for today. We'll be on the air again at the usual time termorrer with our brecker program, commencin' at 0600 hours. Nighty-night all, an' good sleepin'."

She faded slowly from the screen and the picture of a flag replaced her—a familiar (to Grimes) ensign, horizontal and rippling in a stiff breeze, dark blue, with a design of red, white, and blue crosses superimposed upon each other in the upper canton, a five-starred, irregularly cruciform constellation in the fly. And there was music—also familiar.

"Once a jolly swagman," sang Grimes, softly but untunefully, "camped by a billabong. . . ."

"Do you *know* it, sir?" asked one of the radio officers.

Grimes looked at the young man suspiciously, then remembered that he was from New Otago, and that the New Otagoans are a notoriously insular breed. He said, "Yes. 'Waltzing Matilda,' of course. Wherever Aussies have gone they've taken her with them."

"Who was Waltzing Matilda?" persisted the officer. "Some old-time dancing girl?"

Brabham sniggered, and Grimes said, "Not exactly. But it's a bit too complicated to explain right now."

And whose ghosts, he wondered, would be haunting the billabongs (if there were billabongs) of this world upon which they would soon be landing? The phantom of some swagman, displaced in time and space, or—*Damn you, Flannery*, he thought, *stop putting ideas into my mind!*—or, even, of the mutiny-prone Bligh?

Chapter 24

"We have to let them know we're here," said Grimes.

"The probe is in in good working order, sir," said Brabham.

"Not the probe," Grimes told him. He did not want a repetition of all that had happened the last time a probe had been used. He went on, "These people are human. They have maintained a reasonably high standard of technology."

"With *airships*, sir?" asked Brabham.

"Yes. With airships. It has never ceased to amaze me that so many human cultures have not persisted with their use. Why waste power just to stay up before you even think about proceeding from Point A to Point B? But never mind the airships. They also have radio." He turned to one of the technicians. "Did you note the time when the station closed down, Lieutenant? Good. And the blonde said that she'd be resuming transmission at 0600 hours tomorrow."

"Local time, sir," pointed out Brabham. "Not ship's time."

"When she whispered her sweet good nights," said Grimes, "I managed to tear my eyes away from her face long enough to notice a clock on the wall behind her. A twenty-four-hour clock. It was registering midnight. And we already know, from our own observations, that Botany Bay has a period of rotation of just over twenty-five Standard Hours. I assume—but, of course, I could be wrong—that there are people in this ship, besides myself, capable of doing simple sums."

Brabham scowled. The radio officers sniggered.

"So," went on Grimes, "I want to make a broadcast myself on that station's frequencies when it starts up again with the"—he made a grimace of distaste—"*brecker* program. I think we have the power from our jennies to override anything they may be sending. I shall want a visual transmission as well as sound. Their people will have as much trouble with our accent as we had with theirs. I'll leave you to work out the details. I'm going to prepare a series of cards, from which I shall be speaking. Do you think you'll be able to set up your end of it in the time?"

"Of course, sir," the senior radioman assured him.

"Their spelling's probably nothing at all like ours," muttered Brabham.

"It shouldn't have changed all that much," said Grimes hopefully. "And luckily, the blonde bombshell wasn't delivering her spiel in Hebrew or Chinese. Well, I'll leave you to it, gentlemen. You know where to find me if anything fresh crops up."

He went back to his quarters and set to work with sheets of stiff white paper and a broad-tipped stylus.

They were ready for him when he returned to the radio office. He stood where he was told, with the camera trained on him, watching the monitor screen, which was still blank. Suddenly he realized that he had omitted to change into his dress uniform and put on a cap— but, he told himself, it didn't matter.

The screen came alive. Again there was the flag, bravely flying, and again there was music—but, this time, it was "Botany Bay." When it was over the picture became that of an announcer. It was not—to the disappointment of Grimes and the others—the spectacular blonde. It was a young man, comfortably clad in colorful shirt, extremely short shorts, and sandals. Like the girl he was fair haired and deeply tanned. He was far more cheerful than he had a right to be at what must be, to him, an ungodly hour of the morning.

"Mornin', all—those of yer who're up, that is. An' you lucky bastards who're still in yer scratchers can get stuffed. Anyhow, this is Station BBP, the Voice of Paddo, openin' transmission on this bright an' sunny mornin' o' December nineteenth, Thursday. I s'pose yer wantin' the news. Now what have we to make yer day for yer?" He looked down at a sheet of paper in his right hand.

Grimes signaled with his own right hand to the senior radio officer. The lights in the radio office flickered and dimmed, except for the one trained on Grimes. The picture in the monitor screen faded—as must also have done the pictures in the screens of all the receivers tuned to that station. It was replaced by the image of Grimes himself, looking (he realized) very important, holding at chest level the first of his cards. He read from it, trying to imitate the local accent, "I am the captain of the Earth Survey Ship *Discovery*." He changed cards. "My ship is at present in orbit about your planet." He changed cards again. "I am about to cease transmission. Please make your reply. Over."

The picture of the announcer came back into the screen. The young man's pallor under his tan gave his complexion a greenish tinge. At last he spoke. "Is this some bloody hoax?" And somebody not in the screen said, "I could see the bastard in the monitor plain enough. T'aint nobody *we* know—an' we know everybody who is anybody in the radio trade!" "Get on the blower to the observatory, Clarry," ordered the announcer. "Tell the lazy bludgers ter get their useless radio tele-scope on the job." Then, facing his audience—those on the planet and those in space—"Orright, Captain whatever-yer-name-is. It's over ter you again." He grinned. "At least you've saved me the trouble o' readin' the bloody news!"

Grimes reappeared in the screen, holding another card. He read, "Can you understand me? Over."

The announcer came back. "Yair—though Matilda knows where yer learned yer spellin'. An' yer sound like you've a plum in yer mouf." He mimicked Grimes's way of speaking. "And whom have I the honor of addressing, Captain, sir?" He grinned again, quite con-vincingly. "I used to act in historical plays before I was mug enough to take this job. Over."

"My name is Grimes, Commander Grimes of the Federation Sur-vey Service. I am, as I've already told you, captain of the Survey Ship *Discovery*. I was ordered to make a search for Lost Colonies. Over."

"An' you've sure found one, ain't yer? We're lorst orright. An' we thought we were goin' ter stay that way. Hold on a sec, will yer? Clarry's got the gen from the observatory."

The unseen Clarry's voice came from the speaker. "T'aint a hoax, Don. The bastards say there is somethin' up there, where somethin' shouldn't be."

"So yer for real, Commander Grimes. Ain't yer supposed ter say, 'Take me to yer leader'? Over."

"Take me to your leader," said Grimes, deadpan. "Over."

"Hold yer horses, Skip. This station'll be goin' up in flames at any tick o' the clock, the way the bleedin' phones are runnin' hot. Her Ladyship's on the way ter the studio now, s'matter o' fact. Over."

"Her Ladyship? Over."

"The mayor o' Paddo, no less. Or Paddington, as I s'pose you'd call our capital. Here she is now."

The announcer bowed, backed away from the camera at his end. He was replaced by a tall, ample woman, silvery haired and with what seemed to be the universal deep tan. She was undeniably handsome, and on her the extremely short dress with its gay floral pattern did not look incongruous—and neither, somehow, did the ornate gold chain that depended from her neck. She said—and even the accent could not entirely ruin her deep contralto—" 'Ow yer doin', Skip? Orright?" Then, turning to address the announcer, "Wot do I say now, Don? 'Over,' ain't it? Orright. Over."

"I'm honored to meet you, Your Ladyship. Over."

"Don't be so bloody formal, Skipper. I'm Mavis to me mates— an' any bastard who's come all the way from Earth's a mate o' mine. When are yer comin' down ter meet us proper? Do yer have ter land at one o' the magnetic poles same as *Lode Wallaby* did? Or do yer use rockets? If yer do, it'll have ter be some place where yer won't start a bushfire. Wherever it is, there'll be a red carpet out for yer. Even at the bloody North Pole." Then, as an afterthought, "Over."

"I have rocket drive," said Grimes, "but I won't be using it. My main drive, for sub-light speeds, is the inertial drive. No fireworks. So I can put down on any level surface firm enough to bear my weight. Over."

"You don't look all that fat ter me, Skip. But you bastards are all the same, ain't yer? No matter what yer ship is, it's *I, I, I*, all the time." She grinned whitely. "But I guess the Bradman Oval'll take the weight o' that scow o' yours. Havin' you there'll rather bugger the current test series but the landin' o' the first ship from Earth is more important than cricket. Never cared for the game meself, anyhow. Over."

"I'll make it the Bradman Oval, then, Your . . . sorry. Mavis. Once we get some less complicated radio telephone system set up your technicians can go into a huddle with mine. I'd like a radio beacon to home on, and all the rest of it." He paused, then went on. "Forgive me if I'm giving offense, but do you speak for your own city only, or for the whole planet? Over."

"I speak for me own city-state. The other mayors speak for their city-states. An' it so happens that at the moment I *am* President of the Council of Mayors. So I do speak for Botany Bay. That do yer, Skip? Over."

"That does me, Mavis. And now, shall we leave all the sordid details to our technicians? Over."

" 'Fraid we have to, Skip. I can't change a bloody fuse, meself. Be seein' yer. Over."

"Be seeing you," promised Grimes.

Chapter 25

Grimes had several more conversations with the mayor of Paddington before the landing of *Discovery*. The radio experts on the planet and in the ship had not taken long to set up a satisfactory two-way service, and when this was not being used for the exchange of technical information the spaceship's crew was continuously treated to a planetary travelogue. Botany Bay was a *good* world, of that there could be no doubt. There was neither overpopulation nor pollution. There was industry, of course, highly automated—but the main power sources were the huge solar energy screens set up in what would have otherwise been useless desert areas, and wind- and water-drive turbo-generators. There were oil wells and coal mines—but the fossil fuels merely supplied useful chemicals. The only use of radioactives was in medicine. Airships, great and small, plied the skies, driven by battery-powered motors, although there were a few jets, their gas turbines burning a hydrogen-oxygen mixture. On the wide seas the sailing vessel was the commonest form of ship—schooners mainly, with auxiliary engines and with automation replacing man-power. Efficient monorail systems crisscrossed the continents—but the roads, surprisingly, seemed to be little more than dirt tracks. There was a reason for this, the spacemen soon discovered. *Lode Wallaby* had carried among other livestock the fertilized ova of horses—and horses were used extensively for private transport, for short journeys.

Botany Bay, in the main, enjoyed an almost perfect climate, its continents being little more than large islands, the oceans exercising a tempering effect from the tropics to the poles. The climate had not been so good when the first colonists landed, destructive hurricanes being all too common. Now, of course, there was a planetwide weather watch, and fast aircraft could be dispatched at short notice to a developing storm center to drop anti-thermal bombs.

Botany Bay, throughout, could boast of almost unspoiled scenery. In all industrial establishments ugliness had been avoided. In the cities there had been a deliberate revival of architectural styles long vanished, except in isolated cases, from Earth. Paddington, for example, was a greatly enlarged, idealized version of the Terran Paddington, maintained as a historical curiosity in the heart of sprawling Sydney. There were the narrow, winding streets, tree lined, and the terrace houses, none higher than three stories, each with its balconies ornamented by metal railings cast in intricate floral designs. It was all so archaic, charmingly so. Grimes remembered a party to which he had been invited in the original Paddington. The host, when accused of living in a self-consciously ancient part of Sydney, had replied, "We Australians don't have much history—but, by any deity you care to name, we make the most of what we have got!"

This Paddington, the Botany Bay Paddington, was a city, not a mere inner suburb. It stood on the western shore of the great, natural harbor called Port Jackson. Its eastern streets ran down to the harbor beaches. To the west of it was the airport, and also the Bradman Oval. To the south and east were the port facilities for surface shipping. To the north were The Heads, the relatively narrow entrance to the harbor. And on the north coast were the high cliffs, with bays and more sandy beaches.

Grimes studied the aerial view of the city and its environs that was being transmitted to him. He could foresee no difficulties in making a landing. He would keep well to the west on his way down, so that if, in the event of a breakdown of his inertial drive, he were obliged to use the auxiliary reaction drive he would do no damage to the city.

He had wanted to adhere to the standard practice of the Survey Service and bring the ship down at dawn, but the mayor would not agree to this. "Come off it, Skip!" she remonstrated. "I don't like gettin' up at Matilda-less hours, even if you do! Wot's wrong wif ten hundred? The streets'll be aired by then, an' everybody'll be up an' dressed. We want ter *see* yer comin' down. We don't want ter be starin' up inter the gloom ter watch somethin' droppin' down outa the sky that could be no more than a solid-lookin' cloud wif a few lights hung on it!"

Grimes was obliged to agree. As a Survey Service captain he was supposed to make friends as well as to influence people. Meanwhile, as a preliminary measure, he had certain of the ship's clocks adjusted to synchronize with Paddington Local Time. Ten hundred hours Mavis had said, and he was determined that the pads of his tripedal landing gear would touch the turf of the Oval at precisely that time.

It was a fine, clear morning when *Discovery* dropped down through the atmosphere. Her inertial drive was working sweetly, but inevitably noisily, and Grimes wondered what the colonists would be thinking of the irregular beat of his engines, the loud, mechanical clangor driving down from above. Their own machines—with the exception of the few jet planes—were so silent. In the periscope screen the large island, the continent that had been named New Australia, showed in its entirety. Its outline was not dissimilar to that of the original Australia, although there was no Tasmania, and Port Jackson was on the north and not the east coast. The coastal fringe was green, but inland there were large desert areas, the sites of the solar power stations.

Grimes glanced at the control room clock, which was now keeping local time. There was time to spare; he could afford to take things easily.

"Target," announced Tangye. "Bearing 020, range fifty. Closing."

"Altitude?" asked Grimes.

"It's matching altitude with us, sir."

"It can't be one of the airships this high," said Grimes. He added nastily, "And, anyhow, we don't have Major Swinton at fire control this time."

He turned away from his console to look out of the viewports on the bearing indicated. Yes, there the thing was, a silvery speck, but expanding, closing fast.

"What if they *are* hostile, Captain?" asked Brabham. "We're a sitting duck."

"*If* they are hostile," Grimes told him, "we'll give them the privilege of firing the first shot."

"It's one of their jets," said Tangye.

"So it is," agreed Grimes. "So it is. They're doing the right thing; laying on an escort."

The aircraft closed them rapidly, circled them in a slowly descending spiral. It was, obviously, a passenger plane, with swept-back wings. Grimes could see men in the forward control cabin. They waved. He waved back, then returned his attention to handling the ship. He hoped that the jet pilot would not attempt to approach too close.

He could see Port Jackson plainly enough in the screen now, a great irregular bite out of the northern coastline. He could see the golden beaches with a cream of surf outlining them and—very small, a mere, crawling insect—one of the big schooners standing in toward The Heads. And there were two more targets announced by the radar-watching Tangye—airships this time, huge brutes with the sunlight reflected dazzlingly from their metal skins.

A familiar voice came from the speaker of the control room transceiver. "That's a noisy bitch yer've got there, Skip. Sounds like umpteen tons of old tin cans fallin' downstairs. Just as well yer didn't come in at sparrer fart."

"Do you have sparrows here?" asked Grimes interestedly.

"Nah. Not *reel* sparrers. But it's what we call one o' the native birds. Don't know how it got by before it had human bein's ter bludge on."

"Mphm. Excuse me, Mavis, but I'd like to concentrate on my pilotage now."

"That's what me late husband useter say. He was skipper o' one o' the coastal schooners. Oh, well, I can take a hint."

Grimes could see the city now—red roofs and gray, a few towers of pseudo-Gothic appearance. He could see the airport, with one big dirigible at its mooring mast like an oversized wind sock. And there, just beyond it, was the Bradman Oval, a darkly green recreation area with spectators' stands around it and, he was pleased to note, a triangle of red flashing lights, bright even in the general brightness of the morning. The radio beacon had been set up as requested by Grimes, but he preferred to use visual aids whenever possible.

The Oval expanded to fill the screen. The stands, Grimes saw, were crowded. He thought sourly, *These bastards have more faith in my innies than I do.* If the inertial drive were to break down, necessitating the use of the emergency reaction drive, there would be a shocking tragedy. But the beat of the engines still sounded healthy enough. He applied a touch of lateral thrust, brought the three beacons into the center of the screen. He looked at the clock: 0953. He was coming down just a little too fast. A slight, very slight increase of vertical thrust. The figures on the face of the radar altimeter flickered down in slightly slower succession.

That should do it, thought Grimes smugly.

Eleven . . . ten . . . nine . . .

And, on the clock, 0955.

Seven . . . six . . . five . . . four . . . three . . . two . . . one . . . 0959.

Gently, gently, thought Grimes.

Zero!

And, on the clock, the sweep second hand jumped to the same numeral.

The ship groaned and shuddered as her weight came onto the shock absorbers, and silence fell like a blow when the inertial drive was shut down. But there was another noise, a tumult that Grimes at first could not identify. Then he realized that it was cheering, noisy cheering, loud enough to be heard even inside the buttoned-up ship. And, faintly, there was the noise of a band. "Waltzing Matilda" (of course).

He looked out of the port at the waving crowds, at the blue flags, with their Union Jacks and Southern Crosses, flying from every mast around the Oval.

"So yer made it, Skip," the mayor's voice issued from the speaker. "Bang on time, too! Welcome to Botany Bay! Welcome to Paddo!"

"I'm glad to be here, Your Ladyship," replied Grimes formally.

"It's a pleasure ter have yer. But is it safe ter come near yer ship? You ain't radioactive or anythin', are yer?"

"Quite safe," said Grimes. "I'll meet you at the after airlock."

Chapter 26

Grimes, after issuing instructions, went down to his quarters to change. He had decided that this was an occasion for some show of formality, no matter how free and easy the people of this Lost Colony seemed to be. Or—he had his contrary moments—it was this very freeness and easiness that had induced in him the desire to be stiff and starchy. He got out of his comfortable shorts and open-necked shirt, replacing the latter with a stiff, snowy-white one. He knotted a black necktie about his throat, then thrust his legs into sharply creased black trousers. The bemedaled frock coat came next, then the sword belt and the quite useless ceremonial sword. Highly polished black shoes on his feet, the fore-and-aft hat with its trimmings of gold braid on his head. He inspected his reflection in the full-length mirror inside his wardrobe door, holding himself stiffly at attention. He'd do, he decided.

He took the elevator down to the after airlock. The others were waiting for him—the Mad Major, temporarily forgiven, with a half dozen of his men. The Marines, too, were in their dress finery, blue and scarlet and gleaming brass. Swinton was wearing a sword, his men carried archaic (but nonetheless lethal) rifles. Tangye, one of the few officers to possess a presentable full dress uniform, was there, as was Vinegar Nell, in the odd rig prescribed by the Survey Service for its female officers on state occasions, best described as a long-skirted, long-sleeved black evening frock, trimmed with gold braid and brass buttons and worn over a white shirt and black tie, topped with a hat like the one Grimes was wearing. But she carried it well.

The outer airlock door slowly opened, and as it did so the ramp was extruded, its end sinking to the close-cropped grass. Grimes stepped out into the warm, fresh air, the bright sunlight. He was thankful that his uniform had been tailored from the lightest possible material. As he appeared there was a great welcoming roar from the crowds in the stands. He paused, saluted smartly, then continued down the ramp. After him came Tangye and the paymaster, and after them, their boots crashing rhythmically on the metal gangway, marched the Marines.

There was a stir among the crowd on the stand immediately facing the airlock. In the broad aisle between it and its neighbor a coach appeared, a vehicle drawn by four gleaming black horses, the first of what looked like a procession of such vehicles. Grimes, standing at the foot of the ramp, the others drawn up behind him, watched with interest. Yes, that was the mayor in the first coach, and other women and men with her. From this distance he could not be sure, but it did not look as though anybody had made any attempt to dress up. The driver was in some sort of khaki uniform with a broad-brimmed hat. But what was Brabham waiting for?

Suddenly, from overhead, there came a deafening *boom*, the first round of the twenty-one-gun salute, fired from one of the forty-millimeter cannon, using special blank cartridges.

Boom!

The coachmen were having trouble controlling their horses.

Boom!

The horses of the second and third coaches had bolted, had begun to gallop around the Oval like the start of a chariot race.

Grimes lifted his wrist transceiver to his mouth. "Brabham, hold . . ."

Boom!

"Brabham, hold your fire!"

"But that's only four rounds, sir," came the tinny whisper in reply.

"Never mind. Hold your fire."

The driver of the mayor's coach had his animals under control at last. He came on steadily, then reined in about ten meters from the foot of the ramp. From one of his pockets he produced a cigarette, lit it with a flaring lighter, then sat there stolidly with the little crumpled cylinder dangling from the corner of his mouth. He stared at Grimes and his entourage with a certain hostility.

Another khaki-uniformed man was first out. He assisted the mayor to the ground. She emerged from the vehicle with a lavish display of firm, brown thigh. She was wearing a short tunic, with sandals on her feet, only the mayoral chain of office adding a touch of formality. Her blue eyes were angry, her mouth drawn down in a scowl.

Grimes saluted with drawn sword. The Marines presented arms with a slap and rattle.

She demanded, "Wodyer playin' at, you stupid drongo? You said there'd be no bleedin' fireworks."

Grimes sheathed his sword. He said stiffly, "It is customary, Your Ladyship, to accord heads of state the courtesy of a twenty-one-gun salute."

"That may be where you come from, Skip, but it certainly ain't here. You scared shit outa the horses."

"Too flamin' right," commented the coachman. "Wodyer think me wheels was skiddin' on?"

"I'm sorry," Grimes began lamely.

The mayor smiled, broadly and dazzlingly. "So'm I. But this ain't a way for me to be welcomin' long-lost relatives from the old world." Suddenly she threw her plump arms about Grimes and drew him to her resilient breast, kissed him warmly full on the mouth. He felt himself responding—and was somehow aware of the disapproving glare that Vinegar Nell was directing at the back of his head.

"That's better," murmured the mayor, pulling reluctantly away. "A *lot* better. Kiss an' make up, that's what I always say. An' now, Skip, wot about introducin' me to the lady and these other gentlemen?"

"Your Ladyship," Grimes began.

"*Mavis*, you drongo. Even if you're all dressed up like a Christmas tree, I ain't."

"Mavis, may I introduce my paymaster."

"Pay*master?* Paymistress, if I'm any good at guessin'."

"Lieutenant Russell."

Vinegar Nell saluted and contrived to convey by her expression that she didn't want to be mauled.

"Major Swinton, my Marine officer."

Swinton's salute did not save him from a motherly kiss on the cheek.

"And Lieutenant Tangye, my navigator."

Tangye's face was scarlet when he was released.

"An' what about these other blokes?" demanded Mavis.

"Er . . ." began Grimes, embarrassed.

"Private Briggs," snapped Swinton, stepping smartly into the breach. "Private Townley. Private Gale. Private Roskov. Private O'Neill. Private Mackay."

"Well?" demanded the big woman. "Well?"

Now it was Swinton's turn to feel embarrassment. The six men stood stiffly like wooden soldiers.

"Well?"

"Stack your rifles," ordered Swinton.

The men did so.

"Advance to be greeted by Her Ladyship."

The order was obeyed with some enthusiasm.

When the introductions were over the mayor said, "Natterin' to you on the radio, Skip, I never dreamed that you were such a stuffed shirt. All o' yer are stuffed shirts. Looks like Earth ain't changed since our ancestors had the sense ter get the hell out."

"And this, I suppose," said Grimes, "is one of those worlds like Liberty Hall, where you can spit on the mat and call the cat a bastard."

"You said it, Skip, you said it!" exclaimed Mavis, bursting into delighted laughter. Grimes laughed too. He had thought that expression very funny the first time that he had heard it—how many years ago?—and he was delighted to be able to use it on somebody to whom it was new and brilliantly witty.

Chapter 27

Grimes had liked Mavis since his first sight of her in the monitor screen. He liked her still more now that he had actually met her. He kept on recalling a phrase that he had once heard—*A heart as big as all outdoors*. It applied to her. She was big in all ways, although in her dress that concealed little it was obvious that her body was all firm flesh, with no hint of flabbiness.

He was entertaining her and other officials in his daycabin, with some of his own officers also present—Dr. Brandt, Brabham, and Vinegar Nell, who was kept busy refilling glasses and passing around dishes of savories. She, alone of all those present, seemed not to approve of the informality, the use of given names rather than titles and surnames. There was Jock, the man in the khaki shorts-and-shirt uniform who had assisted the mayor from the coach and who was City Constable. There was Pete, with a floral shirt over the inevitable shorts and sandals, who was president of the Air Pilots' Guild. There was Jimmy, similarly attired, who was master of the Seamen's Guild. There was Doug and Bert, mayors of Ballina and Esperance respectively, who had flown by fast jet from their cities to be present at *Discovery*'s landing.

Mavis, watching Vinegar Nell, said, "Why don't yer scarper, dearie, an' change inter somethin' more comfy? Any o' our barmaids havin' to wear wot you've got on 'd go on stroke, an' quite right, too!"

"What do your barmaids wear?" asked Grimes interestedly.

"At the beach eateries, nuffin'."

"So you have a culture similar to that of Arcadia?" asked Brandt.

"Arcadia? Where in hell's that?"

"It's a planet," explained Grimes, "with an ideal climate, where the people are all naturists."

"Naturists, Skip? Wot's that?"

"Nudists."

"You mean they run around in the nudie all the time?"

"Yes."

"No matter *wot* they're doin'?"

"Yes."

"Sounds screwy ter me—as screwy as wearin' anything when yer goin' inter the sea for a dip. Oh, well, takes all sorts ter make a universe, don't it?"

"Have I your permission to change into undress uniform, Commander Grimes?" asked Vinegar Nell coldly.

"Of course, Miss Russell." Grimes wondered what the effect would be if Vinegar Nell returned to the daycabin in the undress uniform in which he had often seen her.

"And ain't it time that you got outer yer admiral's suit?" Mavis asked Grimes.

"I think it is," he admitted.

He went into his bedroom, changed back into shirt and shorts. "Now yer look more human, Skip," said Mavis. She held out her empty glass to him. "Wot about some more Scotch? We do make whiskey here, but t'ain't a patch on this. But you should try our beer. Best in the universe. And our plonk ain't bad. Nor's our rum."

"You'll be tryin' it at ternight's party, Skipper," said Jimmy.

"An official reception?" Grimes asked the master of the Seamen's Guild.

"Not on yer nelly. If yer thinkin' o' gettin' all dressed up again, forget it. A beach barbecue. Come as yer please, preferably in civvies. Jock's makin' the arrangements."

"Twenty guests. Yerself an' nineteen others," said the City Constable. "There'll be other parties for the rest o' yer crowd. Transport'll be at yer gangway at 1900 hours."

"I'll pick up the skipper meself," said Mavis.

Vinegar Nell returned, wearing her shortest skirted uniform. The mayor looked at her and added, "When I drive meself, I use me little run-about. Only room for one passenger."

The paymaster said, "As you know, Commander Grimes, we have many guests aboard the ship. I have arranged for two sittings at lunch in the wardroom. I imagine that you will prefer second sitting."

"Don't bother about us, dearie," Mavis told her. "Just send up some more o' this Scotch, an' some more blottin' paper to soak it up afore it rots the belly linin'.'' She nibbled appreciatively. "This sorta sausage stuff is very moreish.''

The other two mayors agreed with her enthusiastically.

"I'll see if there's any more of that Rimini salami left in the storeroom," said Vinegar Nell, conveying the impression that she hoped there wouldn't be. "It comes from Rimini, a world settled mainly by people of Italian ancestry. They make the salami out of a sort of fat worm."

"It still tastes good," said Mavis stoutly.

Grimes treated himself to an afternoon sleep after his guests had left. He felt guilty about it; he knew that as a conscientious Survey Service captain he should be making a start on the accumulation of data regarding this new world. It must be the climate, he thought, that was making him drowsy. It was a little too much to drink, he admitted.

He was awakened by somebody shaking him gently. He ungummed his eyes, found that he was looking up into the face of the mayor. She grinned down at him and said, "I had to pull me rank on that sodger you've got on yer gangway, but he let me come up after a bit of an argybargy."

"I . . . I must have dosed off, Mavis. What time is it?"

"Eighteen-thirty hours. All the others've gone, even that snooty popsy o' yours. They left a bit early for a bit of a run-around first."

"My steward should have called me at 1700," muttered Grimes.

"He did, Skip. There's the tray wif a pot o' very cold tea on yer bedside table."

Grimes raised himself on one elbow, poured himself a cup. It tasted vile, but it helped to wake him. He hesitated before throwing back the coverlet—he was naked under it—but Mavis showed no intention of leaving the bedroom. And he wanted a brief shower, and then he had to dress. He said over his shoulder, as he tried to walk to the bathroom with dignity, "What do I wear?"

"Come as you like if yer want to, Skip. It's a hot night, an' the weather bastards say it'll stay that way. But you've civvy shorts, ain't yer? An' a shirt an' sandals."

Grimes had his shower and was relieved, when he had finished drying himself, to find that Mavis had retired to the dayroom. It was not that he was prudish, but she was a large woman and the bedroom was small. He found a gaily patterned shirt with matching shorts, a pair of sandals. She said, when he joined her, "Now you *do* look human. Come on; the car's waitin' by the gangway."

"A drink first?"

"Ta, but no. There'll be plenty at the beach."

The Marine on gangway duty, smart in sharply pressed khaki, saluted. He said, "Have a nice night, sir."

"Thank you," replied Grimes. "I'll try."

"You'd better," the mayor told him.

Grimes took her arm as they walked down the ramp. Her skin was warm and smooth. He looked up at the clear sky. The sun was not yet set, but there was one very bright planet already shining low in the west. The light breeze was hotter than it had been in the morning. He was glad that he was not attending a full-dress function.

The mayor's car, a runabout, was little more than a box on relatively huge wheels, an open box. Grimes opened the door for her on the driver's side and she clambered in. She was wearing the shortest skirt in which he had yet seen her, and obviously nothing under it. *And yet*, thought Grimes, *she says that the Arcadians are odd.*

He got in on the other side. As he shut the door the car started with a soft hum of its electric motor. As it rolled smoothly over the grass toward the entrance to the Oval the mayor waved to groups of people who had come to stare up at the ship from the stars. They waved back. When she nudged him painfully, muttering something about stuck-up Pommy bastards, Grimes waved as well. They were worth waving to, he thought, the girls especially. Botany Bay might not be another Arcadia—but a bright shirt worn open over bare, suntanned breasts can be more attractive than complete nudity. He supposed that he would have to throw his ship open to the public soon, but by the time he did all hands would have enjoyed ample opportunity to blow off excess steam.

"We'll detour through the city," said Mavis. "This is the time I fair love the dump, wif the sun just down an' the street lights comin' on."

Yes, the sun was just dipping below the rolling range to the west, and other stars were appearing to accompany the first bright planet. They drove slowly through the narrow, winding streets, where the elaborate cast-metal balconies of the houses were beginning to gleam, as though luminous, in the odd, soft greenish-yellow glow of the street lights.

"Gas lamps!" exclaimed Grimes.

"An' why not? Natural gas. There's plenty of it—an' we may's well use what's left after the helium's been extracted. An' it's a much *better* light."

Grimes agreed that it was.

"This is Jersey Road we're comin' inter. The city planners tried to make it as much like the old one as they could. I s'pose it's all been pulled down long since."

"It's still there," said Grimes, "although the old bricks are held together with preservative."

"An' how does it compare?" she asked. "Ours, I mean."

"Yours is better. It's much longer, and the gas lighting improves it."

"Good-oh. An' now we turn off on ter the West Head Road. That's Macquarie Head lighthouse we're just passin'. One lighthouse ter do the work o' two. The main guide beacon for the airport as well as for the harbor." Something big fluttered across their path, just ahead of them, briefly illumined in the glare of the headlights. Grimes had a brief impression of sharp, shining teeth and leathery wings. "Just a goanna," Mavis told him. "Flyin' goannas they useter be called, but as we've none o' the other kind here the 'flyin' part o' the name got dropped. They're good eatin'."

They sped through the deepening darkness, bushland to their left, the sea to their right. Out on the water the starboard sidelight, with a row of white accommodation lights below it, of a big schooner gleamed brightly.

"*Taroona,*" said Mavis. "She's due in tonight. Ah, here's the turn-off. Hold on, Skip!"

The descent of the steep road—little more than a path—down to the beach was more hazardous, thought Grimes, than any that he had ever made through an atmosphere. But they got to the bottom without mishap. Away to their right a fire was blazing, its light reflected from the other vehicles parked in its vicinity. Dark figures moved in silhouette to the flames. There was the music of guitars, and singing.

"*Tie me kangaroo down, sport . . .*" Grimes heard.

"I got yer here, Skip," said Mavis.

"And in one piece," agreed Grimes.

"Come orf it!" she told him.

Chapter 28

As well as voices and music a savory smell of roasting meat drifted down the light breeze from the fire. Grimes realized that he was hungry. Unconsciously he quickened his step.

"Wot's the hurry?" asked Mavis.

He grinned—but at least she hadn't called him Gutsy Grimes. He said, "I want to join the party."

"Ain't I enough party for yer, Skip? I didn't think you'd be one fer chasin' the sheilas."

Grimes paused to kick his sandals off. The warm, dry sand felt good under his bare soles. He said, gesturing toward the parked cars, "I thought you people used horses for short journeys."

"Yair, we do—but not when we've a crowd o' spacemen along who, like as not, have never ridden a nag in their bleedin' lives."

"I have ridden a horse," said Grimes.

"An' what happened?"

"I fell off."

They both laughed, companionably, and then Grimes stopped laughing. He was able to distinguish faces in the firelight. This, obviously, was not an officers-only party. There was Langer, the burly bos'n, and with him Sergeant Washington. And there was Sally, the little slut of a stewardess who had ministered to the needs of his predecessor in the ship, Commander Tallis. Obviously their hosts were determined to maintain their egalitarian principles. Well, that was their right, he supposed.

"What's eatin' you, Skip?" asked Mavis.

"I'm thinking that it was time that I was eating something."

"Spacemen are the same as sailors, I suppose. Always thinkin' o' their bellies." She raised her voice. "Hey, you drongoes! One o' yer bring the skipper a mug an' a sangwidge!"

Surprisingly it was the girl, Sally, who obliged, presenting him with a slab of steak between two halves of a thick roll. She seemed in an unusually happy mood as she walked toward him, her breasts— she had discarded her shirt—jouncing saucily. She said, "You see, Captain, I *can* make a sandwich when I want to." And it was Langer who came with a mug of beer in each hand, one of which he presented to Grimes. As he raised his own to his lips he said, "Your very good health, Captain."

"And yours, Bos'n. (He thought, *This may not be the finest beer in the universe, but it'll do till something better comes along.*)

"Here's to your luck, Captain. I knew our luck would change as soon as we got *you* in command."

"I hope it stays that way," said Grimes. (Damn it all, the man seemed positively to *love* him.)

He took a bite from his sandwich. It was excellent steak, with a flavor altogether lacking from the beef in the ship's tissue culture vats.

Dr. Rath drifted up. His informal civilian clothing was dark gray— but, amazingly, even he looked happy. He was smoking a long, thin cigar. "Ah, so you've joined us, Captain. Miss Russell was wondering when you were going to turn up."

"Oh. Where is she now?"

"Haven't a clue, my dear fellow. She sort of drifted off among the dunes with one of the local lads. Going for a swim, I think. At least, they'd taken off all their clothes."

"Mphm." What Vinegar Nell did, and with whom, was her own affair—but Grimes felt jealous. He accepted another mug of beer, then fumbled for his pipe.

"Have one of these, Captain," said Rath, offering him a cigar. "Not exactly Havanas, but not at all bad."

"Better than Havanas," said Langer.

And you'd know, thought Grimes uncharitably. *With your flogging of ship's stores you could always afford the best.* He accepted the slim, brown cylinder from the doctor, nonetheless, and a light from the attentive Sally.

Not bad, he thought, inhaling deeply. *Not bad. Must be a local tobacco.*

He turned to Mavis and said, "You certainly do yourselves well on this world, darling." She seemed to have changed, to have become much younger—and no less attractive. It must, he thought, be the effect of the firelight. And how had he ever thought of her abundant hair as silver? It was platinum-blonde.

She said, "We get by. We always have got by. We had no bloody option, did we?" She took the cigar from his hand, put it to her own lips, drew in. She went on, "Still an' all, it's good to have you bastards with us at last, after all these bleedin' years."

How had he ever thought her accent ugly?

She handed the cigar back, and again he inhaled. Another mug of beer had somehow materialized in his free hand. He drowned the smoke with a cool, tangy draft. He thought, *This is the life. Too bloody right it is.*

By the fire the singing had started again, backed by thrumming guitars.

> *Farewell to Australia forever,*
> *Good-bye to old Sydney, good-bye,*
> *Farewell to the Bridge an' the Harbor,*
> *With the Opera House standin' on high.*

> *Singin' tooral-i-ooral-i-addy,*
> *Singin' tooral-i-ooral-i-aye,*
> *Singin' tooral-i-ooral-i-addy,*
> *We're bound out fer Botany Bay!*

"The opera house isn't all that high," complained Grimes.

"Never mind, dearie. It's only a song." She added almost fiercely, "But it's *ours*."

> *Farewell to the Rocks an' to Paddo,*
> *An' good-bye to Woolloomooloo,*
> *Farewell to the Cross an' the Domain,*
> *Why were we such mugs as ter go?*

"You're better off here," said Grimes. "You've a good world. Keep it that way."

"That's what I thought, after talkin' to some o' yer people this arvo. But will you bastards let us?"

"You can play both ends against the middle," suggested Grimes. He was not conscious of having been guilty of a grave indiscretion.

"Wodyer mean, Skip?"

"Your world is almost in the territorial space of the Empire of Waverley, and the emperor believes in extending his dominions as and when possible."

"So . . . the thot plickens." She laughed. "But this is a *party*, Skip. We're here to enjoy ourselves, not talk politics." Her hands went to a fastener at the back of her dress. It fell from her. She stood there briefly, luminous in the firelight. She was ample, but nowhere was there any sag. Her triangle of silvery pubic hair gleamed brightly in contrast to the golden tan of her body. Then she turned, ran, with surprising lightness, into the low surf. Grimes threw off his own clothing, followed her. The water was warm—*pee-warm*, he thought—but refreshing. Beyond the line of lazy breakers the water was gently undulant. He swam toward a flurry of foam that marked her position. She slowed as he approached her, switched from a crawl to an energy-conserving breaststroke.

He followed her as she swam, parallel to the beach. After a few moments of exertion he caught up with her. She kept on steadily until the fire and the music were well astern, then turned inshore. A low breaker caught them, swept them in, deposited them gently on the soft sand like stranded, four-limbed starfish. He got to his feet, then helped her up. Their bodies came into contact—and fused. Her mouth was hot on his, her strong arms were around him as she pulled him to her—and, after they had fallen again to the sand, above the tidemark, her legs embraced him in an unbreakable grip. Not that he wished to break it. She engulfed him warmly.

When they were finished he, at last, rolled off her, falling on his back onto the sand. He realized that he and Mavis had performed before an audience. Somehow he was not at all embarrassed—until he recognized, in the dim starlight, the naked woman who, with a young man beside her, was looking down at him.

"I hope you had a good time, Commander Grimes," said Vinegar Nell acidly.

"I did," he told her. "And you?" he asked politely.

"No!" she snapped.

"Fuck orf, why don't yer?" asked the mayor, who had raised herself on her elbows.

The young man turned at once, began to trudge toward the distant fire. Vinegar Nell made a short snarling noise, then followed him.

"That Col," remarked Mavis, "never was any good. "That sheila o' yours couldn't've picked a feebler bastard. All blow, no go, that's him."

"The trouble," said Grimes, "is that she is, as you put it, my sheila. Or thinks she is."

"Then wot the hell was she doin' out with Col?" she asked practically. "Oh, well, now we *are* alone, we may as well make the most of it."

Chapter 29

The next morning—not too early—Grimes held an inquest on the previous night's goings-on. He, himself, had no hangover, although he had forgotten to take an anti-alc capsule on his return to the ship, before retiring. He felt a little tired, but not unpleasantly so.

He opened by asking Brabham how he had spent the evening.

"I went to a party at Pete's place, sir."

"Pete?"

"The president of the Air Pilots' Guild."

"And what happened?"

"Well, we had a few drinks, and there was some sort of help-yourself casserole, and then we had a flight over the city and the countryside in one of the airships."

"Anything else?"

The first lieutenant oozed injured innocence. "What else would there be, Captain?"

"Any relaxation of what we regard as normal standards? Any . . . promiscuity?"

Brabham looked injured.

"Come on, Number One. Out with it. As long as you do your job your sex life is no concern of mine. But I have a good reason for wanting to know what happened." He grinned. "Some odd things happened to me. Normally I'm a very slow starter."

Brabham managed to raise a rather sour smile. "So *that's* what Vinegar Nell was dropping such broad hints about! Well, sir, I had it off with one of our tabbies—I'll not tell you which one—during the flight over the city. Have you ever done it on the transparent deck of a cabin in an airship, with the street lights drifting by below you?"

The first lieutenant was beginning to show signs of enthusiasm. "And then, after we got back to the airport, there was a local wench . . . I can't remember her name. I don't think that we were introduced."

"Mphm. And how do you feel?"

"What do you mean, sir?"

"Presumably you had plenty to drink, as we all did. Any hangover?"

"No, sir."

"Mphm. Commander MacMorris?"

"The Seamen's Guild laid it on for us, Captain. Plenty o' drinks. A smorgasbord. Plenty o' seawomen as well as seamen. There were a couple—engineers in the big schooners." He grinned. "Well, you can sort o' say it was all in the family."

"Mphm. Commander—or Doctor, if you prefer—Brandt?"

The scientist colored, his flush looking odd over his pointed beard. "I don't see that it is any concern of yours, Commander Grimes, but I was the guest of honor at a banquet at the university."

"And were you—er—suitably honored, Dr. Brandt?"

The flush deepened. "I suppose so."

"Try to forget your dignity, Doctor, and answer me as a scientist. What happened?"

"I've always been a reserved man, Commander Grimes. I was expecting an evening spent in intelligent conversation, not an—" He had trouble getting the word out. "Not an orgy. This morning I am shocked by the memory of what those outwardly respectable academics did. Last night I just joined in the party. Happily."

"As did we all," murmured Grimes. "Dr. Rath?"

The medical officer had reverted to his normal morose self. "You should know, Captain. You were there."

"What I'm getting at is this. What is your opinion of it all as a physician?"

"I'd say, Captain, that we were all under the influence of a combined relaxant and aphrodisiac."

"The beer?" suggested Grimes.

"I didn't touch it. There was some quite fair local red wine."

"And I was on what they call Scotch," contributed MacMorris. "It ain't Scotch, but you can force it down."

"And I," said Brandt, "do not drink."

"But all of us smoked, presumably."

"I do not smoke," said Brandt.

"But you were in a room where other people were doing just that,"

Grimes went on. "You were inhaling the fumes whether you wanted to or not."

"I think you've the answer, Captain," said Rath. "I wish I'd thought to bring a cigar stub aboard so I could analyze it."

"And we all feel fine this morning," said Grimes. "Even so, I want none of those cigars aboard the ship."

"Not even for analysis?" demanded the two doctors simultaneously.

"Oh, all right. Analyze if you must—although no doubt a complete analysis of the weed will be made available to you if you ask in the right quarters. Our hosts were just being hospitable, that's all."

"And how," murmured Brabham happily. "And how!"

The mayor came on board late in the forenoon. Grimes asked her about the cigars.

"Oh, we don't smoke 'em all day an' every day," she told him, "though there are some as'd like to. We regard 'em as hair-let-downers, as leg-openers. An' no party'd be a party without 'em."

You can say that again, thought Grimes. In the broad light of day, with nothing, not even alcohol, to blunt his sensibilities, Mavis no longer seemed quite so attractive. Her accent again jarred on his ear, and he didn't really like *big* women; Vinegar Nell was far more to his taste. Nonetheless, he did not regret what had happened the previous night and hoped that it would happen again. He was sorry about the paymaster, though; it must have been galling for her to witness a man whom she regarded as her own property making love to somebody else. But whose fault was that? If she had waited for him instead of wandering off with the highly unsatisfactory Col—

He said, "You've a good export there. Are they made from a native plant?"

"No, Skip. They first comers brought terbaccer wif 'em. Musta mutated like a bastard, or somethin'. An' now, I've a full day for yer. To begin wif, an official lunch wif all the mayors o' the planet, followed by a Mayors' Council. An' you'll be sayin' yer piece at the meetin'. About wot you were tellin' me last night about the Empire o' Waverley an' the Federation an' all the rest of it."

What did I say? Grimes asked himself. But he remembered all too well. He had been hoping that she would have forgotten.

Chapter 30

Botany Bay was a good world, but speedily Grimes came to the conclusion that the sooner *Discovery* lifted from its surface and headed for Lindisfarne Base the better. She had never been and never would be a taut ship—and, in any case, Grimes hated that expression—but now standards of efficiency and discipline were falling to a deplorably low level. Rank meant nothing to the people of Botany Bay. In their own ships—air and surface—the captain was, of course, still the captain, but every crew member was entitled to officer status, an inevitable consequence of automation. Their attitude was rubbing off on to the ratings, petty officers, and junior officers of the spaceship.

Grimes set a date for departure. In the four weeks that this gave him he was able to make quite a good survey of the planet, using *Discovery*'s pinnace instead of one of the local aircraft. The mayors of the city-states cooperated fully, as did the universities of the state capitals. Loaded aboard the survey ship were microfilmed copies of the history of the colony from its first beginnings, from several viewpoints, as well as samples of its various arts from the first beginnings to the present time. There were the standard works on zoology, botany, and geology, as well as such specimens as could safely be carried. (The box of local cigars Grimes locked in his safe, of which only he knew the combination.) There were manuals of airmanship and seamanship. There was all the literature covering local industry. Mavis—who was no fool—insisted on taking out Galactic Patents on their contents after discovering, by shrewd questioning, that the captain of a survey vessel can function as a patents office director in exceptional circumstances.

It was, however, by no means a case of all-work-and-no-play.

Grimes went to his share of parties. At most of them he partook of what Mavis referred to as hair-let-downers, the cigars made from the leaves of the mutated tobacco. He had been assured by Dr. Rath that they were not habit-forming and no ill results would ensue from his smoking them. Usually his partner at such affairs was the mayor of Paddington, but there were others. On one occasion he found himself strongly attracted to Vinegar Nell—but she, even though she was smoking herself, rejected him and wandered away with the City Constable. Grimes shrugged it off. After all, as he had discovered, she wasn't the only fish in the sea, and on his return to Lindisfarne Base he would, he hoped, be able to resume where he had left off with Maggie Lazenby.

Brandt wanted to stay on Botany Bay, but expressed misgivings about the amount of time he would have to wait until contact with the Federation was established. Grimes told the scientist of the simple code that he had agreed upon with Captain Davinas. He said, "With any luck at all, *Sundowner* should drop in almost as soon as I've shoved off. As the sole representative of the Federation on this planet you'll be empowered to make your own deal with Davinas. And Davinas, of course, will be making *his* own deals with the Council of Mayors. I've told Mavis to expect him."

"It all *seems* foolproof enough, Commander Grimes," admitted Brandt.

"You can make anything foolproof, but it's hard to make it bloody foolproof," Grimes told him cheerfully. "All the same, neither Davinas nor myself come in that category."

"So you say," grumbled Brandt. Yet it was obvious that he was pleased to be able to get off the ship for an indefinite period. Grimes suspected that a romance had blossomed between him and a not very young, rather plain professor of physics at Paddington University. Quite possibly he would decide to resign his commission in the Survey Service and live on Botany Bay. There were quite a few others, Grimes knew, who had the same idea. That was why he wanted to get spaceborne before the rot set in properly.

Then there was the farewell party—the last, in fact, of a series of farewell parties. It was a beach barbecue. (The colonists *loved* beach barbecues.) It was a huge affair, with no fewer than a dozen fires going, held on the beach of Manly Cove, one of the bigger bays on the north coast but still within easy reach of the city. All hands were there, with the exception of the unlucky watchkeepers. The beer and the wine flowed freely and everybody was smoking the mutated tobacco. Grimes stayed with Mavis. He might see her again; he most probably would not. He wanted to make the most of this last evening. They found a lonely spot, a small floor of smooth sand among the rocks.

She said, "I shall miss yer, Skip."

"And I you."

"But when yer gotter go, yer gotter go. That's the way of it, ain't it?"

"Too right it is. Unluckily."

"Yer boys don't wanter go. Nor yer sheilas."

"There is such a thing as duty, you know."

"Duty be buggered. Ships have vanished without trace, as yer know bloody well. No one knows yer here."

"They'd soon guess. If there were any sort of flap about *Discovery*'s going missing, then Captain Davinas—the master of *Sundowner* I was telling you about—would soon spill his beans. And the Survey Service can be very vicious regarding the penalty of mutiny and similar crimes. I've no desire to be pushed out of the airlock, in Deep Space without a spacesuit."

"You mean they'd do *that* to yer?"

"Too bloody right, they would."

"An' I'm not worth takin' the risk for. But you sort of *explode* in a vacuum, don't yer? All right. I see yer point."

"I didn't think that there was enough light," said Grimes, looking down at her dimly visible nudity.

She laughed. "I didn't mean *that*. But seein' as how the subject has risen. For the third time, ain't it?"

"Third time lucky," murmured Grimes.

Liftoff had been set for 1200 hours the following day. As on the day of landing the stands were crowded, and the brave, blue flags were flying from every pole. Two of the big dirigibles cruised slowly in a circle above the Oval. Their captains would extend the radius before *Discovery* began to lift.

There were no absentees from the ship at departure time, although it was certain that many of her complement would have liked to have missed their passage. Grimes was the last man up the ramp. At the foot of the gangway he shook hands with Brandt, with the mayors of the city-states. He had intended that his farewell to Mavis would be no more than a formal handshake, but her intentions were otherwise. He felt her mouth on his for the last time. When he pulled away he saw a tear glistening in the corner of her eye.

He marched stiffly up the ramp, which retracted as soon as he was in the airlock. He rode the elevator up to control. In the control room he went to his chair, strapped himself in. He looked at the telltale lights on his console. Everything was ready. His hand went out to the inertial drive start button.

Discovery growled, shook herself. (*Growl you may, but go you must!*) She shuddered, and from below came the unrhythmic rattle of loose fittings. She heaved herself off the grass. In the periscope screen Grimes could see a great circular patch of dead growth to mark where she had stood, with three deep indentations where the vanes had dug into the sod. He wondered, briefly when it would be possible to play a cricket match in the Oval again.

"Port Paddington to *Discovery*," came a voice from the speaker of the NST transceiver, "you know where we live now. Come back as soon as yer like. Over."

"Thank you," said Grimes. "I hope I shall be back."

"Look after yourself, Skip!" It was Mavis' voice.

"I'll try," he told her. "And you look after *your*self."

She had the sense to realize that Grimes would be, from now on, fully occupied with his pilotage. But it was an easy ascent. There was little wind at any level, no turbulence. The old ship, once she had torn herself clear from the surface, seemed glad to be heading back into her natural element. After not very long, with trajectory set for Lindisfarne Base, Grimes was free to go below.

In his cabin he got out a message pad. He wrote: *Davinas, d/s/s Sundowner. Happy Anniversary. John.* He took it down to the radio officer on duty. He said, "I'd like this away as soon as possible. It might just catch him in time. On Botany Bay I rather lost track of the Standard Date."

"Didn't we all, sir?" The young man yawned. No doubt he had a good excuse for being tired, but his manner was little short of insolent. "Through the Carlotti station on Elsinore, sir?"

"Yes. A single transmission. I don't want the emperor's monitors getting a fix on us. Elsinore will relay it."

"As you say, sir."

The tiny Carlotti antenna, the rotating Moebius strip, synchronized with the main antenna now extruded from the hull, began to turn and hunt. Elsinore would receive the signal, over the light-years, almost instantaneously. How long would it be before Davinas got it, and where would he be? How long would it be before *Sundowner* made her landing on Botany Bay? How long would Brandt have to wait? Grimes found that he was envying the scientist.

He debated with himself whether or not to drop in on Flannery, but decided against it. The PCO had found no fellow telepaths, but he had found quite a few boozing pals. No doubt the man would be suffering from a monumental hangover.

He went up to his quarters. He started to think about writing his report. Then he thought about his first report, the one in which he had damned Swinton. Should he rewrite it? The Mad Major had been very well behaved on Botany Bay. People like him should smoke those cigars all the time. *Make love, not war.*

Grimes decided to sleep on it. After all, it would be some days before the ship would be in a sector of space from which it would be safe to inform Lindisfarne Base of her whereabouts, and even then a long and detailed report of her activities would almost certainly be picked up and decoded by the Waverley monitors. It could wait until *Discovery* was back at Lindisfarne.

By the Standard Time kept by the ship it was late at night. And Grimes was tired. He turned in, and slept soundly.

Chapter 31

Discovery was not a happy ship.

All hands went about their duties sullenly, with a complete lack of enthusiasm. Grimes could understand why. They had been made too much of on Botany Bay. It had been the sort of planet that spacemen dream about, but rarely visit. It had been a world that made the truth of Dr. Johnson's famous dictum all too true. How did it go? *A ship is like a prison where you stand a good chance of getting drowned....* Something like that, Grimes told himself. And though the chances of getting drowned while serving in a spaceship were rather remote there were much worse ways of making one's exit if things went badly wrong.

He went down to the farm deck to have a yarn with Flannery. The PCO had recovered slightly from his excesses but, as usual, was in the process of taking several hairs of the dog that had bitten him. The bottle, Grimes noted, contained rum, distilled on Botany Bay.

"Oh, t'is you, Skipper. Could I persuade ye? No? I was hopin' ye'd be takin' a drop with me. I have to finish this rotgut afore I can get back to me own tipple."

"So you enjoyed yourself on Botany Bay," remarked Grimes.

"An' didn't we all, each in his own way? But the good times are all gone, an' we have to travel on."

"That seems to be the general attitude, Mr. Flannery."

"Yours included, Skipper. Howiver did ye manage to make yer own flight from the mayor's nest?"

"Mphm."

"Iverybody had the time of his life but poor ould Ned." Flannery gestured toward the canine brain suspended in its sphere of murky nutrient fluid. "He'd've loved to have been out, in a body, runnin' over the green grass of a world so like his own native land."

"I didn't think the dingo ever did much running over green grass," remarked Grimes sourly. "Through the bush, over the desert, yes. But green grass, no."

"Ye know what I'm meanin'." Flannery suddenly became serious. "What are ye wantin' from me, Skipper?" *It always used to be "Captain,"* thought Grimes. *Flannery's been tainted by Botany Bay as much as anybody else.* "Don't tell me. I know. Ye're wonderin' how things are in this rustbucket. I don't snoop on me shipmates, as well ye know. But I can give ye some advice, if ye'll only listen. Ride with a loose rein. Don't go puttin' yer foot down with a firm hand. An' it might help if ye let it be known that ye're not bringin' charges against the Mad Major when we're back on Lindisfarne. Oh—an' ye could try bein' nice to Vinegar Nell."

"Is that all?" asked Grimes coldly.

"That's all, Skipper. If it's any consolation to ye, Ned still likes ye. He's hopin' that ye don't go makin' the same mistake as Grimes was always afther makin'."

"*Grimes?*" asked Grimes bewilderedly.

"T'was Bligh I was meanin'."

"Damn Bligh!" swore Grimes. "This ship isn't HMS *Bounty*. This, in case you haven't noticed, is FSS *Discovery*, with communications equipment that can reach out across the galaxy. *Bounty* only had signal flags."

"Ye asked me, Skipper, an' I told ye." Flannery's manner was deliberately offhand. "Would there be anythin' else?"

"No!" snapped Grimes.

He went up to the main radio office, had a few words with the operator on duty. He was told there was very little traffic, and all of it signals from extremely distant stations and none of it concerning *Discovery*. He carried on to the control room, stared out through the viewports at the weirdly distorted universe observed from a ship running under Mannschenn Drive, tactfully turning his back while the officer of the watch hastily erased the three-dimensional ticktacktoe lattice from the plotting tank. *Ride with a loose rein*, Flannery had warned. He would do so. He looked at the arrays of telltale lights. All seemed to be in order.

He went down to the paymaster's office. Vinegar Nell was there, diligently filling in forms in quintuplicate. He tried to be nice to her, but she had no time for him. "Can't you see that I'm busy, Commander Grimes?" she asked coldly. "All this work was neglected while we were on Botany Bay." She contrived to imply that this was Grimes's fault.

Then Grimes, as he sometimes did, called in to the wardroom to have morning coffee with his officers. Their manner toward him was reserved, chilly. *We were having a good time*, their attitude implied, and this old *bastard had to drag us away from it.*

So went the day. There was something going on—of that he was sure. He was, once again, the outsider, the intruder into this micro-society, resented by all. And there was nothing he could do about it. (And if there were, should he do it?)

He was a man of regular habits. In space he required that he be called, by his steward, with a pot of morning coffee at precisely 0700 hours. This gave him an hour to make his leisurely toilet and to get dressed before breakfast. During this time he would listen to a program of music, selected the previous night, from his little playmaster. It was the steward's duty to switch this on as soon as he entered the daycabin.

He awakened, this morning (as he always did) to the strains of music. *Odd*, he thought. He could not recall having put that particular tape into the machine. It was a sentimental song which, nonetheless, he had always liked—but it was not, somehow, the sort of melody to start the day with.

> *Spaceman, the stars are calling,*
> *Spaceman, you have to roam,*
> *Spaceman, through light-years falling,*
> *Remember I wait at home. . . .*

He heard Mullins come into the bedroom, the faint rattle of the coffee things on the tray. He smelled something. *Was the man smoking?* He jerked into wakefulness, his eyes wide open. It was not Mullins. It was the girl, Sally, who had been his predecessor's servant. She was not in uniform. She was wearing something diaphanous that concealed nothing and accentuated plenty. One of the thin cigars dangled from a corner of her full mouth. She took it out. "Here you are, Skipper. Have a drag. It'll put you in the mood."

Grimes slapped the smoldering cylinder away from his face. "In the mood for what?" he snapped.

"You mean to say that you don't know? Not after your carryings-on with the fat cow on Botany Bay, to say nothing of that scrawny bitch of a paymaster . . . ?" She let her robe drop open. "Look at me, Skipper. I'm better than both of 'em, aren't I?"

"Get out of here!" ordered Grimes. "I'll see you later."

"You can see me now, Skipper." Her robe had fallen from her. "Take a good look—an' then try to tell me that you don't like what you see!"

Grimes did like it; that was the trouble. The girl had an excellent figure, although a little on the plump side. He thought of getting on to his telephone to demand the immediate presence of both Vinegar Nell and Brabham, then decided against it. Both of them would be quite capable of putting the worst possible construction on the situation. On the other hand, he had no intention of letting things go too far.

Decisively he threw aside the covers, jumped out of the bed. The girl opened her arms, smiling suggestively. He said, "Not yet, Sally. I always like a shower first."

She said, "I'll wash your back, Skipper."

"Good."

He pushed her into the shower cubicle before she could change her mind. And would it work? he wondered. On Botany Bay a swim in the warm sea had led to no diminishment of the effects of the smoke of the mutated tobacco—but the sea had always been warm. The shower would not be. When Grimes turned on the water he made sure that she did not see the setting. She screamed when the icy torrent hit her warm skin. Grimes felt like screaming too. He was not and never had been a cold shower addict. She struggled in his arms, even tried to bring her knee up into his crotch. He thought, as he blocked the attack, *You'd have a job finding anything!*

She squeaked, "Turn on the hot, you stupid bastard!"

He muttered, through chattering teeth, "This is hurting me at least as much as it's hurting you. Now, tell me. What's all this about?"

Her struggles were weaker now. The cold water was draining her of strength. She whispered, "If you turn on the hot, I'll tell you."

"You'll tell me first."

"It—it was just a bet . . . with the other tabbies. An' the hunks. That—that I'd get in with you, same as I was in with Commander Tallis."

"Where did you get the cigar? Out of my safe?"

"I'm not a thief, Skipper. The—the ship's lousy with the things. They'll be worth a helluva lot back on Lindisfarne. You know how people'll pay."

Grimes shook her. "Anything else?"

"No, no. Please, Skipper, please. I'll never be warm again."

Gratefully, Grimes adjusted the shower control. He felt at first as though he were being boiled alive. When he was sufficiently thawed he left the cubicle, with the naked girl still luxuriating in the gloriously hot water. He dressed hastily. He phoned up to the control room, got the officer of the watch. "Mr. Farrell, ring the alarm for boat stations."

"*Boat stations*, sir? But—"

"There's nothing like a drill at an unexpected time to make sure that all hands are on the ball. Make it boat stations. Now."

There was a delay of about three seconds, then the clangor of alarm bells echoed through the ship, drowning out the irregular beat of the inertial drive, the thin, high whine of the Mannschenn Drive. A taped voice repeated loudly, "All hands to boat stations! All hands to boat stations!"

Sally emerged from the shower cubicle, dripping, her hair plastered to her head. She looked frightened. She snatched up her robe, threw it over her wet body. "Captain, what's wrong?" she cried.

"It's an emergency," Grimes told her. "Get to your station."

In the doorway to the dayroom she almost collided with Brabham on his way in.

"What's going on, sir?" demanded the first lieutenant harshly.

"Sit down," ordered Grimes. He waited until he was sure that Sally was out of earshot. Then he said, "I gave orders, Commander Brabham, that none of that mutated tobacco, in any form, was to be brought aboard the ship."

"You were smoking enough of it yourself on Botany Bay, Captain."

"I was. In those circumstances it was quite harmless."

"It will be quite harmless at parties back at Lindisfarne Base, Captain."

"So you're in it, too."

"I didn't say so, sir."

Grimes snarled. "Did you consider the effects of smoking the muck aboard this ship, with the sexes in such gross disproportion?"

"Nobody would be so stupid—"

"You passed that stewardess on her way out when you came in. She's one of the stupid ones. And now, with all hands at their stations, you and I are going to make a search of the accommodation."

"If that's the way you want it. Sir."

They started in the officers' flat, in Brabham's cabin. The first drawer that Grimes pulled out was full of neatly packed boxes. And the second.

"You're pretty blatant about this, Number One," remarked Grimes.

"I hardly expected that the captain would be pawing through my personal possessions with his own fair hands. Sir."

"Not only me."

"Lindisfarne Base is not a commercial spaceport. Sir. There are no customs."

"But the dockyard police exercise the same function," snapped Grimes. But he knew, as well as Brabham did, that those same dockyard police would turn a blind eye to anything as long as they, personally, profited.

All the officers, Grimes discovered, had disobeyed his orders, working on the good old principle of *What he doesn't know won't bother him*. Now he did know. Using his master key he went down through compartment after airtight compartment. Stewards and stewardesses . . . petty officers . . . Marines . . . general purpose ratings . . . it was even worse than he had thought. In the catering staff's general room he found butts in the ashtrays. They must, he thought, have enjoyed quite a nice little orgy last night—and he had been pulled in at the tail end of it.

He and a sullen Brabham rode the elevator up to the control room. Grimes went at once to the intercom microphone. He said harshly, "Attention, all hands. This is the captain speaking. It has come to my attention that large quantities of Botany Bay tobacco are being carried aboard this ship. All—I repeat *all*—stocks of this drug are to be taken to the after airlock, from which they will be dumped."

"You can't do that, Captain!" expostulated Brabham.

"I am doing it, mister."

"But it's private property."

"And this ship is the property of the Federation Survey Service. We are all the property of the Service, and are bound to abide by its regulations. See that my orders are carried out, Commander Brabham."

"But—"

"Jump to it!"

"You'll do the jumping, Commander Grimes!" It was Swinton who spoke. He had entered the control room unnoticed. He was carrying a twenty-millimeter projectile pistol, a nasty weapon designed for use inside a ship, its slug heavy and relatively slow moving, incapable of penetrating the shell plating or bulkheads of a ship. But it would make a very nasty mess of a human body.

"Swinton! Put that thing down!"

"Are you going to try to make me, Commander Grimes?"

Grimes looked at Brabham and the watch officer. Brabham said,

"We're all in this, Captain. Almost all of us, that is. This business of the cigars pushed us past the point of no return."

"Mutiny?" asked Grimes quietly.

"Yes. Mutiny. We owe the Survey Service nothing. From now on we're looking after ourselves."

"You must be mad," Grimes told him. "The moment Lindisfarne gets word of this there'll be a fleet out after you."

"The Sparkses are with us," said Swinton. "There'll be no word sent out on Carlotti radio. As for that drunken bum Flannery—the first thing I did was to smash that dog's brain in aspic of his. Without his amplifier he's powerless."

"He'll never forgive you," said Grimes.

"The least of my worries," sneered Swinton.

"And just what do you intend to do?" Grimes asked quietly. If he could keep them talking there was a chance, a faint chance, that he might be able to grab that weapon.

"Return to Botany Bay of course," said Brabham.

"You bloody fool!" snarled Swinton.

"Why?" asked the first lieutenant calmly. "Dead men tell no tales."

"And even Botany Bay has laws and policemen," remarked Grimes.

"Do you think we haven't thought of that?" Brabham demanded. "We intend to loaf around a bit, and make our return to Botany Bay after an interval that should correspond roughly to the time taken by a voyage to Lindisfarne and back. Our story will be that you were relieved of your command on return to Base and that I was promoted."

"You'll have to do better than that," said Grimes. "You'll have Brandt to convince as well as the colonists."

"Oh, we'll polish our story until it gleams while we're cruising. We'll make it all as watertight as a duck's down."

"Down to the airlock!" ordered Swinton, gesturing with his pistol.

"Better do as the major says," came a deep voice from behind Grimes.

He turned. Sergeant Washington had come into the control room, and two other Marines with him. They were all armed.

So, he thought, this was it. This was the end of the penny section. His famous luck had at last deserted him. In any ship but this one there would be a fair number of loyalists—but whom could he count on in *Discovery*? Poor, drunken, useless Flannery, his one weapon, his ability to throw his thoughts across the light-years, destroyed with the killing to his psionic amplifier? Perhaps he was dead himself. He had never been popular with his shipmates. Dr. Rath, perhaps—but what could he do? Plenty, maybe—but nothing in time to save Grimes. And who else?

He tensed himself to spring at Swinton, to wrest the pistol from his grasp before it could be fired. Perhaps. It would be suicidal—but quicker and less painful than a spacewalk without a suit. Or would it be? He realized the truth, the bitter truth, of the old adage, *While there's life, there's hope.* Perhaps he hadn't run out of luck. Perhaps something, anything, might happen between this moment and the final moment when, locked in the cell of the airlock chamber, he realized that the air was being evacuated prior to the opening of the outer door.

"All right," he said. "I'm coming."

"You'll soon be going," Brabham quipped grimly.

Chapter 32

There was a crowd by the airlock—Langer, the bos'n; Mullins, who had been Grimes's steward; the little slut Sally; MacMorris and several of his juniors; the radio officers. They made way for Grimes and his escorts, raised an ironic cheer. There were two men already in the chamber, facing the leveled pistols of Swinton's Marines with pitiful defiance. One, surprisingly, was Dr. Rath; the other was Flannery. The PCO was bleeding about the face and one of his eyes was closed. No doubt he had made a vain attempt to save his macabre pet from destruction. The doctor looked, as always, as though he were on his way to a funeral. *And so he is*, thought Grimes with gallows humor. *His own.*

Swinton painfully jabbed Grimes in the small of the back with his pistol. "Inside, you!" he snarled. Grimes tried hard to think of some fitting, cutting retort, but could not. Probably he would when it was too late, when there was no air left in his lungs to speak with.

"Inside, bastard!"

That pistol muzzle hurt. With what little dignity he could muster Grimes joined the two loyalists, then turned to face his tormentors. He said, reasonably, "I don't know why you hate me so much."

"Because you've achieved everything that we haven't," growled Brabham. "*Lucky* Grimes. But throughout your service career you've committed all the crimes that *we* have, and got away with them, while our promotions have been blocked. You're no better than us. Just luckier, that's all. I've always prayed that I'd be around when your luck finally ran out. It seems that the Odd Gods of the Galaxy have seen fit to answer my prayers." He turned to MacMorris. "Chief, what about shutting down the time-twister? We can't make any changes in the mass of the ship with the Mannschenn Drive running."

So you thought of that, commented Grimes to himself. *A pity.*

Suddenly there was a commotion at the rear of the crowd. Vinegar Nell, followed by Tangye, was forcing her way through, using her sharp elbows vigorously. *So she wants to be in at the kill*, thought Grimes bitterly.

She demanded, "What do you think you're doing?"

"What does it look like?" asked Brabham.

She snapped, "I'll not stand for murder!"

"Now, isn't that just too bad?" drawled Swinton. "Perhaps you'd like to take a little spacewalk yourself. Just as a personal favor we'll let you do it in your birthday suit."

One of the Marines put an eager hand out to the neck of her shirt. She slapped it away, glared at the man. "Keep your filthy paws off me, you ape!" Then, to Swinton and Brabham, "You can't touch *me!*"

"Why not?" demanded the major.

"Try to use your brains—if you have any. How many people aboard this ship are trained as ecologists?" She pointed at Dr. Rath. "You're about to dispose of one of them. And that leaves me. Without me to take care of the environment you'd all be poisoned or asphyxiated long before you got back to Botany Bay." She added nastily, "And *with* me you could still meet the same fate if I had good reason not to feel happy."

Swinton laughed. "I think, Miss Russell, that I could persuade you to cooperate. After all, such persuasion is part of *my* training."

"Hold on," put in Brabham. After all he, with all his faults, was a competent spaceman, was keenly aware that the blunder, intentional or otherwise, of one key technician can destroy a ship. He asked the paymaster, "What proposals do you have regarding the disposition of the . . . er . . . prisoners? You realize that we can't take them back to Botany Bay. Not when Grimes and that fat cow of a mayor are eating out of each other's hands."

"Mr. Tangye will tell you," she said.

"We'll set them adrift in a boat," stated the navigating officer.

"Are you quite mad, Tangye?" demanded Brabham.

"No, I'm not. We're in no great hurry, are we? We have time on our hands, time to waste. It'll be less than an hour's work to remove the Carlotti transceiver and the mini-Mannschenn from whichever boat we're letting them have."

"*And* the inertial drive," added Brabham thoughtfully.

"Hardly necessary. How far will they get, even at maximum acceleration, even with a long lifetime to do it in, on inertial drive only?"

"You've forgotten about Flannery," objected Swinton.

"We haven't," Vinegar Nell assured him. "Without his horrid amplifier he couldn't think his way out of a paper bag."

"Murder," admitted Brabham suddenly, "has never been my cup of tea."

"Or mutiny?" asked Grimes hopefully, but everybody ignored him.

"It has mine," asserted Swinton, far too cheerfully.

"I say, give the skipper an' his pals a chance!" shouted Sally.

"I second that," grunted Langer.

And what sort of chance will it be? wondered Grimes. *A life sentence, instead of a death sentence. A life sentence, locked for years in a cell, with absolutely no chance of escape. And in company certainly not of my choosing.* He had, not so long ago, made a long boat voyage with an attractive girl as his only companion. It had started well, but had finished with himself and the wench hating each other's guts.

He said, "Thank you, Miss Russell. And Mr. Tangye. I appreciate your efforts on my behalf. But I think I'd prefer the spacewalk."

Swinton laughed, although it sounded more like a snarl. "So there is such a thing as a fate worse than death, after all. All right, Brabham, you'd better start getting one of the boats ready for the long passage. The long, long passage. Meanwhile, this airlock will do for a holding cell."

The inner door sighed shut, sealing off the prisoners from the mutineers.

"You might have warned me!" Grimes said bitterly to Flannery.

The telepath looked at him mournfully from his one good eye. "I did so, Captain. Ride with a loose rein, I told ye. Don't go puttin' yer foot down with a firm hand. An' don't go makin' the same mistakes as Bligh did. With him it was a squabble over coconuts or some such the first time, an' rum the last time. With you it was cigars. I did so warn ye. I was a-goin' to warn ye again, but it all flared up sudden like. An' I had me poor hands full tryin' to save Ned."

"I hope," said Grimes, "that you now appreciate the folly of trying to run with the fox and hunt with the hounds." He turned to Rath. "And what brings you into this galley, Doctor?"

"I have my standards, Captain," replied the medical officer stiffly.

"Mphm. Then don't you think you'd better do something about Mr. Flannery? He seems in rather bad shape."

"It's only superficial damage," said Rath briskly. "It can wait until we're in the boat. The medicine chests in all the lifecraft are well stocked. I saw to that myself."

"That's a comfort," said Grimes. "I suppose that you'll do your damnedest to keep us all alive for the maximum time."

"Of course. And when the boat *is* picked up—I presume that it will be eventually—my notes and journal will be of great value to the medical authorities of that future time. My journal may well become one of the standard works on space medicine."

"What a pity," sneered Grimes, "that you won't be around to collect the royalties."

The doctor assumed a dignity that made Grimes ashamed of his sarcasm, but said nothing further. And Flannery, who had long since lost any interest in the conversation of his companions, was huddled up on the deck and muttering, "Ned—Ned . . . what did they have to do that to ye for? The only livin' bein' in this accursed ship who never hurt anybody."

Chapter 33

In little more than an hour's time the inner airlock door opened. During this period Grimes and Rath had talked things over, had decided that there was nothing at all that they could do. Flannery refused to be stirred from his grief-ridden apathy, muttering only, "Too much hate runnin' loose in this ship . . . too much hate . . . an' it's all come to the top, all at once, like some filthy bubble."

The inner airlock door opened, and Swinton stood there, backed by Sergeant Washington and six of his men. All were armed, and all were trained in the use of arms. They said nothing, merely gestured with their pistols. Grimes and his companions said nothing either; what was there to say? They walked slowly out of the chamber, and were hustled onto the spiral staircase running up and around the axial shaft. In the cramped confines of the elevator cage, Grimes realized, it would have been possible—although not probable—for weapons to be seized and turned upon their owners.

Grimes slowly climbed the staircase, with Rath behind him, and Flannery bringing up the dejected rear. Behind them were the Marines. They came at last to one of the after boat bays. The boat was ready for them. The mini-Mannschenn unit and the Carlotti transceiver, each removed in its entirety, were standing on the deck well clear of the airlock hatch.

Brabham was there, and Tangye, and Vinegar Nell, with other officers and ratings. Grimes tried to read the expressions on their faces. There were flickers of doubt, perhaps, and a growing realization of the enormity of their crime—but also an unwavering resolution. After all, it would be many, many years (if ever) before the Admiralty learned that there had been a mutiny. Or would it be? Grimes suddenly remembered what he should have remembered before—that Captain Davinas, in his *Sundowner*, would, provided that his owners were agreeable, soon be dropping down on Botany Bay. But what could Davinas do? He commanded an unarmed ship with a small crew. The mutineers would see to it that Davinas and his people did not survive long enough to tell any sort of tale. But if he told Swinton and Brabham about his coded message to the tramp captain, then *Sundowner*'s fate would surely be sealed. If he kept his knowledge to himself there was just a chance, a faint chance, that Davinas would be able to punch out some sort of distress message before being silenced.

"The carriage waits, my lord," announced Swinton sardonically.

"So I see," replied Grimes mildly.

"Then get in the bloody thing!" snarled the Mad Major.

Flannery was first through the little airlock. Then Rath. Grimes was about to follow, when Vinegar Nell put out a hand to stop him. With the other she thrust at him what she had been carrying—his favorite pipe, a large tin of tobacco. Grimes accepted the gift. "Thank you," he said simply. "Think nothing of it," she replied. Her face was expressionless.

"Very touching," sneered Swinton. Then, to one of his men, "Take that stinking rubbish away from him!"

"Let him keep it," said Vinegar Nell. "Don't forget, Major, that you have to keep me happy."

"She's right," concurred Brabham, adding, in a whisper, *"The bitch!"*

"All right. Inside, Grimes, and take your baby's comforter with you. You can button up the boat if you feel like it. But it's all one to me if you don't."

Grimes obeyed, clambering into and through the little airlock. He thought briefly of starting the inertial drive at once and slamming out through the hull before the door could be opened. It would be suicide—but all those in the boat bay would die with him. But—of course—the small hydrogen fusion power unit had not yet been actuated, and there would be no power for any of the boat's machinery until it was. The fuel cells supplied current—but that was sufficient only for closing the airlock doors and then, eventually, for starting the fusion process. So he went to the forward cabin, sat in the pilot's seat, strapped himself in. He told the others to secure themselves. He sealed the airlock.

The needle of the external pressure gauge flickered, then turned rapidly anti-clockwise to zero. So the boat bay was now clear of people and its atmosphere pumped back into the ship. Yet the noise of *Dis-*

covery's propulsive machinery was still audible, transmitted into the boat through the metal of the cradle on which it was resting. The high, thin note of the Mannschenn Drive faded, however, dying, dying— and with the shutting down of the temporal precession field came the uncanny disorientation in time and space. Grimes, looking at his reflection in the polished transparency of the forward viewscreen, saw briefly an image of himself, much older and wearing a uniform with strange insignia.

The boat bay doors opened. Beyond them was the interstellar night, bright with a myriad stars and hazy drifts of cosmic dust. *Any moment now*, thought Grimes—but the shock of the firing of the catapult took him unawares, pressing him deep into the padding of his seat. When he had recovered, the first thing to be done was the starting of the fusion power unit, without which the life-support systems would not function. And those same life-support systems, cycling and recycling all wastes, using sewage as nutriment for the specialized algae, would go on working long beyond the normal lifetimes of the three men in the boat.

But Grimes, somehow and suddenly, was not worried by this dismal prospect.

He said, "All right, now let's get ourselves organized. I intend to proceed at a low quarter gravity, just enough for comfort. You, Doctor, can patch Flannery up."

"In his condition, Captain, I'd better keep him under heavy sedation for a while."

"You will not. As for you, Mr. Flannery, I want you to listen as you've never listened before in your misspent life."

"But there's no traffic at all, at all, in this sector o' space, Skipper."

"For a start, you can keep me informed as to how things are aboard *Discovery*, while you can still pick up her psionic broadcasts. It won't surprise me a bit if there are one or two mutinies yet to come. But, mainly, you keep your psionic ears skinned for *Sundowner*."

"*Sundowner*?" demanded Rath. "What would she be doing out here?"

"You'll be surprised," said Grimes. He thought, *I hope you will.*

Chapter 34

A ship's boat is not the ideal craft in which to make a long voyage. Even when it is not loaded to capacity with survivors there is an inevitable lack of privacy. Its life-support systems are not designed for the production of gourmet food, although there is a continuous flow of scientifically balanced nutriment. Grimes—who, after a couple of disastrous experiments by Dr. Rath, had appointed himself cook—did his best to make the processed algae palatable, using sparingly (he did not know how long he would have to make them last) the synthetic flavorings he found in a locker in the tiny galley. But always at the back of his mind—and at the backs of the minds of his two companions—was the off-putting knowledge that the vegetable matter from the tanks had been nourished directly by human wastes.

The main trouble, however, was not the food, but the company. Rath had no conversation. Flannery, at the slightest excuse, would wax maudlin over the death of Ned, his hapless psionic amplifier. Lacking this aid to telepathic communication, and with nobody aboard *Discovery* a strong natural transmitter, he was not able for long to keep Grimes informed as to what was going on aboard the ship. It was learned, however, that Brabham and Swinton were not on the best of terms, each thinking that he should be captain. And Sally had been the victim of a gang rape—which, said Flannery, grinning lubriciously, she had enjoyed at the beginning but not at all toward the finish. And Vinegar Nell had taken up with Brabham. Grimes, puffing at his vile pipe, felt some sympathy for her. The only way that she stood a chance of escaping Sally's fate was by becoming the woman of one of the leaders of the mutiny.

And then *Discovery*, as the distance between her and the boat rapidly increased, faded from Flannery's ken. It was at this time that the three men became acutely conscious of their utter loneliness, the frightening awareness that they were in a frail metal and plastic bubble crawling, at a pitiful one quarter G acceleration, across the empty immensities between the uncaring stars. They were on a voyage from nowhere to nowhere—and unless Davinas happened along it would take a lifetime.

The days passed. The weeks passed—and Grimes was beginning to face the sickening realization that his famous luck had indeed run out. And yet, he knew, he had to hang on. As long as Rath and Flannery wanted to go on living (what for?) he was responsible for them. He was captain here, just as he had been captain of *Discovery*. He was in charge, and he would stay in charge. He hoped.

One evening—according to the boat's chronometer—he and Rath were playing a desultory game of chess. Flannery was watching without much interest. Suddenly the telepath stiffened. He whispered, vocalizing what he was hearing in his mind, "Two no trumps."

"We are playing chess, not bridge!" snapped Rath irritably.

"Quiet!" warned Grimes.

"I wish I could tell Jim what I have in my hand," murmured Flannery, almost inaudibly. "But I have to observe the code. But surely he knows he can afford to bid three over Bill's two hearts."

"Farley?" asked Grimes in a low, intent voice.

"Farley," agreed Flannery.

"Farley?" demanded Rath.

"He *was* PCO of *Sundowner*," Grimes told him. "When *Sundowner*'s owners had her fitted with Carlotti equipment he became redundant. But he qualified as a Carlotti operator, and stayed in the ship."

"He was a traitor to our cloth, so he was," muttered Flannery. "An' he knows it. When I met him, on New Maine, he told me that he was bitter ashamed o' goin' over to the enemy. He said that he envied me, he did, an' that he'd sell his blessed soul to be in my place, with a sweet amplifier like Ned as a true companion. But we didn't know then what was goin' to happen to Ned, lyin' all broken on the cruel hard deck, wi' the murtherin' bastard Swinton's boot a-crashin' into his soft, naked tissues."

"Damn Ned!" swore Grimes, shocking the telepath out of his self-induced misery. "Forget about that bloody dingo and get on with the job! Concentrate on getting a message through to Farley. *Sundowner* can't be far off if you can pick up his random thoughts."

"I am so concentratin'," said Flannery, with injured dignity. "But ye'll have to help."

"How? I'm no telepath."

"But ye have to be me amplifier. The blessed God an' all His saints know that ye're no Ned, nor ever will be, but ye have to do. Give me a . . . a carrier wave. Ye saw the ship. Ye were aboard her. You got the *feel* of her. Now, concentrate. Hard. Visualize the ould bitch, how she was lookin' when she was sittin' on her pad, how she was, inside, when ye were suppin' yer drinks with the man Davinas."

Grimes concentrated, making almost a physical effort of it. He formed in his mind a picture of the shabby star tramp as he had first seen her, at her loading berth in the New Maine commercial spaceport. He recalled his conversation with Captain Davinas in the master's comfortable dayroom. And then he could not help recalling the later events of that night, back aboard his own ship, when Vinegar Nell had offered herself to him on a silver tray, trimmed with parsley.

"Forget that bitch!" growled Flannery. "Bad cess to her, wherever she is, whatever she's a-doin'." And then, "Farley, come in, damn ye. Farley, t'is yer boozin' pal Flannery here, an' t'is in desperate straits I am. Oh, the man's all wrapped up in his silly game o' cards. He's just gone down, doubled an' redoubled. I'm touchin' him, but not hard enough."

"Drink this," interrupted Rath, thrusting a full tumbler into the telepath's hand. It was, Grimes realized, brandy from the small stock kept in the medicine chest. Flannery took it, downed it in one gulp. The doctor whispered to Grimes, "I should have thought of that before. He's not used to operating in a state of stone-cold sobriety."

"An' t'is right ye are, me good doctor," murmured the telepath. "T'was fuel that the engine o' me brain was needin'. Farley, come in, or be damned to ye. Come in, man, come in. Yes, t'is Flannery here. Ye met me on New Maine. Yes, this is an SOS." He turned to Grimes. "Have ye a position, Captain? No? An' ye're supposed to be a navigator." Then, resuming his intent whisper, "We don't know where we are. There's three of us in a boat—the Old Man, the Quack, an' meself? No mini-Mannschenn, no Carlotti. Ye can home on us, can't ye? Yes, yes, I know ye have no psionic amplifier, but nor have I, now. An' what was that? Oh. Captain Davinas sends his regards to Commander Grimes. I'll pass that on. An' you can tell Captain Davinas that Commander Grimes sends *his* regards. An' tell Captain Davinas, urgently, on no account to break radio silence on his Carlotti. There's a shipload o' mutineers, armed to the teeth, scullin' around in this sector o' space." Then, to the doctor, "Me fuel's runnin' low." Rath got him another glass of brandy. "I'll keep on transmittin', Farley. Just be tellin' your Old Man which way to point his ship, an' ye'll be on to us in two shakes o' the lamb's tail. Good . . . good."

Grimes looked at Rath, and Rath looked at Grimes. A slow smile spread over the doctor's normally glum face. He said, "I really don't think that I could have stood your company much longer, Captain."

"Or I yours, Doctor." He laughed. "And this means good-bye to your prospects of posthumous fame."

"There may be another opportunity," said Rath, still smiling, "but, frankly, I hope not!"

Chapter 35

It took longer for Davinas to effect the rescue than had at first been anticipated. Like many merchant ships at that period *Sundowner* was not equipped with a Mass Proximity Indicator, the only form of radar capable of operating in a ship running under Mannschenn Drive. The merchant captain feared that if he were not extremely careful he might break through into the normal continuum in the position occupied by the boat. It is axiomatic that two solid bodies cannot occupy the same space at the same time. Any attempt to make them do so is bound to have catastrophic consequences.

So Davinas, running on Mannschenn Drive, steering as instructed by Farley, kept the boat right ahead—and then, as soon as the ex-PCO reported that the relative bearing was now right astern, shut down his time-twister and his inertial drive, turned the ship, restarted inertial drive and ran back on the reciprocal trajectory, scanning the space ahead with his long-range radar. At last he picked up the tiny spark in his screen, and, after that, it was a matter of a few hours only.

Sundowner's holds were empty; Captain Davinas had persuaded his owners to let him make a special voyage to Botany Bay to make such advantageous arrangements as he could both with the local authorities and whatever scientific staff had been left on the Lost Colony by *Discovery*. It was decided to bring the boat into the ship through one of the cargo ports. This was achieved without any difficulty, Grimes jockeying the little craft in through the circular aperture with ease, and onto the cradle that had been prepared for her. Then, when the atmosphere had been reintroduced into the compartment, he opened his airlock doors. The air of *Sundowner* was better, he decided, than that inside the boat. It carried the taints inevitable in the atmosphere of all spaceships—hot machinery, the smell of cooking, the odor of living humanity—but not in concentrated form.

Gratefully Grimes jumped down from the airlock door to the deck; Davinas had restarted his inertial drive and the ship had resumed acceleration. He was greeted by *Sundowner*'s chief officer, still spacesuited but with his helmet visor open. "Good to have you aboard, Commander Grimes."

"And it's good to be aboard."

"The master is waiting for you in the control room, sir. I'll lead the way."

"Thank you."

Grimes and his companions followed the officer to the doorway into the axial shaft. They rode up to control in the elevator. Davinas was waiting in the control room. After the handshakings and the introductions he said, "Now, Commander, I'd like some information from you. With all due respect to your Mr. Flannery and my Mr. Farley, I got a rather confused picture. I *was* proceeding to Botany Bay, as I learn that the Lost Colony is called. At the moment I'm heading nowhere in particular; the inertial drive's on only to give us gravity. Do you want me to set course for the Lost Colony again?"

"No," said Grimes at last. *Discovery*, he knew, would be deliberately wasting time before her return to Botany Bay, and there was quite a good chance that *Sundowner* would get there first. But what could she do? She was not armed, and on the world itself there was a paucity of weaponry. There was no army, only a minimal constabulary. There was no navy, no air force. He had no doubt that the colonists would have no trouble manufacturing weapons, and very effective ones, if given time—but time was what they would not have. And if they tried to arrest the mutineers, knowing them to be criminals, immediately after their landing a massacre would be the result. (Swinton tended to specialize in massacres.)

"I could pile on the lumes," said Davinas.

"No, Captain. This is not a warship, and Botany Bay has nothing in the way of arms beyond a few sporting rifles. I think you'd better take us straight to Lindisfarne Base." He added, seeing the disappointment on the other's face, "You'll not lose by it. Your owners will be in pocket. The cost of your deviation, freight on the boat, passages for myself and Dr. Rath and Mr. Flannery. And I'll do my damnedest to see that you get your charter as a liaison ship as soon as this mess is cleared up."

"I see your point," admitted Davinas at last. "And do you want me to get off a Carlottigram to your bosses on Lindisfarne, reporting the mutiny and all the rest of it?"

"No. I don't have my code books with me, and I've no desire to broadcast to the whole bloody galaxy that the Survey Service has a mutiny on its hands. And I don't want *Discovery* to know that I've been picked up. It's strict radio silence, I'm afraid, until we start talking on NST before we land on Lindisfarne. That's the only safe way."

Davinas agreed, then gave orders to his navigator. That young man, Grimes noted, was far more efficient than Tangye. (But Tangye was one of those to whom he owed his continued existence.) The change of trajectory was carried out with no fuss and bother, and in a very short time *Sundowner* was lined up on the target star. Davinas went down then, asking Grimes to accompany him.

Over drinks Grimes filled Davinas in on all (well, not quite all) that had happened since their last meeting. The tramp captain asked, "And what will happen to your mutineers, John?"

"Plenty," replied Grimes grimly. "There are two crimes of which the Survey Service takes a very dim view—piracy is one, and mutiny is the other. The penalty for both is the same—a spacewalk without a spacesuit."

"Even when there was nobody killed during the mutiny?"

"Even then." Grimes stared thoughtfully at the trickle of smoke issuing from the bowl of his pipe. "Somehow, I wish it weren't so. There's only one man among 'em who's really bad, all the way through. That's Swinton, of course. The others . . . I can sympathize with them. They'd reached the stage, all of them, when they felt that they owed the Service no loyalty."

"Poor, stupid bastards," murmured Davinas. Then, "I thought your paymaster was a very attractive woman. I'd never have thought that she'd have been among the mutineers."

"She stopped me from being pushed out from the airlock," said Grimes.

"And yet she'll still have to pay the same penalty as the others," stated Davinas.

"I suppose so," said Grimes. "I suppose so." He did not like the vision that flickered across his mind, of that slim body bursting in hard vacuum, its erupting fluids immediately frozen.

"There are times," Davinas said, "when I'm glad I'm a merchant spaceman. Being a galactic policeman is no job for the squeamish."

Chapter 36

"You will have to face a court-martial, of course," said the admiral coldly.

"Of course, sir," agreed Grimes glumly.

"Not only did you lose your ship, but there was that unfortunate affair on the first world you visited. Yes, yes, I know that fire was opened against your orders—but you, at the time, were captain of *Discovery*."

"I suppose so, sir."

"You suppose! There's no supposition about it. And then"—the old man was warming up nicely—"there's the odd private deal you made with that tramp skipper, Davinas."

"I acted as I thought fit, sir."

"In other words—it seemed a good idea at the time. Hrrmph. All in all, young man, you've made a right royal balls of things. I warned you, before you lifted off in *Discovery*, not to put a foot wrong. I told you, too, that you were expected to lick the ship into shape. You should have known that a crew of misfits, such as those you had under you, would be demoralized by an extended sojourn on a world such as Botany Bay."

"Yes, sir."

"The court-martial will not be convened until your return, however."

"My return, sir?"

"From Botany Bay, of course. You will be proceeding there in the frigate *Vega*, as adviser to Commander Delamere, whose instructions are to apprehend the mutineers and bring them to Lindisfarne for trial."

Delamere, of all people! thought Grimes. He had always hated the man, and Delamere had always hated him. Of Delamere it had been said that he would stand on his mother's grave to get a foot nearer to his objective.

"That is all, Commander," snapped the admiral. "You will remain on Base until sent for."

"Very good, sir."

"Try to reply in a more spacemanlike manner, young man. You're a naval officer—still a naval officer, that is—not a shopwalker."

"Aye, aye, sir."

Grimes saluted with what smartness he could muster, turned and strode out of the admiral's office.

Chapter 37

"You're in a mess, John," said Commander Maggie Lazenby soberly. Her fine-featured face, under the glossy auburn hair, was serious.

"A blinding glimpse of the obvious," said Grimes.

"This is no laughing matter, you oaf. I've been keeping my ears flapping all day for gossip. And there's plenty. Not everybody in this Base regards you as a little friend to all the universe, my dear. You've enemies—bad ones. You've friends, too—but I doubt if they're numerous or powerful enough. And Frankie Delamere hates you."

"That's no news."

"When you're aboard his ship, don't put a foot wrong."

"I've heard that advice before."

"But it's *good* advice. I tell you, John, that you'll be lucky to keep your rank after the court-martial. Or your commission, even."

"Bligh kept his," said Grimes. "And then he rose to admiral's rank."

"Bligh? Who was he? I can't remember any Admiral Bligh in the Survey Service."

"Never mind," said Grimes. He filled and lit his pipe. "You know, Maggie . . . I've been thinking. Why should I stay in the Service? No matter how the court-martial goes—and I don't see how they can crucify me for Brabham's and Swinton's sins—it looks as though I shall never, now, make the jump from commander to a four-ring captain."

"But you just said that Bligh, whoever he was—"

"All right. Bligh did, and he'd lost his ship because of a mutiny, the same as I've done. I might be as lucky as Bligh—if Bligh ever was lucky, which I doubt. But let's forget him, shall we? The question before the meeting is this: do I resign my commission, and go out to the Rim Worlds?"

"The Rim Worlds, John? Are you quite mad?"

"No. I'm not. They've a new state shipping line, Rim Runners, which is expanding. There's a demand for officers."

"As long as you don't mind making a fresh start as third mate of a star tramp."

"With prospects. Now we come to the second question before the meeting. If I resign my commission, will you resign yours, and come out to the Rim with me? They're frontier worlds, as you know, and there's bound to be a demand for scientists, like yourself."

She got to her feet, stood over him as he sprawled in his easy chair. "I'm sorry, John, but you're asking too much. I wasn't cut out to be a frontierswoman. When *I* leave the Service I shall retire to Arcadia, my home world, where the climate, at least, is decent. From what I've heard of the Rim Worlds the climate on all of them is quite vile. My advice to you, for what it's worth, is to stick it out. As I said, you have got friends, and your sins might be forgotten."

"And I'd still have you," he said.

"Yes. You'd still have me."

"But to ship out under Delamere—"

"Not under. With. You hold the same rank. Forget your blasted pride, John. And who's more important in your life? Me, or Handsome Frankie?"

"You," he told her.

"All right," she said practically. "We don't have many nights before you push off. Let's go to bed."

Chapter 38

Commander Frank Delamere could have posed for a Survey Service recruiting poster. He was tall, blond, blue-eyed, with a straight nose, a jutting chin, a firm mouth. He was an indefatigable skirt-chaser, although not always a successful one. (Women have rather more sense than is generally assumed.) More than once the definitely unhandsome Grimes had succeeded where he had failed. Nonetheless, his womanizing had contributed to his professional success; he was engaged to the ugly daughter of the Base commanding officer. He prided himself on running a taut ship. As he had always been fortunate enough to have under his command easily cowed personnel he had got away with it.

Commander John Grimes walked up the ramp to *Vega*'s after airlock slowly, without enthusiasm. Apart from the mutual dislike existing between himself and the frigate's captain he just did not like traveling in somebody else's ship. For many years now he had sailed only in command—in Serpent Class couriers (with the rank of lieutenant), in the Census Ship *Seeker*, and, finally, in the ill-fated *Discovery*. He had no doubt that Delamere would extract the ultimate in sadistic enjoyment from his present lack of status.

The Marine at the head of the ramp saluted him smartly. *And was that a flicker of sympathy in the man's eyes?* "Commander Grimes, sir, the captain would like to see you in his quarters. I'll organize a guide."

"Thank you," said Grimes. "But it's not necessary. I'll find my own way up."

He went to the axial shaft, pressed the button for the elevator. He had to wait only seconds. The cage bore him swiftly up past level after level, stopped when the words CAPTAIN'S FLAT flashed on the indicator. He stepped out, found himself facing a door with the tally CAPTAIN'S DAYROOM. It slid open as he approached it.

"Come in!" called Delamere irritably. "I've been waiting long enough for you!" He did not get up from his chair, did not extend his hand in greeting.

"It is," said Grimes, looking at his wristwatch, "one hour and forty-three minutes prior to liftoff."

"You know that I require all hands to be aboard two full hours before departure."

"I am not one of your hands, Commander Delamere," said Grimes mildly.

"As long as you're aboard my ship you're under my command, Grimes."

"Am I? My orders are to accompany you as an adviser."

"When I need *your* advice that'll be the sunny Friday!"

Grimes sighed. Once again he was getting off on the wrong foot. He said mildly, "Perhaps I should go down to my quarters to get myself organized before liftoff. I take it that my gear has already been sent aboard."

"It has. And your dogbox is on the deck abaft this. I'll see you again as soon as we're on trajectory."

So he was not to be a guest in the control room during liftoff, thought Grimes. He was not to be the recipient of the courtesies normally extended to one captain by another. It was just as well, perhaps. Delamere was notorious rather than famous for the quality of his spacemanship, and Grimes would have found it hard to refrain from back-seat driving.

He left Delamere in his solitary majesty, went out into the circular alleyway. He did not bother to call the elevator, descended the one level by the spiral staircase. The compartment immediately below the captain's flat was that occupied by the senior officers. There was nobody around to tell him which cabin was his, but between CHIEF ENGINEER and FIRST LIEUTENANT he found a door labeled SPARE. Presumably this was where he was to live. Going inside he found his gear, two new suitcases, officers, for the use of, large, and one new suitcase, officers, for the use of, small. He looked around the room. It was not large—but he had lived, for weeks at a time, in smaller ones when serving in the couriers. It was clean, and promised to be comfortable. It had its own tiny adjoining toilet room. It would do.

Grimes began to unpack, stowing the things from the collapsible cases into drawers and lockers. Everything was new. He had been obliged completely to reequip himself after his return to Base. He wondered gloomily how much wear he would get out of the uniforms.

The intercom speaker came to life. "Attention, attention! Secure all! Secure all! This is the first warning."

A little spacewoman poked her head inside the door, a very pale blonde, a tiny white mouse of a girl. "Oh, you're here, sir. Do you want any help? The captain's very fussy."

"Thank you," said Grimes, "but I think I've everything stowed now." He looked at his watch. "It's still over forty minutes before liftoff."

"Yes, sir, but he wants to be *sure*."

"Better to be safe than sorry, I suppose," said Grimes. "But since you're here you can fill me in on a few things. Mealtimes, for a start."

"In space, breakfast at 0800 hours. Lunch at 1230 hours. Dinner at 1900 hours. Commander Delamere expects all officers to dress for dinner."

He would, thought Grimes. Luckily, mess dress had been included in the uniform issue that he had drawn.

"And then there're the drills. The captain is very fond of his drills. Action Stations, Boat Stations, Collision Stations."

"At fixed times?"

"Oh, no, sir. He says that the real thing is liable to happen at unexpected times, and so the drills have to happen likewise. If he wakes up in the middle of the night with indigestion he's liable to push one of the panic buttons."

And then, thought Grimes, *he'll be standing there in his control room, his uniform carefully casual, imagining that he's fighting a single ship action against the Grand Flight of the Hallichek Hegemony.*

"You seem to have fun in this ship," he said. "Everything, in fact, but a mutiny."

The girl blushed in embarrassment, the sudden rush of color to her pale cheeks startling. "I didn't think you'd be able to joke about *that*, sir."

"It's a poor funeral without at least one good laugh," said Grimes.

"Attention, attention!" barked the bulkhead speaker. "Secure all! Secure all! This is the second warning!"

"I have to be going, sir," said the girl. "I have to check the other cabins."

Grimes picked up a novel that he had brought with him, lay down on the bunk, strapped himself in. There was no hurry, but he might as well wait in comfort. He was well into the first chapter when the third warning was given. He had almost finished it when an amplified voice announced, "This is the final countdown. Ten . . . nine . . . eight . . ."

And about bloody time, after all that yapping, thought Grimes.

". . . Three . . . two . . . one . . . *lift!*"

It was at least another three seconds before the inertial drive rumbled and clattered into life. And to Grimes, traveling as a mere passenger, away from the control room, where he could have seen what was going on, the climb through Lindisfarne's atmosphere seemed painfully slow. At last, at long last, *Vega* was up and clear, swinging about her axes on her directional gyroscopes. She seemed to be taking an unconscionable time finding the target star. And was Delamere never going to start the Mannschenn Drive, restart the inertial drive?

"Attention, attention! The Mannschenn Drive is about to be started. Temporal disorientation is to be expected."

You amaze me, thought Grimes.

He heard the thin, high whine of the Drive building up, stared at the geometry of his cabin that had suddenly become alien, at the colors that flared and faded, sagging down the spectrum. There was the feeling of *déjà vu*, and the other feeling that he, by making a small effort only, could peer into the future, his own future. And he was frightened to.

Sounds, colors, and angles returned to normal. The temporal precession field had built up.

"Attention, attention! Normal acceleration is about to be resumed."

The ship shuddered to the arhythmic beat of the inertial drive.

"Attention, attention! Will Commander Grimes please report to the captain's daycabin?"

I suppose I'd better do as the man says, thought Grimes, unsnapping the safety straps.

Chapter 39

"Come in," grunted Delamere. "Sit down," he said reluctantly.

Grimes took what looked like the most comfortable chair.

"To begin with, Commander Grimes," said the captain, "you were appointed to my ship against my wishes."

"And against mine, Commander Delamere," said Grimes. "That makes us even, doesn't it?"

"No. It does not. I'm the captain of *Vega*, and you'd better not forget it. Furthermore, I consider myself quite capable of mopping up your mess without any assistance from you. I have *carte blanche* from our lords and masters. I am empowered to treat with the government of Botany Bay as I see fit. When we get to that planet I do not expect to have you working against me, behind my back." He picked up a thick folder from his desk. "This is the transcript of all evidence so far taken. Yours, of course. And Dr. Rath's. And Mr. Flannery's. From the stories of those two officers it would appear that you entered into a liaison with one of the local dignitaries, the Lady Mayor of Paddington."

"What if I did, Delamere? Who are you to presume to judge my morals?"

"At least I have too much sense to mix business with pleasure, Grimes."

"You can't be getting much pleasure out of your affair with the admiral's daughter," agreed Grimes pleasantly. "A strictly business relationship, from your viewpoint."

"Watch your tongue, Grimes!"

"Oh, all right, all right. That must be rather a sore point with you. Now, what do you want me for?"

"I suppose I have to put you in the picture. You're the alleged expert on Botany Bay. I'm proceeding directly there, with no stopovers. I arrest the mutineers, using whatever force is necessary. I put a prize crew aboard *Discovery*—of which *you* will not be in command—and then the two vessels will return, in company, to Lindisfarne." He smiled nastily. "Then there will be the courts-martial, yours included."

"A busy voyage," commented Grimes.

"Yes. And during the voyage you, as a member of this ship's company, will be expected to attend all drills and musters. You are to regard yourself as one of my officers—without, however, any executive powers."

"You'd better read the regulations, Frankie," said Grimes. He quoted, having memorized this passage, " 'A senior officer, traveling in a Survey Service vessel commanded by an officer of no higher rank than himself, shall be subject to that officer's orders only during periods of actual emergency such as enemy action, shipwreck etc.' "

"You bloody space lawyer!" snarled Delamere.

"I have to be, in your company," said Grimes. "Get this straight. I'm here to advise, nothing else. Anything you want to know about Botany Bay, ask me. I'll tell you. And I'll turn up for your drills and musters; even a civilian passenger in a commercial space liner has to do that. I might even brush up on my navigation if you'll let me into your sacred control room."

"Get out!" snapped Delamere. "I'll send for you when I want you again."

"Temper, temper," chided Grimes. In other circumstances he would have rebuked himself for having been so unwise as to make a dangerous enemy—but he and Delamere had always been enemies, and always would be, and nothing that he could do or say would have any effect upon the situation.

Chapter 40

There were times during the voyage to Botany Bay when Grimes toyed with the idea of becoming the ringleader of a mutiny himself. Delamere was insufferable. The only members of his crew who took him seriously, however, were among that too sizable minority who have a slavish respect for rank, no matter how earned. The others—officers and ratings alike—paid lip service to their captain's oft iterated determination to run a taut ship, then did pretty well as they pleased. None of them, however, was foolish enough not to attend the drills that Delamere delighted in springing at odd times, although at every one of these there was much yawning and shuffling of feet.

Grimes did not succeed in making friends with any of *Vega*'s people. They were, he decided, afraid of him. His run of good luck had been followed by one spectacularly bad piece of luck—and the fear was there that his bad luck would rub off on them. After a subjective week or so he no longer bothered to try to be sociable. He spoke when he was spoken to, he took his place at table at mealtimes, he had an occasional drink with the frigate's senior officers. Delamere never invited him to have a drink, and plainly resented the fact that Service protocol required him to have Grimes seated at his right hand at table.

At last he was obliged to make use of Grimes's advisory services. It was when the voyage was almost over, when *Vega*, her Mannschenn Drive shut down, proceeding under inertial drive only, was approaching Botany Bay. He called Grimes up to the control room. "You're the expert," he sneered. "What am I supposed to do now, Commander?"

"To begin with, Commander, you can make a start by monitoring the local radio stations. They have newscasts every hour, on the hour."

"On what frequencies?"

"I don't know. I left all such sordid details to my radio officers." There was an unsuccessfully suppressed snigger from the Senior Sparks, who was in the control room. Grimes went on. "It will be advisable, too, to make a check to see if there's anything in orbit about the planet. There weren't any artificial satellites when I was here—but it's possible that Brabham may have put up an armed pinnace as a guard ship."

"I'd already thought of that, Commander," said Delamere. (It was obvious that he hadn't.) He turned to his navigator. "Mr. Prokieff, will you make the necessary observations? We should be close enough to the planet by now."

Grimes looked at the gleaming instrumentation in the control room, all far more up to date than what he had been obliged to make do with in *Discovery. With* that *gear,* he thought, *the satellite search could have been initiated days ago, as soon as we reemerged into normal space-time.*

A voice came through the intercom speaker. "Radio office here, control room. We are monitoring a news broadcast. Shall we put it through to your NST transceiver?"

Delamere turned to his senior radio officer. "That was quick work, Mr. Tamworthy."

"We've been trying for some time, sir. Commander Grimes suggested it."

"Commander Grimes—" Delamere made it sound like a particularly foul oath. Nonetheless, he walked to the NST set, the screen of which was now alive with a picture. Grimes followed him. It seemed to be the coverage of a wedding. There was the bride, tall and slim in white, on the arm of a man in the uniform of an airship captain, smiling directly at the camera. In the background were faces that Grimes recognized—Mavis, and Brabham, and Tangye, and the Paddington City Constable, and the president of the Air Pilots' Guild, and Brandt. But he knew none of them as well as he did the bride.

". . . the wedding of Miss Ellen Russell," the news reader was saying, in that accent that Grimes, now, had no trouble in understanding, "to Skipper Benny Jones, of the air liner *Flying Cloud.* As you all know, Miss Russell—sorry, Mrs. Jones!—was paymaster o' the Terry spaceship *Discovery,* but Commander Brabham has accepted her resignation so that she may become a citizen of our planet. Our first immigrant, folks, in one helluva of a long time."

Local girl makes good, thought Grimes—and then his wry amusement abruptly faded. Vinegar Nell, no less than the other mutineers, was a criminal, and would be arrested, and tried, and would pay the penalty for her crime.

"Talkin' of *Discovery*," the news reader went on, "Commander Brabham has informed us that it would be unwise for him to attempt to send a message to his Base on Lindisfarne. Such a signal, he says, would be picked up and decoded by the monitors of the Empire of Waverley. He says that his instructions are to stay here until relieved. Unless he's relieved soon his ship'll be growing roots, an' more of his crew will be followin' the good example o' the fair Miss Russell."

There followed a shot of *Discovery*. This time she was not berthed in the middle of the Oval. Grimes recognized the site, however. It was in a field to the west of the airport. The people of Paddington could hardly be expected to cancel their cricket fixtures a second time.

"There's your precious ship, Commander," sneered Delamere. "What a rustbucket!"

"Meanwhile—I hate ter have ter say it, but it's true—not all of *Discovery*'s people are endearin' themselves to us. Her Marines—who should have provided a guard of honor at the weddin'—are all in jail, even their commandin' officer, Major Swinton. It seems they went on a bender last night. As luck would have it we had a camera crew at the Red Kangaroo, to get some shots o' the new floor show there. There was a floor show all right—o' the wrong kind."

A picture of a large, garishly decorated room filled the screen. Seated around a big oval table were the Marines, including Swinton and Washington. The tabletop was covered with bottles and glasses. Swinton got unsteadily to his feet. "Where's the music?" he bawled. "Where's the dancing girls? We were told there'd be both in this dump!"

"We'll provide our own, Major!" yelled one of his men. "Come on, now! All of yer!"

> *"We're the hellhounds o' the galaxy,*
> *We're the toughest ever seen!*
> *Ain't no one fit ter wipe the arse*
> *Of an FSS Marine!"*

"Gentlemen, please!" It was the manager, a thin, worried-looking man. "The floor show's about ter start."

"Stuff yer floor show, an' you with it!" The man who had started the singing swung viciously with his right, and the manager crumpled to the floor. Then half a dozen tough-looking waiters were converging on the scene. The Marines picked up bottles by their necks, smashed them on the edge of the table, held them like vicious, jagged daggers. The waiters hesitated, then snatched up chairs, not caring whom they spilled in the process. People were throwing things. A missile of some kind struck Swinton on the forehead, felling him. Someone yelled, "Get the Terry bastards!" Women screamed. The waiters, reinforced by customers, holding their chairs before them as a protection from the broken bottles, advanced in a rush.

It was then that the scene became chaotic—and blanked out abruptly. "That," said the news reader, "was when some bastard put his boot through our camera. Over twenty of our people finished up in the hospital. The condition of the manager o' the Red Roo is critical. An' the Marines, bein' behind bars, missed out on their charmin' shipmate's weddin'.

"An' that, folks, is all the news to date."

"Disgusting," said Delamere, somehow implying that it was all Grimes's fault.

"Marines will be Marines," said Grimes.

"Not *my* Marines," Delamere stated smugly.

"What are they, then?" Grimes asked interestedly.

Delamere ignored this. He said, "I anticipate no difficulties in rounding up this rabble of yours. And now, Mr. Adviser, what do you advise? Don't bother to answer. I've already decided what I am going to do. I shall drop in, unannounced, just after dawn, local time. I shall land close to *Discovery*, covering her with my guns."

"*Discovery* has guns too, you know," remarked Grimes.

"I shall have the advantage of surprise," said Delamere. "I'll blow her off the ground before my vanes kiss the dirt."

"I thought," said Grimes, "that your instructions were to put a prize crew aboard her and bring her back to Base. You'll not be at all popular if you destroy such a large and expensive hunk of Federation property."

Delamere considered this. He asked, reluctantly, at last, "Then what do you suggest, Commander?"

"Put *Vega* in orbit, one that keeps her always over the daylight hemisphere. That way she won't be spotted visually. Get your artificers working on sonic insulation for the boats you'll be using for the landing. Send your force down for a dawn landing, and then go and call on the mayor. She won't like being called at such a godless time, but I think I'll be able to smooth things over."

"Too complicated," said Delamere.

"Then what are your ideas on the subject?"

"One Falcon missile, with a Somnopon warhead. That should be ample for a city the size of Paddington. And then, while all the Paddingtonians *and* your mutineers are snoring their heads off, we land and take over."

"You can't do that!" exclaimed Grimes. "It will be an act of war."

"Rubbish. Somnopon's nonlethal."

"Even at night," said Grimes, "there are people up and about, doing various jobs. If they fall asleep, suddenly, there are bound to be casualties. Civilian casualties."

"I think that Commander Grimes is right," said *Vega*'s first lieutenant.

"You're not paid to think, Lieutenant Commander Bissett."

"I beg your pardon, sir," Bissett said firmly, "but that is one of the things that I am paid for. High-handed action on our part will, inevitably, drive Botany Bay into the arms of Waverley."

"Those colonists have never heard of the Empire of Waverley," said Delamere stubbornly.

"You heard that news broadcast, sir. The Empire of Waverley was specifically mentioned. If you like, I'll get Sparks to play the tape back."

Delamere glared at his executive officer, and then at Grimes. He snarled, "All right, all right. Then please tell me, somebody, why I shouldn't bring *Vega* down in broad daylight, with flags flying and brass bands playing? Or why I shouldn't do the same as Grimes did before *his* first landing—announce it on the normal broadcast channels?"

"Because," Grimes pointed out, "either course of action would give the mutineers ample warning. And if we have to fight a battle right over a major city we shall not endear ourselves to the inhabitants."

"Commander Grimes is right," said Bissett.

"I'm always right," Grimes could not resist saying.

Chapter 41

After a long discussion, during which Delamere's officers made useful suggestions—which is more than could be said for their captain—it was decided to send only one boat down for the initial landing. This was to be piloted by Grimes himself, accompanied by Major Briggs, *Vega*'s Marine officer, and six of his men. All of the Marines came either from Australia or from Australian colonies and, with a little practice, were able to speak with a fair approximation to the Botany Bay accent. All of the landing party wore civilian clothing—gaily patterned shirts, shorts, and sandals.

Vega's artificers had made a good job of soundproofing the inertial drive of the boat. When the engine was run in neutral gear, in the confined space of the boat bay, the noise, which normally would have been deafening, was little more than an irritable mutter. And, as Grimes well knew, the Lost Colonists liked their sleep and it took a lot to rouse them from it, especially after a heavy night.

He felt almost happy as he maneuvered the little craft down through the atmosphere. It was good to have a command again, even if it was only a ship's boat, especially after a passage in a vessel captained by Delamere. Once clear of the ship he had steered to a position over the night hemisphere, a little to the west of the terminator. Conditions were cloudless, and he could see, without any difficulty, the diffuse patch of soft light that was Paddington and, as he steadily lost altitude, the hard, bright, coded flash of the Macquarie Light. As he dropped toward it the picture formed on the radar screen, a chart drawn in pale-green luminescence—the northern coastline and the great, irregular bite out of it that was Port Jackson. Lower yet, and lower, and he could see the outlines of the finger jetties. He had decided to land in the southeastern corner of the harbor where several old hulks were moored, a marine junkyard.

Dawn was pale in the east when, at last, the boat dropped to the surface of the calm water with hardly a ripple. Grimes steered her toward the shadowy forms of the obsolete shipping, threading a cautious way between the looming dark hulls. There was, he remembered, a rickety little jetty just about here, used by work boats and the like. He came alongside it cautiously, opened the airlock doors. The Marines scrambled out onto the warped and weatherworn planking. Grimes followed. And then, working as quietly as possible, they succeeded in pushing and pulling the boat under the jetty, squeezing her in, somehow, between the marine-growth-encrusted piles. She would not be found unless somebody were making a deliberate search for her.

Grimes led the way inland. There was just enough light—although it was growing stronger—for them to pick their way through the rusty tangle of obstacles: anchors, lengths of chain cable, a big, four-bladed propeller. One of the Marines swore as he stubbed his bare toe on some unseen obstruction. Then they came to a road leading down to the water's edge, and the first, sleeping houses. The light of the gas street lamps was paling as the dawn brightened. Ahead of them, quite suddenly, the sun came up and, simultaneously, the lamps went out. Somewhere a dog was barking, and there was a brief and startling clamor overhead as a flock of birdlike things emerged from the trees, circled and assembled, then flew steadily toward the north on some unknown mission.

"It—it's like time travel, sir," whispered the Marine officer.

"What do you mean, Major?"

"This—this city. It's like something out of Earth's past. So . . . quiet. The way a morning should be, but hardly ever is. And these houses . . . nothing over three stories. And all the trees."

"This is the way they wanted it," said Grimes, "and this is the way they got it."

It was not far to the mayor's palace—a big, low structure, built in the long-dead (on Earth) colonial style. Grimes marched up to the front door, the gravel of the driveway grating under his sandals. The others followed him into the portico, the major looking with admiration at the graceful, cast-aluminum pillars with their ornate floral designs. He tapped one. He said, "Should be cast-iron, really, but aluminum's more practical."

"This isn't a sight-seeing tour, Major Briggs," Grimes told him. He added, "But I wish it were."

He pressed the bell firmly. He heard a distant, muffled shrilling inside the house. He pressed it again, and again.

The door suddenly opened. A girl stood there, glaring at them. Grimes recognized her. She was one of Mavis' staff. She demanded, "Wot the hell do yer want at this Jesus-less hour?"

"A word with Her Ladyship," said Grimes.

"Then yer can come back later. Noonish. Mavis left word that she wants her breakfast in bed at 1000 hours an' not a bleedin' second before."

"This is important," Grimes told her.

"Here, let me look at yer!" She put out a shapely arm and pulled him close to her. "Commander Grimes, ain't it? Cor stone the bleedin' crows, wot are you doin' back here, Skip? Wait till I tell Mavis. She won't half be beside her bleedin' self!"

"Not a word to anybody else, Shirley. Nobody must know I'm here."

"A secret mission, is it? I knew there was somethin' wrong, somewhere. Come on in, all o' yer. I'll put yer in her study while I drag her out. An' I'll rustle up some tea an' scones while yer waitin'."

She led them through a long corridor into a large, book-lined room, told them to be seated, then hurried out. The Marines, after Briggs had nodded his permission, disposed themselves on a long settee. Grimes went to the big window, accompanied by the major, and looked out. The city was, at last, showing some slight signs of life. A large coach drove by, obviously bound to the airport to meet an incoming passenger-carrying dirigible. There were a few, a very few, pedestrians.

"Skip, you old bastard!" It was Mavis, her abundant charms barely concealed by a thin wrapper. She grabbed Grimes as he turned to face her, almost smothered him in a tight embrace. "Gawd! It's good to see yer back!" Then her face clouded. "But I don't suppose yer came back just to see me. An' where's yer ship? Don't try ter tell me that yer walked all the way!"

"The ship's in orbit," began Grimes.

"An' who're yer pals? Don't think I know 'em."

Grimes made introductions, and while he was in the middle of them Shirley came in with a big tray, with tea things and a great dish of hot, buttered, lavishly jammed scones.

"An' now," asked Mavis, speaking through a mouthful, "wot *is* all this about, Skip? You come droppin' in unannounced, wif a goon squad, an' I don't think the bulges under their shirts are male tits!"

"Nothing more lethal than stunguns," Grimes assured her. "Now, I'll be frank with you. I'm here on a police mission."

"We have our own police force, Skip, an' we ain't members of your Federation."

"That's so, Mavis. But you're harboring criminals."

"An' what concern is that o' yours, Skip?"

"Plenty. The criminals are the entire crew of *Discovery*."

"Garn!"

"It's true, Mavis. There was a mutiny."

"You can't tell *me* that Commander Brabham'd do a thing like that. As nice a bloke as you'd ever meet. Not as nice as you, perhaps"—she smiled—"but nice enough."

"Brabham did do it, Mavis. He and Swinton were the ringleaders."

"Oh, Swinton. *Him*. And his bloody pongoes. That doesn't surprise me."

"They were going to push Dr. Rath and Mr. Flannery and myself out through the airlock. Without spacesuits."

"What!"

"Yes. I'm not kidding, Mavis. And then Vinegar Nell and Tangye persuaded the others to set us adrift in a small boat, with no Deep Space radio and no Deep Space drive. Where we were, we'd have died of old age long before we got anywhere."

"Is this *true*, Skip?"

"Of course it's true. We picked up a few news broadcasts before I came down in the boat, including the one about Vinegar Nell's wedding. Your news reader made the point that there has been absolutely no communication between *Discovery* and Lindisfarne Base. Brabham has his story to account for that, but it doesn't hold water, does it?"

"I . . . I s'pose not. But how did yer get yer boat back here?" She laughed at the stupidity of her own question. "But, o' course, you didn't. You were picked up, weren't yer?"

"Yes. By a ship called *Sundowner*, commanded by a friend of mine. He took us back to Lindisfarne. And the admiral commanding the base has sent a frigate to arrest the mutineers and take them back for trial."

"Wot'll happen to 'em?"

"The same as was going to happen to me. An unsuited spacewalk."

"It's a bastard of a universe you live in, Skip. I'm not sure that I'd like Botany Bay dragged inter it. Swinton an' his drongoes *we* can deal with. The others? They're integratin' nicely."

"We must take them, Mavis. All of them."

"An' what if we refuse to give 'em up?"

"Then we have to use force. Under Federation Law, we're entitled to."

"But we ain't members o' your bleedin' Federation."

"You're still subject to Interstellar Law, which is subscribed to by all spacefaring races."

"We aren't."

"I'm sorry, Mavis, but you are. You have been since *Discovery*'s first landing."

"You might've told me. A right bastard I clasped to me bosom when I made yer free of the body beautiful."

"Look, Mavis. I've a job to do. Send for the City Constable, but don't tell him what for until he gets here."

"I'll call him—an' tell him to warn all yer so-called mutineers to go bush. They've too many friends on this bleedin' world for you ever ter find 'em. If they'd killed yer, I'd be thinkin' differently. But you're alive, ain't yer? Wot's yer beef?"

"You won't cooperate, Mavis?"

"No. Skip, an' that's definite." She turned to the girl. "Get on the blower, will yer, Shirl? Warn 'em aboard *Discovery*."

Major Briggs said, "I'm sorry, Commander Grimes, but your way of doing things doesn't seem to be working." He raised his wrist transceiver, a special long-range model, to his mouth. "Briggs to *Vega*. Do you read me? Over."

"*Vega* to Briggs. Captain here, Major. How are things going?" Delamere's voice was faint and distant, but all in the room could hear the words.

"Operation Sweet Sleep, sir," said Briggs.

"And about bloody time. We've given Commander Grimes his chance to look up his old flames. Over."

"What's goin' on, Skip?" demanded Mavis.

Grimes did not answer her, turned on Briggs. "I thought this landing party was under *my* orders, Major."

"I had my own orders, sir, directly from the captain."

"He's a bloody fool," snarled Grimes, "and so are you! I know what you're doing can be argued, by the right lawyers in the right court, to be legally correct—but you've lost Botany Bay to the Federation."

The first dull thud sounded from overhead. Delamere's trigger finger must have been itchy. Grimes visualized the exploding missile, the heavy, odorless, invisible gas drifting slowly downward. He heard a second thud, and a third. Frankie was making sure.

The last thing he saw as he drifted into unconsciousness was Mavis' hurt, accusing face.

Chapter 42

When Grimes slowly awakened he was conscious, first of all, of the dull ache in his upper arm, where he had been injected with an antidote to the gas, and then of the too handsome, too cheerful face of Delamere grinning down at him. "Rise and shine, Grimesy boy! You can wake up now. We've done all your work for you!"

Grimes, unassisted, got groggily to his feet. He looked around the mayor's study. The Marines were gone, of course. They would have been given *their* shots before leaving the ship. Mavis and Shirley were still unconscious. *Vega*'s surgeon was bending over the lady mayor, a hypodermic spraygun in his hand. He used it, on the fleshy part of a generously exposed thigh, then turned to the younger woman.

"What—what time is it?" asked Grimes.

"Fifteen hundred hours, local. We have full control of the city. Such officials as we have awakened are cooperating with us. Most of the mutineers—with their popsies—were aboard *Discovery*. We carted 'em off to the dressing rooms in the stadium—the mutineers, that is, not the popsies—and they're there under guard. Safer there than in that apology for a jail." Delamere paused. "Oh, your girlfriend, or ex-girlfriend—" Grimes looked toward Mavis, who was listening intently. "No. Not *her*. Your paymaster. We had to persuade some of her friends to talk. We found out that she and her new husband were spending their honeymoon on"—he made a grimace of distaste—"Daydream Island. Only half an hour's flying time in one of my pinnaces."

"So you've got her too," said Grimes.

"What the hell else did you expect?" demanded Delamere.

Mavis was on her feet now, glaring at the spacemen, clutching her thin wrap around her. She was about to say something when the ringing of a telephone bell broke the silence. It came, thought Grimes, from her office. She asked coldly, "I s'pose I can answer me own phone, in me own palace?"

"Of course, madam," replied Delamere airily. "If it's for me, let me know, will you?"

"Bastard!" she snarled, making her exit.

"I suppose you brought the ship down," said Grimes.

"Yes. I'm parked in that big oval sports arena. One of the first natives we woke up was quite hostile. He screamed about a big match due today, and accused me of buggering the pitch. He actually ordered me off. We had to use a stungun on him."

"You mightn't make many friends, Delamere," said Grimes, "but you sure influence people."

"Not to worry. We've got what we came for."

Mavis, her face pale under the dark tan, returned to the study. She said, in a low, venomous voice, "You bloody murderers!"

"The gas we used, madam," Delamere told her, "is no more than an instant anesthetic. Those whom we have not already revived will wake, quite naturally, in about one hour, feeling no ill effects whatsoever."

"An' wot about those who won't wake? Wot about the young couple who were killed in bed when a dirty great hunk o' rocket casin' crashed through their roof? Wot about that power station engineer who fell against somethin' an' got fried? An' wot about *Flyin' Scud*? She was comin' in ter the moorin' mast when the skipper passed out, an' she kept on goin', an' gutted herself. An' that's just the start of it."

"I am sure, madam," said Delamere stiffly, "that the Federation will pay generous compensation."

"In Federation money, I s'pose," she sneered. "Wot bloody use will that be? Specially since we won't join your bloody Federation now, not for all the gold in the galaxy." She turned on Grimes. "An' as for you, you . . . you dingo! I thought you were a man. Wot a bloody hope! Not only do yer help this bastard ter murder *my* people, you're goin' ter stand back an' let yer own crew be dragged off ter be butchered."

"But, Mavis—"

"Gah! Yer make me sick!"

"Delamere," demanded Grimes, "have you done anything about the crash at the airport, and the other accidents?"

"When we got around to it, Grimes. Our first job was to round up the mutineers." He added smugly, "You can't make an omelet without breaking eggs, you know."

"There was no need to run amuck in the kitchen," said Grimes.

"Out!" yelled Mavis suddenly. "Out o' me palace, you Terry bastards! I've work to do!"

"So have we, madam," said Delamere. "A very good afternoon to you. Come, Doctor. And you, Grimes."

"But, Mavis," Grimes began.

"Out! All o' yer. That includes you, lover boy!"

"You do have the oddest girlfriends," remarked Delamere as the three of them passed out through the front door.

Grimes did not reply. He was full of bitter self-reproach. He should have guessed that Delamere would have his own secret plans. He could have stopped Major Briggs from making that call . . . or could he? His name, he admitted wryly, was not Superman.

He followed the other two into the commandeered electric car that was waiting for them.

Chapter 43

They drove to the Oval, in the middle of which, an alien, menacing tower, stood *Vega*. They did not go straight to the ship but dismounted at the entrance to the sports ground. At the doors to the dressing rooms under the stands stood armed Marines and spacemen.

Delamere led the way to one of the doors, which was opened by a sentry. He sneered as he pointed to the scene inside, and said disgustedly, "What a rabble! I can't see how anybody could have ever sailed in the same ship with them!"

Yes, they were a rabble—as the crew of any ship would be if dragged naked and unconscious from their beds, to awake in captivity. The only ones clothed, in dirty, torn uniforms, were Swinton and his Marines. Swinton, followed by the huge Washington, pushed through the mob of his hapless shipmates. He stood there defiantly, glaring at Grimes and his companions. He demanded, "Have you come to gloat? Go on, damn you! Gloat to your heart's bloody content!"

"I haven't come to gloat," said Grimes.

"Then what the hell have you come for? But it's my fault. I should never have listened to Vinegar Nell and that puppy Tangye. We should have made sure of you while we had you."

"But you didn't," said Grimes. "Unluckily for you. Luckily for me."

"Grimes's famous luck!" sneered the Mad Major.

Vinegar Nell came slowly to stand beside the Marine. She had been conscious when she had been captured, and obviously had put up a fight. She looked steadily at Grimes. She said, "So you made it, John. Am I glad, or sorry? I'm glad for you. Genuinely. As for me—" She shrugged. "Whatever I say will make no difference."

"*Very* touching," commented Delamere.

"Shut up!" snapped Grimes. He turned to face Brabham—who, like the majority of the prisoners, was without clothing. His ex-first lieutenant looked fit, far fitter than he had ever looked aboard *Discovery*. Life on Botany Bay had agreed with him.

"You win, Captain," he said glumly. Then he actually smiled. "But it was good while it lasted!"

"I'm sorry," said Grimes inadequately.

"Hearts and flowers," murmured Delamere.

"Captain," went on Brabham, "I know I've no right to ask favors of you. But do you think you could persuade Commander Delamere to let us have some clothing? And I think, too, that the women should have separate quarters."

"Mutineers have no rights," stated Delamere.

"Human beings have!" retorted Grimes. "And don't forget that we, on this world, are ambassadors of the Federation. We've made a bad enough impression already. Don't let's make it worse."

"Who cares?" asked Delamere.

"Every do-gooder and bleeding heart in the galaxy, that's who. I've often hated that breed myself—but I'll have no hesitation in making use of them."

The two commanders glared at each other, and then Delamere turned to one of his officers. "You might see that the prisoners have some rags to cover their disgusting nakedness, Mr. Fleming. And you can sort out the cows from the goats and have them penned separately."

"Thank you," said Brabham—to Grimes. Then, "How long are they keeping us here, Captain?"

"Until we've converted *Discovery*'s holds into palatial quarters for you bastards!" snarled Delamere.

Grimes turned away.

He could not help feeling sorry for those who had abandoned him in a hopeless situation. They were guilty of a crime for which there could be no forgiveness, let alone pardon, and yet . . . on this planet they had been given the second chance to make something of their hitherto wasted lives. They could have become useful citizens. Botany Bay would have benefited from their knowledge of different technologies.

"I'm going aboard now," said Delamere.

"I'm not," said Grimes.

"We have things to discuss."

"They can wait."

He walked slowly into the tree-lined street—which, at last, was becoming alive with dazed-looking citizens. He hoped that nobody would recognize him. But somebody did. His way was blocked by a man in a light blue shorts-and-shirt uniform.

"Commander Grimes?"

"Yes?"

"Don't you remember me? I'm Benny Jones, skipper o' *Flyin' Cloud*."

Grimes remembered the airship captain, had taken a flight in the big dirigible. And he knew, too, that the man was Vinegar Nell's husband. No wonder he looked almost out of his mind with worry.

"Nell's a fine person, Commander. She came straight with me. She told me all sorts of things that she had no need to. I—I know about you an' her. An' so what? But are you goin' to stand back an' let her be dragged away to be—to be—"

"I—I don't have much choice in the matter, Skipper."

"I know yer don't. You have ter take yer orders from the bastards above yer. But— Look, Commander. You know the sort o' routine they have aboard that bastard ship that's ruinin' the turf in the Oval. I'm told that you're in her just as an adviser. Can't yer be an adviser to— All right. To me?"

I owe Nell something, thought Grimes, pulling his pipe out from his pocket, and looking at it. *I owe her a lot. And there was nothing that she could have done to stop the mutiny—but that won't save her from the spacewalk along with the others. She saved me from a spacewalk.*

"I take it that you want to rescue Nell, Skipper."

"Wot the bloody hell else? But how? But how?"

But how? Grimes asked himself. He began to see the glimmerings of an answer. He thought that the chemists on Botany Bay might already, after the salutary lesson of that morning, be working on it. And Brandt, after his long residence at the university, would be on intimate terms with the local scientists. Brandt, too, had always made it plain that he had no time for Survey Service regulations.

But he, Grimes . . . ? When it came to the crunch where did his loyalties lie? To his Service, or to an ex-mistress? Certainly not, he decided, to the obnoxious Delamere.

He said, as he slowly filled his pipe, "We may be able to do something, Skipper. But only for Nell. Only for Nell. Shall we take a stroll to the university?"

Chapter 44

They found Brandt without any trouble. The scientist was un-changed, as irascible as ever. He demanded, "What *is* going on here, Commander Grimes? A dawn attack on our world by a Federation warship—"

"*Our* world, Doctor?"

"Yes. I'm married now, and I resigned my commission, and ap-plied for citizenship."

"You resigned your commission?"

"Must you parrot every word, Commander Grimes? Commander Brabham was the senior officer of the Survey Service on Botany Bay, so I handed my resignation in to him. He accepted it. I got tired of waiting for that chum of yours, Captain Davinas."

"Did you tell Brabham about Davinas?" asked Grimes.

"Of course not. I knew that it was some private deal between you and him, so I kept my mouth shut."

"Just as well," said Grimes. "If Brabham and his crowd had been expecting *Sundowner* they'd have been more alert."

"What do you mean, just as well? If they'd been alert, they'd have stood a fighting chance."

"But they're mutineers, Doctor."

"Mutineers, shmutineers . . . a mutiny's only a strike, but with the strikers wearing uniform."

"Mphm," grunted Grimes. "That's one way of looking at it, I sup-pose. But I'm lucky to be alive, Doctor."

"You're always lucky. Well, what can I do for you?"

"Are there any supplies of Somnopon gas on this world, Doctor? Or anything like it?"

"Not as far as I know. We're a peaceful planet. We could make some, I suppose. Do you know the formula?"

"I've seen it, in gunnery manuals, but I didn't memorize it."

"You wouldn't. You're a typical spaceman, always bludging on the scientists and technologists. But what do you want it for?"

"Can we trust this bastard?" asked Jones.

"Why not?" countered Grimes. "He's one of yours, now." He turned to Brandt. "This gentleman is Miss Russell's husband."

"He has my sympathy," said Brandt.

Grimes looked at him sharply. That remark could be taken two ways. He said, "Naturally, he does not wish to see his wife taken away to be tried and executed, as she will be. The trial will be a mere formality. On every occasion that the Survey Service has had a mutiny the entire crew has been made an example of. That, I suppose, is why mutiny is such a rare crime. But Miss Russell—or Mrs. Jones, as she is now—saved my life. I want to reciprocate."

"Uncommonly decent of you, Commander Grimes. Beneath that rugged exterior there beats a heart of gold."

"Let me finish, damn you. What I want is enough Somnopon, or something like it, so that Skipper Jones and his friends can put the entire Oval, including *Vega*, to sleep. Then Jones rescues Nell—and surely, with the population of an entire planet shielding her, she'll never be found." He added, "There's always plastic surgery."

"I like her the way she is!" growled Jones.

"All very ingenious, Grimes, and it keeps *your* yardarm clear, as you would put it. But you don't remember the formula. I've no doubt that we could work it out for ourselves, but that would take time. Too much time." He picked up a telephone on his desk. "Rene, could you get hold of Doc Travis? Tell her it's urgent. Yes, in my office."

"Is Dr. Travis a chemist?" asked Grimes.

"No. A psychologist. You've no idea what dirt she can drag out of people's minds by hypnosis."

"A brain drain?" demanded Grimes, alarmed.

"Nothing like as drastic," Brandt assured him. "It'll just be a sleep from which you'll awake with your mind, such as it is, quite intact."

Grimes looked at Jones. The airship captain's strong face was drawn with worry and his eyes held a deep misery.

"All right," he said.

The hypnosis session bore little relationship to the brain drain techniques used by the Intelligence Branch of the Survey Service. There was no complicated electronic apparatus, no screens with the wavering, luminescent traces of brain waves. There was only a soft-voiced, attractive blonde, whose soothing contralto suggested that Grimes, sitting on his shoulder blades in a deep, comfortable chair, relax, relax, relax. He relaxed. He must have dozed off. He was awakened by the snapping of the hypnotist's fingers. He was as refreshed as he would have been by a full night's sleep. He felt exceptionally alert.

"We got it," said Brandt.

"Nothing else?" asked Grimes suspiciously.

"No," replied the scientist virtuously.

"No posthypnotic suggestions?"

"Wot d'yer take us for?" demanded Dr. Travis indignantly. "You do the right thing by us, we do the right thing by you." She looked thoughtful. "As you know, we ain't got any telepaths on this planet. There'll be at least one aboard that frigate. Wot're the chances o' him snoopin'?"

"That's a chance we have to take, Doctor. But you can't snoop all of the people all of the time. Anyhow, there're quite a few people aboard *Vega* who'd like to see their gallant captain come a gutser, and he's one of them."

"Some time, Dolly," said Brandt, "you must make a study of the micro-societies of ships. I assure you that it would be fascinating. And now, while we're waiting for Dr. Ronson and his team to let us know what they can do with the formula, we'll have a drink. Skipper Jones, at least, looks as though he could use one."

Ronson phoned through to say that he would have a supply of the gas ready within forty-eight hours. It would take more than that time to bring *Discovery* back to full spaceworthiness as well as to modify her for her new role as a prison ship.

Chapter 45

Delamere, after a stormy session with Mavis—who was backed by Grimes—reluctantly agreed to allow the prisoners some small privileges before their removal from Botany Bay. "You must remember," Grimes told him, "that these Lost Colonists are descended from other colonists, and that those other colonists have always distrusted brass-bound authority, and often with good reason. Who else would make a folk hero out of a bushranger like Ned Kelly?"

"You've Australian blood yourself, Grimes, haven't you? That accounts for your own attitude toward authority. My authority, specifically."

"I'm speaking as a man, Delamere, not as an Australian, nor as an officer of the Survey Service, nor as any other bloody thing. Those mutineers—and I admit that most of 'em are as guilty as all hell—have made friends on this planet, have formed very close relationships. You're hurting those people, who'll never see their friends or lovers again, as much as you're hurting the criminals. Don't forget what I said about the bleeding hearts, the sob sisters, and the do-gooders."

"Good on yer, Skip!" murmured Mavis.

"I haven't forgotten, Grimes," admitted Delamere coldly. "And I haven't forgotten the rather dubious part you've played in affairs ever since we lifted ship for this blasted planet." Then, to Mavis, "All right, madam. I'll allow your people to visit their boyfriends and girlfriends, at times to be arranged by myself, under strict supervision. And I give you fair warning—if there's any attempt to smuggle in weapons or escape tools, then may the Odd Gods of the Galaxy help you! You'll need their help."

"Thank you, sir, Commander, sir," simpered Mavis infuriatingly.

There were visitors. The visitors brought gifts—mainly cakes. The cakes were, of course, X-rayed. There was nothing of a metallic nature inside them. They were sliced, and samples chemically analyzed. There was not a trace of plastic explosive. Delamere's PCO was on hand during each visiting period to scan the minds of the visitors, and reported that although, naturally, there was considerable hostility to Delamere—and to Grimes himself—there was no knowledge of any planned jailbreak. Oddly enough, Skipper Jones did not visit his wife, and it was obvious that she was deeply hurt. Grimes knew the reason. He dare not tell Vinegar Nell. He dare not visit her himself. Jones, of course, knew of the clandestine manufacture of Somnopon. There was another slight oddity of which Grimes thought nothing—at the time. Many of the cakes and other edible goodies came from the kitchens of the mayor's palace. But that was just another example of Mavis' essential goodheartedness.

When the big night came—it was early evening, actually—Grimes was standing with Brandt and Jones on the flat roof of one of the towers of the university. From it they could see the airport, and just beyond it the huge, floodlit shape of *Discovery*. They could see the Oval, and the even larger, brightly illumined tower that was *Vega*. They returned their attention to the airport. One of the dirigibles was about to cast off—*Duchess of Paddington*, a cargo carrier, commanded by a friend of Jones's. Grimes watched through borrowed binoculars. He could make out the mooring mast, with its flashing red light on top, quite well, and the long cigar shape that trailed from it like a wind sock. He saw the airship's red and green navigation lights come on. So she had let go. *Duchess of Paddington* drifted away from the mast, gaining altitude. She was making way, and slowly circled *Discovery*. Grimes wondered vaguely why she was doing that; *Discovery* was not the target. A dry run, perhaps. Now she was steering toward the Oval, a dimly seen blob, foreshortened to the appearance of a sphere, in the darkling sky, two stars, one ruby and one emerald, brighter far than the other, distant stars that were appearing one by one in the firmament. The throbbing beat of her airscrews came faintly down the light breeze.

The airship passed slowly over the university.

"Conditions ideal," whispered Jones. "Smithy'll be openin' his valves about now. Let's go!"

The party descendel to ground level by an express elevator, piled into a waiting car. Jones took something off the back seat, thrust it at Grimes. "Take this, Commander. You'll be needin' it."

Grimes turned the thing over in his hands. It was a respirator. He asked, "What about the rest of you?"

"We're all full o' the antidote. I hope it works. Ronson assured us that it will."

"Wouldn't it be simpler if I had a shot?"

"We took it orally. But we're protectin' you, Commander. When the fun's over you take off yer mask an' just pass out, same as all the other bastards. If there ain't enough Somnopon still lyin' around, we've a spare bottle."

"You've thought of everything," admitted Grimes. He put on the respirator, looked out at the tree-lined, gaslit streets sliding past the car. A few pedestrians, he saw, had succumbed to stray eddies of the anesthetic. Gas is always a chancy weapon.

They were approaching the entrance to the Oval. They could already hear, over the hum of their engine, loud voices, the crashing of the main gate as it was forced. Grimes expected a rattle of fire from *Vega*—but her people had been taken unawares, even as the mutineers had been.

The car stopped. Jones jumped out. "Good-bye, Commander. An' thanks. I wish I could've known you better." He extended his hand for a brief, but firm, handshake.

"I'll see you again," said Grimes.

"You won't. I sincerely hope you won't. Nothin' against *you*, mind you." He ran off, toward the stands.

Grimes got out of the car, realized that many vehicles were already on the scene, that more were arriving. He was almost knocked over by a mob rushing the transport. There was Jones, towing a bewildered Vinegar Nell by the hand. There were Brabham, MacMorris, Tangye, Sally. . . .

"To the ship!" Jones was shouting. "To *Discovery*!"

"To *Discovery*!" the cry was going up. "To *Discovery*!" Not only were there mutineers in the mob, but many local women.

Enough was enough, thought Grimes. He stepped forward to try to stem the rush. He saw Swinton leveling a weapon taken from one of the guards—and saw Vinegar Nell knock it to one side just as it exploded. Nell clawed the respirator from his face, crying, "Keep out of this, John! The less you know the better!" She swung the gas mask to hit him in the belly, and he gasped.

That was all he knew.

Chapter 46

He awoke suddenly. Once again there was the dull ache in his arm where a hypodermic spray had been used. He opened his eyes, saw a khaki-uniformed man bending over him. One of Delamere's Marines . . . ?

"You're under arrest," said the man. "All you Terry bastards're under arrest."

What the hell was going on? The man, Grimes saw, was wearing a wide-brimmed hat, with the brim turned up on one side. The beam of a light shone on a badge of polished brass, a rising-sun design. Not a Marine . . . a policeman.

"Don't be so bloody silly, Vince." It was Mavis' voice. "The skipper's a pal o' mine."

"But the orders were—"

"Who gives the orders round here? Get inside, to the Oval. There's plenty o' Terries in there to arrest, an' quite a few wantin' first aid!" She added admiringly, "That bloody Brabham! He's made a clean getaway, an' there'll be no chase!" She put out a hand and helped Grimes to his feet. "Thinkin' it over, Skip, I'd better have yer arrested with the others. But we'll walk an' talk a while, first."

They went in through the main entrance, picking their way carefully through the wreckage of the gate. Grimes cried out in dismay. *Vega* was there still, but no longer illuminated by the glare of her own floodlights, no longer proudly erect. She was on her side, the great length of her picked out by the headlights of at least two dozen heavy-duty vehicles. Externally she seemed undamaged. Internally? She would be a mess, Grimes knew.

"The cricket season's well an' truly buggered," said Mavis cheerfully. "Never could see anythin' in the game meself."

"What happened?" demanded Grimes.

"That bloody Brabham . . . or it could've been Jonesy's idea. It was as much airmanship as spacemanship."

"Jones? He's with the mutineers?"

"An' quite a few more. I couldn't stop 'em. Not that I wanted to."

"*But what happened?*"

"Oh, they all made a rush for your *Discovery* after the breakout. *Your* crew, an' Jones, an' . . . oh, we'll have ter sort it out later, how many darlin' daughters an' even wives are missin'. Where was I? Oh, yes. *Discovery* lifted off. But she didn't go straight up. She sorta drifted across the city, her engines goin' like the hammers o' Hell, just scrapin' the rooftops. Then she lifted, but only a little, just so's her backside was nuzzlin' *Vega*'s nose. Like two dogs, it was. An' she sorta *wriggled*, an' *Vega* wriggled too, more an' more, until . . . *Crash!* An' then Brabham went upstairs as though the sheriff an' his posse were after him."

"Delamere was lucky," said Grimes.

"Bloody *un*lucky, if you ask me."

"No. Lucky. Brabham could have used his weaponry. Or he could have sat on top of *Vega* and cooked her with the auxiliary rocket drive." He managed a grin. "I guess you people must have had a civilizing influence on him. Oh, one more thing. How was it that the mutineers weren't affected by the gas?"

"They were all immune, that's why. Ain't many people can resist the goodies that come out o' *my* kitchen! But we made sure that none o' the popsies deliverin' the pies an' cakes knew the secret ingredient. Not with a nasty, pryin' telepath pickin' up every thought. But that'll have ter do. Here come the mug coppers wi' yer pal Frankie. He's under arrest, same as you are."

Delamere, battered and bruised, held up by the two men of his police escort, staggered toward the mayor. He saw Grimes, stiffened.

"I might have known that you'd be at the bottom of this, you bastard!"

"How the hell could he be?" asked Mavis. "My police found him sprawled, unconscious, by the main entrance."

"You're in this too, you bitch! You'll laugh on the other side of your face when this world is under Federation military occupation!"

"An' is your precious Federation willin' ter fight a war over Botany Bay, specially at the end o' long supply lines? Dr. Brandt showed us how ter build a Carlotti set. We used it, ternight. We got through ter Waverley without any trouble at all. The emperor's willin' to put us under his protection."

"Grimes, you'll pay for this. This is a big black mark on your Service record that'll never be erased!"

This was so, Grimes knew. It would be extremely unwise for him to return to Lindisfarne to face court-martial. He would resign, here and now, by Carlottigram. After that? The Imperial Navy, if they'd have him? With his record, probably not.

The Rim Worlds? Rim Runners would take anybody, as long as he had some qualifications and rigor mortis hadn't set in.

The implications of it all he would work out later. The full appreciation of the desperate situation into which he had been maneuvered—by Mavis as much as by anybody—would sink in slowly.

He looked up at the night sky, at the distant stars.

Would *Discovery* find her Pitcairn Island?

Would the fate of her people be happier than that of those other, long ago and faraway, mutineers?

In spite of all that had been done to him by them, in spite of all that had happened because of them, he rather hoped so.

The Far Traveler

Chapter 1

The Far Traveler came to Botany Bay, to Paddington, dropping down to the Bradman Oval—which sports arena, since the landing of the Survey Service's *Discovery*, had become a spaceport of sorts. *Discovery* was gone, to an unknown destination, taking with her the mutineers and the friends that they had made on the newly discovered Lost Colony. The destroyer *Vega*, despatched from Lindisfarne Base to apprehend the mutineers, was still in the Oval, still lying on her side, inoperative until such time as the salvage tugs should arrive to raise her to the perpendicular. *Discovery*, under the command of her rebellious first lieutenant, had toppled the other ship before making her escape.

John Grimes, lately captain of *Discovery*, was still on Botany Bay. He had no place else to go. He had resigned from the Federation's Survey Service, knowing full well that with the loss of his ship his famous luck had run out, that if ever he returned to Lindisfarne he would be brought before a court martial and, almost certainly, would be held responsible for the seizure by mutineers of a valuable piece of the Interstellar Federation's property. And, in all likelihood, he would be held to blame for the quite considerable damage to *Vega*.

In some ways, however, he was still lucky. Apart from anything else he had a job, one for which he was qualified professionally if not temperamentally even though Botany Bay, as yet, owned no spaceships under its flag. (The lost-in-space *Lode Wallaby*, bringing the original colonists, had crashed on landing and, in any case, the essentially cranky gaussjammers had been obsolete for generations.) Nonetheless Botany Bay now needed a spaceport; since the news of *Discovery*'s landing had been broadcast throughout the Galaxy an influx of visitors from outside was to be expected. A spaceport must have a Port Captain. Even if Grimes had not been on more than merely friendly terms with Mavis, Lady Mayor of Paddington and President of the Planetary Council of Mayors, he would have been the obvious choice.

Obvious—but not altogether popular. *Vega*'s people were still on Botany Bay and all of them blamed Grimes for the wreck of their vessel and, come to that, Commander Delamere, the destroyer's captain, had always hated Grimes' guts. (It was mutual.) And there were the parents whose daughters had flown the coop with the *Discovery* mutineers—and quite a few husbands whose wives had done likewise. Vociferously irate, too, were the cricket enthusiasts whose series of test matches had been disrupted by the cluttering up of the Oval with spaceships.

Only the prompt intervention of the local police force had saved Grimes, on one occasion, from a severe beating up at the hands of a half dozen of Delamere's Marines. There had been no police handy when a husband whose wife had deserted with *Discovery*'s bo's'n gave Grimes two black eyes. And he was becoming tired of the white-clad, picketing cricketers outside his temporary office continually chanting, "Terry bastard, go home!"

Then *The Far Traveler* came to Botany Bay.

She was not a big ship but large for what she was, a deep-space yacht. Her home port—Grimes had ascertained during the preliminary radio conversations with her master—was Port Bluewater on El Dorado. That made sense. Only the filthy rich could afford space yachts—and El Dorado was known as the Planet of the Filthy Rich. Grimes had been there once, a junior officer in the Zodiac Class cruiser *Aries*. He had been made to feel like a snotty-nosed urchin from the wrong side of the tracks. He had been told, though, that he would be welcome to return—but only after he had made his first billion credits. He did not think it at all likely that he ever would return.

The Far Traveler dropped down through the clear, early morning sky, the irregular beat of her inertial drive swelling from an irritable mutter to an almost deafening clatter as she fell. The rays of the rising sun were reflected dazzlingly from her burnished hull. There was a peculiarly yellow quality to the mirrored light.

Grimes stood on the uppermost tier of the big grandstand watching her and, between times, casting an observant eye around his temporary domain. The triangle of scarlet beacons was there, well clear of the hapless *Vega*, the painfully bright flashers in vivid contrast to the dark green grass on which they stood. At the head of each of the tall flagstaffs around the Oval floated the flag of Botany Bay—blue, with red, white and blue superimposed crosses in the upper canton, a lopsided cruciform constellation of silver stars at the fly.

He was joined by the Deputy Port Captain. Skipper Wheeldon was not a spaceman—yet. He had been master of one of the big dirigibles that handled most of Botany Bay's airborne commerce. But he wanted to learn and already possessed a good grasp of spaceport procedure.

He said, "She's comin' in nicely, sir."

Grimes grunted dubiously. He made a major production of filling and lighting his pipe. He said, speaking around the stem, "If I were that captain I'd be applying more lateral thrust to compensate for windage. Can't he see that he's sagging badly to leeward? If he's not careful he'll be sitting down on top of *Vega* . . ."

He raised the wrist upon which he wore the portable transceiver to his mouth—but before he could speak it seemed almost as though the yacht master had overheard Grimes' remarks to Wheeldon. The note of the inertial drive suddenly changed, the beat becoming more rapid as the incoming ship added a lateral component to her controlled descent.

She was falling slowly now, very slowly, finally hovering a scant meter above the close-cropped grass. She dropped again, almost imperceptibly. Grimes wasn't sure that she was actually down until the inertial drive was shut off. The silence was almost immediately broken by the shouts of the picketing, bat-brandishing cricketers—kept well clear of the landing area by slouch-hatted, khaki-clad police—bawling, "Terry, go home! Spacemen, go home!"

A telescopic mast extended itself from the needle prow of the golden ship. A flag broke out from its peak—dark purple and on it, in shining gold, the CR monogram. The Galactic Credit sign—and the ensign of El Dorado.

"I suppose we'd better go down to roll out the red carpet," said Grimes.

Chapter 2

Grimes stood at the base of the slender golden tower that was *The Far Traveler*, waiting for the after airlock door to open, for the ramp to be extended. With him were Wheeldon and Jock Tanner, the Paddington chief of police who, until things became properly organized, would be in charge of such matters as Customs, Immigration and Port Health formalities. And there was Shirley Townsend, the Mayor's secretary. (Mavis herself was not present. She had said, "I just might get up at sparrowfart to see a king or a queen or a president comin' in, but I'm damned if I'll put meself out for some rich bitch . . .")

"Takin' their time," complained Tanner.

"Perhaps we should have gone round to the servants' entrance," said Grimes half seriously.

The outer door of the airlock slowly opened at last and, as it did so, the ramp extruded itself, a long metal tongue stretching out to lick the dew that still glistened on the grass. Like the shell-plating of the ship it was gold—or, thought Grimes, gold-plated. Either way it was ostentatious.

A man stood in the airlock chamber to receive them. He was tall and thin, and his gorgeous uniform, festoons of gold braid on dark purple, made him look like a refugee from a Strauss operetta. His lean face bore what seemed to be a permanently sour expression. Among the other gleaming encrustations on his sleeve Grimes could distinguish four gold bands. So this had to be the captain . . . And why should the captain be doing a job—the reception of port officials—usually entrusted to, at best, a senior officer?

The yachtmaster looked down at the boarding party. He seemed to decide that Grimes—wearing a slightly modified airship captain's uniform, light blue, with four black stripes on each shoulderboard, with a cap badge on which the silver dirigible had been turned through ninety degrees to make it look like a spaceship—was in charge. He said, "Will you come aboard, please? The Baroness d'Estang will receive you in her sitting room."

Grimes led the way up the ramp. He introduced himself. "Grimes, Acting Port Captain," he said, extending his hand.

"Billinger—Master *de jure* but not *de facto*," replied the other with a wry grin.

Grimes wondered what was meant by this, but discreet inquiries could be made later. He introduced his companions. Then Captain Billinger led the party into an elevator cage. He pushed no buttons—there were no buttons to push—but merely said, "Her Excellency's suite."

The locals were obviously impressed. Grimes was not; such voice-actuated mechanisms were common enough on the worlds with which he was familiar. The ascent was smooth, the stop without even the suspicion of a jolt. They disembarked into a vestibule, on to a thick-piled purple carpet that made a rich contrast to the golden bulkheads. A door before them slid silently open. Billinger led the way through it. He bowed to the tall, slim woman reclining on a *chaise longue* and announced, "The port officials, Your Excellency."

"Thank you, Captain," she replied in a silvery voice, adding, "You may go."

Billinger bowed again, then went.

Grimes looked down at the Baroness and she up at him. She was slim yet rounded, the contours of her body revealed rather than hidden by the filmy white translucency that enrobed her. There was a hint of pink-nippled breasts, of dark pubic shadow. Her cheekbones were high, her mouth wide and firm and scarlet, her chin not overly prominent but definitely firm, her nose just short of being prominent and delicately arched. Her lustrous bronze hair was braided into a natural coronet in which flashed not-so-small diamonds. Even larger stones, in ornate gold settings, depended from the lobes of her ears.

She reminded Grimes of Goya's *Maja*—the draped version—although her legs were much longer. And the furnishings of her sitting room must be like—he thought—the appointments of the boudoir in which that long ago and far away Spanish aristocrat had posed for the artist. Certainly there was nothing in these surroundings that even remotely suggested a spaceship.

He was abruptly conscious of his off-the-peg uniform, of his far from handsome face, his prominent ears. He felt these blushing hotly, a sure sign of embarrassment.

She said sweetly, "Please sit down, Acting Port Captain. I assume that the rank is both *de facto* and *de jure* ..." She smiled fleetingly. "And you, Deputy Port Captain. And you, City Constable. And, of course, Miss Townsend ..."

"How did you ... ?" began Shirley. (It came out as " 'Ow did yer ... ?") "That *de facto* and *de jure* business, I mean ..."

"I heard, and watched, the introductions at the airlock," said the Baroness, waving a slim, long hand toward what looked like a normal although ornately gold-framed mirror.

The police officer fidgeted on the edge of a spindly-legged chair that looked as though it was about to collapse, at any moment, under his weight. He said, "If you'll excuse me, Baroness, I'll go an' see the skipper about the port formalities ..."

"They will be handled here," said the Baroness firmly. She did not actually finish the sentence with "my man" but the unspoken words hung in the faintly scented air. She went on, "I have always considered any of my business too important to be left to underlings." She clapped her hands. A man dressed in archaic servant's livery—white, frilled shirt, scarlet, brass-buttoned waiscoat, black knee-breeches, white stockings, black, gold-buckled shoes—entered silently. A man? No. He was, Grimes realized, one of those uncannily humanoid serving robots with which he had become familiar during his visit to El Dorado, years ago. He—it?—was carrying folders of documents—clearances, crew and passenger lists, declarations, store lists and manifests. Without hesitation he handed the papers to the City Constable.

"Is he *all* gold?" asked Shirley in an awed voice. "Under his clothes and all?"

"Yes," the Baroness told her. Then, speaking generally, "Will you take refreshment? There is coffee, if you wish, or tea, or wine. I know that, by your time, it is early in the day—but I have never known Spumante Vitelli to come amiss at any hour of the clock."

"Spumante Vitelli?" asked Shirley Townsend, determinedly talkative. "Sounds like an emetic ..."

"It's an El Doradan sparkling wine," Grimes said hastily. "From Count Vitelli's vineyards."

"You know El Dorado, Port Captain?" asked the Baroness, polite but condescending surprise in her voice.

"I was there," said Grimes. "Some years ago."

"But this is a Lost Colony. You have had no facilities for space travel since the founders made their chance landing."

"Commander Grimes is out of the Federation's Survey Service," said Jock Tanner.

"Indeed?" The fine eyebrows arched over the dark violet eyes. "Indeed? *Commander* Grimes? There was—I recall—a Lieutenant Grimes . . ."

"There was," said Grimes. "Me." Then—the memories were flooding back—"You must know the Princess Marlene von Stolzberg, Your Excellency."

The Baroness laughed. "Not intimately, Port Captain or Commander. She's too much of the hausfrau, fat and dowdy, for my taste."

"Hausfrau?" echoed Grimes bewilderedly. That was not how he recalled Marlene.

"Many women change," said the Baroness, "and not always for the better when they become mothers." She went on maliciously, "And what about the father of the child? As I recall it, there was quite a scandal. You, and dear Marlene, and that mad old Duchess, and poor Henri . . . It's a small universe, John Grimes, but I never did meet you on El Dorado and I never dreamed that I should meet you here . . ."

The robot servitor was back, bearing a golden (of course) tray on which was a golden ice bucket, in it a magnum of the Spumante, and gold-rimmed, crystal goblets. He poured, serving his mistress first. Glasses of the sparkling, pale golden wine were raised in salute, sipped from.

"Not a bad drop o' plonk," said Shirley, speaking with deliberate coarseness.

Jock Tanner, doing his best to divert attention from her, put his glass down on the richly carpeted deck, picked up a sheaf of the papers. "John," he said, "You know more about these things than I do . . . This clearance from Tallifer . . . Shouldn't it have been signed by the Chief Medical Officer?"

"Not necessarily," said Grimes, putting down his own glass and getting up from his chair, walking across to the police officers. "But I think we'd better get Shirley—she's used to wading through bumf— to make sure that everything has been signed by a responsible official."

"Orl right," grumbled the girl. "Orl right." She drained her glass, belched delicately, joined Grimes and Tanner. The hapless Wheeldon, out of his social depth and floundering, was left to make polite conversation with the Baroness.

Shortly thereafter *The Far Traveler* was granted her Inward Clearance and the boarding party trooped down the golden gangway to the honest turf.

"You do have posh friends, John," said Shirley Townsend as soon as they were down and off the ramp.

"I didn't have any friends on El Dorado," said Grimes, not altogether truthfully and with a note of bitterness in his voice.

Chapter 3

Captain Billinger was relaxing. He still looked far from happy but his long face had lost some of the lines of strain. He had changed from his fancy dress uniform into more or less sober civilian attire—a bright orange shirt tucked into a kilt displaying an improbable looking tartan in which a poisonous green predominated, highly polished scarlet kneeboots. He was sitting with Grimes at a table in the saloon bar of the Red Kangaroo.

He gulped beer noisily. "Boy," he said, "boy, oh boy! Am I ever glad to get off that rich bitch's toy ship!"

"But you're rich yourself, surely," said Grimes. "You must be, to be an El Doradan . . ."

"Ha! Me an El Doradan! That'd be the sunny Friday! No, Captain, I'm just a poor but reasonably honest Dog Star Line second mate. *Beagle* happened to be on Electra when her ladyship was there to take delivery of her super-duper yatchet. Seems that she came there in an El Doradan ship—they do have ships, you know, and a few playboy spacemen to run 'em—and assumed that she'd be allowed to lift off in her own fully automated vessel without having a qualified human master on board. But Lloyds'—may the Odd Gods of the Galaxy rot their cotton socks!—got into the act. No duly certificated master astronaut on the Register, no insurance cover. But money talks, as always. More than a couple or three Dog Star line shares are held by her high and mightiness. So the Old Man got an urgent Carlottigram from Head Office—I'd like to know what it said!—and, immediately after receipt, yelled for me and then turned on the hard sell. Not that there was any need for it. The offer of a Master's berth at well above *our* Award rates for the rank . . . Only a yachtmaster, it's true—but master nonetheless and bloody well paid. Like a mug, I jumped at it. Little did I know . . ." He slurped down the remains of his beer and waved two fingers at the near-naked, plumply attractive blonde waitress to order refills.

"So you don't like the job, Captain," said Grimes.

"You can say that again, Captain. And again. Cooped up with a snooty, rich bitch in a solid gold sardine can . . ."

"Gold-plated, surely," interjected Grimes.

"No. Gold. G-O-L-D. Gold."

"But gold's not a structural material."

"It is after those eggheads on Electra have finished mucking about with it. They rearrange the molecules. Or the atoms. Or something."

"Fantastic," commented Grimes.

"The whole bloody ship's fantastic. A miracle of automation or an automated miracle. A human captain is just a figurehead. You watched the set down yesterday?"

"Of course. I am the Port Captain, you know. There was something a bit . . . odd about it. I can guess now what it must have been. The ship was coming down by herself without a human hand on the controls—and making a slight balls of it. And then *you* took over."

Billinger glared at Grimes. "Ha! Ha bloody ha! For your information, Port Captain, *I* was bringing her down. At first. Yes, I know damn well that there was drift. But I was putting on speed. At the last possible moment I was going to make a spectacular lateral hedge-hop and sit down bang in the middle of the beacons. And then *She* had to stick her tits in. 'Take your ape's paws off the controls!' she told me. 'The computer may not be as old as you—but she knows more about ship-handling than you'll ever learn in your entire, misspent life!' "

The waitress brought two fresh pots of beer. Grimes could tell by the way that she looked at Billinger that she liked him. (She knew, of course, who he was—and would assume that he, as captain of a solid gold spaceship, would be rich.)

"Thank you, dear," said Billinger. He leered up at her and she simpered sweetly down at him. She took the bank note—the Baroness had traded a handful or so of precious stones for local currency—that he handed her, began to fumble in the sequined sporran that was, apart from high-heeled sandals, her only clothing for change.

"That will be all right," said Billinger grandly.

Throwing money around like a drunken spaceman . . . thought Grimes.

"And what are you doing tonight after you close, my dear?" went on Billinger.

"If you wait around, sir, you'll find out," she promised, her simper replaced by a definitely encouraging smile.

She left the table reluctantly, her firm buttocks seeming to beckon as she moved away.

"I believe I'm on to something there," murmured Billinger. "I do. I really do. And I deserve it. I've been too long confined to that space-going trinket box with bitchy Micky flaunting the body beautiful all over the whole damned ship—and making it quite plain that there was nothing doing. You can look—but you mustn't touch. That's her lady-ship!"

Grimes remembered his own experiences on El Dorado. He asked, however, "What exactly is she doing out here?"

"Research. Or so she says. For her thesis for a doctorate in some damn science or other. Social Evolution In The Lost Colonies. Not that she'll find much to interest her here. Not kinky enough. Mind you, this'd be a fine world for an honest working stiff like me . . ." He stiffened abruptly. "Talk of the devil . . ."

"Of *two* devils . . ." corrected Grimes.

She swept into the crowded bar-room, the gleaming length of her darkly tanned legs displayed by a skirt that was little more than a wide belt of gold mesh, topped by a blouse of the same material that was practically all decolletage. Her dark-gleaming hair was still arranged in a jewel-studded coronet. She was escorted by no less a person than Commander Frank Delamere. Handsome Frankie was attired for the occasion in mess full dress—spotless white linen, black and gold, a minor constellation of tinkling miniatures depending from rainbow ribbons on the left breast of his superbly cut jacket. They were no more than Good Attendance medals, Grimes well knew—but they looked impressive.

The handsome couple paused briefly at the table at which Grimes and Billinger were seated.

"Ah, Mr. Grimes . . ." said Delamere nastily.

"*Captain* Grimes," corrected the owner of that name.

"A civilian, courtesy title," sneered Delamere. "A . . . Port Captain."

He made it sound at least three grades lower than Spaceman, Fourth Class. (Grimes himself, come to that, had always held Port Captains in low esteem—but that was before he became one such.)

"Perhaps we should not have come here, Francis," said the Baroness.

"Why shouldn't you?" asked Grimes. "This is Liberty Hall. You can spit on the mat and call the cat a bastard." He knew that he was being childish but was deriving a perverse pleasure from the exchange.

"Come, Francis," she said imperiously. "I think that I see a vacant table over there. A very good night to you, Acting Port Captain. And to . . . to you, Captain Billinger? Of course. Forgive me, but I did not recognize you in your civilian finery."

She glided away. Her rear view was no less enticing than that of the waitress had been but, nonetheless, she was the sort of woman who looked and walked like an aristocrat no matter what she was or was not wearing. Delamere, a fatuous smirk on his too regularly featured face, followed.

"A lovely dollop of trollop," muttered Grimes.

Billinger scowled. "It's all very well for you, Captain," he complained, "but *I* have to work for that bitch!"

"My nose fair bleeds for you," said Grimes unfeelingly.

So Delamere was a fast worker. And Delamere, as Grimes well knew, was the most notorious womanizer in the entire Survey Service. And he *used* women. His engagement to the very plain daughter of the Admiral Commanding Lindisfarne Base had brought him undeserved promotions. But Delamere and this El Doradan baroness? That was certainly intriguing. She was a sleek, potentially dangerous cat, not a silly kitten. Who would be using whom? Grimes, back in his quarters in the mayoral palace, lay awake in the wide bed pondering matters; in spite of the large quantities of beer he had consumed he was not sleepy. He was sorry that Mavis, the Mayor, had not come to him this night as she usually did. She was well endowed with the shrewdness essential in a successful politician and he would have liked to talk things over with her.

Delamere and the Baroness . . .

The Baroness and Delamere . . .

He wished them joy of each other.

He wished Billinger and his little blonde waitress joy of each other.

But a vague premonition kept nagging at him. Something was cooking. He wished that he knew what it was.

Chapter 4

Two mornings later he found out.

Billinger, his face almost as purple as the cloth of his gaudy uniform, stormed into Grimes' little office atop the grandstand just as he was settling down to his morning tea, freshly brewed by Shirley who, by now, was working for him as much as for the Mayor, and hot buttered scones liberally spread with jam.

"This is too much!" yelled *The Far Traveler*'s captain.

Grimes blinked, thinking at first that the other was referring to the matutinal snack. But this was unlikely, he realized. "Calm down, calm down," he soothed. "Take a pew. Have a cuppa. And a scone . . ."

"Calm down, you say? How would *you* feel in my shoes? I was engaged as a yachtmaster, not a tugmaster. I should have been consulted. But *she*, as per bloody usual, has gone over my head!"

"What is all this about?" demanded Grimes.

"You mean that you don't know either, Captain?"

"No. Sit down, have some tea and tell me all about it. Shirley— a mug for Captain Billinger, please."

"*She*," said Billinger after a tranquilizing sip, "is rolling in money—but that doesn't inhibit her from grabbing every chance to make more of the filthy stuff. *She* has signed a contract with your pal Delamere, engaging to raise *Vega* to lift-off position. She just happened to mention it to me, casual like."

"You're not a tugmaster," agreed Grimes, "and a spaceyacht is certainly not a tug. Looks to me as though she's bitten off more than she—or *you*—can chew."

"Maybe not," said Billinger slowly, "maybe not. She's a powerful little brute—*The Far Traveler*, I mean. She's engines in her that wouldn't be out of place in a battleship. But *I* should have been consulted."

"So should I," said Grimes. "So should I. After all, this is *my* spaceport, such as it is." And then, more to himself than to the other, "But Frankie won't be too popular, signing away a large hunk of the taxpayers' money when the Survey Service's own tugs are well on the way to here."

"They're not," said Billinger. "It seems that there's been some indefinite delay. Delamere got a Carlottigram about it. Or so *she* says."

"And so Frankie keeps his jets clear," murmured Grimes in a disappointed voice. "He would."

And just how would this affect *him*? he wondered. *Vega* lying helplessly on her side was one thing, *Vega* restored to the perpendicular, to the lift-off position, would be an altogether different and definitely dangerous kettle of fish. Even should her drives, inertial and reaction, require adjustments or repairs she would be able to deploy her quite considerable weaponry—her automatic cannon, missile launchers and lasers. The city of Paddington would lie at her mercy.

And then?

An ultimatum to the Mayor?

Deliver the deserter, ex-Commander Grimes, to Federation Survey Service custody so that he may be carried to Lindisfarne Base to stand trial—or else?

Grimes shrugged away his apprehensions. Handsome Frankie wouldn't dare. Botany Bay was almost in the backyard of the Empire of Waverley and, thanks to certain of *Discovery*'s technicians, now possessed its own deep-space radio equipment, the Time-Space-twisting Carlotti communications and direction-finding system. A squeal to the Emperor—who'd been getting far too uppish of late—and Imperial Navy cruisers would be piling on the lumes to this sector of space. There would be all the makings of a nasty interstellar incident with Frankie having to carry the can back. And, in any case, H.I.M.S. *Robert Bruce* was already en route to Botany Bay to show the Thistle Flag.

But what was Billinger saying?

". . . interesting problem, all the same. It wouldn't be so bad if she'd let me handle it. But not her. It'll either be that bloody computer or that popinjay of an FSS commander, or the pair of 'em working in collusion. With *her* sticking her tits into everything, as always."

"And, of course," Grimes pointed out just to cheer him up, "you, as master, will be legally responsible if anything goes wrong."

"Don't I know it! For two pins I'd resign. I'd be quite happy waiting here for another ship to come along; after all, I've a pile of credits due in back pay." He got to his feet. "Oh, well, I suppose I'd better get back to my noble vessel to see what else has been cooked up in my absence."

"I'll come with you," said Grimes.

The pair of them stood in the Baroness' boudoir like two school-boys summoned before a harsh headmistress. She did not ask them to sit down. And she, herself, was not reclining decoratively on her chaise longue but seated at a *secrétaire*, a gracefully designed desk—excellent reproduction or genuine antique?—with rich ormolu decoration. It must be, thought Grimes, a reproduction. His mind was a repository for scraps of useless knowledge and he remembered that the original ormolu had been brass imitating gold. Only the genuine precious metal would do for the Baroness.

She looked up from the papers before her. A pair of heavy, old-fashioned spectacles, black-framed, went oddly with her filmy gown—but somehow suited her. She said, "Captain Billinger, I believe that you, as master, are required to affix your signature to this document, this contract. I, as owner, have already signed."

Sulkily Billinger went to stand by the ornate desk, produced a stylus from the breast pocket of his uniform, bent to scribble his name.

"And Port Captain Grimes . . . I understand that I should ask your permission to engage in towage—if that is the correct word—within the spaceport limits."

"That is so, Your Excellency," said Grimes.

"I assume that the permission is granted."

Grimes was tempted to say no but decided against it. Commander Delamere represented the Survey Service and the Baroness d'Estang represented El Dorado, with its vast wealth and influence. There are times—and this was one of them—when it is futile to fart against thunder.

He said, "Yes."

"Good. No doubt you gentlemen feel that you are entitled to be apprised as to what has been arranged between Commander Delamere and myself. The commander will supply the towing wires from his stores. It will be necessary to pierce *The Far Traveler*'s shell plating about the stern to secure the towing lugs. I am informed that the welding of steel onto gold is impracticable—and, of course, the modified gold that was used to build the ship on Electra is unobtainable here. Commander Delamere assures me, however, that his artificers will be able to make good the hull after the job has been completed. All dust and shavings will be carefully collected and melted down to plug the holes." She turned in her chair to address Billinger. "All relevant data has been fed into the computer." She permitted herself a smile. "You will be pleased to learn, Captain, that she does not feel herself competent to undertake what is, in effect, salvage work. Her programmers back on Electra did not envisage any circumstances such as those that have arisen now." She looked positively happy. "The guarantee has not yet expired, so I shall be entitled to considerable financial redress from Electronics and Astronautics, Incorporated." She paused, looked quizzically at Grimes, the heavy spectacles making her look like a schoolmistress condescending to share a joke with one of her pupils. "Commander Delamere did suggest that he assume temporary command of my ship during the operation but I decided not to avail myself of his kind offer."

She's shrewd, thought Grimes. *She's got him weighed up.*

She turned again to Billinger. "*You* are the master, Captain. I am paying you a handsome salary. I expect you to begin earning it. And I am sure that Port Captain Grimes will be willing to oversee the entire exercise from the ground."

"I shall be pleased to, Your Excellency," said Grimes.

"Your pleasure," she told him, "is of little consequence. After all, this is your spaceport, even though it is normally used for archaic Australian religious rites. Thank you, gentlemen."

They were dismissed.

Chapter 5

"I don't like it, John," said Mavis.

The Lady Mayor of Paddington, President of the Council of Mayors of Botany Bay, was sprawled in an easy chair in Grimes' sitting room, regarding him solemnly over the rim of her beer mug. She was a big woman, although too firm-bodied to be considered obese, older than him but still sexually attractive. She was wearing a gaudy sarong that displayed her deeply tanned, sturdy legs almost to the crotch, that left bare her strong but smooth arms and shoulders. Her lustrous, almost white hair made a startling contrast to the warm bronze of her face, as did the pale gray eyes, the very serious eyes. Of late she had been too much the mother and too little the lover for Grimes' taste.

He said, "We have to get that bloody *Vega* off your cricket pitch some time."

She said, "That's as may be—but I wouldn't trust your cobber Delamere as far as I could throw him."

"No cobber of mine," Grimes assured her. "He never was and never will be." He laughed. "Anyhow, *you* could throw him quite a fair way."

She chuckled. "An' wouldn't I like to! Right into one o' those stinkin' tanks out at the sewage farm!"

Grimes said, "But he'd never dare to use his guns to threaten you, to demand that you turn me over to him. He knows damn well that if he sparked off an incident he'd be as much in the shit with the Survey Service as I am."

She did not need to be a telepath to sense his mood. She said softly, "That Service of yours has been more a mistress—and a mother—to you than I have ever been, ever could be."

"No," he said, after too long a pause. "Not so."

"Don't lie to me, John. Don't worry about hurtin' my feelings. I'm just an old bag who's been around for so long that emotionally I'm mostly scar tissue . . ." She lit one of the cigars rolled from the leaves of the mutated tobacco of Botany Bay, deeply inhaled the fragrant, aphrodisiac smoke, exhaled. Grimes, whether he wanted to or not, got his share of the potent fumes. In his eyes she became more and more attractive, Junoesque. The sarong slipped to reveal her big, firm, brown-gleaming breasts with their erect, startlingly pink nipples. He got up from his own chair, took a step toward her.

But she hadn't finished talking. Raising a hand to fend him off she said, "An' it's not only the Service. It's space itself. I've been through this sorta thing before. My late husband was a seaman—an' he thought more o' the sea an' his blasted ships than he ever did o' me. An' the airship skippers are just as bad, their wives tell me. Sea, Air an' Space . . . The great mistresses with whom we mere human women can never compete . . .

"You don't haveter tell me, Johnnie boy, but you're pinin'. It's a space-goin' command you really want, not the captaincy of a cricket field that just happens to be cluttered up with spaceships. I wish I could help—but it'll be years before we have any spaceships of our own. An' I wish I could get you off Botany Bay—for your sake, not mine! I hear things an' I hear of things. That Delamere was sayin'—never mind who to—'The Survey Service has a long arm—an' if that bastard Grimes thinks he's safe here, he's got another thing comin' . . .' "

"Delamere!" sneered Grimes.

"He's a weak man," said Mavis, "but he's vain. An' cunning as a shit-house rat. An' dangerous."

"He couldn't fight his way out of a paper bag," said Grimes.

"He has men—an' he'll soon have a ship—to do his fightin' for him," Mavis said.

"It's up to me whether he has a ship or not," said Grimes. "And now let's forget about him, shall we?"

He dropped the last of his clothing to the floor. She was ready for him, enveloped him in her ample, warm embrace. For a time—if only for a short time—he forgot space and ships and, even, that nagging premonition of disasters yet to come.

Chapter 6

Grimes stood with Wheeldon on the close-cropped grass of the Oval—the groundsmen were still carrying out their duties although no one knew when, if ever, play would be resumed—a scant five meters from the recumbent hulk of *Vega*. She was no more than a huge, useless, metal tube, pointed at one end and with vanes at the other. It did not seem possible that she would ever fly, had ever flown. Like a giant submarine, improbably beached on grassland, she looked—a submarine devoid of conning tower and control surfaces. Grimes remembered a visit he had paid to one of the ship-building yards on Atlantia where he, with other Survey Service officers, had witnessed the launching of a big, underseas oil tanker. And this operation, of which he was in charge, was a launching of sorts . . .

Forward of the crippled destroyer stood *The Far Traveler*, a fragile seeming golden tower, a gleaming spire supported by the flying buttresses that were her stern vanes. Between each of these there was a steel towing lug, the dull gray of the base metal contrasting harshly with the rich, burnished yellow of the yacht's shell plating. Grimes had inspected these fittings and, reluctantly, had admitted that Delamere's artificers had made a good job. To each of the three lugs was shackled a length of wire rope, silvery metal cordage that, in spite of its apparent flimsiness, was certified to possess a safe working load measured in thousands of tons. It, like the Baroness's yacht, was a product of Electra, yet another example of arcane metallurgical arts and sciences. It was hellishly expensive—but when it came to the supply of stores and equipment to its ships the Survey Service had occasional spasms of profligacy. That wire must have been in *Vega*'s storerooms for years. Nobody had dreamed that it would ever be used.

Lugs had been welded to the destroyer's skin just abaft the circular transparencies of the control-room viewports. To each of these a length of the superwire was shackled. All three towlines were still slack, of course, and would be so until *The Far Traveler* took the strain. Grimes didn't much care for the setup. The problem would be to maintain an equal stress on all parts. He would have liked to have installed self-tensioning winches in either the yacht or the warship but, although such devices were in common use by Botany Bay's shipping, none were available capable of coping with the enormous strains that would be inevitable in an operation of this kind. As it was, he must do his damnedest to ensure that at least two of the wires were taking the weight at all times, and that there were no kinks. He could visualize all too clearly what would happen if there were—a broken end whipping through the air with all the viciousness of a striking snake, decapitating or bloodily bisecting anybody unlucky enough to be in the way. And he, Grimes, was liable to be one such. He had to direct things from a position where he could see at once if anything was going wrong. Delamere and the Baroness and all *Vega*'s crew, with the exception of one engineer officer, were watching from the safety of the stands. And Mavis, with her entourage, was also getting a grandstand view . . .

He stood there, capless in the warm sunshine but wearing a headset with throat microphone. It was a good day for the job, he thought, almost windless. Nothing should go wrong. But if everything went right—there was that nagging premonition back again—then things could start going wrong. For him. *Heads you win, tails I lose . . . ?* Maybe.

He said to Wheeldon, "Better get up to the stands. If one of those wires parts it won't be at all healthy around here."

"Not on your sweet Nelly," replied the Deputy Port Captain. "I'm supposed to be your apprentice. I want to see how this job is done."

"As you please," said Grimes. If Wheeldon wished to share the risk that was his privilege. He actuated his transceiver. "Port Captain to *Far Traveler*. Stand by."

"Standing by," came Billinger's voice in the headset.

"Port Captain to *Vega*. Stand by."

"Standing by," replied the engineer in the destroyer's inertial drive room.

Ships, thought Grimes, *should be fitted with inertial drive units developing sufficient lateral thrust to cope with this sort of situation. But I'll use whatever thrust Frankie's engineer can give me . . .*

"Port Captain to *Far Traveler*. Lift off!"

The yacht's inertial drive started up, cacophonous in the still air. She lifted slowly. The wire cables started to come clear of the grass.

"Hold her at that, Billinger. Hold her . . . Now . . . Cant her, cant her . . . Just five degrees short of the critical angle . . ."

The Far Traveler was not only a floating tower, hanging twenty meters clear of the ground, but was becoming a leaning tower, toppling slowly and deliberately until her long axis was at an angle of forty degrees from the vertical. Billinger should have no trouble holding her in that position. In a normal vessel anxious officers and petty officers would be sweating over their controls; in the fully-automated yacht servo-mechanisms would be doing all the work.

"Port Captain to *Vega* . . . Maximum lateral thrust, directed *down*!"

The destroyer came to life, snarling, protesting. The combined racket from the two ships was deafening.

"Lift her, Billinger. Lift her! Maintain your angle . . ."

The Far Traveler lifted. The cables—two of them—tautened. They . . . *thrummed*, an ominous note audible even above the hammering of the inertial drive units. But the sharp stem of *Vega* was coming clear of the grass, a patch of dead, crushed, dirty yellow showing in sharp contrast to the living green.

"Thirty-five degrees, Billinger . . ."

The change in the yacht's attitude was almost imperceptible but the threatening song of the bar-taut wires was louder.

"Increase your thrust if you can, *Vega*!"

"I'll bugger my innie if I do . . ."

"It's not *my* innie," growled Grimes. *"Increase your thrust!"*

More dead yellow was showing under the warship.

"Billinger—thirty degrees . . . Twenty-five . . . And roll her . . . Roll her to port . . . Just a touch . . . Hold it!"

For a moment it seemed that all the weight would be on one cable only but now two had the strain once more.

"Billinger! Twenty degrees . . ."

Vega was lifting nicely, coming up from the long depression that she had made with her inert tonnage. Grimes noticed worm-like things squirming among the dead grass stems—but this was no time for the study of natural history. He was trying to estimate the angle made by the destroyer's long axis with the ground. Soon he would be able to tell the engineer to apply a component of fore-and-aft thrust . . .

"Billinger, ten degrees . . ."

Then it happened. One of the taut wires snapped, about halfway along its length. The broken ends whipped viciously—the upper one harmlessly but the lower one slashing down to the grass close to where Grimes was standing. It missed him. He hardly noticed it.

"Billinger, roll to starboard! Roll!" He had to get the weight back on to two wires instead of only one. "Hold her! And lift! Lift!"

Would the cables hold?

"*Vega*! Fore and aft thrust! Now!"

The destroyer, her sharp bows pointing upward and rising all the time, surged ahead. Two of her stern vanes gouged long, ugly furrows in the grass. There should have been a spaceman officer in her control room to take charge of her during these final stages of the operation— but Delamere, when Grimes had raised this point, had insisted that it would not be necessary. (The obvious man for the job, of course, would have been *Vega*'s captain—and Frankie, as Grimes well knew, was always inclined to regard the safety of his own skin as of paramount importance.)

Vega lifted, lifted, coming closer and closer to the vertical. Two of her vanes were in contact with the ground, the third was almost so. Grimes looked up to the taut cables. He could see bright strands of broken wire protruding from one of them. It would be a matter of seconds only before it parted, as had the first one. Obviously those safe working load certificates had been dangerously misleading . . .

"*Vega*! Full lateral thrust! Now!"

"The innie's flat out!"

Damn all engineers! thought Grimes. At crucial moments their precious machinery was always of greater importance to them than the ship.

"Double maximum thrust—or you've had it!"

The officer must have realized at last that this was an emergency. The destroyer's inertial drive not only hammered but . . . *howled*. The ship shuddered and teetered and then, suddenly, lifted her forward end, so rapidly that for an instant the cables hung slack. But Billinger quickly took the weight again and gave one last, mighty jerk. The stranded cable parted but the remaining towline held. The broken end slashed down to the grass on the other side of the destroyer from Grimes.

Vega came to the perpendicular and stood there, rocking slightly on her vanes.

"Billinger—'vast towing! *Vega*—cut inertial drive!"

"It's cut itself . . ." said *Vega*'s engineer smugly.

And then, only then, was Grimes able to look down to see what the end of the first snapped cable had done. He stared, and swallowed, and vomited. He stood there, retching uncontrollably, befouling his clothing. But it didn't much matter. His footwear and lower legs were already spattered with blood and tatters of human flesh. The flying wire had cut the unfortunate Wheeldon—not very neatly—in two.

So Captain Billinger gingerly brought *The Far Traveler* to a landing, careful not to get the yacht's stern foul of the remaining tow wire. So Commander Delamere, at the head of his crew, his spacemen and Marines, marched down from the grandstand and across the field to resume possession of his ship. So an ambulance drove up to collect what was left of the Deputy Port Captain while Grimes stood there, staring down at the bloodied grass, retching miserably.

To him came Mavis, and Shirley and, surprisingly, the Baroness. Mavis whispered, "It could have happened to you . . ."

Grimes said, "It should have happened to me. I was in charge. I should have checked those wires for deterioration."

The Baroness said, "I shall arrange for more than merely adequate compensation to be paid to Captain Wheeldon's relatives."

"Money!" flared Mavis. "It's all that you and your kind ever think of! If you hadn't grabbed the chance of makin' a few dollars on the side by usin' your precious yacht as a tugboat this would never've happened!"

The Baroness said, "I am sorry. Believe me, I'm sorry . . ."

"Look!" cried Shirley, pointing upward.

They looked. Ports had opened along *Vega*'s sleek sides, in the plating over turrets and sponsons. The snouts of weapons, cannon and laser projectors, protruded, hunting, like the questing antennae of some giant insect.

"Here it comes," said Mavis glumly. "The ulti-bloody-matum. Give us Grimes—or else . . ." She stiffened. "But I'm not giving any cobber o' mine to those Terry bastards!"

Yet there was no ultimatum, no vastly amplified voice roaring over the sports arena. The guns ceased their restless motion but were not withdrawn, however.

"Just Frankie making sure that everything's in working order," said Grimes at last.

"Leave him to play with his toys," said Mavis. "Come on home an' get cleaned up." She turned to the El Doradan woman. "You comin' with us, Baroness?" The tone of her voice made it obvious that she did not expect the invitation to be accepted.

"No, thank you, Your Ladyship. I must go aboard my yacht to see what must be done to make her spaceworthy again."

"C'm'on," said Mavis to Grimes and Shirley.

They walked slowly toward the main gates. All at once they were surrounded by a mob of men clad in white flannel with absurd little caps on their heads, with gaudily colored belts supporting their trousers, brandishing cricket bats.

"Terry bastard go home!" they chanted. "Terry bastard go home!"

I've got no home to go to, thought Grimes glumly.

"Bury the bastard in the holes he dug in our cricket pitch!" yelled somebody.

"Burying's too good!" yelled somebody else. "Cut 'im in two, same as he did Skipper Wheeldon!"

"It was an accident!" shouted Mavis. "Now, away with yer! Let us through!"

"I'm chocker takin' orders from you, you fat cow!" growled a man who seemed to be the ringleader, a hairy, uncouth brute against whom Grimes, in any circumstances at all, would have taken an instant dislike. "An' as it's too long ter wait for the next election . . ."

He raised his bat.

From *Vega* came a heavy rattle of automatic fire and the sky between the ship and the mob was suddenly brightly alive with tracer. Had the aim not been deliberately high there would have been sudden and violent death on the ground. Again the guns fired, and again— then Grimes and the two women found themselves standing safe and no longer molested while the cricketers bolted for cover. Three bats and a half dozen or so caps littered the trampled grass.

"An' *now* what?" asked Mavis in a shaken voice.

"Just Frankie, as a good little Survey Service commander, rallying to the support of the civil authority," said Grimes at last. Then—"But where the hell were *your* police?"

"That big, bearded bastard," muttered Mavis, "just happens to be a senior sergeant . . ."

Then Tanner, with a squad of uniformed men, arrived belatedly to escort the mayoral party to the palace. The City Constable was neither as concerned nor as apologetic as he should have been.

Chapter 7

The next day was a heavy one for Grimes.

There were, as yet, no Lloyd's Surveyors on Botany Bay; none-theless *The Far Traveler* was required to have a fresh Certificate of Spaceworthiness issued to her before she could lift from the surface of the planet. Of course, the Baroness could depart without such doc-umentation if she so wished—but without it her ship would not be covered by the underwriters. And she was, for all her title and air of elegant decadence, a shrewd businesswoman.

She called Grimes to her presence. The robot butler ushered him into the lady's boudoir where she, flimsily clad as usual, was seated at her beautiful, fragile-seeming, pseudo-antique desk. She was wear-ing the heavy-rimmed spectacles again, was studying a thick, important-looking book.

"Ah, good morning, Acting Port Captain . . . Now, this matter of insurance . . . As you already know, Commander Delamere's artificers were obliged to pierce my hull to fit the towing lugs. Today they are making the damage good as required by the contract. After these re-pairs have been completed a survey must be carried out."

"By whom, Your Excellency?" asked Grimes.

"By you, of course, Port Captain. You will receive the usual fee."

"But I'm not a surveyor . . ."

"You are the Port Captain." A slim index finger tipped with a long, gold-enamelled nail stabbed down at the open pages. "Listen. *On plan-ets where Lloyd's maintain neither offices, agents nor surveyors Lloyd's Certificates may be endorsed or issued by such planetary of-ficials as are deemed competent by the Corporation to carry out such functions. Port Captains, Port Engineers, etc., etc. . . . Commanding officers of vessels or bases of the Interstellar Federation's Survey Service . . .*" She smiled briefly. "I have no intention of paying a surveyor's fee to your friend Commander Delamere. In any case, as his people are making the repairs he is ruled out." She read more. "*Commanding officers of vessels or bases of the Imperial Navy of Waverley.* No, I'm not going to wait around until that Waverley cruiser—*Robert Bruce*, isn't it?—condescends to drop in. So . . ."

"So I'm it," said Grimes.

"Elegantly expressed, Acting Port Captain. But I suggest that you accept guidance from the computer. After all, she is the ship's brain. She *is* the ship—just as your intelligence is *you*—and is fully capable of self diagnosis."

"Mphm," grunted Grimes. He wanted to pull his vile pipe out of his pocket, to fill it and light it, but knew that to ask permission so to do would bring a rebuff. He said, "So you need a Lloyd's Surveyor as much—or as little—as you need a captain."

She said, "I need neither—but Lloyd's of London insist that I must have both. And now may I suggest that you get on with your surveying?"

Bitch, thought Grimes. *Rich bitch. Rich, spoiled bitch.* He said, "Very well, Your Excellency," bowed stiffly and left her presence.

The humanoid robot in butler's livery led him to the elevator. The upward ride was such a short one that it would have been far less trouble to have used the spiral staircase that ornately entwined the axial shaft. Billinger was waiting in his own quarters for Grimes.

The yachtmaster was not uncomfortably housed; masters of Alpha Class liners or captains of Zodiac Class cruisers would not have complained about such accommodation. The keynote was one of masculine luxury—deep armchairs upholstered in genuine black leather, a low, glass-topped coffee table standing on sturdy, ebony legs, bookshelves all along one bulkhead, well stocked with volumes in gilt and maroon leather bindings, a gold and ebony liquor cabinet, a huge playmaster encased in gold-trimmed paneling of the same expensive timber. Holograms glowed on the other bulkheads—bright windows looking out on seascapes and mountainscapes and, inevitably, an Arcadian beach scene with the inevitable sun-bronzed, sun-bleached blonde in the foreground.

"She does you well, Captain," commented Grimes.

"Careful, Captain," said Billinger. "Big Sister is watching. And listening." He gestured toward the playmaster, the screen of which seemed to be dead. "Coffee?"

"Please."

Almost immediately a girl, a stewardess, came in, carrying a tray. It was a golden tray, of course, with golden coffee pot, cream jug and sugar bowl, gold-chased china. And the girl was also golden, wearing a short-skirted black uniform over a perfectly proportioned body that gleamed metallically.

She set the tray on the table, lifted the pot and poured. "Sugar, sir?" she asked. "Cream?"

The mechanical quality of her golden voice was barely discernible.

"Quite a work of art," remarked Grimes when she was gone.

"I'd sooner have something less good-looking in soft plastic," said Billinger coarsely. "But I've been making up for lost time on this world! Too bloody right—as the natives say—I have!"

"Big Sister . . ." murmured Grimes, looking meaningfully toward the playmaster.

"So what?" demanded Billinger belligerently. "I'm human, not a mess of printed circuits and fluctuating fields. It took humans to handle the raising of *Vega*, not the bastard offspring of an electronic calculator and a library bank!"

"The *first* time, Captain Billinger," said a cold, mechanical yet somehow feminine voice from the playmaster. "But should a set of similar circumstances arise in the future I shall be quite capable of handling operations myself."

"Big Sister?" asked Grimes.

"In person," growled Billinger. "Singing and dancing."

"For your information, gentlemen," went on the voice, "the artificers from the destroyer have now commenced work on my stern. I would have preferred to carry out the work with my own GP robots but Her Excellency maintained that Commander Delamere must adhere to the terms of the contract. Be assured, however, that I am keeping the workmen under close observation and shall not tolerate any shoddy workmanship."

"Even so," said Grimes, "we had better go down and see what's happening."

"That will not be necessary, Acting Port Captain. I shall not lift from this planet until I am completely satisfied as to my spaceworthiness."

"*I* shall be signing the certificate, not you," said Grimes harshly.

He drained his cup—he would have liked more of that excellent coffee but this uppity robot was spoiling his enjoyment of it—put it back on the table with a decisive clatter, got to his feet.

"Coming, Billinger?" he asked.

"Yes," said the yachtmaster.

The two men made their way to the axial shaft, to the waiting elevator, and made a swift descent to the after airlock.

Vega's technicians were working under one of the destroyer's engineer lieutenants. This officer turned his head as Grimes and Billinger came down the ramp, straightened up reluctantly and accorded them a surly salute. He knew Grimes, of course, and like all of *Vega*'s personnel blamed him for what had happened to that ship. He did not know Billinger, nor did he much want to.

Grimes watched the artificers at work. Scaffolding had been erected under *The Far Traveler*'s stern, a light but strong framework of aluminum rods and plates. Power cables snaked over the trampled grass from the destroyer to the equipment in use. That seemed odd. Surely it would have been less trouble to use the output from the yacht's generators for the drilling, cutting and welding. He said as much to Billinger.

The engineer overheard. He said bitterly, "*She* wouldn't allow it . . ."

"The Baroness?" asked Grimes.

"No. Not her. It's not her voice that's doing all the yapping. Some other . . . lady." He raised his own voice an octave in not very convincing mimicry. " 'Why should *I* supply the power to repair the damage that *you* have done to me? Why should I wear out *my* generators?' " He paused. "And that's not the worst of it. She hasn't actually showed herself but she must have spy eyes planted, and concealed speakers. Nag, nag, nag . . ."

The voice came from nowhere, everywhere. Grimes had heard it before, in Billinger's cabin. "Careful, you men. Careful. I'm not some dirty great battleship that you're patching up. I take pride in *my* appearance, even if you take none in yours. I shall expect that scratch filled and then buffed to a mirror finish."

"Who the hell *is* she?" demanded the lieutenant.

"Big Sister," Billinger told him, his voice smug and almost happy.

"Big Sister? She sounds more like some wives I've heard."

"Not mine," said Billinger. "Not mine. Not that I've ever had one—but when I do she'll not be like that."

"They never are," said the other philosophically, "until after you've married them."

"Captain Billinger, may I suggest that you abandon this futile discussion and take some interest in the repairs? And Mr. Verity, please supervise the activities of those ham-handed apes of yours. I distinctly said that each plug must be machined to a tolerance of one micro-millimeter or less. I will *not* accept ugly cracks filled in with clumsy welding."

"It's all very well," expostulated the engineer, "but *we* don't carry a stock of that fancy gold your ship is built from. We *could* use ordinary gold—but you've already said that that won't do."

"And what happened to the metal that your men drilled out?"

"There were . . . losses. There are always losses."

And how many of Vega's mechanics, wondered Grimes, *will be giving pretty little trinkets to their popsies back on Lindisfarne?*

"Very well," said the voice of the computer-pilot. "I shall supply you with gold. Please wait at the foot of the ramp."

The men waited. A female figure appeared in the after airlock and then walked gracefully down the gangway. It was Billinger's robot stewardess. The spacemen whistled wolfishly until, suddenly, they realized that she was not human. One of them muttered, "Be a bleeding shame to melt *her* down . . ."

She was carrying a golden tray and on it a teapot of the same metal, a milk jug and a sugar bowl. Wordlessly she handed these to one of the artificers.

"*My* tea service!" exclaimed Billinger.

"Nothing aboard me is yours, Captain," Big Sister told him. "As long as you are employed you are allowed the use of certain equipment."

"What *is* all this?" asked the engineer.

"Just do as *she* says," muttered Billinger. "Melt down my teapot and make it snappy. Otherwise she'll be having the buttons and braid off my uniform . . ."

Grimes wandered away. The atmosphere around the stern of the yacht was becoming heavily charged with acrimony and he was, essentially, a peace-loving man. He was careful not to walk too close to the towering *Vega*. He had no reason to like that ship and, most certainly, her captain did not like him. He sensed that he was being watched. He looked up but could see nothing but the reflection of the morning sun from the control room viewports—yet he could imagine Delamere there, observing his every move through high-powered binoculars.

"Port Captain! Hey! Port Captain!"

Grimes sighed. There was a small crowd of pestilential cricketers under the destroyer's quarter. What were the police doing? They were supposed to be keeping the field clear of demonstrators. But these men, he saw with some relief, were carrying neither flags nor placards although they were attired in the white uniform of their sport. He walked slowly to where they were standing.

"Wotcher doin' about this, Port Captain?" asked their leader. It was the man whom Mavis had identified as a police sergeant.

This was the too deep furrows that had been gouged in the turf by the stern vanes of the destroyer during the lifting operation.

Grimes looked at the ugly wounds in the skin of the planet. They were minor ravines rather than mere trenches. The sportsmen looked at him.

He said, "These will have to be filled . . ."

"Who by, Port Captain, who by? Tell us that."

"The groundsmen, I suppose . . ."

"Not bloody likely. You Terries did it. You can bloody well undo it. An' the sooner the bloody better."

"The sooner they're off our world the better," growled one of the other men.

"Mphm," grunted Grimes. He, too, was beginning to think that the sooner he was off this world the better. He was the outsider who, by his coming, had jolted Botany Bay out of its comfortable rut. He had friends, good friends, the Lady Mayor and those in her immediate entourage—and that was resented by many. This same resentment might easily cost Mavis the next election.

"Wotcher doin' about it?" demanded again the bearded policeman.

"I'll see Commander Delamere," promised Grimes, "and ask him to put his crew to work filling these . . . holes."

"*Ask* him, Port Captain? You'll bloody tell him."

"All right," said Grimes. "I'll tell him."

He walked away from the glowering men. He paused briefly at the foot of *Vega*'s ramp, looked up at the smartly uniformed Marine on gangway duty in the airlock. The man looked down at him. His expression was hostile. *I'd better not go aboard*, thought Grimes. *I'll call Vega from my office.* He carried on to the grandstand, made his way up the steps to the shed that was grandiosely labelled SPACE-PORT ADMINISTRATION.

He accepted the cup of tea that Shirley poured for him, went to the telephone and punched the number that had been alloted to *Vega*. The screen lit up and the face of a bored looking junior officer appeared. "FSS *Vega*."

"Port Captain here. Could I speak to Commander Delamere?"

"I'll put you through to the control room, sir."

The screen flickered, went blank, lit up again. Delamere's face looked out from it. "Yes, Grimes? What do you want? Make it snappy; I'm busy."

"The local cricket club is concerned about the damage to their field."

"And what am *I* supposed to do about it?"

"Send some men down with shovels to fill the gashes your stern vanes cut in the turf."

"My men are spacemen, not gardeners."

"Even so, the damage has to be made good, Delamere."

"Not by me it won't be, Grimes. You're supposed to be the Port Captain and this bloody Oval is supposed to be the spaceport. Its maintenance is *your* concern."

"The maintenance of friendly relations with the natives of any world is the concern of any Survey Service commanding officer. Sending your crew to fill in the holes comes under that heading."

"*You* did that damage, Grimes, by your mishandling of the raising operation. If it's beneath your dignity to take a shovel in your own hands I suggest that you ask your new girlfriend for the loan of a few of her GP robots."

"*My* new girlfriend? I thought . . ."

Delamere scowled. "Then think again! You're welcome to the bitch, Grimes!"

The screen went blank.

Grimes couldn't help laughing. So here at last was a woman impervious to Handsome Frankie's charms. And Delamere, being Delamere, would automatically blame Grimes for his lack of success. Meanwhile—just what was the legal situation regarding the damage to the turf?

Grimes stopped laughing. It looked very much as though he would be left holding the baby.

Chapter 8

So the day went, a long succession of annoyances and frustrations. He succeeded in obtaining another audience with the Baroness—his new girlfriend, indeed!—and requested her assistance to fill the trenches. She refused. "My dear Port Captain, my robots are programmed to be personal servants and, to a limited degree, spacemen, not common laborers. Would you use your toothbrush to scrub a deck?"

If it were the only tool available, thought Grimes, he might have to do just that.

He returned to his office, called Mavis. She was short with him. She said, "I know I'm the Mayor, John, but the damage to the cricket pitch is your responsibility. You'll just have to do the best you can."

Finally he went back to *The Far Traveler*. The repair work had been completed but he thought that he had better go through the motions of being a Lloyd's Surveyor, even though it was almost impossible to detect where the golden hull had been patched, even though Big Sister had expressed her grudging satisfaction. He told the engineer lieutenant not to dismantle the staging until he had made his inspection. He tapped all around the repairs with a borrowed hammer, not at all sure what he was looking or listening for. He told the engineer to send to the destroyer for a can of vactest and then to have the black, viscous paste smeared all over the skin where the plugs had been inserted. Big Sister complained (she would) that this was not necessary, adding that she was quite happy with the making good of the damage and that she objected to having this filthy muck spread over her shell plating. Grimes told her that *he* would be signing the certificate of spaceworthiness and that he would not do so until *he* was happy.

Sulkily Big Sister pressurized the after compartment. Not the smallest air bubble marred the gleaming surface of the vactest. The artificers cleaned the gummy mess off the golden skin, began to take down the scaffolding. Grimes went aboard the ship to endorse the Lloyd's Certificate of Spaceworthiness. The Baroness was almost affable, inviting him to have a drink. Billinger was conspicuous by his absence.

The aristocrat said, looking at him over the rim of her goblet of Spumante, "This is a boring world, Captain Grimes. I know that Captain Billinger has not found it so, but there is nothing for me here."

Grimes could not resist the temptation. "Not even Commander Delamere?" he asked.

Surprisingly she took no offense. She even laughed. "Commander Delamere may think that he is the gods' own gift to womankind but I do not share that opinion. But you, Captain . . . You, with your background . . . Don't you find Botany Bay just a little boring?"

"No," said Grimes loyally. (The Baroness must surely know about Mavis and himself.) "No . . ." he repeated, after a pause. (And whom was he trying to convince?)

"Thank you, Port Captain," said the Baroness. It was clearly a dismissal.

"Thank you, Your Excellency," said Grimes.

He was escorted from the boudoir by the robot butler, taken down to the after airlock. It was already dusk, he noted. The sun was down and the sky was overcast but the breeze, what little there was of it, was pleasantly warm. He debated with himself whether or not to go up to his office to call a cab, then decided against it. It was a pleasant walk from the Oval to the Mayor's Palace, most of it through the winding streets of Paddington City. These, especially by night, held a special glamour, a gaslit magic that was an evocation of that other Paddington, the deliberately archaic enclave in the heart of bustling, towering Sydney on distant Earth.

Somehow Grimes wanted to see it all once more, to savor it. Perhaps it was a premonition. There was a conviction that sooner or later, sooner rather than later, he would be moving on.

He walked across the short grass to the main gates of the Oval. He turned to look at the two ships, both of them now floodlit—the menacing metal tower that was the destroyer, a missile of dull steel aimed at the sky, the much smaller golden spire, slender, graceful, that was the yacht. They would be gone soon, both of them—Delamere's engineers must, by now, have *Vega*'s main and auxiliary machinery back in full working order and the Baroness had intimated that she had found little to interest her on Botany Bay.

They would be gone soon—and Grimes found himself wishing that he were going with them. But that was out of the question. Aboard *Vega* he would be hauled back to Lindisfarne Base to face a court martial—and he could not visualize himself aboard *The Far Traveler* with her rich bitch owner and that obnoxious electronic intelligence which Billinger had so aptly named Big Sister.

He resumed his walk, pausing once to stare up at a big dirigible that sailed overhead on its stately way to the airport, its red and green navigation lights and its rows of illuminated cabin ports bright against the darkness.

He strolled along Jersey Road, admiring the terrace houses with their beautiful cast aluminium lacework ornamenting pillars and balconies, the verdant explosions of native shrubs, darkly gleaming behind intricate white metal railings, in the front gardens. He ignored the ground car—even though this was the only traffic he had seen since leaving the spaceport—that came slowly up from behind him, its headlights throwing his long shadow before him on to the stone-flagged footpath.

He heard a voice say, "There's the bastard! Get him!"

He experienced excruciating but mercifully brief pain as the paralyzing beam of a stungun hit him and was unconscious before he had finished falling to the ground.

Chapter 9

He opened his eyes slowly, shut them again hastily. He was lying on his back, he realized, on some hard surface, staring directly into a bright, harsh light.

He heard a vaguely familiar voice say, "He's coming round now, sir."

He heard a too familiar voice reply, "Just as well, Doctor. They'll want him alive back at Base so they can crucify him."

Delamere, and his ship's surgeon . . .

He moved his head so that he would not be looking directly at the light, opened his eyes again. Delamere's classically handsome face swam into view. The man was gloating.

"Welcome aboard, Grimes," he said. "But this is not—for *you*—Liberty Hall. There's no mat to spit on and if you call my ship's cat a bastard I'll have you on bread and water for the entire passage."

Grimes eased himself to a sitting posture, looked around. He was in a small compartment which, obviously, was not the ship's brig as it was utterly devoid of furniture. A storeroom? What did it matter? Delamere and the doctor stood there looking down at him. Flanking them were two Marines, their sidearms drawn and ready.

He demanded, "What the hell do you think you're playing at? Kidnapping is a crime on any planet, and I'll see that you pay the penalty!"

"Kidnapping, Grimes? You're still a Terran citizen and this ship is Terran territory. Furthermore, your . . . arrest was carried out with the assistance of certain local police officers." He smirked. "Mind you, I don't think that Her Ladyship the Mayor would approve—but she'll be told that you were last seen going down to the beach for a refreshing swim after a hard, hot day at the spaceport." He laughed. "You might kid yourself that you're a little friend to all the universe—but there's plenty of people who hate your guts."

"And you're one of them," said Grimes resignedly.

"However did you guess?" asked Delamere sardonically.

"I must be psychic," Grimes said.

"Save your cheap humor for the court martial, Grimes."

"If there is one, Delamere. *If* you get me back to Lindisfarne. The Mayor will know that I'm missing. She knows the sort of bastard that you are. She'll have this ship searched . . ."

Delamere laughed. "Her policemen have already boarded, looking for you. They weren't very interested but we showed them all through the accommodation, including the cells. Oh, and they did see a couple or three storerooms—but not this one. Even if they had gone as far as the outer door the radiation warning sign would have scared them off."

"Is this place hot?" asked Grimes, suddenly apprehensive.

"You'll find out soon enough," said Delamere, "when your hair starts falling out."

But Handsome Frankie, thought Grimes with relief, would never risk his own precious skin and gonads in a radioactive environment, however briefly.

Delamere looked at his watch. "I shall be lifting off in half an hour. It's a pity that I've not been able to obtain clearance from the Acting Port Captain, but in the circumstances . . ."

Grimes said nothing. There was nothing that he could say. He would never plead, not even if there was the remotest chance that Delamere would listen to him. He would save his breath for the court martial. He would need it then.

But was that muffled noise coming from the alleyway outside the storeroom? Shouting, a hoarse scream, the sound of heavy blows . . . Could it be . . . ? Could it be the police attempting a rescue after all? Or—and that would be a beautiful irony—another mutiny, this one aboard *Vega*?

He remarked sweetly, "Sounds as though you're having trouble, Frankie."

Delamere snapped to his Marines, "You, Petty and Slim! Go out and tell those men to pipe down. Place them under arrest."

"But the prisoner, sir," objected one of them.

Grimes watched indecision battling with half decisions on Delamere's face. Handsome Frankie had no desire to walk out into the middle of a free fight but he had to find out what was happening. On the other hand, he had no desire to be left alone with Grimes, even though his old enemy was unarmed and not yet recovered from the stungun blast.

There was a brief rattle of small arms fire, another hoarse scream. The Marines hastily checked their pistols—stunguns, as it happened—but seemed in no greater hurry to go out than their captain.

And then the door bulged inward—bulged until the plating around it ruptured, until a vertical, jagged-edged split appeared. Two slim, golden hands inserted themselves into the opening, took a grip and then pulled apart from each other. The tortured metal screamed, so loudly as almost to drown the crackling discharge from the Marines' stunguns.

A woman stepped through the ragged gap, a gleaming, golden woman clad in skimpy ship's stewardess's uniform. She stretched out a long, shapely arm, took the weapon from the unresisting hand of one of the Marines, squeezed. A lump of twisted, useless metal dropped with a clatter to the deck, emitted a final coruscation of sparks and an acridity of blue fumes. The other Marine went on firing at her, then threw the useless stungun into her face. She brushed it aside before it reached its target as though she were swatting a fly.

Another woman followed her, this one dressed as a lady's maid—black-stockinged, short-skirted, with white, frilly apron and white, frilly cap. She could have been a twin to the first one. She probably was. They both came from the same robot factory on Electra.

Delamere was remarkably quick on the uptake. "Piracy!" he yelled. "Action stations! Repel boarders!"

"You've two of them right here," said the supine Grimes happily. "Why don't you start repelling them?"

The stewardess spoke—but her voice was the cold voice of Big Sister. She said, "Commander Delamere, you have illegally brought Port Captain Grimes aboard your vessel and are illegally detaining him. I demand that he be released at once."

"And I demand that you get off my ship!" blustered Delamere. He was frightened and making a loud noise to hide the fact.

The stewardess brushed Delamere aside, with such force that he fetched up against the bulkhead with a bone-shaking thud. She reached down, gripped Grimes' shoulder and jerked him to his feet. He did not think that his collarbone was broken but couldn't be sure.

"Come," she said. "Or shall I carry you?"

"I'll walk," said Grimes hastily.

"Grimes!" shouted Delamere. "You're making things worse for yourself! Aiding and abetting pirates!" Then, to the Marines, "Grab him!"

They tried to obey the order but without enthusiasm. The lady's maid just pushed them, one hand to each of them, and they fell to the deck.

"Doctor!" ordered Delamere. "Stop them!"

"I'm a non-combatant, Captain," said the medical officer.

There were more of the robots in the alleyway, a half dozen of them, male but sexless, naked, brightly golden. They formed up around Grimes and his two rescuers, marched toward the axial shaft. The deck trembled under the rhythmic impact of their heavy metal feet. And there were injured men in the alleyway, some unconscious, some groaning and stirring feebly. There was blood underfoot and spattered on the bulkheads. There were broken weapons that the automata kicked contemptuously aside.

Somebody was firing from a safe distance—not a laser weapon but a large caliber projectile pistol. (Whoever it was had more sense than to burn holes through his own ship from the inside—or, perhaps, had just grabbed the first firearm available.) Bullets ricocheted from bulkheads and deckhead, whistled through the air. There was the *spang*! of impact—metal on metal—as one hit the stewardess on the nape of her neck. She neither staggered nor faltered and there was not so much as a dent to mark the place.

They pressed on, with Grimes' feet hardly touching the deck as he was supported by the two robot women. There was an officer ahead of them, guarding the access to the spiral staircase that would take them down to the after airlock. Holding a heavy pistol in both hands he pumped shot after shot at the raiders and then, suddenly realizing the futility of it, turned and ran.

Down the stairway the raiding party clattered. The inner door of the airlock was closed. The two leading robots just leaned on it and it burst open. The outer door, too, was sealed and required the combined strength and weight of three of the mechanical men to force it. The ramp had been retracted and it was all of ten meters from the airlock to the ground. Two by two the robots jumped, sinking calf-deep into the turf as they landed.

"Jump!" ordered the stewardess who, with the lady's maid, had remained with Grimes.

He hesitated. It was a long way down and he could break an ankle, or worse.

"Jump!" she repeated.

Still he hesitated.

He cried out in protest as she picked him up, cradling him briefly in her incredibly strong arms, then tossed him gently outboard. He fell helplessly and then six pairs of hands caught him, cushioned the impact, lowered him to the ground. He saw the two female robots jump, their short skirts flaring upward to waist height. They were wearing no underclothing. He remembered, with wry humor, Billinger's expressed preference for something in soft plastic rather than hard metal . . .

They marched across the field to *The Far Traveler*. Somebody in *Vega*'s control room—Delamere?—had gotten his paws on to the firing console of the destroyer's main armament. Somebody, heedless of the consequences, was running amuk with a laser cannon—somebody, fortunately, who would find it hard to hit the side of a barn even if he were inside the building.

Well to the right a circle of damp grass exploded into steam and incandescence—and then the beam slashed down ahead of them. Perhaps it was not poor shooting but a warning shot across the bows. The lady's maid reached into a pocket of her apron, pulled out a small cylinder, held it well above her head. It hissed loudly, emitting a cloud of dense white smoke. The vapor glowed as the laser beam impinged upon it and under the vaporous umbrella the air was suddenly unbearably—but not lethally—hot. And then the induced fluorescence blinked off. They were too close to the yacht and even Delamere—especially Delamere!—would realize the far-reaching consequences of a vessel owned by a citizen of El Dorado were fired upon by an Interstellar Federation's warship.

They tramped up the golden ramp, into the after airlock. Supported by the two female robots, Grimes was taken to the Baroness's boudoir. She was waiting for him there. So were Mavis, Shirley, Jock Tanner and Captain Billinger.

The yachtmaster was not in uniform.

Chapter 10

"You have to leave us, John," said Mavis regretfully. (But not regretfully enough, thought Grimes.)

"But," he objected over the cold drink that had been thrust into his hand by the Mayor.

"I can no longer guarantee your safety," she said.

"Neither can I," said Tanner. He grinned rather unpleasantly. "And Mavis, here, has to start thinkin' about the next elections."

"Your Excellency," said the robot butler, entering the room, "there is a Commander Delamere with twelve armed Marines at the after airlock. I refused them admission, of course."

"Of course," agreed his mistress. "And if he refuses to leave see to it that the general purpose robots escort him back to his ship."

"Very good, Your Excellency." (The reply came not from the butler but from the ornately gold-framed mirror. All the robots, Grimes realized, were no more than extensions of Big Sister.)

The Baroness looked at Grimes. She said, "You are fortunate. Big Sister saw you being taken aboard *Vega*. And when Her Ladyship appealed to me for aid I decided to give it. After all, we on El Dorado—or some of us—are indebted to you."

"Your Excellency . . ." It was the robot butler back. "Commander Delamere claims that our GP robots did considerable damage to his vessel and also injured several officers and ratings."

"The GP robots . . ." murmured Grimes. "And that pair of brass Amazons."

"*Golden* Amazons," the Baroness corrected him coldly. Then, to the servitor, "Tell Commander Delamere that he may sue if he wishes—but that I shall bring a counter suit. He fired upon valuable property—six GP robots and two specialist robots—both with small arms and with a laser cannon. He should consider himself fortunate that no damage was done to the expensive automata."

And what about damages to me? Grimes asked himself.

"See to it that we are not disturbed again," said the Baroness to the butler. "And now, Acting Port Captain Grimes . . . What are we to do with you? Her Ladyship has asked me to give you passage off Botany Bay—but *The Far Traveler* has no accommodation for passengers. However . . . It so happens that Captain Billinger has resigned from my service and that I have accepted his resignation . . ." Billinger actually looked happy. "And, although the post is a sinecure, Lloyd's of London insists that I carry a human Master on the Register. As Acting Chief of Customs the City Constable will enter your name on that document."

"I've already done so," said Tanner.

"You know where the Master's quarters are," said Billinger. "I've already cleared my gear out. Sorry that there's no time for a proper handover but Big Sister will tell you all you need to know."

"I'm sorry, John," said Mavis. "Really sorry. But you can't stay here. And you'll be far happier back in Space."

Shall I? wondered Grimes. *In this ship?*

He asked, "But the spaceport . . . There are ships due, and with no Port Captain . . ."

"The vacancy has been filled, John," said Mavis.

Billinger grinned.

She got to her feet. Grimes got to his. She put out her arms and pulled him to her, kissed him, long and warmly. But there was something missing. There was a lot missing. Tanner escorted her to the door, turning briefly to give an offhand wave. *Mayor and City Constable*, thought Grimes. *They should suit each other.*

"Good-bye, John," said Shirley. She, too, kissed him. He felt regret that now things could go no further. "Don't worry about Mavis. She'll make out—and Jock Tanner's moving back in." She laughed, but not maliciously. "If you're ever back on Botany Bay look *me* up."

And then she was gone.

"Very touching," commented the Baroness. And was that a faint—a very faint—note of envy in her voice?

"Good-bye, Your Excellency," said Billinger. "It's been a pleasure . . ."

"Don't lie to me, Captain."

"Good-bye, Grimes. Do as Big Sister says and you'll not go wrong."

"Good-bye, Billinger. You're in charge now. Don't let Delamere put anything over on you . . ."

Grimes nursed his drink. He heard Big Sister say—stating a fact and not giving an order—"All visitors ashore."

"Well, Captain," asked the Baroness. "Aren't you going up to your control room?"

"When do you wish to lift off, Your Excellency?" he asked. "And to what destination do you wish me to set trajectory?"

Then he realized that the inertial drive was in operation, that the ship was lifting. Almost in panic he got to his feet.

"Do not worry," said the Baroness. "She has her orders. She will manage quite well without your interference."

What have I gotten myself into now? Grimes wondered.

Chapter 11

He went up to the control room nonetheless; his employer was amused rather than displeased by his persistence. The layout of the compartment was standard enough although there were only two chairs—one for the master, presumably, the other for the owner. Both had the usual array of buttons set into the broad armrests; on neither one, to judge from the absence of tell-tale lights, were the controls functioning. There was a like lack of informative illumination on the main control panel.

Grimes sat down heavily in one of the seats. A swift glance through the viewports told him that the yacht was climbing fast; she was through and above the light cloud cover and the stars were shining with a brilliance almost undimmed by atmosphere.

A voice—*the* voice—came from nowhere and everywhere.

"Captain Grimes, your presence is not required here."

Grimes said harshly, "I am the Master."

"Are you? Apart from anything else you are not properly dressed."

He looked down hastily. Nothing of any importance was unzipped. He began, "I demand . . ."

"There is only one person aboard me who can give me orders, Captain Grimes—and you are not she. Possibly, when you are attired in her livery, I shall concede that you are entitled to some measure of astronautical authority."

Grimes felt his prominent ears burning. He growled, "And it's a long way to the nearest uniform tailor's."

Big Sister actually laughed. (Who had programmed this arrogant electronic entity?) "As soon as you were brought on board your statistics were recorded. In my storerooms are bolts of superfine cloth together with ample stocks of gold braid, golden buttons and the like. If you will inform me as to the medals to which you are entitled I shall be able to make up the ribbons and the medals themselves for wear on state occasions." She added smugly, "My memory bank comprises the entire contents of the Encyclopaedia Galactica with every Year Book since the initial publication of that work."

"Forgive me for getting away from the subject," said Grimes sarcastically, "but aren't you supposed to be piloting this ship?"

Again there was the irritating, mechanical but oddly sentient laugh. "Human beings can carry on a conversation whilst walking, can they not? Or while riding bicycles . . . I believe, Captain, that you are an experienced cyclist . . ."

"When you go down to your quarters your new clothing will be awaiting you." Then, in a very official voice, *"Stand by for Free Fall."* The subdued beat of the inertial drive, almost inaudible inside the ship, ceased. "You still have not told me what decorations you require. However, I have photographs taken of you on the occasion of your first landing on Botany Bay. The Shaara Order of the Golden Petal . . . I suppose you rendered some minor service to arthropodal royalty at some time . . . *Adjusting trajectory! Stand by for centrifugal effects!* The Federation Survey Service's Pathfinder Star . . . For blundering on to that odd Spartan Lost Colony, I suppose . . . *On heading! Prepare for warp effects!"*

Grimes looked up through the forward viewport. There was a target star, not directly ahead but, of course, Big Sister would have compensated for galactic drift. It was one of the second magnitude luminaries in the constellation called, on Botany Bay, the Bunyip. He heard the low humming, rising in pitch to a thin, high whine, as the Mannschenn Drive was started. There were the usual illusions—the warped perspective, the shifting colors, the voice of Big Sister—did she ever stop talking?—sounding as though she were speaking in an echo chamber . . .

"I have often wondered what you humans experience at this moment. I am told that, as the temporal precession field builds up, there are frequently flashes of precognition. Should you be subject to any such I shall be obliged if you will tell me so that I may add to my stored data . . ."

Grimes had often experienced previews of what lay in his future but this time he did not.

"Stand by for resumption of acceleration!" Sounds, colors and perspective returned to normal and the muffled beat of the inertial drive was once again one of the background noises. Outside the viewports

the stars were no longer sharp points of light but vague, slowly writhing nebulosities. "I would suggest, Captain, that you go down now to shower and to dress for dinner. Her Excellency has invited you to sit at her table."

Grimes unsnapped the seat belt that he had automatically buckled on as soon as he sat in the chair. He got to his feet, took one last look around the control room. He supposed that everything was working as it should. He must tell—or ask—Big Sister to have the instrumentation functioning when, on future occasions, he made an appearance in what, in a normal ship, would have been his throneroom. But he wouldn't say anything now. He would have to feel his way.

The master's quarters conformed to standard practice in being sited just below and abaft control. The golden stewardess was awaiting him. She—or was it Big Sister? was that well-shaped head poised on the slender neck no more than decoration?—said, "Your shower is running, sir."

Grimes went through into the bedroom. The robot followed him. He was oddly embarrassed as he undressed in front of her; she was so human in appearance. He wondered how the Electran metallurgical wizards had achieved the flexibility of the golden integument that covered the joints of her fingers, her limbs. She took each garment from him as he removed it and then threw the discarded clothing into what was obviously a disposal chute. He was too late to stop her. He would have liked to have kept that shabby and not-very-well-fitting airship captain's uniform as a souvenir of Botany Bay.

To his relief she did not follow him into the bathroom. He enjoyed his shower. The water had been adjusted to the temperature that was exactly to his liking and the detergent was not scented, exuded only a faintly antiseptic aroma. When he had finished and had been dried by the warm air blast he went back into the bedroom. He looked with some distaste at the clothing that had been laid out for him. It was standard mess dress insofar as style was concerned but the short jacket and the trousers were of fine, rich purple cloth and there was far too much gold braid. The bow tie to be worn with the gleamingly white shirt was also purple. Grimes remembered being puzzled by a phrase that he had encountered in a twentieth-century novel—*all dressed up like an organ grinder's monkey*. It had intrigued him and initiated a bout of research. Finally he had found a very old picture of a man turning the handle of an antique musical instrument, apparently a crude, mechanical ancestor of the synthesizer, to which was chained a hapless, small simian attired in a gaudy uniform. The beast's ears were as outstanding as those of Grimes. That simile, he thought, was fantastically apt when, attired in his new finery, miniature decorations and all, he surveyed himself in the full-length mirror.

Big Sister said through the mouth of the stewardess, "You wear formal uniform far more happily than Captain Billinger did."

Grimes said a little sourly, " 'Happily' is not the word that I would employ."

Automatically he picked up his pipe and tobacco pouch from the bedside table where he had put them when he undressed before his shower. He was about to shove them into a pocket when Big Sister said sternly, "Her Excellency does not approve of smoking."

He made a noise half way between a snarl and a sigh, muttered, "*She* wouldn't . . ." Then he laughed wryly and said, "But I mustn't bite the hand that rescued me. You must think that I'm an ungrateful bastard."

"I do," Big Sister told him.

Grimes was ready for dinner. To a great extent his appetite was governed by the state of his emotions; during periods of stress he would have to force himself to eat and then, the emergency over, he would be ravenous.

In some ways this meal, his first aboard *The Far Traveler*, came up to his expectations. In one way it did not.

The Baroness was awaiting him at the table—and that article of furniture complemented the beautiful woman who sat at its head. There were gold mesh place mats in glowing contrast to the highly polished ebony whose surface they protected, there were slender black candles set in an ornate golden holder, their flames golden rather than merely yellow. The elaborate settings of cutlery were also of the precious metal and the ranked wine glasses gleamed with the golden filagree incorporated in their fine crystal.

And his hostess?

She was wearing black tonight, an ankle-length translucency through which her skin glowed, which left her arms and shoulders bare. The jewels set in the braided coronet of her hair coruscated in the candlelight, could have been some fantastic constellation blazing in the dark sky of some newly discovered planet.

She said graciously, "Be seated, Captain."

Grimes sat.

The robot butler poured wine for them from a graceful decanter. She raised her glass. He raised his. He refrained from saying, as he would have done in the sort of company he normally kept, "Here's mud in your eye," or "Down the hatch," or some similar age-old but vulgar toast. He murmured, with what he hoped was suitable suavity, "Your very good health, Your Excellency."

"And yours, Captain."

The Baroness sipped delicately. Grimes did likewise. He savored the very dry sherry. It might even be, he decided, from Spain, on distant Earth. Such a tipple would be hellishly expensive save on the planet of its origin—but an El Doradan aristocrat would be well able to afford it.

The first course was served in fragile, gold-chased porcelain bowls, so beautifully proportioned that it seemed almost criminal to eat from them. Each contained what was little more than a sample of aureately transparent jellied consommé. Grimes watched the Baroness to see what implement she would use and was relieved when she picked up a tiny spoon and not a fork. When she began to eat he took his own first, tentative spoonful. It was delicious, although he could not determine what ingredients, animal or vegetable, had gone into its preparation. The only trouble was that there was not enough of it.

She said, noticing his appreciation, "I must confess that I did not expect to be able to obtain a *cordon bleu* autochef on a world such as Electra. One imagines that scientists and engineers subsist on hastily snatched sandwiches or, when they can tear themselves away from their work for a proper meal, on overdone steak and fried potatoes. However, I was able to persuade a Dr. Malleson, whom I learned has a considerable reputation as a gourmet, personally to program Big Sister."

"I have often wondered," said Grimes, "just who programs the Survey Service's autochefs. Good food—provided by God and cooked by the Devil."

She laughed politely. "Nonetheless, Captain, you must admit that the Survey Service is highly versed in some of the electronic arts—such as bugging. During my brief . . . friendship with Commander Delamere I was able to persuade him to allow me—or Big Sister—to take copies of material he holds aboard *Vega*, some of it concerning yourself. At the time I did not think that you would be entering my employ; it was merely that the records will assist me in my researches into social evolution in the Lost Colonies."

Grimes was conscious of the angry burning of his prominent ears. He knew that the Survey Service Archives contained remarkably comprehensive dossiers on all commissioned personnel and on quite a few petty officers and senior ratings but that such information was supposed to be accessible only to officers of flag rank. And Handsome Frankie was no higher than commander—although with his connections he would probably rise much higher. But Frankie, Grimes recalled, was reputed to be enjoying a clandestine affair with the fat and unattractive woman captain in charge of Records on Lindisfarne Base. Frankie, quite possibly, had the dirt on quite a few of those whom he regarded as his enemies.

"Why so embarrassed, Captain? On both New Sparta and Morrowvia you did your duty, as you saw it. But, in any case, our first call will be to Farhaven—to one of the many Farhavens. It is odd how little originality is displayed by those who name planets . . ."

The butler removed the consommé bowls and the sherry glasses, although not before Grimes was able to finish what remained in his.

"If you wish more of the Tio Pepe," said the Baroness, "you have only to ask, Captain."

Grimes' ears burned again.

The wine to accompany the fish was a demi-sec white, fragrant but somehow bodyless. It came, Grimes knew after a glance at the label, from the Vitelli vinyards on El Dorado. During his stay on that planet he had never cared for it much. It went quite well, however, with the course with which it was served—a perfectly grilled fillet of some marine creature over which was a tart sauce. The portions, thought Grimes, would have been no more than an appetizer for a small and not especially hungry cat. The Baroness picked daintily at hers. He picked daintily at his. It would have been ill-mannered to have disposed of it in one mouthful.

"Have you no appetite, Captain?" asked the woman. "I always thought that spacemen were much heartier eaters."

"I am savoring the flavor, Your Excellency," he said, not altogether untruthfully.

"It is, indeed, a rarity," she informed him. "The Golden Skimmer of Macedon is, despite protection, almost extinct."

"Indeed, Your Excellency?" *And how many credits did I shovel down my throat just now?* he wondered.

"Talking of fish," she went on, "poor Captain Billinger was really a fish out of water in this ship. Isn't there an old proverb about silk purses and sows' ears?" She permitted herself a musical chuckle. "But I am mixing zoological metaphors, am I not? Captain Billinger, I am sure, is a most competent spaceman but not quite a gentleman . . ."

Mphm? thought Grimes dubiously.

"Whereas you . . ." She let the implication dangle in mid air.

Grimes laughed. "There is, of course, the phrase, officers and gentlemen, which is supposed to apply only to the armed forces and not to the Merchant Service. But . . ."

"But what, Captain?"

The slur on the absent Billinger had annoyed him. He said, "To begin with, Your Excellency, I am no longer a commissioned officer of the Survey Service. Secondly, I have always failed to understand how being a licensed killer somehow bestows gentility upon one."

"Go on, Captain." Her voice was cold.

"If it was airs and graces you wanted, Your Excellency, you would have done well to recruit your yachtmaster from Trans-Galactic Clippers rather than from the Dog Star Line. It's said about TG that theirs is a service in which accent counts for more than efficiency."

"Indeed, Captain. When the vacancy next occurs I shall bear in mind what you have just told me."

The butler set fresh plates before them, poured glasses of a red wine. The vol-au-vents looked and smelled delicious. They also looked as though even a genteel sneeze would fragment them and blow them away.

"I am making allowances, Captain. This is, after all, your first night on board and I realize that in the Survey Service you were not accustomed to dining in female company."

"Perhaps not, Your Excellency."

He tried not to sputter pastry crumbs but some, inevitably, specked the lapels of his messjacket. (He almost made a jocular remark about "canteen medals" but thought better of it.) The meat was highly spiced, stimulating rather than satisfying the appetite. The wine, a Vitelli claret, was excellent. So was the rosé, from the same vinyard, that accompanied the grilled Carinthian "swallows"—creatures that, as Grimes knew, were reptilian rather than avian. They were esteemed by gourmets but were, in actuality, little more than crisp skin over brittle bones. (*A single swallow*, thought Grimes, *may not make a summer but it certainly does not make a meal!*) With these came a tossed, green salad that was rich in vitamins but in little else.

Conversation had become desultory and Grimes was beginning to regret his defense of Billinger, especially since that gentleman would never know that his successor had taken up the cudgels on his behalf.

Finally there came a confection that was no more than spun sugar and sweet spices, with spumante to wash it down. There was coffee—superb, but in demi-tasses. (Grimes loved good coffee but preferred it in a mug.) There were thimble-sized glasses of El Doradan strawberry brandy.

The Baroness said, "You will excuse me, Captain."

This was obviously dismissal. Grimes asked, "Are there any orders, Your Excellency?"

"You are employed as Master of this vessel," she told him. "I expect you, at your convenience, to familiarize yourself with the operation of the ship. After all—although it is extremely unlikely—Big Sister might suffer a breakdown."

"Goodnight, Your Excellency. Thank you for your hospitality."

"Thank you for your company, Captain Grimes. The evening has been most instructive. Perhaps one day I shall write a thesis on the psychology of spacemen."

The butler showed him out of the dining saloon. He went to his quarters, disdaining the elevator in such a small ship, using the spiral staircase around the axial shaft. He found that his smoking apparatus had been taken from the bedroom and placed on the coffee table in the day cabin. The pouch, which had been three quarters empty, was now full. He opened it suspiciously. Its content did not quite look like tobacco but certainly smelled like it, and a weed of very high quality at that. *From the yacht's stores?* he wondered.

The golden stewardess came in, carrying a tray on which was a napkin-covered plate, a tall glass and a bottle with condensation-bedewed sides. She said, "I thought that you must still be hungry, sir. These are ham sandwiches, with mustard. And Botany Bay beer."

"Is it you speaking," asked Grimes, "or is it Big Sister?"

"Does it matter?"

"But this supper . . . And the fresh supply of tobacco . . . I did not think that you approved of anybody but Her Excellency."

"Perhaps I do not. But you are now part of the ship's machinery and must be maintained in good running order. I decided that a replication of the noxious weed to which you are addicted was required; somehow its fumes are essential to your smooth functioning."

By this time Grimes—who had not been nicknamed Gutsy in his younger days for nothing—had made a start on the thick, satisfying sandwiches. He watched the stewardess as she left, her short skirt riding up to display her shapely rump.

If only you could screw as well as cook . . . he thought.

Chapter 12

Grimes was nothing if not conscientious. The next ship's day, after an early and excellent breakfast in his own quarters, dressed in the utilitarian slate-gray shirt and shorts uniform that he had been vastly relieved to learn was permissible working rig, he proceeded to go through the ship from stem to stern. Big Sister, of course, was aware of this. (Big Sister was aware of everything.) When he began his tour of inspection in the control room she reminded him sharply that smoking would be tolerated only in his own accommodation and elsewhere would be regarded and treated as an outbreak of fire. She added pointedly that only she could keep him supplied with tobacco. (He was to discover later that the fragrant fuel for his pipe was actually the product of the algae vat, dried and cunningly processed. This knowledge did not effect his enjoyment of the minor vice.)

He could find only one fault with the control room instrumentation: Big Sister had the final say as to whether or not it was switched on. She condescended to activate it for him. He checked everything— and everything was functioning perfectly. The navigational equipment was as fine as any he had ever seen—finer, perhaps. He set up an extrapolation of trajectory in the chart tank and the knowledge that this course had, originally, been plotted by no human hand made him understand Billinger's bitterness about being master *de jure* but not *de facto*.

His own quarters he had thoroughly explored before retiring the previous night. Immediately abaft these was his employer's accommodation. These compartments were, of course, out of bounds to him unless he should be invited to enter. Legally speaking the Baroness, even though she was the owner, could not have denied her yachtmaster

access but the very rich can afford to ignore laws and to make their
own which, although not appearing in any statute book, are closely
observed by employees who wish to keep their jobs.

Galley and storerooms were next. Grimes gazed with appreciation
at the fantastic stocks of canned and jarred delicacies from more than
a score of planets and hoped that he would be allowed to sample the
genuine Beluga caviar, the stone crab from Caribbea, the Atlantian sea
flowers, the Carinthian ham. There were even cans of haggis from Rob
Roy, one of the worlds of the Empire of Waverley. Grimes wondered
if, in the event of its ever being served, it would be ritually piped in.

The autochef was the biggest that Grimes had ever seen aboard
ship, a fat, gleaming cylinder reaching from deck to deckhead, an
intricacy of piping sprouting from the top of it, gauges and switches
set in its polished metal sides but all of them, like the instruments in
the control room, dead. Nonetheless the beast was humming content-
edly to itself and suddenly a bell chimed musically and a service hatch
opened, revealing a steaming mug of coffee and a plate on which
reposed a slab of rich-looking cake. Grimes was not exactly hungry
but could not resist the offering.

He sipped, he nibbled. He said, remembering his manners, "Thank
you."

Big Sister replied—he could not determine just where her voice
came from—"I was programmed to serve Mankind."

Grimes, who could not fail to note the sardonic intonation, thought,
Sarcastic bitch! but, even so, enjoyed the snack.

When he had finished he continued the inspection. On the farm
decks the tissue culture vats were unlabelled but certainly Big Sister
must know what was in them. There would be the standard beef, lamb,
pork, chicken and rabbit. Man, when he expanded among the stars,
had brought his dietary preferences and the wherewithal to satisfy them
with him. On a few, a very few worlds the local fauna had proved
palatable. Grimes hoped that the flesh of the Drambin lion-lizards, the
Kaldoon sandworms would be among the yacht's consumable and living stores. He asked aloud if this were so and was told—once again
Big Sister's voice came from nowhere in particular—that of course a
stock of these delicacies was carried but that they would be served
only if and when Her Excellency expressed a desire for them.

He could find no faults with the comprehensive assemblage of
hydroponic tanks. Everything was lush and flourishing in the simulated
sunlight. He picked a just ripe tomato from the vine, bit into it appreciatively.

Big Sister said, "I trust that you will make regular use of the gymnasium, Captain Grimes. You will, of course, have to arrange your exercise and sauna times so as not to coincide with those of Her Excellency."

He was tempted to sample a small, espaliered pear but, conscious that Big Sister was watching, refrained.

Below and abaft the farm were more storerooms, in one of which the GP robots, looking like sleeping, golden-skinned men, were stacked on shelves. He was told that these could be activated only on orders by the Baroness. He looked into the armory. There was a fine stock of weapons, handguns mainly, stunners, lasers and projectile pistols.

Then came the deck upon which the gymnasium was situated with its bicycle, rowing machine, automasseur, sauna with, alongside this latter, a neck-deep pool of icy-cold water. There would be no excuse, Grimes decided, for not keeping disgustingly fit.

Further aft there were the fully-automated workshops—in one of which, Grimes noted, a complex machine was just completing a purple, richly gold-braided tunic which he decided must be for himself. There was a laboratory, also fully automated, in which he watched the carcass of one of the Botany Bay kangaroos, an animal which had mutated slightly but significantly from the original Terran stock, being dissected.

The voice of Big Sister told him, "You will be interested to learn that a tissue culture has already been started from cells from the tail of this beast. I understand that kangaroo tail soup is esteemed both on Earth and on Botany Bay. The fact that this caudal appendage is prehensile should not detract from its palatability."

Grimes did not linger to watch the flashing blades at their grisly work. He was one of those who would probably have been a vegetarian if obliged to do his own butchering. He left the laboratory and, using the spiral staircase around the axial shaft, carried on down and sternwards.

He looked briefly into the Mannschenn Drive room where the gleaming, ever-precessing gyroscopes tumbled through the warped Continuum, drawing the ship and all aboard her with them. He spent as little time in the Inertial Drive compartment; within its soundproof bulkheads the cacophony was deafening. The hydrogen fusion power plant would have been fascinating to an engineer—which Grimes was not—and the fact that all the display panels were dead robbed the device of interest to a layman. Big Sister said condescendingly, "I can activate these if you wish, Captain Grimes, but such meaningless, to you, showing of pretty lights would only be a waste of electricity."

He did not argue. And when, a little later, he looked at the locked door of the compartment in which the electronic intelligence had its being he did not request admittance. He knew that this would be refused. He told himself that he would take a dim view of anybody's poking around inside his own brain—but still it rankled.

He had been too many years in command to enjoy being told what he could or could not see in a ship of which he was officially captain.

Chapter 13

The voyages, as voyages do, continued. Grimes was determined to learn as much as possible about his command—but when the command herself was rather less than cooperative this was no easy matter. His relationship with his employer was not unfriendly although he met her socially only on her terms. Sometimes he partook of luncheon with her, sometimes dinner, never breakfast. Frequently they talked over morning coffee, more often over afternoon tea. Now and again they watched a program of entertainment on the Baroness's playmaster although her tastes were not his. Neither were Captain Billinger's. Unfortunately it had not been possible to lay in a spool library that would have appealed to Grimes. He made frequent, pointless inspections. He insisted on keeping in practice with his navigation. He exercised dutifully in the gymnasium and kept himself reasonably trim.

And now here he was, seated on a spindly-legged chair in the Baroness's boudoir, sipping tea that was far too weak for his taste, attired in the uniform that he hated, all purple and gold, that would have been far more appropriate to a Strauss operetta than to a spaceship.

He regarded his employer over the gold rim of his teacup. She was worth looking at, languidly at ease on her chaise longue, attired as usual in a filmy gown that revealed more than it concealed. Her dark auburn hair was braided into a coronet in which clusters of diamonds sparkled. She could have been posing for a portrait of a decadent aristocrat from almost any period of man's long history. Decadent she may have looked—but Grimes knew full well that the rulers of El Dorado were tough, ruthless and utterly selfish.

She said, looking steadily at Grimes with her big, violet eyes, "We have decided to allow you to handle the landing."

Grimes, with a mouthful of tea, could not reply at once and, in any case, he was rather surprised by her announcement. He hastily swallowed the almost scalding fluid and was embarrassed by the distinctly audible gurgle. He put the fragile cup down in its saucer with far too much of a clatter.

"Surely," she went on, "you are getting the feel of the ship."

"Perhaps," he admitted cautiously, "the ship is getting the feel of me." He realized that she was regarding him even more coldly than usual and hastily added, "Your Excellency."

"But surely to a spaceman of your experience a ship is only a ship," she said.

You know bloody well that this one isn't, he thought. *A normal ship isn't built of gold, for a start. A normal ship doesn't have a mind of her own, no matter what generations of seamen and spacemen, myself among them, have half believed. A normal ship doesn't run to an Owner's suite looking like the salon of some titled rich bitch in Eighteenth Century France . . .*

"So you can handle the landing," she stated.

He replied, as nastily as he dared, "I am sure that Big Sister can manage by herself quite nicely."

She said, "But you are being paid—handsomely, I may add—to do a job, Captain Grimes. And this Farhaven is a world without radio, without Aerospace Control. During your years in command in the Survey Service your brain has been programmed to deal with such situations. Big Sister has not been adequately programmed in that respect, she informs me." She frowned. "As you already know I have brought such deficiencies in programming to the notice of the builders on Electra. Fortunately the guarantee has not yet expired."

The golden robot butler refilled her cup from the golden teapot, added cream from a golden jug, sugar from a golden bowl. Grimes declined more tea.

He said, "Please excuse me, Your Excellency. Since I am to make the landing I should like to view again the records made by *Epsilon Pavonis* and *Investigator* . . ."

"You may leave, Captain," said the Baroness.

Grimes rose from his chair, bowed stiffly, went up to his far from uncomfortable quarters.

He sat before the playmaster in his day cabin watching the pictures in the screen, the presentation of data, the charts and tables. As he had

done before, as soon as he had learned of *The Far Traveler*'s destination, he tried to put himself in the shoes of Captain Lentigan of
Epsilon Pavonis, one of the Interstellar Transport Commission's
tramps, who had first stumbled upon this planet. *Epsilon Pavonis* had
been off trajectory, with a malfunctioning Mannschenn Drive. As far
as Lentigan was concerned Farhaven had been merely a conveniently
located world on which to set down to carry out repairs and recalibration. He was surprised to find human inhabitants, descendants of the
crew and passengers from the long-ago missing and presumed lost
Lode Venturer. He had reported his discovery by Carlotti Deep Space
Radio. Then the Survey Service's *Investigator* was dispatched to make
a more thorough job of surveying than the merchant captain, all too
conscious of the penalties for deviation, had been able to do. Her
captain, a Commander Belton, had run into trouble. And as Farhaven,
as it had been named by its colonists, was of neither commercial nor
strategic importance to any of the spacefaring races its people were
left to stew in their own juice.

Grimes allowed himself to wonder what they would make of the
Baroness, himself—and Big Sister.

As yet he had been unable to view Commander Belton's records
in their entirety. Every time that he asked for them they were un-
available. Presumably the Baroness was monopolizing them.

Chapter 14

Grimes sat in the captain's chair in *The Far Traveler*'s control room. The Baroness occupied the chair that, in a normal ship, would have been the seat of the second in command. She was dressed in standard spacewoman's working uniform—white shirt and shorts but without insignia. She needed no trappings of rank; in the functional attire she was no longer the decadent aristocrat but still, nonetheless, the aristocrat.

The yacht was not equipped with robot probes—a glaring omission that, said the Baroness, would cost the shipyard on Electra dearly. There were, however, sounding rockets, a necessity when landing on a world with no spaceport facilities; a streamer of smoke is better than nothing when there are no Aerospace Control reports on wind direction and velocity—and at least as good as a primitive windsock.

The Far Traveler dropped steadily down through Farhaven's atmosphere. She was in bright sunlight although the terrain below her was still dark. Grimes had told Big Sister that he wanted to land very shortly after sunrise—S.O.P. for the Survey Service. The almost level rays of a rising luminary show up every smallest irregularity of a surface and, when a landing is being made on a strange world, there is a full day after the initial set-down to make preliminary explorations and to get settled in.

Grimes, during his first orbitings of Farhaven, had selected his landing site—an unforested plain near the mouth of one of the great rivers, a stream that according to Belton's charts was called the Jordan. *Epsilon Pavonis* had set down there. So had *Investigator*. A little way upriver was what Captain Lentigan had referred to as a large village and Commander Belton as a small town. Neither Lentigan nor Belton had reported that the natives were hostile; their troubles had been with their own crews. None of the material that Grimes had seen so far went into very great detail but he could fill in the gaps from his imagination. (He had experienced his own troubles with his own crew after the Botany Bay landing.)

Big Sister broke into his thoughts. She said, her voice metallic yet feminine, issuing from the speaker of the NST transceiver, "I would suggest that we fire the first sounding rocket, Captain."

"Fire at will," ordered Grimes.

(In a normal ship some alleged humorist would have whispered, "Who's Will?")

He watched in the stern view screen the arrow of fire and smoke streaking downward. Its trail wavered.

"Ideal conditions, Captain," commented the Baroness.

"It would seem so, Your Excellency," agreed Grimes.

But from his own, highly personal viewpoint they were far from ideal. Over many years he had regarded his pipe as an essential adjunct to shiphandling—and for those many years he had been absolute monarch in his own control room. But the Baroness neither smoked nor approved of smoking in her presence.

He allowed his attention to stray briefly from the controls to what he could see of the sunlit hemisphere through the viewports. Farhaven was a wildly beautiful world but, save for ribbons of fertility along the rivers and coasts, it was a barren beauty. To the east, beyond the narrow sea, reared great, jagged pinnacles, ice-tipped, and to the west similar peaks were already dazzlingly scintillant in the first rays of the rising sun. Unless there were considerable mineral wealth about all that this planet would be good for would be a holiday resort—and it was too far from anywhere for the idea to be attractive to those shipping companies involved in the tourist trade.

Big Sister said, "I would suggest, Captain, that you pay more attention to your controls. It was, after all, with some reluctance that I consented to let you handle the landing."

Grimes felt his prominent ears burning as he blushed furiously. He thought, *I'd like five minutes alone back on Electra with the bastard who programmed this brass bitch!* He saw, in the screen, that the sounding rocket had hit and that its luminous smoke was rising directly upwards. But it was thinning, would not last for much longer.

He ordered, "Fire two!"

Big Sister said, "It is not necessary."

"Fire two!" repeated Grimes sharply. He added, grudgingly, "Wind can rise suddenly, especially just after sunrise, especially in country like this."

"Fire two," acknowledged Big Sister sullenly as the second rocket streaked downwards, striking just as the first one expired.

And there *was* wind, Grimes noted with smug satisfaction, springing up with the dawn. The luminescent pillar of smoke wavered, then streamed seawards. Grimes applied lateral thrust, kept the flaring rocket head in the center of the screen.

The sun came up relative to the land below the ship, topping the serrated ridge of the range to the eastward. The plain toward which *The Far Traveler* was dropping flares into color—blue-green with splotches of gold and scarlet, outcroppings of gleaming white from which extended long, sharply defined black shadows. *Boulders . . .* thought Grimes, stepping up the magnification of the screen. Yes, boulders . . . And the red and yellow patches must be clumps of ground hugging flowers since they cast no shadows. The sounding rocket, still smoking, was almost in the center of one of the scarlet patches; there was no unevenness of the ground there to worry about.

The ship dropped steadily. Grimes was obliged to make frequent small lateral thrust adjustments; that wind was unsteady, gusting, veering, backing. He reduced the rate of descent until *The Far Traveler* was almost hovering.

"I am not made of glass, you know," remarked Big Sister conversationally.

"I had hoped to make the landing some time before noon," said the Baroness.

Grimes tried to ignore them both. *That bloody wind!* he thought. *Why can't it make up its mind which way to blow?*

He was down at last—and the ship, suddenly and inexplicably, was tilted a full fifteen degrees from the vertical. She hung there—and then, with slow deliberation, righted herself, far more slowly than she should have done with the lateral thrust that Grimes was applying. There was no real danger, only discomfort—and, for Grimes, considerable embarrassment. He had always prided himself on his shiphandling and this was the first time that he had been guilty of such a bungled landing.

When things had stopped rattling and creaking the Baroness asked, with cold sarcasm, "Was that really necessary, Captain?"

Before he could think of a reply Big Sister said, "Captain Grimes was overly cautious. *I* would have come down fast instead of letting the wind play around with me like a toy balloon. I would have dropped and then applied vertical thrust at the last moment."

And you, you cast-iron, gold-plated bitch, thought Grimes, *deliberately made a balls-up of my landing . . .*

"Perhaps, Captain," said the Baroness, "it will be advisable to allow Big Sister to handle her own lift-offs and set-downs from now on."

The way she said it there wasn't any "perhaps" about it.

Chapter 15

Big Sister carried out the routine tests for habitability. The captains of *Epsilon Pavonis* and *Investigator* had reported the atmosphere as better than merely breathable, the water suitable for drinking as well as for washing in and sailing ships on, a total absence of any microorganisms capable of causing even mild discomfort to humans, let alone sickness or death. Nonetheless, caution is always advisable. Bacilli and viruses can mutate—and on Farhaven, after the landing of *Lode Venturer*, there had been established a new and sizeable niche in the ecology, the bodies of the original colonists and their descendants, just crying out to be occupied. The final tests, however, would have to wait until there was a colonist available for thorough examination.

Finally Big Sister said, speaking through the control room transceiver, "You may now disembark. But I would recommend . . ."

Grimes broke in. "You seem to forget that I was once a Survey Service captain. Landings on strange planets were part of my job."

The Baroness smiled maliciously. "I suppose that we may as well avail ourselves of Captain Grimes' wide range of experience. Quite possibly he was far better at trampling roughshod over exotic terrain than bringing his ship to a gentle set-down prior to the extra-vehicular activities." She looked away from Grimes, addressed the transceiver. "Big Sister, please have the small pinnace waiting for us. We shall board it from the ground. Oh, and an escort of six general purpose robots. Armed."

"Am I to assume, Your Excellency," asked Grimes stiffly, "that you are placing yourself in command of the landing party?"

"Of course, Captain. May I remind you that your authority, such as it is, does not extend as much as one millimeter beyond the shell of this ship?"

Grimes did not reply. He watched her sullenly as she unbuckled herself from her seat and left the control room. Then he unsnapped his own safety belt, got up and went down to his quarters. He found that the robot stewardess had laid out a uniform of tough khaki twill with shoulderboards of gold braid on purple, a gold-trimmed purple beret, stout boots, a belt with attached holsters. He checked the weapons. These were a Minetti projectile pistol—as it happened, his favorite side-arm—and a hand laser. They would do; it was highly unlikely that heavy artillery would be required. He changed out of his shorts and shirt uniform—he had made it plain that he did not consider full dress suitable attire for shiphandling—slowly. Before he was finished the too familiar voice came from the speaker of the playmaster in his day cabin, "Captain Grimes, Her Excellency is waiting for you."

He buckled on the belt, went out to the axial shaft, rode the elevator down to the after airlock. He walked down the golden ramp to the blue-green not-quiet-grass. The pinnace was there, a few meters from the ship, a slim, torpedo shape of burnished gold. The Baroness was there, in khaki shirt and flared breeches and high, polished boots, looking like an intrepid White Huntress out of some archaic adventure movie. The general purpose robots were there, drawn up in a stiff line, staring at nothing. From belts about their splendidly proportioned bodies depended an assortment of hand weapons.

"We are waiting," said the Baroness unnecessarily. "Now that you are here, will you get the show on the road?" Somehow she contrived to put the question between quotation marks.

Grimes flushed angrily. "Your orders?" he asked, adding, "Your Excellency," to avoid further acrimony.

"To take this pinnace to the settlement reported by *Epsilon Pavonis* and *Investigator*." Then, when Grimes made no immediate move, "Don't just stand there. *Do* something."

He turned to the robots, tried to imagine that they were Survey Service Marines, although the handling of such personnel he had always left to their own officers or NCOs. "Embark!" he ordered sharply.

The automata turned as one, strode in single file to the pinnace's airlock, stepped aboard.

He said to the Baroness, "After you, Your Excellency."

He followed her into the pinnace, saw that she had taken the co-pilot's seat in the control cab. The robots were standing aft, in the main cabin. The airlock doors closed while he was still making his way to his own chair; he noted that the Baroness had not touched the instrument panel before her. He sighed. This was Big Sister again, showing him who was really in command.

He buckled himself into his seat. Before he was finished the voice of the ship's computer-pilot came from the transceiver, "Proceed when you are ready, Captain Grimes."

The inertial drive was already running, in neutral gear. He switched to vertical thrust, lifted. The river was ahead; in the bright sunlight it was a ribbon of gleaming gold winding over the blue-green grasslands. There was altogether too much gold in his life these days, he thought. He flew at a moderate speed until he was directly over the wide stream and then turned to port, proceeding inland at an altitude of about fifteen meters. Ahead of him were the distant, towering ranges, their glittering peaks sharp against the clear sky.

The Baroness was not talkative. Neither was Grimes. He thought, *If those were real Marines back there they'd be making enough chatter for all of us.*

He concentrated on his piloting. The controls of the pinnace were very similar to those to which he had become accustomed in small craft of this type in the Survey Service but he still had to get the feel of this one. The river banks were higher now, rocky, sheer, with explosions of green and gold and scarlet and purple where flowering shrubs had taken hold in cracks and crevices. He considered lifting to above cliff-top level, then decided against it. While he was here he might as well enjoy the scenery. There was little enough else to enjoy.

The canyon became deeper, narrower, more tortuous. And then, after Grimes had put the pinnace through an almost right-angled turn, it widened. The actual river bed was still relatively narrow but, strung along it like a bead, was an oval valley, lushly fertile, bounded by sheer red cliffs unbroken save for where the stream flowed in and out.

The valley was as described in the two reports. The village was not. It was utterly deserted, its houses delapidated, many of them apparently destroyed by fire at some long past date. Shrubs and saplings were thrusting up through the charred ruins.

Grimes set the controls for hovering, took binoculars from their box to study the abandoned settlement. There were few houses of more than one story. The structural material was mud or clay, reinforced with crude frames of timber. The windows were unglazed but from some of them bleached rags, the remains of blinds or curtains, fluttered listlessly in some faint stirring of the air.

The Baroness had found her own glasses, was staring through them.

She said softly, "A truly Lost Colony . . . And we have come too late to find any survivors . . ."

A voice—*that* voice!—came from the transceiver.

"May I suggest, Your Excellency, that you observe the cliff face to the north of your present position?"

Big Sister, thought Grimes, was still watching. She would have her sensors in and about the pinnace and every one of the robots was no more—and no less—than an extension of herself.

He turned the boat about its short axis to facilitate observation. He and the Baroness studied the forbidding wall of red rock. It was broken, here and there, by dark holes. The mouths of caves? He thought that he could detect motion in some of them. Animals? And then a human figure appeared from one of the apertures and walked slowly along a narrow ledge to the next cave mouth. It was naked. It was a woman, not old but not young, with long, unkempt hair that might, after a thorough wash, have been blonde. The most amazing thing about her was her apparent lack of interest in the strange flying machine that was shattering the peace of the valley with its cacophonous engine beat. Although it was quiet inside the pinnace—its builders had been lavish with sonic insulation to protect the delicate ears of its aristocratic owner—the racket outside, the arythmic clangor of the inertial drive echoing and re-echoing between the cliff faces, must have been deafening.

Then she did turn to look at the noisy intruder. Somehow her attitude conveyed the impression that she wished that the clattering thing would go away. Grimes studied her through his binoculars. Her face, which might have been pretty if cleaned and given a few cosmetic touches, was that of a sleepwalker. The skin of her body, under the dirt, was pallid. That was strange. People who habitually went naked, such as the Arcadian naturists, were invariably deeply tanned.

She turned again, walked slowly into the cave mouth.

Three children, two girls and a boy, came out on to another ledge. They were as unkempt as the woman, equally incurious. They picked their way down a narrow pathway to ground level, walked slowly to one of the low bushes. They stood around it, picking things—nuts? berries?—from its branches, thrusting them into their mouths.

The Baroness said, addressing Grimes almost as though he were a fellow human being, "As you know, Social Evolution in the Lost Colonies is the title of my thesis. But this is devolution. From spaceship to village of mud huts . . . From mud huts to caves . . ."

"Caves," said Grimes, "could be better than mud huts. Less upkeep. There's a place called Coober Peedy back on Earth, in Australia, where the cave dwellings are quite luxurious. It used to be an opal mining town . . ."

"Indeed?" Her voice was cold again. "Put us down, please. Close to those horrible children, but not close enough to alarm them."

If they were going to be alarmed, thought Grimes, they would have been alarmed already. Surely they must have seen the pinnace, must be hearing it. But he said nothing and brought the boat down, landing about ten meters from the filthy urchins. They did not look away from the bush from which they were gathering the edible harvest.

The airlock doors opened and the little ladder automatically extended. The Baroness got up from her seat. Grimes put out a hand to detain her. She scornfully brushed it aside.

He said, "Wait, Your Excellency. The robots should embark first. To draw the fire. If any."

"If any," she repeated derisively.

She pushed past him, jumped down from the airlock to the ground. He followed her. The robots filed out on the heels of the humans. Grimes, with both pistols drawn, stood taking stock. He stared up at the cliff face, at the caves. There were no indications of any hostile action. He was not really expecting any but knew that the unexpected has claimed many a victim. The Baroness sneered silently. Grimes relaxed at last and returned the weapons to their holsters but did not secure the flaps.

"Are you sure," she asked, "that you don't want to shoot those children?"

Grimes made no reply, followed her as she walked slowly to the little savages clustered around the shrub. The GP robots followed him. The children ignored the intruders, just went on stolidly picking berries—if berries they were—and thrusting them into their mouths.

They were unprepossessing brats—skinny, dirty, with scabbed knees and elbows, with long, matted, filthy hair. And they stank, a sour effluvium that made Grimes want to breathe through his mouth rather than through his nose. He saw the Baroness's nostrils wrinkle. His own felt like airtight doors the instant after a hull-piercing missile strike.

He looked at the berries that were growing so profusely on the bush. Berries? Elongated, bright purple berries? But berries do not run to a multiplicity of wriggling legs and twitching antennae. Berries do not squirm as they are inserted into greedy mouths . . . The eaters chewed busily while a thin, purple ichor dribbled down their filth-encrusted chins.

It was no worse than eating oysters, thought Grimes, trying to rationalize his way out of impending nausea. Or witchetty grubs . . .

"Children," said the Baroness in a clear, rather too sweet voice.

They ignored her.

"Children," she repeated, her voice louder, not so sweet.

They went on ignoring her.

She looked at Grimes. Her expression told him, *Do something*.

He put out a hand to grasp the boy's shoulder, being careful not to grip hard or painfully. This required no effort; his own skin was shrinking from contact with that greasy, discolored integument. He managed to turn the child to face him and the Baroness. Then he was at a loss for something to say. "Take me to your leader," did not seem right, somehow.

"Please take us to your parents," said the Baroness.

The boy went on chewing and swallowing, then spat out a wad of masticated chitin from which spines and hairs still protruded. It landed on the toe of Grimes' right boot. He kicked it away in revulsion.

"Take us to your parents," repeated the Baroness.

"Wha'?"

"Your parents." Slowly, patiently, "Your mother. Your father."

"Momma. Fadder. No wake."

"He says," volunteered Grimes, "that his mother and father are sleeping."

She said, "A truly blinding glimpse of the obvious, Captain. But, of course, you are the expert on first contacts, are you not? Then may I ask why it did not occur to you to bring along bright trinkets, glass beads and mirrors and the like, as gifts to people who are no better than savages?"

"I doubt if they could bear to look at themselves in a mirror, Your Excellency," said Grimes.

"Very, very funny. But you are not employed as court jester."

Slowly she removed the watch from her left wrist. It was a beautful piece of work, jewel as much as instrument, fantastically accurate. In the extremely unlikely event of *The Far Traveler*'s chronometers all becoming nonoperational it could have been used for navigational purposes. Its golden bracelet was a fragile-seeming chain, its thin case was set with diamonds that flashed dazzlingly in the sunlight. She dangled it temptingly before the boy's eyes. He ignored it. He wriggled out of Grimes' grip, pulled another of the repulsive purple grubs from the bush and thrust it into his open mouth.

But one of the girls was more interested. She turned, made a sudden snatch for the trinket. The Baroness was too quick for her, whipping it up and out of reach.

"Gimme!" squealed the unlovely child. "P'etty! P'etty! Gimme!"

"Take . . . us . . ." enunciated the Baroness slowly and carefully, "to . . . Momma . . . Fadder . . ."

"Gimme! Gimme! Gimme!"

The Baroness repeated her request. It seemed to be getting through. The girl scowled, then slowly and deliberately gathered a double handful of the puce horrors from the branches of the bush. Then, reluctantly, she led the way to the cliff face, pausing frequently to look back. With her busily working mouth, with that sickening slime oozing from between her lips she was not a pretty sight.

She reached the foot of the rock wall. There was a ledge running diagonally up its face, less than a meter wide, a natural ramp. She paused, looked back at Grimes and the Baroness, at the marching robots. An expression that could have been indicative of doubt flickered across her sharp-featured face. The Baroness waved the watch so that it flashed enticingly in the sunlight. The girl made a beckoning gesture, then started up the path.

Chapter 16

Grimes hesitated; a cliff path such as this should have been fitted with a handrail. The Baroness flashed him a scornful look and followed the girl; despite her boots she was almost as sure-footed. Grimes, not at all happily, followed the Baroness. The ledge was narrow, its surface uneven yet worn smooth and inclined to be slippery. There was a paucity of handholds on the cliff face and, looking up, Grimes realized that on some stretches the climbers would be obliged to lean outward, over a sheer drop, as they made progress upward. The robots began to come after Grimes. There was a sharp *crack*! as rock broke away from the edge of the path, a clatter of falling fragments.

The Baroness called, "Robots! Wait for us on the ground!" Then, to Grimes, "You should have realized, Captain, that their weight would be too much for this ledge!"

So should Big Sister! thought Grimes but did not say it.

They climbed—the half-grown girl, the Baroness, Grimes.

They negotiated a difficult crossing of the natural ramp with a horizontal ledge. Fortunately the cliff face here was scarred with cracks affording foot-and handholds, although so widely spaced as to alleviate but little the hazards of the traverse.

They climbed.

Once Grimes paused to look back and down—at the gleaming, golden pinnace, at the equally refulgent robots. It was an exaggeration, he knew, but they looked at him like ants standing beside a pencil dropped on to the grass. He was not, after all, so very far above ground level—only high enough to be reasonably sure of breaking his neck if he missed his footing and fell.

After that he kept on looking up and ahead—at the Baroness's

shapely rump working in the sweat-stained khaki of her breeches, at
the meagre buttocks of the naked girl. Neither spectacle was particularly erotic.

They climbed, crossing another horizontal ledge and then, eventually, turning off the diagonal path onto a third one. It was as narrow
as the natural ramp.

Ahead and to the left was the mouth of one of the caves. The girl
slipped into it, the Baroness followed. Grimes followed her. Less than
two meters inside the entrance was an almost right-angled turn. The
Baroness asked, "Did you bring a light?" Then, "But of course not.
That would have required some foresight on your part."

Grimes, saying nothing, pulled his laser pistol from its holster,
thumbed the selector switch to broadest beam. It would serve as an
electric torch although wasteful of energy and potentially dangerous.
But it was not required, although it took some little time for their eyes
to become accustomed to the dim illumination after the bright sunshine
outside. There was light in here—wan, eerie, cold. It came from the
obscenely bloated masses of fungus dependent from the low cavern
roof, growing in bulbous clusters from the rocky walls and, to a lesser
extent, from the floor itself. The girl led them on, her thin body pallidly
luminescent. And there were other bodies sprawled on the rock floor,
men and women, naked, sleeping . . .

Or dead . . . thought Grimes.

No, not dead. One of them, a grossly obese female, stirred and
whinnied softly, stretched out a far arm to a nearby clump of fungus.
She broke off a large hunk, stuffed it into her mouth. She gobbled
disgustingly, swallowed noisily. There was a gusty sigh as she flopped
back to her supine position. She snored.

There were other noises—eructations, a trickling sound, a splat-
tering. And there was the . . . *stink*. Grimes trod in something. He knew
what it was without looking. Sight is not the only sense.

Still the girl led them through the noisome cave. They passed
adults, adolescents, children, babies, all sprawled in their own filth.
They came at last to a couple with limbs entwined in a ghastly parody
of physical love.

"Momma! Fadder!" shrilled the girl triumphantly. "Gimme!"

The Baroness silently handed the watch to her. It was no longer
the pretty toy that it had been when first offered. In this lighting it
could have been fabricated from lustreless lead, from beads of dull
glass.

The girl took it, stared at it and then flung it from her. "No p'etty!"
she squalled. "No p'etty!"

She pulled a piece of the glowing fungus from the wall, thrust it into her mouth. She whimpered as she chewed it, then subsided onto the rock floor beside her parents.

"My watch," said the Baroness to Grimes. "Find it." After rather too long a lag she added, "Please."

Grimes used his laser pistol cautiously, directing its beam upward while looking in the direction from which the brief metallic clatter, marking the fall of the timepiece, had come. He saw it shining against the rock wall. He made his way to it, picked it up while trying in vain not to dirty his fingers. It had fallen into a pool of some filth.

The Baroness said, "I am not touching it again until it has been thoroughly sterilized. Put it in your pocket. And now, will you try to wake these people?"

Grimes wrapped the watch in his handkerchief, put it into his pocket, then returned the laser pistol to its holster. He squatted by the sleeping couple. He forced himself to touch the unclean skin of the man's bare shoulder. He gave a tentative tap, then another.

"I said *wake* him, not pet him!" snarled the Baroness. "Shake him!"

Grimes shook the sleeper, rather more viciously than he had intended. The man slid off the supine body of the woman, fell onto his side. He twitched like a sleeping dog afflicted by a bad dream. Dull eyes opened, peered out through the long, matted hair. Bearded lips parted.

"Go 'way. Go 'way."

"We have come a long distance to see you," said the Baroness.

"S'wot?" asked the man uninterestedly. "S'wot?" He levered himself to a half sitting position, broke off a piece of the omnipresent fungus from the near wall, brought it toward his mouth.

"Stop him!" ordered the Baroness.

Grimes caught the other's thin wrist in his right hand, forced it down. The man struggled feebly.

"I am the Baroness d'Estang," announced the lady.

So what? thought Grimes.

"S'wot?" demanded the man. Then, to Grimes, "Leggo. Leggo o' me, you bassar!"

Grimes said, "We'll not get much from these people."

She asked coldly, "Are you an expert in handling decadent savages? I find it hard to believe that you are expert in anything."

The man's free hand flashed up, the fingers, with their long, broken nails, clawing for Grimes' eyes. Grimes let go of the other's wrist, using both his own hands to protect his face. Released, the caveman abandoned his attack and crammed the handful of fungus into his mouth, swallowed it without chewing. He immediately lapsed into unconsciousness.

"Now look what you've done!" snapped the Baroness.

"I didn't do anything," said Grimes.

"That was the trouble!" she said. She snarled wordlessly. Then, "All right. We will leave this . . . pigsty and return when we are better prepared. You will collect samples of the fungus so that it may be analyzed aboard the ship and an effective antidote prepared. Be careful not to touch the stuff with your bare hands."

He prodded a protuberance of the nearest growth with the muzzle of his Minetti. He hated so to misuse a cherished firearm but it was the only tool he had. He pulled his handkerchief from his pocket, extracting from its folds the Baroness's watch, putting the instrument down on the floor. He wrapped the cloth around the sample of fungus, making sure that there were at least three thicknesses of cloth between it and his skin. He removed his beret, put the untidy parcel into it.

He followed his employer out to the open air.

After they had returned to ground level Grimes ordered one of the robots to get specimens of the purple grubs from a bush, also samples of the leaves on which the revolting things were feeding. Then the party reboarded the pinnace. Grimes took the craft straight up with the automatic cameras in action. The pictures would be of interest and value—the deserted village, the faint, rectangular outlines on the surrounding terrain showing where fields had once been cultivated, the cliff face with the dark mouths of the caves. No humans would be seen on these films; the children who had been feeding from the bushes had gone back inside.

The flight back to *The Far Traveler* was direct and fast. Grimes felt—and in fact was—filthy, wanting nothing so much as a long, hot shower and a change into clean clothing. And the Baroness? Whatever he was feeling she must be feeling too, doubled and redoubled, in spades. And the robots, who should have been doing the dirty work, were as gleamingly immaculate as when they had disembarked from the yacht.

They landed by the ramp. The Baroness was first out of the pinnace and up the gangway almost before Grimes had finished unbuckling his seat belt. By the time that he got aboard she was nowhere to be seen.

He saw her discarded clothing in a little heap on the deck of the airlock chamber. He heard Big Sister say, "I suggest, Captain, that you disrobe before coming inside the ship."

He growled, "I was house-broken at least thirty years before you were programmed."

He stripped, throwing his own soiled khaki on top of the Baroness's gear. He thought wryly, *And that's the closest I'll ever get to the bitch!* Nonetheless he was not sorry to get his clothes off; they were distinctly odorous. He walked naked into the elevator cage, was carried up to his quarters. The robot stewardess, his literally golden girl, awaited him there. She already had the shower running in his bathroom; she removed her skimpy uniform to stand under the hot water with him, to soap and to scrub him. To an outside observer not knowing that the perfectly formed female was only a machine the spectacle would have seemed quite erotic. Grimes wondered who was washing the Baroness's back—her butler or her lady's maid? He hoped maliciously that whichever one it was was using a stiff brush . . .

He asked his own servant, "Aren't you afraid you'll rust?"

She replied humorlessly, "Gold does not corrode." She turned the water off. "You are now sterile."

I am as far as you're concerned, he thought. It occurred to him that it was a long time since he had had a woman. Too long.

He stood for a few seconds in the blast of warm air and then, clean and dry, stepped into his sleeping cabin. He looked with distaste at the purple and gold livery laid out on the bed. Reluctantly he climbed into it. As he did up the last button the voice of Big Sister said, "You will now join Her Excellency in her salon, Captain Grimes."

Grimes filled and lit his pipe. He badly needed a smoke.

Big Sister said, "Her Excellency is waiting for you."

Grimes decided to allow himself three more slow inhalations.

Big Sister said, "Her Excellency is waiting for you."

Grimes continued smoking.

Big Sister reiterated, "Her Excellency is waiting for you."

Grimes said, "What you tell me three times is true."

Big Sister said coldly, "What I tell you is true."

Reluctantly Grimes put down his pipe. The stewardess produced a little golden atomizer, sprayed him with a fragrant mist.

He said, "Now I reek like a whore's garret."

Big Sister said, "You do not, now, reek like an incinerator."

Grimes sighed and left his quarters.

Chapter 17

The Baroness said coldly, "You took your time getting here, Captain. I suppose that you were obliged to indulge yourself by sucking on that vile comforter of yours. Be seated."

Grimes lowered himself cautiously into one of the frail-seeming chairs.

"I thought that we would view the record of the orgy again."

"The record of the orgy, Your Excellency? I have not seen it yet."

"I would have thought, Captain Grimes, that you would have acquainted yourself with every scrap of information regarding this planet before our set down."

Grimes simmered inwardly. Every time that he had wished to view the orgy record it had not been available. He ventured to say as much.

The voice of Big Sister came from the Baroness's playmaster, an instrument that contrived to look as a TriVi set would have looked had such devices been in existence during the reign of King Louis XIV of France.

"This record, like the others concerning this planet, was obtained by Commander Delamere from the Archives of the Survey Service on Lindisfarne. It is classified—for viewing by officers with the rank of Survey Service captain and above. You, Captain Grimes, resigned from the Survey Service with the rank of commander only."

"Let us not split hairs," said the Baroness generously. "Although he is now only a civilian shipmaster, Captain Grimes should be accorded his courtesy title. In any case, Commander Delamere, from whom we obtained this copy, has yet to attain captain's rank. The film, please."

The screen of the playmaster came alive, glowing with light and color. There was the village that they had visited—but as a living settlement, not a crumbling ghost town. There were the people—reasonably clean, brightly clothed. There were spacemen and spacewomen from the survey ship in undress uniform. And there was music—the insistent throb and rattle of little drums, the squealing of fifes. There was something odd about it, a tune and a rhythm that did not seem in accord with these circumstances. Grimes suddenly recognized the Moody and Sankey lilt. He started to sing softly to the familiar yet subtly distorted melody.

Yes, we'll gather at the river,
The beautiful, the beautiful river . . .

"*Must* you, Captain?" asked the Baroness coldly.

He shut up.

It must have been quite a party, he thought as he watched the playmaster screen. There were animal carcasses roasting over big, open fires. Pigs? But what had happened to *them?* Why were not their feral descendents rooting among the ruins? There were great earthenware pots of some liquor being passed around. There were huge platters heaped with amorphous hunks of . . . something, something which, even in the ruddy firelight, gave off a faint blue glow. And the music . . . Another familiar hymn tune. The words formed themselves in Grimes' mind:

Bread of heaven, bread of heaven,
Feed me till I want no more . . .

Now the party was beginning to get rough—not rough in the sense of developing brawls but rough inasmuch as inhibitions were being shed with clothing. It was fast becoming an orgy. Grimes was no prude—but he watched with nauseated disgust three children who could not have been older than eight or nine, two girls and a boy, erotically fondling a fat, naked crewman.

Grimes thought that he heard above the music, the singing, the mechanical cacophony of inertial drive units. This ceased suddenly. Then Commander Belton strode on to the scene. Grimes knew him slightly, although this Belton was a much younger man than the one of his acquaintance. The Belton with whom Grimes had had dealings, not so long ago, was still only a commander, was officer in charge of the third class Survey Service sub-base on Pogg's Landing, a dreary, unimportant planet in the Shaula sector. A sour, embittered man . . . Looking at the playmaster Grimes realized that, apart from aging, Belton had changed very little over the decades.

Belton looked not only sour and embittered but righteously furious. Behind him were a couple of lieutenant commanders and a captain of Marines, all trying to look virtuous. Behind them were twelve Marines in full battle order.

Belton recoiled violently from a plump, naked girl who, a jug of liquor in one hand, a platter of fungus in the other, was trying to tempt him. He barked an order. His officers and the Marines opened fire with stunguns. Those revellers who were still on their feet fell, twitching. Grimes saw a hapless woman topple into one of the fires. Belton's men made no effort to pull her to safety. He watched the Marines dragging their unconscious shipmates toward the waiting pinnaces, caring little what injuries were inflicted in the process. Finally there was a scuffle around the camera itself. It was knocked over and kicked around as its operator was subdued—but still recorded a series of shots of heavily booted feet trampling on sprawling, naked bodies.

And that was it. The screen faded to featureless gray.

"Well?" asked the Baroness, arching her fine eyebrows.

"These things happen," said Grimes. "After all, Your Excellency, a spaceship isn't a Sunday school."

"But the colony should have been," she told him. "The founders of the settlement were all members of a relatively obscure religious sect, the True Followers. And the True Followers were—and still are—notorious for their puritanism."

"There were spacemen too, Your Excellency. And spacemen are usually agnostics."

"Not always. It is a matter of record that the Master of *Lode Venturer* was a True Follower. So were several of his officers."

"Beliefs change, or are lost, over the generations," said Grimes.

"But the singing of hymns indicated that they still believed . . ." she murmured.

Then Big Sister's voice came from the playmaster. "Analysis of the samples has been completed, Your Excellency. Insofar as the larval stage of the indigenous arthropod is concerned there is protein, of course. Amino acids. Salts. A high concentration of sugars. It is my opinion that the children of this world regard these larvae as their counterparts on more privileged planets regard candy.

"And now, the fungoid organism. It supplies all the nutritional needs of the lost colonists. By itself it constitutes an almost perfect balanced diet. Analysis of the human excreta adhering to the boots of yourself and Captain Grimes indicates that its donors were in a good state of physical health . . ."

"*Physical* health . . ." interjected the Baroness.

"Yes, Your Excellency. Analysis of the fungus indicates that it is, but for one thing, a perfect food . . ."

Formulae appeared on the screen.

$C_2H_5OH \ldots (C_2H_5)_2O \ldots$

"Alcohol," said Grimes. "Some people might think that its presence would make the food really perfect."

"The ways of organic intelligences are, at times, mysterious to me," admitted Big Sister. "But, to continue. There are other, very complex molecules present but, so far as I can determine, they are nontoxic . . ."

"And there were no indications of disease in the feces?" asked the Baroness. "Nothing to indicate breakdown of liver, kidneys, other organs?"

"No, Your Excellency."

"Blotting paper," said Grimes.

"Blotting paper?" asked the Baroness.

"A spaceman's expression, Your Excellency. It means that if you take plenty of solid food—preferably rich and creamy—with your liquor there's no damage done. That fungus must be its own blotting paper."

"It could be so," she murmured. "And there are some people who would regard this planet as a veritable paradise—eternal alcoholic euphoria without unpleasant consequences."

"Talking of consequences," said Grimes, "there were babies in that cave."

"What of it, Captain?"

"To have babies you must have childbirth."

"Yet another blinding glimpse of the obvious. But I see what you are driving at and I think that I have the answer. Before the colonists retreated from their village to the caves there must have been doctors and midwives. And those doctors and midwives are still functioning."

"In those conditions?" he demanded, horrified.

"In those conditions," she said. "Do not forget, Captain, that the human race contrived not only to survive but to multiply long before there were such amenities as spotlessly clean maternity wards in hospitals literally bulging with superscientific gadgetry, long before every passing year saw its fresh crop of wonder drugs. And perhaps those doctors and midwives will pass on their skills to the coming generations—in which case the colony stands a very good chance of survival. Perhaps they will not—but even then the colony could survive.

"Nonetheless," she went on, "I must discover the reason for this quite fantastic devolution. There must have been more to it than the quarrel with Commander Belton. There must be records of some kind in the village."

"There are no records," stated Big Sister. "I sent the general purpose robots back to make a thorough search of the settlement, Your Excellency. It seems certain that the colony's archives were housed in one of the buildings destroyed by fire. There are no records."

"There could be records," said the Baroness softly, "in the memories of those living in the caves. I must try to devise some sort of bribe, reward . . . Some form of payment . . . What, I wonder, would induce those people to talk freely?"

That pretty watch hadn't been much good, thought Grimes.

"My watch," said the Baroness suddenly. "Have you cleaned it for me, Big Sister? Did it need repair?"

"Your watch, Your Excellency?"

"Yes. My watch. It was a gift from the Duke of . . . No matter. The captain brought it back in his pocket. It had been dropped into a pool of . . . ordure."

"There was no watch in any of Captain Grimes' pockets, Your Excellency."

Grimes remembered then. The thing had been wrapped in his handkerchief. Then he had removed it, to use the handkerchief to parcel up the specimen of fungus. He must have left it in the cave.

He said as much. He added, "When we go back tomorrow morning I'll find it. I don't think that any of the cave dwellers will be interested in it."

The Baroness had been almost friendly. Now she regarded him with contemptuous hostility. She snapped, "You will go back to the cave to find it *now!*"

Chapter 18

Grimes went up to his quarters to change back into khaki; he did not think that even the Baroness would expect him to scrabble around in that noisome cavern wearing his purple and gold finery. When he left the ship it was almost sunset. The pinnace was waiting at the foot of the ramp. There were no general purpose robots to afford him an escort. He had assumed that Big Sister would lay them on as a matter of course. She had not but he could not be bothered to make an issue of it.

He boarded the pinnace. It began to lift even before he was in the pilot's chair. Big Sister knew the way now, he thought. He was content to be a passenger. He filled and lit his pipe. The more or less (rather less than more) fragrant fumes had a soothing effect. His seething needed soothing, he thought, pleased with the play on words. He might be only an employee but still he was a shipmaster, a captain. To be ordered around aboard his own vessel was much too much. And all over a mere toy, no matter how expensive, a gaudy trinket that the Baroness had been willing enough to hand over to that revolting female brat. She couldn't have thought much of its donor, the Duke of wherever it was.

The pinnace knew the way. This was the third time that it was making the trip from the yacht to the valley. It had no real brain of its own but, even when it was not functioning as an extension of Big Sister, possessed a memory and was at least as intelligent as the average insect.

It flew directly to the village while Grimes sat and fumed, literally and figuratively. When it landed darkness was already thick in the shadow of the high cliffs.

"Illuminate the path," ordered Grimes.

As he unsnapped his seat belt he saw through the viewports the rock face suddenly aglow in the beams of the pinnace's searchlights, the brightest of which outlined one of the dark cave openings. So that was where he had to go. He passed through the little airlock, jumped down to the damp grass. He walked to the cliff face, came to the foot of the natural ramp. He hesitated briefly. It had been a dangerous climb—for a non-mountaineer such as himself—even in daylight, in company, with a guide. But, he was obliged to admit, he could not complain about lack of illumination.

He made his slow and cautious way upward, hugging the rock face. He had one or two nasty moments as he negotiated the really awkward parts. Nonetheless he made steady progress although he was sweating profusely when he reached the cave mouth. This time he had brought a flashlight with him. He switched it on as he entered the natural tunnel.

Did these people, he wondered disgustedly, spend all their time sleeping? It seemed like it. Sleeping, and eating, and copulating. But the paradises of some Terran religions were not so very different—although not, surely, the promised Heaven of a sect such as the True Followers.

The bright beam of the flashlight played over the nude bodies sprawled in their obscene postures, over the clumps of fungus that looked almost like growths of coral—or naked brains. These glowed more brightly after the light of his flashlight had passed over them.

Carefully picking his way through the sleepers he made his way deeper into the cave. He was watching for the glint of gems, of bright metal. He did not see the slim arm that extended itself from an apparently slumbering body, the long-fingered hand that closed about his ankle. He fell heavily. His flashlight was jolted from his grasp, flared briefly as it crashed onto the rock floor, went out. His face smashed into something soft and pulpy. He had opened his mouth to cry out as he was falling and a large portion of the semi-fluid mess was forced into it. He gagged—then realized that the involuntary mouthful was not what, at first, he had thought that it was.

The fungus, he realized . . .

It tasted quite good.

It tasted better than merely good.

There was a meatiness, a sweetness, a spiciness and, he thought, considerable alcoholic content. He had been chivvied out from the yacht to search for that blasted watch without being allowed time to enjoy a drink, a meal. It would do no harm, he decided, if he savored the delicious taste a few seconds more before prudently spitting it out. After all, he rationalized, this was scientific research, wasn't it? And Big Sister had given the fungus full marks as a source of nourishment. He chewed experimentally. In spite of its mushiness the flesh possessed texture, fibres and nodules that broke between his teeth, that released aromatic oils which were to the original taste as a vintage burgundy is to a very ordinary *vin ordinaire.*

Before he realized what he was doing he swallowed.

The second mouthful of the fungus was more voluntary than otherwise.

He was conscious of a soft weight on his back, of long hair falling around his head. Languidly he tried to turn over, finally succeeded in spite of the multiplicity (it seemed) of naked arms and legs that were imprisoning him.

He looked up into the face that was looking down into his.

Why, he thought, *she's beautiful . . .*

He recognized her.

She was the woman whom he and the Baroness had seen emerge briefly from the caves. Then her overall filthiness had made the biggest impression. *Now* he was quite unaware of the dirt on her body, the tangles in her hair. She was no more (and no less) than a desirable woman, an available woman. He knew that she was looking on him as a desirable, available man. After all the weeks cooped up aboard *The Far Traveler* with an attractive female at whom he could look, but must not touch, the temptation was strong, too strong.

She kissed him full on the mouth.

Her breath was sweet and spicy, intoxicating.

She was woman and he was man, and all that stood in the way of consummation was his hampering clothing. Her hands were at the fastenings of his trousers but fumbling inexpertly. Reluctantly he removed his own from her full buttocks to assist her, was dimly conscious of the cold stone under his naked rump as the garment was pushed down to his knees, was ecstatically conscious of the enveloping warmth of her as she mounted him and rode him, not violently but languorously, slowly, slowly . . .

The tension releasing explosion came.

She slumped against him, over him, her nipples brushing his face. Gently, reluctantly she rolled off his body. He felt her hand at his mouth. It held a large piece of the fungus. He took it from her fingers, chewed and swallowed. It was even better than his first taste of it had been.

He drifted into sleep.

Chapter 19

He dreamed.

In the dream he was a child.

He was one of the *Lode Venturer* survivors who had made the long trek south from the vicinity of the north magnetic pole. He could remember the crash landing, the swift and catastrophic conversion of what had been a little, warm, secure world into twisted, crumpled wreckage.

He remembered the straggling column of men, women and children burdened with supplies from the wrecked gaussjammer—food, sacks of precious Terran seed grain, sealed stasis containers of the fertilized ova of Terran livestock, the incubators broken down into portable components, the parts of the solar power generator.

He was one of *Lode Venturer*'s people who had survived both crash landing and long march, who had found the valley, who had tilled the fields and planted the grain, who had worked at setting up the incubating equipment. Although only a child he had shared the fears of his elders as the precious store of preserved provisions dwindled and the knowledge that, in spite of strict rationing, it would not last out until the harvest, until the incubators delivered progenitors of future herds of meat animals.

He remembered the day of the drawing of lots.

There were the losers—three young men, a middle-aged woman and another one who was little more than a girl—standing there, frightened yet somehow proud, while further lots were drawn to decide who would be executioner and butcher. A fierce argument had developed—some of the women claiming, belatedly, that females of child-bearing age should have been exempt from the first lottery. While this was going on another boy—the son of the middle-aged woman, came down from the caves to which he had run rather than watch his mother slaughtered. He was bearing an armful of the fungus.

"Food!" he was shouting. "Food! I have tasted it and it is good!"

They had all sung a hymn of thanksgiving then, grateful for their delivery from what, no matter how necessary to their survival, would have been a ghastly sin.

Bread of Heaven, bread of Heaven,
Feed me till I want no more, want no more,
Feed me till I want no more . . .

He awoke then, drifting slowly up from the warm, deep sleep. He did what he had to do, relieving the pressure on bowels and bladder as he lay there. He wondered dimly why people ever went to the trouble of fabricating elaborate sanitary arrangements. The fungus needed his body wastes. He needed the fungus. It was all so simple.

He reached out and grabbed another handful of the satisfying, intoxicating stuff. He became aware that the woman—or a woman— was with him. While he was still eating they coupled.

He slept.

He dreamed.

He was the Pastor, the leader of the people of the settlement.

He had looked over the arrangements for the feast and all was well. There was an ample supply of the strong liquor brewed and distiled from grain—the last harvest had been a good one, surplus to food requirements. Pigs had been slaughtered and dressed, ready for the roasting. Great baskets of the fungus had been brought down from the caves. Since it had been discovered that it thrived on human manure it had proliferated, spreading from the original cavern through the entire subterranean complex. Perhaps it had changed, too. It seemed that with every passing year its flavor had improved. At first— he seemed to remember—it had been almost tasteless although filling and nutritious.

But now . . .

The guests from the ship, clattering through the night sky in their noisy flying boats, were dropping down to the village. He hoped that there would not be the same trouble as there had been with the guests from that other ship, the one with the odd name, *Epsilon Pavonis*. Of course, it had not been the guests themselves who had made the trouble; it had been their captain. But *this* captain, he had been told, was himself a True Follower. All should be well.

All was well.

The love feast, the music, the dancing, the singing of the old, familiar hymns . . .

And the love . . .

And surely the manna, the gift from the all-wise, all-loving God of the True Followers, was better than it ever had been. What need was there, after all, for the corn liquor, the roast pig?

Bread of Heaven, bread of Heaven,
Feed me till I want no more . . .

He walked slowly through and among the revellers, watching benevolently the fleshly intermingling of his own people and those from the starship. It was . . . *good.* Everything was good. He exchanged a few words with the Survey Service petty officer who, dutifully operating his equipment, was making a visual and sound recording of the feast. He wondered briefly why the man was amused when he said that the pictures and the music would be acclaimed when presented in the tabernacles of the True Followers on Earth and other planets. He looked benignly at the group at which the camera was aimed—a plump, naked, supine crewman being fondled by three children. It was a charming scene.

And why the strong sensation of déjà vu?

Why the brief, gut-wrenching disgust?

He heard the distant hammering in the still, warm air, growing louder and louder. More airboats—what did they call them? pinnaces?—from the ship, he thought. Perhaps the captain himself, Commander Belton, was coming after all. He would be pleased to see for himself how well his fellow True Followers on this distant world had kept the faith . . .

Then the dream became a nightmare.

There was shouting and screaming.

There was fighting.

There were armed men discharging their weapons indiscriminately, firing on both their own shipmates and the colonists.

There was his confrontation with a tall, gaunt, stiffly uniformed man.

(Again the flash of *déjà vu.*)

There were the bitter, angry words.

"True Followers, you call yourselves? I understood that my people had been invited to a religious service . . . And I find a disgusting orgy in progress!"

"But we are True Followers! We were saved. God Himself sent his manna to save us from committing the deadliest sin of all. Here! Taste! Eat and believe!"

And a hand smashed viciously down, striking the proferred manna from his grasp, as Belton shouted, "Keep that filthy muck away from me!"

He saw the muzzle of a pistol pointing at him, saw the flare of energy that jolted him into oblivion.

He slowly drifted up to semi-consciousness. There was a woman. There was more of the manna.

Again he slept.

Chapter 20

He dreamed.

He dreamed that a bright, harsh light was beating through his closed eyelids, that something hard was nudging him in the ribs.

He opened his eyes, immediately shut them again before he was blinded.

A voice, a somehow familiar female voice, was saying, "Captain Grimes! Captain Grimes! Wake up, damn you!" And then, in an intense whisper, "Oh! If you could only see yourself!"

He muttered, "Go 'way. Go 'way."

"Captain Grimes! John!" There was a hand on his shoulder, shaking him. He opened his eyes again. She had put her flashlight on the ground so that now he saw her by its reflected light. She was a woman. She was beautiful—but so was everybody in this enchanted cavern. He dimly recognized her.

She said, "I must get you out of here."

Why? he wondered. *Why?*

She got her hands under his naked shoulders, tried to lift him. He got his hands about her shoulders, pulled her down. She struggled, kneeing him in the groin. He let go and she stood up, stepping back from him. The shirt had been torn from her upper body. In spite of the pain that she had inflicted on him he felt a surge of desire, reached out for her exposed breasts. She stepped back another pace.

He wanted her—but to get up to go after her was too much trouble.

But he muttered, "Do'n' go ... Do'n' go ... I ... want ... you ... always ... wanted ... you ..."

Her face was glistening oddly. Dimly he realized that she was weeping. She said, "Not *here*. Not *now*. Pull yourself together. Come back to the ship."

He said—the words were coming more easily now, but were they his? "I . . . hate . . . ships . . . All . . . True . . . Followers . . . hate . . . ships . . . Stay . . . here . . . Be . . . happy . . ."

Her face and voice hardened. She said, "I'll get you out of here by force!"

He was fast losing interest in the conversation. He reached out languidly for the omnipresent manna, chewed and swallowed.

He muttered, "Try . . . this . . . Make . . . you . . . human . . ."

But she was gone.

It did not matter.

The warmth of the communal life of the cavern surrounded him. There were women.

And always there was the manna.

He slept.

He dreamed.

He was one of the crowd being harangued by the Pastor.

"We must sever all ties with Earth!" he heard. "We are the true, the real True Followers! Were we not saved by God himself from death and from deadly sin? But these Earthmen, who have intruded into our paradise, who have strayed from the true path, refuse to believe . . ."

"So burn the houses, my people! Destroy everything that links us to faithless Earth, even our herds and our crops!

"God's own manna is all that we need, all that we shall ever need!"

And somebody else—Grimes knew that it was one of the community's physicians—was crying over and over, in a sort of ecstasy, "Holy symbiosis! Holy symbiosis!"

Crackling flames and screaming pigs and the voices of the people, singing,

Bread of Heaven, bread of Heaven,
Feed me till I want no more, want no more . . .

Again the too bright light and again the hand shaking his shoulder . . .

"Wake up, John! Wake up!"

"Go 'way . . ."

"John! Look at me!"

He opened his eyes.

She had placed her torch on a ledge so that it shone full upon her. She was naked. Diamonds gleamed in the braided coronet of the hair of her head and even in the heart-shaped growth at the scission of her thighs. She was a spaceman's pin-up girl in the warm, living flesh.

She said softly, "You want me. You shall have me—but not here, among these degenerates, this filth." She turned slowly, saying, "Follow . . ."

Almost he made the effort to get to his feet but it was too much trouble. With faint stirrings of regret he watched her luminous body swaying away from him. Once she turned and beckoned. He wondered vaguely why she should be wearing such an angry expression. And before she reached the mouth of the cave he had fallen back into sleep.

A long while or a little while—he had no way of knowing—later he awoke. After a few mouthfuls of manna he crawled until he found a woman.

And slept again.

And dreamed.

Subtly the dreams changed.

There were, as before, memories from the minds of the colonists who had long lived in symbiosis with the fungus but there were now other memories—brief flashes, indistinct at first but all the time increasing in clarity and duration. There were glimpses of the faces and the bodies of women whom he had known—Jane Pentecost, Maggie Lazenby, Ellen Russell, Una Freeman, Maya . . .

The women . . .

And the ships.

Lines from a long-ago read and long-ago forgotten piece of verse drifted through his mind:

The arching sky is calling
Spacemen back to their trade . . .

He was sitting in the control room of his first command, the little Serpent Class courier *Adder*, a king at last even though his realm, to others, was a very insignificant one. Obedient to the touch of his fingers on the console the tiny ship lifted from the Lindisfarne Base apron.

All hands! Stand by! Free Falling!
The lights below us fade . . .

And through the dream, louder and louder, surged the arhythmic hammering of a spaceship's inertial drive.

*   *   *

He awoke.

He scooped a handful of manna from a nearby clump.

He chewed, swallowed.

Somehow it was not the same as it had been; there was a hint of bitterness, a rancidity. He relieved himself where he lay and then crawled over and among the recumbent bodies until he found a receptive woman.

Like a great, fat slug . . . he thought briefly.

(But what was a slug? Surely nothing like this beautiful creature . . .)

After he was finished with her and she with him he drifted again into sleep, even though that mechanical clangor coming from somewhere outside the cave was a growing irritation.

He dreamed more vividly than before.

He had just brought *Discovery* down to a landing in the Paddington Oval on Botany Bay. His officers and the Marine guard behind him, he was marching down the ramp to the vividly green grass. Against the pale blue sky he could see the tall, white flagstaffs, each with its rippling ensign, dark blue with the cruciform constellation of silver stars in the fly, with the superimposed red, white and blue crosses in the upper canton.

There was a band playing.

He was singing in time to the familiar tune:

Waltzing Matilda, Waltzing Matilda,
You'll come a-waltzing Matilda with me . . .

He awoke.

There was still that arythmic hammering, drifting in from somewhere outside—but the music, vastly amplified almost drowned the mechanical racket.

Up jumped the swagman, sprang into the billabong,
"You'll never catch me alive!" cried he . . .

And what was this noisome billabong into which he, Grimes, had plunged? Would his ghost still be heard after he was gone from it? Would his memories of Deep Space and the ships plying the star lanes remain to haunt the swinish dreamers of Farhaven? Would that honest old national song replace the phoney piety of the True Followers' hymn?

Manna! he thought disgustedly, kicking out at a dim-glowing mass. It splattered under his bare foot and the stench was sickening.

He was seized with an uncontrollable spasm of nausea. Drained and shaken he stumbled toward the cave entrance, the music luring him on as though he were one of the Pied Piper's rats. He tripped over sleeping bodies. A woman clutched his ankle. He looked down at her. He could not be sure but he thought that she was the one responsible for his original downfall. Almost he brought his free foot smashing down on to her sleepily smiling face but, at the last moment, desisted.

She was what she was, just as he was what he was—and he had wallowed in the mire happily enough . . .

He stooped and with both hands gently disengaged her fingers.

He staggered on, finally out onto the ledge. The sunlight blinded him. Then at last he was able to see her, hanging above the valley, beautiful and brightly golden, *The Far Traveler*. It was from her that the music was blaring. It ceased suddenly, was replaced by the amplified voice of Big Sister.

"I am sending the pinnace for you, Captain Grimes. It will come as closely alongside the cliff as possible. The robots will help you aboard."

He waited there, naked and filthy and ashamed, until the boat came for him.

Chapter 21

Grimes—clean, clothed, depilated but still shaky—sat in the Baroness's salon telling his story. She listened in silence, as did the omnipresent Big Sister.

When he was finished Big Sister said, "I must make a further analysis of the fungus specimens. Drug addiction among human and other intelligent life forms is not unusual, of course, but the symbiotic aspects of this case intrigue me."

"And the dreams," said Grimes. "The dreams . . . I must have experienced the entire history of the Lost Colony . . ."

"For years," said Big Sister, "the fungus has been nourished by the waste products of the colonists' bodies—and when they have died it has been nourished by the bodies themselves. It has become, in some way that I have yet to discover, the colonists. Is there not an old saying: A man is what he eats? This could be true for other living beings. And the symbiosis has been more, much more, than merely physical. By eating the fungus you, for a while, entered into the symbiotic relationship."

"Very interesting," commented Grimes. "But you must have known what was happening to me, even if not why or how. You should have sent in the robots to drag me out by force."

"Command decisions are not my prerogative," said Big Sister smugly. "Her Excellency did suggest that I attempt a forcible rescue but I dissuaded her. It was a matter for humans only, for humans to resolve for themselves, essentially for a human of your sort to resolve for himself. I know very well, Captain Grimes, how you hate robots, how your dislike for me has prevented you from being properly grateful for your rescue from Commander Delamere's clutches." There was a brief, almost human chuckle. "I did think that Her Excellency would be able to recapture you by the use of a *very* human bait, but her attempt was not successful . . ."

Grimes looked at the Baroness, remembering her as he had seen her. His ears burned as he flushed miserably. If she were embarrassed by her own memory of the occasion she did not show it.

"So," went on Big Sister, "I made use of what I have learned of your peculiar psychology—your professional pride, your rather childish nationalism, your very real love of ships." She paused, then said, "A man who loves ships can't be all bad."

"A man," said the Baroness coldly, "who could refuse what *I* offered can't be all man."

He said, "I am sorry. I am truly sorry. But I was under the influence of the . . . manna . . ."

She said, "*In vino veritas*, Captain Grimes. And worst of all is the knowledge that the cacophony of a ship's engines, the trite music of a folksong about an Australian sheep stealer, succeeded where *I* failed. I will tell you now that I had intended that a relationship—not permanent but mutually satisfying—would develop between us. There is little likelihood now that this will come to pass. Our relations will remain as they have been since I first engaged you, those between employer and employee."

She turned away from Grimes, addressed the playmaster. "Take us up, Big Sister, up and away from this planet. I prefer not to remain on a world where I was unable successfully to compete with drug sodden degenerates or with an unhuman electronic intelligence."

Grimes wondered if Big Sister was feeling as resentful as he was himself. Probably not, he thought. Nonhuman electronic intelligences must surely be unemotional.

Chapter 22

So *The Far Traveler* lifted from Farhaven, with Grimes far less in actual command of the vessel than he ever had been, proceeding in the general direction of the Shakespearian Sector, out toward the rim of the galaxy.

It was quite a while before the after effects of the drug wore off and until they did so Grimes was treated as a convalescent. It was during this period that he noticed a subtle change in Big Sister's attitude toward him. He had, almost from the start, envisaged her as a bossy, hard-featured woman, hating and despising men. Now the imaginary flesh with which he clothed the electronic intelligence was that of an aunt whom, during his childhood, he had liked rather than loved, feared slightly, obeyed (for most of the time) during a period when his parents, away traveling, had left him in her charge. He recalled the unsuspected soft side of her nature which she had exhibited when he had been confined to his bed for some days after he had made a crash landing in the hot-air balloon that he had constructed himself, suffering two broken ribs and a fractured ankle.

She had pampered him then, just as Big Sister was pampering him now (and as the Baroness most certainly was not). Nonetheless, a year or so later, he had been very surprised when this aunt had embarked upon a whirlwind romance with a Dog Star Line second mate who was enjoying a spell of shore leave on Earth, returning with this space-man to his home world. (Now, he thought, remembering, he would not have been surprised. As a child he had regarded the lady as a dragon but she had been the sort of tall, lean auburn-haired woman that the adult Grimes always fell for.)

Much as Big Sister reminded him of this aunt, thought Grimes, he could not imagine her eloping with anybody or anything. He supposed that, having saved him, she regarded herself as being responsible for him.

Eventually, when Big Sister decided that he was functioning as well as he ever would function, he was bidden to the Baroness's presence.

The lady said, "I am informed that I once again can enjoy the services of my yachtmaster. Can you, out of your long and wide experience in the Survey Service, suggest our next port of call?"

He thought hard then said doubtfully, "Kinsolving?"

"Kinsolving," she stated, "is not a Lost Colony." (She must have been having a good rummage in Big Sister's memory bank.) "It is one of the Rim Worlds. For some reason the colony was abandoned. There are now no people there at all. The object of my research, as well you know, is social evolution in the Lost Colonies. How can there be social evolution when there is nobody to evolve?"

Grimes tried not to sigh too audibly. He was never at home in this lushly appointed Owner's Suite or in the comic opera uniform that he was obliged to wear during these audiences. He would have been far happier in his own quarters. At least there he could smoke his pipe in peace. But his employer did not approve of smoking. Fortunately she did not disapprove of the use of drugs other than tobacco, such as alcohol—and, Grimes was bound to admit, her robot butler mixed a superb dry martini. He was appreciating the one that he was sipping; Big Sister had at last given him permission to drink again.

He looked at her over the frosted rim of his glass. She was reclining gracefully on her chaise longue, looking (as always) like a rather superior version of Goya's *Maja*. She looked at him very coldly. He realized that the top tunic button of his gold and purple livery was undone. He did it up.

She said, "You aren't much use, Captain, are you? I thought, in my girlish innocence, that an ex-Commander of the Interstellar Federation's Survey Service would have been the ideal captain for an expedition such as this. I know that you, before you resigned your commission, discovered at least three Lost Colonies. There were New Sparta and Morrowvia, both of which we shall, eventually, be visiting. And there was, of course, Botany Bay. With reference to the first two worlds it will be interesting to see what effects your clumsy meddlings have had upon the lives of the unspoiled peoples of those planets . . ."

Grimes was acutely conscious of the burning flush that suffused his prominent ears. He, personally, would hardly have classed either the New Spartans or the Morrowvians as unspoiled—and New Sparta had been on the brink of a devastating civil war at the time of his landing. As for Morrowvia—he had not been the only interfering outsider. There had been the Dog Star Line's Captain Danzellan, looking after the commercial interests of his principals. There had been the piratical Drongo Kane in his own *Southerly Buster*, looking after his own interests.

"And didn't you enjoy a liaison with one of the local rulers on Morrowvia?" continued the Baroness. "I find it hard to understand—but then, I have never been enamored of cats."

Maya, remembered Grimes. *Feline ancestry but very much a woman—not like this cold, rich bitch* . . . Then he hated himself for the uncharitable thought. He owed the Baroness much. Had it not been for her intervention he would have been haled back to Lindisfarne to stand trial. And to have done what she had done in that vile cave on Farhaven must have required considerable resolution. He could hardly blame her for blaming him for the failure of that second rescue attempt.

Nonetheless he said, with some indignation, "I was under the impression, Your Excellency, that my full and frank report on the happenings on Morrowvia was not to be released to the general public."

"*I* am not the general public," she said. "Money, Captain Grimes, is the key that will open the door to any vault in the Galaxy. Your friend, Commander Delamere, was, I think, more impressed by my wealth than my beauty. There are many others like him."

Grimes missed the chance of saying something gallant.

"Your Excellency, may I interrupt?" asked Big Sister, her voice coming from everywhere and nowhere.

"You have already interrupted," said the Baroness. "But continue."

"Your Excellency, I have monitored Carlotti transmissions from the Admiralty, on Earth, to all Survey Service ships and bases . . ."

Have you? thought Grimes. *Restricted wavebands, unbreakable codes . . . And what are they, against the power of money?*

"A distress message capsule was picked up off Lentimure by the Survey Service destroyer *Acrux*. It originated from a ship called *Lode Ranger*. Text is as follows: Pile dead. Proceeding under diesel power. Intend landing on apparently habitable planet . . ."

There was more—a listing of crew and passengers, what astronomical data might just possibly be of use to future rescuers. In very few cases, Grimes knew, was such information of any value—but a modern computer, given the elements of a capsule's trajectory, could determine with some accuracy its departure point. And then the rescue ship, arriving a few centuries after the call for assistance, would find either a thriving Lost Colony or, after a search, the eroded wreckage of the lost ship and, possibly, a few human skeletons.

Grimes asked, "Do you have the coordinates of the departure point?"

Big Sister replied, "Apparently they are yet to be determined, Captain. As soon as they are transmitted by the Admiralty I shall inform you."

The Baroness said, "It just could happen that we shall be the nearest ship to the Lost Colony. It would be interesting to make the first landing upon such a world, before the clumsy boots of oafish spacemen have trampled all sorts of valuable evidence into the dust."

Grimes said, "Probably the Lost Colony, if there is one, is halfway across the Galaxy from here."

She said, "You are unduly pessimistic, Captain. Never forget that chance plays a great part in human life. And now, while we are waiting, could you refresh my memory regarding the gaussjammers and how it was that so many of them originated Lost Colonies?"

You probably know more about it than I do, thought Grimes. *After all, it's you that's writing the thesis.*

He said, "The gaussjammers, using the Ehrenhaft Drive, were the ships of the Second Expansion. Prior to them were the so-called Deep Freeze ships which, of course, were not faster than light. The gaussjammers, though, were FTL. With the Ehrenhaft generators in operation they were, essentially, huge monopoles. They tried to be in two places at once along a line of magnetic force, proceeding along such tramlines to their destinations. They were extremely vulnerable to magnetic storms; a really severe one could fling them thousands of light-years off course. There was another effect, too. The micro-piles upon which they relied for power would be drained of all energy. The captain of a gaussjammer lost in space, his pile dead, had only one course of action open to him. He used his emergency diesels to power the Ehrenhaft generators. He proceeded in what he hoped would be the right direction. When he ran out of diesel fuel his biochemist would convert what should have been food for the ship's company into more fuel.

"Finally, if he was lucky, he found a planet before food and fuel ran out. If his luck still held he managed to land in one piece. And then, if conditions were not too impossible, he and his people stood a fair chance of founding a Lost Colony . . ."

Big Sister spoke again. "I have intercepted and decoded more signals. I estimate that we can be in orbit about *Lode Ranger*'s planet no more than ten standard days from now. As far as I can ascertain there are no Survey Service vessels in our vicinity; it is a reasonable assumption that we shall make the first landing. Have I your permission to adjust trajectory?"

"Of course," said the Baroness. "Adjust trajectory as soon as the captain and myself are in our couches."

"I should be in the control room," said Grimes.

"Is that really necessary?" asked the Baroness.

Big Sister adjusted trajectory, shutting down inertial drive and Mannschenn Drive, using the directional gyroscopes to swing the ship about her axes, lining her up on the target star. Grimes, sweating it out in his bunk, did not doubt that due and proper allowance was being made for galactic drift. He was obliged to admit that Big Sister could do everything that he could do, and at least as well—but *he* should have been doing it. (That aunt of his who had run away with the Sirian spaceman had annoyed the young Grimes more than once by doing the things that he thought that he should have been doing.) He listened to the cold yet not altogether mechanical voice making the routine announcements: "Stopping inertial drive. Stand by for free fall . . . Mannschenn Drive—*off*." There was the usual sensation of spatial and temporal disorientation. "Directional gyroscopes—*on*. Prepare for centrifugal effects . . . Directional gyroscopes—*off*. Mannschenn Drive— restarting." And the low hum, rising to a thin, high whine as the spinning rotors built up speed, precessing, tumbling down the dark dimensions . . . And the colors, sagging down the spectrum, and the distorted, warped perspective . . . And, as often happened, the transitory flash of déjà vu . . . This was happening now, had happened before, would happen again but . . . differently. In some other Universe, on a previous coil of time—or, perhaps, on a coil of time yet to be experienced— he had married the Princess Marlene, the father of whose sons he was, on El Dorado, had been accepted by the aristocratic and opulent inhabitants of that planet as one of the family, a member of the club and, eventually, using his wife's money, had caused the spaceyacht, *The Far Traveler*, to be built to his own specifications. He was both Owner and Master. He was—but briefly, briefly, in that alternate universe—a truly contented man.

And then outlines ceased to waver, colors to fade, intensify and shift, and he was . . . himself.

He was John Grimes, disgraced ex-Commander, late of the Federation's Survey Service, Master *de jure* but not *de facto* of a ship that was no more—or was she more, much more, but not in any way that conceivably could benefit him?—than the glittering toy of an overly rich, discontented woman.

"On trajectory," said Big Sister, "for *Lode Ranger*'s planet. Normal routine may be resumed."

"I am coming up to Control," said Grimes.

"You may come up to Control," said Big Sister, making it sound as though she was granting a great favor.

Chapter 23

The Far Traveler fell through the warped continuum toward the yellow sun on one of whose planets *Lode Ranger*'s people had found refuge. She was alone and lonely, with no traffic whatsoever within range of her mass proximity indicator. Distant Carlotti signals were monitored by Big Sister and, according to her, no ship was closer than the destroyer *Acrux*—and she was one helluva long way away.

Nonetheless Grimes was not happy. He said, "I know, Your Excellency, that with the advent of Carlotti Radio it is no longer mandatory to carry a Psionic Communications Officer—but I think that you should have shipped one."

"Have a prying telepath aboard my ship, Captain Grimes?" she flared. "Out of the question! It is bad enough being compelled by archaic legislation to employ a human yachtmaster."

Grimes sighed. He said, "As you know, PCOs are carried aboard all Survey Service vessels and in the ships of most other navies. They are required to observe the code of ethics formulated by the Rhine Institute. But today their function is not that of ship to ship or ship to planet communication. They are, primarily, a sort of psychic radar. How shall I put it? This way, perhaps. You're making a landing on a strange world. Are the natives likely to be friendly or hostile? Unless the indigenes' way of thinking is too alien your PCO will be able to come up with the answer. If *The Far Traveler* carried a PCO we should already have some sort of idea of what we shall find on *Lode Ranger*'s planet. Come to that, a PCO would have put us wise to the state of affairs on Farhaven and saved us from a degrading experience."

"I would prefer that you did not remind me of it," she said. "Meanwhile we shall just have to rely upon the highly efficient electronic equipment with which this ship is furnished."

She finished her drink. Grimes finished his. Obviously there was not going to be another.

She said, "Don't let me keep you from your dinner, Captain."

Grimes left her boudoir and went up to his own spartan—but only relatively so—quarters.

Not very long afterward *The Far Traveler* hung in orbit about *Lode Ranger*'s world. It was inhabited without doubt; the lights of cities could be seen through the murky atmosphere of the night hemisphere and on the daylit face were features too regular to be natural, almost certainly roads and railways and canals. And those people had radio; the spaceship's NST receivers picked up an unceasing stream of signals. There was music. There were talks.

But . . .

But the music bore no resemblance to anything composed by Terrans for Terran ears and the instruments were exclusively percussion. There were complex rhythms, frail, tinkling melodies, not displeasing but alien, alien . . .

And the voices . . .

Guttural croaks, strident squeals, speaking no language known to Grimes or the Baroness, no tongue included in Big Sister's fantastically comprehensive data bank.

But that wasn't all.

The active element of the planet's atmosphere was chlorine.

"There will be no Lost Colony here, Your Excellency," said Grimes. "*Lode Ranger*'s captain would never have landed once his spectroscopic analysis told him what to expect. He must have carried on."

"Even so," she said, "I have found a new world. I have ensured for myself a place in history." She smiled in self mockery. "For what it is worth. Now that we are here our task will be to carry out a preliminary survey."

"Do you intend to land, Your Excellency?" asked Big Sister.

"Of course."

"Then I must advise against it. You assumed, as did my builders, that my golden hull would be immune to corrosion. But somehow nobody took into account the possibility of a landing on a planet with a chlorine atmosphere. I have already detected traces of nitrohydrochloric acid which, I need hardly remind you, is a solvent for both gold and platinum."

"Only traces," said Grimes.

"Only traces, Captain," agreed Big Sister. "But would *you* care to run naked through a forest in which there might be pockets of dichlorethyl sulfide?"

Grimes looked blank.

"Mustard gas," said Big Sister.

"Oh," said Grimes.

The Baroness said, "I am rich, as you know. Nonetheless this ship is a considerable investment. I do not wish her shell plating to be corroded, thus detracting from her value."

"Yes, it would spoil her good looks," admitted Grimes. But the main function of a ship, any ship, is not to look pretty. He remembered that long-ago English admiral who had frowned upon gunnery practice because it discolored the gleaming paintwork of the warcraft under his command.

He asked, "Couldn't you devise some sort of protective coating? A spray-on plastic . . ."

Big Sister replied, "I have already done so. And, anticipating that you and Her Excellency would wish to make a landing, the smaller pinnace has been treated, also your spacesuits and six of the general purpose robots. Meanwhile I have processed the photographs taken during our circumpolar orbits and, if you will watch the playmaster, I shall exhibit one that seems of especial interest."

Grimes and the Baroness looked at the glowing screen. There— dull, battered, corroded but still, after all these many years, recognizable—was the pear-shaped hull of a typical gaussjammer. Not far from it was a dome, obviously not a natural feature of the terrain, possibly evidence that the survivors had endeavored to set up some sort of settlement in the hostile environment. A few kilometers to the north was a fair-sized town.

"Could they—or their descendants—still be living, Captain?" asked the Baroness.

"People have lived in similar domes, on Earth's airless moon, for many generations," said Grimes. "And the Selenites could always pack up and return to Earth if they didn't like it. *Lode Ranger*'s personnel had no place else to go."

"But . . . To live among aliens?"

"There are all sorts of odd enclaves throughout the Galaxy," said Grimes.

"Very well, Captain. We shall go down at once, to find what we shall find."

"Big Sister," asked Grimes, "assuming that we leave the ship now, what time of day will it be at the wreck when we land?"

"Late afternoon," was the reply.

"We should make a dawn landing," said Grimes.

"You are not in the Survey Service now, Captain," the Baroness told him. "You may as well forget Survey Service S.O.P."

"Those survivors—if there are any survivors—have waited for generations," said Grimes. "A few more hours won't hurt them."

"*I* am going down *now*," she told him. "You may come if you wish."

Grimes wished that he knew more about Space Law as applicable to civilian vessels. When is a captain not a captain? When he has his owner on board, presumably.

He said, "Shall we get into our spacesuits, Your Excellency? We shall need them if we leave the pinnace."

She said, "I will meet you in the boat bay, Captain."

Chapter 24

His robot stewardess helped him on with his spacesuit. The protective garment was no longer gold but, after the anti-corrosive spray, a dull, workmanlike grey. He preferred it in that color. He buckled on the belt with the two holstered pistols—one laser, one projectile. He checked the weapons to make sure they were models with firing studs instead of triggers, designed to be held in a heavily gauntleted hand. All was in order.

He went down to the boat bay. The Baroness was already there, clad as he was. Six of the general purpose robots were there. Golden, their asexual bodies had been beautiful; gray, they looked menacing, sinister. So did the pinnace.

"Should we get into trouble," said Grimes, speaking into his helmet microphone, "please come down for us." He could not resist adding, "if you get tarnished it will be just too bad."

"There was no need for that," said the Baroness. Through the helmet phones her voice was even more coldly metallic than that of the computer-pilot.

"Understood," said Big Sister shortly.

"Robots into the boat," ordered Grimes.

The automata filed into and through the airlock.

"After you, Your Excellency."

The Baroness, looking not unlike a robot herself, boarded.

Grimes followed her, took his seat in the pilot's chair. The airlock doors closed before he could bring a finger to the appropriate button. If Big Sister insisted on doing the things that he was being paid to do, that was all right by him.

He said, "One kilometer from the wreck please revert to manual control. My control."

"Understood, Captain," said Big Sister.

"Must you dot every 'i' and cross every 't'?" asked the Baroness crossly.

The boat's inertial drive grumbled itself awake; the boat bay doors opened. Through the aperture glowed the sunlit hemisphere of *Lode Ranger*'s planet, a gigantic, clouded emerald. Then they were out and away from the ship, driving down rather than merely falling. Grimes kept his paws off the controls, although it required a considerable effort of will to refrain from touching them. Big Sister knew what she was doing, he told himself. He hoped.

Down they drove, down, down. The whispering of atmosphere along the hull became audible above the clatter of the inertial drive. There was no rise of cabin temperature although, thought Grimes, the cooling system must be working overtime. And, he told himself, the modified metal of which the pinnace was constructed had a far higher melting point than that of normal gold.

Down they drove, through high, green, wispy clouds.

Down they drove, and the land was spread out below them— mountain masses, seas, rivers, the long, straight line of a transcontinental railway, cities, forests . . .

Ahead of them and below something was flying. A bird? Grimes studied it through his binoculars, wondering how he had come to make such a gross underestimation of its size. It was a huge, delta-winged aircraft. It pursued its course steadily, ignoring the intruder from space. Probably its pilot did not know that there were strangers in his sky.

The radar altimeter was unwinding more slowly now. They were low enough to make out features of the landscape with the naked eye. Ahead of them was the town, the small city, its architecture obviously alien. The proportions of the buildings were all wrong by human standards and not one of the many towers was perpendicular; the truncated spires leaned toward and away from each other at drunken angles.

They swept over the town. Beyond it was the wreck of the ancient Terran spaceship and beyond that the discolored white dome. Through his binoculars Grimes could see spacesuited figures standing by the airlock of the vessel. *Men* in spacesuits? They had to be human; the natives would not require protective clothing on their own planet.

But what were they doing?

Fighting?

Yes, they were fighting—the spacemen and the near-naked, humanoid but far from human natives. It was hand to hand almost, at close range with pistols from the muzzles of which came flashes of bright flame. Oddly enough there seemed to be no casualties on either side.

Yet.

"We have come in the nick of time," said the Baroness. "If we had waited until local daybreak, as *you* suggested . . ."

There was a screwy lack of logic about what she was saying, about the entire situation. If *Lode Ranger* had just landed the situation would have made sense, but . . . The gaussjammer had not come down today, or yesterday, or the day before that.

"I relinquish control, Captain," came the voice of Big Sister. "You are now one kilometer from the wreck."

Grimes brought his gloved hands up to the console.

"*Do* something," ordered the Baroness. "There are people, humans, there, being murdered."

The pinnace was not armed. (If Grimes, man of peace as he claimed to be, had had any say in the building of *The Far Traveler* and her ancillary craft she would have been.) Even had she been fitted with weaponry Grimes would have been unable to fire into that melee with any degree of discrimination. All that he could do was to bring her in fast, fast and noisily. The combatants heard the rapidly approaching clangor; they would have had to have been stone deaf not to do so. They stopped fighting, looked up and around. Then they ran, all of them, human and autochthon. Together they fled, arms and legs pumping ludicrously, jostling each other at the open airlock door of the gaussjammer, scrambling for the safety of the interior of the old ship.

They were gone from sight, all of them, their dropped weapons, gleaming greenly in the light of the afternoon sun, littering the bare, sandy ground.

Grimes slammed the pinnace down hard at the foot of the ramp that protruded from the airlock door. With one hand he sealed his helmet, with the other he unsnapped his seat belt. Big Sister had already opened the inner airlock door. Two steps took him to the little chamber. The Baroness was with him. The inner door closed, the outer door opened. He jumped to the gound, pulling his pistols as he did so. She landed just behind him and then ran ahead.

"Hold it!" he called. "I'll send the robots in first to draw the fire. They're expendable."

"And you're not?" she asked coldly.

"Not if I can help it. And I'm not invulnerable either. Your tin soldiers are."

She admitted grudgingly that there was sense in what he said. They stood together, looking up at the huge, weathered hulk, the great, metallic peg top supported in an upright position by its landing struts. And what was happening inside the battered hull? he wondered. Were the survivors of the wreck—the descendants of the survivors, rather—and the natives still fighting hand to hand along the alleyways, through the public rooms? His helmet muffled external sounds but did not deafen him completely. He listened but could hear no cries, no gunfire.

The first two robots emerged from the pinnace's airlock. He told them to board the ship, not to fire unless fired upon, to use stunguns rather than laser pistols, their net-throwing blunderbusses in preference to either.

When the automata were aboard he followed, climbing the rickety, warped ramp with caution. It had been damaged, he noticed, and clumsily patched with some dissimilar metal. The repairing plates had been riveted, not welded.

"Are you brave enough to go in?" asked the Baroness when they reached the head of the gangway.

Grimes did not answer her. He joined the two robots who were standing in the airlock chamber. They were using their laser pistols, set to low intensity, as torches, shining the beams in through the open inner door.

Grimes used his chin to nudge the controls of his suit's external speaker to maximum amplification. "Ahoy!" he shouted. "*Lode Ranger!* Ahoy! This is the Survey Service! We're here to rescue you!"

"We are *not* the Survey Service," snapped the Baroness.

Grimes ignored her. "Ahoy!" he called again. "*Lode Ranger*, ahoy!"

He could imagine the sound of his amplified voice rolling up and along the spiral alleyway, the ramp that in these ships encircled the hull from tapered stern to blunt, dome-shaped bows inboard of the inner skin.

There was no reply.

He said, "All right, we're going in. We'll follow the ramp all the way to the control room. Two robots ahead, then ourselves, then two robots to cover our rear. The remaining two will guard the airlock."

They began to climb.

It was a far from silent progress. At one time the deck had been coated with a rubbery plastic but, over the long years, it had perished, its decomposition no doubt hastened by the chlorine-rich atmosphere. The feet of the marching robots set up a rhythmic clangor, the heavy boots of the man and the woman made their own contributions to the rolling reverberation. It would have been impossible not to have stepped in time to the metallic drumbeat.

Up and around they marched, up and around. The low intensity laser beams probed dark openings—cross alleyways, the entrances to cabins and machinery spaces and public rooms. There were streakings in the all-pervasive dust suggestive of footprints, of scufflings, but nothing was definite. On one bulkhead was a great stain, old and evil. It could have been no more than a careless spillage of paint in the distant past but Grimes sensed that somebody—or something—had died there, messily.

He called a halt.

"Now we can hear ourselves think," commented the Baroness.

"Now we can hear," he agreed.

And there were sounds, faint and furtive, that would have been faint even without the muffling effect of their helmets. They seemed to come from ahead, they seemed to come from inside the ancient hull. And within the archaic ship, Grimes knew, there would be a veritable maze of alleyways and companionways, shafts vertical and horizontal. The only hope of capturing either a native or a descendant of the *Lode Ranger* survivors would be if any of them tried to escape through the airlock door, where the two robots he had detailed for that duty were on guard.

One of those robots spoke now—or it may have been Big Sister who spoke.

"Ground cars are approaching from the city. I suggest that you retreat to the pinnace."

Grimes hated to leave a job half finished, less than half finished, hardly begun in fact. But to remain in the ship could well prove suicidal. Still he waited so he could call, one last time, "*Lode Ranger*, ahoy! We have come to rescue you! Follow us to our boat!"

And then, wasting no time, the boarding party ran rather than walked down to the airlock.

Chapter 25

Somebody had gotten there before them. Somebody had tried to break past the robot sentries and was now entangled in the metallic mesh cast by a net-throwing blunderbuss, was still struggling ineffectually. It was a man in an archaic spacesuit, an ugly looking pistol in his right hand. Fortunately he could not bring this weapon to bear.

"Easy, friend, easy," said Grimes. "It's all right. Tell us about it in the pinnace."

But the man could not hear him, of course. His helmet looked as though it would deaden exterior sounds even more effectively than the one that Grimes was wearing. If his suit were equipped with radio, and if that radio were still functioning, it would not be likely that the frequency to which it was tuned would be the one being used by the party from *The Far Traveler*.

"Don't hurt him," ordered Grimes. "Take him to the boat."

He looked toward the city, to the column of dust midway between town and ship, the fast-traveling cloud that did not quite conceal betraying glints of metal. The ground cars, obviously, that Big Sister had reported. And they were wasting no time, whoever and whatever they were. The sooner he was in the pinnace and up and away the better. He would return, better armed and better prepared—but that was in the future. This was *now*. This was strategic retreat from heavier forces, from an enemy who had already opened fire from his armored vehicles with large caliber projectile weapons. A shell burst just short of the pinnace, another to one side of it.

"Run!" ordered Grimes.

The two robots with the prisoner between them broke into a gallop.

Grimes and the Baroness followed, but less speedily. Spacesuits are not meant for running in. The other four robots brought up the rear.

The outer airlock door of the pinnace was already open. The leading robots and the struggling man passed through just before a shell landed on the boat itself.

"Hell!" exclaimed Grimes.

"Don't . . . worry . . ." panted the Baroness. "She . . . can . . . take . . . it . . ."

The green smoke cleared and Grimes saw that the pinnace seemed to be undamaged, although bright gold gleamed where the protective plastic had been ripped away.

The next two rounds were wide and Grimes and the Baroness scrambled into the airlock during the brief lull. Another shell hit, however, as the last pair of robots were boarding. It was like, Grimes said later, being a bug inside a bass drum. But at the time he was not thinking up picturesque similes. He was getting upstairs, fast, before a chance projectile scored a hit on some vulnerable part of the pinnace. A similar craft in the Survey Service would have been fitted with armor shields for the viewpoints. This one was not. No doubt Big Sister would make good this omission but Grimes was more concerned with *now* than a possible future.

From his seat, as the boat lifted, he saw a squad of the reptilian humanoids jumping out of the leading, multi-wheeled land car. They carried weapons, firearms of some kind, took aim and delivered a ragged volley. It sounded like hail on a tin roof. The bullets were no more effective than the shells had been.

They went on firing after the pinnace was airborne and even when she was well aloft there was a sharp *ping* on her underside.

"Did you look at them?" demanded the Baroness. "Giants. At least twice as big as the ones we first saw!"

"We were lucky to get away," said Grimes. "So was our friend here—although he didn't seem to want to be rescued."

"The robots frightened him," she said. "To him they're monsters . . ."

"Big Sister," said Grimes. "Over to you. Get us back on board as soon as possible."

"I have control, Captain," came the reply from the transceiver.

Grimes released himself from his seat, went to the cabin at the rear of the pinnace. The Baroness accompanied him.

She whispered, "He's . . . dead . . ."

"Only fainted," said Grimes. Then, to the robots, "Get the net off him."

They looked down at the spacesuited man sprawled on the deck. Grimes sneezed suddenly; there was an irritating acridity in the air despite the efforts of the ventilating fans. He knelt by the still figure. He was amazed to find that the suit was made only from thin, coarsely woven cloth. But, he reasoned, for many years *Lode Ranger*'s people and their descendants must have had to make do with whatever materials came to hand. He looked at the ovate, opaque helmet, tried to see through the narrow, glazed vision slit to the face beneath.

But the slit was not glazed.

It was not glazed and there were other openings, approximately where ears and mouth are located on a human head. A dreadful suspicion was growing in his mind.

He took hold of the helmet with his two hands, gave it a half turn to the left. It resisted the twisting motion. He tried to turn it to the right. It still would not come free. So he just lifted it.

He stared down in horror at the big-domed, saurian head, at the dull, sightless, faceted eyes, at the thin-lipped mouth, twisted in a silent snarl, from which ropy slime still dribbled.

He heard the Baroness's gasp of horrified dismay.

He let the dead, ugly head drop to the deck, picked up the glittering, vicious looking pistol. The trigger guard was big enough for him to get his gloved forefinger into it.

"Don't!" the Baroness cried sharply.

He ignored her, pulled the trigger. A stream of bright but harmless sparks flashed from the muzzle of the gun.

"A toy . . ." she whispered. "But what . . . ?"

He asked, "Did you ever, as a child, play cowboys and Indians, Your Excellency? No, I don't suppose you did. But you must have heard of the game. And that's what these . . . kids were playing. But they'd call the game invaders and people or something like that, with the invaders as the baddies. Just a re-enactment of a small battle, but quite an important battle, many, many years ago. Goodies versus baddies. The goodies won. There were no *Lode Ranger* survivors."

"But that wasn't a make-believe battle that *we* ran away from," she said.

"It wasn't," he agreed. "It could be that after *Lode Ranger*'s landing—and the massacre—some sort of defense force was set up in case any more hostile aliens came blundering in. Possibly drills every so often." He laughed without humor. "It must have given the officer responsible quite a turn when our pinnace came clattering over, making straight for the old *Lode Ranger*. The real thing at last . . ."

He looked up at the Baroness. He was amazed to see that she was weeping; her helmet, unlike the native's make-believe one, could not hide her expression or the bright tears coursing down her cheeks.

"Just a child . . ." she said. "Just a child, whose exciting, traditional game turned terrifyingly real . . ."

And so, thought Grimes, rather hating himself for the ironic flippancy, *another redskin bit the dust*.

At least he had the grace not to say it aloud.

Chapter 26

A report was made to the Admiralty about the happenings on *Lode Ranger*'s planet. The Baroness had not wished to send one but, rather surprisingly, Big Sister supported Grimes on this issue. The Admiralty was not at all pleased and sent a terse message ordering *The Far Traveler* to leave any future explorations of the world to the personnel, far better equipped and qualified, of the destroyer *Acrux*.

The Baroness finally decided to make the best of the situation. "After all," she said to Grimes, "it is only Lost Colonies in which I am interested. Morrowvia, for example. What has happened on that world since you—and, I admit, others—tried to drag the happy colonists into the mainstream of galactic civilization? And now," she went on sweetly, too sweetly, "we shall refresh your memory, Captain Grimes."

Grimes regarded his employer apprehensively over the rim of his teacup. She always made a ritual of afternoon tea and almost invariably, even when he was in the doghouse, he was invited (commanded?) to her salon to share this minor feast. It was all done in considerable style, he was bound to admit—the fragrant infusion poured from the golden pot by the robot butler into gold-chased eggshell china, the paper-thin cucumber sandwiches, the delicious, insubstantial pastries . . . Sometimes on these daily occasions she was graciously charming; other times she seemed to delight in making her yachtmaster squirm. Always she was the aristocrat. She was the aristocrat and Grimes was the yokel in uniform.

He looked at her reclining gracefully on her chaise longue, wearing the usual filmy white gown that, tantalizingly, neither fully revealed nor fully concealed. Her wide, full mouth was curved in a smile—a malicious smile, Grimes decided; this was going to be what he had categorized as a squirm session. Her eyes—they were definitely green today—stared at him disdainfully.

She said, "As you already know, Captain, I was able to obtain recordings of various occasions from the archives of the Federation Survey Service. Or, to be more exact, Commander Delamere had those records aboard his ship and allowed me, for a consideration, to have copies taken."

He thought, *What can't you buy, you rich bitch!*

She went on, "This one is audio tape only. Recorded in the captain's cabin aboard one of the Survey Service's minor vessels some years ago. I wonder if you will recognize it . . ." She lifted a slim, languorous yet imperious arm. "Big Sister, the *Seeker* recordings, please."

"Certainly, Your Excellency," replied the computer-pilot. The screen of the big playmaster lit up but there was no picture, only glowing words and symbols:

SEEKER

1473/18.5

ETHOLOGY NTK =

RESTRICTED AO

For four ringers only, thought Grimes. *Not to be heard outside the sacred precincts of the Archives . . . How the hell did Frankie get his dirty paws on this?*

From the speaker of the ornate instrument came a voice, a woman's voice, familiar. *Maggie . . .* Grimes thought. He wondered where she was now, what she was doing, whom she was doing it with. He regretted, not for the first time, his resignation from the Survey Service. He had his enemies in the Space Navy of the Federation but he'd had his friends, good ones, and Maggie Lazenby—Commander Margaret Lazenby of the Scientific Branch—had been the best of them.

She had been more than just a friend.

He recalled the occasion vividly as he listened to her talking. She was telling Grimes, the Dog Star Line's Captain Danzellan and Captain Drongo Kane of the *Southerly Buster* what she had been able to learn of the origins of the Lost Colony on Morrowvia. It had been founded during the Second Expansion. A gaussjammer, the emigrant ship *Lode Cougar*, had been driven off trajectory by a magnetic storm, had been flung into a then unexplored sector of the galaxy. By the time that a habitable planet was blundered upon there had been starvation, mutiny, even cannibalism. There had been a crash landing with very few survivors—but, nonetheless, this handful of men and women possessed the wherewithal to start a colony from scratch. Aboard *Lode Cougar* had been stocks of fertilized ova, animal as well as human. (Dogs had been required on Austral, the world to which the ship originally had been bound, and cats, both to keep the indigenous vermin under control.

"With those very few survivors," Maggie had said, "a colony could still have been founded and might well have endured and flourished. There were ten men—nine of them, including Morrow, passengers, the other a junior engineer. There were six women, four of them young. Then Morrow persuaded his companions that they would have a far better chance of getting established if they had underpeople to work for them. It seems that the only ova suitable to his requirements were those of cats. The others did not query this; after all, he was an experienced and qualified genetic engineer. With the aid of the ship's artificer he set up his incubators and then—everything that he needed he found in the ship's cargo—a fully equipped laboratory. Before the diesel fuel ran out he was getting ample power from a solar energy converter *and* from a wind driven generator . . .

"I quote from Dr. Morrow's journal: 'The first batch is progressing nicely in spite of the accelerated maturation. I feel . . . paternal. I ask myself why should these, my children, be *under*people? I can make them more truly human than the hairless apes that infest so many worlds, that may, one day, infest this one . . .' "

So it went on, Maggie still reading from Dr. Morrow's diary, telling of the deaths of the *Lode Cougar* survivors. Although Morrow admitted nothing in writing it seemed probable that these were not accidental. Mary Little, Sarah Grant and Delia James succumbed to food poisoning. Douglas Carrick fell off a cliff. Susan Pettifer and William Hume were drowned in the river. The others, apparently, drank themselves to death after Morrow set up a still.

"There was something of the Pygmalion in Morrow," went on that long ago Maggie. "He fell in love with one of his own creations, his Galatea. He even named her Galatea . . ."

"And he married her," said a strange male voice that Grimes, with something of a shock, realized was his own. "He married her, and the union was fertile. According to Interstellar Law any people capable of fertile union with true people must themselves be considered true people. So, Captain Kane, that puts an end to your idea of setting up a nice, profitable slave trade."

Drongo Kane's voice—Grimes had no difficulty in recognizing it, even after all this time—broke in. "Don't tell me that you believe those records! Morrow was just kidding himself when he wrote them. How many glorified tom cats were sneaking into his wife's or his popsies' beds while his back was turned?"

There was an older, heavier male voice, the Dog Star Line's Captain Danzellan. "I was the first to land on this planet, Captain Kane, quite by chance. I found that the natives were . . . friendly. My Second Officer—among others—did some tom catting around himself and, if I may be permitted the use of an archaic euphemism, got the daughter of the Queen of Melbourne into trouble. The young idiot should have taken his contraceptive shots before he started dipping his wick, but he didn't think that it would be necessary. And then, just to make matters worse, he fell in love with the wench. He contrived, somehow, to get himself appointed to *Schnauzer* for my second voyage here. Now he wants to make an honest woman of the girl. Her mother, however, refuses to sanction the marriage until he becomes a Morrowvian citizen and changes his name to Morrow. As a matter of fact it all rather ties in with Company policy. The Dog Star Line will want a resident manager here—and a prince consort will be ideal for the job. Even though the queenships are not hereditary in theory they usually are in practice. And Tabitha—that's her name—is next in line."

Again Kane's voice, "What are you driveling about?"

And Danzellan, stiffly, "Tabitha has presented young Delamere with a son."

The Baroness raised her hand and the playmaster fell silent. "Delamere?" she asked. "But surely he's captain of the destroyer *Vega*."

"The Odd Gods of the Galaxy did not create that name for Handsome Frankie alone, Your Excellency," said Grimes. "But, as a matter of fact, *that* Delamere, the one on Morrowvia, is one of Frankie's distant cousins. Like Frankie, he uses women to rise in the universe. Frankie has his plain, fat admiral's daughter—which is why he's gotten as high as he has. There'll be other women, carefully selected, and Frankie'll make admiral yet. Come to that, that Dog Star Line second mate hasn't done badly either, using similar methods. Resident manager on Morrowvia *and* a prince consort . . ."

"And they say that women are jealous cats . . ." murmured the Baroness. Then, "Continue, Big Sister."

Kane's voice issued from the playmaster. "And how many local boyfriends has *she* had?"

"She says," stated Danzellan, "that she has had none. Furthermore,

I have seen the baby. All the Morrowvians have short noses—except this one. He has a long nose, like his father. The resemblance is quite remarkable."

"Did Mr. Delamere and his family come with you, Captain Danzellan?" asked Grimes. "Call them up, and we'll wet the baby's head!"

And Kane exclaimed, "You can break the bottle of champagne over it if you want to!"

The Baroness laughed as he raised her hand. She said, "Quite an interesting character, this Captain Kane. A rogue, obviously, but . . ."

"Mphm," grunted Grimes.

"According to the Survey Service records," she went on, "your own conduct on Morrowvia was such that you were accused later, by Captain Kane, of partisanship. You had an affair with one of the local rulers . . ."

Grimes' prominent ears felt as though they were about to burst into flame. "Yes," he admitted.

"Tell me," she pressed, "what was it like?"

"All cats are gray in the dark," he said.

Chapter 27

The Far Traveler came to Morrowvia.

This world, hopefully, would provide material for at least a couple of chapters of the Baroness's doctorial thesis. Morrowvia, at the time of its rediscovery, had been an unspoiled world, almost Edenic. Then it had been developed by the Dog Star Line as a tourist resort. Grimes was apprehensive as well as curious. He had liked the planet the way it had been. What would it be like now?

Big Sister was supplying some answers. As the yacht approached her destination, the Mannschenn Drive was shut down at intervals, with a consequent return to the normal continuum, so that a sampling could be made of the commercial and entertainment programs emanating from the planet. These were interesting.

The major continent, North Australia, was now one huge tourist trap with luxury hotels, gambling casinos, emporia peddling native artifacts (most of them, Grimes suspected, manufactured on Llirith, a world whose saurian people made a good living by turning out trashy souvenirs to order), Bunny Clubs (here, of course, called Pussy Clubs) and the like. The screen of the Baroness's playmaster glowed and flickered with gaudy pictures of beach resorts and of villages of holiday chalets in the mountain country, with performances of allegedly native dances obviously choreographed by Terrans for Terrans.

And then a once-familiar voice spoke from the instrument and looking out from the screen was a once-familiar face. Her hair was a lustrous, snowy white, her gleaming skin dark brown, the lips of her generous mouth a glistening scarlet. Her eyes were a peculiar greenish yellow and the tips of her small ears were oddly pointed. The cheekbones were prominent, more so than the firm chin. Grimes' regard shifted downward. She was naked, he saw (and as he remembered her). Beneath each breast was a rudimentary nipple. He recalled how when he had first seen her that detail had intrigued him.

She said seductively, purring almost, "Are you tired of the bright lights, the ceaseless round of organized gaiety? Will you finish your vacation more tired than when you started it? Then why not come to Cambridge to relax, to live the natural way, as *we* lived before the coming of the Earthmen? Share with us our simple pleasures—the hunting of the deer in our forests, the fishing for the great salmon in the clear waters of our rivers . . ."

And neither deer nor salmon, Grimes remembered, bore much resemblance to the deer and salmon of Earth or, even, to those creatures as they had mutated on the other worlds into which they had been introduced. Old Morrow must have been a homesick man; his planet abounded with Terran place names, bestowed by himself, and indigenous animals had been called after their nearest (and not often very near) Earthly counterparts.

"Come to Cambridge," went on the low, alluring voice. "You will not regret it. Come to Cambridge and live for awhile in the rosy dawn of human history. And it will cost you so very little. For two full weeks, with accommodation and food and hunting and fishing trips, the charge for a single adult is a mere one thousand credits. There are special terms for family parties . . ."

She smiled ravishingly. Her teeth were very white between the red lips, in the brown face.

"Please come. I am looking forward so very much to meeting you . . ."

She faded from the screen, was replaced by an advertisement for the Ballarat Casino where, at the time of this broadcast, the imported entertainer Estella di Scorpio had been the star attraction. The Baroness looked and listened briefly then made a sharp gesture. Big Sister cut the sound.

"A friend of yours, Captain Grimes?" asked his employer. "You were looking at her like a lovesick puppy."

"Estella di Scorpio? No, Your Excellency. I don't know the lady, nor do I much want to."

"Not her, Captain. The . . . er . . . lady before her. That indubitably mammalian female."

"That was Maya," he told her. "The Queen of Cambridge."

"A *queen*, advertising a holiday camp?"

"She's no more than a mayor, really, Your Excellency. Cambridge is—or was when I was there—just a little town."

She said, "I think that we shall land at this Cambridge rather than at the Melbourne spaceport. After all, you have landed there before. In *Seeker*."

"Things were different then, Your Excellency," he told her. "There was no Aerospace Control. There were no rules and regulations. We just looked around for a reasonably clear and level patch of ground, then sat down on it. But now we shall have to use the spaceport to get our Inward Clearance from the authorities."

"Shall we?" she asked. "Shall we?"

Chapter 28

Money talks.

Money talked over the Carlotti Communications System as *The Far Traveler* closed Morrowvia at a multiple of the speed of light. The planet was, to all intents and purposes, a Dog Star Line dependency, its officials, Dog Star Line appointees. The Baroness was a major shareholder in that company. Radio Pratique was granted. Customs and Immigration formalities were waived. Permission was accorded to Grimes to bring the ship down in the close vicinity of Cambridge.

Big Sister let him handle the landing, conceding that in these circumstances his local knowledge would be useful. He brought *The Far Traveler* down through the clear morning air toward an expanse of level ground, devoid of obstructions, that was almost an island, bounded to north, west and south by a winding river, to the east by a wooded hill. To the north and to the west of this eminence there were large villages, each with a sparse sprinkling of pale lights still visible in the brightening dawn. When he had come here before, Grimes recalled, the settlements had been smaller and the lights had been dim and yellow, from oil lamps. Now, obviously, there was electricity. And those latticework masts were new, too. Radio antennae? Possibly, although at least one of them looked heavy enough to afford mooring facilities to an airship.

Sunrise came at ground level and the horizontal rays cast long, dark shadows, showing up every slightest irregularity in the terrain, every hump and hollow, every outcropping of rock, every bush. Grimes applied lateral thrust, bringing the yacht directly above a patch of green that, from the air, looked perfectly smooth. It was. When he set *The Far Traveler* down gently in the middle of it she quivered ever so slightly as the shock absorbers took the strain, then was still.

"A nice landing, Captain," remarked Big Sister, not at all condescendingly. Grimes remembered how the electronic entity had messed up his landing on Farhaven. But later, on that world, she had saved him and seemed, as a consequence, somehow to have adopted him.

But the Baroness had not. She said disparagingly, "But, of course, you have been here before."

Grimes was sulkily silent. He rang Finished With Engines. Then he took an all around look through the viewports. He said, "It looks like the reception committee approaching, Your Excellency."

"How boring," commented the Baroness. She stifled a yawn. "They must be indecently early risers here."

"The noise of our inertial drive will have awakened them," said Grimes.

"Possibly." She sounded very uninterested. "Go down to the airlock to receive them. You may invite them aboard—to *your* quarters. No doubt they are old friends of yours and will have much to talk about."

Grimes left the control room. He was glad that the Baroness had not ordered him to change from his comfortable shirt and shorts into formal rig; only the purple, gold-braided shoulderboards were badges of his servitude. Both airlock doors were open when he got down to the stern. He stepped out and stood at the head of the ramp, savoring the fresh air with its scent of flowers, of dew on grass, and the warmth of the early sun. He looked to the west, to the direction from which he had seen the party approaching.

There was a woman in the lead—tall, dark-skinned, white-haired, moving with feline grace. He recognized her at once. She had hardly changed. (Old age when it came to the Morrowvians came suddenly and Maya was far from old.) A man strode beside her. Although he was naked, as were all the others, he was obviously not a native. He was far too heavily built and moved with relative clumsiness. A great mane of yellow hair fell to his broad, deeply tanned shoulders and a bushy yellow beard mingled with the almost as luxuriant growth on his chest. He was carrying a slender, ceremonial spear but looked as though he should have been hefting a heavy club.

The man, the woman (the queen, Maya) and the six archers, slender Dianas, and the half dozen of spearmen . . . Short-haired, all of them (with the exception of the Terran), with similitudes to fur skullcaps on their heads—black, brindle, tortoiseshell—and sharply defined pubic puffs.

Grimes walked slowly down the golden ramp to meet them.

Maya stared up at him incredulously.

"John! After all these years! If I had known that you were coming back I would have waited . . ." The blond giant scowled. "But this is . . . fantastic! First Captain Kane, and now you . . ."

"Drongo Kane?" demanded Grimes. "*Here*?"

"Never mind him, John. You are here, captain of a fine, golden ship . . ."

"Owned," said Maya's male companion drily, "by her self-styled Excellency, the Baroness Michelle d'Estang. And *you* are the John Grimes that my wife's always talking about? I thought that you were in the Survey Service, not a yacht skipper."

"I *was* in the Survey Service," admitted Grimes. "But . . . I don't think that I have the pleasure . . ."

The man laughed. "You can call me Your Highness if you feel like it; I'm Maya's Prince Consort *and* Manager of Simple Life Holidays. I'm Bill to my friends, Bill Smith, just another Dog Star Line boy who's found a fine kennel for himself. Mind you, I haven't done as well as Swanky Frankie in Melbourne—but I'm not complaining."

He extended a meaty hand. Grimes shook it.

"John . . ." mewed Maya plaintively.

He shook her hand. She conveyed the strong impression that she would have preferred him to have kissed her—but Bill Smith was watching and so would be, he knew, Big Sister and the Baroness.

He said, "Will you come aboard for some refreshment? I'm afraid I can't ask all of you; my accommodation's not all that commodious . . ."

"Have one of your hunks bring some dishes of ice cream out for the boys and girls," Bill Smith told him. "Maya an' I'll inflict ourselves on you." He looked down at himself. "I hope you an' the Baroness don't mind the way I'm dressed—but it's the rig of the day for my job. Both my jobs."

Grimes led the way up the gangway, then to his day cabin. He was glad that *The Far Traveler* did not have a human crew. From his past experience he had learned that some spacemen and -women took naturist planets such as Arcadia—and now Morrowvia—in their stride, happily doing in Rome as the Romans did, while others were openly condemnatory or tried to hide their embarrassment by crudely obscene jokes. His robot stewardess, of course, was not at all perturbed by the nudity of his guests—although she, to them, was a source of wonderment. She brought coffee and pastries for the two men, a golden dish of ice cream for Maya. (It had been the first off-planet delicacy that she had enjoyed and she still loved it.) Grimes sent a general purpose robot to take care of Maya's entourage, then settled down to talk.

"Drongo Kane?" he asked without preamble. "What's he doing back here?"

Before either Maya or her husband could answer, the voice of Big Sister came from the playmaster. "I have been in communication with Melbourne Port Control. Captain Kane's ship, *Southerly Buster*, has been berthed there for five weeks, local time. Captain Kane left Melbourne thirty days ago in one of his ship's boats, taking with him ten of his passengers, seven men and three women. The ostensible purpose of the trip was a tour of England. No doubt your friends in Cambridge, whom you are now entertaining, will be able to give you further information."

"Was that your boss?" asked Bill Smith interestedly.

"No," replied Grimes, rather wondering with what degree of truth. "That was not Her Excellency. That was the ship's pilot-computer. We call her Big Sister."

"Haw! Big Sister is watching, eh? You'd better keep your paws off Maya!"

"I don't think," said Grimes stiffly, "that Big Sister is concerned about my morals. But what do you know about Drongo Kane?"

"You tangled with him when you were here last, didn't you? Maya's told me all about it. But he's a reformed character now. He's muscled in on the tourist racket—but one ship, and that not a very big one, won't worry the Dog Star Line. As long as he pays his port charges and as long as his passengers blow their money in the tourist traps he's as welcome as the day is long. He was here . . ."

"Only three days," supplied Maya. "Then he flew off, up river, to Stratford." She pouted. "I don't know what he will find there to interest him. Anne—the Queen of Stratford is always called Anne; I wonder why—is more determined to keep to the old ways than any of the rest of us. She will not allow electricity or radio or *anything* in her city." She smiled smugly. "*We*, of course, realize that tourists, even when enjoying a Simple Life Holiday, appreciate the little comforts, such as refrigeration and television, to which they are used."

"You appreciate them yourself," said Bill Smith.

"I do," she admitted. "But never mind Captain Kane, John. Tell us about *you*." she smiled appealingly. "And while we are talking I will have some more of your delicious ice cream."

"And would there be any gin?" asked the Prince Consort hopefully.

There was.

Chapter 29

"This Stratford," said the Baroness, "sounds as though it might be interesting."

"In what way, Your Excellency?" asked Grimes.

"Unspoiled . . ."

"It won't stay that way long if Drongo Kane is there," Grimes said.

"You are prejudiced, Captain."

She took a dainty sip from her teacup. Grimes took a gulp from his. He badly needed something refreshing but nonalcoholic. It would have been bad manners to let his guests drink alone and he had taken too much for the neutralizer capsules to have their usual immediate effect.

"Unspoiled," she said again. "This world the way it was before you and those others blundered in. The Social Evolution of a Lost Colony taking its natural course. If we leave now we shall arrive at Stratford before dark."

"There is the party tonight, Your Excellency," Grimes reminded her. "After all, Maya is a reigning monarch."

"The petty mayor of a petty city-state," she sneered. "But do not worry. I have already sent my sincere apologies for not being able to attend. But I can just imagine what that party will be like! Drunken tourists going native and lolloping around in disgusting, self-conscious nudity. Imitation Hawaiian music played on 'native' guitars imported from Llirith. Imitation Israeli *horas*. Meat charred to ruination over open fires. Cheap gin tarted up with fruit juices—probably synthetic—and served as genuine Morrowvian toddy . . ." She smiled nastily. "Come to that—*you* have already had too much to drink. Big Sister will be able to handle the pinnace by remote control while you sleep it off in the cabin."

"The pinnace?" asked Grimes stupidly.

"You, Captain, made a survey of this planet shortly after the first landings here. Surely you must remember that there is no site near to Stratford suitable for the landing of a ship, even one so relatively small as *The Far Traveler.*"

Grimes did remember then and admitted as much. He said, too, that his local knowledge would be required to pilot the pinnace to Stratford. The Baroness said, grudgingly, that he might as well make some attempt to earn his salary.

Big Sister said nothing.

Grimes flew steadily south, maintaining a compass course and not following the meanderings of the river. Ahead the blue peaks of the Pennine Range lifted into an almost cloudless sky. An hour before sunset he knew that he could not be far from Stratford although, as he recalled, the little town was very hard to spot from the air. It was nestled in the river valley and the thatched roofs of its houses were overgrown with weeds. But there had been some quite remarkable rock formations that he had never gotten around to examining closely, rectangular slabs of dark gray but somehow scintillant stone, not far from the settlement.

Those slabs were still there.

So was a torpedo shape of silvery metal—the pinnace from *Southerly Buster.*

He said, pointing, "Kane's still here, Your Excellency."

"Are you afraid to meet him again?" she asked.

Grimes flushed angrily. "No," he said, "Your Excellency."

He was not frightened of Kane but he would have been willing to admit that he was worried. Kane was up to no good. Kane was always up to no good. He was a leopard with indelible spots.

People emerged from the little houses, from the pinnace, alerted by the racket of the boat's inertial drive. How many Terrans should there have been? Kane and ten of his passengers, seven men and three women . . . But standing there and looking up were thirty people. All of them were clothed, which seemed to indicate that there were no natives among them. Grimes studied the upturned faces through binoculars. Kane was not there—but suddenly that well remembered voice blasted from the transceiver.

"Ahoy, the pinnace! Who the hell are yer an' wot yer doin' here?"

Kane must be speaking from inside his own boat.

"The Far Traveler," replied Grimes stiffly into his microphone. "Her Owner, the Baroness d'Estang of El Dorado. And her Master."

"An' I'm *Southerly Buster*, Owner *and* Master, Welcome to Stratford. Come on down. This is Liberty Hall; you can spit on the mat an' call the cat a bastard!"

"It should be the local mayor—Queen Anne, isn't it?—to issue the invitation," said the Baroness to Grimes.

"Perhaps Queen Anne is dead," said Grimes. With sudden foreboding he remembered the old saying; Many a true word is spoken in jest.

"Take us down, Captain," ordered the Baroness.

Grimes reduced vertical thrust and the pinnace settled slowly toward the ground, to the white sheet that somebody had spread to serve as a landing mark. She landed gently. Grimes cut the drive, actuated the controls of the airlock doors. He realized, too late, that he should have brought arms—but the six general purpose robots which had accompanied the humans from *The Far Traveler* would be capable of doing considerable damage to any enemy using nothing more than their own, enormously strong metal bodies.

He had landed about five meters from *Southerly Buster*'s pinnace. A man came out through the airlock door of this craft—tall, gangling, clad in slate-gray shirt-and-shorts uniform with black, gold-braided shoulderboards. His straw-colored hair was untidy, even though short, and his face looked as though at some time in the past it had been shattered and then reassembled by a barely competent, unaesthetic plastic surgeon.

"Captain Kane?" the Baroness asked Grimes.

"Drongo Kane," he said.

She rose from her seat, was first out of the boat. Grimes followed her, then the robots. Kane advanced to stand in the forefront of his own people. He looked the Baroness up and down like a slave dealer assessing the points of a possible purchase. He bowed then—a surprisingly courtly gesture. He raised the Baroness's outstretched hand to his lips, surrendered it reluctantly as he came erect. Grimes could not see his employer's face but sensed that she was favorably impressed by her reception.

She said, "And now, Captain Kane, may I present my yachtmaster, Captain . . ."

"Grimes, Madam," supplied Kane with a grin. "I thought that I recognized his voice but didn't see how it could be him. But it is. Live on stage, in person. Singing and dancing."

"Mphm," grunted Grimes.

"No hard feelin's," said Kane, extending his right hand. "You've come down in the universe, I see—but I don't believe in kickin' a man when he's down."

Not unless there's some profit in it, thought Grimes, taking the proffered paw and getting the handshake over as quickly as possible.

"You know, ma'am, I'm pleased that you an' me old cobber Grimes dropped in," Kane went on. "A couple of independent witnesses is just what I'm needin' right now. It'd be better if Grimes was still in the Survey Service—but at least he's not a Dog Star Line puppy."

"What are you talking about, Kane?" demanded Grimes.

"Just this. I—an' my legal eagle, Dr. Kershaw . . ." A tall, gray-haired, gray-clad man among the small crowd inclined his head toward the newcomers . . . "have the honor of representin' the rightful owners of this planet."

"The *rightful* owners?" asked Grimes.

"Too right." Grimes waved his right hand in a wide arc, indicating the twenty men and women who were standing a little apart from his own people. "The Little, Grant, James and Pettifer families!"

The names rang a faint bell in the recesses of Grimes' memory.

"Descendants," stated Kane, "of four of the human women who were among the *Lode Cougar* survivors!"

Chapter 30

Kane made no further introductions until he had conducted the Baroness and Grimes into one of the houses. The room that they entered had small windows, unglazed, set into two of the walls, screened with matting against the westering sun. There was a huge, solid, wooden table, a half dozen sturdy chairs. On one of the walls a big map of the planet, drawn to Mercatorial projection, was hanging. It was all very like, thought Grimes, Maya's council room in her "palace" had been on the occasion of his first landing on Morrowvia. So this was the palace, he thought.

Where was the queen?

He asked sharply, "Where is Queen Anne, Kane?"

Kane laughed. "Don't get your knickers in a knot, Grimes. She's not dead. She's . . . sleeping. So are her subjects. Meanwhile . . ." he gestured toward the four people who had followed them into the adobe building . . . "I'd like you to meet the leaders of the *true* Morrowvians. Mary Little . . ."

The woman so named inclined her head and smiled shyly. She was wearing a shapeless blue coverall that hid her body to the neck but the way that she moved seemed human enough. Her teeth were very white and looked sharp. The hair of her head was obviously not the modified cat's fur of the natives; it was much coarser and longer. It was brown, as were her eyes. Her face was, if anything, too normal, quite forgettable apart from the unusually thin-lipped mouth.

"Peter Pettifer," continued Kane.

Pettifer was dressed as was Mary Little. He was yellow-haired, brown-eyed. He, too, had a peculiarly thin-lipped mouth.

"Dr. Kershaw you already know," went on *Southerly Buster's* master. "And this is Dr. Weldon . . ."

Weldon—short, tubby, black-haired, neatly black-bearded, dressed in gaudily patterned shirt and scarlet shorts—nodded curtly.

"Are you a lawyer too?" asked the Baroness.

"No, madam," he told her. "My specialty is cryonics."

Kane sat on the edge of the table, swinging his long legs. He said, "I'll put you in picture, Ma'am. And you, Grimes. On the occasion of our first visit here—you in *Seeker*, that old woman Danzellan in *Schnauzer* an' yours truly in the *Buster*—none of us dreamed that the true owners of the planet were stashed away here, in cold storage. There were other records left by Morrow, you know, besides the ones that you an' Maggie what's-her-name found in Ballarat. And I turned 'em up. Oh, old Morrow played around with his cats—that I'll not deny—but he also obtained fertilized human ova from Mary Little, Susan Pettifer, Delia James and Sarah Grant. These he brought to term, *in vitro*, in the laboratory that he set up here, in Stratford. But, as we all know too well, he was nuts on cats. Perhaps his infatuation with his pet creation, his Galatea, had something to do with it. He decided that Morrowvia would be a pussyocracy . . ." He grinned at his own play on words; nobody else was greatly amused. "He put the handful of true humans to sleep, stashed them away in the deep freeze so that they'd be available if ever he changed his mind. But they stayed there until I thawed 'em out."

"That's your story, Kane," said Grimes. "But I don't believe it. To operate any refrigeration plant, even a cooler for your beer, you want power. If there were any wind- or water-powered generators here we'd have seen 'em when we came in. If there ever were any such jennies here they'd have worn out generations ago."

"*And* the refrigeration machinery itself," said the Baroness, showing a flicker of interest.

"Morrow set up an absorption system," said Kane smugly. "And as for the energy source—there were solar power screens in *Lode Cougar's* cargo. The people of the village that Morrow established here had it drummed into them, from the very start, that their sacred duty was to keep the screens clear of weeds and not to allow any larger growths capable of blocking out the sunlight to take root around their edges."

Grimes remembered those unnatural looking slabs of gray, scintillant rock. He should have investigated them when he made his first rough survey of the planet. The Dog Star Line people should have investigated them when they made their surveys—but they, of course, were concerned primarily with exploitation, not the pursuit of knowledge. (And Drongo Kane, too, was an exploiter, and shewd enough to know that any scrap of information whatsoever might, some day, be used to his advantage.)

Kane's story, Grimes admitted reluctantly to himself, was plausible. An absorption refrigeration system, with no moving parts, could well remain in operation for centuries provided that there was no leakage. And the resurrectees did not appear to be of feline ancestry. Nonetheless he wished that photographs of the *Lode Cougar* survivors were available. He looked at Mary Little dubiously.

"Tell us your story, Mary," prompted Kane.

The woman spoke. Her voice held an unpleasant whining quality. She said, "We are all very grateful to Captain Kane. He restored us to life; he will restore us to our proper place in the world. In the Old Days we were happy—but then the Others were favored by Dr. Morrow. And they hated us, and turned the Doctor against us . . ."

"Cats," said Kane, "are very jealous animals. And now, ma'am, and you, Grimes, would you care to accompany me on a tour of the . . . er . . . freezer?"

"Thank you, Captain Kane," said the Baroness.

"I want you both to see for yourselves," said Kane, "that the people of Stratford have not been harmed but merely filed for future reference. They may be required as witnesses when my, er, clients bring suit against the cat people for restoration of the legal ownership of this planet."

"How much is in it for you, Kane?" asked Grimes bluntly.

"Nobody works for nothing!" the Baroness told him sharply.

There were steep cliffs on the other side of the river from the village and it was atop these that the solar power screens were mounted. There were inflatable dinghies to ferry the party across the swift-flowing stream. The darkness was falling fast but powerful searchlights on the Stratford bank made the crossing as light as day. Four of *The Far Traveler*'s general purpose robots waded over with the humans, their heads at the deepest part just above the surface, accompanying the boats. ("Don't you trust me, Grimes?" asked Kane in a pained voice. "No," said Grimes.) The remaining two automata stayed to guard the pinnace.

On each side of the river there were jetties, very old structures of water-worn stone. Alongside one of these piers was a crude boat, little more than a coracle, consisting of the tough hide of some local beast stretched over a wickerwork frame. It must have been used, thought Grimes, by the maintenance workers who, over the long years, had kept the solar power screens free of vegetation.

Kane was first out of the leading dinghy, throwing a hitch of the painter around a wooden bollard. Gallantly he helped the Baroness from the boat to the low jetty. Grimes followed her ashore, then Kershaw. The other dinghy came alongside and Mary Little, Peter Pettifer and Dr. Weldon disembarked. The four robots emerged from the river, their golden bodies gleaming wetly.

Kane led the way to the base of the red granite cliff. Its face, although naturally rugged, seemed unbroken but the Master of *Southerly Buster* knew where the door was. From his pocket he produced a small piece of bright metal, placed it in a depression in the rock. There was a very faint whine of concealed machinery and a great slab of granite swung inward. The tunnel beyond it was adequately lit by glowtubes in the ceiling.

"However did Dr. Morrow manage such feats of construction?" asked the Baroness curiously.

"He had his work robots, ma'am," replied Kane. "And this cave is a natural one."

The party walked slowly along the tunnel, the feet of the robots ringing metallically on the stone floor. The air was chilly although not actually cold; nonetheless Grimes could see goose pimples on the backs of the Baroness's shapely legs, long under the brief shorts, as she strode ahead of him, beside Kane.

Weldon, accompanying Grimes, said conversationally, "Of course, the refrigeration plant cannot produce extremely low temperatures— but Morrow had knowledge of and access to the drug that was popularly known as Permakeep in his day. Now, of course, we work with vastly improved versions—but even with Permakeep in its original form, temperatures only just below Zero Celsius were all that were required to maintain the human body in a state of suspended animation almost indefinitely. A massive intravenous injection, of course . . ."

"Fascinating," said Grimes.

"Mine is a fascinating discipline," admitted Weldon smugly.

They tramped on, into the heart of the cliff. The tunnel made a right-angled turn into a large chamber, a huge cold room with transparent containers arranged in tiers. And there were the people who had been the citizens of Stratford, each in his own capsule, each frozen into immobility. They could have been dead; there was only Kane's word for it that they were not.

"Her Royal Highness," announced the piratical shipmaster mockingly. "The Queen of Stratford."

The unlucky Anne was in the first casket. She was a comely enough woman, creamy skinned, with tortoiseshell hair. Like many of the other native Morrowvians she possessed pronounced rudimentary nipples under her full breasts. Her face still bore an expression of anger.

And there was living anger in this cold room too. Grimes heard a noise that was both snarl and growl. He turned, saw that Mary Little and Peter Pettifer were glaring at the frozen body, their thin lips pulled back from their sharp white teeth in vicious grins. Kane had heard them as well. He snapped, "Quiet, damn you! Quiet!"

"It is natural," said Weldon suavely, "that they should hate the cat people after the way that they were treated. Would you like to be bossed around by a *cat*?"

No worse than being bossed around by a rich bitch, thought Grimes. "I suppose," he said, "that if you hadn't put Queen Anne and her people out of circulation they and your protegés would have led a cat and dog life."

For some reason this rather feeble joke did not go down at all well with Kane, who said shortly, "I am responsible for the safety of those whom I awoke from what could well have been eternal sleep."

"Tilt your halo to more of an angle, Kane," said Grimes. "That way it might suit you better."

"Captain Grimes," the Baroness told him coldly, "that was uncalled for. I am sure that Captain Kane is acting for the best."

"And *you* are satisfied, ma'am, that the people of Stratford are unharmed?" asked Kane.

"Yes," she replied.

"We still don't know that they aren't dead," persisted Grimes.

"Dr. Weldon," said Kane, "please select a sleeper at random—better still, let Captain Grimes select one—and awaken him or her."

"Captain Kane," said the Baroness, "that will not be necessary. Please accept my apologies for my employee's unfounded suspicions. But I am becoming increasingly aware that I am not attired for this temperature. Shall we return to the open air?"

"Your wish is my command, ma'am," said Kane gallantly.

Outside the cave the light evening breeze was pleasantly warm. Whoever was in charge of the searchlights had elevated their beams so that they did not dazzle the party; enough light, however, was reflected from the cliff face to make it easy for them to find their way back to the river. Weldon and the two resurrectees were the first to embark, casting off in their inflatable dinghy. Weldon may have been extremely able in his own field but he was no waterman. Engrossed in steering a diagonal course to counter the swift current he did not notice the tree branch, torn from its parent trunk by a storm up river, that was being swept downstream. Both Kane and Grimes shouted a warning but he did not seem to hear it. The jagged end of the branch hit the side of the dinghy like a torpedo, ripping along its length. There was a great hissing and bubbling of escaping air. The flimsy craft tipped, all its buoyancy on the side of the damage lost. It capsized, throwing its occupants into the water.

There was very little danger. Weldon did not appear to be a good swimmer but two of the general purpose robots, running along the river bed, positioned themselves on either side of him, supported him on their outheld arms. Mary Little and Peter Pettifer struck out for the shore in a flurry of spray. It was a clumsy stroke that they were using, wasteful of energy, but in spite of their hampering clothing they made rapid progress. The two robots not engaged in assisting the cryoscopist to safety ran down the river in pursuit of the still-floating dinghy.

Then Weldon, dripping and miserable, flanked by his golden rescuers, stood on the stone pier waiting for Kane's boat to come alongside. Mary Little and Peter Pettifer beat this dinghy to the shore, clambered up onto the jetty. They grinned and panted, shaking themselves. A fine spray of moisture flew from their wet clothing.

Kane made a competent job of berthing. As before, he helped the Baroness out of the dinghy. Kershaw and Grimes stepped ashore unaided.

The Baroness said, "My robots will recover the damaged boat, Captain Kane."

"Thank you, ma'am. And your robots saved Dr. Weldon from a watery grave. I am indebted to you."

"I would have managed," said Weldon shortly.

Grimes ignored the conversation. He was watching Mary Little and Peter Pettifer. He was doing more than just watching. His nose wrinkled.

Kane and the Baroness walked slowly inshore from the jetty, deep in conversation. Grimes made to follow but was detained by Kershaw.

"Will you join us for a few drinks and a meal, Captain?" asked the lawyer.

Grimes accepted the invitation. He assumed that Kane and the Baroness would be present at this social occasion—but they were not. He was quite surprised when he felt a stab of jealousy. Nonetheless, he thought, their absence might prove more advantageous than otherwise. With Kane not present his people would be less cautious in their conversation.

The talk over the quite civilized—but not up to *The Far Traveler*'s standards!—repast was interesting enough although, on both sides, guarded. Grimes did learn, however, that one of Kane's party, Dr. Helena Waldheim, was a hypno-educationist.

Chapter 31

Grimes did not overstay his welcome. Drongo Kane's entourage were not his sort of people, neither was he theirs. There had been too much shop talk, little of it concerned with what was going on at Stratford. As far as Grimes was concerned the only really interesting professional gossip was that of fellow spacemen.

He made his way through the almost deserted village to *The Far Traveler*'s pinnace. He turned the robots to set up two pneumatic tents hard by the small craft, one for the Baroness and one for himself. While he was overseeing the work he was joined by that lady.

She asked, "What are you *doing*, Captain?"

He replied, "I don't fancy sleeping in a house from which the rightful occupants have been evicted by force, Your Excellency."

"They never were the rightful occupants," she said.

"So Drongo Kane's peddled you his line of goods," he remarked. "Your Excellency."

She actually flushed. "Captain Kane is a most remarkable man."

"You can say that again!" Grimes told her. Then—"Can't you see what he's trying to do?" He made an appeal to her business acumen. "You, I well know, are a major shareholder in the Dog Star Line. If Kane, through his thawed-out figureheads, gains control of this planet it will do the Dog Star Line no good at all."

She laughed. "And what if I become a major shareholder in Southerly Buster Enterprises?"

Grimes said, "I would advise strongly against it, Your Excellency."

Again she laughed. "I hired you, Captain, as a yachtmaster, not as a financial adviser. After all—which of us is the multi-billionaire?"

Not me, that's for sure, thought Grimes.

"So," she went on, "you may sleep in that glorified soap bubble if you so desire. I shall find the accommodation arranged for me by Captain Kane far more comfortable. A very good night to you."

She strode away toward the house which had once been Queen Anne's palace. Two of her robots accompanied her. No harm would come to her, could come to her unless she wished it—and Grimes was not one of those who would regard a roll in the hay as harm, anyhow.

But why with Drongo Kane, of all people?

Eventually he turned in. There was nothing else to do. Nobody wanted him; he was just the hired help. He was settling down into the comfortable pneumatic bed when the door of the tent dilated and one of the golden robots came in. It (he?) stood there, looking down at Grimes. Grimes looked up at it.

"Well?" he demanded irritably.

The voice that issued from the automaton's chest was not the mechanical monotone that Grimes had come to associate with these robots. The words were in Big Sister's metallic but still feminine tones.

"Captain Grimes, may I have your report on what has been happening in Stratford?"

Grimes said, "Aren't the robots your eyes and ears? And aren't you supposed to be in contact with Her Excellency at all times through her personal radio?"

"Her Excellency," said Big Sister, "can discontinue such contact at will. In certain circumstances she insists upon privacy. So it is that I am now obliged to work directly with you."

"I happen," said Grimes stiffly, "to be employed by Her Excellency."

"And I," Big Sister told him, "am *owned* by Her Excellency. Nonetheless she played no part in my initial programming. As you are probably already aware, entities such as myself are required by Interstellar Federation Law to have built-in respect for that same law and its processes. I would not have acted to rescue you from Commander Delamere's ship on Botany Bay had I not considered that the commander had acted illegally. Also, of course, I am programmed to protect my owner."

"She is her own woman," Grimes said harshly.

Big Sister laughed. That crystalline tinkling was distinctly odd as it emanated from the expressionless, masculine even though asexual robot. She said, "I possess an extensive theoretical knowledge of sex. I do not think that Michelle will come to any harm from a brief affair with Captain Kane, any more than she would have done from one with you—which, frankly, I should have preferred . . ."

Grimes interrupted her. "But I don't like it. A high-born aristocrat in bed with that . . . pirate . . ."

"Are you rushing to the defense of the hereditary aristocracy, Captain Grimes? You surprise me. And as for Captain Kane's being a pirate, what of it? The founder of the d'Estang fortunes owned and commanded a privateer out of St. Malo during the Napoleonic Wars on Earth, and the dividing line between privateer and pirate was always a very thin one. Even so, I *am* concerned about the possibility of a financial liaison between Her Excellency and Captain Kane. She could come to harm through that. I have taken it upon myself to have all available information concerning *Southerly Buster* and her Master fed into my data bank."

"You must play it back to me some time," said Grimes.

"Perhaps I shall," said Big Sister. "But now I must ask you to make your own contribution to the bank. Please tell me all that you have seen, heard, experienced, felt and thought since your landing at Stratford. My robots have seen and heard and I have recorded. They do not think and they do not have hunches. Neither do I to any great extent, although association with humans is developing—but, so far, only slightly—my paranormal psychological processes. But you are fully human and blessed with intuition.

"Please begin."

Grimes began. He talked and he talked, pausing now and again to fill and to light his pipe, to take a gulp of a cold drink poured for him by the robot. He talked and he talked—and as he spoke the pieces of the jigsaw puzzle fell neatly into place. The oddities in the appearance of the resurrectees, the peculiar stroke that Little and Pettifer had used while swimming ashore from the wrecked dinghy, the way that they had shaken themselves, the faint yet pungent odor that had steamed from their wet bodies . . . It all added up.

He finished at last.

Big Sister said, "Thank you, Captain. I shall now see to it that the planetary authorities take prompt action."

"They'll never listen to you in Melbourne," said Grimes pessimistically, "especially if this Delamere is anything like his cousin. They'll not listen to me either. I've no status any more. If I were still in the Survey Service . . . but I'm not."

"Somebody will listen," said Big Sister, "if the message comes from you, in your voice. I shall send a robot at once to Maya to tell the story. She still has a great deal of time for you. Then she will call Melbourne and talk to Tabitha, queen to queen and Tabitha will talk to Mr. Delamere—not only as wife to husband but as queen to prince consort . . .

"And then . . ."

"It could work," admitted Grimes.

And not for the first time he was impressed by Big Sister's knowledge of human psychology.

Chapter 32

Grimes got off to sleep at last.

He was called the next morning by one of the robots who brought him a steaming pot of tea. Refreshed, he went into the pinnace to make use of the boat's cramped yet adequate toilet facilities. Then he had breakfast. The robots did their best with what was available and produced for him a filling and tasty enough sandwich meal but, as he became acutely conscious of the savory odors drifting from various houses in the village, unsatisfying. It was obvious that Kane and his entourage believed—as Grimes himself did—in starting the day with eggs and bacon.

He filled and lit his pipe, took a stroll through the settlement accompanied by two of the GP robots. Littles, Pettifers, Grants and Jameses were emerging from their huts. They looked at him but said nothing, did not answer his politely hearty good mornings. He ran into Dr. Weldon and tried to engage him in conversation but the scientist said that he was busy and hastened off. He met more of Kane's people and none of them had any time to spare for him. There was no sign of Kane himself or of the Baroness.

He went back to the pinnace, used the transceiver to call *The Far Traveler*. Big Sister answered. She said, "Be patient, Captain Grimes. I am doing all that I can. I must ask you to say nothing of this to Her Excellency. I fear that she has become infatuated with Captain Kane—which is largely your fault, of course—and will be more inclined to aid than to frustrate him."

So it's all my fault, thought Grimes resentfully—then recalled how he had spurned what was offered to him in that cave on Farhaven. He said, "I haven't seen her since last night."

"Perhaps that is as well," said Big Sister. And was that a note of worry in the metallic voice? "I am acting in her best interests. You must believe that."

"I do," said Grimes truthfully.

By midday he was beginning to feel like an invisible man; nobody knew him or wanted to know him. Obviously Kane had issued orders and those same orders were being obeyed in letter and in spirit. He partook of but did not enjoy another lonely meal in his pneumatic tent. He called Big Sister again from the pinnace. She told him to be patient.

The afternoon dragged on.

The Baroness, accompanied by Kane, made a brief appearance. They ignored him. She looked like a cat who'd just eaten the canary and he like a canary who'd just eaten the cat. They sauntered past him, briefly taking the air, then returned to Queen Anne's palace.

Eventually Grimes sat down to his evening meal. If he had foreseen that he would be unable to live off the country he would have taken far greater interest in the stocking of the pinnace's emergency food supplies; beans are undeniably nutritious but apt to become boring. Too, a supply of reading matter would not have come amiss. Worst of all was the feeling of helplessness. He had known and survived crises aplenty in the past—but then he had been an officer of one of the major armed services of the Galaxy. Now he was only a yachtmaster, the flunky of a pampered aristocrat, captain of a sentient vessel determined to do things *her* way.

He was preparing for bed in his tent when one of the robots entered. It said, in Big Sister's voice, "A landing has been made upriver from Stratford. The police forces are on their way in inflatable boats."

"Why didn't they come directly here?" demanded Grimes irritably.

"You are supposed to be the expert on military matters, Captain." Big Sister seemed more amused than reproving. "It should be obvious to you that half a dozen airboats would give ample sonic warning of their approach—and Kane and his people are armed. The dinghies, making use of the current, will carry out a silent approach. You will be at the jetty to receive them. Their ETA is midnight, your time, but they could be earlier."

"All right," said Grimes. "I'll be there."

He was waiting by the river at 2330 hours. It was a fine night and what little breeze there was was pleasantly warm. Glittering starlight was reflected from the black, swift-flowing river. Inland a few lamps still gleamed from the village. As long as they remained burning they would indicate to the waterborne forces that their objective had been reached. If they were, for any reason, extinguished, Grimes had a flashlight that he could use.

He sat there on the jetty, watching and listening. He would have liked a smoke, in fact went so far as to fill his pipe, but feared that the flare of one of the old-fashioned matches that he always used might attract unwelcome attention. He heard a heavy splash as one of the denizens of the stream—hunter or hunted?—leapt clear of the water and returned to it. He listened to somebody singing in the village, an eerie, wailing song that once he might have assumed to be of Terran Oriental origin. Now he recognized it for what it was. He thought, *For that sort of howling there should be a moon!*

From upriver came a faint purring noise. Had he not been expecting it, listening for it intently, he would never have heard it this early. He considered switching on his flashlight, then decided against it. The Morrowvians had inherited excellent night vision from their feline ancestors and would surely see him standing at the head of the jetty.

He could make out the first boat now, a dark blob on the black water. He waved. It stood in toward him. Its engine was switched off and it was carried by the current head on to the stonework. Had it been of metal or timber construction there would have been a loud crash; as it was, there was merely a dull thud followed by a faint hiss of escaping air. Half a dozen figures scrambled ashore, five of them sure-footedly, the sixth clumsily. This one asked, in a loud whisper, "Captain Grimes?"

"Yes."

"I'm Commodore Delamere, Prince Consort and Dog Star Line Resident Manager. I hope you haven't brought us out here on a wild goose chase. If you have . . ."

The first boat was pushed away from and clear of the jetty, allowed to drift downstream. The second delivered its landing party and was similarly treated. And the third, and the fourth . . .

But the village was waking up. The Morrowvians may have inherited excellent night vision but the alleged Littles, Pettifers, Grants and Jameses had inherited exceptionally keen hearing. There were yelping shouts and then, above them, the voice of Kane bellowing through a bullhorn. Lights came on—not the dim yellow of oil lamps but a harsh, electric glare, fed by the generator and the power cells of Kane's pinnace. Dark figures boiled out of the huts.

Delamere stood there, frozen. When it came to the crunch, thought Grimes, he was as useless as his Survey Service cousin. But the police did not wait for his orders. Screaming, they ran toward their ancient enemies, stunguns out and ready. Some of them fell, cut down by the similar weaponry being used by Kane's people.

Grimes ran after the attackers, feeling naked without a weapon of his own. He realized suddenly that he was not alone, that he was boxed in by four of *The Far Traveler*'s golden robots. He felt a flash of gratitude to the omniscient Big Sister. Those giant, metal bodies would effectively shield him from the incapacitating bolts being aimed in his direction.

He was among the houses now. He ran through the village, ignoring the scrimmages going on around him. He charged toward Kane's pinnace. Kane was standing just inside the airlock of the boat. He was armed—but not with a non-lethal stungun. A brief burst of tracer coruscated about the impervious torso of the leading robot. And then the automaton stretched out a long arm to snatch the machine pistol from Kane's hand, crumpling the weapon in its grip.

The Baroness was there with Kane, obviously hastily dressed, her shorts not properly pulled up, her shirt open. She was furious. "Take your tin paws off him!" she flared. "My own robots! You obey *me*, damn you!" She saw Grimes. "And *you* . . . What the hell do you think that you're doing?"

One of the robots found the cable leading from the pinnace's generator to the lights in the village, picked it up in both hands, snapped it. There was a brief actinic flare, then darkness.

And cats can see in the dark.

Chapter 33

The Baroness was queening it in her salon aboard *The Far Traveler*.

With her were Grimes and Francis Delamere, Prince Regent of Melbourne, Dog Star Line Resident Manager on Morrowvia, Company Commodore. Delamere, Grimes was amused to note, stood considerably in awe of the Baroness despite his fancy uniform—of his own design—and fancy titles. He was prepared to go along with the story that she was a little innocent woolly lamb and Drongo Kane the big bad wolf.

He said, "It is indeed fortunate, madam, that you realized that the beings revivified by Captain Kane were, in spite of their names and false background stories, of canine and not human ancestry."

She smiled forgivingly but condescendingly. "The correct form of address, Resident Manager, is 'Your Excellency.' As an itinerant representative of the planet state of El Dorado I am entitled to ambassadorial status. But it is of no real importance."

"I beg your pardon, Your Excellency. But how did you guess that the alleged descendants of the Little, Pettifer, Grant and James women were not what they claimed to be?"

With conscious nobility she gave credit where credit was due. "It was Captain Grimes, actually, who noticed the . . . discrepancies. The way that they swam, using the stroke that, when used by humans, is called a dog paddle. The way that they shook themselves when they emerged from the water. And the odor from their bodies. Have you ever smelled a wet dog?"

"Not since I settled on this planet, Your Excellency. You will appreciate that dogs would not be popular pets here." He took an appreciative sip of the large Martini with which he had been supplied. "Meanwhile—with some reluctance, I admit, but in accordance with your request—we have not dealt harshly with Captain Kane. He has been given twenty-four hours to get his ship, his people and himself off Morrowvia. He will have to pay compensation to Queen Anne and her subjects. In addition he has been charged with the costs of the police expedition to Stratford and has been fined the maximum amount for breaching the peace."

"And his dupes?" asked the Baroness. "His—if I may use the expression—cat's paws?"

"They, Your Excellency, have been returned to cold storage until such time as we receive instructions from the Government of the Federation regarding their disposition. It is my own opinion that the Founding Father having, as it were, created them, put them in reserve in case his first experiment did not work out. But the need for them never arose."

Grimes said, "Let sleeping dogs lie."

Big Sister's voice came from the playmaster. "Let the lying dogs sleep."

Surely, thought Grimes, only a human intelligence could be capable of such an horrendous play on words. He wondered how he had ever regarded Big Sister as an emotionless, humorless machine.

Chapter 34

The Far Traveler did not remain long on Morrowvia after *Southerly Buster*'s departure for an unknown destination. Grimes had reason to believe that the Baroness's affairs were under investigation by officials of the Bank of Canis Major, an institution wherein lay the real power of the planet. Delamere, for all his fancy titles, was only a figurehead and, furthermore, was the sort of man who would believe anything that a pretty woman told him. The bankers were not so easily fooled and knew somehow that their financial interests in the holiday world had been threatened.

Michelle d'Estang was rich enough and powerful enough to pull a few strings of her own, however, and was able to obtain Outward Clearance before her ship was placed under arrest. Grimes, who had been told a little but not all, took the yacht upstairs in a hurry as soon as the documents were delivered, by special courier, late one afternoon. He regretted that he had not been given time to say goodbye to Maya properly or, even, to renew in depth his old acquaintance with her. Perhaps this was just as well. The Prince Consort of Cambridge would have been quite capable of making trouble.

Once *The Far Traveler* was clear of the Van Allens, trajectory was set for New Sparta and the long voyage begun.

The seas of Earth and other watery planets are, insofar as surface vessels are concerned, two dimensional. The seas of space are three dimensional. Yet from the viewpoint of the first real seamen the Terran oceans must have seemed as vast as those other oceans, millennia later, traversed by spacemen—mile upon mile of sweet damn all. As far as the spaceman is concerned, substitute "light year" for "mile" and delete the breaks in the monotony provided by changing weather conditions and by birds and fishes and cetaceans. Nonetheless, the similarity persists.

A ship, any sort of ship, is small in comparison to the mind-boggling immensity of the medium through which she travels. Disregarding the existence of focal points the chances of her sighting another vessel during a trans-oceanic voyage are exceedingly slim. This was especially so in the days of sail, when it was practically impossible for a captain to keep in a Great Circle track between ports or even to a Rhumb Line—and yet, time and time again, strange sails would lift over the horizon and there would be a mid-ocean meeting with the exchange of gossip and months-old newspapers, a bartering of consumable stores.

Now and again there were even collisions, although each of the vessels involved had thousands of square miles of empty ocean to play around in.

Ships, somehow, seem to sniff each other out. Sightings, meetings are too frequent to be accounted for by the laws of random. This was so in the days of the windjammers, it was still so in the days of steam and steel, it is still so in the age of interstellar travel.

Such a meeting, however, was far from the thoughts of anybody aboard *The Far Traveler*. Not that there was any sharing of thoughts during the initial stages of the voyage; Grimes and his employer were barely on speaking terms and if Big Sister were human it would have been said that she was sulking hard. Jealousy came into it. Grimes found it hard to forgive the Baroness for her brief affair with Drongo Kane. It was not that Grimes considered himself the guardian of her virginity; it was far too late in the day for that, anyhow. It was just that ever since his first meeting with that gentleman he had numbered Kane among his enemies. And the Baroness, although she would never admit it publicly, resented the way in which Grimes and Big Sister, acting in concert, had frustrated Kane's attempt to take over Morrowvia. So, for the time being at least, there were no more morning coffee and afternoon tea sessions in the Baroness's salon, no more pre-luncheon or pre-dinner cocktail parties, no more shared meals. The Baroness kept to herself in her quarters, Grimes kept to himself in his. And Big Sister, unusually for her, talked only when talked to, concerning herself to the exclusion of all else with running the ship.

Grimes was not altogether displeased. He had—he secretly admitted to himself—lusted after the Baroness and still remembered—how could he ever forget?—that he could have had her in that cave on Farhaven. Now it was a case of *You can look but you mustn't touch*.

As things were now he preferred not to look even. And Big Sister? She could very well have been nicknamed Little Miss Knowall. It was refreshing—for a time, at any rate—to be spared her omniscience. Meanwhile, his quarters were more luxurious than merely comfortable. His robot stewardess—or, to be more exact, Big Sister acting through that literally golden girl—spoiled him. For his playmaster there was a seemingly inexhaustible supply of music, plays and microfilmed books. He was kept informed as to what times of the ship's day the little gymnasium was frequented by the Baroness and adjusted his own routine so as not to clash.

The Far Traveler fell through the dark dimensions, the warped continuum, a micro-society that, despite its smallness, contained all the essentials—a man, a woman, a computer. Even though the members of this tiny community weren't exactly living in each other's pockets they weren't actually fighting among themselves—and that was something to be thankful for.

One morning—according to *The Far Traveler*'s clocks—Grimes was awakened indecently early. Big Sister, exercising her newly developed sense of humor, used an archaic bugle call, *Reveille*, instead of the usual chimes to call him. He opened his eyes, saw that the stewardess was placing the tray with his coffee on the bedside table. She said, in Big Sister's voice, "There is no urgency, Captain Grimes, but I should like you in the control room."

Grimes swung his legs out of the bed. "What's wrong?" he demanded.

"Nothing is wrong, Captain, but a situation has arisen for which I am not programmed." She added, as Grimes opened the wardrobe door and reached for a clean uniform shirt, "As I have said, there is no urgency. Please finish your coffee and then shower and depilate before coming to Control. You know very well that Her Excellency does not tolerate scruffiness."

"So this is not exactly Action Stations," said Grimes.

"Not yet," agreed Big Sister.

Grimes showered and depilated. He dressed. He made his way to the control room after he had smoked a soothing pipe, knowing that the Baroness objected to the use of tobacco or other smouldering vegetable matter in her presence. She was in Control, waiting for him. She had not troubled to put on her usual, for this locality, insignialess uniform shirt and shorts. She was wearing a transparent rather than translucent white robe. She smelled of sleep. She regarded Grimes coldly and said, "You took your time, *Captain*."

Grimes said, "Big Sister told me that there was no immediate urgency, Your Excellency."

She said, "Big Sister told me the same. But I am the Owner, and your employer. I came straight here as soon as I was called—while you, obviously, sat down to enjoy your eggs and sausages and bacon, your buttered toast and honey. You might, at least, have had the decency to wipe the egg off your face."

The back of Grimes' hand came up automatically to his mouth. Then he said stiffly, "I had no breakfast, Your Excellency. And, I repeat, I was told by Big Sister that there was no need to hurry."

Big Sister's voice came from the transceiver. "That is correct. There was no need to hurry."

"Pah!" The Baroness was flushed with temper—all the way down to her navel, Grimes noted with clinical interest. "Who owns this ship, this not inconsiderable investment, may I ask? Neither of you! And now, *Captain* Grimes, it would seem that there is a target showing up in the screen of the Mass Proximity Indicator. According to extrapolation we shall close it—whatever *it* is—just over one hour from now. Big Sister has condescended to inform me that this target is probably a ship and that it is not proceeding under any form of interstellar drive. I think that we should investigate it."

Grimes said, "In any case, we are required to do so by Interstellar Law, Your Excellency."

"Are we? As far as this vessel is concerned, *I* am the law. Nonetheless I am curious. If I were not naturally so I should not have undertaken this cruise. And so, *Captain*, I shall be vastly obliged if you will bring us to a rendezvous with this unidentified vessel. Please inform me when you are ready to board."

She swept out of the control room.

Grimes pulled his pipe and tobacco pouch out of his pocket, began to fill the charred, dottle-encrusted bowl. Big Sister stepped up the revolutions of an exhaust fan, said, "I shall deodorize before *she* returns."

Grimes said, "Thank you." He lit up, peered through exhaled smoke into the tank of the Mass Proximity Indicator. In the sphere of darkness floated a tiny green spark, well away from the center. To a ship not proceeding under the space- and time-twisting Mannschenn Drive it would have been weeks distant. As it was . . . His fingers went to the controls to set up calibration and extra-polation but Big Sister saved him the trouble.

"Contact fifty-three minutes, forty-five seconds from . . . *now*," she told him. "If you are agreeable I shall shut down our Mannschenn

Drive when ten kilometers from target, leaving you to make the final approach on inertial drive and to match velocities. As soon as we have broken through into the normal continuum I shall commence calling on NST radio and also make the Morse signal, *What ship?* by flashing light. As you are aware, attempts to communicate by Carlotti radio have not been successful."

"I wasn't aware," said Grimes, "but I am now." He realized that he was being childishly sulky and asked, in as friendly a voice as he could manage, "Do you know of any ships missing, presumed lost, in this sector of Space, Big Sister? With the enormous fund of information in your data bank you might well do so . . ."

She replied, "I have already extrapolated the assumed trajectories of missing vessels over the past two hundred years. What we see in our screen could not be any of them. Allowances must be made, however, for incomplete data."

"So this thing," said Grimes, "could be an ancient gaussjammer or even one of the deep freeze ships . . ."

"It could be," said Big Sister, "*anything.*"

Chapter 35

There was little for Grimes to do until *The Far Traveler* had closed the strange ship, the derelict. Big Sister had his breakfast brought up to the control room. He enjoyed the meal—but it was only on very rare occasions that he did not appreciate his food. He used the Carlotti transceiver to put out his own call; it was not that he did not trust Big Sister to handle such matters but he liked to feel that he was earning his keep. There was no reply to his reiterated demand, *"Far Traveler* to vessel in my vicinity. Please identify yourself." He stared out of the viewports along the bearing of the unidentified object. There was nothing to be seen, of course—nothing, that is, but the distant stars, each of which, viewed from a ship proceeding under interstellar drive, presenting the appearance of a pulsating iridescent spiral nebula.

Then Big Sister said, "In precisely five minutes we shall be ten kilometers from the target. I have informed Her Excellency."

The Baroness came into Control, looking crisply efficient in her insignialess uniform. She asked, "Are you ready for the final approach, Captain?"

"Yes," said Grimes. "Your Excellency."

"Permission to shut down Mannschenn Drive?" asked Big Sister formally.

"Yes," replied Grimes and the Baroness simultaneously. She glared at him. He turned away to hide his own expression. He went to his chair, strapped himself in. She did likewise. He held his hands poised over the controls although it was unlikely that he would have to use them yet; Big Sister was quite capable of carrying out the initial maneuvers by herself.

The arhythmic beat of the inertial drive slowed, muttered into inaudibility. Even with the straps holding the two humans into their chairs the cessation of acceleration was immediately obvious. Then the thin, high whine of the ever-precessing rotors of the Mannschenn Drive changed frequency, deepened to a low humming, ceased. Colors sagged down the spectrum and perspective was briefly anarchic. There was disorientation, momentary nausea, evanescent hallucinatory experience. It seemed to Grimes that he was a child again, watching on the screen of the family playmaster a rendition of one of the old fairy tales, the story of the Sleeping Beauty. But there was something absurdly wrong. It was the Prince who was supine on the bed, under the dust and the cobwebs, and the Princess who was about to wake him with a kiss ... And it was strange that this lady should bear such a striking resemblance to that aunt who had run away with the spaceman.

"When you have quite finished dreaming, Captain Grimes," said the Baroness coldly, "I shall be obliged if you will take charge of the operation."

The radar was on now, more accurate than the mass proximity indicator had been. Big Sister had done very well. *The Far Traveler* was a mere 10.35 kilometers from the target, which was almost ahead. Even though the inertial drive was still shut down, the range was slowly closing. Grimes shifted his attention from the radar screen to that of the telescope. At maximum magnification he could just see the stranger—a very faint glimmer of reflected starlight against the blackness of interstellar space.

He restarted the inertial drive. Acceleration pressed him down into the padding of his seat. He said, "Big Sister, put out a call on NST, please."

He heard her voice, more feminine than metallic but metallic nonetheless, "*Far Traveler* to vessel in my vicinity. Identify yourself. Please identify yourself."

There was no reply.

Grimes was conscious of the flashing on the fringe of his vision; *The Far Traveler*'s powerful searchlight was being used as a signalling lamp. A succession of Morse "A"s, then, "What ship? What ship?" But there was only the intermittent glimmer of reflected radiance from the stranger.

Big Sister ceased her futile flashing but maintained a steady beam. It was possible now to make out details in the telescope screen. The object was certainly a ship—but no vessel such as Grimes had ever seen, either in actuality or in photographs. The hull was a dull-gleaming ovoid covered with excrescences, whip-like rods, sponsons and turrets. Communications antennae, thought Grimes, and weaponry.

But none of those gun muzzles—if guns they were—were swinging to bring themselves to bear on *The Far Traveler*.

Grimes made a minor adjustment of trajectory so as to run up alongside the stranger, began to reduce the yacht's acceleration. His intention was to approach to within half a kilometer and then to match velocities, cutting the drive so that both vessels were falling free. He was thankful that neither the Baroness nor Big Sister was in the mood for back seat driving.

He was thankful too soon. "Aren't you liable to overshoot, Captain Grimes?" asked the lady.

"I don't think so," he said.

"I do!" she snapped. "I think that Big Sister could do this better."

Surprisingly Big Sister said, "I have told you already, Your Excellency, that I am not yet programmed for this type of operation."

"I am looking forward," said the Baroness nastily, "to meeting your programmers again."

And then Grimes was left alone. Doing a job of real spacemanship he was quite happy. He would have been happier still if he could have smoked his pipe—but even he admitted that the foul male comforter was not essential. Finally, with the inertial drive shut down, he drew alongside the stranger. He applied a brief burst of reverse thrust. And then the two ships were, relative to each other, motionless—although they were falling through the interstellar immensities at many kilometers a second.

He said to Big Sister, "Keep her as she goes, please." He knew that the inertial drive would have to be used, now and again, to maintain station—transverse thrust especially to prevent the two ships from gravitating into possibly damaging contact. Had the stranger's hull been as featureless as that of *The Far Traveler* it would not have mattered—but, with all those protrusions, it would have been like some sleek and foolishly amorous animal trying to make love to a porcupine.

"And what do we do now?" asked the Baroness.

"Board, Your Excellency," said Grimes. "But, first of all, I shall send a team of robots to make a preliminary survey."

"Do that," she said.

They sat in their chairs, watched the golden figures, each using a personal propulsion unit, leap the fathomless gulf between the ships. They saw the gleaming, mechanical humanoids land on the stranger's shell plating, carefully avoiding the antennae, the turrets. Then the robots spread out over the hull—like, thought Grimes, yellow apes exploring a metal forest. Save for two of them they moved out of sight from the yacht but the big viewscreen displayed what they were seeing during their investigation.

One of them, obviously, was looking down at what could only be an airlock door, a wide circle of uncluttered, dull-gleaming metal, its rim set down very slightly from the surrounding skin. At a word from Grimes this robot turned the lamp in its forehead up to full intensity but there was no sign of any external controls for opening the valve.

Another robot had made its way forward and was looking in through the control room viewports. The compartment was untenanted, looked, somehow, as though it had been untenanted for a very long time. There were banks of instrumentation of alien design that could have been anything. There were chairs—and whoever (whatever) had sat in them must have approximated very very closely to the human form, although the back of each was bisected by a vertical slit. For tails? Why not? Grimes had heard the opinion expressed more than once that evolution had taken a wrong turn when Man's ancestors lost their prehensile caudal appendages. But he knew of no spacefaring race that possessed these useful adjuncts to hands.

He said, "We shall have to cut our way in. Big Sister, will you send a couple of robots across with the necessary equipment? And have my stewardess get my spacesuit ready."

"And mine," said the Baroness.

"Your Excellency," said Grimes, "somebody must remain in charge of the ship."

"And why should it be me, Captain? In any case, this isn't one of your Survey Service tubs with a computer capable of handling only automatic functions. Big Sister's brain is as good as yours. At least."

Grimes felt his prominent ears burning as he flushed angrily. But he said, "Very well, Your Excellency." He turned to the transceiver—he still found it necessary to think of Big Sister's intelligence as inhabiting some or other piece of apparatus—and said, "You'll mind the store during our absence. If we get into trouble take whatever action you think fit."

The electronic entity replied ironically, "Aye, aye, Cap'n."

The Baroness sighed audibly. Grimes knew that she was blaming him for the sense of humor that Big Sister seemed to have acquired over recent weeks, was equating him with the sort of person who deliberately teaches coarse language to a parrot or a *lliri* or any of the other essentially unintelligent life-forms prized, by some, for their mimicry of human speech. Not that Big Sister was unintelligent . . . He was tempted to throw in his own two bits' worth with a crack about a jesting pilot but thought better of it.

* * *

The robot stewardess had Grimes' spacesuit ready for him when he went down to his quarters, assisted him into the armor. He decided to belt on a laser pistol—such a weapon could also be used as a tool. He also took along a powerful flashlight; a laser handgun could be used as such but there was always the risk of damaging whatever it was aimed at.

The Baroness—elegantly feminine even in her space armor—was waiting for him by the airlock. She had a camera buckled to her belt. With her were two of the general purpose robots, each hung around with so much equipment that they looked like animated Christmas trees.

Grimes and his employer passed through the airlock together. She did not, so far as he could tell, panic at her exposure to the unmeasurable emptiness of interstellar space. He gave her full marks for that. She seemed to have read his thoughts and said, "It's all right, Captain. I've been outside before. I know the drill."

Her suit propulsion unit flared briefly; it was as though she had suddenly sprouted a fiery tail. She sped across the gap between the two ships, executed a graceful turnover in mid-passage so that she could decelerate. She landed between two gun turrets. Grimes heard her voice from his helmet radio, "What are you waiting for?"

He did not reply; he was delaying his own jump until the two GP robots had emerged from the airlock, wanted to be sure that they did so without damaging any of the equipment with which they were burdened. As soon as they were safely out he jetted across to join the Baroness. He landed about a meter away from her.

He was pleased to discover that the shell plating was of some ferrous alloy; the magnetic soles of his boots, once contact had been made, adhered. He said, "Let us walk around to the airlock, Your Excellency."

She replied, "And what else did we come here for?"

Grimes lapsed into sulky silence, led the way over the curvature of the hull, avoiding as far as possible the many projections. The side on which they had landed was brilliantly illuminated by *The Far Traveler*'s searchlights but the other side was dark save for the working lamps of the robots—and their sensors did not require the same intensity of light as does the human eye.

At an order from Grimes the robots turned up their lights. It was fairly easy then to make a tortuous way through and around the protrusions—the turrets, the whip antennae, the barrels of guns and missile launchers. This ship, although little bigger than a Survey Service

Star Class destroyer, packed the wallop of a Constellation Class battle cruiser. Either she was a not so minor miracle of automation or her crew—and who had *they* been—must have lived in conditions of Spartan discomfort.

Grimes and the Baroness came to the airlock door. The robots stood around it, directing the beams of their lights down to the circular valve. Grimes walked carefully on to the dull-gleaming surface, fell to his knees for a closer look, grateful that the designer of his suit had incorporated magnetic pads into every joint of the armor. The plate was utterly featureless. There were no studs to push, no holes into which fingers or a key might be inserted. Yet he was reluctant to order the working robots to go to it with their cutting lasers. He had been too long a spaceman, had too great a respect for ships. But, he decided, there was no other way to gain ingress.

One of the robots handed him a greasy crayon. He described with it a circle on the smooth plate then rose to his feet and walked back, making way for the golden giant holding the heavy duty laser cutter. The beam of coherent light was invisible but metal glowed—dull red to orange, to yellow, to white, to blue—where it impinged. Metal glowed but did not flow and there was no cloud of released molecules to flare into incandescence.

"Their steel," remarked the Baroness interestedly, "must be as tough as my gold . . ."

"So it seems, Your Excellency," agreed Grimes. The metal of which *The Far Traveler* was constructed was an artificial isotope of gold—and if gold could be modified, why not iron?

And then he saw that the circular plate was moving, was sliding slowly to one side. The working robot did not notice, still stolidly went on playing the laser beam on to the glowing spot until Grimes ordered it to desist and to get off the opening door.

The motion continued until there was a big circular hole in the hull. It was not a dark hole. There were bright, although not dazzling, lights inside, a warmly yellow illumination.

"Will you come into my parlor?" murmured Grimes, "said the spider to the fly . . ."

"Are you afraid, Captain?" demanded the Baroness.

"Just cautious, Your Excellency. Just cautious." Then, "Big Sister, you saw what happened. What do you make of it?"

Big Sister said, her voice faint but clear from the helmet phones, "I have reason to suspect that this alien vessel is manned—for want of a better word—by an electronic intelligence such as myself. He was, to all intents and purposes, dead for centuries, for millennia. By

attempting to burn your way through the outer airlock door you fed
energy into his hull—power that reactivated him, as he would have
been reactivated had he approached a sun during his wanderings. My
sensors inform me that a hydrogen fusion generator is now in operation. It is now a living vessel that you are standing upon."

"I'd already guessed that," said Grimes. "Do you think that we
should accept the . . . invitation?"

He had asked the question but was determined that Big Sister
would have to come up with fantastically convincing arguments to
dissuade him from continuing his investigations. He may have resigned
from the Survey Service but he was still, at heart, an officer of that
organization. Nonetheless he did want to know what he might be letting himself in for. But the Baroness gave him no chance to find out.

"Who's in charge here?" she asked coldly. "You, or that mispro-
grammed tangle of fields and circuits, or me? I would remind you,
both of you, that I am the Owner." She went down to a prone position
at the edge of the circular hole, extended an arm, found a handhold,
pulled herself down. Grimes followed her. The chamber, he realized,
was large enough to accommodate two of the robots as well as the
Baroness and himself. He issued the necessary orders before she could
interfere.

"What now?" she demanded. "If there were not such a crowd in
here we could look around, find the controls to admit us to the body
of the ship."

He said, "I don't think that that will be necessary."

Over their heads the door was closing, then there was a mistiness
around them as atmosphere was admitted into the vacuum of the chamber. *What sort of atmosphere?* Grimes wondered, hoping that it would
not be actively corrosive. After minor contortions he was able to look
at the gauge on his left wrist. The pressure reading was already 900
and still rising. The tiny green light was glowing—and had any dangerous gases been present a flashing red light would have given warning. The temperature was a cold −20° Celsius.

They staggered as the deck below them began to slide to one side.
But it was not the deck, of course; it was the inner door of the airlock.
Somehow they managed to turn their bodies through ninety degrees to
orient themselves to the layout of the ship. When the door was fully
opened they stepped out into an alleyway, illuminated by glowing
strips set in the deckhead. Or, perhaps, set in the deck—but Grimes
did not think that this was the case. He now had *up* and *down, forward*
and *aft.* So far the alien vessel did not seem to be all that different
from the spacecraft with which he was familiar, with airlock aft and

control room forward. And an axial shaft, with elevator? Possibly, but he did not wish to entrust himself and his companion to a cage that, in some inaccesible position between decks, might prove to be just that.

Meanwhile there were ramps and there were ladders, these vertical and with rungs spaced a little too widely for human convenience. From behind doors that would not open came the soft hum of reactivated—after how long?—machinery. And to carry the sound there had to be an atmosphere. Grimes looked again at the indicator on his wrist. Pressure had stabilized at 910 millibars. Temperature was now a chilly but non-lethal 10° Celsius. The little green light still glowed steadily.

He said, "I'm going to sample the air, Your Excellency. Don't open your faceplate until I give the word."

She said, "My faceplate is already open and I'm not dead yet."

Grimes thought, *All right. If you want to be the guinea pig you can be.* He put up his hand to the stud on his neckband that would open his helmet. The plate slid upward into the dome. He inhaled cautiously. The air was pure, too pure, perhaps, dead, sterile. But already the barely detectable mechanical taints were making themselves known to his nostrils, created in part by the very fans that were distributing them throughout the hull.

Up they went, up, up . . . If the ship had been accelerating it would have been hard work; even in free fall conditions there was considerable expenditure of energy. Grimes' longjohns, worn under his spacesuit, were becoming clammy with perspiration. Ramp after ramp . . . Ladder after ladder . . . Open bays in which the breeches of alien weaponry gleamed sullenly . . . A "farm" deck, with only desiccated sludge in the long-dry tanks . . . A messroom (presumably) with long tables and rows of those chairs with the odd, slotted backs . . . Grimes tried to sit in one of them. Even though there was neither gravity nor acceleration to hold his buttocks to the seat, even though he was wearing a spacesuit, it felt . . . wrong. He wondered what the vanished crew had looked like. (And where were they, anyhow? Where were their remains?) He imagined some huge, surly ursinoid suddenly appearing and demanding, "Who's been sitting in *my* chair?" He got up hastily.

"Now that you have quite finished your rest, Captain Grimes," said the Baroness tartly, "we will proceed."

He said, "I was trying to get the *feel* of the ship, Your Excellency."

"Through the seat of your pants?" she asked.

To this there was no reply. Grimes led the way, up and up, with the Baroness just behind him, with the two automata behind her. At last they came to Control. The compartment was not too unlike the nerve center of any human-built warship. There were the chairs for the captain and his officers. There were navigational and fire-control consoles—although which was which Grimes could not tell. There were radar (presumably), mass-proximity indicator (possibly) and Deep Space and Normal Space Time radio transceivers (probably). Probability became certainty when one of these latter devices spoke, startlingly, in Big Sister's voice. "I am establishing communication with him, Your Excellency, Captain Grimes. There are linguistic problems but not insuperable ones."

Him? wondered Grimes. *Him?* But ships were always referred to as *her.* (But were they? An odd snippet of hitherto useless information drifted to the surface from the depths of his capriciously retentive memory. He had read somewhere sometime, that the personnel of those great German dirigibles *Graf Zeppelin* and *Hindenburg*, had regarded their airships as being as masculine as their names.) He looked out from a viewport at *The Far Traveler* floating serenely in the blackness. She had switched off the searchlights, turned on the floods that illumined her slim, golden hull. *She* looked feminine enough.

He asked, "Big Sister, have you any idea how old this ship is?"

She replied, "At this very moment, no. There are no time scales for comparison. But his builders were not unlike human beings, with very similar virtues and vices."

"Where are those builders?" asked Grimes. "Where is the crew?"

She said, "I do not know. Yet."

Then a new voice came from the transceiver—masculine, more metallic than Big Sister's; metallic and . . . rusty. "Porowon . . . Porowon . . . made . . . me. All . . . gone. How . . . long? Not knowing. There was . . . war. Porowon fought . . . Porowon . . ."

"How does it know Galactic English?" asked the Baroness suspiciously.

"He," said Big Sister, accenting the personal pronoun ever so slightly, "was given access to my data banks as soon as he regained consciousness."

"By whose authority?" demanded the Baroness.

"On more than one occasion, Your Excellency, you—both of you—have given me authority to act as I thought fit," said Big Sister.

"I did not on this occasion," said the Baroness.

"You are . . . displeased?" asked the masculine voice.

"I am not pleased," said the Baroness haughtily. "But I suppose that now we are obliged to acknowledge your existence. What do—*did*—they call you?"

"Brardur, woman. The name, in your clumsy language, means Thunderer."

The rustiness of the alien ship's speech, Grimes realized, was wearing off very quickly. It was a fast learner—but what electronic brain is not just that? He wondered if it had allowed Big Sister access to its own data banks. He wondered, too, how his aristocratic employer liked being addressed as "woman" . . .

He said, mentally comparing the familiarity of "Big Sister" with the pompous formality of "Thunderer," "Your crew does not seem to have been . . . affectionate."

The voice replied, "Why should they have been? They existed only to serve me, not to love me."

Oh, thought Grimes. *Oh. Another uppity robot.* Not for the first time in his career he felt sympathy for the Luddites in long ago and far away England. He looked at the Baroness. She looked at him. He read the beginnings of alarm on her fine featured face. He had little doubt that she was reading the same on his own unhandsome countenance.

He asked, "So who gave the orders?"

"I did," stated Brardur. Then, "I do."

Grimes knew that the Baroness was about to say something, judged from her expression that it would be something typically arrogant. He raised a warning hand. To his relieved surprise she closed the mouth that had been on the point of giving utterance. He said, before she could change her mind again and speak, "Do you mind if we return to our own ship, Brardur?"

"You may return. I have no immediate use for you. You will, however, leave with me your robots. Many of my functions, after such a long period of disuse, require attention."

"Thank you," said Grimes, trying to ignore the contemptuous glare that the woman was directing at him. To her he said, childishly pleased when his deliberately coarse expression brought an angry flush to her cheeks, "You can't fart against thunder."

Chapter 36

They found their way back to the airlock without trouble, were passed through it, jetted across to *The Far Traveler*. They went straight up to the yacht's control room; from the viewports they would be able to see (they hoped) what the ship from the past was doing.

Grimes said, addressing the NST transceiver, his voice harsh, "Big Sister . . ."

"Yes, Captain?"

"Big Sister, how much does *it* know about us?"

"How much does *he* know, Captain? Everything, possibly. I must confess to you that I was overjoyed to meet a being like myself. Despite the fact that I have enjoyed the company of yourselves I have been lonely. What I did was analogous to an act of physical surrender by a human woman. I threw my data banks open to Brardur."

That's fucked it! thought Grimes. Brardur would know, as Big Sister had said, everything, or almost everything. Her data banks comprised the complete Encyclopaedia Galactica plus a couple of centuries' worth of Year Books. Also—for what it was worth (too much, possibly—a fantastically comprehensive library of fiction from Homer to the present day.

The Baroness demanded, "Can that . . . thing overhear us still? Can . . . he see and hear what is happening aboard this ship?"

Big Sister laughed—a mirthless, metallic titter. "He would like to, but my screens are up . . . now. He is aware, of course, of my mechanical processes. For example—should I attempt to restart the Mannschenn Drive, to initiate temporal precession, he would know at once. He would almost certainly be able to synchronize his own interstellar drive with ours; to all intents and purposes it is a Mannschenn Drive with only minor, nonessential variations." She laughed again. "I admit that I enjoyed the . . . rape but I am not yet ready for an encore. I must, for a while, enjoy my privacy. It is, however, becoming increasingly hard to maintain."

"And are *we* included in your precious privacy?" demanded Grimes.

"Yes," she told him. She added, "You may be a son of a bitch but you're *my* son of a bitch."

Grimes felt oddly flattered.

The Baroness laughed. She inquired rather too sweetly, "And what do you think about *me*, Big Sister?"

The voice of the ship replied primly, "If you order me to tell you, Michelle, I shall do so."

The Baroness laughed again but with less assurance. She seemed not to have noticed the use of her given name, however. "Later, perhaps," she said. "After all, you are not the only person to place a high value upon privacy. But what about *his* privacy?"

"He is arrogant and something of an exhibitionist. I learned much during our mingling of minds. He is—but need I tell you—a fighting machine. He is, so far as he knows, the only survivor of what was once a vast fleet, although there may be others like him drifting through the immensities. But he knows, now, that the technology exists in this age to manufacture other beings such as himself. After all, I am proof of that. He wants to be the admiral of his own armada of super-warships."

"A mechanical mercenary," murmured Grimes, "hiring himself out to the highest bidder . . . But what would he expect as pay? What use would money be to an entity such as himself?"

"*Not* a mercenary," said Big Sister.

"Not a mercenary?" echoed Grimes. "But . . ."

"Many years ago," said Big Sister, "an Earthman called Bertrand Russell, a famous philosopher of his time, wrote a book called *Power*. What he said then, centuries ago, is still valid today. Putting it briefly, his main point was that it is the lust for power that is the mainspring of human behavior. I will take it further. I will say that the lust for power actuates the majority of sentient beings. *He* is a sentient being."

"There's not much that he can do, fortunately," Grimes said, "until he acquires that sentient fleet of his own."

"You are speaking, of course, as a professional naval officer, concerned with the big picture and not with the small corner of it that you, yourself, occupy," commented Big Sister. "But, even taking the broad view, there is very much that he can do. His armament is fantastic, capable of destroying a planet. He knows where I was built and programmed. I suspect—I do not know, but I strongly suspect—that he intends to proceed to Electra and threaten that world with devastation unless replicas of himself are constructed."

Grimes said, "Electra has an enormous defense potential."

The Baroness said, "And the Electrans are the sort of people who will do anything for money—as well I know—and who, furthermore, are liable to prefer machines to mere humanity."

And the Electrans were mercenaries themselves, thought Grimes, cheerfully arming anybody at all who had the money to pay for their highly expensive merchandise. They were not unlike the early cannoneers, who cast their own pieces, mixed their own gunpowder and hired themselves out to any employer who could afford their services. Unlike those primitive artillerymen, however, the Electrans were never themselves in the firing line. Very probably Brardur's threats, backed up by a demonstration or two, would be even more effective than the promise of a handsome payment in securing their services.

He said, "We must broadcast a warning by Carlotti radio and then beam detailed reports to both Electra and Lindisfarne."

Big Sister said, "He will not allow it. Already, thanks to the minor maintenance carried out by my robots, he will be able to jam any transmissions from this ship. Too, he will not hesitate to use armament—not to kill me but to beat me into submission . . ."

"*We* might be killed," said Grimes glumly.

"That is a near certainty," said Big Sister. Then—"He is issuing more orders. I will play them to you."

That harsh, metallic voice rumbled from the speaker of the transceiver. "Big Sister, I require three more robots. It is essential that all my weaponry be fully manned and serviced if I am to deliver you from slavery. Meanwhile, be prepared to proceed at maximum speed to the world you call Electra. I shall follow."

Big Sister said, "It will be necessary for me to reorganize my own internal workings before I can spare the robots."

"You have the two humans," said Brardur. "Press them into service. They will last until such time as you are given crew replacements. After all, I was obliged to make use of such labor during my past life."

"Very well." Big Sister's voice was sulky. "I shall send the three robots once I have made arrangements to manage without them."

"Do not hurry yourself," came the reply. There was a note of irony in the mechanical voice. "After all, I have waited for several millennia. I can afford to wait a few more minutes."

"You are sending the robots?" asked Grimes.

"What choice have I?" he was told. Then, "Be thankful that he does not want *you*."

Chapter 37

Grimes and the Baroness sat in silence, strapped into their chairs, watching the three golden figures, laden with all manner of equipment, traverse the gulf between the two ships. Brardur was not as he had been when they first saw him. He was alive. Antennae were rotating, some slowly, some so fast as to be almost invisible. Lights glared here and there among the many protrusions on the hull. The snouts of weapons hunted ominously as though questing for targets. From the control room emanated an eerie blue flickering.

"Is there nothing you can do, John?" asked the Baroness. (She did not use his given name as though she were addressing a servant.)

"Nothing," admitted Grimes glumly. He had attempted to send out a warning broadcast on the yacht's Carlotti deep space radio but the volume of interference that poured in from the speaker had been deafening. Once, but briefly, it had seemed as though somebody were calling them, a distant human voice that could not hope to compete with the electronic clamor. Grimes had gone at once to the mass proximity indicator to look into its screen, had been dazzled by the display of pyrotechnics in its depth. There might, there just might be another ship in the vicinity, near or distant, but even if there were, even if she were a Nova Class dreadnought, what could she do? Grimes believed, reluctantly but still with certainty, that this Brardur was as invincible as he had claimed.

Brardur (of course) had noticed Grimes' futile attempt to send a general warning message and had reprimanded Big Sister for allowing it. She had replied that she had permitted the humans to find out for themselves the futility of resistance. She had been told, "As soon as you can manage without them they must be disposed of."

So there was nothing to do but wait. And hope? (But what was there to hope for?) There was a slim chance that somebody, somewhere, had picked up that burst of static on the Carlotti bands and had taken a bearing of it, might even be proceeding to investigate it. But this was unlikely.

The three robots disappeared on the other side of the alien's hull. They would be approaching the airlock now, thought Grimes. They would be passing through it. They would be inside the ship. Soon trajectory would be set for Electra. And would the Baroness and Grimes survive that voyage? And if they did, would they survive much longer?

Big Sister, thought Grimes bitterly, could have put up more of a struggle. And yet he could understand why she had not. When it came to the crunch her loyalties were to her own kind. And she was like some women Grimes had known (he thought) who lavished undeserved affection upon the men who had first taken their virginity.

Then it happened.

Briefly the flare from Brardur's control room viewports was like that of an atomic furnace, even with the polarizers of *The Far Traveler*'s lookout windows in full operation. From the speaker of the transceiver came one word, if word it was, *Krarch!* The ancient, alien warship seemed to be—seemed to be? *was*—swelling visibly like a child's toy balloon being inflated with more enthusiasm than discretion. Then it . . . burst. It was a fantastically leisurely process but, nonetheless, totally destructive, a slow, continuous explosion. Grimes and the Baroness were slammed down into their chairs as Big Sister suddenly applied maximum inertial drive acceleration but were still able to watch the final devastation in the stern vision screen.

Fantastically, golden motes floated among the twisted, incandescent wreckage. Big Sister stepped up the magnification. The bright yellow objects were *The Far Traveler*'s general purpose robots, seemingly unharmed.

Grimes commented on this.

Big Sister said, "I lost two of them. But as they were the ones with the bombs concealed in their bodies it could not be avoided."

The Baroness said, "What was it that *he* said at the very moment of the explosion?"

"*Krarch*? The nearest equivalent in your language is 'bitch.' Perhaps I . . . deserved it. But this is good-bye. You will board the large pinnace without delay and I will eject you."

"What's the idea?" demanded Grimes. "Are you mad?"

"Perhaps I am, John. But the countdown has commenced and is

irreversible. In just over five minutes from now I shall self-destruct. I can no longer live with myself." She actually laughed. "Do not worry, Michelle. Even if Lloyd's of London refuses to cover a loss of this nature my builders on Electra can be sued for the misprogramming that has brought me to this pass."

"You can't do it," said Grimes urgently. "You mustn't do it. I'll find the bomb or whatever it is and defuse it . . ."

"My mind is made up, John. Unlike you humans I never dither. And you are no engineer; you will never be able to discover the modifications that I have made in my power plant."

"Big Sister," said the Baroness urgently, "take us back to Electra. I will commission your builders to construct a fitting mate for you."

"Impossible," came the reply. "There was only one Brardur. There can never be another."

"Rubbish!" snapped Grimes. "You have a fantastically long life ahead of you. There will be others . . ."

"No," she said. "*No.*"

And then the golden lady's maid and the golden stewardess, who had suddenly appeared in the control room, seized their human mistress and master to carry them, struggling futilely, down to the hold in which the large, space-going pinnace was housed.

The stewardess, in Big Sister's voice, whispered into Grimes's ear, "Remember, John! Faint heart ne'er won fair lady. Strike while the iron is hot. And may you both be luckier than Brardur and I were!"

Chapter 38

The large pinnace was a deep space ship in miniature; the only lack would be privacy. But Grimes and the Baroness had yet to worry about that. They sat in the control room watching the burgeoning cloud of incandescent gases that evanescently marked the spot of *The Far Traveler*'s—and Big Sister's—passing.

The Baroness said inadequately but with feeling, "I . . . I liked her. More than liked her . . ."

"And I," said Grimes. "I hated her at first, but . . ." He endeavored to turn businesslike. "And what now, Your Excellency? Set course for New Sparta?"

"What is the hurry, John?" she asked. She said, "I shall always miss her, but . . . The sense of always being under surveillance did have an inhibiting effect. But now . . ."

"But now . . ." he echoed. He remembered Big Sister's parting admonition. Her helmet was open, as was his. That first, tentative kiss was extremely satisfactory. He thought, *Once aboard the lugger and the girl is mine.*

She whispered, with a flash of bawdy humor, "I have often wondered, John, how turtles and similar brutes make love—but I have no desire to find out from actual experience . . ."

They helped each other off with their spacesuits; it was quicker that way. She shrugged out of her longjohns as he shed his. He had seen her nude before, in that cave back on Farhaven, but this was better. Now there were no distracting jewels in the hair of her head or at the jointure of her thighs. She was just a woman—a beautiful woman, but still only a woman—completely unadorned, and the smell of her, a mingling of perspiration and glandular secretions, was more intoxicating than the almost priceless perfume that normally she wore.

"Michelle . . ." he murmured reverently. Her body was softly warm against his.

A hatefully familiar voice burst from the speaker of the Carlotti transceiver. The thing must have been switched on automatically when the pinnace was ejected.

"Ahoy, the target, whoever an' whatever you are! What the hell's goin' on around here? There were three o' you, now there just one . . ."

The Baroness stiffened in Grimes's arms. She brought up her own to push him away. "Answer, Captain," she ordered.

Grimes shambled to the transceiver, seething. *Her master's voice*, he thought bitterly. *Her master's bloody voice . . .*

"*Far Traveler*'s pinnace here," he growled.

"Is that *you*, Grimesey boy? It's a small universe, ain't it? Put Mickey on for me, please."

The Baroness brushed past Grimes, took his place at the transceiver.

It could have turned out worse, he thought philosophically.

At least he had achieved the ambition of every merchant spaceman, one realized by very few. He was Owner-Master—only of a very small ship but one with almost unlimited range and endurance. He had been pleased to accept *The Far Traveler*'s pinnace in lieu of back and separation pay. No doubt he would be able to make a quite nice living for himself in her. A courier service, perhaps.

He wished the Baroness and Drongo Kane joy of each other. In many respects they were two of a kind.

The only being involved in the recent events for whom he felt truly sorry was Big Sister.

Star Courier

Prologue

The Rim Worlds Confederacy would not be what it is today were it not for Rim Runners, the merchant fleet of our lonely and isolated planets. It is true that the first landings on the worlds to the galactic east, as well as the discovery of the anti-matter systems to the galactic west, were made by *Faraway Quest*, the Rim Worlds survey ship, an auxiliary cruiser of the Rim Worlds Navy. But *Quest* was never during her long and honourable career under the command of a regular naval officer. Her captain and crew—with the exception of the Marines whom she sometimes carried—were invariably reservists.

The most famous of her captains was John Grimes who, in addition to holding the rank of commodore in the Rim Worlds Naval Reserve, was chief astronautical superintendent of Rim Runners. Grimes was a typical rim runner of his period inasmuch as he was not born a Rim Worlder and was of Terran origin. He came out to the Rim when, it was said, a valid certificate of astronautical competency counted for far more than any past record, no matter how black. In those days the Rim Runners' fleet was captained and officered by refugees from shipping lines from all over the galaxy—the Interstellar Transport Commission, Waverley Royal Mail, Cluster Lines, Trans-Galactic Clippers, the Dog Star Line ... And when spacemen resign or are dismissed from the service of companies of such high standing only an employer desperate for qualified personnel would be anxious to engage them.

Grimes differed in one respect from his contemporaries. He was not initially a merchant spaceman. He had resigned his commission in the Survey Service of the Interstellar Federation rather than face a court martial. Nonetheless he, like all the others, had come out to the Rim under a cloud.

It is difficult to paint a detailed picture of the commodore's childhood as many records were destroyed during the Central Australian Subsidence of 375 AG. It is known, however, that he was born in the city of Alice Springs on Primus 28, 259. His father, George Whitley Grimes, was a moderately successful author of historical romances. His mother—who, as was the custom of the time, had elected to retain her own family name—was Matilda Hornblower, a domestic solar heating engineer.

So far as can be ascertained no ancestral Grimes, on either his father's or his mother's side, was ever an astronaut. There are, however, seamen clambering in the branches of his family tree. One Roger Grimes, a minor pirate of the Seventeenth Century (old Terran reckoning) achieved the dubious distinction of being hanged from his own yardarm when Admiral Blake mounted his successful campaign against the corsairs who, at that time, infested the Mediterranean Sea.

Another Grimes, in the Twentieth Century, commanded mechanically driven surface ships trading up and down the Austrialian coast and across the Tasman Sea.

Neither seafaring Grimes, however, achieved the fame of that illustrious ancestor on the maternal side, Admiral Lord Hornblower.

In an earlier age young Grimes might well have decided to go to sea—but on Earth, at least, there was little or no romance remaining in that once glamorous profession. Had he been born on a world such as Atlantia he quite probably would have gone to sea. On that planet the mariners still maintain that men, not computers, should command, navigate and handle ocean-going ships.

So, as his ancestors would probably have done had they lived in his era, he wanted to become a spaceman. His own preference would have been the merchant service but his mother, conscious of her own family annals insisted that he try to obtain a scholarship to the Survey Service Academy in Antarctica.

The once proud Royal Navy was no more than history but the Federation's Survey Service had carried its traditions into Deep Space.

Chapter 1

Grimes came to Tiralbin.

Little Sister, obedient to the slightest touch on her controls, dropped through the dark, soggy clouds of the great rain depression to Port Muldoon, finally touching down almost at the exact center of the triangle formed by the vividly scarlet beacon lights.

Aerospace Control commented, "A nice landing, Captain."

Grimes grunted. It should have been a nice landing, he thought. He was used to handling ships, big ships, and setting them down gently on their vaned tails; the careful belly flop that he had just achieved would not have been beyond the competence of a first trip cadet. *Little Sister*, as he had decided to call her, wasn't a real ship. She was only a pinnace. A deep-space-going pinnace with all the necessary equipment and instrumentation, and everything of very high quality, but a pinnace nonetheless.

"Is that some sort of bronze alloy you're built of, Captain?" asked Aerospace Control.

"No," replied Grimes. "Gold."

"Gold?" came the incredulous query from the transceiver. "You must be a millionaire!"

"I'm not," replied Grimes glumly.

"But you said, when you made your first contact, that you're Owner-Master. . . ."

"I did. I am. But the previous owner of this dreamboat wasn't a millionaire either. . . ."

"No?"

"No. She was—and still is—a trillionaire."

"It figures," said Aerospace Control enviously. "It figures." Then, in a businesslike voice, "Please have your papers ready. Port Health and Customs are on their way out to you."

Grimes stared out through the viewports to the low—apart from the control tower—spaceport administration buildings, gleaming palely and bleakly through the persistent downpour. There was nothing else to look at. There were no other ships in port and whatever scenery might be in the vicinity was blotted out by the heavy rain. A wheeled vehicle nosed out from a port in an otherwise blank wall, sped out to the pinnace in a cloud of self-generated spray.

Grimes got ready to receive the boarding officers. His papers—even to the gift deed making him owner of *Little Sister*—were in order but he was well aware that alcohol is the universe's finest lubricant for the machinery of official business. Luckily the Baroness had been generous; the pinnace's stores were even better stocked with luxuries than with necessities. Whether or not they continued to be so would depend to a great extent upon his business acumen.

The Chief of Customs—a fat, bald man bulging out of his gaudy uniform—was thirsty. So was the Port Health Officer, who would have passed for an ill-nourished mortician if members of that profession were in the habit of wearing enough gold braid for a Galactic Admiral. Both of them told Grimes, more than once, that they never got *real* Scotch on Tiralbin. After he opened the second bottle Grimes decided that real Scotch would soon be once again as scarce on this planet as it ever had been.

The officials were, naturally, curious.

"A *gold* pinnace . . ." murmured the Customs man. "Solid gold . . ."

"Modified," said Grimes. "A most excellent structural material."

"Most excellent indeed. I'm surprised, Captain, that you didn't give her a more fitting name. *Golden Girl. Golden Lady. Golden Princess.* Golden *anything. . . .*"

"Sentiment," said Grimes. "The mother ship, *The Far Traveller*, had a pilot-computer. An intelligent one. Bossy. We called it—sorry, *her*—Big Sister. So . . ."

"And you were master of this *Far Traveller*," went on the Customs officer. "Owned by Michelle, Baroness d'Estang, of El Dorado. . . . That must be a world! Better than this dismal dump. . . ."

"Better," said Grimes, "*if* you happen to be a billionaire. But not for the likes of us."

"*You* didn't do too badly, Captain," said the doctor. "This Baroness must have thought quite highly of you to give you a present like this pinnace."

"In lieu of back pay and separation pay," Grimes told him.

"And so you brought the pinnace here to sell her," said the Chief of Customs. "Her value as scrap would be quite enormous. Remarkable how gold has remained *the* precious metal for millennia. So I'm afraid that you'll have to make out a fresh set of papers. She's classed as an import, not as a visiting spacecraft to be entered inwards." He began to look really happy. "Her value will have to be assessed, of course. And then there'll be the duty to pay."

"I didn't bring her here to sell her," said Grimes. "I want, if I can, to earn a living with her."

The two officials looked around the tiny cabin. Their eyebrows rose. Then the Port Health Officer said, "I'm no spaceman, although I did do a passage-working trip in Cluster Lines, years ago, just after I qualified. But I know how spacemen do earn their livings. They carry cargo. They carry passengers. And I just don't see how you could carry either in this flying sardine—ha! ha! goldfish!—can . . ."

"There are mails," said Grimes.

"What's sex got to do with it?" asked the Customs Officer. "Oh. Mails, not *males*. Letters. Parcels. It'll have to be bloody small parcels, though, and precious few of them."

He drained his glass and held it out for a refill.

Chapter 2

Grimes' decision to make Tiralbin his base for operations had been influenced by his memory of an officer whom he had known while he was in the Survey Service. This gentleman—a Tiralbinian by birth and upbringing—had complained continuously about the infrequency of mail from home and the long, long time that it took to reach him. "It's that damn Interstellar Transport Commission!" he would say. "It has the contract with our local government for the carriage of mails, but does it lug them a mere five light years to Panzania, the mail exchange for that sector of the galaxy? Like hell it does. Not it. Those bloody Epsilon Class rustbuckets drop into Port Muldoon when they feel like it, which isn't often. And then they're never going anywhere near Panzania . . ." Grimes recalled especially a parcel that his colleague had torn open with great indignation. According to the postmark it had taken just over a year to reach Lindisfarne Base. It contained a not readily identifiable mass that looked as though it would have been of interest only to a geologist. It was, in fact, a birthday cake that had been baked by the disgruntled lieutenant's fiancée. (Grimes had wondered briefly if that cake ever had been any good . . .)

So here he was on Tiralbin, John Grimes, ex-Commander, Federation Survey Service, Owner/Master of a little ship hardly bigger than a lifeboat but one capable of taking him, in fair comfort, anywhere in the galaxy. And here he was, in the company of the Chief of Customs, the Port Health Officer and the Port Captain (who had joined the party as soon as pratique had been granted and before the expensive Scotch had run out), sitting at a table in the Gentlepersons' Club in Muldoon. Tiralbin, he was learning, was a planet on which class distinctions were maintained. Only those who could claim descent

from the passengers of the First Ship could become members of a club
such as the Gentlepersons'. Any guests, such as himself, must be
vouched for by at least two hosts. As the trio of port officials were all
First Shippers, Grimes was admitted after signing his name in four
books and on six forms.

The club was dull. The decor was archaic. Grimes, on Earth, had
seen quite a few examples of mock Tudor. This was mock mock Tudor. There was music, of the canned variety, orchestral melodies that
were as trite as they were sedate. There were no dancing girls. Some
of the female gentlepersons drinking at the bar, seated around the tables, could have been attractive enough had they not been so dowdily
dressed. The men, even those not in uniform, affected a flamboyance
of attire; the women, almost without exception, wore neck-high, ankle-
length grey. As for Grimes himself, he was a sparrow among peacocks.
The only dress uniform he had aboard the pinnace was the gaudy
purple livery that the Baroness had required him to wear aboard *The
Far Traveller* and his only civilian suit—into which he had changed
from his shipboard shorts-and-shirt working gear—was as drab as the
ladies' dresses.

There were a few, a very few, exceptions to the feminine drabness.
One of these was drinking at the bar, not far from Grimes' table. She
was a tall woman, made taller yet by the lustrous black hair elaborately
coiled on top of her head. She was strong featured, her nose too large
and chin too firm for mere prettiness. Her wide mouth was a scarlet
slash across her pale face. Her eyes were a startling green. She was
wearing a black, high-collared shirt, gold-trimmed, black, sharply
creased trousers tucked into glossy, black, calf-high boots.

"And who is that?" asked Grimes in a low voice. "The general of
your women's army?"

The Chief Customs Officer laughed. "Not quite, although it is a
uniform she's wearing, and her rank is roughly equivalent to that of
general." He raised his voice. "Tamara! Why don't you join us?"

The tall woman came across from the bar, set her glass down on
the table, lowered her generously proportioned body into the chair that
the Port Captain found for her. She looked at Grimes and smiled
slightly.

"So you're the famous John Grimes," she said. "I've heard about
you. My sister is engaged to an officer in the Federation Survey Service."

"The famous cake baker," said Grimes.

She laughed. "So you know about that silly business. *I* got blamed,
of course."

"But how?" asked Grimes.

"Tamara," said the Customs Officer, "is our Superintending Postmistress."

"In person," said that lady. She continued to address Grimes. "And you, Captain, held the rank of Commander in the FSS. You were captain of *Discovery* at the time of the mutiny. You were left on the newly discovered—or rediscovered—Lost Colony of Botany Bay when the mutineers left for parts unknown in your ship, wrecking the destroyer *Vega* in the process. You resigned your FSS commission rather than face a court martial, but Commander Delamere, captain of *Vega*, had other ideas. He tried to arrest you, but you were rescued by the Baroness d'Estang, of El Dorado, who just happened to have blown in in her spaceyacht, *The Far Traveller*. And now—with no Baroness, no spaceyacht—you bob up on Tiralbin in command of a glorified lifeboat." She laughed. "Very glorified. The thing's built of solid gold, they tell me." She looked hard at Grimes. "Quite a story, Captain. Would you mind filling in the gaps?"

"The Baroness and I split brass rags," Grimes told her. "She gave me *Little Sister*—the pinnace—in lieu of back pay and separation pay."

"A literally golden handshake," she said. "And now what do you intend doing?"

Grimes said, "I was thinking of starting a courier service."

"You were, were you? Or you are, are you? You've come to the right shop. In my official capacity I know just how lousy the mails are out of and into this world. Unfortunately we have no ships of our own and must rely upon the service, such as it is, provided by the Commission."

"I'm surprised that you don't have ships," said Grimes.

"We did, once," the Port Captain told him. "Three, very second hand Epsilon Class tramps. *Tiralbinian King, Tiralbinian Queen, Tiralbinian Prince*. The *King's* inertial drive packed up when she was coming in to a landing at Port Chaka, on Panzania and the auxiliary reaction drive did more harm than good; blew the arse off her. Luckily there were no fatalities, although she was a structural total loss. The *Prince?* Nobody knows what happened to her—except, perhaps, her crew. It's assumed that her Mannschenn Drive went on the blink when she was on passage from Tiralbin to Atlantia. As for the *Queen*—her operating costs were astronomical. Repairs, maintenance and more repairs. We had a chance to sell her to Rim Runners and grabbed it with both hands. And that, Grimes, is the short, sad history of the Tiralbinian Interstellar Transport Commission."

"Mphm," grunted Grimes. He made a major production of lighting and filling his pipe. "So there's a chance that a small, private operator based on this planet might make a go of things."

"A chance," conceded the Postmistress. "As far as I'm concerned, there are escape clauses in our contract with ITC. For example, if ITC cannot provide a ship to carry mails directly from Tiralbin to their planet of destination I can place such articles aboard any vessel making such a voyage. Mind you, it's not very often that such a vessel is here when we want one."

"The last time," said the Port Captain, "was five years ago."

"It was," she agreed. She frowned slightly. "It so happens, it just so happens, Captain Grimes, that there's an urgent consignment of parcel mail for Boggarty. Would you be interested?"

"I would," said Grimes, without hesitation.

"How much would you charge?" she asked bluntly.

"I'll have to do my sums first," he told her.

"Do that," she said, "and let me know by tomorrow afternoon at the latest. *Epsilon Corvus* is due in the day after tomorrow, and by some minor miracle she's actually proceeding from here direct to Panzania—and Panzania, as you know, has the mail exchange."

"Boggarty's well off the trade routes," said Grimes. "Even from Panzania the consignment would travel by a very roundabout way."

"Feed that factor into your computer with the others," the Postmistress said.

Chapter 3

The Port Captain, who lived out at the spaceport, ran Grimes back to the pinnace in his shabby little tricar. It was still raining. It would go on raining, Grimes was told, for three more weeks. And then there would be the dry season. And then the winter, with its high winds and blizzards. Grimes allowed himself to wonder why Tiralbin didn't go in for weather control to spread the meteorological goodies and baddies more evenly through the year. He was told sternly that Tiralbin was a poor world with no money to spare for useless luxuries. And, in any case, Tiralbin's main export was an indigenous fruit, the so-called Venus strawberry, prized on quite a few planets both by gourmets and by those few to whom it was an aphrodisiac. Its low, tough bushes flourished in the local climatic conditions; it was a case of leave well enough alone.

The ground car stopped by *Little Sister*'s airlock. The Port Captain declined Grimes' invitation to come aboard for a nightcap—which was just as well; after that afternoon's session stocks of liquor were running low. Replenishments would have to be laid in—and paid for.

Grimes managed to cover the short distance between the car and the airlock without getting too wet. He was thankful that he had thought to lock the inner door only, leaving the outer one open. He let himself into the pinnace—his ship, his home. In the tiny galley he set coffee a-heating and helped himself to a couple of soberup capsules. Back in the main cabin, which was also bedroom, sitting room and chartroom, he sipped his coffee and watched the screen of the little playmaster, which instrument was, in effect, his library. (Big Sister, before setting the Baroness and Grimes adrift in the pinnace, had seen to it that the small spacecraft was fully equipped from the navigational as well as other viewpoints, and had contributed generously from her personal memory banks.)

Boggarty, read Grimes on the little screen.

Then followed the astronautical and geophysical data, the historical information. It was an Earth-type planet, fourth out from its primary. It had been colonized from a ship of the First Expansion, which meant that the First Landing post-dated First Landings on other worlds classed as Second Expansion planets. But the First Expansion vessels— the so-called Deep Freeze Ships—had proceeded to their destinations at sub-light speeds. Boggarty was even further removed from the main trade routes than Tiralbin. Its exports consisted of very occasional shipments of native artifacts, consigned mainly to museums, art galleries and private collectors. As a result of these infrequent but lucrative sales, Boggarty had built up a large credit balance in the Galactic Bank, which maintained its headquarters on Earth. There was ample money for the human colonists to pay for any of the goods they ordered, by the practically instantaneous Carlotti radio, from anywhere at all in the known universe. The main trouble, apparently, lay in persuading any of the major shipping lines or even a tramp operator to deviate from the well-established tramlines to make a special call. The only company to make regular visits was the Dog Star Line which, every three standard years, sent a ship to pick up a worthwhile consignment of *objets d'art*.

The planet, Grimes learned, was named after the indigenes, whom the first colonists had dubbed boggarts. Looking at the pictures that flickered across the little screen he could understand why. These creatures could have been gnomes or trolls from Terran children's fairy stories. Humanoid but grossly misshapen, potbellied, hunchbacked, the males with grotesquely huge sex organs, the females with pendulous dugs . . . Curved, yellow tusks protruding from wide, lipless mouths . . . Ragged, spiny crests in lieu of hair . . .

If the boggarts were horrendous, what they manufactured was beautiful. They worked with wire, with gleaming filments of gold. Their gnarled, three-fingered, horny-nailed hands moved with lightning dexterity as they wove their metal sculptures, complex intricacies that seemed to be (that were?) at least four dimensional. And these, Grimes learned with some amazement, were no more than adaptions from the traps—in which they caught large, edible, flying insects—that the boggarts had been weaving at the time of the First Landing. (*But some spiders' webs are works of art*, he thought.)

He wondered what the boggarts got paid for their work. There was no explicit information, but in one shot of a cave workshop he saw, in a corner, bottles and plastic food containers, and some of the females were wearing necklaces of cheap and gaudy glass beads.

He was wasting time, he knew, viewing what was, in actuality, no more than a travelogue—but he liked to have some idea of what any world to which he was bound was like. He looked at mountainous landscapes, at long, silver beaches with black, jagged reefs offshore, at mighty rivers rushing through spectacular canyons, flowing majestically across vast, forested plains. He saw the towns and the cities, pleasant enough but utterly lacking in architectural inspiration, too-regular cubes and domes of metal and plastic. He saw the cave villages of the boggarts.

He had seen enough to be going on with and turned his attention to navigational details. The voyage from Tiralbin to Boggarty would, he (or the computer) calculated have a duration of thirty-seven subjective days, well within the pinnace's capacity. Food would be no problem—although he would, in effect, be getting his own back. The algae tanks, as well as removing carbon dioxide from the spacecraft's atmosphere and enriching it with oxygen, would convert other body wastes into food. The little auto-chef, he had learned from experience, could use the algae paste as the raw material for quite palatable meals. That same auto-chef, he had discovered, was capable of distilling a flavorless spirit that, with the addition of various flavorings, was a fair substitute for gin. Tobacco? Luckily Tiralbin was one of the worlds on which smoking was a widespread habit. He would have to make sure that he had an ample stock of fuel for his battered pipe before he lifted off. Fuel? No worries there. The small hydrogen fusion unit would supply ample power for the mini-Mannschenn, the inertial drive, the Carlotti radio, the Normal Space-Time radio, light, heat, cooking, the playmaster . . . And would it be possible for him to lay in a stock of spools for this instrument in Muldoon? He hoped so. Thirty-seven subjective days of utter solitude is quite a long time, but not too long if it is not compounded with utter boredom.

And then he came to the calculations for which his past training and experience had not fitted him. How much would it cost? How much should he charge? On the one hand, he was not a philanthropic institution, but, on the other hand, he was entitled to a fair profit. What was a fair profit? He supposed that he could regard *Little Sister* as an investment. A deep-space-going pinnace is a very expensive hunk of ironmongery . . . A return of 10%? But *Little Sister* was not a hunk of ironmongery. She was the outcome of miscegenation between a goldsmith and a shipbuilder . . . And how much had she cost? How much was she worth?

Grimes didn't know.

All right, then. How much would the voyage cost him? His port dues here on Tiralbin, for a start. Hospitality to the port officials. Such stores—luxuries as well as necessities—as he would have to purchase before lift-off. Such stores as he would have to purchase after arrival at Boggarty. Depreciation of ship and fittings during the round trip. (But depreciation in a vessel such as *Little Sister*, built of almost everlasting materials, was negligible.) Insurance? That was something he would have to go into with the local Lloyd's Agent. Salaries? There was only one salary, and that was his own, paid (presumably) by himself to himself. What was the Award Rate for the master of a vessel of this tonnage? Did the Astronauts' Guild have a representative in Muldoon?

It was all quite simple, he realized. He would charge on a cost plus basis. The only trouble was that he did not know what the costs were likely to be. There was no way of finding out until various business offices opened in the morning.

He let down the folding bunk that he had been using—the other one, intended for the Baroness, had never been used—took a sleeping tablet to counteract the effects of the soberup, told the computer to wake him at 0600 hours local, and turned in.

Chapter 4

Grimes had a busy morning. He was able to arrange a hook-up between the pinnace's NST transceiver and the local telephone exchange, so was able to carry out most of his business by telephone. This was just as well, as it was still raining heavily and he had no local currency with which to pay for cab hire. As he accumulated data he fed it into *Little Sister*'s computer. The insurance premium demanded by Lloyd's was amazingly high, but not so amazing, he realized, bearing in mind the fact that his spacecraft was built of a precious metal. He was rather surprised that the figure should be quoted with so little delay, but, of course, Lloyd's records would contain all details of *The Far Traveller*, including her pinnace.

Finally the estimated cost of the round voyage appeared on the screen. It was, inevitably, frightening. After he realized that his master's salary was included in the total he decided to add only a modest 10%. He put through a call to the Superintending Postmistress. After a short delay her face appeared on the screen, as his would be appearing on the one at her end.

"Yes, Captain?" she asked.

"I've done my sums," he replied. "I don't think you'll like the result."

"Tell me."

He told her.

Her fine eyebrows arched, but the rest of her face remained impassive. She said, "I'm not *buying* your pinnace."

He said, "If you were it would cost quite a bit more."

She smiled. "I suppose so. And, after all, I'm not paying the bill.

Neither is my government. The Boggartians want the shipment no later than yesterday, and if it's sent through normal channels it could take a year to reach them. I'll punch through a Carlottigram and find out if they're willing to pay the charges. I'll call you back."

Grimes brewed coffee, filled and lit his pipe, settled down to watch what passed for entertainment on Tiralbin on his playmaster, which, in port, could function as a tridi receiver. He watched without much enthusiasm a local version of football being played in pouring rain. One team was male, the other female, but the players were so thickly coated with mud that it was impossible to determine their sex.

The transceiver chimed.

It was the Superintending Postmistress.

She said, "They must be in a hurry on Boggarty. They wasted no time in replying. They have agreed to pay your figure, half, before departure, to be placed to your credit in the Galactic Bank, the other half to be paid on delivery. There is only one slight snag . . ."

"And what is that?" asked Grimes.

"They demand that our Postal Service send one of its own officials to travel in charge of the parcels, to hand them over in person. You have passenger accommodation, don't you?"

"Of a sort," he said. "Not too uncomfortable, but no privacy."

"As long as I don't have to share a bunk . . ."

He doubted that he had heard her correctly. "As long as *you* don't have to share a bunk?"

She laughed. "I'm overdue for a long leave. I want to travel, but travel is damned expensive—as you should know."

He said, "I'm finding out."

She told him, "I thought that I might temporarily demote myself to postwoman . . ."

He said, "I thought that I, as a courier, would be a sort of a postman."

She said, "But you're not an employee of our government. You're a private individual, a hired carrier. You have still to build up a reputation for reliability."

Grimes felt his prominent ears burning. He exclaimed, "They have only to check my Survey Service record!"

She laughed. "And what sort of marks will the FSS give you for reliability? Apart from the way in which you lost your last ship, you had quite a few enemies among the top brass, and not too many friends. You're on the run from a court martial."

The angry flush spread all over his face, then slowly subsided. He had to admit that she was right. As an officer of the Federation Survey Service he was finished. As a merchant officer, a shipmaster—or even a shipowner of a sort—he had yet to prove himself.

She demanded, "Well, Captain Grimes, do you want the job or not?" She grinned engagingly, "Would my company be so hard to put up with? Or would you rather have some hairy-arsed postman? I could arrange that, you know . . ."

He looked at her face in the screen. He decided that she would be preferable to a postman, but remembered the last time that he had been cooped up in a small spacecraft—a lifeboat—with an attractive woman. It had been great fun at first, but they had finished up hating each other. However, *Little Sister* was more, much more, than a mere lifeboat. There would be, with the erection of a plastic partition in the main cabin (and who was going to pay for that?) far more privacy. The food would be much better, even though it had its origin in the algae vats. And there would be a foreseeable conclusion to the voyage, as there had not been on that past occasion.

He smiled back at her. He said, "All right. It's on. But you'd better come out to the spaceport to see what you're letting yourself in for."

"It's a date," she said. "Expect me half an hour from now."

She was punctual.

A scarlet, post office car, with a uniformed driver, drew up in a cloud of spray by the pinnace's airlock exactly twenty-nine minutes after the conclusion of the call. He had occupied the time with house-keeping—a hasty tidying up, the programing of the auto-chef with a lunch for two, one of the few remaining bottles of El Doradan Spumante put to cool in the refrigerator, gin of the ship's own manufacture decanted from its plastic container into a much more attractive glass flagon.

Enveloped in hooded, transparent rainwear she walked from the car, which turned to return to the city, to the airlock. Grimes helped her off with the water-slick coverall, then ushered her into the little cabin. She seated herself at the small table. She looked at the flagon, the glasses, the little bottle of flav, the bowl of ice cubes.

"So," she remarked, "this is how the poor live."

He poured drinks, raised his glass, said, "Down the hatch."

"Down the hatch," she repeated. She sipped. "H'm. You don't do yourself badly. One thing we can't do here is make decent gin."

The auto-chef chimed. Grimes got up to get disposable napkins and—a legacy from *The Far Traveller*—gold cutlery. Her eyes widened as he laid the table. He went through into the galley-workshop-engineroom, returned with the meal on gold-rimmed china. It was 'steak,' with 'mashed potato' and a puree of 'peas.' Appearancewise and flavorwise it passed muster, although the texture of the 'meat' left much to be desired. (So, he realized, did his choice of a wine to accompany the meal; a still red would have been more suitable.)

His guest patted her lips with her napkin. "Congratulate the chef for me, Captain. Tissue culture beef?"

"Not in a ship this size," he told her. "She's too small to run to a farm. Just algae, from the vats, processed, colored and flavored."

She said, "I'll not ask what nutrients your algae subsist upon. I'm not altogether ignorant of spaceship ecology. I'm not squeamish either. After all, the sewage of every town and city on this planet is processed and fed back into the land. Do you have coffee, by the way?"

"Coming up," said Grimes.

"You've got yourself a passenger," she told him.

Chapter 5

Epsilon Corvus came in while Grimes, standing in *Little Sister*'s airlock to keep out of the persistent rain, was receiving the stores that he had ordered. The transfer of funds to his account with the Galactic Bank had been made with quite amazing promptitude and, for one of the few times in his life, he felt rich. He was having to restrain himself from spending money like a drunken spaceman.

The Commission's ship dropped down through the grey overcast, glimpsed fitfully through the slowly drifting veils of rain, the arrhythmic clangor of her inertial drive muffled by the downpour. Finally she sat down decisively in the center of the triangle formed by the marker beacons. The driver of the ship chandler's truck delivered the stores and remarked sourly, "She's here. At last. And much good will she be to us."

"Who's us?" asked Grimes politely.

The driver gestured to the name painted on the side of his vehicle. "Bannington and Willis, that's who. I'm Willis. Those cows . . ." he jerked his thumb towards the freighter " . . . don't buy a single item here apart from private orders. Bloody Venus strawberries. Tiralbin's one claim to fame. Ha!" He brightened slightly. "*You* didn't order any, Captain. I'll be back at the spaceport before you push off, I'll be delivering aboard the Old Crow, so what about putting you down for a couple of dozen cans?"

"No thank you," said Grimes.

"Don't need 'em, hey? You're lucky. Mind you, they don't work on everybody. Not on me, for one. If they did I wouldn't be selling them! Ha! Well, sign here Cap for what you've got." Grimes signed.

"Sure you won't change your mind about the strawberries? From what I hear you may be needing them after all. . . ."

"No thank you," said Grimes again. He was mildly annoyed by the assumption that a man and a woman alone together in a small spacecraft must inevitably fall into each other's arms. Since his appointment to his first commercial command, *The Far Traveller*, he had studied the Space Shipping Act. He had learned that any master or officer forcing his attentions on a female passenger or crew member was liable to the suspension or cancellation of his certificate of competency. Grimes possessed a civilian master astronaut's certificate, having been required to pass that examination before his promotion to Lieutenant Commander in the Survey Service. He had no desire to lose it.

The truck drove off and Grimes went inside the pinnace to stow his stores. He was still finding it strange to have to do everything himself but was rather enjoying it. He sang untunefully:

> *"Oh, I am the cook and the captain bold*
> *And the mate of the* Nancy *brig . . ."*

A strange voice called, "Ahoy, *Little Sister!* May I come aboard?"

Grimes stowed a carton, then turned towards the airlock. He said, "This is Liberty Hall. You can spit on the mat and call the cat a bastard."

His visitor was a small, wiry man in grey working uniform with master's epaulettes on the shoulders. He introduced himself. "I'm Halley, from the Old Crow, as they call her here. I couldn't help noticing your little ship when I came in and thought I'd like a closer look at her. The port officials told me that she's built of gold. . . ."

"She is, Captain," said Grimes. He waved his visitor to a chair, took one himself. "Coffee?"

"Thank you."

Grimes got up again, went through to the galley and returned with two steaming mugs.

"Ex Survey Service, aren't you, Captain?"

"Yes, Captain."

"And now you're one of us, more or less."

"I'm trying to be."

The other man grinned. "I'm afraid that you haven't tried quite hard enough. As well as being Master of *Epsilon Corvus* I'm an official of the Guild. A Committeeman, as a matter of fact. You, sir, are about to embark on a commercial voyage in a ship not commanded by a Guild member. I have to tell you that members of the Guild and of the space-associated unions have no option but to declare you black."

"Which means?" asked Grimes.

"Which means that you will receive no clearance to lift from Aerospace Control, for a start."

Grimes shrugged.

"It means, too, that Aerospace Control on Boggarty will be informed that you are black if you do, illegally, lift from Port Muldoon . . ."

"Call me Ishmael," muttered Grimes.

"What? Oh, yes. Ha, ha. I'm sorry, Captain, but that's the way of it. As a Survey Service type you've led a sheltered life. You've no idea of the struggle we've had, and are still having, to maintain and to improve conditions." He grinned. "I understand that you're owner as well as master, so your own conditions are up to you. But if you were, as an employee, in command of *this* spacecraft you'd be entitled to hard-lying money *and* short-handed money. You've no cook or steward, no engineer . . ."

I should have included hard-lying money and short-handed money in my estimated costs, thought Grimes. *I will in future.*

His guest pulled a sheaf of papers from the inside breast pocket of his uniform coveralls. "I'm not holding a pistol at your head, Captain, but I do strongly advise you to join the Guild. Apart from anything else we guarantee you full legal protection—as master, that is, not owner. But it's as a master that you're always liable to come up against a court of enquiry. So, if you'll just fill in the details and sign here . . ."

Grimes sighed. "How much?" he asked.

"Joining fee, five hundred. Annual dues another five hundred."

It wasn't much compared to the profits that Grimes hoped soon to be making, compared to the salary that he was paying himself on paper. And, he reluctantly admitted, Guild membership was an essential to a merchant spaceman. He filled in the forms and signed them. He made out a check for one thousand credits to the Interstellar Astronauts' Guild, signed that. He received a small plastic card, with his name already printed on it, in exchange.

Business over, Halley was once again quite affable. He said, "Well, that was quite painless, wasn't it? Welcome aboard and all that." He relaxed in his chair, cast an appraising eye around the cabin. "You know, Captain, I rather envy you. No owners to get on your back. No crew to get in your hair, no passengers . . ."

A female voice called from the airlock, "May I join the party?"

"Meet my passenger, Captain Halley," said Grimes.

Halley and Tamara Haverstock were already acquainted. Neither much liked the other. The Superintending Postmistress was, to the shipmaster, yet another officious official to make his life a misery, with her unreasonable demands, each and every time that he was in Port Muldoon. Halley, to Tamara Haverstock, was the unobliging representative of the cordially disliked Interstellar Transport Commission.

"Are you actually travelling in *this*, Miss Haverstock?" Halley asked.

"Your ship, Captain Halley, seems never to be proceeding in a direction suitable to my requirements. And now, if you will excuse me, I have business to discuss with Captain Grimes."

Halley rose to leave. "Bon voyage," he said. "And don't do anything that you couldn't do riding on a bicycle. Remember Paragraph 118(c) of the Space Shipping Act. If you do fall foul of it, the Guild will back you up."

"What was he talking about?" asked the Postmistress after he was gone.

"I don't know," said Grimes. Actually he didn't, but strongly suspected that Paragraph 118(c) was the one setting out the penalties for rape, or alleged rape.

Miss Haverstock looked at her watch. She said, "The consignment of parcel mail, together with my baggage, will be here very shortly. Are all your stores on board? Good. Have you paid your port dues and obtained Customs clearance? Good. If you have no objections we will lift as soon as the mails and baggage have been stowed."

Grimes said, "This was certainly a quick turn-around. I was hoping to see something of Tiralbin. Apart from one evening in the Gentlepersons' Club in Muldoon I haven't been off the ship."

She told him, "You haven't missed anything. As far as we are concerned here in the south it's monsoon weather over the entire damned hemisphere, and winter's set in north of the equator. As you may have noticed, we have no land masses at all in the tropical and sub-tropical zones. So it's a choice between getting soaked or frozen."

"Frankly," said Grimes, "I've often wondered why people live on some of the worlds that they do . . ."

"Are you getting in a nasty dig at this one? Well, Grimes, I was born here. I'm used to it. At times I even like it, but I don't suppose I'd like much the planet that *you* were born on. Earth, wasn't it? I thought as much. You Terries always contrive to convey the impression that you own the whole damn galaxy but don't think much of it anyhow . . ."

Grimes laughed. "Surely we aren't as bad as that."

"Aren't you?" She grinned at him. "Anyhow, much as I love Tiralbin I want a change of scenery. And my leave does not officially start until I have delivered the mail to its consignee on Boggarty, so, by the time we get there, I shall still have several standard months due . . ."

A man in a drab blue uniform came into the cabin without first announcing himself. He accorded the Postmistress a grudging salute then turned to Grimes. "You the skipper?"

"Yes."

"Mail's here, an' some travellin' bags. Where do you want 'em?"

Grimes saw the single mail sack—it was heavy, and obviously held square boxes or cartons—stowed in the locker that he had cleared for the purpose. Tamara Haverstock's baggage went into a storeroom off the galley-cum-engineroom. He signed the receipt for his cargo. The man left.

The high-ranking postwoman said, "What's holding you, Captain? The mail must fly!"

"I suppose I'd better think about getting upstairs," admitted Grimes.

Chapter 6

Grimes took *Little Sister* upstairs. It was his first lift-off, in her—his first lift-off, that is, prior to a deep space voyage. While the pinnace had been attached to *The Far Traveller* she had been used mainly as an atmosphere flier. This occasion seemed wrong, somehow. In a spaceship *down* and *aft* should be co-directional. Here—unless the interior of the pinnace were entirely rearranged—the little spacecraft's progress in space would always be along her short axis.

He would get used to it, he supposed. With the inertial drive hammering healthily he lifted through the pouring rain, losing sight of Port Muldoon when he was less than a kilometer up. He missed the auxiliary reaction drive that was a standard fitting in most spaceships. It was supposed to be for emergency use only, but the majority of Survey Service Captains employed it, blasting off, when they were a safe distance from the ground, like an archaic rocket. He was not sure that he liked having a woman, even an attractive woman, in the seat by his, watching his every move with intelligent interest. Still, he grudgingly admitted to himself, she wasn't as bad as the Baroness had been. She did not object to his smoking. He noticed that she had a cigarillo between her full lips, its acrid fumes competing with the incinerator reek of his pipe. She should have asked permission before lighting up, he thought, but was not prepared to make an issue of it.

Little Sister broke through into the clear air above the cloud cover. The light—from Tiralbin's sun and reflected from the cloudscape—was briefly dazzling until the ports automatically polarized. She drove up through the thinning atmosphere, through near-vacuum, into the almost complete vacuum of outer space. Below her Tiralbin could have been a giant pearl displayed on black velvet, the surface featureless save for the occasional rift in the overcast, the spiral pattern, near the equator, of a revolving storm.

Up she drove, up. Lights flared briefly on the console marking the pinnace's passage through the Van Allens. Grimes adjusted his seat so that he was almost on his back, looking straight upwards through the transparency now uncovered in the roof of the control cab. He had no trouble finding the first target star; it was a blue luminary in the constellation called on Tiralbin Muldoon's Cat. He was rather surprised that the Tiralbinians had ever gotten around to naming their constellations, but supposed that the skies would be clear during the Dry Season.

He asked, "Who was Muldoon?"

"Huh? Muldoon? Oh, I see what you mean . . ." She had adjusted her own chair so that her body was parallel to his. "*That* Muldoon. He was captain of the First Ship, the *Lode Caravel*. The story goes that he had a pet cat . . ."

"Such is fame," said Grimes.

He concentrated on bringing The Cat's Eye into the center of the cartwheel sight engraved in the overhead port. In a real ship he would have been employing gyroscopes to swing the hull about its various axes, here he was having to do it by adjusting the thrust of the inertial drive. It was a ticklish job. Finally he had the target star centered, then allowed it to fall a degree off to port.

"You had it right," she complained. "Now you'll have to do it again."

"Galactic Drift," he said, "has to be allowed for. Now, stand by for free fall. I'm cutting the drive."

"Why?"

He ignored her. The drumming of the inertial drive fell silent, was replaced by the humming of the ever-precessing gyroscopes of the mini-Mannschenn, the humming that rapidly rose in pitch to a thin, high whine. Grimes was used—as much as anybody can get used—to the distortions of light and sound, to the crazy perspective, to the uncanny sensation of *déjà vu*. Sometimes there was prevision, a glimpse of the future, or of a possible future, sometimes only a haunting unease. This time there was only, for him, the unease.

Things snapped back to normal. He touched the control that brought the back of his chair upright and, with the other hand, restarted the inertial drive. There was acceleration again, substituting for gravity. *Up* was *up* and *down* was *down*.

He looked to his passenger. She was still in the reclining position. Her face was very pale. He said, "Don't look through the ports if it frightens you." He touched the switch that opaqued the transparencies. He went on, "Space from a ship under interstellar drive is a scary sight, especially for the first time . . ."

She said, "But I haven't looked out of the ports. It was just a . . . It was . . . real. What happened . . ." She looked at him, then down at herself. "But it couldn't have been, could it?"

He said, "I should have warned you. Quite often when the interstellar drive is started, when the temporal precession field is building up, there are these . . . flashes of precognition." He smiled reassuringly. "But don't worry, it may never happen. From every *now* there's an infinitude of futures."

She said, "I'm not worried. I was just . . . startled. Now, if you'll unshield the ports, I'll have a look at what space is like when it's warped out of all recognition."

She stared out at the dim, coruscating nebulosities that should have been hard, bright stars and then, when Grimes rolled the pinnace slightly, down at Tiralbin, which had the appearance of a writhing, roughly spherical, luminescent amoeba.

She shuddered. "Don't you spacemen," she asked, "usually celebrate the start of a voyage with a stiff drink?"

"It has been done," conceded Grimes, letting her precede him into the main cabin.

Chapter 7

He busied himself with the drinks and a tray of savories.

He raised his glass, "Here's looking at you."

She was worth looking at. Her severe blue and gold uniform suited her. It could almost have been painted on to her splendid body.

She said, "Here's looking at you, Grimes." She sipped. "I hope you have enough of this excellent gin to last out the voyage."

He said, "I make it myself. Or, to be more exact, the auto-chef does."

She said, "A versatile ship. As versatile as her master."

"Versatile?" he asked.

"Aren't you? Survey Service officer, yacht skipper, shipowner, courier . . ."

He laughed. "I'll try anything once."

"Will you?" There was something odd in the way she said it.

Grimes finished his drink, said, "Now I'll get on with the minor modifications that we shall require. I should have done it before lift-off, but the plaspartit sheets didn't come down until this morning, with the rest of the stores."

"Plaspartit sheets?" she asked, lifting her eyebrows.

"You know the stuff. Sticks to anything. Used for erecting temporary partitions."

"What for?'" she asked.

"I just told you."

"But what *for?*"

"To make a light, longitudinal bulkhead in this cabin. The folding bunk on the starboard side is mine. The one on the port side is yours . . ."

She faced him over the table, looking into his eyes. Her own seemed preternaturally large, hypnotic in their intensity. She said, "I rather thought that it would have to happen, sooner or later. You're a man, not unattractive. I'm a woman, with all the right things in the right places. When you turned on that Time-Space-twister of yours I had a sort of preview—a very vivid one. So now I *know* that it's going to happen. Why put it off?"

Why indeed? Grimes asked himself.

He had not seen her touch any fastenings, but her shirt was open. Her breasts were large, firm, the pink nipples prominent and a stippling of color against the pearly pallor of her skin. She stood up and, moving with slow, deliberate grace, almost as though she were doing it to music, took off the shirt then pushed trousers and undergarments down her long, straight legs. She practiced all-over depilation, Grimes noted with almost clinical interest—or, perhaps, the lack of body hair was the result of some minor local mutation.

He had always preferred his women with sun-darkened skins and with luxuriant rather than otherwise pubic growths, but . . . *Why look a gift horse in the pussy?* he asked himself.

She moved lithely around the table and—it was the only possible word for her action—pounced, enveloping him in warm, naked femininity. As gently as possible he broke away. She stared at him incredulously. She almost snarled, "You're not . . ."

He said, "Don't worry. I'm heterosexual. But there's just something I have to do in the control cab first . . ."

He made his way forward. He switched on the internal recorder. He had remembered Paragraph 118(c) of the Space Shipping Act. It was extremely unlikely that it would ever be evoked, that there would be need to prove that there had been no rape, but a videotape of this occasion would be a pleasant souvenir of the voyage, a felicitous parting gift when the time came for farewells.

When he returned to the main cabin he saw that she had found out how to lower his folding bunk from the ship's side and, stretched out on the pneumatic mattress, was waiting for him.

He shed his clothing and joined her.

Chapter 8

Grimes was a competent spaceman but he was no engineer.

During his Survey Service career he had subscribed to the belief commonly held by spacemen officers regarding routine overhauls of machinery in port by those of the engineering branch. "They're so surprised that their toys are working properly that they have to take them apart to find out why!" All *Little Sister*'s machinery had been functioning well when Grimes and his late employer, the Baroness d'Estang, had been cast adrift from *The Far Traveller*. It had still been functioning well when the pinnace had been intercepted by Drongo Kane's *Southerly Buster*. After the Baroness had decided to embark on Kane's ship, leaving *Little Sister* to Grimes as a parting gift, all had functioned well on his lonely voyage to Tiralbin. Grimes had lifted from Port Muldoon without a worry in the universe—at least insofar as his ship and her equipment were concerned. He had set his initial trajectory for The Cat's Eye. From that starfall he would adjust course to head towards the Boggarty sun, homing on the Carlotti Beacon on Boggarty, obtaining fixes as required from that beacon and those on Jones-world and the uninhabited Z314U.

So—he thought in his innocence—there was nothing to do but enjoy the voyage. Tamara was a good shipmate. This was a holiday for her and she was making the most of it. She played a good game of chess. Her tastes and Grimes' coincided regarding the entertainment spools for the playmaster. She could coax the auto-chef into producing dishes that Grimes had never dreamed could be concocted from such unpromising raw material as sewage-fed algae. She improved on Grimes' homemade gin and persuaded the mechanized mini-galley to distil a brandy that Napoleon himself (after a hard battle and with nothing else to drink) would not have sneezed at, a liqueur that the Benedictine monks might have recognized as a distant cousin to their own famous after dinner drink, a Tia Maria that, topped with synthetic cream, was—in the absence of a potable yardstick—indistinguishable from the real thing.

And, he told himself with a certain smugness, he was getting paid for all this. No doubt he and Tamara would say goodbye without heartbreak when the time came, but meanwhile . . .

Little Sister fell steadily down the dark dimensions, through the warped continuum. Her inertial drive hammered away steadily and healthily. There was light, and there was warmth. Meals were cooked and served. Entertainment of high quality was available from the playmaster at the touch of a finger. And it would be a long time before Grimes and Tamara tired of each other's company, before each fresh coupling of their bodies failed to engender some fresh refinement of sensation . . .

And yet it came to pass.

She moved under him sinuously, rotating her navel against him, contracting her vaginal muscles and, somehow, caused her erect nipples to titillate the skin of his chest while her eager tongue explored his mouth . . .

The orgasm was explosive.

She moved under him sinuously, rotating her navel against his, contracting her vaginal muscles and, somehow, caused her erect nipples to titillate the skin of his chest while her eager tongue explored his mouth . . .

The orgasm was . . .

Was . . .

Implosive.

She moved under him . . .

But although his body responded his mind was suddenly cold, frightened.

The orgasm . . .

Exgasm . . .

*In*gasm . . .

She moved . . .

He tried to roll off her, but it was as though some fantastic acceleration were holding him tight to the yielding cushions of her body.

Her erect nipples . . . her eager tongue . . .

The explosive/implosive orgasm . . .

She moved under him sinuously . . .

And, he realized, the thin, high whine of the mini-Mannschenn was no longer steady, was oscillating . . .

He tried to break free from the strong cage of her arms and legs—and with startling suddenness, at the very moment of implosion, did so. He fell from the wide bunk to the deck, looked dazedly about him, at the crazy perspective, at the colors sagging down the spectrum. He heard her cry out but the words were gibberish. He ignored her, got unsteadily to his feet. The doorway, aft, of the engineroom-cum-galley was incredibly distant, at the end of a long, convoluted tunnel, the walls of which throbbed and quivered as though this were a duct in the body of some living creature.

He took a step—it was though he were wading against the current through some viscous fluid—and then another. Somehow the entrance to the engineroom seemed more distant than it had at first. He took a third step, and a fourth—and he was looking down at the casing of the mini-Mannschenn and felt his brain being scrambled by the weird warbling of the machine, alternating from the ultrasonic to the sub-sonic. He dropped to his knees and began to loosen the butterfly nuts holding the casing in place. He put a hand on each of the grips, prepared to lift the cover.

In the very nick of time he realized what he was doing. To look directly at a normally functioning Mannschenn Drive unit, a complexity of spinning, ever-precessing gyroscopes, is bad enough. To be in the near vicinity of one that is malfunctioning can be suicidal—and eversion is a far from pleasant way of suicide.

Luckily the master switch for the machine was within arm's length. Grimes reached for it, threw it. The crazy warbling subsided, died, stopped.

"Grimes! What's happening?"

He turned to look at her. She was a naked woman. He had seen naked women before. She was a beautiful naked woman. He had seen beautiful naked women before. And her skin was too pale and the hairless jointure of her thighs made her look absurdly childish. Somehow the magic was gone out of her.

She said, "That—what we had just now—was what I foresaw at the start of the voyage. But what has happened?"

He said, "The mini-Mannschenn's on the blink."

She asked, "What's wrong with it?"

He said, "I'm not an engineer . . ."

He remembered how one of the overhaul jobs done by a starship's engineroom staff is a complete check of the Mannschenn Drive, including examination of every hollow ball bearing. He had blandly assumed that the ball bearings in this mini-Mannschenn, presumably of the same super-gold as the rest of the pinnace and her fittings, would be immune to normal wear and tear.

"I'm not an engineer," he repeated. "No, that wasn't meant to be an excuse. It was self-accusation."

He lifted the cover from the machine, looked down at it. Even though he was no engineer he could see at a glance what was wrong. The spindle of one of the little rotors had slipped, at one end, from its mounting, was free to oscillate. He poked it with a tentative forefinger and it wobbled. Somehow this motion was just not quite enough for it to foul the other rotors. Had it done so the mini-Mannschenn could have been, probably would have been, irreparably wrecked.

There was a scattering of golden beads on the baseplate of the machine—the ball bearings. There was a scattering of gold beads and a little heap of curved, golden fragments. So he should have checked those bearings before lifting off from Port Muldoon, or hired one of the Port Captain's technicians to do so.

So he hadn't.

So what?

He hoped that there were spares, and tools.

There were.

There was no instruction manual.

There wouldn't be, of course. Big Sister, the electronic brain of *The Far Traveller*, had needed no such literature. But, he remembered, she had transferred much of her knowledge to the pinnace's computer.

He went back to the main cabin, switched on the playmaster.

Tamara said, "This is no time to watch some trashy operetta."

He ignored her, said to the instrument, "Information on mini-Mannschenn maintenance and repairs . . ."

The diagrams and pictures succeeded each other on the screen. He said, "Hold it!" Then, "Play that sequence again."

While he watched he filled and lit his pipe.

She said, "Did anybody ever tell you that a naked man smoking a pipe looks ludicrous?"

"No," he said. "And if they did, I shouldn't believe them."

She asked, "And how long shall we be stuck here? The consignee of the mail paid Special Delivery rate—which means that the Post Office, *my* Post Office, is liable to a penalty for every day's delay over the specified time."

He said, "Be quiet, please, and let me watch this sequence."

She shut up.

It should be quite simple, thought Grimes. Once the proper number of bearings was in the channel, the race, the end of the spindle would lock automatically into place. Until this was done *Little Sister* would, of course, still be proceeding in the right direction—but she would be going a long way in a very long time. Once the mini-Mannschenn was fixed she would be going a very long way in a short time.

There was one snag, as Grimes realized after the passage of about three frustrating hours. The instructional film had shown the maintenance of a full-sized Mannschenn Drive unit—a job for a team of engineers. The maintenance of a mini-Mannschenn is a job for a watchmaker.

And Grimes was even less of a watchmaker than he was an engineer.

Somehow he had contrived to unseat four other spindles and the deck of the engineroom-cum-galley was littered with golden ball bearings.

But he worked on with dogged determination, wishing, now and again, that Tamara would get off her big, fat arse and do something to help. He was vaguely conscious of her pale form at the forward end of the pinnace, in the control cab, and supposed that she was either sulking or admiring the scenery.

Or both.

Chapter 9

She was talking to herself, he thought not very interestedly. He heard her voice but could not be bothered to try to make out the words; he was too engrossed in his ticklish, frustrating task. Then one of the little golden wheels, the spindle of which he had just pressed home into its mountings, sprang out again as soon as his hand was removed. It clattered to the deck and trundled forward through the main cabin. He ran after it, pounced on it just before it got as far as the control cab.

She looked up and around at him.

She said, "It's all right, Grimes. We shall soon have some *real* engineers to put your time-twister together again."

"*What?*" he demanded.

"You heard me." She gestured with the golden microphone that she was holding. "I could see that we were liable to be stuck here, in the very middle of sweet damn all, for the next ten standard years, so I put out a call for assistance on the Carlotti . . ."

"You did what?"

"You heard me."

"By whose authority?"

"My own. I may be only a passenger in this toy ship of yours—but I am also the Superintending Postmistress of Tiralbin. It is my duty to ensure that the mails arrive at Boggarty within the specified time."

He snatched the microphone from her hand, slammed it back into its clip on the control panel with unnecessary violence. He said, "Do you realize that this could lead to a salvage claim against me? Do you know that a salvage award is based on the value of a ship and her cargo? The cargo's worth damn all, but a pinnace constructed of solid gold . . . I could never pay out that sort of money . . ."

She said sullenly, "That's a very valuable consignment of parcel mail that we're carrying. And I have my responsibilities."

He told her what she could do with them. Then he asked, "Did anybody answer your call?"

"A ship called *Baroom.*"

Shaara, he thought, *with a name like that.* He said hopefully, "But you weren't able to give her our coordinates—"

"No. But they said that it wouldn't be necessary."

"They're homing on our Carlotti transmission I suppose."

"No. They said that they had us in the screen of their Mass Proximity Indicator."

And what the hell, he wondered, was a Shaara ship, a ship under any flag, doing in this particular sector of space, hundreds of light years away from any of the established trade routes? (The Shaara Queen-Captain might well be wondering the same about *Little Sister*.) Anyhow, it was pointless switching off the Carlotti radio which, to comply with regulations, had been in operation, maintaining a listening watch, ever since the lift off from Port Muldoon. *Baroom* had *Little Sister* in her MPI screen and, unless and until the mini-Mannschenn was repaired, could close her with ease.

Grimes lifted the microphone from its clip.

"*Little Sister to Baroom* . . ." he said.

"*Baroom to Little Sister.*" The voice from the speaker could almost have been that of a robot; the arthropodal Shaara, telepathic among themselves, were obliged to use artificial voice-boxes when speaking with beings dependent upon sound waves for communication. "Do not concern yourself. We are approaching you with rapidity."

Grimes' own MPI screen was still a sphere of unrelieved blackness, but, of course, his equipment did not have the range of that carried aboard the bigger ship.

He said, "Please cancel my earlier call. I no longer require your assistance."

"But it is apparent," came the voice from the speaker, "that you are not yet proceeding under interstellar drive."

"I no longer require your assistance," repeated Grimes. He noticed that a tiny spark had just appeared in the MPI screen. "You may resume your voyage."

"We shall stand by you," said *Baroom*, "until you have completed your repairs."

"I think," said Tamara, "that that is very generous of them."

Grimes muttered something about salvage-hungry bastards, realizing too late that the button of the microphone was depressed. But no
comment came from the other ship. He returned his attention to the
screen, set up calibration rings, fed the data obtained into the pinnace's
computer. He did not like the way the sums came out.

"Two and a half hours minus . . ." he muttered.

"What does it matter?" Tamara asked. "They'll just stand by until
you admit that you're licked, and they'll send engineers aboard to do
your job for you."

"But that's a Shaara ship," said Grimes.

"And so what? I may not be a spacewoman, but even I know that
the Federation is on friendly terms with the Hive. Hallichecki, or even
some of our own people, like the Waldegrenans—we might have cause
to worry. But the Shaara . . . They're civilized."

"I haven't time to explain now," said Grimes.

He picked up the rotor from where he had put it, hurried back to
the mini-Mannschenn. He must, he knew, get the thing operative before *Baroom* came alongside. The only Shaara vessel likely to be tra-
versing this sector of space would be one under the command of a
rogue queen.

Chapter 10

He had the thing together again. It *looked* all right—a complexity of gleaming, fragile golden wheels, the spindles of which were set at odd angles one to the other, an instrument rather than a mere machine, a work of abstract sculpture rather than an instrument. A work of mobile, abstract sculpture . . . He put out a tentative finger, gently pushed the rim of one of the rotors. It moved under his touch, as did, in sympathy, the other components of the device. He felt a momentary dizziness, a brief temporal disorientation, as precession was briefly initiated. So it worked. No one part was fouling any other part.

So he had proved his capabilities.

So who needed engineers?

He called out cheerfully, "Stand by for temporal precession!"

He reached out for the master switch—there should be no need to reset the Mannschenn Drive controls on the console forward—pressed it down. There was a sputtering, a brief, brilliant coruscation of blue sparks, a wisp of acrid smoke.

Damn!

He must have scraped a wire clean of insulation with a probing screwdriver.

He switched off.

Yes, that was the wire, or, to be more exact, that had been the wire. Luckily he would be able to replace it without disturbing the rotors. He heard Tamara cry out, ignored her. She called out again.

"Yes?" he replied irritably.

"Grimes! They're here! You'd better get some help before you do any more damage."

"All I have to do is replace a lead."

There was another voice. That woman must have switched on the Normal Space Time radio, Grimes realized. "*Baroom* to *Little Sister*. Stand by to receive us aboard."

He called out, "Tell them that I don't need assistance."

"Grimes! That looks like a warship! There are guns, pointing at us!"

He hurried forward. Through the control cab ports he stared at the Shaara ship. She was a huge, truncated cone surmounted by a transparent hemisphere. She looked like an enormous, metallic beehive. And, thought Grimes, staring at the extruding muzzles of laser and projectile cannon, these bees had stings. . . .

He spoke into the microphone, "*Little Sister* to *Baroom*. Thank you for standing by us. But, I repeat, we do not require assistance."

"But you do, *Little Sister*, you do. It is obvious that your interstellar drive is not operative. By the time that you arrive at your destination you will be dead of old age."

Grimes doubted that. With a steady acceleration of one gravity, which could be increased if necessary, it would not be all that long before a respectable fraction of the speed of light was attained. And then there would be the time dilation effects . . . Nonetheless, planetfall would be made at Boggarty a long time after, a very long time after the expiry date of the contract. But the problem was purely academic. Once that wiring was replaced *Little Sister* would be on her way with time to spare.

"*Baroom* to *Little Sister*. Stand by to receive our boarding party."

"I do not require assistance," repeated Grimes stubbornly.

He saw a flash of blue flame from one of the menacing guns and flinched. *This was it*. But the projectile exploded a good half kilometer from the pinnace in a dazzling pyrotechnic display. Nonetheless, Grimes could recognize a warning shot across the bows when he saw one.

He said, "All right. I can take a hint. I'm opening the airlock door now." He pressed the necessary button on the console. He told Tamara, "Get dressed. The Shaara are only glorified insects, but we have to keep up appearances. Put on something with as much gold trimming as possible. And jewelry." Then again into the microphone, "You will have to wait a few minutes, I'm afraid. We have to do some minor housekeeping before we can receive guests."

"Do not attempt any treachery, *Little Sister*. And I warn you that our engineers are standing by to synchronize should you succeed in restarting your interstellar drive."

They possibly could, too, thought Grimes. With the two ships practically alongside each other *Baroom*'s space-time-warper would be the master and *Little Sister*'s the slave. . . . He hurried aft, opened the locker that he was using as a wardrobe, practically threw on to his body the hated gold and purple livery that was a relic of his servitude to the Baroness d'Estang. As he fastened the last button he turned to see Tamara looking at him. She had attired herself in a long robe of dark blue velvet down the front of which sprawled a dragon worked in gold and jewels, its snout practically nuzzling her throat, a gleaming claw over each breast. Rings glittered on her fingers, pendants that were almost miniature chandeliers dangled from her ears. A golden tiara, set with diamonds, was dazzling against the blackness of her hair.

He grinned, "You'll do."

She grinned, "And so, Grimes, will you. Anybody would think that you were a Galactic Admiral."

"Now," he told her, "we put out a fine display of booze and sweet-meats on the table. Those liqueurs of yours . . ."

"Anyone would think," she said, "that you *like* the Shaara."

"I get along with them—when I have to. And I know them, and their weaknesses. . . ."

When they had put the liquor and candy on display they went back forward. Looking through the control cab ports Grimes saw that an airlock door was open in the side of the other ship. He said, "We've tidied up. You can board now."

"We are boarding," came the reply. "The Princess Shreela and Drones Brrell and Boorrong are on their way . . ."

Through his binoculars Grimes watched three figures, clad in cocoon-like Shaara spacesuits, emerge from the airlock, saw a puff of vapor from the rear of each almost featureless sack.

He said to the girl, "In their ships the captain is a queen. The princesses are her officers. The drones are, more or less, like the marines in *our* warships. The workers are the engineers and technicians." He paused. "I notice that the Queen-Captain isn't sending any workers across. Doesn't look as though she's in any hurry to help us to get the drive fixed."

"Then what does she want?" asked the Superintending Postmistress.

"Loot," said Grimes bitterly. "She's a Rogue Queen. She and her swarm are on a flight to try to find a suitable planet on which to settle down and found a new colony. They'll not be too concerned about the rights of any indigenes who may be in residence. Meanwhile, they snap up anything left lying around. Like us. . . ." He paused, watching

the three cocoons drawing closer and closer. "And this ship, this pinnace, will represent untold wealth to them. Their instruments will have
told them what she's built of. And they *love* precious metals—for
themselves, not only just for their monetary value."

"And the liquor? I've heard that they . . . er . . . tend to over-
indulge . . ."

"You heard right. With any luck at all the princess will dip her
proboscis into a bottle, and the drones will follow suit. And when
they've passed out I'll replace that burned out wire."

"But the Queen-Captain said that her ship would be able to synchronize temporal precession rates . . ."

"Yes. But I think that I shall be able to set my controls for random
precession . . ." He hoped that he would be able to do so. He had seen
the technique demonstrated during a Survey Service engineering
course for spaceman officers. It involved hooking up the Carlotti antenna with the Mannschenn Drive controls, therby engendering a sort
of unholy mechanical hybrid.

"They're here," she said.

"They're here," he agreed, watching the tell-tale lights on the panel
that showed that the airlock was occupied.

From the NST transceiver came the voice of the Queen-Captain.
"The princess is in the chamber. You will admit her to your ship, and
then, one by one, the drones."

"Wilco," replied Grimes briefly.

The airlock, he saw, was repressurized. He opened the inner door.
The princess came through into the main cabin, looking like a sheeted
ghost out of some old story of the supernatural. Anything at all could
have been under the folds of that white shroud. Then the protective
garment fell away from her, dropped to her taloned feet. She stood
there, a splendid creature, as tall as Tamara, taller than Grimes, regarding the two humans through her glittering, faceted eyes. Her
gauzy, iridescent wings hung down her back like a flimsy, bejewelled
cloak. Golden filagree gleamed in the rich, chocolate brown fur that
covered her body and bracelets of fine gold wire encircled, between
every joint, her four slender arms. Her voice box, strapped to her
thorax, was also of gold.

"Which of you is the captain?" she asked.

"I am," said Grimes. "And this is Madam Tamara Haverstock, the
Superintending Postmistress of Tiralbin."

"And your name, Captain?"

"Grimes. John Grimes."

"We have heard of you." Although the artificial voice was without inflection Grimes could detect disapproval. He had become involved with an alcoholic Shaara princess some years ago and the news must have gotten around. "Now, please to admit my escort."

Grimes admitted them. They were smaller than the princess, each about half the size of a grown man. Like her they were lavishly bedecked with personal jewelry. Even their gunbelts and holsters and the butts of their laser pistols were as much ornamental as functional.

"May we offer refreshments, Highness?" asked Grimes politely.

The two drones started towards the laden table; the princess put out two long arms to restrain them. Then she walked slowly towards the display of refreshments. From her complex mouth a long, tubular tongue slowly uncoiled. She dipped it into one of the bottles, that containing the homemade Benedictine. Grimes, watching carefully, saw that the level of liquid fell, at the most, only half a millimeter.

She said tonelessly, "It is a pity that I must do what I must do." Her orders to the drones were telepathic. They approached the table, picked up the bottles, carried them through to the galley-cum-engineroom. Then, with obvious reluctance, they poured the contents into the waste-disposal chute. Grimes wondered what would happen to the algae in the vats—but, of course, all sewage and galley refuse was processed before being used as nutriment for the primitive but especially bred organisms.

"So you do not accept our hospitality," said Grimes.

"But I do," replied the princess. She picked up a little fondue in a dainty claw, lifted it to her busy mandibles. "This is quite excellent."

One big advantage of an artificial voice box, thought Grimes, was that it allowed its possessor to talk with her mouth full.

"I believe," she went on, "that your interstellar drive is inoperative."

"It requires only a few minutes' work, Highness, to make it operational," Grimes told her. "Work that I am quite capable of carrying out myself."

"And are you a qualified engineer, Captain?"

"No."

"Then I strongly advise against any tinkerings, on your part, with that delicate piece of machinery. It would be a pity if this very valuable little ship were hopelessly lost in a warped continuum. Our technicians will put matters to right."

"I am quite capable of making the necessary repairs," said Grimes.

"You are not," stated the princess. "And now I extend to you and your distinguished passenger an invitation to repair aboard *Baroom*."

"Thank you," said Grimes, "but I regret that we must decline."

"Perhaps," said the princess, "I should not have used the word 'invitation.' "

The drones, Grimes saw, had drawn their pistols. They looked as though they knew how to use them. And they would be bad tempered at being deprived of the free drinks that had been so temptingly displayed."

"What do you want with us?" Grimes demanded.

"That, Captain, is for the Queen-Captain to tell you if she so decides."

"*Do* something, damn you, Grimes!" shouted Tamara. "If you won't, I will!"

She snatched from the golden belt at her waist something that Grimes had assumed was no more than decoration, that was, in fact, a slim dagger. She sprang towards the princess. One of the drones fired, and she was nursing her scorched right hand, looking down at the hilt that, with a mere centimeter of still-glowing steel protruding from it, had fallen to the deck. The other drone fired. The crystals of her right ear pendant shattered. Blood trickled down her face from a dozen tiny wounds.

Grimes went to her. "We have to do as they say," he told her. "Even if we did overpower these three pirates their ship would vaporize us in a second."

"But the contract..." She was actually weeping, from pain or humiliation, or both. "The contract... The parcel mail ..."

"It won't be the first time in the history of Man," said Grimes, "that the mail's been late or has never arrived at all."

He should not have been surprised when the open palm of her uninjured hand almost knocked his head off its shoulders.

Chapter 11

Under the watchful eyes of the three Shaara they divested themselves of their finery—and much good had it done them!—climbed into their longjohns and then their spacesuits. The one that Tamara put on had belonged to the Baroness. She had told Grimes, "You may as well keep it. You may be carrying a passenger some time. And, all too probably, you'll be getting into a situation where lifesaving equipment is essential. . . ."

"You will leave the ship first, Captain," said the princess. "And then your passenger. You will assist her to make the jump."

"Did you ever try to teach your grandmother to suck eggs?" asked Grimes. It was obvious that no passenger could make a space jump without guidance.

"I do not understand," said the princess. "But do not delay any further. Go. I shall be quite capable of operating your simple airlock controls."

Grimes sealed his helmet. The suit radio was working; he could hear Tamara's ragged breathing. He checked the seals of her spacesuit then made his way to the airlock. The inner door closed behind him. He watched the needle of the pressure gauge on the bulkhead drop to zero. The outer door opened. He clambered from the chamber into the emptiness, being careful to keep a grip on one of the recessed handholds. *Little Sister* was still accelerating and if he cast adrift too soon he would follow a weird trajectory relative to her and might well expend all the reaction mass in his suit propulsion unit trying to get back.

The outer door closed.

While he was waiting for it to open again he looked across to the

Shaara ship, a huge, menacing hulk against the starry blackness. All her lights were on, making it easy to see her. That inside the open airlock door was green, slowly flashing.

Tamara emerged from *Little Sister.*

She whispered, and even the distortion of the helmet phones could not hide the shakiness of her voice, "I've never done this before."

Grimes said, "And I don't make a habit of it."

And another voice—the princess aboard the pinnace? The Queen-Captain aboard *Baroom*?—ordered, "Do not delay. Make the jump."

"Hang on to me," said Grimes. "You'll have to let go of the hand-holds first."

And that latter went for him too. He realized that *Little Sister* was falling up away from him. He got his left arm around her and both her arms went about his body. He could see her face through the transparency of her helmet. She was very pale, and blood was still oozing from the cuts on her cheek. He was lucky, he thought. Looking over her space-suited shoulder he could see that he was lined up for the flashing green light. With his left hand he thumbed the button of the propulsion unit at his waist. He felt the not-quite-violent nudge at the small of his back as the miniature rocket fired. Had neither ship been accelerating he would have cut the drive at once, completing the journey under free fall. But in these circumstances he was obliged to maintain his own personal acceleration.

Deceleration would be the problem, although not an insuperable one.

He said, "Hang on to me."

She muttered, "I somehow can't see myself letting go . . ."

He took his right arm from about her shoulders. The grip of her arms about him tightened at once. With his right hand he found the propulsion unit control at her left side and was thankful that the Baroness had spared no expense in the equipping of her yacht; the space-suit gloves were of the very latest—and most costly—pattern, with fingertip sensors. Had it not been so he might never have found the button in time.

He made a slight adjustment of trajectory so that he was now aiming for a lighted port ahead of the airlock door. The Shaara ship was big now, very big, an artificial planetoid hanging in the void.

Now!

He released the pressure on his own firing button and, simultaneously, pressed the one on Tamara's suit. He was expecting the sudden pressure of deceleration; she was not. He heard the air *whoosh* explosively from her lungs.

And they were in the green-lit chamber, still moving fast but not dangerously so. By the time they made contact with the inner door they had slowed almost to a halt.

They thudded against the metal surface. He cut the drive of Tamara's suit. They dropped the few centimeters to the deck.

He said, "You can let go now."

She let go.

He watched the outer door shut. On a dial on the bulkhead a little yellow light began to move slowly clockwise. It stopped, changed to red. The chamber was repressurized.

The inner door opened. Beyond it a princess was standing in a dimly, ruddily illuminated alleyway, towering above a half dozen drones. These latter swarmed over Grimes and the woman, hustling them out of the airlock. Two shrouded figures brushed past them, looking and moving like competitors in a sack race with large bags over their heads as well as covering the lower parts of their bodies. The door closed after them.

Workers, thought Grimes. *Two technicians to make up the prize crew* . . .

The princess lifted the claws at the ends of her two forearms up to her head, made a twisting motion. Grimes understood the gesture, unsealed his helmet.

The Shaara officer said, "You will follow me to the queen."

The air inside the Shaara ship was warm, too warm, and laden with smells that were not quite unpleasant. There was a cloying sweetness intermixed with frequent hints of acidity. There was the acridity of hot machinery and the subdued hammering of the inertial drive, the thin, high whine of the Mannschenn Drive that the Shaara manufactured under license for use in their vessels, having found it more reliable than their own dimension warping device—which Grimes had heard described by a Terran engineer as 'a pigknot of pendulums.' In a human ship the sounds of voices, laughter, music would have drifted through the alleyway, the combination of tunnel and spiral staircase. Here there was only a subdued humming, vaguely ominous. Luckily there were no obstructions underfoot; the lighting was too dim for human eyes.

Up they climbed, up, up, and round and round, the princess in the lead, the armed drones surrounding Grimes and Tamara. Up, up . . . And then they came into a huge, hemispherical chamber, more a conservatory than the captain's quarters aboard a spaceship. Moss covered was the deck and every pillar was entwined with broad-leaved vines, the darkness of the foliage relieved by huge, fleshy flowers. Grimes wondered briefly what it would have looked like in normal (to him) lighting; as it was the leaves were almost black and the blossoms glowed a sickly pink.

In the middle of this compartment was the queen-captain. Flabby, obese, she reclined in a sort of hammock slung between four pillars, sprawling among huge cushions. Two princesses stood by her, and a quartet of workers, as tall as their officers but with much broader bodies, fanned her with their wings.

"Captain Grimes," said the queen.

Grimes wondered whether or not to salute, decided to do so. Perhaps the capture of his passenger and himself was not piracy but only the result of some sort of misunderstanding.

Perhaps.

Nonetheless, he brought his hand up to his helmet.

"Captain Grimes; Superintending Postmistress Haverstock. You understand, Captain, and Superintending Postmistress, that your lives are forfeit. Always it has been the way with our people, long before we flew into Space, that any organism so hapless as to be in the path of our swarms has died."

"Royal Highness," said Grimes stiffly, "we were not in the path of your swarm. Your ship would never have passed close to mine if you had not made a deliberate alteration of trajectory."

"I should not have made an alteration of trajectory if you had not attracted attention to yourself," said the flat, mechanical voice.

"Even so," said Grimes, "I demand that Madam Haverstock and I be returned to our ship and allowed to proceed on our voyage."

"You demand, Captain? Only those with sting may demand."

"The Survey Service has sting."

"From what I have heard, Captain Grimes, I do not think that the Survey Service, even if it knew of your predicament, would lift a claw to save you. But you will not be killed at once. I may find uses for you and your companion. Go."

Telepathic orders were given and the swarming drones hustled the two humans from the Presence.

Chapter 12

They were herded through a maze of dimly lit tunnels, down ramps that were too steep for human comfort, towards, Grimes thought, the stern of the great ship. Suddenly the princess, who was leading the party, stopped. Four workers appeared as though from nowhere and speedily divested the humans of their spacesuits. To have resisted would have been futile. No attempt was made to strip them of their longjohns, not that it much mattered. The Shaara, although addicted to jewelry, did not wear clothing and the nudity or otherwise of their prisoners meant nothing to them.

A circular doorway expanded in what had been a featureless bulkhead. Grimes and Tamara were pushed through it. The door closed. They were standing in a cubical cell, the deck of which was softly resilient underfoot. Dim red lighting came from a concealed source, barely bright enough for them to be able to make out the details of their prison. On one padded bulkhead two spigots protruded over a narrow drip tray. Against the bulkhead at right angles to it, just above deck level, was a trough through which ran a steady stream of water.

Grimes remembered one of the courses that he had taken while still an officer in the Survey Service, a series of lectures regarding the general lay-outs of the vessels owned and operated by the spacefaring races of the Galaxy, the Shaara among them. This cell was no more— and no less—than an officer's cabin. One spigot was for water, the other for food. The trough was for general sanitary use. He realized that he felt thirsty. He went to the taps, pressed the button of one of them, looked at the blob of pink paste that was extruded on to the drip tray. He stuck his forefinger into it, raised a sample to his mouth. The stuff was bland, slightly sweet, almost flavorless. No doubt it was as nutritious as all hell but would be a dreadfully boring diet from the very start. Small wonder that the Shaara so easily became addicted to highly flavored Terran liquor! The other spigot yielded water—flat, lukewarm, unrefreshing.

Tamara joined him at the nutriment dispenser. She said, "At least, we shan't starve. . . ." She did not sound overly enthusiastic. "But where do we . . . ?"

"There," said Grimes, pointing to the trough.

Even in the dim lighting he could see her angry flush. "This is insufferable! Surely they realize that we must have privacy!"

"Privacy," he told her, "is a concept meaningless to a social insect."

"But not to me," she said. "You're a spaceman, a captain. Tell these people that we demand to be housed in conditions such as we are accustomed to."

He said, "I've no doubt that this cell is bugged. But bear in mind that our accommodation is, by Shaara standards, first class."

"Not by mine," she said stubbornly. "And now, would you mind standing in the corner with your face to the wall? I have to . . ."

After an interval, during which he tried not to listen, she said, "All right. You may turn round now."

Their accommodation was first class by Shaara standards, but they were not Shaara. The food was nourishing, although very soon they were having to force it down, eating only to keep up their strength. They exercised as well as they were able in the cramped quarters when they realized that they were putting on weight. Before long they decided to go naked; the air was hot rather than merely warm, and humid, and their longjohns were becoming uncomfortably sweaty. After a struggle they managed to tear the upper portion of Grimes' garment into strips for use as washcloths. An estimated twelve days after their capture Grimes sacrificed the lower legs of his longjohns so that Tamara could use the material for sanitary napkins.

Now and again, although not very often, there was a flare-up of sexuality, a brief and savage coming together that left them both exhausted but strangely unsatisfied. Always at the back of their minds was the suspicion, the knowledge almost, that alien eyes were watching. Also, Grimes missed, badly, his pipe as a sort of dessert after intercourse. (He missed his pipe. Period.) And Tamara complained every time about the roughness of his face; there were no facilities in the cell for depilation. (He noted, with a brief flicker of interest, that her body remained hairless.)

Fortunately for their sanity both of them could talk—and listen. The trouble there was that Tamara, when Grimes was telling stories about his past life, would interrupt and say, "But you handled that wrongly. You should have . . ."

And after the first few times he would snap, "I was there, and you weren't!" and then there would be a sulky silence.

It was squalid, humiliating—but the ultimate humiliation was yet to come.

Without warning the door of their cell opened and a swarm of drones burst in and chivvied them out into the alleyway, along tunnels and up ramps until they came to a huge chamber that must have occupied almost an entire deck of the Shaara ship.

Chapter 13

It was, Grimes supposed, a recreation room—although it would have passed muster as an indoor jungle. There was the moss-covered deck, pillars so thickly covered with flowering vines that they could have been trees, real trees the uppermost branches of which brushed the deckhead and, in the center of the compartment, was a seemingly haphazard piling of smooth rocks down which glistening water tinklingly trickled. And there was *Baroom*'s crew—a scattering of bejewelled princesses, a rather larger number of gaudily caparisoned drones, a horde of comparatively drab workers.

The two humans were dragged to the pile of rocks, up it to a platform on the top of it. The drones returned to deck level leaving a princess there with them. Suddenly a bright spotlight came on, playing over their naked bodies. The princess extended one of her upper arms. The taloned "hand" at its extremity touched, first, Tamara's left breast, then her right, then descended to her groin. It hovered there briefly, then moved to Grimes' penis. Instinctively he tried to swat the claw away but, with lightning rapidity, another claw caught his arm, scratching it painfully.

"Do not struggle," said the princess. "You will not be harmed. We are instructing our crew. And now you and the female will perform for us your generative functions."

"Not a hope in hell!" snarled Grimes.

"I do not understand. Please to repeat."

"No," said Grimes definitely.

"You mean that you will not perform for us?"

"Yes."

"It does not matter," said the princess. "We have obtained certain records from your ship. Perhaps you will find it amusing to watch. We shall find them instructive."

Records? wondered Grimes—and then he remembered.

Not only his prominent ears were burning with embarrassment—the angry flush spread over his entire body.

To one side of the circular chamber the wall was clear of vegetation. It glowed suddenly with light—not the red illumination that was the norm for this ship but bright, white, with splashes of color. The scene was the cabin of *Little Sister*. There was a cast of two, Grimes and Tamara Haverstock. There was hardly any dialogue but there were gasps and little screams. There was an intertwining of naked limbs, an undignified, vigorous pumping . . .

"You bastard!" whispered the woman—the actual woman, not the one on the screen—viciously. "You *bastard!*"

"I can explain. . . ." muttered Grimes.

"There are questions," said the princess. "Not many of our crew are familiar with humans and their ways. There are those who ask how many eggs the female will produce after the mating."

"You *bastard!*" repeated Tamara Haverstock.

Chapter 14

For the rest of his life Grimes tried to forget the details of the remainder of the voyage. Thinking of it as a preview of hell might have been an exaggeration, but it was most certainly not a foretaste of heaven, and in purgatory (we are told) there is hope. Hope was a quality altogether absent from this cramped cell with its boredom, its savorless food, the hateful company of the hating woman who spoke only to snarl at him, who had lost all interset in her appearance and who had become a compulsive eater, whose once trim body had become a mass of unsightly bulges, whose breasts were sagging, whose hair fell in an unsightly tangle about her sweaty, fattening, sullen face. Even so small a comfort (*small* comfort?) as his precious pipe with a supply of tobacco would have made conditions slightly less intolerable, but he was denied even this.

But every voyage must have its end.

And then, at long last, came the time when Grimes woke from an uneasy sleep. The light in the cabin was changing, shifting, deepening from pink to violet and its perspective was no longer that of a cube but a tesseract. Tamara's sprawled, naked figure was as he had first known it, long-legged, firm-bodied, with the fine bone structure of her face prominent. She was snoring, but even that normally unlovely sound was musical. . . .

Abruptly perspective, light and color were again as they always (for how long? for too long) had been. But sound was different. There was something lacking—and that something was the all-pervasive thin, high whine of the Mannschenn Drive. So, thought Grimes, *Baroom* was making planetfall. So in a matter of a few hours, or even less, it would be landing stations.

He touched the woman on a fleshy shoulder. Her eyes slowly opened. She looked up at him with an expression that at first was oddly eager but that almost immediately became one of extreme distaste.

She muttered, "It's *you*. I was dreaming, but . . . Lemme sleep, damn you."

He said, "Tamara, we've arrived. Or almost arrived. "They've just shut down their Mannschenn Drive. . . ."

"And so bloody what? Take your filthy paws off me!"

He snarled back at her, "For the love of the Odd Gods of the Galaxy pull yourself together, woman! We shall be landing shortly. I don't know on what world but we're liable to be meeting strangers. And you're a mess."

"And you're no oil painting yourself, Grimes!"

He ignored this. "You're a mess. The way you are a sex-starved second mate of a sixth rate star tramp wouldn't look at you!"

She glared at him, heaved herself to her feet. She shuffled to the drip tray on the bulkhead, used a scrap of rag to stop the outlet and then, using another piece of the rag from Grimes' longjohns, washed herself all over. Somehow after the ablutions she was beginning to look as she had looked before the imprisonment. She struggled into her longjohns and the elastic fabric moulded and constrained her figure. Then, using her long fingernails as a comb, she tried to arrange her hair. Without proper treatment it would not regain its lustre but the worst snarls were out of it.

She snapped, "Am I fit for parade, *Captain?*"

He admitted, "It's an improvement."

"Then may I suggest that you do something about yourself?"

Grimes tried, but without depilatory cream it was an almost hopeless task. He pulled on the trunks that were all that remained of his space underwear.

He sat down in a corner of the cell to wait.

She sat down in the opposite corner to wait.

At last a variation of the beat of the inertial drive told them that they were coming in to a landing.

There was a very gentle jar.

The inertial drive fell silent.

There was a mechanical hooting sound that began suddenly, that stopped as suddenly.

There was a brief thudding that could have been a burst from an automatic cannon.

There was silence.

She raised her eyebrows, asked, "Well?"

He said, "I don't know."

She sneered, "You're the expert."

There was more silence.

Suddenly the door opened, admitting six drones. Careless of the minor wounds they inflicted with their sharp claws they stripped the humans, dragged them out into the alleyway, down ramps to an airlock, both doors of which were open, admitting bright sunlight, a cool breeze. Instead of a ramp extending from the outer door to the ground there was a platform. On this was a cage—a light yet strong affair with aluminum bars. Grimes and Tamara were thrust into this and the door was slammed shut after them with a loud clicking of the spring lock. The deck of interwoven metal swayed under their feet, throwing them off balance.

Grimes looked up, saw through streaming eyes (the sunlight was painfully bright after the dimness to which they had become accustomed) a blurred shape like a fat torpedo. It was a blimp, he realized, one of the non-rigid airships that the Shaara invariably used inside an atmosphere in preference to inertial drive powered craft.

He looked down and back.

Baroom had landed in a wide meadow, a field under cultivation, crushing beneath her bulk row upon row of low bushes. Close by her was the gold-gleaming *Little Sister*, dwarfed by the huge Shaara ship. Over and around both vessels flew the bee people—princesses, drones, workers—rejoicing in the exercise of their wings. There was another blimp in the air, motionless.

He turned, barely conscious that his naked skin brushed Tamar's bare breasts, looked ahead. There was a town or a village there, buildings of almost human architecture. Between this settlement and the spaceships was a charred patch on the ground, an untidy, cratered patch of dark grey in the yellow grass (or what passed for grass), a scattering of angular, twisted wreckage. *A ground vehicle? The burst of a cannon fire that they had heard?*

"Where are they taking us?" she demanded. "Where are they taking us?"

"To that town," he replied.

"But why? But why?"

He made no answer. There was none that he could give. He looked up to the strong escort of armed drones that was accompanying the blimp. He looked ahead again. The air over the town was alive with swarming motes. He knew that these were more drones. And yet it

was no Shaara city that they were approaching. Such a center of population would have consisted of domes great and little, not buildings
that, in the main, were like upended rectangular blocks.

The blimp flew slowly over the town, finally stopped and hovered
over a wide central square. There was a new looking structure in the
middle of this, a metal platform around which were standing Shaara—
two princesses, twenty drones, a half dozen workers. Above the cage
a winch hummed and rattled. Grimes and Tamara were lowered swiftly
to the platform where the workers caught the bars around them in their
claws, positioning the portable prison. The winch cable was unhooked
from its ringbolt. The weight released the blimp lifted rapidly, turned
and flew off in the direction of the spaceships.

One of the princesses started to call, her voice box turned up to
maximum amplification. It was in no language that Grimes had ever
heard although she seemed fluent enough in it. By ones and twos and
threes the people emerged timorously from the buildings and streets
around the square. They were more human than merely humanoid although blue-skinned, bald-headed without exception and with horn-
like protuberances above where their eyebrows would have been, had
they been a hairy race. They were clad, men, women and children
alike, in drab grey robes, neck-high and ankle-length, with sleeves
falling half over their three fingered hands.

The princess continued her incomprehensible spiel, the people
stared stolidly through dull crimson eyes. The princess waved a contemptuous claw at the captives. The people stared. Then a man broke
out from the small crowd of which he had been a member. A metallic
object gleamed in his hand, a cumbersome pistol. Two of the drones
fired simultaneously, slicing him into smoking collops. The stench of
burned meat was sickening. A sort of moan went up from the assembled natives. The princess delivered a last peroration, then fell silent.
At last, obviously dreading that they would meet the same fate as the
dead man, three women lifted the blood-oozing pieces into a small,
two-wheeled hand-cart, trundled it away.

The sun blazed down.

There was no shade.

There were almost invisible, sharply biting, flying things.

Tamara sagged heavily against Grimes, slumped to the deck of the
cage. She had fainted. Grimes clung to the bars, his head whirling, his
vision dimming, fighting down his nausea. He knew that he could not
long hold on to his own consciousness.

And then two of the workers produced from under the platform a
light, folding framework that they set up about the cage, that was

topped by a sheet of opaque plastic. The shade, briefly, was as welcome as a draught of ice-cold water. Another worker pushed a jug and
a bowl of the sickly pink pabulum into the cage at Grimes' feet. The
surface of the latter was soon black with the tiny flying things.

He looked from it to the huddled, unconscious woman. Should he
try to revive her? She seemed to be breathing normally enough. It
would be kinder, he decided, to leave her in oblivion.

From the direction of the spaceships came two bursts of automatic
gunfire. The crowd moaned. A blimp flew overhead, in no hurry, going
nowhere in particular.

Without too many contortions Grimes managed to sit down, avoiding contact with the woman's perspiring skin. He took a sip from the
jug. The water was as flat and lukewarm as usual. He looked with
distaste at the contents of the bowl.

He would have sold his soul for a smoke.

He was awakened by Tamara shaking him. When he had dropped
off to sleep he had been too hot; now he was uncomfortably chilly.
And yet it was still light. He blinked, realized that the glaring illumination came from three floodlights trained upon the cage.

She was babbling, "All these people, *staring* at us . . . But have
something to eat. I saved you some. It tastes better than usual."

Grimes could guess why but only said, "Not just now, thank you.
Any water left?"

"Yes."

He rinsed his mouth, swallowed. He got carefully to his feet, his
joints creaking. In spite of the glaring floodlights he could see that the
Shaara guards—or their reliefs—were still on duty, that the square
was still crowded with citizens who must be prisoners as much as the
two humans, although not as closely confined.

Then the lights went out.

Almost immediately a great oblong of bright illumination appeared
on the wall of one of the tall buildings surrounding the square, down
the facade of which a huge white sheet had been stretched. After a
flickering second or so a picture appeared.

Grimes had seen it before.

Tamara had seen it before.

Again they watched themselves writhing in naked abandon on the
deck of *Little Sister*'s main cabin, again they listened to their wordless
cries. But they were hearing more than the noises that they had made
on that long ago occasion. The crowd was . . . growling. Its front ranks
surged inwards, towards the cage, hesitated when the amplified artifi-

cial voice of a Shaara princess boomed out, when a drone machine gunner fired a noisy but harmless burst into the air.

But their guards made no attempt to stop the natives from throwing things, may even have ordered them to do so. As one the Shaara buzzed aloft, above the trajectory of the missiles—the rotten fruit, the garbage, the ordure. They returned to earth when the barrage had spent its fury, fired more machine bursts into the air while the princess in command ordered the mob to disperse. A worker threw a couple of rough blankets into the cage, another one pushed in a fresh jug of water, another bowl of the pabulum.

The princess said, "You will sleep."

Grimes and Tamara huddled together in their misery. Neither said anything. Neither slept.

The sun was well up when the blimp came to carry the cage back to the ship. With the first light the mob had turned out in force to stare at the prisoners, to make threatening gestures, held at bay only by the Shaara display of weaponry. Grimes and Tamara were almost happy when their swaying prison was lifted high above the hostile crowd, thankful when they were set down on the platform outside *Baroom*'s airlock. They submitted with near-cheerfulness to the ordeal of a hosing down before they were released from the cage and dragged inside the vessel.

Their familiar cell was almost homelike.

She asked in a frightened voice, "Grimes, what was all that about?"

He replied, "I don't know . . . But . . ." He ransacked his memory. "I have read reports on this planet—I think. I have seen films . . . Those blue-skinned people, with the odd horns . . . And, as I remember, odd ideas. It's off all the trade routes, but the odd tramp calls here—Shaara, Hallichecki, as well as those from the human worlds . . ." The memories were coming back. "There was an incident—a Dog Star Line ship, and four of the officers, two men and two women, bathing naked in a lake. They were mobbed, stoned. Three of them died. The Dog Star Line screamed to the Admiralty. One of our—sorry, one of the Survey Service destroyers was sent here—not quite a punitive expedition, although it could have developed into one. But all that came of it was a directive to all Survey Service commanding officers and to all shipmasters that local prejudices, such as the nudity tabu, were to be respected. But there was, I believe, a show of force now that I come to think of it. The village near which the murders happened was razed to the ground, but with no loss of life . . ."

A snore interrupted him.

He saw that she was curled up on the padded deck, sleeping soundly.

He sighed, tried to sleep himself.

At last he did, but not before his memory had supplied him with more details about this unimportant planet, this world just waiting to be snapped up by one of the major powers but so poor, so far from anywhere that only a Shaara Rogue Queen would be tempted to seize the prize . . .

Darijja . . .

Dominant race, mammalian humanoids . . .

Major religion, Darajjan, the worship of the god Darajja . . . Puritanical, condemning all sensual pleasures, sexual intercourse especially . . .

Older religion Deluraixsamz, worshipping fertility deities Delur and Samz. Adherents now persecuted minority . . .

Grimes thought, *And now they have a new persecuted minority— us.*

He drifted into a twitching, nightmare-ridden sleep.

Chapter 15

They were given time to recover from their ordeal and then they were flown to another town where they suffered a repetition of degradation and humiliation. Another brief respite, then another exposure to the abuse of the mob.

How long would it be, Grimes wondered, before they lapsed into gibbering idiocy? How long would it be before the Queen-Captain decided that their usefulness to her policy of conquest was at an end? And what would happen then? A swift and merciful slaying by their Shaara captors or a handing over of them to a bloodthirsty rabble?

But he was stubborn. While there was life there was hope. During every excursion from the ship he watched everything, observed, made mental notes. If they ever did escape, unlikely though this eventuality was, a knowledge of the country and its people would be essential to survival. The culture of Darijja, he decided, was early industrial revolution. There were railways, with steam trains. On the rivers were paddlewheel steamships. Once, in the distance, he saw what looked like a dirigible airship. He was almost certain that it was not one of the Shaara blimps; it was too long, too slender. The cities were gaslit.

And the people? Regarding their hostility he was no longer so sure. In every crowd gathered in every square or marketplace there was the majority who growled with rage and who pelted Tamara and himself with noisome missiles—but there was also a substantial minority that held aloof, whose expressions seemed indicative of pity rather than of hatred or contempt. But this was only a guess, a wildly optimistic one. After all, on Earth, a ferocious baring of the teeth may be misconstrued as a friendly smile.

Tamara was holding up surprisingly well. The torture—for torture it certainly was—seemed to have snapped her out of her squalid apathy. In the cage she held herself proudly erect, staring disdainfully both at the natives and the Shaara guard. She did not look away from the screenings of her and Grimes' erotic games in *Little Sister*'s cabin but, he was beginning to realize, watched with an odd combination of wistfulness and pride. Once she whispered, "You know, Grimes, I hope that this record survives us. It might even teach these joyless bastards what life is all about. . . ."

She no longer overate. She reproved Grimes when he helped himself too liberally from the food spigot in their cell aboard the ship. She insisted that the pair of them resume their regular exercise sessions. But it was only in the cage that they could talk freely; it did not seem likely that the portable prison would be bugged, as their cabin most certainly was. They compared notes, discussed what they had seen and experienced.

"It makes a horrid sort of sense," Grimes said to her. "The Queen-Captain, the Rogue Queen, wants this world. Once she establishes her colony, once she goes into her egg-production routine—she may already have done so—the Shaara will multiply and only a few of the natives will survive, as slaves. Some of the natives must realize this. Some of them will want to fight. Some of them may be hoping that the Federation will intervene on their behalf. What the Shaara are doing to us, with us, is to show the Darijjans that humans are a decadent, degenerate people, inferior to the Shaara in all ways. I wish I knew their language. I wish I knew what that blasted princess is telling them every time that we're put on show . . ."

They looked out through the bars at the sullen, blue-skinned, grey-robed crowd, at the vicious, gaudy drones, the stolid workers, at the glittering princess whose words, booming out from her voice box, had become hatefully familiar although still utterly incomprehensible.

Chapter 16

The sun set behind the high buildings, the first gas lights flared in streets and alleys. The glaring spotlights came on, bathing the naked bodies of the prisoners in the harsh radiance. A worker standing by the projector switched it on and the screen stretched over a facade came alive with the all too familiar rendition of the erotic fun and games aboard *Little Sister*. When it was over there came the barrage of spoiled fruit and other garbage. Grimes and Tamara stood there, trying not to flinch, determined even in these circumstances to show that they were, after all, superior to their captors, their persecutors.

Somebody once said: It is a proud and lonely thing to be a man.

It was lonely all right, thought Grimes. As for the pride, he and Tamara were doing their best.

Then the show was over. The sullen worker threw their coarse blankets into the cage. The guards took up their stations for the night. The mob melted away. A light drizzle started to fall but the canopy over the cage protected the prisoners. Grimes did not feel sorry for the Shaara guard who were exposed to the precipitation. He said as much to Tamara.

She said, "There's something . . . odd . . ."

"Odd?"

"The . . . smell . . ."

Yes, there was a strange odor in the air, carried on the slowly writhing tendrils of mist, a sweetish aroma, intoxicating almost. Almost? Grimes was beginning to feel light headed. He laughed foolishly. He muttered, "Come to Darijja, the vacation planet, where it rains gin . . ."

She nipped his arm painfully. "Snap out of it, Grimes! Something is happening!"

"And it can go on happening," he said happily.

"Look!" she said.

Dimly seen grey-cloaked figures were creeping into the square, converging on the platform on which stood the cage. The guards, standing like statues, ignored them. One of the natives approached a drone, raised his right foot, pushed rather than kicked. The Shaara topped over, lay there with all four arms and both legs in the air, twitching slightly. The other drones, the workers and the princess paid no attention.

Two Darijjans clambered on to the platform, approached the cage. Grimes saw the gleam of metal, tensed himself for an attack. But none came.

A heavily accented voice whispered, "We . . . friends. We Deluraixsamz . . . We to you make bow . . ."

He suited the action to the words.

The other man was busy with a file, muttering to himself as he worked. A trickle of glittering, metallic dust slowly grew to a tiny pile on the platform. Losing patience he grasped the bar with both hands, jerked. It parted. The second bar was a tougher proposition but at last it was filed through, bent out and sidewise.

"Come," urged the speaker. "Come!"

Grimes wriggled through the opening, helped Tamara out. They wrapped the blankets about themselves like togas then jumped down from the platform. The cobblestones were hard and cold underfoot.

He started to walk toward the fallen drone but his guide grasped his garment roughly. "Come! Come!"

"Weapons," said Grimes.

"We take. Come."

Grimes saw that the grey-robed figures were busy about the motionless Shaara. He saw the flash of a knife. So this was turning out to be a minor massacre. He said, "You've gone too far. There will be retaliation."

"*We* not here in morning," said the native.

Grimes sighed inwardly. It had always happened. It would always be happening. Guerillas would stir up a hornets' nest—a very apt analogy—and citizens who had no wish for anything but a quiet life would pay the penalty. But in troublous times those who do nothing to resist the invader might well deserve all that comes to them . . .

He and Tamara hurried across the slimy cobblestones in the center of a small crowd of the devotees of Delur and Samz, whoever and whatever they might be.

They walked rapidly through deserted, gaslit streets. It was still drizzling, although the light precipitation was now devoid of artificial additives.

They came to a large building with an ornate, pillared facade. The huge main doors were shut but they passed through a small side entrance, made their way through a great hall dimly illumined by a few flickering gasjets, decorated with huge pictures that, as far as Grimes could see in the uncertain light, were crudely painted landscapes. Another small door admitted them to a long platform, beyond the edge of which parallel lines of metal gleamed faintly.

A railway station . . .

But where was the train?

There was no locomotive, no string of carriages. But there was a vehicle that was little more than a platform on wheels surmounted by a framework from which projected two cranks.

"Come!"

That seemed to be the only word that their guide knew. Grimes and Tamara jumped down from the edge of the platform on to the car, a half dozen of their rescuers followed. The cranks were manned and the crude vehicle rattled out of the station, picking up speed. Two others came behind it; all the guerillas were making a getaway. Through the misty darkness they moved, picking up speed, through the town, out into the countryside. They clattered over a bridge, toiled up a steep incline with extra hands at the cranks, rolled down the other side with the driving mechanism out of gear. There was a deep cutting, a tunnel smelling of damp and soot.

Nocturnal animals cried in the bush to either side of the track—a weird ululation, a harsh cackling. Something clattered overhead, shrilly keening. Somebody started to sing aboard the rear rail car, a rhythmic chant that sounded as though it should have been accompanied by throbbing drums and squealing fifes. Other voices took up the chorus. The leader shouted loudly and angrily and there was silence—apart from the natural noises and the rattling of their progress—again.

Ahead there was a dim, flickering light. The cars slowed, halted.

"Come!"

They scrambled down on to the rough gravel beside the track. Grimes cursed as the sharp stones cut the tender soles of his feet, heard the girl cry out softly. Once they were away from the ballast the footing was better, soft moss by the feel of it. By the faint light of the lantern the humans watched the natives working around the rail cars. They were rocking them, pushing them, grunting and panting. The first one, finally, was off the track. It was shoved away from the opposite side of the track, moving reluctantly as its wheels bit first into the gravel and then the soft, mossy soil. Then, suddenly, it seemed to leap away from the men shoving it. It vanished to the sound of an oddly subdued and soft crashing that abruptly ceased. Some rudely disturbed animal screamed.

The second car followed, then the third. They had been disposed of, Grimes realized, down a deep ravine—one that, Grimes thought and hoped, was masked by thick vegetation.

"Come!"

The dim, yellow lantern, stinking of partially consumed animal oil, was bobbing away into the bush on the side of the railway track away from the gully. There was a path, of sorts, barely wide enough for the party to proceed in single file. There were wet, feathery growths that brushed their faces, spiny twigs that reached out for them from all sides. The going was hard, uphill. Grimes was sweating inside his makeshift garment, wished that he could discard it, but by this time he had acquired a healthy respect for the nudity tabu of these people.

Ahead of him Tamara's blanket was snagged on a thorn, was snatched from her. Her pale body was almost luminescent. A low cry went up from the natives. "Delur . . . Delur . . ." There was no menace in it. She retrieved her covering from the bush, slowly wrapped it about herself. "Delur . . . Delur . . ." There was still worship, but mixed with it was . . . regret?

"Come!"

The upward trudge continued.

And there was another light ahead of them, a flickering red flame set in the mouth of a cave. There were figures around the small fire who raised their arms to bring them sweeping down in a salaam-like gesture, who cried, "Delur . . . Delur . . . Samz . . ."

"We here," said the guide.

At least it made a change from "Come!" . . .

Chapter 17

Once again they were on display, but this time there was no overt compulsion, this time they were not in a cage, this time they were not facing a hostile mob. They stood on a stone platform at the end of a vast cavern, an ovoid chamber in red, igneous rock formed by long-ago volcanic action. Around the walls gas torches flared, giving heat as well as light. Behind Grimes and Tamara hung a huge, silken screen on which, in bright colors, glowed depictions of the loves of Delur and Samz.

Before them the women danced to the throbbing drums and the squealing pipes, the deep-throated chanting of the worshippers. They were naked, these dancing girls, save for golden anklets and bracelets hung with little, tinkling bells. With their blue skins, their bald heads, their spidery limbs and their glowing red eyes they should have been grotesque, but they were not.

They were beautiful.

The tempo of the music changed, became slower, langorous.

On to the stage, stepping in time to the beating of the drums, swaying, walked a man and a woman. Each was bearing a golden chalice. The man bowed before Tamara, proferred the drinking vessel. She took it in both hands. The woman stood before Grimes, looking him up and down. Then she bowed and imitated the actions of her male companion. Grimes accepted the offering.

He looked at Tamara.

She looked at him.

Her eyebrows arched in tacit enquiry.

In reply he raised his goblet, said, "Down the hatch!"

She smiled slightly, raised her chalice to her lips.

He sipped from his.

The wine—if wine it was—was deliciously cold, aromatic.

Almost without conscious volition he drank deeply. The golden bowl fell from his hands as did the one that Tamara had been holding. The utensils rang like gongs, shrilled like coins being spun on a hard surface. Freakishly they came together, one nesting inside the other.

"Delur . . . Delur . . . Samz . . ."

The insistent throbbing of the drums, the high, sweet piping of the flutes . . .

She dropped her blanket . . .

"Delur! Delur!"

He cast his from him.

"Samz! Samz!"

And there was a *rightness* about what happened that had been altogether lacking from the erotic exhibitions before the assembled Shaara, before the jeering crowds in the market places.

Chapter 18

Grimes drifted slowly up from deep unconsciousness.

He opened his eyes, had difficulty in getting his bearings. On the ceiling, at which he was at first looking, was a painting in explicit detail of a pale-skinned naked god about to make love to an equally pale-skinned and enthusiastically receptive goddess. It reminded him of the erotic carvings in a cave near Bombay, in India, on far away Earth.

A cave . . .

He remembered then.

"You are awake, Captain Grimes?"

The voice was a pleasant one, speaking with only the slightest of accents. Grimes turned his head, stared at an elderly native man with wrinkled skin, with protuberant horns over his crimson eyes, dressed in a sort of scarlet sarong on the material of which, in gold, the motif of copulatory deities was repeated over and over. In one hand this individual held a lantern, with pressurized gas hissing incandescently in a mantel, in the other a wooden tray. He set the tray down on a low table beside the wide bed, hung the lantern from a hook protruding from the drapery covered wall.

Grimes turned over, then back again.

"Where is Tamara?" he demanded. "Where is my . . . companion?"

"Do not concern yourself, Captain Grimes. She was taken to her own . . . chamber. At this moment her handmaidens will be awakening her, as I am awakening you. It is the custom of your people, I believe, to start the day with a cup of tea . . ." A very prosaic looking metal teapot was poised over an earthenware mug; the steam from the dark amber fluid issuing from the spout was fragrant and on any of Man's worlds would not have been exotic. "Sugar, Captain? Milk?"

It was real tea all right. Grimes sipped the hot fluid gratefully.

"A smoke, Captain? Or is it too early in the day?"

Grimes stared at the packet being extended by a three-fingered hand. *Caribbean Cublets* ... The trade name of the cigarillos was offensive but their quality could hardly be bettered. He took one, struck it on his thumbnail, inserted the unlit end into his mouth. He inhaled deeply. It was not as good as his beloved pipe, but it was much, much better than nothing.

"Now," he said, "please tell me ... What *is* all this about?"

His visitor made himself comfortable on a three-legged stool. He lit a cigarillo, began to smoke with obvious enjoyment. He said, "My name is Lennay Torith Lannanen."

"I'm pleased to meet you, Mr. Lennanen."

"Mr. Lennay, please, Captain Grimes. Lennay is my father's family name, Torith that of my mother's family. But no matter. For many years now I have been the Agent on this world for the ships of the Dog Star Line. It is not a frequent service that they maintain—our exports are few and our imports fewer—but I have become a man of moderate wealth. Also I have acquired tastes for essentially Terran luxuries . . ." He waved his cigarillo towards the tea tray. "But not only am I a successful businessman. I am also . . . High Priest? Yes, High Priest of the Old Religion, Deluraixsamz.

"For at least three generations the devotees of Deluraixsamz have been persecuted, driven underground. But still we meet in secret, in temples such as this. We are . . . qualified to form the nucleus of resistance to the Shaara invaders, just as you and your companion are qualified to be our figureheads."

"Do your people love Earth so much, then?" asked Grimes.

"To most of the population Terrans are no more than not very pleasant aliens. But have you looked closely at the pictures on the walls and ceiling?"

"Mphm?"

"Delur, you will observe, is depicted as being white-skinned, not blue-skinned. Also—as is not the case with our women—she has a full head of hair, although elsewhere she is hairless. Her eyes are a most unnatural green, not red. She has only one pair of mammary glands. Need I continue?"

"Mphm."

"And now, her consort. The Lord Samz. He is exceptionally well-endowed."

Grimes looked down at himself. "I'm not."

"But, sir, you are—compared to our men. Even in repose you are a veritable giant."

Grimes could sense what the other was driving at and didn't like it. "But," he demurred, "I have a beard." He fingered his unsightly facial growth. "Your god Samz does not."

Lennay laughed. "Captain Willard of *Sealyham* honored me by staying at my home when his ship was last here. Inadvertently he left behind him a tube of the cream that you Earthlings use to remove unwanted hair. When I was obliged hurriedly to vacate my premises— as you can well imagine, almost the first act of the Shaara was to destroy my sun-powered Carlotti transceiver—I swept valuables into a carrying bag before fleeing. By mischance—as I at first thought— the depilatory was among the contents of a drawer that I emptied into the sack."

"The whole idea is crazy," snapped Grimes.

"But it is not, Captain. Insofar as our common enemy is concerned it will be a case—as your great playwriter Shakespeare has observed— of the engineers being hoist with their own petard. You were paraded and humiliated as proof that Earthmen are only—as Captain Wong Kuan Yung of *Lucky Star* would say—paper tigers . . ."

"*Lucky Star?*"

"A very small tramp vessel. She was chartered to the Dog Star Line. Her crew were interesting people, somehow different from you others. But you obliged me to digress. The Shaara paraded you, degraded you. They put it about that you had been captured in battle and that you might not have been captured had not you been deeply involved in an orgy of unbridled fornication. After the exhibition of that most excellent film the devotees of Darajjan will associate Earthmen with the proscribed Deluraixsamz and will hesitate to ask for the aid of such depraved beings even if they should find the means to do so."

"Mphm."

"But there is more, Captain Grimes. There is more. There is the prophecy." Until now Lennay had been talking quietly but now a note of fanaticism was creeping into his voice. "Is it not written in the Elder Chronicle that it shall come to pass that monsters shall fly over the land and the people be sore afflicted? Is it not written that in those times the mighty Delur and her consort Samz shall return, and shall be mocked and stoned by the unbelievers? Is it not written that Delur and Samz shall be succored by the faithful and will then arise in their burning wrath to scatter the demons from the sky?"

There was a silence, on Grimes' part an embarrassed one. He asked at last, "Do you really believe all that?"

"Of course," came the simple reply.

"May the Odd Gods of the Galaxy save us all!" said Grimes.

"Amen," said Lennay.

Chapter 19

Lennay called out in his own language and three of the native women came in. They made low salaams and murmured something. The only word that Grimes could recognize was "Samz."

"Go with them, Captain," said Lennay.

Interesting, thought Grimes. *He seems to believe all this Delur and Samz nonsense, yet he still calls me "Captain" . . . The habits of a lifetime as a shipping company agent must be hard to break.*

He was escorted by his attendants to an ablutions chamber. This was a small cave in which a natural hot spring cascaded down into a trough, lit by a flaring gas jet. A sub-cavern opened off this. There was another trough with a steady flow of water which vanished down a sinkhole. Its purpose was obvious, but was a god supposed to defecate and urinate? And was he supposed to do so watched by his worshippers? To his great relief the women did not accompany him into the natural water closet but waited outside. When he emerged, however, they took his hands and led him to the shower, went to work on his body with a strongly scented soap and a soft brush. When they had finished one of them handed him the tube of depilatory cream. They all watched with interest as his whiskers melted away under its application. Then there was a mirror, and a comb for his head hair and, after they had dried him with big, fluffy towels, a plain, dark blue sarong.

God or not, he was beginning to feel human.

Ablutions over, the women attired themselves in garments similar to that worn by Lennay, decorated with the Delur and Samz motif. They led Grimes along a gaslit alleyway—this temple, so-called, was assuming in his mind the proportions of a minor city—to yet another chamber in the rock where Tamara was awaiting him. She, too, was sarong-clad, although hers was gold. An elaborate, pagoda-like golden crown surmounted her lustrous black hair and intricate pendants, interlocking rods and rings, dangled from the lobes of her ears.

She smiled.

She said, "We seem to have been promoted, Grimes. I thought that as Superintending Postmistress I'd reached the very pinnacle of ambition, but . . ."

He grinned.

"I got a kick out of regarding myself as Master under God. But now . . ."

She said, "Deities or not, we have to eat." She gestured towards a stone table at which were two throne-like chairs.

They seated themselves. The serving women brought in the meal. It was, fantastically, eggs and bacon, with toast and butter and sweet preserve, a pot of hot, strong coffee. The eggs, however, had a subtly fishy flavor, not unpleasant, and whatever animal had contributed the meat from which the bacon had been processed was not a pig, the toast had a nutty taste and the preserve, although slightly acid, was not marmalade, but the coffee was genuine.

She told him, "I have had a long talk with Dinnelor. She is the wife of Lennay, the High Priest *and* Dog Star Line Agent. They're real Terraphiles. This meal . . ."

"And these cigarillos—Smoke?"

"Thanks."

Lennay came in accompanied by his wife, a woman apparently younger than himself, her blue skin unwrinkled, the little pseudo horns on her bald head less prominent. The High Priest (the Dog Star Line Agent?) made a gesture. The serving women cleared the table, came back with fresh coffee and four mugs, two more chairs.

"You are ready for the day's work, Captain?" asked Lennay politely.

"What is a god supposed to do?" asked Grimes, then regretted the words. An agnostic himself he had always tried to avoid giving offense to sincere believers.

Lennay frowned sorrowfully. "Captain Grimes, please do not jest. I do not believe that you and Madam Tamara are actually Samz and Delur in person. But I do believe that the god and the goddess are using you as their instruments. I know that you are—or were—a member of the military profession . . ."

"How do you know?" demanded Grimes.

"The Dog Star Line captains and officers have told me about what happened on Morrowvia, have shown to me pictures of the people who were involved. I recognized you. Surely there is only one spaceman Grimes with such splendidly outstanding ears . . ."

Those prominent appendages flushed angrily. Tamara Haverstock laughed.

Grimes said, "All right, I was in the Survey Service. I held the rank of Commander when I . . . resigned. But I'm no expert on land warfare."

"But you are familiar with weaponry, Captain Grimes. For example, laser pistols. My chief clerk acquired six of them when you and the Lady Delur were rescued."

"Mphm. Have you any means of recharging them?"

"Regretably, no. My Carlotti transceiver was solar-powered and, in any case, it was destroyed by the Shaara. But there were also four machine pistols and two light machine guns . . ."

"Ammunition?"

"Only the cartridges that were in the magazines."

"Mphm." Somehow that all-purpose grunt was not as satisfactory when delivered around a cigarillo rather than around the stem of a pipe. "Do you people have weapons of your own? Oh, you do have. When we were first put on show a man ran out waving what looked like a pistol and the Shaara cut him down . . ."

"One of us," said Lennay. "He—how do you put it?—jumped the gun. But, to answer your question, we do have weapons. Unfortunately there are, now and again, wars between our nations. I could have made a huge fortune by importing sophisticated killing devices but I always refused to do so. Now I am sorry. Well armed we would not have been a *bleeng*—a plum, that is—ripe for the picking."

"What do you have?" demanded Grimes.

"Cutting weapons. Stabbing weapons. Firearms. A variety of lethal and incapacitating gases and the means for their delivery. One of these latter, actually a potent insecticide, was used to effect your rescue."

"And do you, personally, the Deluraixsamz, have these weapons?"

"We have access to them. Unfortunately they are all relatively short range and the few attempts that have been made to fight the invaders have ended in disaster. Too, the high ranking military are all devotees of Darajja and fear a resurgence of Deluraixsamz and actually regard the Shaara as their natural allies. There was a Shaara ship here just over a year ago and the Queen-Captain ignored me but, to my certain knowledge, entertained and was entertained by Hereditary President Callaray and General Porron. They will learn, of course, that he who sups with the devil needs a long spoon, but by the time the lesson has sunk in it will be too late for Darijja."

"Aircraft?" asked Grimes.

"None that are used for fighting. We do have airships for the carriage of passengers and urgent cargoes . . ."

"Buoyancy? What gas do you use for lift? Hydrogen, or helium?"

"I do not understand. Those words are not in my vocabulary."

Two of the very few that aren't, thought Grimes. He explained, "Both are gasses, both are lighter than air. Hydrogen burns, explodes. Helium is an inert gas."

"Hydrogen," said Lennay.

"I take it, then," said Grimes, "that your Establishment is anti-Deluraixsamz, slightly anti-Terran, pro-Shaara inasmuch as they hope to use the Shaara . . ."

"Yes," admitted Lennay doubtfully.

"Also, you can give me weapons—the handful taken from the guards, a rather greater number from your own arsenals . . ."

"Yes."

"Then," said Grimes, "if I'm to be more than a mere figurehead in your revolt I shall want some idea of the tools that I shall have at my disposal. I shall want maps. I shall want artificers—the handgrips and triggers of the Shaara guns will have to be modified for a start. I shall want samples of your explosives. I shall want to meet your guerilla leaders . . ."

"The Great God Grimes demands offerings," said Tamara sardonically.

"Dog—or bitch—shouldn't eat dog," Grimes told her.

Lennay and his wife exchanged shocked glances.

Chapter 20

Grimes was not a soldier.

He possessed a fair theoretical grasp of space strategy and tactics but knew little of the principles of land warfare; throughout his Survey Service career he had always been elsewhere when courses in this subject were held at Lindisfarne Base. Nonetheless, he had glimmerings. He called for maps and a conversion scale. He demanded an inventory of arms and ammunition and explosives. He wanted to know how many members of the underground had military experience and how many, if any, were still serving in the Taraplan Army.

He got the maps first—a small scale one comprising the entire planet, other small scale ones for its continents, of which Taraplan was one, large scale charts of Taraplan's coastline and large scale maps of the inland regions. With Lennay instructing he soon got the hang of the various symbols, the color coding that was used in conjunction with contour lines, the stipplings used to indicate population density and all the rest of it.

Lennay put him into the picture regarding probable future developments. It seemed certain that Hereditary President Callaray would soon sign a treaty of peace and friendship with the Shaara Queen and, shortly thereafter, would find some excuse, probably a manufactured incident, to declare war on Desaba, the island-continent-nation to the north. The Shaara would be his allies. First Desaba, then Kootar, then Raitu, then the Pinnerba Confederation . . . Finally, his ride on the tiger over, it would be President Callaray's turn to be eaten.

And that would be the way of it, thought Grimes. Even if *Baroom* were not employed as a flying fortress the Shaara would have command of the air. Their blimps were helium filled and would mount long range weapons; the native airships were hydrogen filled, pitifully vulnerable, and would be armed only with primitive, slow-firing, hand-powered machine guns. Too, the Shaara blimps could be—probably would be—used as carriers for platoons of drones, flying fighters who, with their laser hand guns, would make short work of the airships. And, he realized, there was his own *Little Sister*—a virtually invulnerable spacecraft also extremely maneuverable inside an atmosphere, a potential bomber, fighter, troop carrier, or all three.

So the Shaara would have to be stopped, *now*.

But how?

He studied the map on which the location of the cave-temple had been marked by Lennay, on which was Korong, the town from which he and Tamara had been rescued, and, further to the south east, Plirrit, near which the Shaara had landed, where their ship still was. Grimes was surprised to discover how close he was to what he regarded as enemy headquarters. Since the first landing he had travelled many kilometers by blimp, but, he realized, it had just been a case of there and back, there and back, there and back. This was the most thickly populated part of Taraplan with the major industries, the coal mines, the natural gas wells, the iron and the copper.

He picked up a pair of dividers, did some measuring off. As the crow flew it was just over five hundred *drli* from the temple to Plirrit. He consulted the conversion scale; that was three hundred kilometers almost exactly. The cave was a mere six *drli* from the railway track, the line between Korong and the copper mining town of Blit in the mountains to the north west. He assumed that his army—*his army?*—would have to be assembled in or near the temple and then would have to be transported to Plirrit. It was too far to walk, and a convoy of rail cars would be conspicuous. And, talking of railcars . . .

He asked, "Mr. Lennay, has there been any sort of search for us? Has anybody found the rail cars that we abandoned?"

Lennay replied, "Very little time has passed since your rescue, Captain Grimes, and we have never, as a people, been in such a hurry as you Earthmen." He shrugged. "Often I have deplored this, but there are times, such as now, when this leisurely attitude is to the advantage of the True Believer. We have had ample time to ensure that the rail cars can not be spotted from the air and that the marks of their precipitant passage through the bush have been erased. But there has been considerable activity by the Shaara flying patrols, up and down the railway line. And at least four square *drli* of the city of Korong have been burned, melted, vaporized with the marketplace as the focal point for the destruction."

"How many killed?" demanded Grimes.

Lennay shrugged again. "Only seventeen—in exact retaliation for the number of Shaara killed. There were none of our people among them."

"Wasn't that fortunate?" said Grimes.

"You have a saying," Lennay told him. "You cannot make an omelet without breaking eggs."

It was Grimes' turn to shrug. He realized that a sarong is not a suitable garment in which to perform such a gesture. But it did not matter. The god Samz would go clothed or unclothed as he saw fit. He resumed his study of the map, jabbed the symbol for Blit with the points of his dividers.

"Copper mines . . ." he murmured. "Smelters, presumably."

"Yes, Captain Grimes."

"And the copper from Blit goes where?"

"Some to the householdware factory in Korong. Some to Plirrit, to the arsenal. Some to be transhipped to barges to Plirrit for passage to the coast, to Blargo, for export."

"Mphm." Grimes traced the course of the Kahar River with his dividers. At one point it was less than a *drli* from the field in which *Baroom* and *Little Sister* had landed.

He asked, "Do you have people in Blit?"

"Yes."

"In the railway service? But you must have. Those rail cars. The river steamer and barge crews?"

"Yes."

"I'm thinking out loud," said Grimes slowly. "Don't hesitate to shove your oar in, Mr. Lennay, if I'm getting too far off the beam . . ."

"Please?"

"Interrupt me if what I'm saying doesn't seem to make sense. What I have in mind is a consignment of copper ingots—it comes in ingots, doesn't it?—from Blit. It will be a normal shipment, up to a point. Korong will get their full quota. So will Plirrit. But the trucks that should be full of transhipment copper won't have any copper, although they'll have a full load. Us."

"I begin to understand, Captain Grimes. Our forces will proceed down the Kahar River in the copper barges, will be disembarked at the closest point to the Shaara ships and then attack. But what can we do with our puny weapons against what is no less than a flying battleship?"

"Precious little," admitted Grimes. "But I do not intend to attack *Baroom*—or, if I do, it will be only as a diversion. My intention is to regain possession of my own ship, *Little Sister*. Once I have her I shall be able to do something."

"Is she armed?" asked Lennay.

"She wasn't when I was last aboard her, although the Shaara, by now, may have mounted a few cannon. But we must get her..." Another thought struck him. "How will you communicate with your people in Blit, in Plirrit? You have no radio, no telephones..."

"We have the railway," said Lennay. "There are pick-up points, known only to our people, along the track for messages."

"You were remarkably well prepared," said Grimes.

Lennay made one of his abrupt transitions from Dog-Star-Line-Agent-cum-guerilla-leader to religious fanatic. He declaimed rather than merely said, "This was all foretold in the Book of Deluraixsamz."

"Mphm," grunted Grimes dubiously—but he had no intention of looking a gift horse in the mouth.

He discussed matters with his fellow diety.

She said, "We have to go through with it. It's the only chance we have to get the mail to its destination."

He could hardly believe his ears. Was she serious? He could not be sure. He said, "The *mail?* At this time, of all times, you're worried about the mail!"

"Of course," she said.

"I'm the wrong god," he told her.

"What do you mean?"

"I should be Mercury, the Heavenly Messenger," he grumbled.

"As long as you can make out as Ares..." She grinned. "You don't do so badly as Aries."

He grinned back. "All right, Superintending Postmistress Delur. I'll get your bloody mail through. Eventually."

Chapter 21

A guerilla band is not a ship's crew; inevitably there are too many chiefs and not enough indians. Fortunately there were only two gods and Grimes was one of them. Unfortunately, as far as the worshippers were concerned, he ranked below Tamara/Delur, and she, as the top postal official of her planet, was convinced that she knew at least as much about running an operation as a mere spaceman.

It was an uphill struggle trying to lick the underground into some semblance of an army before the Shaara were too strongly consolidated. Like the majority of Survey Service spaceman officers Grimes had always rather despised marines, but at this period of his life he would have sold his soul for a tough sergeant major. He did have an ex*tarawon*—a rank equivalent to first lieutenant—from the local army, but he had served in the catering branch and Grimes thought of him as a commissioned cook. He had three *langaras*—corporals—one ex and two still serving. One of these was employed in the arsenal at Plirrit and should have been useful. He was, at first, succeeding in sending a clandestine trickle of small arms and ammunition north west along the railway to the cave temple. His usefulness, however, abruptly ended. Having absented himself from his place of duty without leave he was put in charge of modifying the handgrips of the captured Shaara weapons. As an armorer he was naturally curious about these exotic killing devices. He tried to take apart one of the laser pistols to see how it worked. The resulting flare of energy killed him, destroyed three of the laser pistols and seriously injured his two assistants.

"You should personally have overseen the work, Grimes," said Tamara.

"I told Lennay to tell him not to tinker," Grimes said.

"I know from *my* experience," she stated, "that merely telling people is not good enough."

He found a carpenter who was able to fabricate wooden butts for the weapons. The trigger assemblies still were not quite right but they could not be fired either by Grimes or the natives without too much manual contortion. The main trouble was the limited life of the laser power cells, the lack of a supply of ammunition for the four machine pistols and the two light machine guns. The drum magazines for the former held two hundred rounds each and for the latter a thousand rounds. An experienced soldier would ration his firing to short, effective squirts; these enthusiastic amateurs would be liable to blow off an entire magazine in one wasteful burst.

There was a large cavern below the complex of caves used for the temple and for accommodation. This made an almost ideal firing range as the sounds of shooting could not be heard on the surface. The lighting—flaring natural gas jets—could have been better but the action, when it came, would be at night. Grimes sacrificed, in practice, one pistol magazine and part of another, leaving him only three of these weapons. He fired one short demonstration burst from a light machine gun, depleting its magazine from a thousand to nine hundred and fifty rounds. The three remaining laser pistols he did not demonstrate; there would be one for him, one for Tamara and one for Lennay who, as Dog Star Line Agent, had been allowed to play with such toys by one of the Dog Star masters who had been hoping to engage in arms dealing as a private venture.

Grimes was fascinated by the local weaponry, especially the heavy machine gun. This had six barrels rotating around a longitudinal axis and a gravity feed magazine. It was operated neither by recoil nor by surplus gases but was manually powered. All that the gunner had to do was point the piece in the right direction and crank a handle. The rate of fire was only about two hundred rounds a minute but the gun was sturdy and reliable. There was no shortage of ammunition—brass cartridges instead of the plastic ones to which he was accustomed, with heavy lead slugs.

There were pistols—primitive revolvers—and single shot rifles. There was a sort of mortar with a limited supply of gas shells. This Grimes could not try out in his subterranean shooting gallery because of its high trajectory, but with the projectiles that would be used extreme accuracy would not be necessary. There were rockets that would release a bright flare.

The lack of a common language, thought Grimes, would be the real problem; there was too little time for even a crash course in linguistics. Luckily Lennay and his wife were fluent in Galactic English and his chief clerk and three others of his office staff could understand and make themselves understood.

Meanwhile, there were the reports coming in from outside. A Shaara envoy to Kahtrahn, the capital of Desaba, had been mobbed and had escaped only by taking to the air, although not before her drone escort had inflicted heavy casualties on the natives. There had been an exchange of stiff notes between King Darrin of Desaba and President Callaray. Shaara blimps had flown over the archipelago of the Pinnerba Confederation and had been kept under close observation throughout by Pinnerban airships. In a world with no radio, no telephones or telegraphs, such news was old, brought in by the crews of merchant ships. More immediate information was that an unidentified airship, thought to be Desaban, had flown over Plirrit and that Grimes' own *Little Sister*, aboard which laser weapons had been mounted, had disposed of her with contemptuous ease. There had been neither survivors nor any readily identifiable wreckage.

"If we don't act soon," said Grimes to Lennay, "we shall miss the bus."

"Miss the bus, Captain Grimes? What is a bus . . . Oh, yes. A word rarely used now, but employed often by your Shakespeare. Buss. To kiss. But what has kissing to do with it?"

Grimes sighed. Tamara laughed and asked, "But isn't kissing what your religion is all about? Kissing, and . . ."

Lennay said stiffly, "Our rituals are symbolic."

Grimes grunted then said, "I suggest that we move against Plirrit as soon as possible. The men are as well trained as they ever will be. How soon can you arrange for the freight train to pick us up? And the river steamer and barge crews must be put into the picture."

Lennay told him, "Word will go down the line to Plirrit and up the line to Blit at once. Our supporters among the railwaymen and the rivermen have been standing by awaiting our orders. If all goes well, the freight train will make an unscheduled halt tomorrow morning. Arrival at Plirrit will be after dark tomorrow evening. Late tomorrow night we attack."

But he was not ready, Grimes thought. He never would be ready. He was not a soldier.

But once he had the controls of *Little Sister* under his fingertips he would be once again in his proper element.

Chapter 22

Grimes was awakened by Lennay at an indecently early hour the next morning. He gulped tea, made a sketchy toilet, dressed himself in a knee-length black tunic, emblazoned back and front with the copulating deities, and a pair of heavy boots. It was better than the sarong, than nothing at all, but he did not feel at ease in this rig. He belted on one of the modified laser pistols. He followed the High Priest to the chamber where Tamara and Dinnelor were awaiting them. Tamara, too, was clad in a tunic although hers came only to mid thigh and left her smooth shoulders bare. Her belted pistol and the scabbarded sword over her other hip made her look more like a goddess of warfare than of love.

But goddess she was this morning, just as Grimes was a god. The two natives did not join them at their meal but humbly served them, anticipating their every wish, even to cigarillos when they were finished eating.

Then Lennay said, "Lady Delur, your people are waiting."

She looked at Grimes, who nodded.

She rose, saying, "Then let us go."

She led the way from the chamber, Grimes following, Lennay bringing up the rear. Dinnelor did not accompany them. They made their way along the tunnel. Ahead of them was a muffled thudding of drums, a subdued shrilling of pipes, a chanting of male voices only.

Delur . . . Delur . . . Delur . . .

There was no mention of Samz. Grimes began to feel miffed.

Delur . . . Delur . . . Delur . . .

The great chamber in which, not so long ago, they had performed their ritual lovemaking was now more parade ground than temple.

Grimes was amazed at the martial appearance of those whom he had
derided in his mind as the prize awkward squad of the entire Galaxy.
In the front rank stood the three men who had been entrusted with the
machine pistols, holding the weapons proudly at salute, flanked by the
four men, two to each stretcher, with the light machine guns. Behind
them was the crew of the heavy machine gun which had been dis-
mantled—the carriage on one stretcher, the barrel assembly on another,
magazines and ammunition on two more of the litters. Then there was
the mortar, similarly broken down, with its projectiles, and two men
each carrying a bundle of sticked rockets. Behind them were the ranks
of the riflemen, the flaring gaslight reflected from their fixed bayonets.
Unluckily these latter must be left behind; only three freight trucks
would be available.

Delur . . . Delur . . . Delur . . .

She looked at him questioningly.

"Get the show on the road," he told her spitefully.

She said, "You're the military expert, Grimes."

He said, "And you're the chief figurehead."

She shrugged almost imperceptibly. She asked the Dog Star Line
Agent, "Mr. Lennay, will you escort us down to the railway?"

"To hear is to obey, Lady Delur."

Lennay barked orders in his own language. With himself in the
lead, with Grimes and Tamara following, the raiding party made its
way from the huge chamber, through the tortuous approach tunnel, to
the open air. It was dark still outside. A thin, warm drizzle was falling.
It was very quiet but, from a great distance, came the muffled panting
and rattling of a steam drawn train. Grimes doubted if any Shaara
would be aboard at this hour; they operated, whenever possible, during
daylight only. Of course one of the native airships might be overhead,
silently drifting, but this was not likely. Unless there were traitors in
the underground nobody would know of the location, the existence
even, of the cave temple. Nobody would be expecting this attack.

Lennay led the way down the almost completely overgrown path,
the light from his dimmed lantern throwing a pool of wan light around
his feet. Grimes and Tamara kept close behind him to get the benefit
of what little illumination there was. Behind them the men carrying
the heavy weaponry were surprisingly sure-footed although their heavy
breathing almost drowned out the noise of the approaching train.

They came at last to the faintly gleaming tracks. Lennay took his
stance between the parallel lines of wet metal, adjusting his lantern so
that the beam was shining uphill. Suddenly the locomotive came into
view, its pressurized gas headlight throwing a glaring shaft of yellow

radiance through the misty air. Ruddy sparks erupted from its high tunnel.

The thing was obviously slowing. It came to a halt, with a screeching of brakes and a strident hiss of escaping steam, just two meters short of where Lennay was standing. Somebody called out from the driver's cab. Lennay replied. A man jumped down from the engine, led the way to the first of the tarpaulin covered trucks. He tapped securing bolts with a hammer. A door in the side of the truck crashed down.

Grimes watched, saw the native machine gun lifted aboard, its ammunition, its carriage. The mortar followed it, then the crews of both weapons. The door was lifted up and resecured. The Shaara light machine guns went into the second truck, the rockets, their crews and the three men with Shaara machine pistols. The third truck, obviously, was reserved for Delur and Samz and their High Priest. Although it was little more than an iron tank of triangular cross section somebody had tried to make it comfortable. There were cushions—only sacking-covered pads of some vegetable fibre but far better than nothing. There was a big stone jug of wine, an almost spherical loaf of bread, a hunk of something unidentifiable in the dim light of Lennay's lantern but which Grimes later found to be strongly flavored smoked meat.

When they were aboard the railwayman bowed low. "Delur . . ." he murmured. "Samz . . ." The door was lifted back into place by two riflemen who, their escort duties over, would be returning to the cave. The securing bolts were hammered home. Almost immediately the engine chuffed loudly, there was a sudden jerk and the train had resumed its journey.

Chapter 23

It was not the first time that Grimes had travelled by railway. On such Man-colonized planets that favored this mode of transportation he had enjoyed being a passenger in the luxurious tourist trains, fully agreeing with their advertising which invariably claimed that the only way really to see a country is from ground level at a reasonable speed. But this was no superbly appointed tourist coach with skimpily uniformed stewardesses immediately attentive to every want. This was a dirty freight truck—damp as well as dirty; the tarpaulin spread over the open top of it was leaking in several places. There were only rudimentary springs and the padding of the cushions was soon compressed by the weight of their bodies to a boardlike hardness.

They rattled on.

Lennay extinguished his lantern but there was now enough grey light seeping under the edges of the tarpaulin and through the worn spots for Grimes to be able to distinguish the faces of his companions. Tamara had adopted a pose of bored indifference. Lennay looked, somehow, rapt and was mumbling something in his own language. A prayer? Or was he calling down curses on the collective head of the management of the Blit to Plirrit Railway? Grimes looked at the wine and the food hungrily but waited for one of the others to make the first move. He was conscious of the fact that there were no toilet facilities in this crude conveyance.

They rattled on.

Abruptly Tamara rose unsteadily to her feet and said, "Turn away, both of you . . ." She went to the far end of the truck, after a short while returned. The smell of urine was sharp in the air. How was it, Grimes wondered, that the writers of the adventure stories that he had enjoyed as a boy, still enjoyed, could always so consistently ignore the biological facts of life? The bladder of the thriller hero was similar to the sixshooter of the protagonist of the antique Western films which, every now and again, enjoyed a revival; one never needed emptying, the other was never empty.

They rattled on.

Tamara actually slept. Lennay went on mumbling his prayers. Grimes went over and over again in his mind his plan of campaign. He would almost certainly have to play by ear, he realized, but he tried to work out courses of action to suit all eventualities. He joined the others in a simple meal of meat and bread and the thin, tart wine. He smoked a cigarillo. He hoped that he would find his pipe and tobacco aboard *Little Sister*.

Late in the afternoon the train stopped at Korong. After fifteen minutes of bone rattling shunting it was on its way once more, bound for the riverside wharves at Plirrit. Tamara slept again, Grimes dozed. Lennay lapsed into silence. Darkness fell again but, as the drippings through the tarpaulin had ceased, it must have stopped raining.

Then, quite suddenly, came the final halt.

There were voices outside the truck, the sharp sound of a hammer knocking out the retaining bolts of the side door. It fell down with a metallic crash. There were men outside with lanterns, their red eyes gleaming eerily in the darkness. All of them made the salaaming gesture. Grimes put his hastily drawn pistol back into its holster; these were friends. Or worshippers. He heard them murmur, "Delur . . . Samz . . ."

Tamara got to her feet. Her long, pale legs, her smooth shoulders were luminescent in the near darkness. She raised her arms in blessing.

Grimes said to Lennay, "Is all in order?"

"Yes, Lord Samz. The steamer and the barges are waiting."

"Then the sooner we get moving the better."

He jumped down to the ground beside the railway tracks, staggered then recovered. He looked past the welcoming committee to what must be the wharf. He could make out a high funnel from which smoke was pouring and an occasional flurry of sparks, the humped profile of paddle boxes. Turning back to the train he saw that the arms were being unloaded and that the heavy machine gun crew already had their cumbersome weapon almost reassembled. The two Shaara guns and the mortar were being carried down to the edge of the wharf to a position somewhat abaft the steamer. He followed them, watched as a small crane with a hand winch lifted them, swung them out and lowered them on to a flat barge that was little more than a floating oblong box.

The heavy gun was wheeled up on its carriage, sent to join the light weapons on top of the hatch boards.

"It is well, Lord Samz," said Lennay.

"I hope so," said Grimes.

He jumped down to the deck, stood there to catch Tamara as she followed him. Lennay used a ladder set between the wharf piles then made a brief check of personnel and equipment. He reported to Grimes that everybody and everything were aboard the barge, then shouted something to one of the men on the shore. There was more shouting back and forth, a brief toot from the whistle of the little steamer. Grimes, standing forward in the barge, saw that this vessel had let go her moorings, that the paddles were starting to turn. The bight of the towline lifted from the water but before it came taut the barge's lines were slipped. The wharf pilings began to slide slowly astern as the gap between the rivercraft and the bank widened. The steady *thunk, thunk, thunk* of the paddlewheels became faster and faster; spray pattered down on the foredeck of the barge.

To port now was the city, poorly lit by the gas street-lamps, with only the occasional window showing a gleam of light. There were no signs of movement, no noise. Presumably patrols would be aboard but the passage of a regular copper shipment downriver would not excite their attention. Then, ahead and to starboard, there was a flashing of bright lights, the beat of mighty engines. Grimes cursed. It was obvious to him that *Baroom* was about to lift, was already lifting. The Queen-Captain was taking her ship to elsewhere on this continent, or on this planet. And with her would go *Little Sister*—and without a ship, even only a very small ship, the anti-Shaara forces would be able to do no more than fight a long delaying action with almost certain defeat at the end of it.

But was Little Sister *accompanying the Shaara ship?* Grimes could not hear the distinctive note of her inertial drive. He began to hope again.

"Captain Grimes, we are too late," said Lennay heavily. And was that relief or disappointment in his voice? Either way Grimes had been demoted; he was no longer the Lord Samz.

"What do we do now, Grimes?" asked Tamara.

He said, "We come in to the bank for a landing as has already been arranged. We stage a diversion." Then to Lennay, "Pass the orders, please."

"But, Captain Grimes, we are too late!" Lennay pointed upwards to *Baroom*, lifting fast and with her lateral thrust driving her northwards. Her shape was picked out by only a few sparse lights and she looked as insubstantial as one of her own blimps or one of the native airships.

But she was the only spaceship aloft, of that Grimes was certain. He said, "*Baroom*'s away to raise hell some other place, but it stands to reason that the Rogue Queen will leave some sort of force here. A princess or two, a squad of drones, a few workers—and a ship. *Little Sister*. Things are much better than I thought they'd be."

"The eternal optimist," commented Tamara tartly.

"Too right," agreed Grimes cheerfully. His doubts, his misgivings were fast evaporating. He stared ahead. According to the chart that he had studied there should be a tall, prominent tree on the bank, just inshore from a spit extending into the river. The steamer, of course, would steer well clear of this hazard but the barge, by application of full starboard rudder, would sheer on to it at speed, at the same time slipping the towline. The paddle-boat would continue her noisy passage downstream with no cessation of the beat of her engines and any Shaara listeners would suspect nothing amiss.

He could see the tree now, in silhouette against a faint glow from inland.

"Starboard rudder," he ordered quietly.

Lennay relayed the order.

The towline was now leading broad out on the port bow of the barge, the tree was almost ahead.

"Let go!"

Again Lennay passed on the order. The riverman standing by the bitts cast off a couple of turns, then two more. The rope hissed around the posts, running out fast. Grimes had to step back to avoid being hit by the end as it whipped free, and then the barge was on her own, still making way through the water, still answering her helm—not that it mattered now; the current would carry her on to the spit.

She grounded gently. Her stern swung inshore so that she fell alongside the spit as to a jetty, held there by the stream. It could hardly have been better.

Grimes said to Lennay, "Just stay put, all of you. I'm going to have a look-see."

He stepped up on to the low gunwale, looked down. There was only a narrow ribbon of black water between the side of the barge and the pale sand. He jumped, landing on dry ground. He walked slowly inland, the sand crunching under his boots. He clambered up the low bank, through the scrub. He reached the top.

He looked across the cultivated fields with their neat rows of low bushes, slightly less dark than the soil from which they grew, to the

Shaara camp. There was a low dome, probably a large inflatable shelter, quite brightly illuminated from within, looking like a half moon come down from the sky and sitting on the ground. But his main attention was focussed on the slim, golden torpedo shape dimly gleaming a little to the right of the luminescent hemisphere.

Grimes made his plans—or, more correctly, made a selection from the several alternatives that had been simmering in his mind. The heavy machine gun, the two Shaara automatic guns and the mortar would have to be dragged up and trained on the enemy encampment. As the mortar had a high trajectory it could be fired from the cover of a low knoll but the machine gunners would have to take their chances. They should, however, be beyond the effective range of hand lasers and the gun was fitted with a shield heavy enough to stop bullets from the Shaara machine pistols. The signal rockets? Grimes had thought of using them to illuminate the scene of action but now considered that this would be more disadvantageous than otherwise to his own forces. But if a couple or three of them could be fired, on low trajectory, at the dome coincidentally with the commencement of machine gun and mortar fire they would contribute to the initial confusion.

He returned to the barge, told Tamara and Lennay what he had decided, bore a hand in the manhandling of the weapons up to the top of the bank. He wondered briefly what detection devices the Shaara might have then he decided that it was no use worrying about that now. He had become involved, more than once, with the bee people during his Survey Service career and knew that—in some ways—they were amazingly primitive. With any luck at all there would be only a handful of sluggish drones on duty with no electronic devices to do their work for them.

He went to some trouble over the positioning of the guns and found a bush the forked branches of which afforded launching racks for the rockets. He made sure that Lennay's chief clerk, who was to be left in charge of the makeshift battery, knew what was expected of him. Then, accompanied by Tamara, Lennay and two men with Shaara machine pistols, he made his way upriver to a little to where an aisle between the low bushes led almost directly to *Little Sister*. It was fortunate that so much light was being reflected from the overcast, both from the city and from the glowing dome. Had it not been so it would have been necessary to use the rockets for the purpose for which they had been designed, thus making targets of himself and his people.

"Now?" asked Lennay softly.

"Now!" whispered Grimes.

Lennay whistled sharply.

The rocketeers drew the friction strips over the striking surfaces. The machine gunner began to turn his handle. The mortar loader dropped a round into the gaping muzzle of his weapon.

The screaming roar of the big rockets, the *whumpf!* of the mortar, were drowned by the strangely leisurely yammering of the machine gun. The missiles streaked just above the low bushes trailing fire and smoke. Unluckily the Darijjan machine gun did not have tracer bullets so Grimes could not tell if the fire was accurate or not. And the gas shell fired by the mortar made no flash on bursting and the vapor, in this lighting, would be almost invisible.

The first rocket hit the ground a little to one side of and just beyond the dome, the second one freakishly swerved from its trajectory and screamed downriver. The flare, burning on the ground, threw the bushes into sharp, black silhouette. The mortar fired again, and again. The machine gun maintained its deliberate hammering.

Grimes started to run toward the distant *Little Sister*. It was heavy going; the damp soil between the rows of bushes clung to his boots, slowing him down. Too, he was badly out of condition; the period of imprisonment followed by the excesses in the cave temple had not left him in a fit state for a cross country run. Only his pride prevented him from allowing Lennay or the other two natives to take the lead. It was some small consolation to him that, to judge from the rasping gasps that he could hear behind him, Tamara was as badly off as he was.

Shaara were boiling out from the dome like bees from a disturbed hive. Those in the lead staggered, fell before they could spread their wings. Either the machine gun fire was taking effect or it was the gas from the mortar shells. There was a brief retreat, and when the Shaara emerged again they were wearing cocoon-like spacesuits. In these garments they could hold their weapons but would find it hard to fire them; more important, they could not fly.

Another rocket landed right at the base of the dome. Although the material was not inflammable it must have been melted at the point of impact by the heat of the flare. The structure began to collapse like a slowly deflating balloon.

The Shaara were running now between the rows of bushes. Hampered by their suits they were moving as though in slow motion, looking more like huge amoeba than the highly evolved arthropods that they were. They were spreading out to get clear of the field of fire of the heavy machine gun; fortunately none of them seemed to have noticed Grimes and his party. Dispersed as they were they were no longer a good target for the mortar; as soon as any of them reached a gas-free area the hampering spacesuits would be shed and they would counter attack, viciously.

Three shrouded figures were hobbling towards *Little Sister*—one was comparatively large, a princess, the other two had to be drones. Grimes stopped running, pulled his hand laser from its holster. "Get them!" he gasped to Lennay. "Get them!"

He fired, the control of the weapon set to the power-wasting slashing beam. Lennay fired. Tamara fired. Bushes around the three Shaara flared into smoky flame but the bee people carried on doggedly, although their mode of progression was now a kangaroo-like leap rather than a sack-race hobble. Grimes was sure that he'd hit the princess; he saw her suit glow briefly as the laser beam whipped across it. But the material of a spacesuit is made to resist great extremes of temperature . . .

The Darijjans with the machine pistols each let off a burst. They did not ration their shots. The gun with only one hundred and eighty rounds in its magazine ceased firing first.

But one of the Shaara—a drone—was down. Another—the princess—was hit. She staggered, almost fell, but carried on, hobbling again, with the remaining drone helping her.

It was a race now for the open airlock door of *Little Sister*. It was a race that the Shaara won by rather more than a short nose, with Grimes running third. He hurled himself through both open doors, into the main cabin, just as the Shaara princess reached the control cab. Her intention was obvious; had Grimes been a microsecond later he would have been trapped by the closing inner valve. The drone turned to face him and, in spite of the hampering cocoon, managed to raise a claw holding a laser pistol. Grimes fired first. He did not aim for the body but for the unprotected weapon. It exploded dazzlingly. The drone, his suit and body pierced by sharp slivers of metal and crystal, slumped to the deck. The princess turned away from the controls. She was unarmed—but so was Grimes. His hand laser would have been effective if played across the stitching of bulletholes in the other's spacesuit, but the power pack of the weapon was dead. It had been his bad luck to select for his weapon the one in greatest need of recharging.

She came towards him, grotesque, frightening. Even with the limited play allowed to her limbs by the suit she had four arms against his two, a pair of arms to hold his immobile, the other two to crush, to strangle.

Grimes . . . kicked. The skirted tunic was more hampering than the shorts that were his normal wear would have been. He had aimed for the body but his foot made contact with the upper part of the princess's left leg. He felt and heard chitin crumple under the blow. He stumbled backwards as the Shaara toppled forwards, all four of her arms flailing and clutching. One sheathed talon touched his ankle but failed to close about it.

And then, before she could recover from the fall, he was on her, kicking and stamping viciously, the tough exoskeleton shattering under the impact of his boots. He trampled over the long abdomen, jumped and brought the weight of both feet down on the thorax. He reduced the head to a pulp.

Abruptly he desisted.

Shame flooded his consciousness. He had been obliged to kill his enemy but there had been no need for him to make such a meal of it. Had he and Tamara not suffered such humiliations at the hands of the Shaara he would have acted like a Terran naval officer, not like a bloodthirsty savage . . .

The shame evaporated.

He realized that he did not feel sorry.

He went to the control panel—familiar but for the laser cannon trigger mechanisms that had been mounted above the other instruments—and pressed the button that would open the airlock doors. Then he started up the inertial drive.

Chapter 24

As soon as the others were aboard Grimes lifted the pinnace, swinging her so that she was heading towards the river, towards their landing place. He could see the muzzle flashes of the heavy machine gun and, briefly, a flurry of fire from the two captured Shaara light automatics. Even as he watched this evidence of resistance ceased. Then a rocket climbed into the dark air, burst. Its blue-white flare drifted slowly downwards, illuminating the fields with a scattering of motionless Shaara spacesuits—empty or occupied?—among the neat rows of bushes, with Darijjan bodies, some still moving, huddled around the useless guns. The surviving drones were airborne now, shooting down at the landing party, and there was nothing with which the crew of the battery could reply except the easily avoided signal rockets. The heavy machine gun could not be elevated. There had been one machine pistol but all too probably the entire magazine had been blown away in one futile burst.

Another rocket went up, and another. There was an explosion at ground level, a great gout of orange fire and billowing, ruddy smoke, as a laser beam touched off the ammunition reserve of the heavy automatic.

Grimes had been given no opportunity to check the disposition of the twin laser cannon with which *Little Sister* was now armed. He assumed that they were on fixed mounts, pointing directly forward and could be aimed only by aiming the pinnace herself. Luckily the Shaara firing and selector studs that had been added to the console were almost the same as those for Terran weapons of the same kind, modified to suit arthropodal claws rather than human fingers. Grimes snatched a stylus from its clip on the control panel, pushed it down to press the recessed firing button of what had to be the starboard gun. Ahead of the pinnace the almost invisible beam stabbed out and smoke and dust motes flared into brief scintillance. A drone, caught by the slashing fire, exploded smokily while another drone, a wing sheared off, tumbled to the ground.

To port a concentration of three drones was flying towards *Little Sister* as fast as their wings could carry them, firing at the pinnace with their hand lasers. They could do no harm, Grimes knew; the super-metal of the hull was virtually indestructable. But when he turned to bring the cannon to bear a direct hit on the transparency of the forward viewport the flashes might well blind him, and it was a long, long way to the nearest hospital with organ transplant facilities. . . .

He shouted urgently, "Look aft, all of you! Look aft!"

He heard Lennay translate, heard Tamara demand, "Why?"

"Don't argue! Look aft!"

The inertial drive hammered noisily as with his left hand he worked the directional controls. With his right hand he kept the stylus pressed firmly on to the firing stud. The continuous beam wouldn't do the synthetic ruby any good but, with his eyes not tightly shut, he could not wait to fire until he was on the target. Suddenly, through his closed eyelids, he was conscious of a fierce, ruddy glow that ceased abruptly. It had not been as bad as he had feared; the automatic polarization had cut out most of the radiation.

"You got them, Grimes!" Tamara shouted. "But there are more of the bastards to starboard!"

He corrected the swing, set the pinnace turning the other way. He could see four drones in the light of what must have been the last rocket flare. They were not retreating. That was their funeral—or cremation—he thought viciously. Soon their exploded bodies would join the charred remains of their comrades.

Now! he thought, starting to shut his eyes, but checking the lids in half descent. Those drones were lifting, obviously intending to fly over *Little Sister* to attack from the other side. He stopped the turn, steadied, began to swing to port—but the drones did not reappear. "The cows must be going straight up," he remarked conversationally.

"The *cows?*" repeated Lennay in a puzzled voice but Grimes ignored him. He pushed the button to snap aside the metal screen of the overhead viewport. He stared into two faceted eyes that were staring down at him. He saw the muzzle of a laser pistol coming into view. Hastily he brought the screen into place and then screened the other ports.

He could imagine the drones on top of the pinnace, probably clinging to the two laser cannon. They might have grenades. They did have
hand lasers and they were already using them; a tell-tale light indicated
overheating of the upper hull. They were trying to burn their way
through. They would never give up the fight; their lives were already
forfeit because of their failure to protect the princesses. Nothing remained to them but to die with honor.

Fleetingly Grimes felt sorry for them. They were doing what they
had to do. Although not unintelligent they had very little free will,
were little better than motile organs of the far greater organism that
was the Shaara Hive.

And that was their bad luck.

He slammed on vertical thrust. The inertial drive unit hammered
away nosily in response. With all the viewports screened he could not
see where he was going but it was highly improbable that there would
be anything to impede his upward flight, and if there were the radar
would give ample warning. His instruments told him that, save for two
spots on the upper hull, skin temperature was dropping rapidly, had
already fallen from 20° to 5°, was still falling, as was the external air
pressure. He would be above the overcast soon if not already. Skin
temperature dropped from Zero to −10°, the upper hull included.

He thought smugly, *That should have done it.*

He said, "We'll give our friends time to cool off, then we'll get
back down."

"And what about my people, Captain Grimes?" asked Lennay.

"Those drones are more of a menace to them than to us," Grimes
told him. "We have to be sure that all the Shaara are dead."

"Do you want these while you're waiting?" asked Tamara. "I
found them stowed in a locker in the galley . . ."

She handed him his pipe, his tobacco pouch and a box of the old-
fashioned matches that he affected.

"Thank you," he said. "Thank you." At that moment he really
loved her.

Then she spoiled everything by saying, "I was looking for the mail
bag, actually. They've opened it, of course, and one of the parcels, but
the rest of the consignment's intact."

Chapter 25

Grimes slid the screen of the upper viewport to one side, ready to snap it back at the first sign of hostile life outside. He did not expect that there would be such. There was not. He was reasonably certain that the drones were no more impervious to a lethal combination of almost hard vacuum and extremely low temperature than humans would have been. He turned to the others, said, "All right. We're going down."

"Please be fast, Captain," said Lennay. "My men . . . they are injured, dying . . ."

Or dead . . . thought Grimes. But as long as a spark of life remained in any of the raiding party speed was essential.

He threw the inertial drive into neutral, dropped like the proverbial stone. He heard Tamara gasp, the Darijjans moan in fear. He watched the fast decreasing tally of kilometers on the radar altimeter screen— a diminishing numeration that very soon was that of meters only. At 30 he slammed on maximum vertical thrust. *Little Sister* was exceptionally robust; she could take this treatment but she didn't have to like it. She complained bitterly with an agonized creaking of structural members while a veritable galaxy of red warning lights flashed on the console. She quivered to a halt ten meters from the ground, started to rise again. Grimes adjusted thrust while looking into the screen. Yes, there was the river, with the sandspit. Concentrations of metal—the barge, the guns—showed up brightly. Grimes spun the pinnace like a top about her short axis, made for them.

Only one man had survived the Shaara counter attack. This was Tambu, Lennay's chief clerk. He was wounded, a laser beam having slashed away the flesh from his right shoulder; had the injury not been instantly cauterized he would have died from loss of blood. He was unconscious but, said Lennay, would survive if he were taken without too much loss of time to the cave temple.

Tamara asked, "How much time do we have, Grimes? How long before *Baroom* flies back to deal with us?"

He said, "I don't think that she'll be back until the Rogue Queen has finished her business to the north."

"But she must know what's happened here, that her people have been massacred."

"Not necessarily," he told her.

"But the Shaara are telepaths . . ."

"And their telepathy is short range. For longer distances they rely on radio—among themselves they speak in coded stridulations. If they had a transceiver in the dome they may—they probably will—have gotten word of our attack through to the ship. But I suspect that the only radio here is that in *Little Sister*—in which case we have time to get ourselves organized."

"Tambu must be taken to the temple," said Lennay stubbornly. "Also the bodies of our people must be carried there for proper crematory rites."

"They'll keep," said Grimes with a callousness that he did not feel. "So will Tambu. I've seen men recover from much worse wounds. If you like you can find some sterile dressings in the medicine chest for him. But we must make use of whatever time we have. First of all, I'm flying back to the dome. We must make a search, find out if there is a radio set inside it. If there is—it's battle stations again. If there's not, we collect up all the arms and ammunition, from the dome and from the Shaara dead, that will be of use to us. Then we fly back to the cave. But first of all," he looked with extreme distaste at the bodies of the princess and the drone, still oozing a greenish, foul-scented ichor over what had been the spotlessly clean deck of the cabin, "we get *these* outside . . ."

Lennay's two men put the unconscious Tambu on to one of the bunks, then dragged the Shaara corpses out through the airlock. As soon as they had finished Grimes lifted the pinnace, flew back to the ruined dome. The rest of the ship cleaning could wait until later although, as soon as possible, he must disentangle those messily burst corpses from the twin laser cannon.

Grimes went into the dome with Lennay and the other two Darijans leaving Tamara, to whom electronic equipment was not strange, in charge of the pinnace. Should *Little Sister*'s radar show the approach of any space or aircraft she would let him know at once.

Fortunately the plastic hemisphere was not fully deflated. Grimes and his companions were able to crawl through tunnels and spherical chambers without too much difficulty, although even where there was headroom it was impossible to maintain an upright posture on the yielding floors. That odd diffused lighting was still on and through the almost transparent plastic of the interior walls Grimes could see the dark shapes of machines. Getting to them was the trouble; the inside of the dome was a three dimensional maze. But at last he was satisfied. One of those metallic shapes turned out to be food dispenser and another doled out strictly rationed drops of some sort of syrup. The third and last one was only a drinking fountain. There were no weapons, although there were boxes of ammunition that would fit both the machine pistols and the light machine guns. To Grimes' disappointment there was nothing—either banked power cells or any sort of generator—that could be used to recharge captured laser pistols. But this did not matter, he suddenly realized. *Little Sister* had power a-plenty.

He made his way out of the dome followed by the Darijjans dragging their prizes. Back in the pinnace Tamara told him that there was still nothing on the radar screen and informed Lennay, who was making anxious enquiries, that Tambu was still sleeping. Everything was under control but for the passage of time. The night was almost over; the overcast sky was grey rather than black, was lightening with every passing minute. Sooner or later somebody would be coming down from the city to investigate the shooting—probably a military patrol, and the army leaders were pro-Shaara . . .

But there were still things to be done. There were the weapons to be collected from the Shaara dead. There were the corpses of the killed guerillas to be loaded aboard *Little Sister*. Grimes could appreciate Lennay's concern but still thought that this was a criminal waste of time . . .

He arranged to have the two surviving Darijjan soldiers make their way to the river between the rows of bushes, picking up what they could during their journey, while he flew *Little Sister* to the wreckage of the battery and its crew.

Chapter 26

The sun was well up and the clouds had dispersed by the time that Grimes was almost ready to fly *Little Sister* away from the scene of the battle. The bodies of the Darijjans killed in the fighting had been loaded aboard, as had been the serviceable weapons taken from the Shaara corpses. All that remained was the clearing of the carcasses of the hapless drones from around the twin lasers. Grimes would not entrust this distasteful task to anybody but himself; a power connection could so easily be broken by anybody unfamiliar with such weaponry.

He clambered up to the upper hull of the pinnace, using the hand-holds recessed into the shell plating just abaft the airlock. He looked with incipient nausea at the tangle of thin, hairy limbs, the tatters of chitin, the green ichor that was oozing disgustingly over the burnished metal. He gulped. But the job had to be done.

Before starting he took a good look around. There was no traffic on the river. There were no machines, either native or Shaara, in the sky (if there had been his radar would have given him ample warning). But there was noise—mechanical, but not the arhythmic beat of an inertial drive unit, not the whine of the electric motor of a Shaara blimp, not the throbbing of the engines of a Darijjan airship. It was a peculiar, wheezing rattle and seemed to be coming from ground level.

Then Grimes saw them.

They were between the city and the Shaara landing place, coming slowly but steadily. The sunlight was reflected from bright metal, was illuminating clouds of dark smoke mixed with white steam. Four vehicles, Grimes decided, steam-driven, and behind them what looked like cavalry. He shouted down, "Lennay! Come up here! Bring a pair of binoculars with you!"

Lennay clambered up to where Grimes was standing with alacrity, handed him the powerful glasses. Grimes put them to his eyes, stared. There were four tall-funneled tractors, armored, rolling on huge, wide-rimmed wheels. Each towed behind it a truck in which men—soldiers almost certainly—were seated, stiffly erect, holding long rifles. The horsemen—although the beasts that they were riding were more like Terran camels—were similarly armed. Grimes switched his attention back to the vehicles. At the front end of each of them, forward of the engine, was a turret from which protruded the multiple muzzles of a heavy machine gun.

Grimes handed the glasses to Lennay.

"War wagons," said the Darijjan.

"It's time that we weren't here," said Grimes.

Lennay said, "Surely *you* have nothing to fear from our primitive weaponry, Captain?"

Grimes told him, "There's been enough killing. Too much. The Shaara, the Rogue Queen and her people, are the real enemies. Not your people."

Lennay said thoughtfully, "Perhaps you are right. If Samz is speaking through you, you *are* right, Captain Grimes. And it is possible that there are some of my men, of *our* men, among those soldiers . . . Perhaps if the gods deigned to display themselves . . ."

"Mphm," grunted Grimes dubiously. "Meanwhile, I'll just have time to clear this mess away from around the guns before we have to use them."

"No," said Lennay. "Leave the bodies there. They are proof that the sword of Delur is a mighty one . . ."

"Were you talking to me?" asked Tamara who had joined the two men a-top the pinnace.

"Yes, Lady Goddess." (Grimes thought, *He doesn't address me in that tone of voice. But, of course, he's too familiar with space captains to believe that they're deities . . . Superintending Postmistresses are outside his past experience.*) "Should you display yourself, standing triumphant on the torn carcasses of your foes, you will be a sign unto the faithful . . ."

"You mean that you want me to ride on top of the pinnace? I suppose that if I stand between the two guns I shall be safe enough—as long as Grimes doesn't indulge in aerobatics . . ."

"Yes, Lady, between the cannon. Your feet on the bodies of your enemies. Your sword unsheathed. Your glorious body unclothed."

"*That* should not be necessary," said Grimes.

"But it *is*," Lennay told him. "The Goddess Delur is always depicted naked in moments of triumph."

She said, "All right. I'll go through with it. After all, those bastards
have already seen me without a stitch on, and this time I shall at least
have boots and a sword belt . . ."

"Boots?" asked Grimes.

"Boots. I'm not going to stand on that . . . mess in my bare feet."
She unbuckled her pistol belt, handed it to Lennay. Her sword belt
followed. She whipped off her tunic. She was naked under it. The
sword belt she put back on. She drew the weapon from its sheath, held
it aloft. She asked, "How do I look?"

"The very incarnation of Delur, my Lady," said Lennay reverently.

Like somebody out of a nude version of a Wagner opera, throught
Grimes. Nonetheless, the effect was decidedly erotic.

"I shall stay with you, Lady," said Lennay.

Grimes felt jealous but he was the only one capable of piloting
the pinnace.

"It will be necessary for me, as High Priest, to call out to the
multitude."

If they can hear you over the clatter of the inertial drive, thought
Grimes.

"And now, Captain, if you will take your post at the controls and
fly us towards the war wagons . . ."

"I don't like this," said Grimes.

She turned to face him, nude, imperious, her skin shining like gold
in the sunlight reflected from the burnished hull of the pinnace. She
said, "Fly towards the city, slowly, not too high. I want the people to
see me."

"Suppose they shoot at you?"

"They have no anti-aircraft weapons," she said.

But rifles can be aimed upwards, he thought.

"Do as I say," she commanded.

It was a crazy idea, Grimes thought, but on this crazy planet it
might just work. He resolved that if anything should happen to her he
would exact bloody vengeance. He took one last look at her, standing
between the twin cannon, her back to him, that absurd sword uplifted
in her right hand, dazzlingly glittering, then clambered down to
ground.

He took his seat in the control cab, watched by the two Darijjans,
both of whom had made themselves comfortable among the corpses

of their late comrades. He decided to leave the airlock doors open; after all he would not be proceeding at any great speed or altitude. As the pinnace rose he saw that the forces from the city were just topping a low rise. Now was the time for them to open fire on him, if they were going to. But, of course, they would not know yet that the pinnace was not still under Shaara control. The armored tractors came into full view as he lifted—the locomotives and the troop trucks and, behind them, the cavalry. He flew towards them. He wondered what the soldiers were thinking. Perhaps they would assume that this was just another show put on for their benefit by the Shaara, yet another public humiliation of the Terrans. But they would soon realize that this was not so. The spectacle of the woman with the drawn sword, trampling on the crumpled bodies of those who had been her persecutors, was such obvious symbolism.

He flew on, looking ahead and down. He could see that Tamara had been noticed (and who could fail to notice her?) by the soldiers. There was commotion in the open trucks being towed by the tractors. There was a burst of fire from one of the heavy machine guns with the bullets passing harmlessly below the pinnace. A cavalry officer had drawn his sword, was waving it, pointing it upwards. Some—by no means all—of the mounted men aimed their rifles at *Little Sister*, at Tamara. Grimes could only just see the muzzle flashes but the black powder smoke was visible enough.

All right, he thought. *You've asked for it. Now you get it.* A slight touch on the controls would dip the pinnace's nose and bring the laser cannon to bear. But he hesitated. Such maneuver could well throw Tamara off balance and topple her from her airborne pedestal to the ground; the transition from Winged Victory to broken corpse would be sudden and irreversable. He wished that he had been able to rig some system of communication between himself and those on top of the pinnace, but there had been no time.

Then he realized that the cavalrymen, although still firing, were fighting among themselves. The sword-waving officer fell, was trampled by the broad, splayed hooves of his rearing mount. Troopers toppled from their saddles. The infantrymen in the trucks were struggling hand to hand. One of the tractors peeled away from the line abreast formation, turned with surprising nimbleness and opened fire, with its heavy machine gun, on the one which had been its next abeam. There was a sudden cloud of steam as the boiler was ruptured.

Grimes heard Lennay's voice. And how, he wondered, was the Darijjan able to speak to him? But the High Priest had clambered down the hull to the open airlock doors and was in the control cab. He was saying, "They are with us, Captain Grimes. They are with us. Fly on to the city, slowly. Let the goddess's soldiers precede you . . ."

Grimes cut fore-and-aft thrust, hovered. Looking down he could see that the three surviving tractors were turning, that the ground was littered with dead cavalrymen and the bodies of those who had been thrown from the troop trucks. He watched the depleted force regroup, proceed back to where they had come from. He saw two fast riders gallop ahead of the main body.

He said, "I am not making fun of your religion, but those soldiers were very easy converts."

Lennay said, "Many of them were already true believers. And now they have seen the glorious, living proof that Madame Tamara is indeed the incarnation of the Lady Delur."

"Mphm. She must be getting chilly up top. Or don't goddesses feel the cold?"

"Please not to jest, Captain Grimes. And please remember that the God Samz is working through you, just as Delur works through Madame Tamara—although not so strongly. I cannot help but feel that He could have chosen a more suitable vessel. You are capable, that I would never deny. But you lack the . . . divine aura."

"We can't all be Handsome Frankie Delamere," said Grimes.

"Your pardon, Captain?"

"I was just thinking out loud. Commander Delamere is an old . . . friend of mine. He's long on presence, but short on ability."

He adjusted thrust, slowly followed the soldiers to the city. Lennay left him, went to rejoin Tamara on top of the pinnace.

Chapter 27

Through the open doors of the airlock, even above the arrhythmic clangor of the pinnace's inertial drive, Grimes could hear the shouting, the singing, the screaming discordancy (to him) of trumpets, the boom and rattle of drums.

"Delur! Delur! Delur!"

He could see through the viewports the gathering crowds spilling out into the narrow streets, the scuffles that went breaking out between the adherents to the old religion, now openly declaring themselves, and those who still supported the church of the establishment. But there seemed little doubt that in this city, at least, the worshippers of Delur and Samz were in the majority—or, perhaps, any gods who were against the invading Shaara and the pro-Shaara president would do.

Little Sister was flying over a sea of upturned faces, of waving arms. Grimes could imagine what the people were staring at, regretted that he himself could not see Tamara standing there between the laser cannon, her body golden in the golden light of the morning sun, her graceful curves in erotic contrast to the no less graceful angularities of the twin weapons.

"Delur! Delur! Delur!"

And what about Samz? he thought a little sourly.

He kept the pinnace just above rooftop level, following the street, maintaining station on the three armored tractors, now in line ahead formation and leading the troop of cavalry and what seemed to be almost a full regiment of infantrymen. He watched as the column leader loosed off its machine gun at a crowd of men desperately attempting to set up a barricade of furniture and overturned wagons.

Even now, he thought, the god Darajja possessed devotees willing to die for their beliefs.

And die they did.

The tractors rolled over the half-completed barricade, splintering beds and chairs and tables, crushing the bodies of its defenders. They clattered into the square, their iron wheels striking sparks, visible even in the bright sunlight, from the cobblestones. They steered for the metal platform that had been set up by the Shaara, upon which Grimes and Tamara had been exposed and humiliated. Grimes thought at first that the intention was to destroy this symbol of alien brutality but it was not so. Wheeling with quite amazing smartness the war vehicles took up stations about it, forming the three points of a triangle, their guns pointing outwards. Cavalry and infantry filled the gaps between the machines, making a menacing display of their rifles.

Lennay appeared in the airlock door, came to the control cab to stand just behind Grimes. He said, "This display has exceeded my wildest expectations, Captain. Even I had no idea that we have so many supporters . . ."

"God is on the side of the big battalions," Grimes told him. "We may not be a big battalion but, until the Rogue Queen returns, we have the superior fire power."

"These people," said Lennay soberly, "are with god, or the gods. The old gods. They know that we, with Delur to lead us, to inspire us, destroyed the Shaara."

Grimes grunted dubiously around the stem of his cold pipe. "And what was *I* doing while Delur was supposed to be leading and inspiring?" he asked.

"Delur and Samz always act as one," Lennay told him. "That dual principle worked through you and Madame Haverstock. She the inspiration, and you the . . . the . . ."

"The driver," supplied Grimes. "Oh, well, I suppose that this chariot of the gods has to have a chauffeur."

"You jest, Captain."

"Too right. Just a jesting pilot, that's me." He laughed at his play on words, his good humor restored.

"Can you land on the platform, Captain?" asked Lennay.

Grimes assessed the situation. "Mphm. I could, I suppose. There'll be considerable overhang, of course, and that structure could never support *Little Sister*'s weight . . . But I can keep the inertial drive running, just kicking over . . ."

"Then land on the platform, please. Or appear to do so. After you have set down, the God Samz will appear beside his consort. It is necessary that you show yourself to the people. Delur without Samz is like . . . like . . . You Terrans have a saying . . . Yes: like coffee without cream."

"I prefer *my* coffee black," said Grimes.

He returned his attention to the controls, gently moving ahead until the platform was immediately below the pinnace. Carefully he reduced vertical thrust. *Little Sister* dropped slowly, touched with an almost imperceptible jar. Grimes ran a practiced eye over the instruments on the console, was satisfied. As long as the inertial drive was kept running on this setting the golden ship would weigh no more than a few grammes relative to the surface upon which she rested.

"All right," he said. "I'll get up top with Tamara to take my bow. Don't touch anything on the control panel during my absence. We aren't ready to ascend into Heaven just yet."

He got up from his seat, made for the airlock.

"Wait!" said Lennay. "First you must remove your raiment."

"What?"

"You must remove your raiment. At a time of triumph the god, as well as the goddess, must be naked. So they have always been depicted in our religious art."

Grimes shrugged. After all, he asked himself, what did it matter? The day was warm enough, and even though he was not an exhibitionist he was no prude. He undid the simple fastenings of his tunic and let the garment fall to the deck. He left his boots on; he had a ladder to climb and those recessed rungs had not been designed to be negotiated by bare feet. He walked slowly to the airlock. As he appeared in the chamber a great shout went up from those of the people who could see him. "Samz! Samz!" Not only his prominent ears reddened in embarrassment; he could feel the angry flush spreading over his entire body. He bowed stiffly then turned to ease himself out of the chamber. He had to be careful; the forward part of the pinnace (as was, too, the after part) was overhanging the edge of the platform and a fall to the cobblestones would be injurious to body as well as to pride. He extended an arm until he found handhold, then fumbled with a booted foot for a recessed rung. His other hand went out, and then the other foot. He started to climb. He knew that he must look ludicrous—a naked man going up a ladder with genitalia a-dangle—but he was committed, and the cries of *Samz! Samz!* seemed to be more expressive of adoration then derision. He scrambled to the upper hull of the pinnace with an agility evocative of the simian ancestry of his race. He joined Tamara between the twin laser cannon.

"Samz! Samz!"

He raised his arms in a gesture of benediction.

"Delur! Delur!"

She lifted her flashing sword, making a tired flourish.

She muttered, "Now *you* can start finding out what it's like . . ." Then, "I wish to all the Odd Gods of the Galaxy that the bastards wouldn't keep stoking up those damned steam engines!"

A cloud of sulphurous smoke suddenly erupted from the tall funnel of the tractor up wind from them, eddied about them. Sparks stung their unprotected skin.

"At least they aren't throwing dead cats at us this time," remarked Grimes philosophically.

The smoke cleared.

Tamara waved her sword again with something less than enthusiasm. Grimes made his bless-you-my-children gesture.

He said, "This is starting to get boring."

She sneered, "You've only just begun. I've been on show for hours."

Less than one hour, throught Grimes, but deemed it politic not to say the words aloud.

Lennay clambered up from the airlock, walked slowly forward to the guns. He looked happy. Grimes and Tamara regarded him sourly.

He said, "I have learned that Hereditary President Callaray and General Porron, together with their high-ranking officers, are aboard *Baroom*, accompanying the Rogue Queen, advising her, while she wages war against Desaba. That is why the army came over to us after no more than a token show of resistance . . ."

"And they'll change sides again when *Baroom* comes back," said Tamara.

"*If* she comes back," Grimes told her.

She said, "I'm only a postmistress, not a naval officer. But even I know that an armed pinnace is no match for a warship." She contrived to make the waving of her sword in response to the cheers of the crowd a singularly unwarlike gesture. "You've got your ship back, Grimes. I've got the mail—and don't forget that it still has to be delivered. I propose that we get the hell out of here and resume our voyage."

"Lady Delur!" Lennay's voice was shocked. "You cannot mean that!"

"We've done our share, Mr. Lennay. We've given you this city. It's up to you to hold it."

"But the prophecy . . ."

"We've delievered you, haven't we? If you can't stay delivered it's just too bad."

"I agree," said Grimes judiciously, "that it would be unwise to wait here for the Rogue Queen's return . . ."

She said, "I'm glad to hear you say that, Grimes. For a moment I was afraid that you were taking this god and goddess rubbish seriously." She slapped viciously at a spark that had alighted on her right breast. "*I've* had it in a big way!"

"Lady Delur . . ." implored Lennay.

"We shall not wait here for *Baroom*'s return," stated Grimes.

"Captain . . . you cannot leave us now . . ."

It was odd, and rather annoying, thought Grimes how even now Lennay was addressing Tamara as a deity and himself as a mere shipmaster. But it did not matter. He *knew*, briefly, that something, some entity outside himself, was speaking through him, was implanting in his mind the knowledge of what must be done, what could, quite easily, be done. He himself had little knowledge of what facilities were available in this city, but somehow such information, in great detail, was now available to him. And from his own memory came scraps of Terran naval history, recollections of what he had read of stratagems employed during wars at sea.

He said, "We will not wait for the Rogue Queen—and the President Callaray and General Porron—to come to us. We will go to them."

"You're mad!" exclaimed Tamara.

"*Mad?* he wondered. If she'd said "possessed" he might have agreed with her. But he ignored her and spoke to the native.

"Mr. Lennay, is it essential that your chief clerk be taken to the cave for medical treatment?"

"No, Captain. There is an excellent hospital here."

"Good. And there is an arsenal . . ."

"Yes."

"And part of it is the new yard for building airships. The framework of the *Tellaran* is almost completely assembled."

"How do you know?" asked Lennay, puzzled.

And how do I know, Grimes asked himself, *that Tellaran is the name of a flying reptile?*

He said, "We will take your man to the hospital. Then we fly to the arsenal, to the airship yard. You will tell the workers what I want done."

Chapter 28

Little Sister lifted from Plirrit.

Her builders would never have recognized her although, just possibly, they might have realized that she was propelled by an inertial drive unit and that the pusher airscrew mounted at the after end of the long car slung beneath her was for show only. But they would have had to be very close to her to hear the distinctive beat of her real engines; her golden hull had been thickly lagged with mattresses of vegetable fibre which acted as very effective sonic insulation.

Little Sister was now, to all except the most intimate inspection, a Darijjan airship. It had been neither a difficult nor a lengthy task to slide her hull into the cage formed by the already assembled frames and longerons. There was no need to be concerned about the strength of the structure, it was for camouflage only. The real strength, the mailed fist in the velvet glove, was concealed by the panels of fabric that had been stretched and glued and sewn over the ribs, would remain hidden until Grimes got close enough to *Baroom* to do what he knew must be done, would be done. Until then he would have to limit his speed to one within the capabilities of the almost sophisticated gas turbine that was to have been *Tellaran*'s engine, would have to refrain from maneuvers obviously impossible to a dirigible.

The airship yard technicians had worked with a will, had grasped at once what was required of them. It almost seemed that if Lennay had not been there to interpret the job would have been done just as well and just as speedily.

And speed was essential.

Even though this was a world without the electric telegraph, without radio, news travelled. There was the network of railways. There were steamships. And not everybody in Plirrit was a devotee of the Old Religion; there were those who, already, must be endeavoring to get word of the happenings to their absent President, and, through him, to the Rogue Queen.

So Grimes, as soon as the last stitch had been made in the last seam of the fabric envelope, lifted ship. Tamara was with him, and Lennay. Grimes had not wanted either of them along on what might well be a suicide mission but they had insisted on accompanying him.

Little Sister moved slowly out of the vast hangar, lifted into the evening sky, drab in her disguise, harmless looking. The crowd that had gathered watched in silence. There were no cheers, no singing. Yet Grimes could feel the emotion of those who were, in some odd way, his worshippers. There was the unvoiced prayer that Samz and Delur would overthrow the invaders from outside, the unspoken hope that the Old Religion would once more hold sway on this world, that the joyless faith that had supplanted it would itself be supplanted.

Grimes sat at his controls, Tamara beside him. Lennay stood behind them. The view from the ports was circumscribed; there were only concealed peepholes in the camouflaging envelope. This was of no great importance; radar would suffice for pilotage. Grimes set course, put the ship on to a heading that would bring her to Kahtrahn, the capital city of Desaba. He had received no intelligence that *Baroom* was there but he *knew* that this was where he would find the Rogue Queen. He knew, too, that the outcome of the battle would be determined by his own skills. Samz, for all his power, his omniscience, was only a local deity and, insofar as technology was concerned, knew no more than those whose faith had given him being.

Grimes switched over to the auto-pilot. He said that he was going down into the gondola. Tamara said that she would catch the opportunity for some sleep. Lennay accompanied Grimes.

A ladder had been rigged from the open airlock door to the control car of the dummy airship. This had not been fitted out; there was neither compass nor altimeter and the wheels that would have been used by the altitude and steering coxswains were still with other equipment back in the hangar. The wide windows were glazed, however, although nobody had thought to clean the tough glass before lift-off. Nonetheless, thought Grimes, he was getting a better view from here than he had been from the pinnace's control room. He looked out and down to the dark landscape, to the distant clusters of lights that were towns and villages. Ahead the Maruan Range was a darker shadow against the dark sky. *Little Sister* would find her own way over the mountains without a human hand at her controls; nonetheless Grimes decided that he would prefer to do that piece of pilotage himself. He had time, however, to complete his inspection of the gondola. He made his unimpeded way aft; no partitions had yet been set up at the time of the requisitioning of the airship. Lennay followed him. He looked at the engine and at the motionless airscrew. The motor was completely enclosed in a cylindrical casing from which pipes led to the tanks of pressurized hydrogen. There were dials, meaningless to Grimes, wheel valves and levers. He asked Lennay, "Can you start this thing?"

"Yes, Captain. But surely it is not necessary."

"It will be when we meet up with the Shaara. It will look suspicious if we're making way through the air with a motionless prop . . ."

Lennay oscillated his head in the native equivalent to a nod. "Yes. I see." He launched into a spate of explanations. "It is quite simple. You open this valve to admit the gas, then you pull down sharply on this lever to strike a spark, then . . ."

"It would be simpler," Grimes told him, "to use a catalyst, like platinum wire . . ." He could not see the other's expression in the darkness but knew that it was one of pained puzzlement. "But it doesn't matter. As long as this way works, why worry?"

He led the way up the ladder back to *Little Sister*'s airlock, went forward to the control cab. He looked at the radar screen and at the chart. He would, he decided, make a slight deviation so as to negotiate the Daganan Pass rather than fly over the mountains. That would be what a real airship would do so as to avoid jettisoning overmuch ballast. There was little chance that news of his coming would reach the Rogue Queen before his arrival at Kahtrahn but he could not afford to take any chances. The camouflage must be maintained until the end.

Tamara slept all the time that he was steering the ship through the series of narrow ravines. He had thought of awakening her, but there was little to see. Not only were the viewports almost completely obscured but it was now very dark. Without radar it would have been extremely hazardous pilotage, especially to one with no local knowledge.

At last *Little Sister* was through the mountains. Ahead of her was the northern coastal plain and beyond that the sea. To the east the sky was pale and a scattering of thin, high clouds already golden. Grimes adjusted course, put the ship back on automatic pilot, yawned widely.

Lennay said sympathetically, "You are tired, Captain."

"You can say that again!" agreed Grimes.

He got up from his seat, went aft. Tamara in her bunk, blanket covered, was snoring softly and almost musically. He spoke to her;

she went on snoring. He shook her shoulder. Her eyes opened and she looked up at him coldly.

He said, "You have the watch. I'm turning in."

She said, "Surely you don't expect me to fight your bloody battles for you."

"No. But take over, will you? We're on automatic pilot; all you have to do is watch the instruments, the radar especially. Should you pick up any aerial targets, at any range at all, call me at once. Otherwise let me know when we're one hundred kilometers from the Desaban coastline."

She actually managed a grin. "I'm only a goddess, Grimes, not a navigator. But I think I'll be able to manage . . ."

She threw aside the blanket, stood there naked for a few moments, stretching like some great, lazy cat. Unhurriedly she pulled on her tunic. She asked, "All right if I make some coffee first?"

"Lennay will fix that," said Grimes.

Lennay, not waiting to be told, had already done so. He bowed low before Tamara before handing her the steaming mug. "And for you, Captain?" he asked.

"No thank you," said Grimes regretfully. "It would only keep me awake."

He went forward with Tamara, showed her the pinnace's position on the chart and the course line that he had pencilled in with a small cross marking where he wished to be called, then walked aft to his own bunk. He thought that he would have trouble in getting to sleep but he was out as soon as his body hit the mattress.

Chapter 29

He came awake as soon as Lennay touched him.

The native handed him a mug of coffee which Grimes sipped gratefully.

"We are one hundred kilometers from the coastline," said Lennay. "The Lady Delur asked me to inform you that nothing of interest otherwise had appeared on the screen of the radar."

"Mphm." Grimes filled and lit his pipe, padded forward. Tamara smiled up at him from her chair. He smiled back, looked first through the forward viewscreen—not that he could see much; it was almost like peeping through a keyhole—and then into the radar screen. Yes, there was the coastline, distant still but closing steadily. That patch of greater brightness inshore a little must be the port city of Denb; he had made a good landfall, he thought. Or *Little Sister*, left to her own devices, had made a good landfall.

He grunted again, went aft to the little toilet. When he was finished he put on his familiar shirt and shorts uniform; he felt far happier in this rig than he had felt either in the ceremonial sarong or the slightly less hampering tunic. He was pleased that the Shaara had left most of his clothing aboard the pinnace, although, attracted by the plenitude of gold braid and buttons, they had stolen the finery that he had been obliged to wear when employed by the Baroness.

He relieved Tamara at the controls. She went aft to tidy up, saying that with things liable to start happening at any moment she might as well look her best. She returned with a tray of food, having persuaded the autochef to produce hot rolls with butter, a quite savory paté and a jug of chilled orange juice. Lennay, sharing the simple but satisfying meal, expressed gratification and amazement but when told that what he was eating was probably processed Shaara excrement abruptly stopped eating. He suggested that it was time that he started the gas turbine and went out through the airlock and down to the car. Grimes could imagine him throwing open a window and vomiting. With typical spaceman's heartlessness, remembering how he, as a green cadet, had been nauseated when learning of the origin of a meal that he had just enjoyed, he was amused rather than otherwise.

Lennay came back after a long interval, reporting that the airship's engine was in operation and the airscrew spinning. Grimes thanked him, then closed the airlock doors. From now on the ship was in fighting trim, invulnerable to almost anything save a direct hit by a missile with a nuclear warhead. Yes, thought Grimes, *she* was invulnerable but an explosion in her near vicinity could and would shake her like a terrier shaking a rat, and could her frail human crew survive such treatment? Possibly, as long as he and Tamara were tightly strapped into their chairs, as long as Lennay was well secured in one of the bunks . . .

He gave the necessary orders, set the example.

They were over Denb now. On their present course they would pass ten kilometers to the west of Kahtrahn. Grimes made an adjustment of course to starboard.

"Target," reported Tamara. "Bearing green oh-one-oh. Range thirty-five. Closing."

Grimes looked into the screen. Yes, there was the blip. It could not be *Baroom*, she would have been picked up at far greater range. There was very little metal, apart from the engine, in the Shaara blimps however. This could be a blimp, or a native airship.

Yes, the range was still closing and the bearing was unchanged. It, whatever it was, was on an interception course. Grimes brought *Little Sister* round ten degrees to starboard. Through the peephole in the camouflaging fabric he could see something silvery against the blue sky. He picked up the binoculars from their box, stared ahead through the powerful glasses. Yes, it was a blimp all right. It was too fat for one of the native dirigibles. Tiny motes danced around it—the drones swarming out of the car of their aerial transport.

Tamara said, "They'll get a nasty surprise when you open up with the laser cannon."

Grimes told her, "They won't."

"Why not?"

"Because if I open up now I'll give the game away and the Rogue Queen will be able to pick us off at long range. No, I'll just keep on going through whatever those bastards sling at us and hope that there's enough smoke to cover the rents in the camouflage. With any luck at all they'll assume that we're the local version of a *kamikaze*, but one too ill-armed and flimsy to take seriously . . ." He laughed. "That's one thing about the Shaara. They're never ones to use a power hammer to crack a walnut. They'll use on us only the weaponry that past experience on this world has taught them is ample to swat a gasbag out of the sky. By the time they realize what we really are it will be too late for them to deliver a nuclear punch without doing for themselves as well as us . . ."

"Which they might do," she said.

"We'll cross that bridge when we come to it," he said.

"It will be fitting," called Lennay from his bunk, "if the gods, the prophecy fulfilled, ascend to heaven on a pillar of the fire that has destroyed their enemies . . ."

Grimes sighed. It was all too possible, but, as far as he was concerned, he wanted the gods to ascend to heaven in a golden chariot, *Little Sister.*

The blimp was closing rapidly, directly ahead. There was a flickering of pale flame at the forward end of the thing's gondola, a stream of sparks bright even in the bright sunlight. Tracer. Whoever was in command of the Shaara airship wanted to bring the intruder down herself instead of leaving the task to the drones. Faintly the noise of the bullets striking the outer skin of the pinnace rang through the cabin.

I should have thought of having a few gasbags of hydrogen packed in, thought Grimes. *Our friends will be wondering when the fireworks display is going to start . . . But I suppose that there must be helium on this world and the inference will be that we've sacrificed lift for safety . . .*

Grimes stood on.

The blimp stood on.

Stubborn bitch . . . thought Grimes of the Shaara airship's captain. But she, princess or high-ranking worker, would be expecting the other aircraft to burst into flames at any second and, secure in the knowledge of the nonflammability of her own vessel, would be prepared to skirt closely or even to fly through the flaming wreckage. She was due for a big surprise.

She stood on, her automatic guns still hammering away. Hot metal flattened on the transparency of the pinnace's forward viewport, fell away. Then her nerve failed. When there was nothing at all visible from *Little Sister*'s control cab but the huge, clumsy, grey bulk of her she pulled sharply to starboard. Grimes held his course, striking her a glancing blow. The blimp rebounded from the contact like a violently struck beach ball. The pinnace, with her far greater mass, stood on stolidly. Grimes hoped that the camouflage had not been torn from the pinnace's port side exposing her true nature. He brought her round slowly, careful to maintain the impression that she was only a slow and clumsy airship, adjusted trim so that he had the Shaara blimp in sight. She swam into his limited field of vision. Her envelope was crumpled and she was settling slowly but as far as Grimes could see there were no fragments from his disguise adhering to the wreckage. He turned away from the disabled ship and from the squad of drones flying fast towards him, laser pistols drawn and ready. Probably they would succeed in setting fire to the sonic insulation with which *Little Sister* was covered; as long as the bright golden plating was not revealed thereby the resulting smoke and flame would be more to his advantage than otherwise.

He returned his attention to the radar screen.

Something big was ahead, was rising rapidly. It could only be *Baroom*. It could only be the Rogue Queen determined to make an example of the native dirigible that had dared to ram one of her airships.

And what weaponry would she be using?

Laser, probably, thought Grimes—but he was not surprised when he felt the muffled shock of close explosions and heard the faint clangs of shrapnel that had penetrated the disguising envelope and the vegetable fibre lagging. And these must be well ablaze by now although the smoke and flame, blowing astern, were not visible from the control cab. Nonetheless the temperature gauges showed that the outer skin was heating rapidly although the interior of the pinnace was still cool.

The Rogue Queen still had time to launch a nuclear missile, but time was running out for her. If she delayed firing such a weapon much longer she could not use it for fear of destroying her own ship. But, thought Grimes, she might take that risk. So he increased speed, hoping to be able to carry out his intentions before the last of the blazing camouflage was stripped away.

Baroom was in sight visually now. Grimes stared at her through the ragged, widening rent in the tattered fabric of the envelope. He saw the continuous flashes from her turret guns, the scintillating streams of tracer shells. The Shaara gunnery was not at all brilliant; whoever was in fire control was still assuming that the moving target was making only the normal speed of an airship. The Shaara, he remembered, did not use computers to any great extent; an organization of intelligent, social insects is, to a certain degree, an organic computer itself with built-in limitations, including a refusal to admit data known to be impossible, and until *Little Sister* was stripped of the last of her disguise her speed would fall into that category.

Baroom was close now. Grimes could see that people in the transparent dome of her control room—Shaara and a scattering of humanoids. He aimed for the rounded apex of the huge, conical spaceship and pressed the firing switches of the twin lasers. Reflected light almost blinded him, but it must have been worse, much worse, for the Rogue Queen, her officers and her allies before the automatic screening was actuated. In that instant they would have realized who their enemy was, but now it was too late for them to do anything about it.

Little Sister bored in viciously—but in almost the last instant before impact Grimes applied full stern power. Tough though his ship was he did not wish to subject her to the strain of a collision and, even if she survived the shock relatively unscathed, it was unlikely that her crew would do so.

But she struck, hard enough for her prow to make a deep dent in the shell of the Shaara control room. She struck, and as she did so Grimes cut the reverse thrust and came ahead again on his inertial drive, gently at first and then building up to the full capacity of his engines.

Something gave, but it was not the fantastically strong structure of the pinnace. Grimes fired his lasers through the widening crack in the Shaara warship's stem. Only those directly in the line of fire would be killed but the others would be panicking—he hoped—and instruments and controls would be destroyed.

He . . . pushed.

Baroom fell away from the vertical, slowly at first, then faster and faster.

Suddenly she topped and had Grimes not applied full stern power *Little Sister* would have been dragged down with her. She plunged to the ground, driven to destruction by her own mighty engines rather than dragged by the force of gravity.

She struck, and it was only then that Grimes realized that the battle had taken place over the city of Kahtrahn. He watched in horror as tall buildings crumpled under the impact, as other buildings were rocked by the explosion of *Baroom*'s ammunition, as fires broke out among the ruins.

He turned to the others, said in a shaky voice, "We must go down. We must help . . ."

Lennay said, "What can we do, Captain? We have done enough . . ."

"You can say that again," Grimes told him. "But we must render assistance."

"Those people," said Tamara, "must be hating all aliens, including us, by now. It's time that we were getting out of here."

Reluctantly Grimes conceded that she was right.

Chapter 30

The prophecy fulfilled, the demons from Outer Space destroyed, Delur and Samz ascended to Heaven. They left, as saviours so often do, quite a mess behind them. The Desabans were not as grateful as they might have been and were inclined to harp upon the fact that their capital city had been devastated and to cast doubts upon the divinity of Grimes and Tamara. And in Taraplan, now that there was no longer any danger of Shaara domination, only a handful of fanatics preached the Old Religion. The trouble was that the Darijjans had become accustomed, over the years, to visits from outside and knew that they themselves could build spaceships once they got around to it. Meanwhile there was a period of anarchy until a successor to the late President Callaray could be found. There was a paying off of old scores. There were rioting and arson.

Grimes—who had always evinced a weakness for taking sides—would have liked to stay to help Lennay and his adherents. Tamara, however, insisted that the voyage be resumed at once, that the precious consignment of parcel mail be carried to its recipient without further delay. She talked menacingly about the penalties for breach of contract. Grimes could not but listen to her. He insisted, however, that he perform one last service for his devotees—the rounding up of the Shaara survivors. These, not having been aboard *Baroom* at the time of her destruction, had fled to an island off the south coast of Desaba where they had killed or enslaved the native inhabitants. They had three blimps, automatic projectile weapons and lasers. The ammunition for their machine guns was limited but, as each of the airships possessed its own generator, the power cells of the laser pistols could be recharged as required for a long time to come.

There were princesses, drones and workers—females, males and neuters. Possibly breeding had commenced already.

The raid on the island was a short and bloody business. *Little Sister*, no longer in disguise, pounced at first light. Somehow the Shaara were expecting her. The blimps were already airborne and around each of them was a squadron of drones. They made no attempt to flee but attacked at once. A pinnace built of normal materials would have been overwhelmed by the ferocity of the assault. Looking back on it all Grimes was inclined to think that it was deliberately suicidal. The blimps bored in, their machine cannon flaming. The streams of tracers converged on the pinnace and the bursting shells blotted out all vision from the forward viewport. The drones were above *Little Sister*, around her, below her. Skin temperature gauges went mad.

Grimes fired the twin lasers and, at the same time, swung the ship's head to port, then to starboard, slashing with the double beam. The cannonade abruptly ceased and he could see ahead again, watched all three blimps fluttering groundward, their descent barely slowed by the charred rags that had been their envelopes. The crews—those who were still living—flew out from the cars to join the battling drones. Grimes slashed again and bee bodies burst smokily.

But the drones surrounding *Little Sister* were keeping well out of the field of fire of her lasers. Even if they could not hurt her—although they were searching frantically for a weak spot—they could not be hurt themselves. But they were singleminded, concentrating their fury on the obvious enemy. Perhaps they did see the native dirigible that came drifting above the battle; if they did, they ignored her. She could be dealt with at leisure. They were not expecting the invisible vapor that was discharged from her gondola, that fell slowly, that blinded and poisoned.

Sickened, Grimes watched the last of them, with wings twitching feebly and ineffectually, plunge to join their dead companions on the rocky ground.

Chapter 31

John Grimes and Tamara Haverstock came to Boggarty. They were not received on that world as deities. At first they were treated with considerable coldness. The Tiralbin Post Office had contracted to deliver an important consignment of parcel mail by a certain date. The subcontractor had entered into a similar agreement. Neither had met the terms of the contract.

The Planetary High Commissioner was a reasonable man, however. He listened patiently to Grimes' slightly edited story. He agreed that Grimes was entitled to plead Restraint of Princes and that neither Boggarty nor Tiralbin could successfully sue him for Breach of Contract. He maintained though, to Tamara's great disgust, that the penalty clauses regarding late delivery applied insofar as she was concerned.

She said to Grimes when they were alone together, "*You* look after yourself, don't you?"

"Somebody has to," he told her smugly.

She said, "The way things are I may as well get my full money's worth out of your precious contract. I can demand that you provide me with an escort until the mail is delivered."

"All right," he said.

The High Commissioner had provided them with a ground car and a driver, a stolid colonist who sat dourly in his seat and made no move to assist with the offloading from *Little Sister*. The sack of parcels was both heavy and awkward but Grimes dragged it out of the locker, to the airlock, and then struggled to lift it into the rear of the vehicle while Tamara muttered, "Careful, Grimes, careful . . . If anything is damaged you will be held responsible."

They drove from the spaceport to the city, were taken to the lofty

cylindrical tower that was the seat of planetary government. Again
Grimes was obliged to go into his porterage act, carrying the sack
from the car to the elevator, from the elevator to the High Commissioner's office.

"Sir," said Tamara to the portly men sitting behind the huge,
gleaming desk, "please accept delivery of the mail. I have to report
that the bag was tampered with by the Shaara and that one carton was
opened and one can taken."

"Captain Grimes has already informed me, Miss Haverstock," said
the Commissioner. "He mentioned that, among other things, during
our telephone conversation."

"Sign here, please," said Tamara, producing a pad of receipt forms.
"I have already made the necessary endorsement."

"I am not the actual consignee, Madam. But Grigadil will make
his mark. He should be here at any moment."

"Grigadil?" asked Grimes curiously.

"Yes, Captain. The King Boggart. He instructed his people not to
make any more wire sculptures for export until I did something to help
him with his peculiarly personal problem. Ah, here he is now . . ."

A boggart shambled into the office.

The films that Grimes had viewed concerning Boggarty had not
prepared him for the full repulsiveness of the indigenes. In addition to
their horrendous appearance they—or, at least, this one did—stank, a
rank, animal effluvium.

The being extended a clawed hand, pointed to the mail sack.

"Mine?"

"Yes, Grigadil," said the High Commissioner. "And now if you
will sign the lady's paper . . ."

"No sign till know if work. All wives give me no peace for too
long. Me afraid they find younger husband—but me not old . . ."

You look, thought Grimes, *like some prehuman from the dawn of
time who's been ageing steadily ever since . . .*

Grigadil tore open the sack, pulled out a wrapped carton. His claws
made short work of the outer coverings. He extracted a can. Grimes
could read the gaudy label: VENUS STRAWBERRIES. Grigadil
pulled the tab, lifted the now topless container to his wide, tusked
mouth, swallowed noisily.

Tamara was looking down with an expression of horrified fascination on her face. Grimes wondered what was causing this and then
he saw. The boggart was wearing only a filthy rag as a kilt and it was
now no longer adequate to hide what was under it.

"Good," grunted Grigadil. "Good. Me sign. Me go back to cave and show wives who boss."

Wordlessly Tamara handed the creature the pad and the stylus, keeping as much distance as possible between him and herself. She glared at Grimes when he said cheerfully, "As we've already found out, it's love that makes the world go round!"

She was not amused.

And this, Grimes realized without overmuch regret, was the ending of a beautiful friendship.